ALSO BY CHLOE WALSH

Boys of Tommen

Binding 13

Keeping 13

Saving 6

Redeeming 6

Taming 7

Releasing 10

Releasing 10

CHLOE WALSH

Bloom books

Published by Bloom Books, an imprint of Sourcebooks
P.O. Box 4410, Naperville, Illinois 60567-4410
(630) 961-3900
sourcebooks.com

Cataloging-in-Publishing data is on file with the Library of Congress.

Printed and bound in the United States of America.
LB 10 9 8 7 6 5 4

Disclaimer

Disclaimer

This book is a work of fiction. All names, characters, places, and incidents either are products of the author's imagination or are used fictitiously. Any resemblance to events, locales, or persons, living or dead, is coincidental.

The author acknowledges all song titles, song lyrics, play titles, film characters, trademarked statuses, and brands mentioned in this book are the property of, and belong to, their respective owners. The publication/use of these trademarks is not authorized, associated with, or sponsored by the trademark owners.

Chloe Walsh is in no way affiliated with any of the brands, songs, musicians, or artists mentioned in this book.

Author's Note

For the survivors.

Author's Note

Releasing 10 is the sixth installment in the Boys of Tommen series.

Some scenes in this book may be **extremely** upsetting; therefore, reader discretion is advised.

Please be aware this story tackles incredibly harrowing topics revolving around childhood abuse, sexual trauma, and suicide that, while incredibly important to speak out about, may **not** be suitable for younger readers. Please be mindful of emotional triggers and proceed with caution.

Because of its explicit sexual content, graphic violence, mature themes, triggers, and bad language, it is suitable for mature readers.

It is based in the South of Ireland, set during the timeframe of 1991–2005, and contains Irish dialogue, slang, language, and cultural stances relevant to that period in history. As such, these are not the personal opinions of the author.

Because the earlier books in the Tommen series centered around the Lynch family, their duets were released in order; however, from book five onward, the order in which the books release will rotate between characters in line with the ongoing storyline.

A detailed pronunciation guide and glossary can be found on the following pages.

Parts, stages, and sections are used instead of the standard chapter headings as the method of navigation in this book.

Thank you so much for joining me on this adventure.

Lots of love,
Chlo xxx

Pronunciations

Aoife: E-fa
Edel: E-dell
Sean: Shawn
Gardaí: Gar-Dee
Caoimhe: Kee-va
Sadhbh: Sigh-ve
Sinead: Shin-aid
Neasa: Nasa
Eoghan: Owen
Tadhg: Tie-g (like Tiger but without the 'r' at the end)
Feis: Fesh
Scoil Eoin: Skull Owen
Poitín: Putt-een
Gardaí Síochána: Guard-ee Shuck-awna
Gardaí: Guard-ee

Glossary / Irish Slang

a bit of talent: a good-looking person.

a forklift wouldn't shift her: I'm not kissing her.

a slab of beer: a box of 24 bottles of beer.

allergic: can't stand something/someone.

the Angelus: every evening at 6pm in Ireland, there is a minute silence for prayer on the television.

any chance of the ride: would you like to have sex with me.

ask me bollox: politely no, and leave me alone.

ask the back of me sack: I'm not doing it for you.

as thick as two short planks: a stupid person.

ate the box off her: cunnilingus.

ate the head off me: told me off.

away for slates: to do well.

back her into me, Bridie: let's have sex.

ball-hopper: a jokester.

balm out: to lie down and relax.

bang on: decent person/correct.

bate: exhausted.

beor: a woman/girl.

the best part of him ran down his mother's leg: he's a fool.

biro: ink pen.

bluey: porno movie.

bog roll: toilet roll.

the bog: the toilet.

bonnet: hood of the car.

boot: trunk of the car.

box of fags: packet of cigarettes.

box the head off ya: I will punch you.

break your melt: test your patience.

breast in a bun: chicken burger.

bulb off someone: look like someone.

Burdizzo: castration device.

camogie: the female version of Hurling.

chancer: an opportunist.

Child of Prague: a religious statue farmers place out in a field to encourage good weather (an old Irish superstition).

chipper: a restaurant that sells fast food.

Clonamore: town next to Ballylaggin.

come here till I kill ya: come here and let me hit you.

cooker: oven/Stove/Hob.

cop on: behave yourself.

corker: beautiful woman.

couldn't get his hole in a polo factory: unlucky in love.

cracking: brilliant.

crack on: do something/get going.

craic: fun.

the craic was ninety: Having a lot of fun and banter.

Culchie: a person from the countryside or a county outside of Dublin. Usually used as a friendly insult.

cute hoor: a clever/slick person.

daft: silly.

daft as a brush: very silly.

deadly: great.

dicky day: children's allowance day.

did you fla her last night: did you sleep with her.

doing a foxer: working for cash in hand.

doing a line: dating.

dolled up to the nines: dressed up and looking good.

don't be scabby: don't be mean.

don't piss down my back and tell me it's raining: don't lie to me.

dosser: someone not doing what they should be doing.

drive on: keep going.

Dub: a person from Dublin.

eejit: fool/idiot.

'een': added to the end of your name, usually by older relatives, ie; Johneen, Jackeen, Juleen, Mikeen, Tadhgeen.

era/yerra: dismissing something.

Fair City: popular Irish television soap.

fair fucks to ya: well done.

fair play: nice one.

fanny: vagina.

the fear: waking up with a hangover

feeking: having sex.

feeling raw: feeling poorly.

feis: a tradition Gaelic arts and culture festival/event.

fla: an attractive person.

fortnight: two weeks.

frigit: someone who has never been kissed.

funt up the hole: kick up the ass.

GAA: Gaelic Athletic Association.

gaff: house.

Gardaí Síochána: Irish police force.

Garda: policeman.

gas: funny.

gas man: funny man.

gatting: drinking.

getting the ride: having sex.

get your hole: have sex.

give us a sconce: let me see it.

the goolies: the testicles.

geebag: derogatory word for a woman.

giving out: scolding/complaining.

gobshite: fool/idiot.

godloon sham: good lord man.

going halves on a bastard: Having unprotected sex.

gowel: stupid person.

grinds: Tutoring.

hatchet craic: Great fun.

haunted: lucky.

haven't seen ya in yonks/donkeys years: I haven't seen you in a long time.

he didn't lick it off a stone: he's like his family.

he got a ration of passion last night: didn't go all the way.

he slipped her the mickey last night: he had sex with her last night.

he thinks he's the dogs bollocks: he loves himself.

he'd drink it out of a wellington boot: an alcoholic.

he'd drink the cross off a donkey: a heavy drinker.

he'd rob the eye out of your head and piss in the hole: don't trust him.

he's A1: he's a lovely person.

he hasn't hands to bless himself: he's clumsy.

he's some me feiner: he's self-absorbed.

hole: often said instead of ass/bottom.

houl your whisht: stop talking.

how bad: that's good.

how's a bit of your father: let's have sex.

how's your belly for a lodger: having unprotected sex.

hup out dat: good job, keep going.

hurling: a hugely popular, amateur Irish sport played with wooden hurleys and sliotars.

hurry up, will ya? my nan's faster than ya and she's ten years dead: speed up.

I hope you die roaring: I don't like you.

I was christened, not pissed on: call me by my name.

I will in my hole, Jack Shea: I absolutely will not.

I will yeah: I absolutely won't.

I wouldn't kick him out of bed for eating a bag of crisps: he's attractive.

I wouldn't give ya the steam off my piss: I don't like you.

I wouldn't get up on him to get over a wall: an unattractive man.

I wouldn't ride ya into battle: I don't find you attractive.

I'd rather shit in my hands and clap: I'm not doing it.

I'll lamp him: I'll hit him.

I'll leave your face like a painter's radio: fellatio.

I'll let you go: I'm finished talking to you.

I'll redden your hole for ya: I will slap you.

I'm scarlet for ya: I'm embarrassed for you.

I've a crow to pluck with ya: you're in trouble with me.

if he fell into a barrel of tits, he'd come out sucking his thumb: he's unlucky

if I'd a garden full of mickeys, I wouldn't let her look over the wall: I'm not attracted to her.

if there was work in the bed, he'd sleep on the floor: lazy person.

if wit was shit you'd be constipated: you're not funny.

if you fall off that wall and break your legs, don't come running to me: a mother's warning not to do something stupid.

Jackeen: a person from Dublin. A term sometimes used by people from other counties in Ireland to refer to a person from Dublin.

the jacks: the bathroom.

jagging: hooking up but not yet in a committed relationship.

jammy: lucky.

jammiest: luckiest.

jocks: men's boxer shorts.

jointed: a crowded place.

junior cert: the compulsory state exam you take in third year—midway through your six-year cycle of secondary school.

jumper: sweater.

kip: messy place.

kit off/tog off: change into or out of training clothes.

knickers: women's underwear.

langer: idiot.

langers: group of idiots and/or to be extremely drunk.

laying pipe: having sex.

leaving cert: the compulsory state exam you take in your final year of secondary school.

leg it: run.

liathroidi: testicles.

lifted: arrested.

like shit out of a goose: moving fast.

living over the brush: living together but not married.

lurching: wrapped around someone at the disco.

mank/manky: something disgusting.

massive: beautiful

meeting: kissing.

messages: groceries.

mickey ring: condom

mickey/willy: penis.

mind the pennies and the pounds will mind themselves: save your money.

minerals/fizzy drinks: soft drinks

mog: an ugly person/stupid person.

mope: idiot.

nearly never bulled a cow: nearly doesn't cut it.

not a hope: I'm not doing that.

now you're taking the hand: asking for too much.

odd with someone: being annoyed.

off your rocker: crazy person.

old doll/aul doll: wife/girlfriend.

on the hop: skipping school.

on the lash: on a night out drinking.

on the piss: going out drinking.

poitín: Irish version of moonshine/illegal, home-brewed alcohol.

pound shop: dollar store.

poxy: lucky.

press: cabinet.

primary school: elementary school—junior infants to sixth class.

    playschool: pre-school/nursery.

    junior infants: equivalent to kindergarten.

    senior infants: equivalent to second year of kindergarten.

    first class: equivalent to first grade.

    second class: equivalent to second grade.

    third class: equivalent to third grade.

    fourth class: equivalent to fourth grade.

    fifth class: equivalent to fifth grade.

    sixth class: equivalent to sixth grade.

puking your ring out: vomiting.

pure: very.

pure daycent: excellent.

pure scanty: extremely mean.

rank: not good.

raw baby: a brand-new baby.

Rebel County: nickname for County Cork.

relax. Johnny's got ya covered: condom.

ridey: a good-looking person.

Rolos: popular brand of chocolate.

rosary, removal, burial: the three days of a Catholic funeral in Ireland.

runners: trainers/sneakers.

Sacred Heart: the name of Shannon, Joey, Darren, Claire, Caoimhe, Lizzie, Tadhg, Ollie, Podge, and Alec's mixed primary school.

same mare, different jockey: same mother, different fathers.

sap: sad/pathetic.

scaldy: something disgusting.

scanty: doing something mean.

Scoil Eoin: the name of Johnny, Gibsie, Feely, Hughie, and Kevin's all-boys primary school.

scoring: kissing.

scut: rascal.

secondary school: high school—first year to sixth year.

    first year: equivalent to seventh grade.

    second year: equivalent to eighth grade.

    third year: equivalent to ninth grade.

    fourth year: transition year, equivalent to tenth grade.

    fifth year: equivalent to eleventh grade.

    sixth year: equivalent to twelfth grade.

septic: someone horrible/vain.

sesh: drinking session in a bar/house party with music.

shades: police.

she'd get up on a gust of wind: a promiscuous woman.

she didn't get those knees from saying prayers: promiscuous woman.

she'd rip up the floorboards to get a bit of pipe: a promiscuous woman.

she'd talk the hind legs off a donkey: a chatterbox.

she had a face like a jockey's bollocks, but you don't look at the mantelpiece when you're poking the fire: she was unattractive, but I still went for it.

shift/shifting: kissing.

shifting jackets: lucky piece of clothing, usually a jacket, when trying to pick up a girl.

shook: feeling sick/hungover.

shook like a hand at mass: trembling.

skip the fancy stuff and horse it into me: skip foreplay and have sex.

skitting: laughing.

solicitor: lawyer.

sound: another way to say cheers/a decent person.

spanner: idiot.

spuds: potatoes.

stall the ball: hold on.

stick your mickey in your ear and shag some sense into yourself: cop on.

stop crying or I'll give ya something to cry about: a mother's warning.

strop: mood-swing/pouting/sulking.

St. Bernadette's: the name of Aoife, Casey, and Katie's all-girls primary school.

St. Stephen's Day: Boxing Day/December 26th.

swot: nerd/academically gifted.

take a gander: take a look/walk.

that's mint: that's cool.

that's the berries: that's great.

there's fierce taspy on that fella: that boy is a rascal.

the tide wouldn't take her out: an ugly person.

turn on the heating: turn on the central heating in the house.

up the pole/poled: pregnant.

wedding tackle: penis.

well, fuck me sideways: I'm shocked.

wellies: rubber boots worn in the rain.

what's on the menu? breakfast, lunch, and dinner: cunnilingus.

wheelie bin: trash can.

where ya born in a field: close the door.

whisht: be quiet.

will you go away with him: will you kiss him.

will you meet my friend: will you kiss my friend.

will you shift her: will you kiss her.

wise up: behave yourself

with his lad out: with his penis on display.

yer: your.

yer wan would get up on a razor blade: a promiscuous woman.

yoke: thing.

yolk: nickname for an illegal drug.

you big, feckless eejit: you are stupid.

you made a balls of it: you messed it up.

you make a good door but a bad window: get out of my way.

you put the heart crossways in me: you scared me.

you're about as useful as tits on a bull: calling someone useless.

you're as tight as a duck's hole: you're stingy.

your wan: that woman.

strop: mood-swing\pouting\sulking.

St. Bernadette: the name of Aoife, Casey, and Katie's all-girls primary school.

St Stephen's Day: Boxing Day, December 26th.

swot: nerd\academically gifted.

take a gander: take a look\walk.

that's mint: that's cool.

that's the berries: that's great.

there's fierce taspy on that fella: that boy is a rascal

the tide wouldn't take her out: an ugly person.

turn on the heating: turn on the central heating in the house.

up the pole\poled: pregnant.

wedding tackle: penis.

well, fuck me sideways: I'm shocked.

wellies: rubber boots worn in the rain.

what's on the menu: breakfast, lunch, and dinner combined.

wheelie bin: trash can.

where ya born in a field: close the door.

whisht: be quiet.

will you go away with him: will you kiss him.

will you meet my friend: will you kiss my friend.

will you shift her: will you kiss her.

wise up: behave yourself.

with his lad out: with his penis on display.

yer man

yes ya would get up on a razor blade: a promiscuous woman.

yoke: thing.

yolk: nickname for an illegal drug.

you big, feckless eejit: you are stupid.

you made a balls of it: you messed it up.

you make a good door but a bad window: get out of my way.

you put the heart crossways in me: you scared me.

you're about as useful as tits on a bull: calling someone useless

you're as tight as a duck's hole: you're stingy

your wan: that woman.

PART 1

The Formative Years

JUNE 12, 1991

Lizzie

"WHAT'S WRONG WITH HER?"

"Nothing." Mammy continued to cradle me to her chest. "She's perfect."

"Why isn't she talking by now?" Caoimhe didn't look happy. She didn't sound happy either. "Lizzie is three, Mam. Three. And she's not doing anything she's supposed to be doing."

"She's fine, Caoimhe," Mammy said, using an extra happy voice. "She'll catch up." She kissed my cheek, and I burrowed in close to her chest. I loved her smell and the way she held me tight. I liked to press my ear against her chest and listen to her heart thump.

Thump, thump, thump.

I smiled and touched her face. She had the best face. She had kind eyes. They were blue, just like mine. I knew the color. I knew all the colors and wanted to tell my sister that. I just…couldn't get the words to come out.

My voice wouldn't work.

"Do you think she's slow?" Caoimhe asked, sounding sad, and I wanted to make her feel better because I wasn't slow at running. I was super fast. "Does she need, like, a special school or something?"

"This is not a conversation for little ears." Mammy's voice was cross now, and I didn't like it. Burrowing in deeper, I hid my face in her cardigan. "So please, just go and do your homework. We can talk about this tonight when your father gets home."

"I want to go home."

"We are home, Caoimhe."

"No, I want to go back to our real home," she shouted. "I hate it in England, Mam. I don't have any friends, and everyone at school teases me for the way I talk."

"They're idiots," Mammy told her. "Ignore them."

"That's easy for you to say," my sister said before turning to me. "You ruined every-thing," she screamed. "I wish you were never born."

"Caoimhe!"

"I'm not sorry, Mam, because it's true!"

"Look at me, pretty girl," Mammy said after my sister had stomped out of the room. "Show me those big, blue eyes."

I did.

"There you are." Smiling warmly, she brushed my hair off my face. "You are perfect, do you hear me?"

I nodded.

"You are my baby, and I will always look after you." She tickled under my chin and smiled. "And you must never let anyone make you feel like there is something wrong with you." She tickled my chin again. "Do you understand me, Lizzie?"

I nodded again.

"Good." She smiled again. "I love you, sweetheart."

OCTOBER 31, 1991

"BE NORMAL WHEN MY FRIENDS COME OVER," CAOIMHE SAID. "DON'T DO ANYTHING embarrassing, okay?" She turned around to look at me. "No screaming fits or throwing yourself around on the floor."

I nodded in understanding.

"God." She shook her head. "I wish you would just speak, Lizzie!"

I shrugged.

"How am I supposed to know you even understand me if you won't *talk*?"

I didn't like it when I made her mad.

It made me feel bad.

It made my face grow hot.

It made my nails get scratchy.

"No," Caoimhe warned, attention moving to my scratchy nails. She stood up from her dressing table and walked over to the bed. "You are not allowed to do that." Crouching down in front of me, she took my hands in hers and looked in my eyes. "You are *not* allowed to hurt yourself."

I'm sorry, I wanted to tell her. *I don't know how to make it stop.*

Instead, I reached up and touched her cheek.

Her blue eyes started to water. "Please talk to me." Sniffling, she swept me up in her arms and held me to her chest. "Please, Liz, just one word. I'm begging you."

I'm trying.

NOVEMBER 12, 1991

Lizzie

"CONSIDERING HER FREQUENT VIOLENT OUTBURSTS AT NURSERY AND TAKING INTO account the strong family history, I would like to start Elizabeth on a treatment plan."

"When you say treatment, are you talking about counseling?"

"And medication."

"She's three and a half," Mammy strangled out. "All three-year-olds throw tantrums for Christ's sake."

"Those aren't tantrums, Catherine, and you know it," Daddy replied. "Give it to us straight, Doc. What's the diagnosis?"

"It's too early to tell."

"But you have a theory, don't you?" he pushed. "You think she has it, doesn't she?"

"Not necessarily, but there is evidence to suggest Elizabeth is experiencing psychotic episodes. What concerns me is her lack of awareness and the frequent blackout episodes." He twisted a pen between his fingers. "She appears to have no memory of what she does."

"You don't know that," Mammy snapped, smoothing my hair with her hand. "You won't know that until she starts talking."

DECEMBER 21, 1991

Lizzie

"THIS IS AN AIRPLANE," MAMMY EXPLAINED, WAVING HER HAND AROUND IN FRONT of us. "It's going to fly us home to Ireland."

I narrowed my eyes.

I *knew* what an airplane was.

"Don't look at me like that," she laughed. "How am I supposed to know you know these things."

I gave her another look, telling her with my eyes that I wasn't stupid.

"Okay, okay," she chuckled, holding her hands up. "I'm sorry for doubting you, sweetheart."

I smiled.

"Oh, you like surprising me, don't you?"

I grinned.

"Clever girl," she praised, hooking her arm around my shoulders. "You're as sharp as a razor in there, aren't you?"

Nodding, I looked over to where Daddy was sitting with Caoimhe and frowned.

I knew they were cross with me.

I just didn't know why.

"Don't worry," she whispered, tightening her arm around me. "They love you, too, sweetheart. Just like Mammy loves you."

JANUARY 6, 1992

Lizzie

"No," Caoimhe argued. "No way. I'm not moving schools again."

"Caoimhe, love, we've talked about this. Please try to understand."

"I'm not fucking moving again," she screamed. "I have friends at St. Joseph's, and you promised I could go back to my old school when we came home." She shook her head and backed toward the door. "You promised, Mam!"

"We tried, Caoimhe," Mammy told her, looking sad. "But the principal said it's not possible to re-enroll you. They don't have the space, love."

"It's not fair," my sister cried, sobbing loudly. "My life is fucking over!"

"Don't say that," Mammy said, trying to coax. "You'll be just as happy over at St. Theresa's."

"But it's an all-girls school," Caoimhe cried. "Run by the nuns."

"It's only for a year and a half, and then you'll go off to secondary school and meet up with all your old friends."

"I fucking hate you!" Caoimhe cried. I was still sitting on the step when she barged past me. "Get out of the way," she screamed, shoving me with her foot. "You're always in the fucking way, Lizzie!"

"Caoimhe!" Mam shouted, following after her. "Don't you dare take it out on your sister!"

I wanted to tell her I was sorry, but I couldn't get the words out.

"It's not your fault, Lizzie." Mammy smiled and crouched down in front of me. "You haven't done anything."

I reached up and cupped her cheek in my small hand.

Sniffling, she closed her eyes and covered my hand with hers. "I'm not crying, sweetheart," she said, answering the question in my head.

She was.

I could feel the wet on my hand.

"Be a good girl and go on up to bed now." When she opened her eyes, she was smiling a big smile. "And remember that Mammy loves you very much."

I love you, too, Mammy.

FEBRUARY 10, 1992

Lizzie

"WHAT IS WRONG WITH THAT CHILD!"

"Mike, she doesn't understand."

"She's disturbed, Catherine. A blind man can see that."

"How can you say that about your own flesh and blood?"

"I can't take it, Catherine. I'm sorry."

"You're a fucking coward, that's why."

"It's killing me to watch her like this."

"And you don't think it's killing me, Mike? The difference is I would never leave her."

"I'm not leaving her, but I have to get out of this house or I'm going to lose my mind right along with her."

"Some father you are, turning your back the minute things get tough."

"Catherine."

"Go on, then! Run away, Mike. We'll be better off alone than with a spineless coward."

JUNE 9, 1992

Lizzie

"HAPPY BIRTHDAY TO YOU, HAPPY BIRTHDAY TO YOU, HAPPY BIRTHDAY TO LIZZIE, happy birthday to you."

My parents and Caoimhe all huddled around me, smiling and singing birthday songs.

It made me feel happy.

I liked it.

Daddy was even smiling as he took pictures on his camera.

"Blow out your candles," Mammy said, pointing to the pink birthday cake in front of me. "And make a wish, sweetheart."

Leaning forward, I took a big breath and blew it out as hard as I could.

When the flames on the candles went out, they all cheered.

For me.

I smiled happily.

"Does she even know it's her birthday?" Caoimhe asked then, and it made me cross. Of course I did. I had a birthday cake, didn't I? She laughed before adding, "She probably doesn't even know what age she's turning."

Planting my hands on my hips, I turned to my sister and glared. "Four."

Caoimhe's eyes widened in surprise. "What did you just say?"

"Four," I repeated, still cross with her. "I'm not silly." I pointed to the candles on my cake. "One, two, three, four."

Now, Mammy and Daddy were looking at me with big, wide eyes.

"Did she just…"

"Yes, she definitely did."

"Oh my God."

"She can talk."

"Never mind talking. She can count."

"Say something else," Caoimhe commanded, sounding excited. "Come on, Liz, tell us something else."

I frowned at her. "Like what?"

"Oh my God!" Caoimhe squealed, jumping from foot to foot as she clapped her hands. "She actually answered me!"

I always answered her, but she just couldn't hear me.

None of them could.

"Am I talking out loud?" I asked, confused. "You can hear me?"

All three of them nodded.

They looked so happy.

They were smiling at me.

"What's my name?" my sister asked, still bouncing.

"Caoimhe Young."

"Oh my God," she cried out, clapping her hands again. "What's your name?"

"Lizzie Young."

My sister yelped excitedly before pointing at our parents. "And who are they?"

"Mammy and Daddy," I replied, frowning when I saw they were both crying. "Are you sad?"

"No," Daddy choked out, throwing his arms around me. "We're happy."

OCTOBER 11, 1992

"She ruined my life!" Caoimhe screamed. "I can never show my face at school again."

"Caoimhe!"

"Everyone is talking about me."

"No, they're not."

"Yeah, they are, Mam, and it's all her fault."

"Caoimhe, please."

"I'm not going to school tomorrow if she's there."

"You're in sixth class, Caoimhe. Your sister is in junior infants. You're on opposite sides of the school."

"I don't care! I'm not going if she's there."

"Oh yes you are."

"She shouldn't even be at my school because there's something fucked-up wrong with her!" Throwing her schoolbag on the floor, she turned to glare at me. "Why did you have to come to my school?" Releasing a furious scream, she looked at our parents. "Why couldn't you have sent her somewhere else?"

"Caoimhe, you need to settle down," Mam said, moving to stand between us. "She's only four, sweetheart, and she's come leaps and bounds this year. Don't be angry with her."

"Angry with her?" Caoimhe's eyes bulged. "I fucking hate her, Mam!"

"Caoimhe!"

"She's a fucking lunatic, Mam."

"Don't you dare call your sister that word."

"Why not? It's the truth. Half the time she's a mute, and the other half, she's screaming her head off and attacking anyone who gets near her." My sister threw her hands up and screamed. "She attacked another child in her classroom, for fuck's sake. My friend's baby brother! She drew blood. You can't honestly think that's normal behavior."

"That's enough!" That was Daddy. He walked over and wrapped his arm around Mammy's shoulder. "Don't raise your voice to your mother. You know she's not well."

"Yeah, from another plague she brought into our lives," Caoimhe spat. "First Lizzie and now cancer!"

"Don't you dare say that about your mother!" Daddy roared. He led Mammy over to her armchair and helped her sit down before turning back to Caoimhe.

Meanwhile, I made a beeline for my mother, feeling scared and cross and worried all at once. Climbing onto her lap, I burrowed into her chest, but it felt different now. Flat and bony. Not soft like it used to be.

"It's okay," Mammy whispered, wrapping her arms around me. Her skin looked yellow now, not peach like it used to, and her head was shiny and bald.

"Now, I've been cutting you slack because I understand how hard the past couple of years have been on you, but you've overstepped your mark, young lady," Daddy told Caoimhe. "I understand your frustrations, and I feel for you, but taking it out on your sick mother is not the way to handle this, Caoimhe."

Breaking down in front of him, my sister covered her face with her hands and screamed, "I wish I was dead!"

NOVEMBER 4, 1992

Lizzie

"LIZZIE, SWEETHEART, ARE YOU UP?" MAMMY WALKED INTO MY ROOM AND SIGHED when she saw me still in bed. "We talked about this." Closing the space between us, she sat on the edge of my bed and gently stroked my hair. "You have to get up for school, baby."

"I'm so tired," I croaked out, feeling like my arms and legs didn't work anymore.

"That's because your body is getting used to the new medication," Mammy explained. "You'll feel better soon."

"I don't want to be me anymore."

"Why would you say that?"

"Because I'm bad."

"You're not bad, sweetheart."

"Yes, I am." I blinked back the tears filling my eyes. "That's why you give me those tablets. I heard Caoimhe and Daddy talking about it. It's because I'm crazy."

"No, Lizzie, no." Mam cupped my face in her hands. "You are not crazy, sweetheart. Do you hear me? You are perfect just the way you are."

"Then why do they hate me?" I sobbed, turning my face away. "Why does everyone look at me funny?"

"They don't hate you, sweetheart, and nobody looks at you funny."

"They do." I sniffled. "I know."

NOVEMBER 27, 1992

Lizzie

CURLING UP IN A BALL ON THE COUCH IN THE SITTING ROOM, I COVERED MY EARS AND tried to block out the shouting, but I could still hear them.

"It's for the best, Catherine," Daddy shouted from the kitchen. "Trust me, I've been through this before."

"I don't care," Mam argued back. "I am not medicating that child another day."

"She needs the medication."

"She needs a childhood!" Mam cried. "She's our baby, our child, and I refuse to continue this farce."

"You want to talk about farces, Catherine? Really?"

"She is not taking another pill. Do you hear me? It stops right now."

"And when she acts out again? What then?"

"We'll handle it."

"I won't move Caoimhe again," he warned. "It's not fair on our other daughter. You do remember her, don't you?"

"That's not fair, and you know it."

"No, what's not fair is living my whole life the way I have and having to repeat the cycle all over again."

"What were we supposed to do?"

"Well, I know what you should have done!" he roared. "You should have fucking—"

"Oh my God, stop! I can hear you from upstairs." That was Caoimhe. "What's wrong?"

"Your mother thinks it's a good idea to take your sister off her meds."

"Are you insane?" That was Caoimhe. "Mam, she has to take them."

"Don't start."

"She is an actual human when she's on them, Mam. Take her off them and she'll go right back to being a feral monster."

"Caoimhe!"

"I'm sorry, but it's true. Dad's right. She needs to be on those tablets. The doctors said it themselves. Multiple doctors, Mam. Multiple times."

"Maybe we're not looking at this the right way," Dad added. "Maybe a residential school would be her best fit."

"I am not sending her away."

"Not permanently."

"No way. It's not happening!"

Scrambling to my feet, I bolted upstairs to my bedroom as fast as I could. I quietly closed the door and sank down on the floor, hand still gripping the circular knob.

I had to make my family love me.

If I didn't, they were going to send me away.

"*Stop fighting it,*" a voice in my head commanded, and I flinched when the watery image of a woman's face flashed before my eyes. "*Just give in. It'll all be better then.*"

Oh no.

The voice was back.

The scary voice.

The one that made me wet the bed.

The one that made me fight.

Clamping my hands over my ears, I hummed loudly to drown it out.

I had to make the voice go away.

DECEMBER 25, 1992

Lizzie

"*I KNEW COMING HOME WAS A BAD IDEA, MIKE. I BLOODY KNEW WE WERE ASKING FOR trouble, and I was right!*"

"*Calm down, Catherine. You can't let yourself get worked up like this. You're in the middle of chemo, love. You need to take it easy.*"

"*How in the name of God am I supposed to calm down when that woman was in my house? I can't breathe thinking about what could've happened today, Mike!*"

Flushing the toilet, I climbed onto the booster step placed in front of the sink, the one that helped me reach the tap, and reached for the orange bar of soap.

"*I tried to warn you in England, but you wouldn't listen. You were hell-bent on doing things your way when I fucking begged you not to. Now, you're getting a small glimpse into what life was like for me, what life is going to be for us.*"

"*Don't think like that!*"

"*I can't help it. I can see it coming down the tracks like a freight train, and we're stuck.*"

"*It's a small chance, Michael, not a guarantee. So don't you dare throw it back in my face. How dare you resent me for doing the right thing!*"

"*The right thing for who?*"

"*For our family!*"

"*Maybe for you, but it was never the right thing for me.*"

"*How can you stand there and say that to me?*"

"*Because that's how I feel, Catherine. That's my truth. I didn't get to have a say in any of this because you took my choices away from me!*"

I turned on the water and giggled when the soap squished between my hands, like a slippery fish.

"*We have to move, Michael. We can't stay here anymore. She's too dangerous.*"

"*I'm not moving again. This is my family home, Catherine. The house my parents raised me in. This is where I belong.*"

"*Well, I'm going back to Cork to my family home—where I belong, where that monster can't find us!*"

"Back to the back-ass of nowhere in Ballylaggin? And where do you expect me to work? Or do you expect me to pack up my family farm and take it with me?"

"You know I have money, Michael. That's never been something we've had to worry about. For Christ's sake, our children's children won't even have to worry. My father saw to that when he left me the family estate in his will."

"I'm not living off your family's generational fucking wealth, Catherine."

"But it's perfectly fine for us to live off the farm you inherited from your father?"

"Have you considered Caoimhe's schooling? She's halfway through sixth class and has switched primary schools three bloody times already, and that's not even considering what another move will do to Elizabeth. You heard what her teacher said. She's barely managing junior infants as it stands, and she has the other children terrified from her outbursts."

"It's called trauma, Michael, and you of all the people in the world should understand how she feels."

"Don't go there..."

"She's an extremely bright girl, and you'd know that if you paid her a minute of your time. Do you remember even one of the many positive things our daughter's teacher had to say about her? No, of course you don't, because you only hear the negative when it comes to Lizzie."

"Can you blame me?"

"How dare you! There is nothing wrong with our daughter, but there is something very wrong with her father. What a coward you are, letting your fear blind you from loving our little girl."

"That's rich coming from the woman who hasn't walked in my shoes."

"In case you've forgotten, I'm the one looking after Lizzie. I'm the one taking her to every appointment, not you."

"I've paid every doctor you've taken her to, haven't I?"

"And I've already told you that I have more than enough money to pay for them. There's more to being a father than writing checks."

Humming under my breath, I wrestled with the soap, trying to squish it between my hands. My eyes looked at me from the mirror and I frowned. I didn't like to look at my eyes for too long. They scared me when they changed colors. They talked to me when they got dark. Inside my head. Whispers, whispers, whispers.

"And were you planning on leaving your cancer behind ya when you up and run again? Hmm? Because you're halfway through your third round of chemo and in no fit state to leave the house, let alone the county!"

"They have hospitals in Cork, too, you know, and at least that horrible creature won't find us in my hometown."

"I'm not moving again, Catherine. I refuse to."

"Fine, if you want to be stubborn and stay here to tend your farm, then go right ahead. But I'm going home, where it's safe, and I'm taking our girls with me."

"Look, can we just talk about this calmly before jumping the gun?"

"What's to talk about? That monster found us, she took my child, and I'm leaving before she can do it again."

"Yes, but she didn't hurt her. She took her for a couple of hours and brought her back."

"Without telling her mother she was taking her! Jesus Christ, Michael, the girls don't even know the woman. Don't you understand how dangerous this was? Anything could have happened to Lizzie!"

"Liz?" Caoimhe poked her head around the bathroom door and smiled. "There you are."

I frowned when I saw her. She never smiled at me. She was always cross with me.

"Nothing happened. She brought her back without a mark on her."

Caoimhe's smile turned into a sad one. "Come on." She held her hand out for me. "Come with me."

"Why?" I asked, feeling confused.

"This time. What happens next time? What if she takes a turn and decides to…"

"Because I want to play with you," she said, giving me a big smile. "Hurry up."

Excited now, I tossed the slippery soap into the sink and turned off the tap before jumping down. Drying my hands on my pajamas, I followed my sister across the landing and into her room.

Caoimhe was almost twelve, which meant she had a big bed like our parents. I was four and still had to sleep in a small bed, but I didn't mind because I still got to sleep with all my teddies.

"Are you okay?" she asked, waiting for me to come inside before closing the door behind us. "You weren't listening to that, were you?"

"Mammy's cross," I replied, making a beeline for her giant bed. Caoimhe never let me go into her room anymore, not since I started junior infants and she was always cross with me, so I was excited to be here now. "Daddy's cross, too."

"Yeah, I know." She walked over to her boom box and switched it on. When the familiar song drifted from the speakers, I smiled.

"This one's my favorite," I told her, sitting cross-legged in the middle of her bed. Before I started big school, she used to let me hang out with her all the time. That's how I knew about all the pop stars and singers.

"I know." She looked over her shoulder and smiled at me. "You remember the name of the band, don't you?" Her tone was teasing now. "You better not have forgotten the name of the best band in the world."

"Fleetwood Mac," I said proudly before pointing at the stereo. "And that's their album called *Rumours*." She played it all the time and I knew the words of the songs better than the prayers I learned at school.

"Excellent," she praised, turning up the volume when the shouting from downstairs got louder. "And who is our witchy queen?"

"Stevie."

"And our guitar king?"

"Lindsey."

Caoimhe's smile grew bigger. "And what's my favorite song?"

"'Landslide.'"

"And Mam's?"

"'The Chain.'"

"And what's yours?"

"'Silver Springs.'"

"And who else do we love?" My sister pointed to the T-shirt she was wearing, the one with the smiley face on it. She was wearing a pair of baggy jeans with holes in the knees, too, and her wrists were covered with bangles and bracelets. She also had a silver, moon-shaped necklace pendant around her neck, and I wanted to look just like her when I was bigger. "I'll give you a hint," Caoimhe said, still pointing to her shirt. "It starts with Nir..."

"Nirvana!" I filled in, feeling excited because she looked so happy with me. I liked it when people were happy with me. It made me feel warm in my belly, not like the burning-hot feeling when I made them sad. Like Daddy. He was always sad when he looked at me, and that didn't feel good. Not good at all.

"Am I bad, Caoimhe?"

"What?" My sister's brows scrunched together, and she gave me a funny look. "Where did you hear that?"

I shrugged. "Don't know."

"No, Liz." Caoimhe heaved out a big breath and climbed onto the bed with me. "You're not bad." Her hands were warm when they pulled me onto her lap, but her voice was sad. It made the burning feeling grow. The one that made me want to scream. The one that made me want to scratch my skin. "You're just complicated."

"How come you don't want me in your school?" I turned in her lap to look at her. "Do you hate me?"

"No," she whispered, sounding super sad. "I just get frustrated, that's all."

"Because of me?"

She nodded.

"I'm sorry."

"No, Liz, I'm sorry." Her arms tightened around me, making me feel warm and happy. Making the burning, itchy pressure in my throat go away. "I need to have more patience with you."

"Does Daddy hate me?"

"No." She pulled me closer. "He's just worried because of Grandad and Nell."

"Who's Nell?"

"Remember that weirdo who showed up to dinner today with the Christmas presents?" Settling me between her legs, she freed my hair from my ponytail. "The one Mam got upset with for taking you to the river?"

I thought about the lady that came to our house today and smiled. "We fed the ducks."

"That's Dad's sister." She continued to brush my hair out with her fingers. "Nell."

"I didn't know Daddy had a sister," I replied. "She never came here before."

"That's because his sister is a rip-roaring lunatic," Caoimhe explained, braiding my hair. "Just like her dad was before he died."

"Her dad?"

"Grandad Young."

"What's a lunatic?"

"Someone who's crazy and hears voices." Caoimhe sighed. "That's why Grandad drowned in the river when Dad was a kid. The voices told him to jump in."

"But I hear voices." My eyes widened. "I can hear your voice right now."

"Not real voices," Caoimhe chuckled, still working on my hair. "Pretend voices." She poked my temple with her finger. "Inside your head."

"But the lady wasn't rip-roaring at me," I replied, scrunching my brows up. "She wasn't talking to any voices when we were feeding the ducks."

"Probably because she was too busy thinking about a way to feed *you* to the ducks," she replied, sounding worried now. "You're lucky she didn't throw you in."

"But I can't swim yet."

"I know." Her voice was sad again. "That's why Mam is so upset. She thought you weren't coming back today."

"Because the lady took me to feed the ducks?"

"Because she took you to the river." Caoimhe shivered. "You must never be alone with her."

"Never?"

"Never ever, and if she ever comes back and tries to take you away, then you have to run, Liz."

"Run?"

"Run." Finishing with my braid, she turned me around to face her. "As fast as you can."

"How did the voices get into Grandad and the lady?" I asked, shuffling closer to my sister.

"I don't know." She shrugged. "I think they were just born with it."

"Can they get better?" Nestling into her chest, I reached up and touched her cheek; my favorite way to snuggle. "Can the doctors take the voices away?"

"Well, Grandad's up in heaven with holy God now, so he's not suffering anymore."

"Suffering?"

"I mean the voices are gone and he's all better."

"Holy God fixed Grandad?"

"Yep," she replied. "Because when you go to heaven, all of your pain goes away."

I smiled to myself.

That was a nice thought.

"Does Daddy hear the voices, too? Is that why he gets so cross with me?"

"No, Dad's fine." She sighed heavily. "And he's not cross with you, I promise. He's paranoid of history repeating itself. He's just scared, that's all."

"Of me?"

"No, Liz, he's not scared of you. Dad's just… It's really complicated, and you're too little to understand any of this." Sighing heavily, she stroked my cheek with her thumb and smiled again, but this time she looked even sadder. "When you're a grown-up, I'll explain everything to you."

"But I want to know now."

"Trust me, you don't."

"But you're not a grown-up," I pointed out. "So how come you get to know?"

"Because I learned about it the hard way." She sounded sad again. "I wish I didn't have to know any of this crap."

"What about the lady?" I asked then. "Does she want to go to heaven so holy God can make the voices go away? Like her daddy?"

"No, because when Nell was in the hospital, the doctors found a way to keep the voices out."

"How?"

"By giving her special medicine."

"So she's better?"

"No, Liz, she's not," Caoimhe muttered. "Because she doesn't take it."

I thought about the medicine in the bathroom cabinet, the bottle with the name

22

Elizabeth Young on it, and how Mammy took one out every day and gave it to me. "Am I sick like the lady?" The hot feeling grew inside of me, gobbling up the earlier excitement. "There's something wrong with me, isn't there?"

I knew there was.

I heard the voices, too.

They whispered in my ear when I was alone in my bed at night.

"No." Caoimhe's voice was hard now. She sounded cross. Like Daddy. "Those tablets are for growing pains, silly."

"No." I shook my head. I knew what the growing pains tablets looked like. "The growing pains tablets are pink."

My sister was lying.

I didn't like it.

It made me feel dizzy.

"Liz."

"I hear them, too, Caoimhe." I sprang up to look at her, feeling itchy all over. "I see things, too. When I'm sleeping. The monster comes to take me. It keeps pushing me down with its sharp nails—"

"Lizzie, you need to stop talking," she warned, covering my mouth with her hand. "Don't ever say that out loud again." She looked down at me with angry eyes. "You are *fine*. There is *nothing* wrong with you. You don't hear voices. You aren't sick. It skipped over you, just like it skipped over me and Dad. You're just a regular kid, and all these weird, little quirks will fade away."

I shook my head, feeling confused and hot all over.

My skin was itching.

My fingers were scratchy.

I could feel the hot screams in my throat.

"There is *nothing* wrong with you," my sister repeated, keeping her hand over my mouth to stop me from screaming. "So you better start acting like it or you'll end up where *she* did."

DECEMBER 31, 1992

Lizzie

"ARE WE THERE YET?" I ASKED FROM THE BACK SEAT OF DADDY'S CAR. STRAINING MY neck, I tried to look over the boxes that were piled around us, but I couldn't see my parents.

"If you ask that question one more time, I'm going to open your door and throw you out," my sister grumbled, elbowing my side. The car was so packed with boxes that we had to sit right next to each other. Caoimhe was wedged so close to me that her elbow was resting on top of mine. "I think I preferred it when you were a mute."

"Caoimhe!" Mam and Dad both scolded from the front seat.

She elbowed me again before switching on her Walkman and resting her arm on top of mine. She turned the volume up so loud that I could hear the song "Do They Know It's Christmas?" blasting from her headphones.

Narrowing my eyes, I elbowed her back and rested my arm on top of hers before turning my attention to the window.

"It's snowing," I cried out excitedly, eyes glued to the white snowflakes falling around us. "Are we there yet?"

"Give me strength," Dad muttered under his breath, while Mam laughed softly.

"Do you see that signpost, sweetheart? Look out the window."

I searched until my eyes landed on a huge signpost on the side of the road.

Ballylaggin

County Cork

"I see it," I exclaimed, bouncing on my seat. "Is this it? Are we here?"

"Nearly," Mam replied, sounding happy. "Just another few minutes in the car."

Pressing my face to the window, I looked out and smiled. The snow was sticking to the ground. It was beautiful. "This is where you're from, Mammy?" I asked, spotting a group of children throwing snowballs at each other in a park.

"Yes, sweetheart," Mam replied. "I was born and raised here in Ballylaggin."

"Ballylaggin." I repeated the word slowly, making sure I said it right.

It was a big town, with long streets of shops and pubs. Christmas lights were everywhere, in the windows of the houses and hanging over the streets. Red-and-white flags hung from all the shops and some of the houses, too. The Cork flag, I remembered. That was Mammy's flag. Daddy's flag was blue and yellow for Tipperary.

"There's a cinema!" Caoimhe yelped. Ripping off her headphones, she leaned over me and pressed her face to the window. "And a leisure center."

"I know," Mam laughed, sounding happier than usual.

"Does it have a pool?"

"Yep," Mam replied. "And a bowling alley."

Daddy kept driving until we were out of the town and back in the countryside. He turned down a smaller road and then slowed down in front of a giant gate.

"Whoa," Caoimhe gasped, and then started to read the shiny plaque attached to the ginormous stone pillar. "Old Hall House, Robin Hill Road, Upper Northwest, Ballylaggin."

"Robin Hill Road," I snickered, watching as the gates creaked open. "That's funny."

Dad drove through the opening, and I could hear gravel crackling beneath the tires. He drove up a winding lane, with trees on either side, until we reached the house.

"We're here," Mam announced with another happy sigh when Dad parked the car. "Welcome home, girls."

I opened the car door, but Caoimhe climbed over my lap and got outside first. "Whoa," she breathed, twirling around in a circle. "This is ours, Dad?"

"No," Dad said quietly, rounding the passenger side to open Mam's door. "It's your mother's."

"Well, it sure beats the hell out of the farm," Caoimhe laughed, still twirling. "Lizzie, come and look."

Scrambling out of the car, I raced over to my sister, kicking gravel as I rushed to get to Caoimhe, who was climbing over a wooden fence.

"We have a courtyard and a meadow," she called back excitedly. "And barns and stables." She climbed over another gate and screamed out. "Omigod, we have an orchard!"

"Is it a palace?" I asked, still trying to climb over the first gate.

"No, it's an estate," Caoimhe called back. "And it's all ours!"

"Girls!" Dad barked. He was standing in front of the big house with his arm around our mother. "Get over here now!"

Jumping down from the wooden gate, I rushed back to my parents, too happy to care that Daddy was cross again.

"This is it, girls," Mammy said with a bright smile when she turned the key in the giant door and Daddy pushed it open for her. "Our family home."

"Holy crap," Caoimhe said, pushing past me to get inside the big house before I could. "We're rich!"

Hurrying inside, I skidded across the tiled entrance hall, running through room after room in search of my sister. There were so many rooms. Too many to count. In our old house, we had one staircase that went up to our bedrooms, but in this house, there was a staircase going up and another one going down, and then another one going up even farther.

I didn't know what to make of it.

Lost in a maze of rooms and hallways, I finally found my parents in the kitchen. It was the biggest one I'd ever seen in my life. When I spotted them sitting at the kitchen table, I moved to go to them, only to stop when I realized that Caoimhe was there, too, and she was talking about me.

Hiding behind the door I had come through, I listened carefully. Their voices were hushed, but I could still hear them.

"She'll be in junior infants, and you'll be in sixth class," Mam was saying. "You won't be anywhere near each other."

"I have sacrificed everything for my family, but I draw the line on this," Caoimhe replied. "I've done everything you guys have asked of me. You packed us up and moved us down here, and I didn't put up a fight. But this is where it stops."

"Caoimhe, *please*."

"I love my sister, I do," Caoimhe argued. "And I understand why we've had to do what we've done, but you guys need to put me first this time. I don't have a chance of fitting in if you send her to Sacred Heart with me."

"I agree," Dad chimed in.

"Michael!"

"Caoimhe's right," he said in a hushed voice. "This is the least we can do for her given what we've put her through."

"And what about Lizzie? Hm?" Mam argued, sounding upset. "When school starts back up, we just don't send her?"

"Exactly."

"But I've already enrolled her at Sacred Heart."

"Then I will unenroll her," Dad replied. "It's for the best, Catherine. You know it is."

"She needs to be in school, Michael."

"And what about when she attacks another child?" Caoimhe strangled out. "And I'm the one everyone's staring at because I have a crazy sister."

"She's not crazy."

"She's not normal, either, Mam," Caoimhe argued. "If you really want to help Liz,

26

you should listen to Dad about finding a residential school for her. One that can help with her—"

"Over my dead body!"

"She can start in September, when Caoimhe has gone off to secondary school," Dad offered. "That'll give us plenty of time to get you back on the mend and get Elizabeth the help she needs."

Mam started to cry then. "This is all so unfair."

"No, what's unfair is our lives being pulled apart," Dad said with a weary sigh. "We've done things your way so far, Catherine, but I'm with Caoimhe on this. Elizabeth stays home."

APRIL 30, 1993

Lizzie

"CAOIMHE, I DIDN'T MEAN IT." HOVERING IN MY SISTER'S BEDROOM DOORWAY, I clasped my hands together and sniffled. I wanted to tell her that I was sorry for ruining her birthday party, but she wouldn't listen to me. "I didn't mean to—"

"Get out!" she screamed, throwing a can of deodorant at me. "I fucking hate you, Lizzie!"

I covered my mouth with my hand to stop myself from screaming again. Like I had in front of her friends earlier. I didn't mean to do it. I didn't know why it happened.

"I hate her!" Caoimhe cried, throwing herself face down on her bed. "I wish she wasn't here!"

"Don't say that," one of her friends from school said while he rubbed her shoulder. He was the only boy at her party. "I have younger brothers and sisters, too, and they throw tantrums all the time."

"Not like her, they don't," Caoimhe wailed into her pillow.

"You clearly haven't met Joey," the boy replied. "Shh, come on, it's not the end of the world."

"I can't even have a birthday party without her ruining it." She cried harder. "I wish she was dead!"

Me too.

"She pulled my hair," I tried to explain, through my tears. "She hurt me."

The boy turned back to look at me. "I know," he said in a gentle voice. "She's telling the truth, you know." He looked at Caoimhe. "I saw Saoirse Murphy pull her ponytail when you were blowing out the candles on your cake."

"And that gives her the right to scratch her eyes out?" Caoimhe snarled, sitting up to glare at me. "She's my friend and you made her bleed." She choked out a sob. "You can forget it if you think Dad will ever send you to school in town now. You'll be lucky if you're not shipped off to residential!"

"Caoimhe, come on, she's only little."

"What? You know I'm right," Caoimhe spat back, shaking all over. "I told you everything, Darren. You know what she cost me." Sniffling, she turned to glare at me again. "You better hope the cancer doesn't kill Mam, because if it does, you'll be out of this house before she's cold in the ground, and good fucking riddance."

"Jesus Christ, Caoimhe!"

"I don't care, Darren," she screamed. "She's a fucking lunatic!"

"Caoimhe, I'm sorry—"

"Get her out of here, Darren," she screamed. "Please get her the fuck away from me before I kill her myself!"

"Maybe you should go downstairs for a little bit." Darren looked at me again, this time with sad, blue eyes. His voice was kind when he said, "Your sister's just upset, okay? She doesn't mean any of this."

Sniffling, I nodded. "I'm sorry."

"It'll be okay." He gave me a reassuring smile. "I promise."

SEPTEMBER 19, 1993

Lizzie

"Hello, sweetheart," Mam said when I walked into the kitchen after school and found her baking cookies. "Did you have a good day at school?"

I shook my head.

"Ah, now, don't say that," Mam mused, placing a tray of cookies in the oven. She closed the oven door and turned to smile at me. "Surely there was one good part."

There wasn't.

There were only ten other children in my class, and some of them wore nappies. They were all younger than me and all we did in class was color pictures and play with toys. Then I got taken out to the "therapy rooms" to talk about my feelings, or play with toys, or do strange exercises, or practice my words. I knew my words, and it made me cross that the teachers acted like I didn't. They watched me all the time and wrote in a secret book about me.

I hated it there.

The best part of the day was coming home to her.

"I don't want to go to preschool," I told her, making a beeline for my mother. "I'm five. I want to go to big school and make friends. Like Caoimhe."

"St. Anthony's isn't a preschool, Lizzie," Mam replied in a gentle voice. "It's a private school for boys and girls of all ages that need a little extra help."

"But I don't need extra help," I complained, leaning against the counter. "I know all my letters and numbers. I can write my name and do my sums, and I can read, too."

"I know you can, clever girl." She was still smiling, but it was a sad one. "But Dr. Wolfe thinks a year at St. Anthony's will help you."

I narrowed my eyes. "I hate Dr. Wolfe." He was old and cranky, and he always looked at me funny. "He thinks I'm bad." Same as Daddy.

"No, he doesn't," Mam said, correcting me. "He's trying to help you."

Yeah, with tablets that made me feel sleepy.

"St. Anthony's isn't forever," Mam offered with another sad smile. "It's just a stepping stone."

"To what?"

"To getting you back on track," she replied, crouching down to stroke my cheek. "You need to start talking to people again."

"I'm talking to you."

"Other people," Mam encouraged. "Teachers and other children. You were doing so well last year." She smiled sadly. "I know you're bright, sweetheart, but the teachers can't know if you don't show them."

"I don't want to talk to them," I replied. "They're always cross with me."

"Now, I'm sure that's not true."

"It is," I argued. "I'm always in the corner."

"Okay." Mam chewed on her lip, looking worried. "I'll talk to them again."

It wouldn't matter.

She talked to them last time and I still ended up in the corner.

"I'm bad."

"No, you are not."

"Everyone thinks I am."

"Well, I'll let you in on a little secret." She crooked her finger, gesturing for me to come closer. When I did, she whispered in my ear, "Anyone who thinks you're bad is a stupid fucker."

My eyes widened in surprise. "You cursed."

"I did," she chuckled, tucking my hair behind my ear. "Don't copy me."

Snickering, I stroked the white curls on her head. "Your hair looks funny."

Mam laughed. "That's because it's growing back."

"It looks like puffy clouds," I replied, tugging on one of the curls. "I missed you."

"I missed you more, baby." She wrapped her arms around me and pulled me in for a hug. "I'm sorry I couldn't pick you up from school today." She peppered my cheek with kisses. "I had a hospital appointment."

Hospital.

That was a bad word.

I didn't like it.

Uh-oh.

"Don't worry," she said, soothing me and rubbing her nose against mine. "The doctors are very happy with Mammy."

"Really?"

She nodded.

I beamed back at her. "Then my wish came true."

"What wish, sweetheart?"

"I used my birthday wish on you," I replied happily. "To make you better, and it *worked*."

"I had the best day ever!" Caoimhe squealed then, barreling into the kitchen in her new school uniform. "It's official, Mam: I *love* school!"

"Well, there's a first time for everything." Mam winked at me before standing up and walking over to my sister. "All right, out with it. What boy has put that smile on your face?"

"Who says a boy has anything to do with my smile?" Caoimhe laughed, bouncing around happily. "Maybe I just love Tommen."

Mam arched a brow. "Caoimhe Catherine Young."

"Okay, okay, his name is Mark, and he's a blow-in to Ballylaggin like me," she gushed. "Recently moved to Clonamore with his dad—you know Clonamore, don't you, Mam? It's the town over from Ballylaggin. A ton of kids from the area go to Tommen."

Our mother opened her mouth to respond, but my sister kept going before she had a chance.

"Well, his mam passed away last year, and his father decided they needed a change of scenery, so they moved down to Cork from Roscommon." She smiled the biggest megawatt grin. "He's in my class at Tommen."

"What about Darren?" I looked up at her. "Is he in your class, too?"

"No." She sighed sadly. "Darren had to go to BCS."

"How come?"

"Because his family doesn't have a lot of money, and Tommen is a private school and it costs a *lot* to attend."

"That's not fair."

"I know." Tossing her schoolbag on the floor, she spun around in circles on her way to the fridge. "Anyway, Mark's a first year like me, and his dad is going out with Sadhbh Gibson. You remember Sadhbh, don't you? I babysit Gibs and Beth all the time."

"Yes, Caoimhe, I remember Sadhbh." Mam rolled her eyes. "I drive you to and from her house every weekend, dear."

"Well, Mark and his dad live in Clonamore, but they're going to be moving into town once Joe and Sadhbh iron everything out. Can you believe it? He's going to be living with the kids I babysit! It's like fate has intervened on my behalf because he is seriously fine."

"Caoimhe," Mam scolded at the same time I asked, "What does *fine* mean?"

"It means beautiful," my sister explained with a dreamy sigh. "He's tall and has black hair, and he plays rugby and has the best curly mullet."

I frowned. "What's a mullet?"

"It's a haircut," Mam filled in, pulling out her ironing board.

"Yeah." Caoimhe agreed, handing our mother her shirt from the basket of ironing. "Like Slater from *Saved by the Bell*."

I knew all about *Saved by the Bell*. It was my sister's favorite TV show. We watched it every day after school. "I like Zach."

"Zach's cute," she said, agreeing with a thoughtful nod. "But Slater's sexy." She covered her chest with her hand and swooned. "And so is Mark!"

"Caoimhe!" Mam scolded again. "Honestly, love, little ears are listening."

"Sorry, sorry, but I can't help it," my sister gushed, smiling bigger than I'd ever seen. "He's just so tall, Mam. Like almost six feet."

"Yes, pet, you already said."

"And he has gorgeous black hair and green eyes, and he plays rugby."

"You've said that, too, Caoimhe."

"I know, but it bears mentioning again." Caoimhe clutched her chest and sighed dreamily. "He's so handsome, Mam, like you wouldn't believe—and he asked me out. Me, Mam. Out of all the girls at school, he picked me." Grinning from ear to ear, she wiggled her hips and squealed. "I think I might love him."

"Oh, Caoimhe," Mam scolded with a laugh, as she pressed the shirt she was ironing. "You've known the boy a month."

"The heart wants what it wants, Mam," my sister replied, clutching her chest again. "And my heart wants Mark Allen." She shuffled around then, doing a funny dance in the kitchen. "I have never been more excited to get to school."

"Well, if he's that special to you, invite him over for dinner this evening."

"Really?" Caoimhe's eyes widened. "You really mean that?"

Mam smiled. "Why not?"

"Oh my God, I love you!" she squealed, throwing her arms around our mother. "You're the best mam in Ireland." She peppered Mam's cheek with kisses. "You guys are going to love him, I promise!"

SEPTEMBER 19, 1993

"WHAT'S WRONG WITH YOUR SISTER?" MARK ASKED AFTER DINNER WHEN I WALKED into the kitchen and saw them kissing.

"Selective mutism," Caoimhe replied, filling a glass of water from the tap. "Don't take it personal. She's like this with everyone except family." She took a sip before adding, "That's why she goes to school in the city and does all that therapy I was telling you about." She shrugged. "She can talk perfectly fine when it suits her."

"Why, though?" He looked at me and then my sister before asking, "Why doesn't she speak like a normal kid?"

"The psychiatrists said it's because of past trauma."

"What kind of past trauma?"

"It's not… I'm, uh, it's a private family matter," Caoimhe replied, cheeks turning red. "But at the rate she's going, she'll be thirty before she graduates." She took another sip before adding, "All you need to know is Liz won't rat us out to my folks."

Mark turned his attention to me and smiled. "Hey, munchkin."

He called me munchkin.

I liked it.

"She won't tell your father we were kissing, right?" he asked, looking over his shoulder at my sister. "She can keep her mouth shut?"

"Duh." Caoimhe rolled her eyes and popped a grape into her mouth. "I just told you she doesn't rat. Besides, she barely talks to our father."

"She's mute with him, too?"

"Sometimes."

"Did he hurt her or something?"

"No," Caoimhe snapped, sounding angry now. "Why would our dad hurt her?"

"Sorry, I was just asking," he replied, holding his hands up. "I didn't mean to upset you."

Caoimhe seemed to brush it off quickly because she started looking at Mark with gooey eyes again. "She likes you."

"How can you tell?"

"She's smiling. Trust me, she wouldn't smile like that if she didn't like you."

"She looks like a little angel." Mark smiled and crouched down in front of me. "Do you like me, munchkin? Hmm? Are you going to talk to me?"

"Oh, no, no, no. She might look like one, but don't let that angelic face fool you," Caoimhe laughed. "She screams like a banshee when she feels like it."

"I bet I can get her to talk," he said, tucking my hair behind my ear.

"You can try." Caoimhe scoffed. "But no doctor has been able to fix her."

"Would you like that, munchkin?" Mark asked, hand on my shoulder. "Would you like me to fix you?"

Nodding, I smiled back at him.

Yes, please.

"Where is she?"

"I know she's in here."

"I can smell her!"

Snickering, I rolled under my bed, trying to escape the smelly-sock monster, but it was no use.

"Gotcha!" A sock-covered hand shot under the bed and grabbed my leg. "Nom, nom, nom, just what I'm hungry for," Mark teased in the funny smelly-sock monster voice, while he dragged me out from under the bed. "A tasty, little munchkin just for me."

Screaming with excitement, I tried to scramble away but Mark was too fast for me. Hooking an arm around my belly, he pulled me onto his lap and pretended to gobble me up with his sock-hand.

"You are, hands down, the best boyfriend in the world." Leaning against the doorframe, my sister smiled at us. "Thanks for being so patient with her."

"We don't mind, do we, smelly-sock monster?" Mark said, and then he used the funny monster voice to say, "No, we don't mind. We love gobbling up little munchkins."

"Well, now that you've made my sister's night, how about you make mine?" She winked at him and inclined her head toward the door. "Before your dad picks you up."

"Sorry, munchkin, but the boss has spoken." He set me down on my bed and ruffled my hair. "I'll play with you the next time I come over, okay?"

Nodding happily, I watched him leave, while hoping Caoimhe brought him back soon.

My very first friend.

NOVEMBER 15, 1993

Lizzie

"WHAT THE HELL ARE YOU DOING?" DAD DEMANDED, JERKING UP OFF THE CHAIR when I climbed onto his lap. "You can't climb onto my lap without any clothes on." He looked furious when he wrapped my towel around my shoulders and covered me up. "Get back upstairs and put your clothes on, and don't ever come downstairs without your clothes on again, or I'll redden your ass for you."

"Calm down," Mam instructed when I bolted past her. "She's just after getting out of the bath."

"She's five years old, Catherine, not a baby," Dad replied. "She's too old to be running around naked and she should know that."

"Michael, she was only trying to give her father a hug."

"Caoimhe never carried on like that."

"Don't compare them. The girls are like night and day."

"Don't I fucking know it."

"Michael!"

"Talk to her, Catherine. Explain to the girl that she can't be doing these things. For Christ's sake, what if Caoimhe had Mark over?"

"Maybe if you worried a little less about Caoimhe and a little more about Elizabeth, then she wouldn't be crying out for your attention."

"And maybe if you didn't pander to her every need, she would open her mouth and speak for herself."

"How dare you!"

"I'm just saying, if you backed off and let her be more independent, she might act like it."

"Don't you dare try to push this all on my shoulders. There is a reason our daughter has issues, and that reason lies on your doorstep, not mine!"

"So now you're blaming me for something I have no control over?"

"Kind of like how you're blaming me for not being able to fix her?"

"This was a mistake."

"Don't say that."

"I'm going for a pint."

"No, don't walk away. We have to talk about this."

"There's nothing to talk about. It is what it is, and we are where we are. End of story."

"Michael, please!"

The front door slammed shut.

"That's it. Don't cry. Shh, shh…"

"That's because you're a bad girl. God is punishing you…"

"He sent me to make you clean…"

"Tell me you want it…"

Panicking, I bolted up the staircase, not stopping until I was under the covers in my bed.

Bad girl.

Bad girl.

Bad girl.

Clenching my eyes shut, I tried to push the voices out of my head, but they wouldn't go.

DECEMBER 25, 1993

Lizzie

It was late on Christmas night when my bedroom door opened inward, and Mark slipped into my room.

I smiled when he locked the door behind him because that meant he was going to fix me again.

I liked Mark a lot. He smelled nice and was super funny, and he always played with me when he came over, even when Caoimhe didn't want me to hang out with them. She wanted to go smooching in the woods at the back of our house instead, where our parents couldn't see them. They did it all the time, and Caoimhe even brought him over when our parents weren't home.

They always made me promise not to tell. That was easy-peasy for me because I was good at keeping secrets.

After all, I kept lots of secrets for them.

Especially Mark's secret superpower.

I never told anyone because Mark said that would make it stop working, and I didn't want to get sick again. He said I would if he didn't keep fixing me.

Mark and his daddy had come over to our house for dinner, and they were sleeping over because his daddy drank too much whiskey with my daddy.

"Are you ready for me, munchkin?" Mark whispered, moving to my bed.

"I've been waiting up for you," I told him, proud of myself for staying up so late without getting caught. "Just like you said."

"That's my girl." Grinning, he sat down on the edge of my bed. "Look what I got for Christmas." He held up a shiny camera and said, "I'm going to take some pictures of you, munchkin. Special pictures just for me, okay?"

Nodding eagerly, I did everything he told me to.

"You're such a pretty little thing," Mark told me when he finished taking my picture. "How are you feeling tonight, munchkin?"

"Great."

He frowned and touched my forehead. "Oh no."

"What?"

"It's getting worse."

My eyes widened. "It is?"

He nodded sadly. "Do you know what happens if you don't get better?"

"What?"

"Your hair will fall out like your mammy's, and you'll get sicker and sicker like her."

"I will?" I gripped my head, feeling scared. "But I don't want to lose my hair."

"You might die."

I started to cry.

"You mustn't tell anyone you know the truth," he whispered, stroking my cheek. "It would make it worse."

"It would?"

"Oh yes, talking about it makes the sickness spread inside of your body."

"Make it stop!"

"I can try if you want me to?"

"You said you could make it better," I cried, gripping his arm. "Please fix me."

"Okay, but you're going to have to be a very good girl." He sighed sadly. "Can you do that for me? Can you be a brave girl and do everything I tell you?"

"I can." I nodded eagerly. "I swear."

"And you can keep it a secret?"

"I promise, I won't tell."

"We might have to try something different tonight, munchkin."

"Like what?"

He thought about it for a long time, tapping his chin before saying, "I could try the really special hug."

"Yes." I nodded eagerly. "Do it."

"Are you sure?" He arched a brow. "It might feel strange."

"Will it make me better?"

"Oh yeah," he said coaxingly. "It'll make you feel so much better, munchkin."

I agreed. "Then do it."

"Okay." He sat on my bed and placed his hand on my leg. "I'm going to need you to take off your nightie for this, munchkin." He smiled. "It's how boys and girls do the special hug. We have to take all of our clothes off."

I didn't think twice about it. I didn't want to get sick like Mammy. I wanted to be fixed, and Mark could fix me. He promised he could. Whipping off my nightie, I looked up at him and waited for him to tell me what to do next.

"You can watch," he said, when he started taking off his clothes. "You like to look, don't you, munchkin?"

My eyes widened in surprise when I saw the thing sticking up between his legs. "What's that?"

"That's what's going to make you better, munchkin," he said. "Do you want to touch it?"

I didn't think so.

It looked strange.

And scary.

"That's okay," he chuckled, climbing onto my bed. "We can work up to that."

"Work up to what?" I asked, lying down on my mattress for my special hug and opening my legs just how Mark liked me to.

"Never mind." Pushing my legs apart farther, he knelt between them and sighed happily. "You're such a good little girl, munchkin."

"I am?"

"You are," he confirmed, walking his fingers up my thigh.

"That tickles."

"It does?" He smiled. "Do you like it when I tickle you?"

I shrugged, feeling scared.

"I know a secret tickle," he whispered, moving his hand up higher. "Do you want me to show you?"

PART 2

The Foundations of Friendship

BURST BALLS, BATTLE-AXES, AND BREAKUPS

Hugh

OCTOBER 27, 1994

"One of these days, I'm going to catch you little toe-rags," Mr. Murphy snarled from the side of the garden wall on Thursday evening after school. "And when I do, I'll string the pair of you up by your bollocks. Do ya hear me? That's the last flower bed of mine you'll destroy with your fucking ball!"

"Aw, crap, he's going to burst it, isn't he?"

"He's bluffing, Hughie."

With my back plastered to the garden wall, I glared at the smaller boy beside me, the one with a head of golden curls, who was laughing into his hand.

"He never bluffs, Gibs," I whisper-hissed, elbowing him. "And stop laughing."

"What?" he replied, laughing hard, as the rain drizzled down on us. "It's *funny*."

"No," I argued. "What's funny is the stupid yellow raincoat you're wearing."

"Hey! I'm a handsome boy in yellow."

"You're a troublemaker is what you are," I snapped back. "And now I'm in trouble *again*. Because of you. *Again*."

"Oh, stop worrying, you big baby." Looking thoroughly amused, he wiped a rain drop from his cheek. "Don't be so touchy."

"Easy for you to say," I grumbled. "When you're not about to lose your third football in a week."

I knew it would happen. Old Murphy was the worst neighbor on our street, and every kid from Avoca Greystones knew what happened if your toy went over his garden wall. It didn't come back. I was lucky to live on the other side of the street from the old crank, but Gibsie lived two houses up from him.

"Don't be cross with me, Hughie," he pleaded, looking up at me with those big puppy-dog, gray eyes that got him out of trouble. "You're my big brother."

I rolled my eyes to the heavens, but I knew he was right. We might not have had the same parents, but Gerard Gibson *was* my brother.

Our parents were best friends since primary school and had ended up buying houses in Avoca Greystones, a twelve-house estate on the upper north side of their hometown of Ballylaggin. We lived at number four, while the Gibsons lived across the street at number nine.

Aside from the four months I'd been alive longer than him, I'd never known a world without the curly-haired troublemaker beside me. It was strange because I didn't think of him as a friend like Patrick Feely, my best friend from school. I thought of Gibsie in the same way I thought about my little sister Claire. Gibs didn't have to be careful with my feelings and I didn't have to be careful with his. We could argue, fight, and say the worst things to each other and still be okay because we were brothers, and brothers always came back together in the end.

"Don't be sad." Gibs patted my shoulder in support, dragging me from my thoughts. "The war's not over. We can get this one back."

"I bet he has the knife out already." I sighed heavily. "That was my favorite ball."

"Are ye listening, ye little hoors from hell?" Old Murphy continued to threaten, sounding closer now. "When I get my hands on the pair of you, I'll wring your necks. Especially the fat one!"

Now, I was the one to cover my mouth to smother my laughter while Gibsie scowled in outrage. "That *fucker.*"

"That's right, ya little overfed tank," Old Murphy taunted, sounding farther away now. "I'll put manners on you yet!"

"That *fucker!* Mam says I'm stocky, not fat, and Dad says it'll fall off when I get taller," Gibsie said, defending himself but looking outraged. "I'm big-boned, *Hughie.*" Now he was the one to elbow me to stop me from laughing. "We can't all be beanpoles."

"I know, I know," I coaxed, trying to stop my face from smiling. "And don't mind Old Murphy. He's only jealous because he's old and bald."

"Really?"

"Really."

"Okay, go and check," he instructed me then, gesturing to the wall we were hiding behind. "See what he's doing now? If he goes back inside, you can sneak through the gate and get your ball."

"Why don't *you* go in?" I shot back. "You kicked the ball in there." *Again.* "You wrecked his petunias." *Again.* "You're the culprit." *Again.*

"Yeah, but I can't scale the wall like you," Gibsie explained, looking up at me with mischievous eyes. "Come on." He hooked his hands together and stooped down low. "I'll give you a boost up."

"I'm four months older than you," I grumbled, using his hands as a step to hoist myself up. "But you're four times more trouble." Gripping on to the concrete ledge of

Mr. Murphy's side-garden wall, I slowly heaved myself up and peeked over just in time to see the gray-haired monster plunge his penknife into my ball.

And that was that.

Another one bites the dust.

Sighing in disappointment, I dropped back down to the ground and shook my head when Gibsie looked at me with a hopeful expression. "Nope," I replied grimly. "Rest in peace, ball."

"Oh, that's it." Balling his hands into fists at his sides, Gibsie glared at the wall separating us from the killer of joy and cupped his mouth with his hands before shouting, "You better take some photos of those flower beds, Murphy, because you can't guard them forever, you big, bald, battle-axe, bollo—"

"Don't make it worse," I warned, slapping a hand over his mouth before he could finish. "We're already dead as it stands." Hooking an arm around him, I backed us away from the neighbor's wall, careful to avoid Mrs. Grady's flower bed as we trudged through her backyard. "If he tells our parents we swore at him, we're double dead."

Waving back at Mrs. Grady, who was smiling at us from her kitchen window, I steered Gibs around her prized roses, taking special care not to upset them. Mrs. Grady was even older than Old Murphy, but she wasn't a grouch like him. She used to be our babysitter until she broke her hip during the summer. Even though she couldn't mind us anymore, she still let us play in her garden and invited us in for tea and scones.

"Oh, this is war," Gibsie grumbled when we were back on the street. "Just wait until next week." He balled his small hands into fists at his sides. "We'll get that fucker on Halloween night, Hughie."

Veering off the footpath when we reached his house, I trudged up the driveway after him, feeling disappointed over my ball.

"I'll get you a new ball for your birthday," Gibsie promised when we walked into his house. "Dad's taking us to his place for the weekend, so he'll take me to the shop to get you a new one."

"Forget about the ball," I replied, feeling even worse now that I knew he was leaving for the weekend. "Will you be at school tomorrow? Miss Lawlor said she's bringing sweets because it's our last day before Halloween break."

"I'll be there," he promised, walking through the hall to the kitchen. "I'll just go from Dad's house instead."

"Will you be back for my birthday party on Monday?"

"Of course."

"And trick-or-treating afterward?"

"Oh *yeah*." He rubbed his hands together with glee and moved for the cake sitting

44

on the kitchen island. "I've been storing trays of eggs under my bed for revenge on the ball-stabber."

I grinned. "Excellent."

"Gerard Joseph Gibson, if you don't take your hands off Hughie's birthday cake, you won't have fingers to pick your nose with," Sadhbh warned, appearing from behind the open fridge door.

"How dare you," he huffed, looking outraged, with his hand hovering inches above the frosting on the birthday cake. "I don't pick my nose."

"No, you don't pick your nose, Gibs," Joe chimed in when he strolled into the kitchen with Bethany snoozing on his shoulder. "You use it for storage, don't ya, son?"

"That was one time, Dad," Gibsie argued back. "And one bead."

"It was four beads," I corrected with a laugh, remembering the incident during arts and crafts at school last week. "And you had to go to the hospital to have them removed."

"I wanted to see how many would fit," he defended. "Is that so bad?"

"Yes," all three of us chorused, causing my friend to sulk in typical Gibs fashion.

"Honestly, Gerard, I shouldn't have to tell you this, but no foreign objects are to enter your nostrils." Waving a wooden spoon around like a weapon, Sadhbh shooed her son away from the number-seven-shaped birthday cake. "Or your ears!"

"I'll pop upstairs and grab their weekend bags," Joe told his wife but made no move to go upstairs until Sadhbh nodded her approval.

"When's Dad moving back home?" Gibsie asked when his father had left the room. "I hate it here without him."

Me too, I wanted to chime in, but my parents had warned me to not interfere.

According to Mam, Sadhbh and Joe were going through a separation, and we needed to stay out of it and keep our opinions to ourselves for Gibs's and Bethany's sakes.

I had plenty of opinions of my own about the crap going on in the house across the street from mine. Especially about the asshole Sadhbh was kissing instead of Joe, but I did as my mother asked.

Keith Allen.

Puke.

"Gerard." A weary sigh escaped Sadhbh. "We've talked about this, pet."

"No, we haven't," Gibs argued back. "Telling me Dad's moving out isn't talking about it, Mam. It's telling, not talking. There's a difference."

"Nothing has changed," his mother said, trying to coax him and going to his side. "Your father and I still love you and your sister very much." She patted his curly hair and stroked his cheek. "We're still a family, love."

"Except we're not." Gibsie's voice cracked, and he pulled away from his mother before swiping his cheek with the back of his hand. "And everything *has* changed."

"We *are* still a family," Sadhbh repeated in a sterner tone. "Our family just looks different to how it used to."

"Yeah, because *you* broke it!" Gibs choked out, backing away from his mother. "You and your asshole boyfriend."

My eyes bugged and I quickly clamped a hand over my mouth to stop the words *oh shit* from slipping out.

His mother sucked in a sharp breath. "Gerard!"

"What?" Gibs glared defiantly at his mother. "I'm not lying."

"Don't speak to me like that," she commanded, voice cracking. "I'm still your mother."

"Well, I wish you weren't!" Gibs screamed before bolting out of the kitchen, leaving me alone with his mam.

"I, ah…" Pushing my chair back, I stood awkwardly and gestured to the kitchen doorway. Feeling uncomfortable, I shrugged and offered Sadhbh a half-hearted smile. "I should probably go home."

With tear-filled eyes, Sadhbh offered me a pained smile before quickly turning around so I couldn't see her face. "Okay, love."

"I'm, ah…thanks for the cake." I shook my head and moved for the door. "And, uh…sorry."

Not waiting for a response, I pulled a Gibsie and bolted out of their house, breaking my personal sprinting record in my rush to get across the street to the safety of my house.

"I think you made your mam cry," I announced breathlessly when I reached my driveway and found Gibsie hopping a basketball off the garage wall.

"Good," was all he replied before throwing the ball at the wall once more.

"You don't mean that."

"Don't I?"

"No, you don't," I said, trying to persuade and narrowly avoiding a furiously thrown basketball as it flew past my head at top speed and crashed loudly against the wheely bins behind me.

"How do you feel about running away?" Gibs asked then, retrieving the ball before aiming at my head once more. "I think we could do it."

"I'm not running away with you again." This time I caught the basketball he flung at my head. "The last time we tried that, you pissed in my sleeping bag." I threw the ball back at him as hard as I could. "With me in it."

"It was an accident," he bit out, launching the ball at my head again. "Let it go."

"I will," I snapped back, slapping the ball away from my face before it connected. "When you stop throwing the ball at my head."

"I'm mad!"

"I *know*."

"I hate that asshole!"

"I *know*."

"I don't want to live with her!"

"I *know*."

"I want to be with my dad!"

"I *know*."

Chest heaving from temper, Gibs glared at me through tear-filled, gray eyes for what felt like forever before exhaling a ragged breath. "I just want everything to go back to normal, Hugh."

"I know, Gibs." I sighed heavily. "Me, too."

"It's not going to, is it?"

"No, Gibs." I slowly shook my head. "I don't think so."

Looking thoroughly defeated, Gibs walked to the edge of the footpath at the end of my driveway and sank down. Hooking his arms around his knees, he stared across the street at his house.

I didn't know what to say to make him feel better and I hated it. Because I *wanted* to help. I wanted to make it all better for him. I wanted to bring his dad home and put his family back together again.

But I couldn't.

All I could do was sit beside him and keep him company.

"Sorry for trying to take your head off," Gibs said once he had finally calmed down.

"It's grand."

"Do you still want me to come to your party Monday?"

"Of course."

"And go trick-or-treating when our friends leave?"

"Yes, Gibs."

"And I'm still sleeping over afterward?"

"Yep."

"And we're still sneaking out to egg that asshole's house once our parents are asleep?"

"Oh *yeah*."

"Good." A smile tugged at his lips, and he nudged my shoulder with his. "So when's your sister getting back from the hairdresser with Sinead?"

Rolling my eyes, I gave Gibs a dirty look, even though I was secretly glad that he was back to his favorite topic. "Would it kill you to pretend I'm your favorite for one day?"

"I don't know, Hugh. I'm not that good of a liar," he chuckled, and just like that, he was back to the jokester I knew. "Is your mam still making you invite Claire's friends to your party?"

"Yes." My shoulders slumped in defeat. "But I'm writing my invitations tonight, and she'll be at work, so maybe I can get away with not having to invite them."

"Who does she want to invite again?"

"Can't remember their names." I shrugged. "But I know there's four of them."

His eyes widened. "Four?"

"Yep."

"And we have to play with all *four* of them?"

"Yep."

"The entire time?"

"Yep."

"Jesus," Gibsie groaned. "What are we supposed to do with four girls?"

"Five," I replied grimly. "You forgot to count my sister."

"But Claire's one of us, so she doesn't count," he offered. "And besides, we like playing with her."

"No, Gibs, *you* like playing with her."

"Maybe it won't be so bad," he offered then, clearly trying to cheer me up. "They might be like your sister."

"Yeah." I shuddered. "And I can't think of anything worse."

TROUBLE COMES A-KNOCKING

OCTOBER 27, 1994

"Thanks, Lizzie," Shannon whispered from her perch beside me. We were sitting on the bench outside the principal's office, waiting for our parents to come out from their meeting. "But you shouldn't have done it." She looked up at me with big, blue eyes. "You're going to get in deep trouble because of me."

"I don't care," I told her. "He hurt my friend. He made you cry."

"Yeah, but you made him bleed," she replied, chewing her lip. "You're going to get punished."

I knew that.

I saw how angry my dad looked when he went into the office with our teacher and the principal. How they all looked. All the angry faces all looking at me.

I didn't feel bad, though.

I didn't feel like screaming.

Instead, I felt warm.

My thoughts were nice and slow.

It always happened when I sat next to Shannon Lynch.

It made me want to sit with her forever.

"Thank you," she offered, shoulders shaking. "I've never had a friend stick up for me before."

"I'll always stick up for you," I promised. "And Claire," I hurried to add, thinking about the curly-haired girl in our class who had become my friend since starting big school last month. Claire was loud and funny, and she made me feel happy. Shannon was quiet and calm and made me feel safe.

I was nervous when I started at Sacred Heart Primary School. It was a lot different from the school I used to go to that helped me to get my words out when they got stuck in my throat. But the grown-ups said I was doing such a good job that I was *finally* ready to go to *this* school now. I wasn't sure what any of it meant, but I was nervous about moving schools and starting in junior infants. All the other kids in my class were four and five, and I was afraid they might think there was something wrong with me.

When our teacher walked me over to a round table and sat me next to a small girl with dark brown hair, I felt out of place. But when Shannon smiled and told me this was her second time in junior infants and that she was turning six next March, I felt better. That feeling only grew when I realized that I already knew her big brother, Darren. He was friends with Caoimhe, and I'd even met him a couple of times. He looked just like Shannon and was just as nice as her, too.

A little while later, the teacher brought another girl over to sit with us. She wasn't shy like Shannon or strange like me. This girl looked like sunshine. Everyone wanted to sit with Claire Biggs and be her best friend, but she only wanted to sit with us and be *our* best friend.

"Why does your mammy have a scarf on her head?" Shannon asked then, distracting me from my thoughts.

"She doesn't have any hair," I replied, swinging my legs back and forth. "It fell out when she got sick."

"Oh." Her small hand covered mine. "I'm sorry."

"It's okay." I smiled back at her. "She got sick before and it grew back." I shrugged. "Once she's better again, she'll get it back again."

Shannon looked at me for a long time before whispering, "You're different, Lizzie Young."

"I am?"

She nodded and smiled. "You're special."

"Is that bad?"

"No." She shook her head, still smiling. "You remind me of Joe."

"Your brother?"

"Yep." She nodded again. "And that's a very good thing."

———————————

"Calm down, Mike," Mam said for the tenth time since we left my school. Sitting in the front seat next to Dad, she placed her hand on his knee and said, "It's not the end of the world," before turning around to wink at me.

Clasping my hands together tightly, I smiled back at my mother. I loved looking at her face. Mam had kind eyes, dark blue like Caoimhe's, and she had my favorite voice. It was soft and gentle and wrapped around me like a hug. Daddy had blue eyes, too, but they looked pale and sad. Like mine.

"Calm down?" Dad shook his head, and I felt the car speed up. "Catherine, she bit a boy in her class. Like a feral fucking dog." He sounded so angry. I didn't like it. "What's the point in spending a fortune on therapists when she reacts like that at the drop of a hat?"

"He pushed Shannon," I heard myself say, growing angry. "He was being a bully, Daddy."

"Did he push you?" Dad demanded, glaring at me in the rearview mirror. "Did he put his hands on you?"

Shaking my head, I turned to look out my window. "No, Daddy."

"Then you had no right to put your hands on him," Dad replied. "You're lucky you weren't expelled for that stunt, Elizabeth. God knows, they had bloody good reason to."

"But he *pushed* Shannon," I argued back, feeling my skin grow hot as my eyes followed the raindrops splattering against the window. "He pushed my *friend*." Was I saying it wrong? Why couldn't he hear me? "He's a mean boy, Daddy," I added, hands balling into fists on my lap. "He pulled Claire's hair last week, and he made her cry on the first day of school, too."

"Enough!" Dad snapped, banging his fist on the steering wheel. "I mean it. Don't try to excuse your behavior because there is no justifying biting another child viciously enough to make him bleed!"

Breathing hard and fast, I glared at the back of his seat, trying so hard not to scream. To not jump out of my seat and scratch him. I didn't want to make my mother sad again, but I could feel it growing inside of me.

"Jesus Christ, I thought you were past all this," Dad continued to shout at me. "You know right from wrong, Elizabeth, so why can't you just behave yourself? You're six years old, for Christ's sake. You're too big in the tooth to be throwing tantrums. Why can't you just be normal, huh? It's not that fucking hard—"

"That's enough, Michael," Mam warned, cutting him off. "Lower your voice."

"Lower my *voice*?" He turned his head to glare at my mother before driving through the enormous gates of my sister's school. "You'd want to wake up, Catherine. The way that young one carries on isn't normal. She's old enough to be in first class, but instead she's in junior infants and miles behind the rest, all because she can't fucking control herself."

"I said that's enough," Mam snapped, sounding just as cross now. "You've had your say, as has the principal. Now let it be."

"She deserves a lot more than a few hard truths, but of course, that won't happen because you're blinded by your soft spot for her." Shaking his head, Dad pulled the car into one of the parking spots and flicked the button to make the wipers go faster. "I thought the doctors said the new medicine would be working by now?"

"It *is*."

"Well, tell that to the poor lad with teeth marks on the side of his face," Daddy shouted again. "I knew it was a bad idea taking her out of St. Anthony's. I fucking knew it. She had all the help she needed up there, with teachers equipped to handle the likes of her. But oh no, you had to have your way again, didn't ya? Because this is the Catherine and Elizabeth show, isn't it? Never mind what the rest of the family want—"

"Michael!" Mam snapped back, voice rising. "Now is not the time for this conversation."

"I never should've listened to you or those fucking doctors," he grumbled. "I'm so sick of living like this, Catherine, really I am."

Covering my ears, I clenched my eyes shut and tried to swallow my voice down, while I tried to push *hers* out.

Come back to me.

I'm waiting.

I'll find you.

Don't fight it.

"Oh my God, it's lashing down out there," Caoimhe's declared loudly, yanking the door wide-open. The sound of my sister's voice made *her* go quiet in my head.

Breathing fast, I kept my eyes shut, too afraid to open them in case I saw *her* again—the scary lady, with the claws, the one with the voice that crawled inside my head at bedtime. Or when I got mad. She crawled out of the water, dripping wet, with her hair in clumps and her long claws. She was the lady I saw from my window sometimes. The one the doctors said wasn't there. The one my family said was a figment of my imagination. I wasn't supposed to see her. *But I did.*

"Elizabeth!" Dad said and the warning tone in his voice had my eyes snapping open.

I didn't see the scary lady's face, but I did see my dad's. I was good at reading faces. It was my special power. And right now, my daddy was telling me with his eyes to *behave.*

"Scoot into the middle, Liz," Caoimhe instructed, tossing her schoolbag onto the floor beneath my feet before climbing in beside me. "Mark's coming home with us, remember?"

Yeah, I remembered.

"How's it going, munchkin?" Mark's familiar voice pulled me from my memories, and I turned to see him climb into the back seat of my dad's Jeep, next to me. He smiled at me when he fastened his seat belt and ruffled my hair before turning his attention to my parents.

I covered my mouth with my hand to hide my giggle.

Mark always called me *munchkin*, and I liked it.

Dad started the car back up and I listened as the four of them chatted the whole way home. Nobody talked to me, but I didn't mind. I was used to it.

When Mark draped his arm over my lap to hold my sister's hand, I shivered all over. He noticed and gave me the special wink. The secret one he saved just for me. For when he was fixing me. It made me feel special, and I beamed back at him.

COERCION IN THE KITCHEN

Hugh

OCTOBER 27, 1994

"How are my favorite men?" Mam asked when she walked into the kitchen on Thursday night.

"All the better for seeing you," Dad replied with a wink. He leaned back on his chair at the table and gave Mam his full attention. "How was work, love?"

"Busy," Mam replied with a cheerful sigh, still wearing her hospital scrubs. "Is my baby in bed?"

"Thankfully," I muttered from my perch beside my father. It took way longer than usual to get Claire to go to sleep tonight, and that bugged me because it meant I got less alone time with Dad.

"It was my fault," Dad told Mam with a chuckle. "I left Claire and Small Gibs alone with a Black Forest gateau."

"Rookie mistake, Biggs."

"Don't remind me."

"Did you boys have a nice evening?" Mam asked with a knowing smile. When she was on the day shift at the hospital, she didn't get home until almost ten at night, but Dad *always* let me stay up late with him. Even if it was a school night. The key was to get Claire to bed by 8 p.m. and then spend the next two hours watching sports, reading stories, or doing whatever I wanted to do.

Tonight, we spent our quality time writing out birthday party invitations to hand out to my friends at school tomorrow before we went on midterm break for Halloween. I was about to turn seven next week, so I didn't need Dad's help to write the invitations, but I *did* want him to watch. I worked hard on my handwriting, even during the school holidays, and it showed. When Dad told me how proud he was, it made me want to work even harder to make him even prouder.

"Oh good, you've made a start on your party invites," Mam said, spying the stack of neatly stacked envelopes on the table in front of me. "Wow, that's a lot of invites, sweetheart."

"I invited the entire class," I explained. "Twenty-six."

"Twenty-six?" Mam's brows shot up. "Lovely." Her voice sounded squeaky when she mumbled, "Twenty-six boys running through my house sounds…lovely."

"It turns out that we have a genius on our hands, Sinead," Dad announced, wrapping an arm around me. "He won't be seven for another week and he wrote every word of those invitations himself. And have you listened to him read lately? He was reading *The Hobbit* the other night, and I've never heard anything like it. The school were right to have him tested, Sinead. He's leaps and bounds ahead of the pack." He squeezed my shoulder. "This young fella of ours is going to do great things."

Mam smiled indulgently at me. "Is that so?"

My face turned beetroot red, and I beamed with pride.

I knew I was considered *bright* at school, but hearing my dad say it out loud made me really believe it. The teachers told me often, and even though they didn't tell me the results of those special one-on-one tests I was taken out of class for, I knew it had to be good.

"He's a fine artist, too." Dad continued to harp on, much to my delight. "Which will only stand to him if he decides to follow in his old man's footsteps." He squeezed my shoulder again. "Isn't that right, son?"

"Hold your horses, Peter Biggs," Mam interjected with a chuckle. "Your son is only seven." She arched a brow. "I think it's a little early to steer him down the architecture and property development route, don't you, love?"

"Not when he has the reading comprehension of a teenager," Dad replied. "Or can master a Lego set faster than any child we know."

"Pete, let the child be a child," Mam instructed, moving for the fridge. "Hugh has a long life ahead of him. His childhood is only a small fraction of that, so let's not make it even shorter, sweetheart."

"Jesus, you're right, Sinead. I shouldn't be talking about that kind of stuff to him. I just got a bit carried away with…" My father let his words trail off before roughly clearing his throat. His face was red, like he was embarrassed. "Never mind all that talk, son. Let's just look forward to your birthday, hmm?"

"Oh, and don't forget to make invitations for Claire's friends," Mam called out. "I know I have their names written somewhere." She searched through the notes and hand-drawn pictures stuck to the fridge before snatching up a yellow sticky note. "Here we go."

"Dad," I groaned, turning to my father, who was sitting beside me. "*Please.*"

Dad held his hands up. "Your mother's the boss, son."

"Claire is only inviting four friends," Mam added. "You can handle it."

"*Why*, Mam?" I whined, turning to look up at her when she placed the sticky note on the table in front of me. "None of my friends from school have to invite their sisters' friends to their parties. Why do I have to be the only boy in class that has *girls* at his party?"

"Because, apparently, you're the only boy in class with a mother who is raising him to be a gentleman," Mam replied, stroking my chin with her thumb before returning to the fridge. "Write the invitations."

"But we're in first class." I continued to plead my case. "What are we supposed to do with four junior infant *girls*?"

"Five," Mam chimed in happily. "You forgot to count your sister."

"Oh God, that's even worse." I dropped my head on the table and covered the back of my head with my hands. "Fuck."

"Watch your language in front of your mother," Dad warned, elbowing my arm in warning. "And sit up straight when you're talking to a lady."

"Sorry," I mumbled, not feeling one bit sorry but doing what he said. "So there's no way out of it?" I heard myself ask, feeling defeated. "No way at all?"

"Not a single one, son. Now, hurry up and get those written before bed," Mam instructed, turning on the microwave. "Claire's on your bus tomorrow, so you can hand them out yourself to the girls."

"Please God, no!"

Mam laughed. "It won't kill you, Hugh."

"It might."

"You heard your mother," Dad chimed in, covering his mouth with his hand. "She's raising a gentleman."

Knowing that I was beaten, I sighed in defeat and reached for the sticky note that contained the names of my sister's stupid friends.

"Shannon Lynch, Marybeth and Cadence O'Neill, and Lizzie Young," I read the list of names on the paper and glared. "Ugh."

"Is that young Caoimhe's sister?" Dad asked, leaning in to get a better look at the names. "Caoimhe Young who babysits for Sadhbh?"

"It sure is," Mam replied. "Speaking of babysitting, I've taken her phone number from Sadhbh. I was thinking we could book her for a night for our gang."

Dad's eyes lit up. "Jesus, it's been forever since we've had a date night, love."

"Since before Mrs. Grady had her hip done," Mam replied with a grin. "Caoimhe comes highly recommended by Sadhbh, and the O'Reillys up the road can't speak highly enough of her."

"Jeez, it would be fantastic if it works out," Dad mused, scratching his chest. "With Mrs. Grady out of action, we're lost for a sitter during the school holidays."

"Let's hope it does work out," Mam replied. "She seems to be a hit with all kids, and even our Small Gibs is infatuated with her."

"I hate it when you guys call him that," I grumbled. "You do it all the time and it's so annoying. He's not *Small Gibs*. He's just *Gibs*."

"Sorry, son," Dad laughed. "But Joe Gibson will always be the original Gibsie."

"And has been since we were children," Mam agreed with a chuckle.

"Which makes his son *Small Gibs*."

"Whatever. I don't care about babysitters—but Joe is *Joe*, and Gibs is *Gibs*," I huffed, turning my attention to the invitation I was being *forced* to write. "Marybeth and Cadence are Pierce's twin sisters, so I'm only writing one invitation for them."

"Make it a nice one," Mam replied. "Best handwriting."

"Don't look so sorrowful, Hugh," Dad laughed, ruffling my hair. "In a few years, you'll be begging me and your mother to let you have girls over."

"You know, Granny Biggs made your father invite me to his birthday party when we were only little." Mam walked over and hugged Dad from behind. "And look at us now."

"That's right, she did," Dad mused, pressing a kiss to my mother's hand. "And it was the best coerced invitation I ever wrote."

Mam beamed at him. "And we haven't spent more than a week apart in three decades."

"So you never know, son," Dad teased. "One of these names could be the name you say on your wedding day."

Shuddering, I gaped at him in horror. "Is that supposed to make me feel *better*?"

BULLIES, BIRTHDAY INVITATIONS, AND BIG BROTHERS

Lizzie

OCTOBER 28, 1994

"Are you nearly ready?" Claire called out from the other side of the bathroom door. "We're going to miss the bus home. It's leaving early, remember? Teacher said twelve o'clock on the dot."

"I'm coming," I called back while I stepped out of my knickers and balled them up. I didn't want to get in trouble again, and that's what would happen if the grown-ups knew I had an accident. Worried, I looked for the bin, and once I found it, I shoved the cotton fabric to the bottom, covering it up with toilet paper.

Flushing the toilet, I unlocked the door and rushed to the sink to wash my hands, calling out the word *sorry* to my friend as I moved. "I had to go really bad."

"That's okay," Claire replied, still holding my bag for me. "Don't forget the soap."

"I won't," I replied, pouring a dollop onto my palm. "Hey, do you ever wee red stuff?"

"Ew, no!" Her brown eyes widened to saucers. "Do you?"

"Sometimes." I focused on washing the suds off my hands. "When it's stingy."

"You get stingy wees?"

Nodding, I moved for the towel and dried my hands. "Do you?"

Claire shook her head. "Nope."

"Oh." Smiling, I snatched my bag up and weaved my arms through the straps. "Ready."

Giggling, we broke into a sprint to see who would get to the school gate first. Claire was tall like me, with long legs to make her run faster, but I still touched the gate before her.

"You're a rocket," she laughed when she caught up with me. "Like a super-superfast rocket."

"You're both rockets," Shannon offered, as she waited among the crowd of other children waiting outside the gates of the school for their bus. "I can't run as fast as either one of you."

"Oh sugar!" Claire exclaimed loudly. "I almost forgot." Digging inside her school-bag, she retrieved an envelope and handed it to Shannon before quickly turning to look at me. "You're getting one later, I promise."

"I am?" I asked, feeling a wave of excitement wash through me. I had no idea what it meant, but I was happy to be included.

"It's a birthday invitation."

"But your birthday is in August," Shannon and I both said in unison.

"My brother's birthday," Claire explained, scrunching her nose up. "He's stinky and super annoying, but he's okay, I guess."

"Okay," I chuckled, while Shannon pocketed the envelope without opening it.

"So can you come?"

I said yes at the same time Shannon said no.

Claire started to smile and say yay, before it morphed into a sad, "How come?"

Shannon shifted from foot to foot, looking uncertain, but didn't answer. "I'm not allowed to go to birthday parties?"

"Why not?" we both asked.

"Because she's a scab," one of the fourth-class girls sneered before roughly shoving Shannon out of her way. "Now, move, *scabby*."

"Hey!" Claire huffed, placing a steadying hand on our friend's shoulder when she staggered from the force of the bigger girl's push. "That was mean."

"Oh, was it?" the dark-haired girl mocked in a mean tone. "Why don't you go and cry about it, *curly sue*."

"Her name is Claire," I growled, feeling my body tremble with anger as I moved to stand with my friends. "So why don't you fuck off!"

Everyone around us gasped.

"Holy shit," one of the bigger boys snickered, while more laughed and pointed.

"You cursed," Claire whisper-hissed in my ear. "You said the f-word, Liz."

"Yeah, I did," I agreed, deciding to stand my ground, even when a crowd formed around us. We were outside of school, but even if someone told a teacher on me, I didn't care. I was used to having grown-ups shout at me. I was used to disappointing people. "I can say worse," I added, scowling up at the bully. "I can do worse, too."

"You live over on Avoca Greystones, right?" a different girl asked Claire.

"Yeah," Claire replied, nodding warily. "So?"

"So those are really nice houses," the girl replied. "Why would you invite a Lynch to your house?"

Everyone around us started to laugh.

Shannon's eyes started to fill with tears.

"Because she's my *friend*," Claire defended, grabbing Shannon's hand. "That's why."

"Yeah, well, if I were you, I wouldn't let that scab inside your front door." The girl flicked her ponytail over her shoulder before adding, "You do know she's from Elk's Terrace, don't ya? She'll probably rob your family blind the minute your backs are turned."

"I also heard she has nits," the original bully chimed in. "So you girls might want to think about that before standing so close to her. You don't want head lice, do you?"

"Why don't you shut the hell up," I screamed, rushing forward and shoving the girl as hard as I could.

Instead of pushing me back, the girl laughed in my face. All her friends laughed, too. Because they were bigger than us. That made me even madder.

I couldn't control the anger building up inside of me, and what's more, I didn't want to. Shannon was a good friend to me. Being around her helped me keep my mind clear and get my voice out. It didn't matter to me where she lived. She was kind and sweet and made me feel safe. I wanted to scratch these girls' eyes out. I wanted to make them bleed, make them pay for hurting my friend.

"Lizzie, don't," Shannon pleaded, wrapping her small hand around mine. "Let's just walk over here and wait for your bus."

"Yeah, *Lizzie*," the bully sneered. "Listen to scabby Shannon who can't take the bus because her scabby parents are too poor to pay for it."

The kids around us all started to laugh, and it made me shake with anger. "Take it back," I warned, breaking free from my friends and balling my hands into fists at my sides. "Take back what you said right now!"

"Or what?" she goaded, leaning down to smirk in my face. "What are you going to do, looney tune?"

"Heads up!" I heard a boy call out moments before the bully staggered away from us.

"Omigod!" Gripping her head, the girl started to scream like a banshee. "My head, my head!"

Shocked, I turned to see Joey Lynch coming down the steps that led from the pitch to the school gates with a hurley slung over his shoulder.

Shannon's big brother was only in second class, but the older boys still moved out of his way. Because they were afraid of him. Because he got into a *lot* of fights at school. Even more than me.

"I said heads up." Joey yanked the school gate open with such force that it clattered against the wall. He didn't need to shove through the crowd to get to his sister; everyone scampered out of his way. "It's not my problem if you're deaf."

"Maybe you should have better aim," the bully wailed, still holding her head, while the friends that had been with her all rushed for the bus pulling up.

"Maybe you shouldn't stand so close to my baby sister," Joey replied, purposefully stepping in front of us and blocking her from view.

"You really hurt me, *Joey Lynch*," the girl continued to wail, full-on crying now. "I'm telling my brother on you."

"I never laid a finger on ya, *Loretta Crowley*," he replied with a careless shrug. "But go right ahead and tell your whole fucking family for all I care."

"She called Shannon a scab," Claire blurted out, tugging on the sleeve of Joey's white school shirt. "And she pushed her, too."

"Oh, did she now?" Joey replied, keeping his eyes locked on Loretta. "That was a mistake, wasn't it, Loretta?"

"I'm not afraid of you," she replied, but she backed up several steps. "You're a scumbag."

"Yeah," Joey agreed with a dangerous chuckle, closing the space she put between them. "But I'm a scumbag that'll tear your fucking world apart if you touch my sister again."

Whoa.

"Tell your brother to come find me," he said before proceeding to hook the sliotar he'd hit her with onto his hurley with expert precision. "I'll be waiting for him. And as for you?" Catching the white, leather ball midair, he tucked it into the pocket of his school trousers and added, "You better take note of *this* warning because it's the last one you'll get, ya hear?"

Loretta sucked in a loud breath before turning around and running in the direction of the school buses.

Ha!

Good enough for you.

I didn't even try to hide the laugh that escaped me.

I was thrilled.

"Shan," Joey said then, turning his attention to his sister. "You good?"

"All good, Joe," she mumbled, quickly moving to his side.

Nostrils flaring, he stared down at his sister for a long moment before saying. "Good." And then, without looking at me or Claire, he nodded stiffly. "Let's go."

"Uh, bye, guys," Shannon called out before hurrying after her brother, who was striding off in the direction of town. "See you after Halloween break."

"Bye," we both called back before turning to gape at each other.

"That was so cool!" I laughed as we hurried toward our bus. "He made her cry."

"That was so scary," Claire offered, brown eyes wide. "Shannon's brother looked super-mad at everyone." She frowned before adding, "He even looked mad at us."

"That's because he's always mad," one of the twins from our class said when we lined up behind them for the bus. I wasn't sure if it was Marybeth or Cadence because they looked *exactly* the same. I didn't mind either way. They were both nice.

"With everyone," the other twin agreed at the same time I said, "I think he's great."

"*Ooh*," the first twin snickered, covering her mouth with her hand. "Lizzie has the hots for Shannon's brother."

"What's the hots?"

"It's when you look at a boy and your face gets hot."

"No it's not."

"Uh-huh, yeah it is."

"I think I have the hots for Joey, too," the second twin confessed. When her cheeks turned bright pink, I decided this one had to be Cadence. She was the twin that blushed whenever a teacher asked her a question. "My face gets hot when I see him on the playground."

"Me, too," Marybeth agreed. "It's because he's pretty, like Casper."

Claire frowned. "The ghost?"

"Yep," the twins said in unison, before both adding, "but the real boy Casper."

The line moved, and my friends climbed up the steps of the bus, while I followed behind.

When I reached the aisle and saw how full the bus was, I felt something strange in my belly. Normally, we took a smaller one home from school at 2 p.m. that was just for junior and senior infants, but because today was Halloween break and everyone had finished at 12 p.m., we had to take the bus with the bigger kids. This bus was one of the big ones, and it picked up children from other schools, too. I didn't like it.

When one of the twins pulled Claire down to sit beside her, and the other sat with someone else, the feeling in my belly got worse.

Finding an empty row across the aisle, I set my schoolbag down on the outside seat and took the seat near the window before the bus took off.

Everything was so loud.

The other children.

The roar of the engine.

The laughter around me.

The vibrations beneath my seat.

Too loud.

Too much.

Uncomfortable, I placed my hands on my lap and focused on picking at the small sliver of skin hanging from my nail as the bus driver made his trek through town.

Caoimhe called those pieces of skin *upstarts* and told me not to pick them or they would get worse, but that never stopped me.

Eyes trained on the wobbly piece of skin, I plucked and yanked at it until it gave way and tore off. When the stinging sensation started in my finger, I felt my shoulders relax. A small red dot appeared from the cut, the same color as the dots in my underwear earlier, and I watched in fascination as it slowly trickled down my finger.

Like a tiny river of blood, the voice whispered from the dark corner of my mind, *you belong to the water, little bee.*

Oh no.

No, no, no.

My body stiffened and I looked around in panic, wondering if anyone else had heard it. Nobody seemed to. They were all chatting and laughing with each other and not looking in my direction. The bus had stopped again, and some children were getting off while even more were getting on.

All boys this time.

Loud, noisy boys.

Panicking, I pulled my sleeves down, hiding my fingers under the fabric of my school jumper. Because I wanted to keep picking. I wanted to scratch and tear and peel my skin off because it made me feel calm. But I wasn't supposed to do that anymore. Because it was bad. The doctors said so.

So I used my sleeves to hide my hands from my eyes.

From my mind.

Because I *wanted* to be a good girl.

Like Mark promised I would be.

"Yay! You did it!"

My head snapped up when I heard Claire's excited squeal, and I spotted her talking to one of the older boys who had just gotten on. She was talking excitedly to the boy, but I wasn't so sure he was listening to her because he had headphones over his ears. The really cool ones with the metal headband, like Caoimhe got last Christmas. The headphones were attached to a black lead that connected to the silver Walkman in his other hand.

"You are the best big brother ever!" she continued to squeal, clapping her hands together. The twins were both kneeling up on their seats, too, but I couldn't tell them apart this time because they were both blushing.

"This is Marybeth," Claire told her brother, pointing to the twin next to her before pointing to the one in front. "And this is Cadence."

When her brother held an envelope out to them, the twins beamed up at him before both diving for it at the same time.

It quickly became a tugging match between the sisters, and I zoned out, focusing on Claire's big brother instead. I knew she had one, I even knew his name—Hugh—but Claire told us he was stinky and looked like the troll on the cover of storybook *The Three Billy Goats Gruff*.

Claire told a lie.

Her brother did *not* look like the troll.

He was wearing a dark green jumper with the Scoil Eoin crest on it and gray school trousers, and he was tall. Like super tall. He had blond hair like his sister, but his hair was a darker shade and cut tight at the back and sides, leaving a messy mop of wavy curls on top.

"That's Lizzie," Claire announced then, pointing in my direction as the bus pulled off again. "She's right over there, see?"

Claire's brother looked my way then, and I felt a sudden wave of warmth flush through my body. Not the angry warm feeling or the scary warm one that happened at nighttime. No, this was a *different* kind of warm. Like the warm I felt when I saw Shannon's brother at school. Except *nicer*.

So much nicer.

Her brother started to walk toward me, and I felt my body lock tight, while the warm feeling grew hotter and hotter.

When he reached my seat, he slid his headphones down to rest on his neck before offering me a hopeful smile. "Lizzie?"

Whoa.

Claire was a big, fat liar.

Nodding eagerly, I grabbed my schoolbag off the seat and smiled up at him, hoping and praying he would sit down.

He *did*.

"Thanks," he said, placing his bag on the floor with mine. "I'm Hugh."

"I know." Excitement bubbled inside me when he turned to face me. "Claire told us you looked like a troll." Twisting sideways on my seat, I leaned in close and took a whiff. "Claire said you were stinky." I pulled back and frown. "But you're not." He smelled like soap and strawberries. "I like how you smell."

"Uh, okay?" Hugh replied with a small laugh. "Thanks, I think?"

His eyes were big, and warm, and brown, and safe. Not the same dark brown as Claire's eyes. Hers were much darker. Her brother's eyes were brown like the color of my daddy's whiskey.

Whiskey eyes.

"What's that?" I asked, pointing at his headphones that were still playing music.

"This?" He held the device up. "It's a Walkman."

"I know that, silly." Giggling, I reached up and tapped one of the earphones. "What's the song?"

"Oh." He pulled the headphones off his neck and handed them to me. "It's called 'Send Me on My Way' from Rusted Root."

Holding the speaker part to my ear, I listened carefully to the melody playing. It was a happy one. It made me smile. "I like it."

"Yeah," he agreed when I handed the headphones back to him. "Me, too."

Attention riveted on the boy sitting next to me, I studied every amber-colored fleck and pattern in his eyes. Thick, dark lashes fanned out from his eyelids, the same color as his big pupils.

Hugh Biggs had whiskey eyes that didn't look away.

Instead, they stayed right on mine, warm and kind and chasing away the scary feeling in my head. Caoimhe always told me to stop staring so hard at people. She said it was creepy and weird. But this boy didn't seem to mind.

"Your eyes are nice," I told him, feeling my heart flip-flop when I looked at him. "I like them."

"Uh, thanks?" His cheeks reddened. "I like yours, too."

"Your face is red."

He shifted in discomfort. "So is yours."

"I know why." I beamed back at him. "It's because I give you the hots."

"Uh." He looked surprised and his face turned even redder. "I, uh…"

"It's okay." Grinning, I grabbed his hand and pressed it to my cheek. "See? You give me the hots, too."

"Uh…yeah, maybe," he mumbled, pulling his hand away. "Here," he said then, thrusting an envelope into my hands, brown eyes watching me warily. "It's an invitation to my birthday party." His cheeks started to turn pink. "I hope you can come."

"I can," I blurted out, gripping the envelope for dear life. "I'll come."

"You don't even know what day it is," he chuckled, giving me a peculiar look. "It's on Halloween, so you might be busy with your family."

"I'm not," I hurried to say, unsure if I was busy or not. I didn't know and I didn't care. All I knew for sure in this moment was that I *was going* to his birthday party. "I'll be there."

"It's a fancy dress party."

"Oh." I scrunched my nose up. "I don't like dressing up."

"Yeah, me either," he sighed. "But my mam makes us because of my birthday being on Halloween." He offered me an apologetic smile. "Some of the lads in my class will have pound shop masks and bin bags on, so don't worry about fancy costumes," he added before bursting into laughter.

"What?" I grinned and shifted closer. "What's so funny?"

"I'm just thinking about my friend," he explained, still chuckling. "He's dressing up as Peter Pan." He choked out another hearty laugh, and this time a snort escaped. "He has green tights and everything."

His laughter caused me to laugh along with him, and I shivered when a rippling feeling settled in my belly. "What are you dressing up as?"

"Dr. Grant from *Jurassic Park*."

"Dr. Grant," I repeated to myself, tucking that information safely away. "So, no tights then?"

"Definitely not," he mused, brown eyes twinkling with amusement. "You really don't have to dress up." His tone was gentle when he added, "You don't have to do anything you don't want to."

"Really?"

"Yeah." He looked at me for a long time before he shook his head and stood up. "I better go back to my friends." Reaching for his bag, he slung it over his shoulder and offered me a smile. "See ya later."

"See ya," I replied, even though I wanted to tell him to come back.

Hugh shook his head and turned to leave, only to swing back around and lean in close. "I think you're right," he whispered, breath fanning my cheek.

I turned to ask him what he meant, but he was already walking away. Pulling up on my knees, I rested my chin on the back of my seat and watched Claire's brother join a group of boys wearing the same uniform as him at the back of the bus.

Grinning, I watched Hugh take a seat next to a dark-haired boy who wrapped his arm around his neck and put him in a headlock. They both started laughing and wrestling each other, while the other boys cheered them on.

When Claire's brother broke free from his friend's headlock, he craned his head up and looked in my direction.

When his eyes landed on mine and he grinned, my heart flip-flopped again. I quickly sank back down on my seat and exhaled a shaky breath. Feeling my face burn with heat, I clutched his invitation to my chest and *smiled*.

THIS IS LIZZIE?

Hugh

WHEN I BOARDED THE BUS AFTER SCHOOL ON FRIDAY, I FELT LIKE A SOLDIER BEING sent on a dangerous mission. Because I just *knew* that anyone my crazy sister attached herself to was going to be a menace, and I had to invite *four* of them to my party. To their *faces*. Worse, Joe picked Gibsie up after school, so I didn't have him on the bus to back me up, and Feely was enjoying my embarrassment too much to step in and help. One of her friends didn't take the bus, so Claire had taken her invitation to school with her this morning to hand over, but that still left three of them.

I spotted Pierce's twin sisters sitting with Claire, so with a grim expression on my face, I trudged down the aisle, stopping when I reached them. They turned to look at me at the exact same time, smiling the same smile and speaking the same words at the same time.

I knew they couldn't help being identical, but it creeped me out so bad.

Jesus, I was so grateful I didn't have to live with *two* Claires.

With three down and one to go, I had every intention of finding the last girl, handing over the invitation as fast as possible, and then booking it back to my friends. What I *didn't* intend on was freezing up in the middle of the aisle when my sister pointed out *her*.

Holy crap.

This was my sister's friend?

This is Lizzie?

I used to think my sister had the lightest blond hair I'd ever seen, but this girl's hair was *white*. Like *snow white*. Her skin was so pale it was almost see-through, like one of Claire's porcelain dolls. She didn't have a single freckle on her face, either. Not even one.

And her blue eyes, the ones locked on my face? Well, I had never seen eyes like *that* before.

I blinked a few times, not entirely sure if I was seeing her properly because this girl didn't look like the other girls on the bus. She didn't look like anything I'd ever seen before.

She sort of resembled a ghost.

Or an angel.

Something different.

Something special.

The girl didn't look away from me when she caught me looking. Instead, she continued to stare back at me.

Somehow, and I wasn't sure how, I managed to gather the nerve to walk over and ask, "Lizzie?" Because if Claire had pointed out the wrong girl, I was going to be embarrassed.

God, please let this be the right girl.

When she nodded and offered me the seat next to her, I almost fell into it. This confused me because I never wanted to sit with girls, but I *wanted* to sit with this girl. I *wanted* to look at her, too.

Her long, poker-straight hair wasn't tied up with any fancy ribbons or bows like the other girls. Instead, she had it tucked behind her ears to keep it out of her way. She wasn't wearing tights like the other girls, either. She wore white socks that stopped below her knees. Her coat was black, not pink or colorful, and both her knees were littered with bramble scratches. Everything about this girl was different, but it was her eyes that really caught my attention. They were so light, they looked like pale-blue icicles with jagged lightning bolts of gray darting through them.

When I introduced myself and we started to talk, I couldn't hear a word of it. I had no clue what was coming out of my mouth. I was too distracted by the sound of my pulse drumming in my ears and the way my eyes enjoyed looking at this girl. It honestly couldn't be helped because sitting in front of me was the prettiest girl in the world. When she leaned in and sniffed my neck, I thought she might be the strangest, too. I didn't pull away, though, and I didn't feel awkward or embarrassed when she paid me a compliment. Instead, I felt *pleased*. Because I quickly realized that I *wanted* her to admire me.

Like I was definitely admiring her.

When I handed her the invitation to my party and she agreed to come, my stomach flipped like a pancake. I tried to be cool about it, but I could hardly breathe. The way she smiled at me made my skin prickle and heat up. I wasn't sure how long it took me to get back to my friends, but when I did, I felt like I'd just staggered off a fairground ride. A really fast one that spun me ragged and made me dizzy.

When the lads started teasing me about her, I found myself not caring one bit. Instead, I laughed off their taunts, feeling smug instead of embarrassed.

Because they didn't know what I did.

They didn't have the strangest girl in Ballylaggin coming to their birthday party.

My eyes locked on hers from across the bus and I smiled.

Or the prettiest.

HE SMELLS LIKE SOAP AND STRAWBERRIES
Lizzie

I WAS SO HAPPY THAT I THOUGHT I MIGHT EXPLODE INTO A HUNDRED MILLION pieces. I had been waiting for Halloween to arrive ever since Friday, and it was finally *here*. Excitement bubbled inside of my belly, making it difficult to sit still for my sister.

"You're like my own personal doll," Caoimhe said from her perch behind me, where she was fixing my hair for the party.

"My hair is getting long," I noted, looking at our reflections in her vanity mirror.

"Mm-hmm," she agreed, flicking her waist-long, blond braid over her shoulder. "Almost as long as mine."

"Almost."

"What time is Claire's mam picking you up?"

"Half past two." A shiver of excitement rolled through me. "What time is it now?"

"Almost two," my sister replied. "You know, you don't have to bring the invitation with you, Liz."

"I know. I just...like it." Still clutching the invitation in my hands, I read it out loud for the hundredth time. "To Lizzie, you are—"

"Invited."

"I know how to read, Caoimhe," I grumbled before quickly carrying on, "to my seventh birthday party—"

"At two o'clock, on the thirty-first of October."

"Hey," I snapped, covering the invitation with my hand so she couldn't see it. "I said I can read it myself."

Huffing out a breath, I retrained my focus on the invitation.

"From Huge," I said slowly, concentrating on saying it right. "From Hu...ge..." A laugh escaped my sister, and I narrowed my eyes in challenge. "It's a hard name, okay!"

"Yes, it is," she agreed, trying to smother her laughter. "And it's Hugh, just so you know. Not *Huge*."

"I knew that," I grumbled, fingers trailing over the handwritten invitation. "Hugh. I like his name." A small smile grew across my face. "I like his handwriting, too. He's neat."

"He *is* neat," she agreed, leaning over my shoulder to inspect the invitation.

"I'm neat, too," I offered. "Not as neat as him, though."

"Yeah, well, you're only six. He's seven."

"I'll be seven in June."

"So? It's not a competition."

"He does joint writing." I held the invitation up to her face for a closer look. "Look at how good his *g* is." I pointed to the perfectly curved letter. "It's the best *g* I've ever seen." I glanced up and caught her eye in the mirror. "You have to show me how to do it."

"Oh my God, Liz, chill." Setting the hairbrush down, my sister retrieved a bottle of perfume from the vanity and squirted it on my hair. "You don't need to learn everything right now. Just turn your mind off and enjoy being a kid."

"But I can't turn my mind off," I protested. "It never stops talking to me."

"*No.*" Smoothing my hair, she gave me a warning look. "You *don't* say things like that."

Swallowing down my words, I nodded my head in understanding.

I knew what that look meant.

It was the same one Dad gave me.

Shut my mouth and keep it in my head.

"See how much we get along when you're not being crazy?" Caoimhe offered then, fixing my outfit. "I swear, this past year has been the best since you were born." She smiled at me in the mirror. "Honestly, you're like a different person since they changed your meds."

"I got in trouble at school last week," I reminded her. "I bit a boy in my class."

"Okay, *aside* from that," she chuckled. "Overall, you've been kicking ass."

I smiled proudly.

I liked it when Caoimhe was happy with me.

I wanted everyone to be happy with me.

"I hate my new doctor," I replied, grimacing at the thought of the lady with the bright-pink lipstick. "She keeps asking me questions."

"Yeah, well, if you don't want to answer them, just lie."

"Lie?"

She nodded. "Tell her what she wants to hear."

"But I'm not supposed to tell lies."

"White lies are fine." She grinned. "I tell white lies all the time."

"You do?"

She nodded. "Yup."

"About what?"

"About my age when I want to do things that I'm too young for." She grinned again. "And my…" A sad look came over her then and she sighed. "About lots of things."

"Do you tell me lies?"

"Only to keep you safe."

I frowned. "Huh?"

"It doesn't matter." She ruffled my hair again. "I am proud of you, you know. You're talking like a normal human being and not freaking out every ten seconds. You've finally started primary school, made yourself a couple of little buddies, and you've even managed to snag yourself a party invite." She winked. "Maybe there's hope for you yet."

"He's really pretty," I sighed, feeling my mind drift back to Claire's brother. "He's got brown eyes and he's tall, and he smells like soap and strawberries, and he doesn't look like a troll at all."

"Aw," Caoimhe gushed, pressing her hand to her chest. "You like him, don't you?"

"Yep." I pointed to my clothes then and asked, "Are you sure this is the right costume?"

"Oh yeah," Caoimhe confirmed, perching sunglasses on my head like a hairband. "You look *amazing*, Liz."

Mammy was supposed to help me get ready, but she had to go to the hospital last night. For another sleepover. Daddy went to visit her this morning and left Caoimhe in charge.

"When's she coming home?"

"Who?"

"Mam."

"Soon."

"Today?"

My sister shook her head. "Just soon, Liz."

"I'm not stupid, Caoimhe," I growled, feeling my body heat up. "I know something's happening to Mam," I choked out, balling my hands into fists at my sides. "I just…I don't understand."

"Be glad you don't, Liz." Sighing heavily, she wrapped her arms around me from behind and hugged me tightly. "Listen, when you're old enough to understand, I'll explain everything to you, but until then, just enjoy being a kid."

I can't, I wanted to scream. *I'm too scared.*

"It's bad, isn't it?" I pushed, stomach sinking. "Mammy's really sick this time, isn't she?"

"She was sick last time, too, and she got better," my sister replied in a tight voice. "Mam's a fighter. She'll beat it again."

"Why does it keep happening to her?"

"I don't know."

"But it keeps coming back, Caoimhe."

"Yeah, Liz, I *know*."

"Is she going to die?"

Caoimhe sighed heavily again. "Nope, enough of the heavy for one day." Releasing me from her bear hug, Caoimhe straightened up and blew out a shaky breath. "Today is a good day, busy Lizzie bee." Plastering on a wide smile, she walked over to her boom box and grabbed a cassette from her impressive stack of music. "It's Halloween. You're going to your first birthday party, where there will be countless hours of fun and dancing. Meanwhile, I'm spending the day with my boyfriend, therefore…" Pausing, she switched up tapes and fiddled with the buttons on the deck until the sound of "Twist and Shout" from Chaka Demus & Pliers blasted from the speakers. "I feel a little pre-dance celebration is in order."

"Oh my God." Unable to stop myself, I snickered into my hand when Caoimhe chicken danced toward me. "You are so strange."

"Oh, *I'm* strange?" Laughing, she grabbed my hand and danced me across the room. "Talk about the pot calling the kettle black, Baby Sister."

Unable to resist the temptation of dancing with Caoimhe, I pushed my scary feelings deep down inside and replaced them with a bright smile. One just like hers.

The sound of our doorbell ringing a moment later caused my sister to scream. "Oh my God. It's him!" Squealing with excitement, she dropped my hands and dove for her vanity table. "He's early!" Swiping up her favorite brown lipstick, she carefully drew on her lips before patting them together. Turning back to look at me, she fluffed out her hair. "Well?" she asked, pouting her lips and striking a pose. "How do I look?"

Caoimhe was wearing a loose, strappy, plaid-green dress that stopped way above her knees, her favorite Dr. Martens, and arms full of bangles. Her hair was half-up, half-down, with parts of it crimped.

"You look like a grown-up," I replied, feeling jealous because my hair was straight and boring.

The doorbell rang again, and my sister burst into action. "Oh my God, I better go and let him inside," she said, rushing toward me with her pinky finger extended. "Okay, you promise to not tell on me?"

I hooked my finger around hers. "I promise."

"Dad would kill me if they knew I brought Mark over when they're not home, so you can't say anything." She chewed on her lip. "Seriously, you can't tell, Liz."

"I won't."

"Because you know how pissed they got when I brought Dar over when they were out." She snickered. "Dad was so pissed when they got home, and he found us in my room."

"I miss Darren," I replied, thinking about Shannon's big brother. The one who looked just like her. "He was nice."

"Yeah, I miss Dar, too," she agreed. "We've drifted since starting secondary school, but he'll always be one of my best friends."

"How come you drifted?"

"He goes to BCS now," she explained. "And he can't stand…well, let's just say he's not the biggest fan of the friends I've made at Tommen."

"How come he was never your boyfriend?" I shrugged. "You knew him first."

"I used to want him to be." She clasped her hands together and sighed. "But it didn't happen that way." She smiled brightly then. "But Mark *is* my boyfriend, and he's superfine, and super-sexy, and I'll be super-dead if Dad finds out he was here when I'm babysitting you, so you can't tell." She gave me a worried look. "I mean it, Liz. You *have* to keep your mouth shut."

"I know, I know." I rolled my eyes and grumbled, "I can keep a secret, Caoimhe." I always did.

JELLY SNAKES AND THE PERFECT G

Hugh

OCTOBER 31, 1994

"HUGH!" ROBBIE MAC, WHO WAS DRESSED AS THE RED POWER RANGER, BARKED FROM his perch at my kitchen table. He pointed to the two girls dressed in princess costumes sitting on either side of him and mouthed the words *do something.*

My birthday party was in full swing, and my house was packed to the rafters with friends. Unfortunately for Robbie, Pierce's creepy twin sisters had taken a shining to him. I wasn't sure what he thought I could do about it. One thing I wasn't going to do was swap places with him. I'd already spent enough of my time with Claire hanging off my arm. I had no plans on volunteering myself for two more.

Pretending like I couldn't hear Robbie, I pushed past a group of lads battering a piñata and headed outside. I rolled my eyes when I passed Danny Callaghan from my class, who was dressed as the Blue Power Ranger, pointing and laughing at Robbie. "Look, lads, Robbie has a *girlfriend.*"

What an asshole.

Relieved when I found Peter Pan and Zorro in the driveway, I made a beeline for them.

"What the hell are you doing?" I demanded when I reached them and caught sight of the slobber dribbling down Peter Pan's chin. "What the fuck is in your mouth, Gibs?"

"…elly…akes…" Gibs tried to slur around a mouthful of what I could only describe as goo.

"He's trying to break the world record," Zorro snickered.

"For *what*?" I demanded, gaping at Feely. "Being an eejit?"

"…elly…akes…" Gibs repeated, using his fingers to push the goo back into his mouth.

"Gibsie thinks he can break the world record of putting the most jelly snakes in his mouth," Feely explained through fits of laughter.

"What's the record?" I asked.

"He doesn't know."

"Then how can he break it?"

"…uther…un…" Gibsie instructed, holding his palm out. "…uther…un…eely…"

"No clue, lad," Feely laughed, handing over another jelly snake to an expectant Gibs. "But it's keeping him quiet."

"He might choke," I warned, eyeing him warily.

"He might," Feely agreed.

"How many has he got so far?"

"Nine."

"Nine?" My eyes widened in wonder. "No fucking way." I gaped at Gibsie. "You're eating them, aren't you?" I narrowed my eyes in suspicion. "You can't fit nine jelly snakes in your mouth, you little liar."

"…ope…" Gibs shook his head and gagged, causing more dribble to leak from his mouth. "…oh…uck!"

The moment he clutched his stomach and started to heave, Feely and I dove out of the way. It wasn't our first time dealing with his upchuck reflux.

"Oh my God." Howling with laughter, Feely clutched his side and pointed at our dopey friend who was purging his gob of jelly. "He looks like Mouth from *The Goonies*."

Groaning in dismay, I clutched my stomach and took in the sight of Gibsie's latest misadventure sprayed all over my driveway. "You are *sick*, Gerard Gibson."

"See? I told you I didn't eat them," Gibs declared proudly when he was finished expelling his snakes. "See, Hugh?" He pointed to each slobbery jelly on the concrete and counted. "Nine full-sized bad boys without a toothmark on them."

"Congratulations," I replied with a shudder. "You have the biggest mouth in Ballylaggin."

The sound of a car horn honking caused all three of us to turn toward my mother's car as it pulled up on the footpath outside our house.

"Well, it's about time!" Gibsie declared with a dramatic sigh before proceeding to use Feely's black cape to clean the dribble off his chin.

"Dammit, Gibs!" Feely shoved him away before quickly peeling off his cape and throwing it at him. "You *are* sick."

"Peter Pan!" My sister's high-pitched scream of excitement pierced the air moments before she came barreling past both me and Feely.

Looking every inch the fairy in her Tinker Bell costume, Claire launched herself at the snake-stuffer himself. "I missed you so much!"

When Gibsie straightened up to his full height, he took my sister with him, causing her feet to lift off the ground. "I missed you more, Claire-Bear."

"He was only gone to his dad's house for the weekend," I reminded her, feeling more uncomfortable with my sister's interactions with my best friend by the day.

Before Joe moved out, they'd spent every spare waking hour of the day together, but now that Gibs had to split his time between Sadhbh's and Joe's, they were even more annoying.

Gibs was *always* looking at her, and on the rare occasion he wasn't, Claire was looking at *him*.

Our mothers called it harmless puppy love, but I wasn't so sure about that.

I had a niggling feeling they would always look at each other like that.

I wasn't sure what to think about it.

"I wouldn't touch him if I were you," Feely warned, keeping a wide berth of them both, while he readjusted his black sombrero. "He just puked nine jelly snakes."

"You did?" My sister's eyes widened to saucers, and she looked up at my oldest friend like he hung the moon. "The most you did last time was seven!"

"I told you I'm going to get in that *Guinness World Records*, Claire-Bear." Proud as a peacock, Gibs set her down on her feet and swiftly reached for her hand. "Come on. There's a tray of brownies in the kitchen with our names on them."

"Claire, haven't you forgotten someone?" Mam called out in a frazzled tone, but it was too late. My sister had already disappeared inside the house with Gibs in search of sugar.

"Ah, crap," Feely muttered under his breath. "Another one."

Meanwhile, my heart started to thump violently in my chest.

She's here.

"I'm sorry about Claire, sweetheart." Rounding the car, Mam opened the back passenger door and smiled. "She doesn't have a spark of sense between her two ears."

"It's fine, Mrs. Biggs," a familiar voice replied. "I'm used to it."

"Call me Sinead," I heard my mother instruct. "And my husband's name is Pete. None of that Mr. and Mrs. Biggs talk, ya hear, love?"

"Just keep backing up," Feely whisper-hissed, moving backward in the direction of the house. "Maybe your mam won't see us."

"Yeah," I tossed back with a forced laugh but made no move to follow him. I had no intention of running away from *this* girl.

"Hugh? Oh good. Come here, love. You can bring Lizzie inside."

Yes!

"Sorry, lad, you're on your own." Snickering, Feely bolted for the door. "I have four sisters," he called over his shoulder. "I suffer enough."

"Hugh!"

"Yeah, Mam, I'm coming," I called back, feeling my palms sweat with every step I took toward the car.

I would never admit it to a soul, not even Gibs, but I *wanted* to see Lizzie Young again. I'd thought about her a lot over the weekend and hoped she would come today. Now she was here, I felt nervous and sick and excited all at once.

"Ah, here's my birthday boy," Mam said when I reached them. She wrapped an arm around my shoulders and pulled me to her side. "I promise this one has much better manners than his sister."

Usually, but right now, I didn't have a word left in my head to fulfill my mother's promise because all my words had flown clean out of my head, and all I could do was stand there and take in the sight of her.

Last week, on the school bus, when I told her my party was fancy dress, I could tell she wasn't a fan, but she was here right now, rocking the coolest costume I'd ever seen.

"You're Dr. Sattler," I finally found my voice and said, eyes raking over her costume with approval. "From *Jurassic Park*."

Unlike the other girls, who were dressed in princess costumes and fairy wings, this girl wore khaki shorts, brown hiking boots, a blue vest, and a pink button-up shirt tied in a knot at her waist. Attached to the brown belt around her waist was a plastic walkie-talkie and a yellow lanyard.

The fact that Lizzie showed up to my party in full costume made me feel special, but knowing that she was matching me? Well, I didn't know how to handle the way that made me feel.

"Happy birthday, Hugh," she said, extending her hand to me. "I mean, Dr. Grant."

"Jesus." The word slipped out of my mouth without permission, and I shook my head, feeling off balance. "I mean thank you…" I cleared my throat, trying to bury the sudden crack in my voice and took her small hand in mine. "And, uh, hi."

"I best go inside and help your father deal with the horde," Mam interrupted, releasing her hold on me. "Hugh, be a good boy and look after Lizzie, will you?" Grabbing several shopping bags off the bonnet of the car, she moved for the front door. "This is her first time at a birthday party, so don't leave her on her own, love."

I arched a brow in surprise. "I'm your first birthday party?"

"You're my first," she confirmed with a shy smile. "I still have your invitation." Releasing my hand, she reached into the pocket of her shorts and retrieved the invitation I had written her. "I like your *g*."

"My *g*?"

"Uh-huh." Nodding eagerly, she unfolded the invite and pointed to where I had signed my name. "You work hard on your handwriting."

I *did* work hard on my handwriting. In fact, I worked hard on everything when it came to school. Not because I had to—learning came easily to me—but because I *wanted* to. English. History. Geography. Nature. Science. Irish. Religion. It didn't matter. I soaked it all in. Everything about the world fascinated me, and I read more books than anyone else in my class, but she couldn't know that. So *how* did she know that?

"You don't have to stay with me, by the way," Lizzie added, tucking the invitation back into her pocket. "I know your mother asked you to, but you can go back to your friends if you want." She smiled again. "I'm not afraid to be on my own."

"No." I shook my head, taking it all in. Taking all of *her* in. "I don't want to do that."

"You don't?"

"No," I confirmed. "I want to stay."

A slow blush crept across her cheeks. "With me?"

Nodding slowly, I kept my attention locked on the strange girl in front of me, while an even stranger pressure grew in my chest. "You're really tall," I noted, taking in how she came up to my nose in height. "For a girl."

"It's my legs." She raised one foot then, giving me no choice but to catch it midair. "My sister says I have giraffe legs."

Her sister was right. "Are you a fast runner?"

"Yep," she replied proudly. "Fastest in my class."

"Thought so," I replied, setting her foot back down. "You're matching me."

"I know." Grinning, she reached up and tipped my hat. "I thought you might like it."

"I do," I replied, feeling my face grow hot again.

"Do you want your present?"

My brows shot up in surprise. "You got me a present?"

"Of course."

"Why?"

"Because it's your birthday."

"But you don't even know me."

"So? You don't know me and you still invited me to your party." With that, she quickly whirled around and moved for my mother's car. "I got you two presents," she explained before opening the car door and climbing inside. "Well, I got you one, and I made you the other."

Intrigued, I followed her to the car and watched as she rummaged around in the back seat. "I don't have a brother, so I'm sorry if you hate it."

"I won't hate it," I replied, taking the parcel from her hands. "And thank you."

"You're welcome." She blew out a loud breath and smiled. "That's the one I bought."

"You want me to open it now?" I asked, feeling another flush of heat spread up my neck when her blue eyes locked on mine.

"Yep."

"Okay then." I shrugged. "Scoot over."

She obliged and I climbed into the back seat beside her, parcel in hand.

"You really didn't have to," I paused to say, midway through unwrapping her gift. "Just so you know."

"Just open it already." Pulling up onto her knees, she watched me with excitement dancing in her eyes. "Go on."

Doing as she asked, I ripped off the rest of the wrapping paper, only to gape in wonder at the computer game in my hands. "*Mortal Kombat II.*" I shook my head in disbelief and clutched the box. "This game *just* came out."

"Yeah, well, Claire told me that you have a Sneeze," she hurried to explain, sounding unsure. "She said you play it all the time. I wasn't sure if you had this game."

"SNES."

"Hm?"

"It's called a SNES," I explained, retraining my attention on the girl sitting beside me. "Super Nes." When she continued to stare blankly at me, I clarified. "Super Nintendo Entertainment System. It's a game console, and I do play it all the time."

"So that game will work on your Sneeze?" she asked, pointing to the game in my hands.

"My SNES," I corrected gently, still in shock. "And it definitely will."

"So you like it?"

"I more than like it." In fact, I'd been hoping to use my birthday money to get it. "Thank you." I shook my head, feeling a mixture of confusion and gratitude. "Seriously, thank you so much."

Relief flashed in her eyes, and she beamed back at me. "You're welcome."

"This is a really big gift," I said slowly, keeping my eyes on hers. "You know that, right? It costs a *lot* of money."

"It's just a game, Hugh," she replied. "My mam said it was fine."

Jesus, her family must be loaded.

"Here." Reaching behind her back, she retrieved a green envelope and thrust it onto my lap. "I made this one."

Setting the game aside so I wouldn't be distracted, I focused all my attention on the envelope with my name on it.

Careful not to tear the homemade card inside, I removed it slowly, dutifully ignoring the cloud of glitter that sprinkled all over my lap in the process.

I lived with Claire, after all. Glitter was a given.

"This is great," I told her, inspecting every inch of her work. It must have taken her hours. Every spare inch of card was filled with color and paint. "You have lovely handwriting." I smiled at the scraggly *g* in my name, where she had attempted cursive. "You're neat."

"Not as neat as you."

"Well, I practice a lot."

"I bet I practice more."

"And I read."

"I bet I read more."

"Oh yeah?" My lips twitched and I tried not to smile, but she was cute when she challenged me. "I doubt that."

"Oh yeah?" Her eyes narrowed once again in challenge. "Try me."

"Okay then." Grinning, I began to reel off the names of every book I could remember, while this strange little girl accepted my challenge by responding with the names of the main characters in every book. And I mean *every single book*. From there, she stunned me with her ability to not only count but add and subtract in her head, without a copybook to work out the sums. She could spell every single word I threw at her, even the difficult ones I planned to catch her out with. Except the only thing that caught me out was *surprise* when she spelled every word without breaking a sweat.

"How do you know all this?" I asked, attention glued to this girl and everything that came out of her mouth because I had never felt more impressed by another person in my life. It wasn't just her outfit that matched mine, but her brain did, too. "Claire doesn't know a quarter of the things you do."

She grinned victoriously. "Told you I'm smart."

"Yeah." I eyed her warily. "You don't act like you're in junior infants."

She shrugged and tossed back, "You don't act like you're in first class."

"That's because I'm smarter than most seven-year-olds."

"Yeah, and I'm smarter than most six-year-olds."

"You're six?" My brows rose in surprise. "When were you born?"

"June 9, 1988."

"So I'm less than a year older than you?"

"Seven months and twenty-two days." She smirked. "I counted."

"Then how come you're in junior infants? Shouldn't you be in seniors?" I frowned. "Or first class like me."

"Uh, yeah." The light in her eyes quickly faded and she dropped her gaze to her lap. "I know."

"Did you get held back or something?" I asked, even though I found it hard to believe. It wouldn't make sense to make a girl as bright as her repeat a year of school.

"I used to go to a different school in the city," she replied, voice small now. I followed her gaze to where she was clasping her hands together so tightly the skin was turning white. "But when I moved to Sacred Heart, they put me in juniors." She chewed on her bottom lip. "I'm not slow," she hurried to add, digging her fingernails into her hand. "I swear I'm not..."

"I know you're not, okay?" I replied, reaching down to peel her hands apart. "And who cares if you're the oldest in your class?" She didn't seem to realize that she was scratching herself, but I noticed. "You're younger than most of my class and still way smarter."

Her head snapped up, and her blue eyes locked on mine. "I am?"

"Yeah." I nodded, wanting to take the worry away for her. I could see it in her eyes, and I didn't like it. "You are."

When the fear in her eyes was replaced with hope and her small hand tightened around mine, I felt a tingling sensation surge through me. While my brain seemed confused by the tingling, my heart assured me that it was an important feeling.

That *she* was important.

"My words used to get stuck," she explained then, still holding my hand. "It was hard for me to get them out."

"Like a stutter?" I asked, feeling doubtful. There was a boy in my class at school who had a really bad one. Lizzie didn't seem to have any problem pronouncing her words.

"Nope, not a stutter. They just got stuck," she replied, looking up at me with those pale blue eyes. "But I can get them out now."

"Well, that's good." I smiled. "Because you have a nice voice."

Her eyes lit up. "I do?"

Aw, crap.

She pulled her hand from mine then and clutched her stomach. "Uh-oh."

"What?"

"It's my belly," she explained. "It keeps twisting around."

I eyed her warily. "Like in a pukey way?"

"No, not pukey." She paused for a moment before saying. "More like hiccups."

"In your throat?"

"No, hiccups in my belly," she corrected. "And butterflies in my throat."

I frowned. "So...you have flutter-cups?"

"Oh my God, yes!" She nodded eagerly. "I have flutter-cups!"

"Fuck." I couldn't stop the laugh that escaped me. "You're so strange."

"Say it again."

"Fuck?"

She grinned. "Fuck."

"How are your flutter-cups?"

"Still there, but it's okay," she laughed. "They don't hurt."

"That's good to know," I replied. *Because I think I caught them, too.*

"What did you mean on the bus?" she asked then. "About me being right."

Aw double crap.

"Uh…I'll tell you later." Pushing the car door open, I sprang out before I embarrassed myself further. "Come on." Smiling, I waved at her to follow me. "Let's go inside and play."

STARS ARE BETTER THAN SQUARES

OCTOBER 31, 1994

AFTER THE CAKE WAS EATEN, WE WERE ALL SENT INTO THE LOUNGE TO PLAY BECAUSE it was raining too heavy to go back outside. Cadence played with a few dolls from Claire's toy box, while the bigger boys wrestled and jumped around to the music playing. Claire and Gibsie were bouncing on the couch, playing the Five Little Monkeys Game.

I wasn't sure what to do.

I didn't know how to talk to everyone.

I missed Shannon.

I wished she had come to the party.

She didn't like to talk a lot, and I liked that about her. Sometimes it was nice to *not* talk and still be friends.

Sitting on the window seat, I dangled my legs off the side and watched everyone. It was so loud. It made my head feel dizzy. Like it was spinning. I felt hot, too, like I was in front of the fire.

My attention switched from one side of the room to the other. I wanted to run away, but we couldn't go outside, so I sat on my hands to stop them from scratching. Shaking my head, I tried to smile, to not feel so cross, but I didn't like this.

It was too loud.

My mind kept flicking back to when my piece of cake fell on the floor and Marybeth laughed.

She was talking to Hugh now.

I narrowed my eyes.

Something in my belly grew.

Something angry.

Something hot.

My breathing got faster and faster until I felt like screaming.

Oh no. No, no, no, no…

I clamped a hand over my mouth to stop myself.

Don't scream.

Be a good girl.

"Hey." Hugh sat down on the window seat next to me. "Not having a good time?"

I couldn't answer him.

I was breathing too fast.

I was trying too hard to keep the scream in.

"Hey, hey…" He leaned in close and looked at me with concern. "You okay?"

I still couldn't answer him.

All I could do was keep my hand over my mouth and breathe through my nose, while I shook my head.

"Can you breathe?"

I shook my head again, eyes growing wild and fearful.

"You're okay." Twisting sideways on the seat to face me, he placed his hand on my shoulder and gently steered me until I was sitting with my back to the room, facing the window. "It's probably just a panic attack." He reached for the hand I wasn't using to cover my mouth and gripped it tightly in his. "Just breathe."

All I could do was stare at him in horror. Because while I didn't understand what was happening to me, I knew what would happen next, what always happened next, and I didn't want my friends to see this.

I didn't want *him* to see this.

"There you go." His voice was gentle and kind. "Nice and slow." He squeezed my hand again. "You're okay."

Was I?

I didn't think so.

I wanted to scream. I wanted to tear every picture frame off the walls. I wanted to run away as fast as I could. I wanted to… I wanted to… I wanted to keep looking into his *eyes*.

Focusing all my attention on the boy sitting beside me, I let my eyes roam over his face.

Golden skin.

Yellow hair.

Kind smile.

Eyes like Daddy's whiskey.

Soap and strawberries.

Hugh Biggs.

"There you go," he finally said with a smile, breaking me from my deep concentration. "Look at you."

84

I looked down and was surprised to see that he was holding both of my hands. My hand wasn't on my mouth, and I wasn't screaming.

Confused, I stared down at my hands before flicking my eyes back to his. "I'm okay?"

He nodded and smiled. "You're okay."

I glanced around the room.

Everyone was still playing.

Nobody was looking at me.

Nobody was shouting at me.

I wasn't bad.

I swung my attention back to him. "How did you do that?"

"Do what?"

"Make it stop."

"The panic attack?"

I nodded, not sure if that's what it was but needing to know either way. "How did you make it stop?"

"I didn't do anything, Lizzie," he replied, still smiling, still holding my hands. "You did that yourself."

I didn't.

I knew I didn't.

He looked down at our joined hands that were resting on his lap. "Hmm."

"What?"

"That's the second time I've held your hand." His cheeks reddened. "I've never held a girl's hand before today."

"You haven't?"

He shook his head slowly, still not letting go of my hands. "Have you?" His cheeks flushed, and he quickly added, "Ever held hands with another boy?"

"No." I shook my head. "You're my only boy." I felt my skin grow hot. "Only you."

His lips twitched into a shy smile, like he was pleased with my answer.

"I like you, Hugh Biggs," I blurted out, feeling the heat bursting out of my chest. "I think."

I watched him carefully for a reaction, and when he tried and failed to hide a smile, I felt my heart slam against my chest.

"I don't think I like you, Lizzie Young." He looked out the window when he whispered, "I *know* I do."

———————————

Several hours later, when almost everyone from the party had been collected, I was still waiting for my dad to come. I didn't mind, though. In fact, I secretly hoped he forgot to pick me up. I wanted to stay right here with my new friends.

Well, Claire wasn't a brand-new friend, but her brother and his friends were. The dark-haired boy was called Patrick Feely, and he was super nice but kind of shy. The other boy's name was Gerard Gibson, and he was so *funny*.

Sitting around in a circle on the floor, the five of us played a game of Pass the Whisper, where we had to pass the same whisper to each other and the last person to hear the whisper said it out loud. Gibsie was the last person in our game, and he never got the whisper right. Instead, he said the strangest things that made me laugh so hard my belly ached.

"Lizzie, sweetheart, your father just called me," Sinead Biggs said, walking into the lounge when we were halfway through another round of Pass the Whisper.

Sitting on the couch, she gestured for me to come to her, which I quickly did. I liked her a lot. She had brown eyes like Claire and a gentle voice.

"Your father is running late," she said when I sat down next to her. "I didn't know your mother's in the hospital, sweetheart."

"Your mam's in hospital?" Claire asked, looking over at us from her spot in the circle. "Is she okay?"

I shrugged. "She has cancer."

Her eyes widened. "What's that?"

"Caoimhe's at home, and your father asked me to drop you home to her, but I have a better idea." Sinead took my hand in hers and smiled. It was a nice smile. Like how my mother smiled at me. "How would you like to go trick-or-treating with us first?"

"Yay, yay, yay!" Claire squealed before I could answer. "Please come, Lizzie." Jumping to her feet, she ran over to the couch and climbed up beside me. "It's so much fun, and we always get a ton of sweets."

"Okay!" I laughed, shaking from the force with which my friend was tugging on my arm. "I'll come."

"Yay, yay, yay," Claire cried out happily, still pulling on my arm. "Can she stay, Mam? Can Lizzie sleep over, too?" She leaned over me to grab her mother's shoulders. "Please, Mam, please. Hughie always gets to have friends sleep over." Scrambling over me, Claire plopped down on her mother's lap and started to beg. "Please, Mammy, *please*! Hugh gets to have Patrick and Gerard sleep over tonight. I want Lizzie."

Nobody had ever said that about me before.

But Claire did.

She said she wanted *me*.

My heart thumped with excitement.

"She can stay in my room, and I'll share my teddies with her, I promise," Claire continued to plead. "Please, Mammy, she's my bestest friend."

"Well, it's fine by me, but maybe we should ask Lizzie what she wants to do first, hmm?" Sinead laughed. "How about it, sweetheart?" She turned to smile at me. "Would you like to stay for a sleepover with this crazy ball of energy?"

"Yes!" I practically screamed, unable to hold in my excitement. "Yes, please!"

"Are you keeping lookout?"

"Yeah."

"Are you sure?"

"Yeah, just do it, Hughie."

"What if someone sees us, Gibs?"

"I've thrown two cartons already, and nobody caught me."

"Yeah, but you're lucky, and I'm always caught."

"Oh my God, just do it, you big baby."

"Fuck you, Feely. You do it."

"Why me? I don't have a problem with Old Murphy."

"Yeah, only because the fucker didn't burst your balls."

"Guys, stop cursing."

"What if he comes out this time?"

"Let's just go back inside, okay? Before we get caught."

"Hell no, we have a mission to complete."

"Maybe Baby Biggs is right, lads. Your mam will flip if she finds out we snuck out and took the girls with us."

"Shut up, Feely. We don't need that kind of negative talk. Now, throw the fucking egg, Hughie!"

"I'll throw it." Snatching up two eggs from the tray, I crept out from behind the car we were hiding behind and ran up the driveway of Hugh and Gibsie's mortal enemy. Launching the eggs as I hard as I could, I scrambled back to our den as fast as I could.

"Holy shit," Hugh whispered, looking at me with wide eyes. "You really *are* fast."

"Told ya," I replied, feeling my belly flip-flop when he looked at me like that. He had done it a lot when we were trick-or-treating earlier, and I liked it then, too.

"That was Tomb Raider–style badass," Gibsie exclaimed, holding up his hand for a high five. "You got his windows."

"This is fun." Snickering, I high-fived him before grabbing more eggs. "Let's do it again."

"This is superbad," Claire groaned, covering her face with her hands. "We're going to be in so much trouble."

"Okay," Hugh said, pulling down his mask to hide his face. "I'm going to do it." Grabbing the last two eggs from our very last tray, he broke off in a crouched run toward the house, while Gibsie cheered him on from the den.

However, the moment he reached the garden and reared back to throw his eggs, the porch light flicked on, and an old man appeared. "I've got ya now, ya little bollocks," the man snarled, grabbing Hugh by the collar of his shirt. "Take off that mask and let me see who I'm dealing with!"

"Oh fuck," Gibsie groaned, scrambling out from our cover to defend our friend, but I got there first.

Bolting out from behind the car, I rushed at the old man who was stringing Hugh up by the collar and threw myself at him. "Let him go," I hissed, smashing him with the eggs I was still holding before biting down on his arm.

"Jesus Christ," the old man yelped, releasing my friend and cradling his hand to his chest.

I moved to rush the man again, but a hand grabbed mine and pulled me away. *Hugh's hand*, I realized, as we ran full speed after our friends in the opposite direction of his house.

"Holy shit," Hugh laughed, still holding my hand, as we ran for our lives from the crime scene. "I can't believe you bit Old Murphy."

"I'm sorry," I called back, running as fast as I could to keep up with him. "Please don't be mad at me."

"Mad at you?" He pulled me behind a wall at the end of their street. "Liz, you just saved me from being grounded for a month." He was breathing hard from running. "I'm not mad at you. I'm grateful."

"You are?" I replied, panting for breath, as we hid from sight. "Really?"

"Really." Hugh squeezed my hand and smiled down at me. "Thanks for saving me back there."

"Anytime," I replied, grinning back at him.

"That was so badass," Gibsie panted, climbing out of the bushes, with Patrick and Claire in tow. Jogging over to us, he slung his arm over my shoulder and laughed. "Lads, we have to keep this girl."

"Agreed," Hugh and Patrick said in unison, while Claire clapped her hands and bounced around excitedly. "See? I told you guys she was the bestest."

"You were right, Claire-Bear," Gibsie replied, giving her a big smile. "A star is better than a square."

I scrunched my brows up. "A square?"

"Yeah, we're a square, see?" Gibsie pointed to the four of them before pointing to me. "You make a star."

"Yay," Claire squealed, clutching her chest. "I'm so happy."

"Okay, guys, all in." Gibsie held his hand out, and we all piled our hands on top of his. "Team Gibson on three."

"No fucking way," Hugh argued. "There are two Biggses in this group, so it should be Team Biggs on three."

"Hold up," Patrick warned. "We need to vote first."

"Fine," Hugh said, holding his hand up. I blushed with heat. "All in favor of Liz joining the gang, raise your hands."

Everyone raised their hands.

I beamed with happiness.

"Then it's official," Hugh said, turning to smile at me. "You're one of us now."

"I am?"

"That means we keep each other's secrets and stick together, no matter what."

My heart leapt. "No matter what?"

"Yeah, Liz." Hugh smiled. "No matter what."

THE BIRDS, THE BEES, AND BULLING COWS

Hugh

NOVEMBER 1, 1994

"WELL, OUR WEDDING IS GOING TO BE SUPERSPECIAL." CLAIRE CONTINUED TO HARP on all the way through breakfast the following morning. "Gerard will wear a tuxedo, and I'll wear a big, white princess dress like Cinderella." She hoofed half a pancake into her mouth and continued. "And we'll have a horse and carriage like Barbie and Ken, and we'll have our honeymoon on the moon."

"Don't forget the babies, Claire-Bear," Gibsie chimed in from his perch beside her, while he too inhaled his stack of pancakes. "We're having ten babies, aren't we?"

"Yes, Gerard, but the babies come after the honeymoon," my sister reminded him. "When we do the smooching and you give me the special hug."

I arched a brow. "The special hug?"

"Uh-huh," she replied, with an eager nod. "You know, like the special hug Daddy gave Mammy to put us in her tummy."

"Jesus Christ," I muttered, dropping my head in my hands, while the girl sitting beside me snickered into her hand.

"They're so strange," Lizzie whispered in my ear, causing the hair on my arms to shoot up.

"Tell me about it," I whispered back, daring myself to take a peek at her. Yep, my heart still slammed at the sight of her this morning.

"That's not how it works," Feely informed everyone at the table. "Bulls have balls like boys have, and cows have vaginas like girls have." He then proceeded to clear his throat, armed and ready with enough farm-life knowledge to shatter their innocence. "The balls store sperm, and the sperm has to shoot out of the penis and go into the cow's vagina to impregnate her."

Gibsie's and Claire's mouths dropped open in unison.

"We call that bulling a cow," Feely continued between mouthfuls of cereal. "The bull would have to mount the cow to put her in calve, or she would need to be artificially inseminated."

"What's that?" Lizzie asked, looking just as wide-eyed now as Gibs and Claire.

"Please don't, Feely," I begged, having heard this exact speech from his father when I went on a playdate to his house last spring and ended up in the calving shed.

"The farmer would collect the sperm from the bull, load it into the insemination gun, and shoot it into the cow's vu—"

"Okay, Feely!" I yelled, loud enough to block his voice out. "La, la, la, la! That's enough for one day, lad."

"Ew," Claire groaned, looking at Gibsie in horror. "Just ew."

"Maybe we'll just have pets," Gibsie offered, looking queasy. "Because I don't think I want to shoot you with the bull gun, Claire-Bear."

"Agreed," she croaked out, hooking her pinky finger around his. "Let's just have cat babies instead."

"What's this about bull guns, young man?" a familiar voice asked, causing Gibsie to leap out of his chair.

"Dad!" Bolting across the kitchen, he threw himself at his father. "You're here!"

"Yeah, well, Pete mentioned something about taking his gang swimming," Joe replied, wrapping Gibsie up in his arms.

Gibsie may have had the same blond hair as his mam, but that's where the resemblance stopped. He was every inch Joe Gibson's son in both looks and personality.

"I figured we could tag along with them." Joe kissed Gibsie's head and set him back down on his feet. "What do you say, son?" He ruffled his son's curls. "How do you fancy getting up-to-speed on that doggy paddle of yours?"

"What about the bakery?"

"Closing shop for one day won't hurt," his father replied with a smile. "Besides, I'd rather hang out with my main man."

Nodding his head, Gibsie beamed for a solid ten seconds before bursting into tears. "I don't know why I'm crying," he tried to tell his father, through floods of tears. "I'm happy, Dad, I promise."

"It's okay, buddy," Joe soothed, tucking Gibsie's face into his chest. "You're allowed to cry. You've had a hard year."

"Yeah." Sniffling, Gibs wrapped his arms around his father's waist and clung to him. "Thanks, Dad."

"That's Gibsie's dad," I whispered in Lizzie's ear. "His mam kicked him out a while back."

"Oh." She looked at me with lonesome blue eyes. "That's so sad."

"I know," I whispered back. "Gibs misses him a lot."

Dad strolled into the kitchen then, phone in hand. "Patrick, son, your sister is outside in the car waiting for you," he told my friend before turning to look at me. "I've just had an interesting conversation with Donal Murphy down the street."

Aw, crap.

Feely, who was halfway out of his chair, froze on the spot before slowly sitting back down.

"Oh, really?" I replied, not daring to look at any of the others. If I did, Dad would know. "What did he want?"

"He's been ringing around all the neighbors," Dad explained, scratching his chin. "Apparently, some kids egged his house last night, and some wild, young one even took a chunk out of his arm."

Lizzie's breath hitched and I quickly snatched her hand up under the table. I couldn't look at her, because I would be busted if I did, so I just smoothed my thumb over the back of her hand reassuringly.

"No way," Gibsie thankfully chimed in, feigning surprise. He was a far better liar than I was. "Where did it happen?" he asked, rejoining us at the kitchen table.

"His front porch," Dad told us. "There were others with her, but they all wore masks, so he can't be sure who the culprits are."

I mentally sagged in relief.

"Is that Old Murphy?" Joe asked then, looking at Dad. "The cranky, old bastard down the street, with a penchant for terrorizing the neighborhood?"

"That's the one," Dad replied, trying not to smile. "I assured him that it couldn't have been any of our gang because they were all tucked up in bed." He looked to us. "Isn't that right, *gang*?"

We all nodded eagerly. "That's right."

"Well, I hope that 'wild, young one' took a fine big chunk out of him," Joe drawled, winking at us. "Might lighten the old crank up a bit."

BACK TO ROBIN HILL ROAD

Lizzie

NOVEMBER 1, 1994

When I arrived home the day after Hugh's party, my sister was the one to greet me at the door. My dad was still at the hospital with my mam, and even though I was really worried about her, I couldn't stop smiling.

Because I'd had the best day of my life yesterday. This morning, too. With my *friends*. I didn't want to go home, but I knew I couldn't stay at their house forever. I would miss my mother too much. But now that she wasn't here, I just felt lonely again.

Still, knowing I now had five friends of my own helped keep the smile on my face.

Hugh.

Claire.

Gibsie.

Shannon.

Patrick.

And *me*.

"Meds," Caoimhe reminded me the moment the front door closed. "Right now, missy." Catching me by the hand, she led me to the kitchen, where she rummaged in one of the cabinets for the pill bottle with my name on it. There were lots of them. "Here we are," she mused, popping open the cap and handing me a pill. "You know what to do."

Sighing heavily, I walked over to the sink and retrieved a glass from the draining board. Filling the glass with tap water, I chugged back the medicine and then opened my mouth for my sister's inspection.

"Good girl," she said approvingly before giving me a hug. "Now, tell me about your sleepover."

"I had the best time ever," I told her, feeling excited all over again. "And I made new friends. I have five now, Caoimhe. Five friends! Claire, Shannon, Patrick, Gibsie, and Hugh!"

"Go on." Lowering herself down on a chair at the kitchen table, she rested her chin in her hand and smiled. "Give me all the juicy details."

"We had the party, and then we did the trick-or-treating and watched *Hocus Pocus*, and we had a midnight snack, and we..." I stopped myself just in time and skipped over the egging part. "Stayed up super late, and then Sinead made us pancakes for breakfast." Flopping onto the chair next to her, I sighed happily. "I think I love him."

"Which one?"

"Hugh," I sighed, clutching my chest. "He's so nice, Caoimhe. Like so, so nice, and he's pretty, and he holds the door for me, and he gave me an extra pillow from his room, and he cut my pancake when I couldn't do it." I heaved out another sigh, missing him already. "He's just so *sweet*."

My sister laughed. "So the crush is in full force."

"How's Mam?" I asked then. "Is she coming home soon?"

"Dad called and said she'll be home in a day or two," she told me. "She's feeling much better."

I sagged in relief. "Thank God."

"I know," she replied, giving my hand a squeeze. "Now, how do you feel about throwing on a scary movie in the sitting room and sharing your trick-or-treating haul with your big sister?"

———————————

Later that night, when I was tucked up in bed, I heard the familiar sound of my bedroom door opening inward, and I looked up from my storybook to see Mark in my doorway.

"Hey, munchkin," he said, closing and locking the door behind him. My stomach sank. "What are you doing up so late?"

"Reading." A wave of panic swept over me, and I felt my body stiffen when he walked toward me. "Why are you here?"

"I came over to keep your sister company," he explained, coming to sit on the side of my bed. "She fell asleep on the couch, so I thought I'd come and check on you."

He was always checking on me.

It used to be okay, but I wasn't so sure anymore.

I didn't think I wanted him to keep checking on me.

I didn't want him to fix me again.

Not ever again.

"Is my daddy home yet?"

"Nope." He smiled and tucked my hair behind my ear. "It's just us, munchkin."

"When is *your* daddy picking you up?"

"I'm sleeping over tonight," he explained, hand resting on my shoulder. "Your dad's staying at the hospital with your mam, so they're none the wiser."

"Oh." My panic grew. "Okay."

"So your sister told me something today and I'm not happy about it."

"What?"

"Caoimhe said you slept at a boy's house last night."

"Hugh." I felt myself smile. "He's really nice."

"Hmm." Mark didn't look happy. "I don't know how I feel about you cheating on me, munchkin."

"What do you mean?" I asked, confused.

"I don't want to share you."

A shiver racked through me. "Share me?"

"You're my special girl, remember?" He placed his big hand on my leg. "And I don't want you being anyone else's special girl."

My face grew warm.

"You're blushing." He leaned in again, closer this time, and whispered, "I like it when you blush for me."

I wasn't blushing; I was frightened. But if I told him, he would get cross with me, and it always hurt extra bad when he was cross. It was better to not make him angry. I shivered, feeling strange in my belly again.

"You know what I think, munchkin?" He walked his fingers up my leg. "I think you need some of my special medicine again." His eyes trailed over me. "You don't want to end up like your mother, do you?" He slid his hand under my nightdress. "Sick and rotting in a hospital bed?"

I shook my head, feeling sad. "But it hurts."

"Only for a little while," he coaxed, wrapping his big hand around my throat. "You can handle it." He pushed me onto my back and dragged my nightie up to my waist. "Like the other times."

Shivering, I clenched my eyes shut and thought happy thoughts.

I thought of *Hugh*.

MILADY AND THE BRAVE KNIGHT

Hugh

NOVEMBER 19, 1994

THIS WAS A TERRIBLE IDEA.

I knew it when Liz slipped halfway up the tree and fell back on me, causing us both to fall on our asses. And I knew it now, as I balanced on a limb and watched her wobble like a newborn foal.

I was dead meat if anything happened to her.

If my mother didn't kill me, my sister would.

"Careful," I called out, unable to mask my concern. I should have known better than to agree to go climbing when it had been raining all day yesterday. Yeah, it was dry today, but the branches of the trees were still slippery. Problem was, I seemed to lose all common sense when Lizzie Young was nearby.

This morning, for example, I was supposed to be at rugby training, same as every Saturday, but Liz had had a sleepover with Claire last night, and when she asked me if I wanted to hang out this morning, I blew training off without a second thought.

Climbing out on a particularly shaky limb of the tree, the same one I was on, Liz balanced with *no* grace and held a stick out in front of her. Grinning mischievously, she swung the stick around with a flourish before aiming it at my heart. "I challenge you to a duel, brave knight."

"A brave knight would never duel with a lady." I mimicked the British tone she had used, and then, with an exaggerated bow, I tipped my imaginary hat to her. "Milady."

"Come now, good knight, and make haste," she challenged, edging farther out on the limb, to poke me in the chest with her stick. "For I have little time for such unpleasant remarks."

"I couldn't possibly, milady," I replied, placing my imaginary sword at her feet. "Now, I must beg of you to retreat before you come to harm."

Lizzie narrowed her eyes and broke character. "Come on! Fight me, Hughie."

"You're going to fall and break your ass," I laughed, thoroughly amused by her antics. "Back up before you kill yourself."

"Oh yeah?" Tossing her stick away, she winked and jumped off the limb.

"Lizzie!" I roared, heart stopping dead in my chest as I gaped down in horror at the blond pancaked on the lawn several feet beneath me. "Are you okay?"

The sound of her laughter was music to my ears, and when she rolled onto her back and held her thumbs up, I felt my entire body sag in relief.

"You're shit at being a lady."

"That's because I don't want to be a lady," she called back with a grin. "I want to be a knight like you."

"Hey, Liz, are you sure you don't want to come to ballet with me?" Claire called out from the patio door, clad in a pink tutu and white tights. "Mrs. Good lets kids come to class to try it out to see if they like it."

"Uh…that's okay?" Lizzie called back, looking horrified, while I covered my mouth to smother my laugh.

Sprawled out on my lawn in a pair of denim dungarees and an oversized plaid shirt, Liz couldn't have looked less like my sister if she tried.

I loved it.

"Hugh, can I have a word, love?" Mam called then, joining my sister in the doorway.

"Yeah, Mam," I called back, maneuvering down the tree with expert precision. Feeling mischievous when I reached the ground, I retrieved Liz's "sword" from the lawn and placed it at her feet. "Milady."

She grinned up at me from her perch on the grass. "Brave knight."

I offered her a dramatic bow before rushing over to my mam. "What's up?"

"Come inside for a minute," Mam said, then told Claire to go out and play with Liz until they had to leave for dance class.

"Is something wrong?" I asked, watching my mother carefully. "Mam?"

She started with, "How's Lizzie doing? Is she doing okay? Has she said anything to you or Claire?"

My brows furrowed. "Like what?"

Mam sighed. "I've just gotten off the phone to her mother."

"So?"

"Lizzie's mam is very sick, Hugh." She placed a hand on my shoulder. "She's going through her third battle with cancer."

"Okay," I replied, frowning. "Is she not getting better?"

"Yes and no," my mother replied, sighing heavily. "But Catherine's recovery is a slow process and has taken a toll on her family—especially Lizzie. Catherine's very worried about how it's affecting her."

"But Liz never says anything about her family," I replied, frowning. "I thought everything was okay and her mam was getting better."

Mam nodded, taking in my answer before asking me another question. "Has she ever spoken to you about her feelings?"

"What kind of feelings?"

"Scary feelings or scary voices," Mam replied in a careful tone. "Or maybe her worries?"

"Huh?" I shook my head in confusion. "What do you mean?"

"Never mind." She smiled brightly. "That's all I needed to know."

"What's going on, Mam?" I asked, feeling worried now. "Is Lizzie okay?"

"Yes, love, she's fine," my mother said, trailing her hand through my hair. "I've told Catherine that we're happy to have her over whenever she needs to while she recovers, so expect Lizzie to be here a lot over the coming months."

"Really?" Excitement sparked to life inside of me, mixing with the confusion I was feeling from this conversation. "That's great."

"You're a good boy, Hugh, and I know you're so emotionally mature that I don't need to ask, but please keep an eye out for her." Mam stroked my cheek and smiled sadly. "She's a very fragile little girl who needs looking after."

"I'll do it," I vowed, casting a glance out the patio window to the blond girl twirling around in circles in her denim dungarees. "I'll look after her, Mam, I promise."

SWIMMING IN THE DEEP END

Lizzie

DECEMBER 3, 1994

BUBBLING WITH EXCITEMENT, I HELD MY MOTHER'S HAND ALL THE WAY FROM THE changing room to the pool. Mam was still feeling sick and couldn't go in the water, but she *still* came when Sinead Biggs invited us today. She said it was a special treat for all of us.

I couldn't wait to get in the swimming pool, and I could see my friends splashing in the water. But I was trying really hard to be a good girl and not make a mistake because Daddy was here, too, and if I was bad, I wouldn't get to come to the pool again.

I had to behave myself.

No mistakes.

"Catherine?" Sinead asked, rising from a deck chair at the side of the pool when I approached with my mother. "I'm Sinead Biggs. It's lovely to finally meet you."

"Likewise," Mam replied, shaking her hand. "Thank you so much for being so good to Lizzie. I'm forever in your debt."

"Not at all," Sinead replied, helping Mammy onto a chair next to hers. "Lizzie is a pleasure. She's welcome at our home anytime."

"My son takes the open-door policy in the literal sense," another woman chuckled from a nearby deck chair. "I swear Sinead sees more of Gerard than I do." Leaning over the seats, she extended her hand to my mother. "Sadhbh Gibson. You're Caoimhe's mother, aren't you? She's a credit to you, Catherine. Truly."

"Thank you so much." Mam smiled and shook her hand. "And it's wonderful to finally meet you ladies."

The three of them started chatting, and I smiled, feeling happy for my mother. It was nice to see her smiling again. Sadhbh and Sinead didn't stare at her headscarf or give her sad looks. They treated my mother like she was a part of their gang.

Just like how their kids treated me.

"You're here," I heard Hugh call out moments before his hand snaked around my ankle. He grinned up at me from the water. "What are you waiting for?"

Looking around, I searched for my father, and when I couldn't find him, I backed right up before running and jumping into the water.

"Are you crazy?" Hugh laughed, watching me paddle toward him. "You can't jump in the deep end yet. You're too small."

"If you can do it, I can do it."

He grinned back at me. "Then why are you sinking?"

I narrowed my eyes. "Because I've never not touched the bottom before."

Chuckling, he swam over to me. "Hold on to me."

I quickly did just that and let him steer us to the edge of the pool. "Here. Use my hand to push up," he instructed, giving my foot a boost with his hand.

When I got out, I sat back down on the edge and smiled at him. "I have a crush on you." At least, that's what Caoimhe said it was. I didn't know what was happening until I explained all about the flutter-cups. She laughed and told me that I had my first crush.

His cheeks turned bright pink. "You're not supposed to say that, Liz."

"But I do," I told him.

"Yeah, but." He looked around before saying, "The guys will laugh at us if they hear you say things like that."

"So?"

"So…" He seemed to think about it for a moment before shaking his head. "I don't know what comes after so."

I grinned at him. "Do you have a crush on me, too?"

"Jesus." Blushing, he dipped under the water, reappearing a few seconds later and a lot farther away.

"Wait!" I called after him. "You didn't answer me."

"Yes," he called over his shoulder as he swam back to our friends. "My answer is yes!"

I sprang to my feet and clutched my chest, unable to stop the grin on my face from spreading.

Because he had a crush on me, too.

Hugh Biggs liked me back.

"Come back for me," I called out, jumping back into the water and kicking my legs.

I didn't feel the same fear others felt when their heads went underwater or when water went up their nose. The more pain I felt, the calmer my mind grew.

"You are a crazy girl," Hugh laughed, hooking an arm around me when he swam back to me. "What would you have done if I didn't swim back for you?"

"I knew you would," I laughed, wrapping my arms around his neck as he swam us over to the shallow part.

"Oh yeah?" he teased, releasing me when I could stand. "How?"

"Because I trust you," I told him. "You make me feel safe."

That seemed to confuse him because his brows furrowed together. "You'll always be safe with me."

"I know." I splashed him with my hand. "No matter what, right?"

"Yeah, Liz," Hugh chuckled, splashing me back. "No matter what."

BRAZEN BOYFRIENDS AND BRAVE BROTHERS

Hugh

DECEMBER 17, 1994

"I KNOW YOUR SISTER" WERE THE FIRST WORDS THAT CAME OUT OF MY SISTER'S MOUTH when Lizzie's sister stepped foot through our door on the last Saturday before Christmas. "She's my best friend at school, but Gerard's my best friend at home."

"Is that so?" Caoimhe laughed, allowing Claire to drag her upstairs to see her doll collection.

"We'll be home for half one," Mam told me, while applying her lipstick in the mirror. "If you need anything or feel unhappy about something, I want you to call Sadhbh, okay?"

"I'm not calling Sadhbh," I replied, scrunching my nose up in disgust. "She's got that man sleeping over again."

"Hugh," Mam admonished. "It's not our business, remember?"

"Yeah, whatever, but Joe's way better," I grumbled.

"You would say that," she chuckled. "He's your godfather who spoils you rotten."

"No, I'm saying it because it's the truth," I shot back with a huff. "I'll call Joe if I need a grown-up."

"Joe has the kids this weekend," Mam reminded, adjusting her dress. "So please just call Sadhbh if you need to."

"I'll call Grandad Healy and that's my final offer," I replied, standing firm.

"Fine, you can call Grandad," Mam conceded with a chuckle. "Oh, and Caoimhe asked if her Mark Allen can come over to watch a movie when you guys are gone to bed. I told her that he could but has to leave by eleven, so just keep an eye on everything, okay?"

"Mark Allen?" I gaped at my mother. "As in Sadhbh's boyfriend's *son*?"

"Hugh."

"Ugh!" I growled, scowling "Why would anyone want to watch a film with *him*?"

"That's not your business, either."

I'd met Mark a few times and Gibs wasn't lying when he said the guy was a creep.

He thought he was so much tougher and cooler than us because he was a teenager, when in fact, all he was better at doing was being a fucking creep. "I hate that guy!"

"Hugh!"

"You taught me not to lie, Mam," I reminded her.

"I also taught you to have manners," she shot back with a smirk. "Now, I know Caoimhe's the babysitter, but you're the man of the house when Dad's not home, so I expect you to look after your sister."

"Jesus, Mam, you look beautiful," I told her, eyeing the tight, sparkly red dress she had on. "You're way skinnier than I thought you were."

"Why thank you, son," Mam chuckled, squeezing my cheek. "What a little charmer you are."

"He gets that from his old fella," Dad chimed in, appearing from the kitchen with both his and Mam's coats flung over his arm. "Right, love, let's get cracking. The taxi's outside."

"Wait, wait, wait, I think I've forgotten something," Mam laughed as he carted her to the door. "I need to kiss my babies before we go."

"Your big baby is right here," Dad drawled, opening the front door and lifting Mam down the porch steps. "And you can kiss him in the taxi."

"Ugh," I groaned, slamming the door behind them. "Good riddance."

———————————

Two hours later, I had to admit that being babysat by Caoimhe Young was way better than Mrs. Grady. I felt bad for thinking it, but it was the truth. Caoimhe had plenty of energy to keep up with Claire, which meant that I didn't have to chase her around the house in case she was on the loose, had the scissors, or had gotten into Mam's makeup. Instead, Caoimhe did all those things while I got to play my computer game in peace.

"We made you cookies," Claire squealed, blowing my bedroom door inward then, and I mentally cursed myself for being a jinx. Goddammit. "Come on, Hugh. Come downstairs and taste them."

I didn't want to eat anything my sister had put her grubby, little fingers on. I was all too familiar with the creepy crawlies that she collected in jars with Gibs, but knowing Claire, she would try to feed them to me in my sleep if I didn't give in. It was a battle I couldn't win, so I switched off my game and trudged downstairs to the kitchen.

As I expected, the cookies looked like something the neighbor's dog shat out, but I picked one up and took a bite to placate the curly-haired demon pirouetting around the kitchen.

"Mm," I mumbled, rubbing my stomach. "It's delicious." It wasn't, but it wasn't terrible either. "Good job."

Caoimhe rolled her eyes and laughed. "My sister was right; you *are* sweet."

My cheeks reddened and I practically choked down my mouthful of cookie to answer her. "Liz said I was sweet?"

"Uh-huh." Grinning, she leaned her hip against the island and dried her hands with the tea towel. "Among other things."

"Like what?" I blurted out, trying and failing to play it cool. "I mean, uh, she said stuff about me?"

"*Aw*, look at you blushing over my sister," Caoimhe crooned. "This is too cute."

"Hugh's in love," Claire chimed in then. "He wants to smooch your sister."

"Claire!" I snapped, feeling my face grow hotter. "Stop it. You know I don't."

"Liar, liar, pants on fire," Claire teased, while she danced over to our babysitter. "He's always asking me questions about her."

"Oh *really*?" Caoimhe's eyes danced with mischief. "What kind of questions, Claire?"

"Like what's her favorite color, and does she like dinosaurs, and who's her favorite author, and does she talk about him at school," my sister replied with a snicker. "He even draws her pictures, and writes little notes, and makes me bring them to school for her."

Groaning, I fought the urge to run upstairs and die from my shame in private.

"Lizzie draws pictures for Hughie, too," Claire continued, spilling my secrets, as she led Caoimhe into the lounge. "And she writes notes with love hearts on them, and I have to bring them home for him."

"Omigod," Caoimhe gushed, sinking down on the couch next to Claire. "That is the sweetest thing I've ever heard."

"I think Hughie is Lizzie's boyfriend," Claire offered. "Like Gerard is my boyfriend."

"No, I'm not," I argued, feeling all sweaty and awkward, as I hovered in the archway. "And Gibsie isn't yours, either." I shook my head, feeling flustered. "He's just a boy who's your *friend*. Same as me and Liz."

"Nuh-uh, Hughie," my sister argued back, gesturing for me to come and sit next to her. "Gerard says he's going to marry me when I'm a big girl."

"Aw." Caoimhe laughed. "My little Gibs told you he would marry you?"

"Yep." Claire smiled proudly. "Except we're getting kittens after the honeymoon and not bull guns."

"Shoot me," I muttered, sinking down on the couch. "Seriously."

"Do you have one?" Claire asked then, climbing onto her lap. "A boyfriend?"

"Yep, I sure do," Caoimhe replied, smiling. "Actually, I think you guys might know my boyfriend: Mark Allen."

"Ew." Claire reared back, looking horrified. "Just ew."

Caoimhe laughed. "You don't approve?"

My sister shook her head. "His daddy was kissing Gerard's mammy when he wasn't supposed to," she explained, scrunching her little nose up. "Gerard says they were being cheaters on his daddy."

"Oh boy." Caoimhe sighed. "Well, that's not good, is it?"

"Nope. That's a bad thing."

"Sometimes grown-ups do bad things," she agreed. "But just because the grown-ups do bad things, doesn't mean the kids are to blame."

Claire looked confused, but I knew *exactly* what she was trying to do.

"It's not Gibsie's fault, is it?" Caoimhe clarified in a gentle tone.

"Nope."

"Exactly." Caoimhe smiled at her. "Then how can it be Mark's fault?"

This seemed to throw my sister, and she frowned. "Huh."

I arched a disbelieving brow and snorted.

"Got something to say, Hugo Boss-Man?"

"Yeah, Gibsie's a child," I told her. "Mark's a bully."

"A bully to who?"

"Gibsie."

Caoimhe's eyes met mine and I could see that she didn't believe me. "You're wrong about him. Mark's really great once you get to know him."

No fucking thanks.

"Do you love him?" Claire asked, dragging our babysitter's attention back to her. "Does he hold the door for you?"

"Yep," she told my sister with a smile. "He does lots of nice things for me."

"Really?"

"Uh-huh."

"What kinds of nice things?"

"Right, I'm off to bed," I declared, standing up and waving them off.

If staying up late meant listening to my babysitter gush about her asshole boyfriend to my gullible sister, then I'd rather not.

When I reached my bedroom window, I looked across the street to Gibsie's window. It was dark. The van parked in the driveway across the street made me glad he was at his dad's house for the weekend.

Kneeling at my bedside, I blessed myself and quickly recited my prayers before climbing into bed. It took a lot longer than usual to fall asleep, and I thought about switching on my television but decided against it. If I did that, I'd be tempted to play on my Sega, and if that happened, I'd be up all night.

A little while later, the sound of the front door opening and closing filled my ears and I strained to hear the muffled voices.

There was a male voice.

This confused me because I knew my dad's voice and that wasn't him.

Rolling onto my side, I tried to drift off, feeling my eyes grow heavy, but a strange feeling in my stomach gnawed at me.

That's when my mother's words drifted into my mind.

Mark Allen.

He was coming over to watch a movie.

Goddammit!

Throwing off the covers, I climbed out of bed and stomped downstairs to check. When I reached the lounge and locked eyes on the familiar, dark-haired teenage boy sitting on my couch, with my sister on his lap, a wave of unease washed over me.

I couldn't explain why I felt so uncomfortable or why the hairs on the back of my neck shot up whenever I laid eyes on him. But it *always* happened. I felt like Peter Parker with Spidey senses, and mine told me that Mark Allen was *not* good. Not good at all.

"Claire!" I barked, stalking into the lounge. "No." Not stopping until I was right in front of them, I grabbed my sister's hand and yanked her off his lap. "You don't sit on strangers' laps."

"It's okay, though, because he's going to be Gerard's brother soon," my sister explained, looking up at me with big, brown eyes. "So he's not a stranger."

"I don't care." Keeping ahold of her hand, I walked my sister to the other end of the couch and lifted her onto it before turning back around. "Don't touch my sister again," I warned, standing in front of her. "Not ever again."

"Whoa, Hugh, it's okay," Caoimhe said from her perch beside Mark. "We were just watching a movie. Your mam said it was okay." Smiling, she gestured to the bully with his arm around her. "Do you want to watch the film with us?"

"Are you going to bed?" I asked my sister, ignoring Mark when he tried to speak to me.

"Nope." Claire smiled and pointed at the television. "I'm staying up for *Look Who's Talking.*"

"Fine." I nodded and plopped down beside her. "Then so am I."

"You're being super rude," Claire whispered in my ear.

I knew I was, and I was worried about getting in trouble from my parents.

I tried to be good, to do the right thing, but I couldn't stop myself tonight.

I didn't like it.

It felt all wrong.

"Don't sit on his lap," I whispered back.

"How come?"

I don't know. "Just don't, okay?"

"Okay."

"I mean it." I held my pinky finger up to her. "Promise me."

"I promise," she replied hooking her finger around mine before proceeding to curl up in a ball on my lap.

Normally, I would kill my sister for hugging me, but not tonight.

Instead, I wrapped my arm around her shoulders and kept her close.

RINGING IN THE NEW YEAR

Lizzie

DECEMBER 31, 1994

"ARE YOU OKAY?" I ASKED GIBSIE, EVEN THOUGH I ALREADY KNEW THE ANSWER.

It was New Year's Eve, and we were sitting at my kitchen table, while his mother and Keith sipped champagne with my parents.

"Yeah, I'll be okay," Gibsie replied, sounding sad. "Thanks for inviting me to your party, Liz."

It was my parents' party, not mine. They'd decided to throw a party this New Year's Eve to thank their friends for all their support during the year.

Mam was out of bed and dressed up in a beautiful dress, and Dad looked actually happy tonight. The kitchen was filled with grown-ups whose names I didn't know, while Caoimhe and Mark had the living room jam-packed with friends from school.

Reaching over, I placed my hand on Gibsie's and whispered, "Keith's a fucker."

That made him smile, so I racked my brain for more curse words. "Keith's a stupid, son-of-a-bitch, fucker pup."

Now, he full belly laughed. "He *is* a fucker pup."

I grinned. "Yep."

When the doorbell sounded, Gibs and I both looked at each other before making a run for the front door.

"He's here," I squealed at the same time Gibs cheered, "She's here!"

Butting Gibsie out of the way with my hip, I grabbed the door handle a second before him and grinned in victory. Call it silly, but I wanted to be the one to open the door when Hugh came to my house. I wanted to be the first person to see his face. In fact, I wanted to see his face all the time. Every day.

When I yanked the door open and was greeted by the Biggs family, I had to force myself to not throw myself at Hugh.

I wanted to.

So bad.

Because I thought about him *all* the time. My face felt hot when he smiled at me, and I wanted to spend all my time being near him. Even when I was supposed to be playing with Claire, I always searched for him and secretly hoped that he would come into the room and join us. I loved the things he talked about. He was so smart and was always teaching me things. About stars and constellations, about nature, books, movies, music. He was like my own personal encyclopedia on life itself.

"Gerard!" Claire squealed, rushing past me to throw her arms around our friend. "You look super nice in your shirt."

"Thanks, Claire-Bear," he chuckled, looking more relaxed than he had all night now that she was here. "You look like a princess." Draping an arm over her shoulders, they followed her parents into the kitchen, while I remained rooted to the spot, attention riveted on the only boy I ever wanted to look at.

He was wearing a red plaid shirt that was tucked into dark jeans, with brown boots. His hair was neatly combed, but it still flopped forward like Junior from the movie *Little Giants*.

Hugh grinned at me. "Hi."

I beamed back at him. "Hi."

"Thanks for the invitation." He held up the familiar card and winked. "Nice *g*."

My face flushed with heat. "I've been practicing."

"I can tell." Smiling, he stepped inside, and his arm brushed against mine as he moved, making the flutter-cups go crazy.

Unable to stop myself, I leaned in close and took a whiff. Just like I remembered: freshly cut grass, soap, strawberries, and Hugh.

"Did you just smell me again?" he asked with a small laugh.

"I like how you smell."

"I took a bath this evening." Raising his arm to his nose, he took a whiff of his armpit and shrugged. "It's the same soap as always."

"Does your mam put bubbles in?"

"Yep."

"I like bubbles."

"Same."

"I don't like baths anymore."

"Why not?"

"They're stingy."

He frowned. "Stingy?"

I nodded. "Yep."

Confusion filled his eyes. "I don't get stung."

I shrugged. "Maybe it's just my bath."

"Maybe." His gaze drifted over me, and I felt my body warm up. "You look really nice." Smiling, he flicked the bow on my hair and teased, "Very un-Lizzie of you."

"My sister made me wear it." Blushing, I closed the door behind him. "Thanks for coming."

"Your house is huge," he told me. "Like seriously huge."

"Yeah." Standing in the hallway, I clasped my hands together and stared at him. "It's really old."

"Yeah, it looks it." He seemed interested in the walls of our entryway. "It's really cool."

"Really?"

"Yeah." His eyes met mine for a moment and my face grew hot again. "My dad's an architect, so I sort of love these kinds of places." He turned around slowly, eyes focused on the carvings in the ceiling. "Georgian?"

"Uh, my dad's name is Michael," I corrected. "And he's in the kitchen."

Hugh frowned at me for a brief moment before a huge smile spread across his face. "You are so cute."

My eyes widened. "I'm cute?"

His lips twitched but he didn't answer, deciding to change the subject by asking, "So, how about it, milady? Fancy giving your brave knight a tour of the palace?"

"You're so weird." Snickering, I grabbed his hand and pulled him toward the staircase. "Let's go."

"Hey, did you know that your mother's great-great-great-great-great-grandfather fought in the Siege of Cork in 1690?"

"That's a lot of greats, Hugh." Sprawled out on my bedroom floor, I rested my chin in my hands, while I watched Hugh comb through a book he'd found in the library room.

"And your family is one of the few Catholic-Irish families to retain their land and wealth during the plantation?"

"Did he die?"

"Who?"

"My great-great-great-great-great-grandfather."

"Nope, but it says here that he lost a leg." Carefully turning the dusty page, he continued to read. "Liz, your mam is wealthy." He leaned in closer to read the handwritten diary entries. "And not just regular wealthy." He turned his head to look at me. "She has *generational* wealth."

I shrugged. "I don't know what any of that means."

"It means her children's children won't ever have to worry about money." He frowned before chuckling to himself. "I guess that means your kids."

"But I don't have any kids?"

"Not now, but when you're a grown-up, you'll have a bunch" he explained, returning his attention to the book. "And they'll be filthy rich."

"Oh." I thought about it for a moment, decided I didn't care, and went right back to staring at him. "I think I like being around you more than your sister," I admitted. "Does that make me a bad friend?"

"Nah," Hugh replied, turning his head to look at me again. "I get it."

"You do?"

"Yep." Nodding, he closed the book and rested his chin on his hand. "You like the peace and quiet, and my sister is the opposite of quiet."

My eyes widened in surprise. "I *do* like the quiet."

"Me, too," he agreed. "Besides, you're the baby of your family, aren't you? And Caoimhe's way older than you."

"Yep."

"So quiet is what you're used to," he continued to explain. "I'm the oldest of the four of us, so I'm used to the noise, but I don't like it."

My brows furrowed in confusion. "But there's only two of you."

"Gibsie's basically the middle child, and Beth's the baby." Lips twitching into a small smile, he added, "He's practically my brother."

"So you guys sort of adopted him?" I grinned. "Like Master Splinter did with the turtles."

His brown-eyed gaze flicked to me and his smirk deepened. "Pretty much."

He was pretty. So pretty. "Hey, Hugh?"

"Hm?"

"I like you."

"I like you, too, Liz," he replied, pulling himself into a sitting position. "I wish you were in my class at school and *not* my sister's."

Mirroring his actions, I sat cross-legged, facing him, and smiled. "I want to be with you all the time."

"Yeah." His cheeks reddened when he nodded. "I want that, too."

"Hey, Hugh?"

"Yeah, Liz?"

"You know the way Gibsie is going to ask Claire to marry him when they're grown-up?" I shifted closer until our knees were touching. "Do you think you might ask me to marry you?"

Hugh stared at me for a long time before saying, "If I asked you, would you say yes?"

"Yes." I nodded eagerly. "I would definitely say yes."

He smiled. "That's good to know."

"Hey, Hugh?"

"Yeah, Liz."

I pointed to the watch on his wrist. "Happy New Year."

Hugh stared down at the face of his watch for a long moment before turning his attention back to me. And then, with red cheeks, he leaned in close and kissed my cheek. "Happy New Year, Liz."

PART 3

Devastating Departures

MOVING ON AND MOVING IN

Hugh

APRIL 1, 1995

Sitting on the footpath on our side of the street, we watched as a big, white van pulled into number nine. Keith and Mark Allen climbed out of the van. Rounding the back of the van, Keith opened the door and the two of them started to retrieve their moving boxes.

"Do you think it's an April Fool's prank?" Feely asked in a hopeful tone.

"I wish," I replied.

"This fucking sucks," Gibsie muttered, balancing the small, curly-haired toddler on his lap.

"Big, fat donkey balls," Liz agreed with a sigh.

"Guys, don't curse," my sister scolded. "Not in front of Beth."

"Come on, Claire," I argued. "If we can't curse today, when can we?"

She shrugged but didn't respond.

Because she couldn't.

Because this was the worst day ever.

A few minutes later, Sadhbh came running out of the house. The smile on her face was bigger than any smile she had ever given Joe.

When she threw her arms around Keith Allen, it caused the boy sitting on the footpath beside me to bury his face in his sister's neck and groan. "This is the worst fucking day of my life."

"Gib," Beth babbled, pulling on his hair. "Gibby."

"It's okay, Beth," I coaxed, shifting the toddler onto my lap. "Gibs is just tired."

Feeling bad for my friend but not knowing what to say, I nudged his shoulder with mine, wanting him to know that I was sorry that his mother was replacing his father with this man.

Meanwhile, my sister made no such promises with herself. "Ew," she groaned from her perch on the other side of our friend. "That's just…ew!"

Scrunching her small nose up in disgust, Claire reached over and hooked her skinny, little arm around Gibsie's shoulder. It didn't reach, of course—she was too little—but the gesture was there, and for some weird reason, her comfort was better received than mine. Because Gibs dropped his head on her shoulder, letting her be the one to comfort him.

I knew he was crying, I could see his shoulders jerking, but he never made a sound. It was the kind of quiet crying I saw in silent movies my grandparents used to watch. Somehow, that made it worse than if he had been screaming like a bull.

Acting like she was Gibsie's personal bodyguard to the ordeal, Claire used her free hand to cover his eyes. I wasn't sure what she was trying to do in the moment, shield him from the kissing or shield the world from him.

I glanced at Feely, who was sitting on the other side of Claire, and he shrugged back at me, looking as uncertain as I felt.

None of us knew what to do.

That's when a small hand entwined with mine, sending a spark of heat through my body.

The moment I turned my head to the left and my eyes locked on Lizzie's pale-blue ones, the familiar surge of electricity I had grown used to feeling when she was nearby surged through me. It even happened when I was alone and *thought* about her.

I used to think it would fade once I got used to seeing her, but having seen her almost every day for the past six months, it was safe to assume that it wasn't going to.

I was beginning to understand why Gibs wanted to be with Claire all the time. If she made him feel the way Liz made me feel, I didn't blame him.

Before Liz, I never really believed that a girl could be your best friend, but she was living proof of it. I preferred her company above all others and spent all my free time with her.

Claire and Gibs were so damn lucky to live across the street from each other. Lizzie lived outside of town. Her house was six miles from mine, and I wasn't allowed to cycle over there yet. She came over with her sister when Caoimhe babysat, and she slept over most weekends, but it *still* wasn't enough because when she had to leave, I didn't feel like myself until she came back to me.

"Poo," Bethany said then, reaching up to pull on my hair. "Poo, Poo."

"It's Hugh," I corrected, while my friends all laughed. "Can you say Hughie, Beth?"

"Pooey," she replied, smiling back at me with big gray eyes. "Poo, Poo, Pooey."

Even Gibsie laughed this time.

At least I was useful for something.

EXCEPT HE DIDN'T

Lizzie

APRIL 21, 1995

"Thank you for inviting me to your house," Shannon said in a quiet voice from the back seat of Claire's dad's car on Friday after school. "I'm really grateful."

"That's okay, Shan." Claire squeezed her hand. "I'm so happy you're coming over." She leaned over Shannon to pat my knee. "You, too, Liz."

I smiled back at them but didn't respond because I was so tired. Everything felt heavy on my shoulders and the scary lady was extra loud in my head today.

I had felt it coming for a while now.

My happiness kept getting lower, and lower, and lower until it hit the bottom.

Now, everything was dark and sad.

I wasn't even cross.

I just felt empty.

Trying to distract myself, I peered at Claire's parents. Her dad was driving, and her mam was in the passenger seat. He was holding her hand and sometimes he would pick it up and kiss it.

"Rock 'n' Roll Kids" was playing on the radio, and I knew all the words because Ireland had won the Eurovision Song Contest with it earlier this year.

I couldn't get myself to care, though.

It didn't matter if I knew the words or not. It didn't matter if the girls talked to me or not. Nothing mattered to me. All I wanted to do was crawl into bed and go to sleep.

When we got to Claire's house, I trailed after my friends and tried my best to keep up with their conversations, but it was exhausting.

The scary lady kept whispering in my head.

Her claws were pushing me under the water.

It felt like my head was underwater and I could see her, but it was blurry and faded.

I was too tired to fight her back in my head.

She was sitting on my shoulder now, but they couldn't see her.

When I told the girls I needed to use the bathroom, it was a lie. I didn't need to go. I just needed to *go*. Climbing into the tub, I curled up in a ball and covered my head.

"Be a good girl and open your mouth."

Get out.

"If you bite me, I'll kill her. Do you want that?"

Get out.

"That's it. You like that, don't you?"

Get out!

"Stop crying. I can feel you enjoying it."

Please get out of my head.

"Fuck me, you're getting so good at that."

Stop hurting me!

"That's it. It's not so bad, is it?"

No!

"Clean yourself up."

Please make it stop!

"That's your fault, not mine..."

I didn't hear the bathroom door open and close, but I *did* hear Hugh's voice when he shouted, "Liz? Are you okay?"

Forcing myself to sit up, I lifted my head to look at him. "Hi."

"Hi." Crouching down next to the tub, Hugh rested his elbows on the rim and stared at me. "What are you doing in the bath?"

"Resting," I whispered, too numb to feel embarrassed. "I'm tired."

"Are you sick?" Reaching out, he pressed his palm to my forehead and frowned. "You're not warm."

"Don't," I begged when he moved his hand. Shivering, I snatched it back up and held it to my cheek. "I can feel you."

"Yeah, well, I would hope so," he offered, giving me a rueful smile. "I am touching your face."

"No, I can *feel* you," I squeezed out, trying to make him understand. "I can feel *me* when I feel *you*."

He didn't say anything to that, but he didn't pull his hand away, either. Instead, he knelt beside me and kept his hand on my cheek.

"Listen, I'm doing homework in my room, but you can come with me and sleep in my bed if you want?" he offered after a long silence. "Claire and Shannon are out back in the treehouse, so they won't mind."

"You can sleep in my bed..."

I knew what that meant.

But it was okay.

Because I loved Hugh Biggs.

My heart was sure I did.

And Hugh would never hurt me like *he* did.

Nodding, I took the hand he offered me and climbed out of the tub. Keeping a firm hold of his hand, I soaked in the warmth as he led me into his room.

It would be okay.

Because he was kind.

He wouldn't make me cry.

He wouldn't make me bleed.

"You can rest here," Hugh said in a gentle voice, stopping in front of a big double bed. "It's comfier than the tub."

Climbing onto the mattress, I rolled onto my back and settled into the familiar position, arms at my sides and legs open, waiting for this boy to do what Mark told me all boys did.

Except he *didn't*.

Instead of taking off my clothes, Hugh covered me with a blanket and stepped away.

Confused, I turned my head to watch him sit cross-legged in front of a stack of schoolbooks on his bedroom floor.

Pulling up on my elbows, I peered down at him, not understanding any of this.

Was I bad?

Did I do something wrong?

Was he cross with me?

He didn't *sound* cross.

In fact, he was humming a song under his breath while he scribbled in his copybook. I knew the song. It was the one playing on his Walkman the first day we met—"Send Me on My Way" by Rusted Root.

My heart slammed hard against my rib cage then, and with it came a flood of emotion. Feelings: they bombarded my heart, rushing through me like a river.

I was feeling.

I could *feel* again.

I didn't have to scream to make the lady go away, either.

She disappeared when he found me in the tub.

She was afraid of Hugh.

Because he was good.

Because he was brave.

A brave knight.

A wave of relief washed over me, and I gripped the blanket draped over me, allowing my heavy eyelids to close.

Mark didn't fix me this time.

Hugh did.

And he didn't have to hurt me to do it…

FIRST HOLY COMMUNION AND FIRST DEAD BODY

Hugh

MAY 6, 1995

WHEN OUR FAMILIES BOARDED THE BOAT ON SATURDAY AFTERNOON, I REMEMBERED thinking it was one of the best days of my life. Looking fancy in our First Holy Communion suits, Gibsie and I leaned over the side of the boat, watching the dolphins chase us as we sailed out to sea.

I remembered spending most of our time planning all the ways we could spend our fortunes. We knew we had made a *lot* of cash today. Our mothers had stacks of thick envelopes shoved into their handbags.

All filled with money and all for us.

It should have been the best day of our lives, but instead, it became our worst day.

One moment, Gibs and I were arguing with our sisters over a stupid toy laser beam, and the next, one of them had fallen overboard.

Everything happened so fast, and yet time seemed to slow down.

One minute, Bethany was there and the next she wasn't.

Time seemed to stand still for a long beat before Sadhbh's high-pitched scream shook the earth's core.

It was the worst, scariest noise I'd ever heard in my life.

"Bethany!" Sadhbh screamed. "Joe, I can't swim. Please, I can't swim, Joe!"

"I'll get our baby." We were shoved out of the way then, and I watched as Joe Gibson barreled past us and jumped overboard, while screaming his daughter's name. "Bethany!"

"Daddy's coming, Beth," Sadhbh continued to scream, and it made my skin crawl because it sounded like impending doom. "Hold on, baby girl. Daddy's on the way!"

Panic stricken, I grabbed *my* sister and pulled her back from the edge, where she had been leaning over and crying hysterically.

Everyone was screaming and I didn't know what to do. I was scared to look at Sadhbh's face because the noises coming out of her were truly terrifying.

Instead, I kept a firm grip on the small, curly-haired girl and thanked Jesus he had spared *my* sister.

Because this was bad.

I knew it was.

Beth couldn't swim, she was only a toddler, and the current was too strong. It wasn't a swimming pool she needed to be rescued from—it was the wild Atlantic Ocean, and she hadn't surfaced once since she fell in.

"Beth, hold on!" My attention snapped to Gibsie's frantic screams, and I locked eyes on him climbing over the side of the boat. "Dad, I'm coming!"

"Gibs, no!" I roared, pushing past my sister, but it was too late.

He was already disappearing beneath the waves.

"Hold on, Gibs!" I called out, before sucking in a deep breath and launching myself over the side.

But I didn't hit the water because someone grabbed me by the back of my shirt. "No!" My father's voice boomed in my ears, as he roughly dragged me backward and tossed me in a heap on the deck. "Stay!" he ordered before jumping overboard.

"Dad!" I screamed, scrambling onto my hands and knees to get to him. "Dad!"

In a nanosecond, my mother was on me, wrapping her arms around me in a ferocious bear hug to stop me from following my dad.

"No, Mam," I cried, pushing and lashing to break free. "Gibs can't swim properly."

"He can't swim yet!" Claire screamed, repeating my words, as she barreled toward the side of the boat where our friend had disappeared. "You gots to do something!" She argued, pushing and slamming her small fists against Keith's leg. "You gots to save them!"

"I can't swim," Keith cried, holding on to Sadhbh, who seemed to be in a state of delirium. "I'm so sorry. I can't swim."

Meanwhile, Mark stood to the side, with his arms folded across his chest.

Like a statue.

Like a devil.

Doing *nothing*.

Managing to free myself from Mam's grip, I bolted over to the side of the boat and screamed when Joe broke the surface with both of his children.

Relief.

It flooded me.

Gibsie's limp body was sprawled over his shoulder, while he clutched his toddler daughter to his chest. Neither one of them were moving.

Gibsie's eyes were closed, and Bethany's hair was draped over her face in wet, golden clumps.

Panic quickly set in.

Oh no.

Oh no, no, no…

"Gerard!" Claire screamed, sounding more frightened than I'd ever heard her. "Just hold on, okay? I'm here, Gerard! Don't go to sleep!"

"Are they okay?" Sadhbh continued to scream over and over, as she collapsed in a heap on the bed of the boat. "Are they breathing?"

"I'm coming, Gibs," Dad called out, breathing hard, as he frantically swam out toward his best friend. "I've got ya, buddy."

"Pete," Joe called back, struggling to keep all three of them afloat from the relentless assault of wave after wave.

We shouldn't have come out today, I thought to myself.

The water was too choppy. The conditions were all wrong. I'd heard my dad say as much to my mother this morning.

Still, I clung to the hope that everything would be okay.

Hope was quick to dwindle when, a moment later, a huge wave crashed over the four of them, causing Joe to lose his hold on Gibsie.

"Gerard!" Claire screamed, trying to climb over the side of the boat to get to him. Thankfully, Mam had a firm hold on her. "Daddy, you gots to find him! Please! Please! Gerard! Over there, Daddy." Claire screamed in a feral tone, pointing to where our friend had been swallowed up by the merciless waters. "It sucked him down there, Daddy!"

"I'll find him, Gibs," Dad vowed, clearly the fresher of the two of them, as Joe was fading fast. "I promise I'll find your son." Dad glanced over to where my sister was screaming and pointing at and nodded. "I'll bring him back."

"Don't let him die, Pete."

"I won't," Dad promised. "Take Beth back in. I'll get the boy."

Another wave crashed over them then, and just like that, Bethany sank under the water like her brother had, followed by her father.

Swallowed up by the waves like a lifeless, floating doll.

The image of her pink dress was the last that I saw of her.

She wouldn't come back up that day.

Neither would Joe.

"He gots him!" Claire screamed then, rekindling the dying flame of hope inside of me. "Daddy gots Gerard!"

I couldn't look because I knew it would be bad.

I was too fucking scared to see him *not* alive.

My oldest friend in the world.

"Hugh, I need you to listen to me." Turning me in her arms, my mother held my shoulders as she spoke. "I need you to be brave, okay?"

Blinking the tears away, I nodded. "I will."

"I need you to do everything I tell you. No matter what, son."

Sniffling, I offered her another nod. "I will."

"I need to help your father now, and I need *you* to look after your sister, okay?"

I choked out a sob and nodded in understanding.

"Good boy." Leaning in close, Mam pressed a hard kiss to my forehead and then climbed over the side of the boat and lowered herself into the choppy water.

"Mammy, no!" Claire screamed frantically when our mother went into the water. "Come back!"

Swimming out to our father, Mam battled against the waves pushing against her, not stopping until she reached my father.

Taking the lifeless boy from his arms, she treaded water, giving my father a chance to regather some strength.

And then, by some miraculous intervention, they managed to work together to bring my oldest friend's lifeless body back to the boat.

"He's dead," Sadhbh continued to wail, collapsing in a heap on the floor in Keith's arms. "They're all dead."

I couldn't concentrate on her, though.

Not when my entire focus was on my mother as I waited for the instructions to come.

"Hugh," Mam said, as she clung to the side of the boat, breathing hard from the effort it was taking to stay afloat in these conditions.

Handing off Gibs to my father once more, she looked up at me from the depths of the water and said, "I need you to hold your friend." Her eyes were pleading when she added, "I need you to use all your strength and hold him for me, okay? Whatever you do, don't let go."

"I won't," I promised through tears, as I leaned over the side and grabbed Gibsie's shoulders. I tried to heave him over, but he weighed so much more than normal that I couldn't.

"I've got you, Hugh," Claire cried, wrapping her limbs around my legs. "I won't let go."

"Don't let go," Dad ordered as he heaved himself out of the water and onto the boat. "Good lad."

"I won't." I hissed through my teeth from the effort it was taking to hold on, especially with the current pulling and the waves crashing over him. But if the ocean wanted Gerard Gibson, then it was going to have to take my arms with him because I would never let go of him.

Scrambling to where I was dangling over the side, Dad grabbed the back of Gibsie's shirt and helped me heave him onto the boat.

"Gerard!" Sadhbh screamed, scrambling toward him on her hands and knees, while my father collapsed in a heap from exhaustion. "Oh, baby, breathe." Trailing her hands all over his lifeless body, Sadhbh started pushing and shoving at his chest, desperate to make his heart start beating again.

But it wasn't beating.

And he wasn't breathing.

He wasn't even the right color.

He was a grayish-blue color.

He was dead.

I knew it.

Ignoring the madness around me, I retrained my attention back on my mother, who was still in the water. Leaning over the side, I reached out both hands to help her back onto the deck. "My brave boy," she panted when she was safely back on the boat. I wasn't sure if it was the ocean water in her eyes or tears, but she gave me the saddest smile and brushed my cheek with her icy-cold fingers before rushing to Gibsie.

"Breathe," Sadhbh continued to scream, pushing on Gibsie's chest, while my father blew into his mouth.

"Come on, kid, breathe."

It wasn't working.

"Come on, son, come back to me."

It didn't seem to make a difference.

"Breathe, Gibs. Breathe, lad!"

He wouldn't *breathe*.

"Move aside," I heard my mother instruct as she knelt in front of my lifeless friend and began to resuscitate him. The proper way. Because my mam was smart like that. She always knew what to do.

Whatever hope Gibs had was in my mother's hands now.

She was a nurse in the ICU.

She would know what to do.

How to make him breathe again.

"I'll start the engine," Keith declared hoarsely. "I've called the paramedics. They'll meet us on the shore."

"No, no, no!" Sadhbh screamed, pulling and tearing at her hair, as she dashed to the side of the boat where her daughter had fallen overboard. "My baby! My baby's in there! We can't leave her!"

"Gerard's going to die if we don't get him help," Keith argued back. "We have to go, Sadhbh, love."

"He's already dead."

"Shut up, Mark."

A few moments later, when the sound of the motor running filled the air, and the vibration rattled through my body, a pair of small arms came around me, and I didn't hesitate to fold her into my body, holding on for dear life to *my* baby sister.

"Joe!" Sadhbh screamed, sounding feral. "Joe!"

"It's okay, love. They'll give you something for the shock when we get back to land."

"Bethany! Joe! No, no, no, don't do this. Don't leave them behind!"

I felt more gratitude for Claire in this moment than I ever had in the five years since she'd arrived into my world. Because she was here, on this boat, with her heart beating. "I love you, Claire," I heard myself cry, holding her so tight, I was sure I was hurting her skinny, little body, but I didn't care. She was alive and I had to feel that in this moment. After holding Gibsie's lifeless body, I had to touch something *alive*. "I love you. I love you. I love you!"

"I loves you, too," Claire sobbed, clinging to me just as tightly, smothering my face with her wild curls. "Don't ever go away, Hughie."

"I won't," I whispered, burying her face in my neck, needing to protect her from what was unfolding around us.

The hopeless feeling that was festering inside of me continued to grow and inflate and consume me until the sound of a choking cough filled my ears.

"That's it, lad," my father cried out. "Come on, come back to us."

Another choking cough filled my ears, but I didn't get my hopes up.

Because what if I was wrong?

What if I was imagining the sound?

"Quick, roll him onto his side, Pete, he's asphyxiating," Mam instructed. "That's it, Gibsie, love. Good boy. Cough it all up."

"Quick, warm him up before his body goes into hypothermia."

"Gerard," Claire cried out, and it was only then that I dared to look.

That I dared to hope.

Scrambling out of my lap, Claire crawled on her hands and knees to where our friend was lying on his side, in the recovery position, facing us. His eyes were blank, but they were open and focused entirely on my sister's face.

"We've got you, Gerard," she continued to tell him, hunched down close to his face, with her small hand touching his hollow cheek. "You came back to me."

He was a deathly bluish-gray color and trembling violently beneath the bundle of coats and blankets the grown-ups had thrown over him, but his chest was moving.

He was *breathing*.

In that moment, I vowed to never sit back and do nothing.

I would never be a statue like Mark or incapable like Sadhbh and Keith.

For the rest of my life, I would help.

I would save people.

I would bring them back to life.

Like my father brought Gibs back from his watery grave.

Like my mother brought his heart back to life.

BEST FRIENDS FOREVER

Lizzie

JUNE 24, 1995

OVER A MONTH HAD PASSED SINCE THE FUNERAL, BUT SADNESS WAS ALL AROUND US. Like a monster, it swept everyone up and gobbled them whole.

I wanted to help Gibsie, but I didn't know how. I wasn't sure of the words I needed to say, or if he even wanted to hear them. I knew I wouldn't have. If my mother got swept out to sea, I wouldn't ever want to wake up again.

It made me so sad to think that Gibs couldn't ever get his daddy and sister back. My daddy and sister were always cross with me, but I still got to see them every day, while Gibsie would never see his again.

He went back to school right after, which I thought was so brave. Claire said he could have taken the rest of the school year off, but he didn't do that. Instead, he got back up and faced the day. It made me proud to be his friend. It made me think I could be brave like him someday, too.

Since the funeral, Caoimhe spent a lot more time babysitting Claire and Hugh because Pete was so sad and Sinead needed the help.

Gibsie's daddy was Hugh's daddy's best friend since primary school, and Pete didn't want to get out of bed anymore. Not with his bestest friend in the world up in heaven.

Sinead told me that I could come over whenever my sister was babysitting because it was good for her kids to have their friends around them.

I happily agreed because I didn't want to be away from any of them, including Gibsie, who spent most of his time at their house.

When Dad dropped Caoimhe to Avoca Greystones this morning for her babysitting shift, I made sure I was right there with her.

Clambering up the familiar staircase, I skipped down the landing, making a beeline to Claire's bedroom door, only to hesitate when I reached it.

Because something deep inside was telling me to go to the other door.

Go to Hugh.

I couldn't explain what that was, but it was strong and forceful and willing me to put one foot in front of the other.

I thought about knocking but decided against it, twisting the doorknob and slipping inside instead.

Glancing around his bedroom, I felt a little dizzy. Giddy even. It felt like I had stepped into someone's "good room" and I wasn't supposed to touch any of the shiny crystalware, but I *wanted* to.

That's what Hugh's bedroom always felt like to me.

I wanted to touch everything.

All his books and trophies and Lego.

Even when I wasn't supposed to.

He had a signed jersey framed over his bed, with Roy Keane's signature on it, and I thought that might be his most important possession.

I wanted to touch that most of all.

He was tidier than Claire. Everything had a place in Hugh's room. It was almost bare in comparison to the countless dolls, stuffed animals, and toys that lined the walls of Claire's room. He was simplistic and structured.

His smell was all around me and it was my favorite smell in the whole world.

Soap, grass, strawberries, and Hugh.

Closing the space between me and the bed, I trailed my fingertips over the Hugh-shaped figure beneath the duvet. "It's me."

Silence greeted me.

Sighing sadly, I glanced out the window next, peering at the house across the street, before returning my attention to the boy under the duvet.

Wordlessly, I kicked off my sandals and smoothed a hand over where I thought his cheek might be before reaching for the covers.

Peeling them back, I quickly climbed in beside him and covered us back up, concealing us from the summer sunshine. "Hi."

This time he answered. "Hi."

Nestling in close to his warm body, I rested on my side, facing him.

Even though he was doing his very best to cloak himself in darkness, sunlight still managed to beam its way through, cloaking him in a glorious, shiny hue.

Exhaling heavily, I reached up and pressed my hand to his cheek, feeling the wetness from where his tears had dripped.

Sniffling, he reached up and covered my hand with his, never saying a word.

That was the thing about me and Hugh: sometimes we never needed to speak at all.

We just knew what the other was feeling.

Right now, he was sad.

He was so sad because of Joe and Bethany.

But he was even sadder that his dad wasn't coming out of his bedroom.

You see, Hugh liked to fix problems, and he was usually really good at it, but this was something he couldn't fix.

It was a problem for the grown-ups, not us kids.

Snuggling in closer, I leaned in close until my nose rubbed against his.

That made him smile.

Another sniffle escaped him, but this one held the air of finality to it, like he was finished crying—or at least he had decided he was.

Removing the hand he was resting on top of mine, he placed it on my cheek instead. "I love you."

My heart thumped like a drum in my chest because this was the first time he said those words out loud. "You do?"

Nodding slowly, he stroked my cheek with his thumb and exhaled a shaky breath. "I just thought you should know." A shiver racked through him. "In case anything happens and I don't get to tell you."

"What's going to happen?"

"Maybe nothing." He exhaled a shaky breath and whispered, "But you never know what tomorrow could bring."

"I know what tomorrow will bring, Hugh," I replied. "You and me. Same as yesterday and same as today. Being best friends forever." Smiling, I leaned in close and brushed his nose with mine. "No matter what."

"Yeah, Liz." His lips grew into a small smile. "No matter what."

BIRTHDAY CELEBRATIONS AND FUTURE WARNINGS

Hugh

JULY 4, 1995

BECAUSE MY HOUSE WAS THE UNOFFICIAL HEADQUARTERS FOR EVERYONE TO HANG out, it meant that I didn't spend much time at friends' homes. Even Feely's. I could count on two hands the number of times I'd been to his farm, but today was his birthday, and he'd only invited myself and Gibsie over to celebrate.

Unfortunately, Gibs was still deep in his "not leaving Claire's side" phase, which meant I was the only guest. To be fair to Feely, he didn't push Gibs, and neither did I.

He was doing remarkably well considering his world had fallen apart two months ago. Neither one of us wanted to tip him over the edge. If Claire's company was what he needed right now, then he could have it with our full blessing.

"You know I don't eat that," Feely said, dragging me from my thoughts. I peered at the plate in front of him and my stomach growled in appreciation when my eyes took in the sight of a juicy steak. "I'm a vegetarian, Dad."

"You're a bollocks is what you are," his father shot back before dumping another massive steak onto *my* plate. "Now, Hughie, lad, tuck into a feed of prime Irish beef for yourself."

I wanted to.

Badly.

But I didn't want to be used as a pawn in Paddy Feely's attack on his son. Especially on his birthday.

"Actually, I'm a vegetarian, too," I lied, mentally devastated to abandon the glorious piece of meat on my plate. Feely caught my eye, and he gave me a grateful smile.

"Jesus Christ," the old man muttered, shaking his head. "There's something fucking wrong with the youth of today."

"Paddy," Mary scolded, pouring a mountain of steaming spuds into a bowl on the middle of the table. "Could you give it a rest? It's our son's birthday. Let the lad eat what he wants for one day, will ya?"

"Would ya take one look at him, Mary?" Paddy continued, using his fork to point at his son across the table. "He's like a ghost."

"He's just pale."

"And scrawny."

"Because he's growing like a beanstalk."

"Because he's lacking in iron. And do ya know where iron comes from, Mary? Red meat is where iron comes from," he ranted, shaking his head. "Did ya ever hear the likes of it in your life? A beef farmer with a vegetarian for a son?"

"You're just old-fashioned," his wife argued. "There's nothing wrong with not eating meat."

"I blame his sisters for putting notions in his head," he continued, not one bit dissuaded by my presence. "They babied the lad and made him soft. Putting musical instruments in his hands instead of a shovel and pike!"

"He's brilliant," I heard myself point out, feeling pissed off with the old man. Feely's dad wasn't intimidating or physically aggressive, just a contrary old fucker set in his backwards ways. Both Feely's mother and father were pushing on in years. They were both gray and wrinkled and sort of looked like they should be his grandparents. "Your son is the best singer at school."

That was no word of a lie. Feely could hit the high notes in "Queen of the May" better than any of us in the school choir, which meant he got roped into singing for Holy Communion every year. And his rendition of "Oíche Chiúin" was tremendous. My friend could turn his hand to any manner of instruments, be it the bodhran or guitar, the keyboard or the fiddle. He was so superior to the rest of us that I often wondered why the teachers forced the rest of us eejits to crow behind him when we clearly brought him down.

Last year, Gibs pitched a fit about favoritism, so they let him tinkle on a triangle while crooning out "Kumbaya, My Lord," but that's as close as Feely ever came to losing his leading role.

"A lot of good that'll do him when he's farming the land," his father scoffed, retraining his attention on his son who could have easily been his grandson. "You'll do well to remember that, boyo. Don't be getting any notions of grandeur because this is your lot." He pointed out the kitchen window to the sprawling, green countryside that was his family's farm. "That's your future."

Borrowing a pair of his wellies after dinner and with a cattle prod in hand, I trailed through the farm with my friend, feeling so fucking sad for him but knowing better than to verbalize my thoughts.

"Are you all right, lad?" I finally asked him once enough time had passed.

"I'm grand," he replied, brushing it under the carpet like only Feely could, while he herded the milked cows out of the parlor and back down the path to the field. "He just doesn't get me."

"Well, I think you're brilliant," I offered. "I think you should keep playing."

"Yeah," he replied flatly, smacking one rogue cow on the hind to move her on when she starting holding up the others. "It is what it is, Hughie."

His shoulders were slumped, his head was bowed, and I knew he was drowning in his father's words of warning.

Now, I was no Patrick Feely. In fact, I couldn't sing for shit and was *always* put in the far back in the choir, but I decided to break into song right now, because he needed me to.

Crowing like a lark, I belted out the first song that came to mind, which just so happened to be Christy Moore's "Don't Forget Your Shovel."

Thankfully my attempt to cheer him up was a success. He choked out a laugh. Encouraged by his hearty chuckles, I upped the stakes, mimicking his father's hobbled walk as I scuffled toward him.

"You're a dope," he laughed, nudging my shoulder with his when I reached him.

Grinning, I threw my arm around him and continued to croon the words until he gave in and sang along with me.

And that's how we spent the rest of his birthday, knee-deep in cow shit on his father's farm, singing about shovels and holes in buckets.

I WAS TRYING TO PROTECT YOU

Lizzie

SEPTEMBER 9, 1995

THE SCREAMING STARTED SHORTLY AFTER OUR PARENTS LEFT TO JOIN THEIR FRIENDS at the pub and grew louder and louder until I couldn't take another high-pitched wail.

Our bedrooms were both on the second floor and a good distant apart, but Caoimhe was screaming so loud that I could hear her all the way from mine.

I knew I wasn't supposed to go near my sister's room when he was over — she made it crystal clear that I was to stay out — but I couldn't stand the sound of her shrill screams.

I knew what they meant.

He was using his special powers.

That scared me because it meant my sister was sick like me. Worried, I climbed out of bed and padded down the hall to her bedroom door. Pressing my ear against the old wooden frame, I listened carefully to the noises coming from the other side of it.

"Oh my God!"

"You like that?"

"Fuck, yes, just like that."

"Mm, that's it, baby. Just like that."

"I can't, I can't…"

"Take it. Fucking take it, you bad girl!"

"Don't stop!"

"Turn over."

"But I don't—"

"I said turn the fuck over. Now!"

"Okay, but be gentle this time… Ahhh!"

My sister screamed so loud that it made me scream even louder. Panicked, I lost all control over my voice and pushed the door inward, afraid that she might be sick like our mam.

"Lizzie, what the hell are you doing!" Caoimhe roared, but I couldn't do anything but stand in the doorway and scream. She was leaning, face-down over the side of her bed, and he was standing behind her. They didn't have any clothes on and he was giving her the special medicine. The one that he made me take, even when I didn't want to.

My heart sank.

She *was* sick.

"Oh my God, Lizzie, get the fuck out!" Caoimhe screamed, pulling at her duvet to cover herself. "Now!"

I tried to tell her that I was sorry, that I didn't mean to break the rules, but she was going to be okay because Mark could fix her.

I opened my mouth, but nothing came out.

My eyes flicked to Mark.

He wasn't looking at me with a cross face.

He was looking at me with a small smile.

I shivered.

"Are you deaf as well as fucking dumb?" This time Caoimhe screamed so loud at me that I felt tears in my eyes. "I said get the hell out."

Turning on my heels, I bolted from her room as fast as my legs could carry me.

"Don't roar at her like that," I heard him shout, but I didn't stop to listen. Instead, I ran straight to my bed and dove under the covers. Covering my mouth with my hands to stop my screams from getting out, I rocked back and forth under the covers, trying to comfort myself.

It would be okay.

Caoimhe wouldn't die.

Mark gave her the medicine.

He used his special powers to fix her.

It was good.

This is good.

I clenched my eyes shut when I felt the tears trickling down my cheeks.

––––––––––

Later that night, when my door opened and my sister walked in, I felt confused because she never visited me at nighttime.

Stiffening, I hid under the covers and tried to make myself as small as I could.

"Don't hide, Liz," she said, and her voice wasn't cross like before. "I'm not mad. I'm sorry." Sniffling, I peeked up at her when she sat on my bed. "I shouldn't have called you names," she told me with a heavy sigh. "But you walked in, and I panicked."

I wanted to ask if she felt better now.

I wanted to ask if she was going to be okay.

"I know it might have looked like Mark was hurting me earlier, but I promise he didn't. The opposite, in fact." Her cheeks turned pink as she spoke. "He was making me feel good, Liz. That's what boys do for girls they love. They make them feel good. And Mark makes me feel really, *really* good. But you don't have to worry about any of this now," she continued, rubbing my arm. "Not until you're a big girl like me and find a special boy who loves you."

If boys only did that to girls they loved, did that mean Mark loved me?

Because I didn't want Mark to love me.

I wanted *Hugh* to love me.

"Please try to forget about what you saw tonight." She blew out a shaky breath and looked at me pleadingly. "And please, please, *please* don't tell anyone, and especially not Mam and Dad."

"Did he make you better?" I croaked out.

"Hmm?"

"Mark," I strangled, trying not to shiver. "Did he make you feel better?"

"Oh." Her cheeks turned pink again and she nodded eagerly. "Yep, he made me feel all better."

"Okay." I heaved out a relieved breath. "I'll keep your secret."

SCORING TRIES AND MISSING FATHERS

Hugh

OCTOBER 30, 1995

"WHERE'S GIBS?" I ASKED WHEN I WALKED INTO THE KITCHEN AFTER AN U10'S RUGBY game on Monday evening.

"Upstairs with Claire," Mam replied, balancing on a chair while she tried to pin a pinata to the ceiling—something my father always did. "How did the match go?"

"We won, thirty-five to six," I replied, dropping my gear bag by the door. "I scored a try and kicked ten points in conversions."

"Good job," she praised, smiling over her shoulder at me. "Did you thank Patrick's mother for dropping you home?"

"Yes, Mam, I always thank Mary," I shot back, trying to keep the sting out of my tone, but the bitterness inside of me was hard to navigate. "Dad said he'd come to this one."

Mam sighed heavily. "Hugh."

"He said he'd get out of the bed and *come* to *this* one," I repeated, tone harder. "The whole reason I play rugby is because *he* wanted me to."

"Hugh, love, I know you're feeling let down, but your father's struggling right now."

"We're all struggling, Mam," I argued, unwilling to give him another pass on being absent. "Joe was Gibsie's father, and Beth was *his* baby sister, but you don't see him taking to the bed for five bloody months, now, do you?"

"Your father is a *good* man." She parroted back the same words she'd been singing since he checked out on us. "He loves us more than a boy your age can comprehend, but he is grieving, and we need to understand that."

"*I'm* grieving," I choked out. "*Claire's* grieving. *You're* grieving. Why does his grief trump ours?"

"It doesn't, but your father's been diagnosed with severe depression and PTSD, sweetheart, and I know those are only words to you, but it's not something he can just snap out of."

"Why not?" I demanded, feeling beyond hurt that the man I'd grown up adoring just checked out on me. "Just tell him that he has to get back up."

"Just because you can't see your father's illness, doesn't mean that it's any less deserving of empathy," she replied, tone hardening. "Now, I understand you're going through a lot, we all are, but that doesn't give you the right to speak badly of your own flesh and blood, and I won't have another bad word said about your father. Is that clear?"

"Crystal," I muttered, knowing now was the time to throw my white flag in. My mother worshipped the ground my father walked on and would go to bat for him no matter what. I used to think it was the same for Dad, but this year had me opening my eyes to a lot of ugly truths.

"Good boy," Mam said in an approving tone. "Now, what do you think of my work?"

"It looks great." Folding my arms across my chest, I leaned against the island and sighed in dismay. Every wall in the kitchen was decorated with a concoction of ghouls, goblins, and balloons. "But you know I'm not having a party this year."

"Uh, yes, you are."

"No, Mam, I'm not. I didn't hand out invitations to the lads or anything."

"Then I guess it's a good thing your mother has 'the lads' home phone numbers, isn't it?"

"Tell me you didn't?" I half begged, half groaned. "Please tell me you didn't do it."

"I sure did, baby boy," she chirped from her perch, happy as a clam with herself. "The lads will be here tomorrow at two, like every other Halloween we've had since the surgeons removed you from my stomach."

"Thanks for that," I deadpanned, moving for the kitchen table. "What a lovely visual."

"Be glad you only have to visualize and not experience it," she laughed. "Now, perk up because we are going to have a massive celebration tomorrow."

"There's nothing to celebrate," I muttered, dropping into a chair.

"I beg your pardon," she feigned outrage. "How about the birth of my first and only son?"

"Mam, come on." Slumped over the table, I rested my chin on my hand and sighed. "What's that word that queen over in England used about having the year from hell?"

"Annus horribilis?"

"That's exactly what this year is for us," I told her. "1995 is our annus horribilis."

"You know what, son? I think you might be too clever for your own good," Mam mused, hanging a plastic skeleton from the ceiling. "I doubt there's another mother in Ballylaggin whose child quotes Latin."

I shrugged, too pissed off and sad to appreciate the compliment.

PART 4

Crushing Realizations

THAT'S A BAD TOUCH

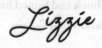

AUGUST 31, 1996

"Hey, Hugh," I asked on the last day of our summer break, shattering the long-stretched silence we'd been basking in. Sprawled out on the flat of my back in the treehouse, with my legs resting on Hugh, who was lounging in a beanbag, I tilted my head to one side to look at him. "Have you changed your mind?"

"About what?" he replied, attention riveted to the book he was reading.

"About being a doctor when you grow up?" I filled in, setting down my copy of *Five on a Treasure Island*.

"Nope," he replied, turning over a page. "It's still the plan."

"And you want to fix hearts, right?"

"I want to be a cardiologist."

"And that's a heart surgeon, right?"

"Yep."

I pulled up on my elbows to get a better look at him. "Why?"

"Because there's too many broken hearts around here."

My eyes widened. "In Ballylaggin?"

He peered over his book at me and smirked. "In the world, Liz."

"Oh." I nodded in understanding. "What about my heart?"

He laughed softly. "Your heart works just fine."

"But what if it breaks?"

"That won't happen."

"How come?"

He turned another page before saying, "Because I won't break it."

"But what if someone else breaks it?"

"Not going to happen."

"How come?"

"Because I've got it locked away safe and sound."

"Oh." I snickered then, feeling mischievous. "What about your heart?"

"What about it?"

"What if it gets broken?" I teased. "You can't fix your own heart, silly."

"Then you better keep it safe."

"I will," I vowed, holding out my pinky finger. "No matter what."

Sighing heavily, he closed his book and leaned forward to hook his pinky around mine. "You're a little menace, you know that?"

"How come?"

"Because you're always distracting me."

"Hey, *you* called me to come over to play, mister." Feeling playful, I pounced on his lap and wrestled him onto the floor before attacking him with the tickles. "Besides, it's bad manners to call your best friend a menace."

"Ah, mercy, mercy!" he roared through fits of laughter when I got him right under his arms. I knew his weak spot. *Ha.* "You win, you win, Liz!"

"You scream like a girl," I snickered, pinning his hands above his head.

"And you wrestle like a boy," he mused, still chuckling. "So I guess we even each other out, huh?"

Straddling his lap, I kept him pinned beneath me and smiled. "You make me feel good in my belly."

"That's the flutter-cups," he replied with a grin.

It wasn't the flutter-cups.

It was something else.

It was the other feeling.

The one *he* put in me.

"Do you want to know a secret?"

Hugh nodded.

"I know someone with superpowers."

"What kind of superpowers?" he replied, still smiling up at me.

I wanted to tell him, but I was scared of what would happen if I did. I didn't want to die. I didn't want him to hurt me. He said he would if I told anyone about the special powers.

"I'm not allowed to say." I sighed sadly. "It's a secret."

"You can tell me," Hugh replied, brown eyes locked on mine. "I'll keep your secret, Liz."

"But it's not my secret," I mumbled, feeling confused. "And I might get in trouble."

"Why would you get in trouble?"

"Doesn't matter." Shaking off the sad feeling, I focused my attention on Hugh. My happy thought. My happy feeling. "You make a comfortable throne, brave knight."

He winked. "Anything for you, milady."

Feeling happy again, I let go of his hands and moved to climb off his lap, only to freeze when Hugh yelped out in pain. "What's wrong?"

"Nothing, nothing, I'm fine," he groaned, squirming around on the treehouse floor with his hands pressed to his crotch. "You just kneed me right in the nuts."

"What's the nuts?"

"The testicles," he clarified through clenched teeth, as his face turned a deep shade of red. "Fuck, that hurt so bad."

"It hurts?"

He nodded stiffly, still squirming. "It'll pass in a bit."

"Don't worry. I know how to fix that thing." I reached for the waistband of his shorts and tried to pull them down. "I'm good at it."

"What? Wait! Liz, no!" Jerking away from me, Hugh bolted to the opposite side of the treehouse. "What are you doing?"

"I know how to fix it," I explained, crawling back over to him. "I can make you feel better."

"No, Liz!" He held out his hand to stop me. "You can't."

"I can't?"

"No," he repeated, shaking his head. "You *can't*."

"Oh." Kneeling with my hands at my sides, I looked up at him, feeling like my whole world was about to crumble. I didn't know what I'd done to make him so upset with me, and that devastated me. Tears prickled my eyeballs. I was so bad. "I'm sorry, Hugh."

He eyed me warily. "Why did you do that?"

I shrugged, unsure of how to answer. "Don't know."

"You *can't* do that, Liz."

I couldn't?

"You are *not* allowed to do that," he repeated in a stern voice. "You are *never* allowed to touch someone like that."

I felt my face grow hot.

"And no one is allowed to touch *you* like that," he added. "Especially not under your clothes. Only grown-ups are allowed to touch other grown-ups like that."

I stared at him in confusion.

I didn't understand.

Was I bad?

Did he hate me?

What was he saying?

"That's a bad touch," Hugh continued to explain. "And nobody is allowed to do that to a kid."

"I'm sorry," I blurted out, tears trickling down my cheeks. "I didn't mean to give you the bad touch."

"It's okay," he replied with a sigh. "And technically, you didn't."

But I tried to.

And it was bad.

Hugh said so.

And Hugh would *never* lie to me.

I trusted him most in the world.

He was my best friend.

"How do you know?" I asked then. "About the bad touch?"

"My mam told me all about it," he explained. "Why? Didn't your mam tell you?"

I shook my head.

He frowned. "Really?"

I shook my head, feeling clueless. It felt like I was sitting in class and everyone else knew the answer except me. I felt stupid. It was a bad feeling. It made my skin grow hot.

"Okay, well, there are parts of your body that are just for you," Hugh started to explain. "For boys, their private part is their penis. For girls, their private part is their vagina. And *nobody* is allowed to touch your vagina. Not your friends. Or your family members. And especially not grown-ups."

"What if you're sick?" I asked, feeling like my world was crashing down around me.

Hugh frowned. "Sick?"

"What if you're sick and need the medicine to get better?" I pushed, digging my nails into my hands. "What if you're bad and need to be fixed?"

"Liz, if you get sick, then you go to the doctor, and they can give you medicine for that," Hugh explained with a frown. "Do you understand?"

No. "Yes."

He eyed me warily. "Are you sure?"

No. "Yes."

"Okay." Hugh looked at me for a long moment before blowing out what sounded like a relieved breath. "Good, because there are monsters out there that like to do bad things to kids."

"Monsters?"

"Yeah." Hugh nodded. "Anyone who hurts children is a monster in disguise."

My eyes widened in terror.

"You don't need to be scared or anything," he was quick to assure me. "You just need to know about this stuff, so you know when to tell a grown-up." He smiled. "Okay?"

"Okay." I nodded my head before bursting into tears. I wanted to throw myself out of the treehouse and hit my head fifty times on the way down because I would rather be dead than do something bad to Hugh.

I couldn't explain the devastation that washed over me in this moment.

"It's okay, Liz, it's okay." He hurried to soothe me, wrapping his arms around me. "You're only a kid. You didn't know."

"I just wanted to f-fix you. M-make you f-feel better," I cried into my hands. "I d-didn't know it was b-bad, Hugh. I'm so s-sorry."

"I know, and it's okay," he coaxed, wrapping me up in his arms. "I'm not mad at you."

"I sh-should g-go h-home."

"No, you shouldn't," he said, tightening his hold on me. "You should stay right here with me because I'm your best friend and I love you and there's nobody else I want to play with."

That made me cry harder.

Because I didn't want to be here anymore.

Because I did a bad thing to Hugh.

I couldn't explain the horror I felt.

I was bad.

Bad.

Bad.

Bad.

"Why are you crying?" Caoimhe asked when she walked into my bedroom that evening. "Liz?"

"Go away," I hissed in between sobs, while I buried my face in my pillow and tried to stop the world from spinning. Because it hurt. Everything was hurting me, and I needed it to *stop*.

"What's wrong?" she demanded, not listening.

Why didn't she listen?

Why didn't *anyone* listen to me?

"I said go away, Caoimhe," I choked out, louder now, as the anger growing inside me threatened to take over. "Leave me alone!"

"No." She still didn't listen. "Not until you tell me why you're wailing like a banshee."

"Because I didn't know, Caoimhe!" I screamed at the top of my lungs, losing all control of my feelings. Springing up on my bed, I grabbed my pillow and flung it at her. "I didn't fucking know!"

"What?" my sister demanded, looking alarmed. "What didn't you know?"

"Get out of my room, you fucking bitch!" I screamed—louder than I ever had in my life. "I'm warning you!"

"Whoa, fuck you right back," she spat. "Sorry for caring. More fool me for caring enough to come check on you, you crazy, little bitch."

"Nobody told me!" I screamed, pulling on my hair so hard a clump of it came away in my hand. So I threw that at her, too. "And it hurts, and it's not making me better, and it's all your fault!"

"What the hell are you talking about?" my sister demanded, looking at me with a horrified expression. "Lizzie Young, you better cop yourself on right this instant and stop pulling your hair!"

She reached out a hand to grab my hand, and that's when I lost it. "I fucking hate you!" Launching myself at my big sister, I grabbed her by the hair and dragged her onto my bed. "This is all your fault!" Using all my strength, I scratched and tore at her face with my nails. "You did this to me! It was you!"

"Dad!" Caoimhe started to scream as she tried to fight me off her. "Dad, help me! Dad, quick! The demented freak is attacking me!"

"Fuck you!" Tightening my grip on her hair so she couldn't run away, I straddled her chest and kept tearing at her face. "You let the monster in!" I scratched her again, deep enough to make blood come out. "You let the monster play tricks on me!"

"Lizzie!" I heard my father roar, and then he was dragging me off my sister. "What in the name of Jesus is wrong with you?" he demanded, holding me so tight to his chest that I couldn't break free. "Stop it, will ya?"

"She just attacked me, Dad." Scrambling to her feet, Caoimhe held her face in her hands and burst into tears. "She's fucking insane."

"It's her fault, Daddy," I tried to protest through my screams as I pointed to my sister, while he held me off the ground in a ferocious bear hug. "She let the monster get me!"

"What's happening?" Mam demanded, coming into my room. "What's going on, girls?"

"What's happening is this girl needs a tranquilizer," Dad snapped, wrestling to keep ahold of me. "I'm having her committed, Catherine."

"Michael, just calm down." Mam tried to plead, coming to stand between all of us. "Let's just sit down and talk about this as a family."

"What's to talk about?" Caoimhe wailed, pointing to the blood dripping down her cheeks. "She's feral, Mam, and needs locking up."

"It's her fault, Mammy! Caoimhe let the monster in," I started to plead, but my father cut me off when he roared at the top of his lungs.

"Enough!" Setting me back down, he grabbed my shoulders and shook me so hard that my teeth chattered. "There is not a monster, and your sister never hurt you!" He shook me again. "There is no scary lady and the voices in your head aren't real!" My head snapped back and forth as he roared into my face. "You have a sickness of the mind; do ya hear me? All this madness is inside of *you*, Elizabeth!"

"Michael, stop shaking her like that!"

"You are going to a specialist, and you are going to do and take whatever they give ya to keep that madness at bay," he continued, ignoring my mother who was trying to pull his hands away. "Or so help me God, I will put you on a boat and send you—"

"Michael!" Mam screamed—louder than I'd ever heard. "Don't you dare!"

"It's happening, Catherine," he warned, giving me a look of revulsion. Releasing my shoulders, he moved straight for Caoimhe. "From this day forward, we're going to do things *my* way."

WHERE'S YOUR SISTER?

Hugh

"Thanks for coming on short notice, love," Mam said when Caoimhe walked into our kitchen on Saturday evening. "I've been called into work and Pete's, uh, well, he's still under the weather."

Under the weather.

What a load of shit.

My dad wasn't under the weather.

My dad had checked out.

"I told her I'm old enough to watch Claire," I offered, still feeling annoyed over the fact that I needed a babysitter when Feely got to stay by himself when his parents weren't home. "I don't need a babysitter anymore."

"You might be able to look after yourself, but your sister certainly isn't," Mam interjected with a look that said *don't start.*

"I know you're well able, Hughie," Caoimhe mused, ruffling my hair. "I'm just here to keep your sister out of trouble, okay?" She smiled. "You do you, kiddo."

"Claire and Gibs are playing in her room, and Pete's upstairs if you need him," Mam said, giving her a grateful look. "The kids have had dinner, but there's cash in the jar for a pizza later if you guys fancy one."

"We'll be grand," Caoimhe assured her, walking my mother to the front door. "Be safe."

"I always am, love."

I waited for the front door to close behind my mother before I began my interrogation. Because I had a crow to pluck with our babysitter. "Where's your sister?"

"You know where my sister is, Hugh." Stepping around me, Caoimhe made her way back to the kitchen. "I've told you a million times."

"Yeah, but you haven't told me when she's coming home," I argued, trailing after her. "Lizzie's been in the hospital for a long time, Caoimhe." I could hear the concern in my own voice as I spoke. "I want to know when she's coming home."

"Soon."

I hadn't seen my best friend in weeks and being told *soon* whenever I asked when she was coming home was driving me crazy. In fact, I felt like screaming. What the hell did *soon* mean anyway? Did the word refer to two hours or two days or two bloody weeks? It was a pointless fucking word that meant *nothing* to me.

"I want to visit her," I pressed, glaring at her. "Liz would want me to come."

"I already told you that she's not allowed visitors right now."

"Yeah, but you haven't told me why!" I shouted, losing my patience. "In fact, you haven't even told me what's wrong with her!"

"She's sick, Hugh. Like I've said."

"With *what*?" I argued back, unwilling to give an inch.

"It's private."

"Private *isn't* a medical illness, Caoimhe."

"Jesus Christ, Hugh, it's complicated, okay?"

"Yeah, well, I can handle complicated," I snapped back. "I'm not your thick-as-shit boyfriend."

"Hey!" Now, she was the one to shout at me. "Don't bring Mark into this."

"Fine." I folded my arms across my chest. "Stop treating me like I'm a kid and I won't."

"You *are* a kid, Hugh," she retorted. "A freakishly brainy one but *still* a *kid*."

"I'm not going to let it go, you know," I warned the teenager in my kitchen. "I'm not Claire or Gibs. You can't butter me up with cookies or distract me with ladybirds." I narrowed my eyes. "And if you don't tell me what's wrong with my best friend, I'll find out my own way."

She arched a disbelieving brow. "Are you threatening me, Hugh Andrew Biggs?"

"How could I do that when I'm just a *kid*?"

Caoimhe stared at me for a long, unblinking beat until she relented with a frustrated growl. "All right, genius, you think you're mature enough for this shit-bomb of a conversation." She sighed in resignation and pointed to the table. "Sit your ass down and let's find out."

With my elbows resting on the kitchen table, I held my head in my hands and listened to every word that poured from my babysitter's mouth.

"The kind of sickness my sister has isn't one you can see," Caoimhe continued, tapping her temple. "It's all in her mind. She hears voices in her head, and it causes her to flip the fuck out." Leaning back in her chair, she pointed to the scar on her cheek. "She did that to me with her nails. My baby sister."

"What did you do to her first?"

"Nothing," Caoimhe snapped back, folding her arms. "That's the whole point, Hugh. She's crazy."

"No, she's not." I shook my head, refuting her claim. "Don't say that about my friend."

"Oh yeah? Well, your *friend* is *my* sister, so I think I know her a little better than you," she shot back angrily. "She might have you and your friends fooled with her sweet disposition, but it's a mask." Her voice was thick with emotion when she said, "I've tried to help her a thousand times and all she does is throw it back in my face. Or worse, blame *me* for her problems." She choked out a pained laugh before pointing to her face again. "This right here is the result of her freaking out and blaming me for bringing monsters into her room." She shook her head. "I mean, what am I supposed to say to that? Sorry about the invisible monsters that only exist in your head, dear sister."

I had no clue what to say in response, but I knew for sure that I *didn't* like her tone, so I decided to tell her just that. "You shouldn't talk about your sister like that. It makes you sound bitter and cruel."

"Yeah, well, sue me," Caoimhe replied, wiping a tear from the corner of her eye. "Because I'm fifteen and a half, and my life's a living hell. I have an angry father in denial, a batshit crazy sister, and a mother who's had cancer so many times, she probably won't see me finish college, so maybe I deserve to feel a little bitter."

"Who else knows about this?" I asked, resisting the urge to defend Liz, but I knew that if I said anything else, Caoimhe would end the conversation. And I had questions. Lots of them. "Aside from your family, I mean."

"Lizzie's school, her doctors and therapists, my boyfriend—oh, and your mam knows, too."

My brows shot up in surprise. "My mother knows?"

Caoimhe nodded. "Sinead's been fantastic to our entire family."

"Oh," I replied quietly, absorbing every word she spoke into my brain for future analysis. "So have the doctors at the hospital figured out what's happening to Liz? Is there a name for it?"

"Not yet, but I'm sure they'll find a fancy medical term to smack on her forehead and call her. After all, there are hundreds of pretty words to label someone crazy." Placing her palms on the table, Caoimhe rose to her feet and gave me a half-hearted smile. "The watered-down version of the dysfunctional Young family."

DOCTOR, DOCTOR, WHERE AM I?

Lizzie

"*Depression.*"

> "*Post-traumatic stress disorder.*"

> "*No, no, no, your daughter is displaying all of the characteristics of social agoraphobia.*"

> "*Actually, I'm beginning to think we're steering toward a panic disorder.*"

> "*It's clinical depression.*"

> "*She needs to take more exercise. Endorphins are a natural mood booster.*"

> "*I would like to schedule her for an MRI, to rule out anything sinister.*"

> "*Major depressive disorder. There's no doubt in my mind.*"

> "*It's a chemical imbalance.*"

> "*At this time, we're considering the possibility of borderline personality disorder.*"

> "*Nonsense, she's perfectly functioning. Fresh air and healthy food is all she needs.*"

> "*She doesn't produce serotonin naturally, so we need to help her with that. Prozac is a gentle SSRI, suitable for children.*"

> "*She's far too young to even consider schizophrenia, but due to the strong genetical link, we can't rule it out.*"

> "*Depressive disorder...*"

Numb to the bone, I sat on the chair between my parents, with my suitcase at my feet, listening as my parents bounced questions at Dr. Christmas. At least, that's what I called him in my head because he looked just like Santa Claus.

I'd tried to remember all the doctors' and nurses' names, but it was too hard. There was always a new name to match a new face to match a new pair of ears that *didn't* listen to me.

I couldn't remember how long I'd been here or if I was even here right now.

It could be another dream.

I had lots of those.

Bad ones with monsters that crawled out from under my bed in the night and scary ladies that scratched holes in my head. But the medicine in the hospital made me too sleepy to worry.

Now, when the monsters came out at night, I let them have me. I didn't fight back anymore. Instead, I opened the door and let them come inside me.

My body.

My mind.

It didn't matter to me.

Because it *wasn't* real.

The doctors said so.

The monsters were all in my head.

"After a great deal of investigation and having spent many hours working with Elizabeth, I'm confident to say that, while it's rare, your daughter meets the criteria for early-onset bipolar disorder. There are a wide range of treatments available, but at this time, given her swift improvement, I would like Lizzie to continue with the current prescribed medication." He cleared his throat before adding, "Of course, this will need to be adjusted as she grows, and you should be aware that adolescence is a particularly difficult period for children. Some studies suggest patients with the disorder encounter early pubertal timing in relation to their peers, including early menstruation. Rapid cycling between manic and depressive episodes is not uncommon, not to mention intense waves of hypersexuality that tend to come hand in hand with severe highs."

My father bowed his head, while my mother started to cry.

"It's not a death sentence," the doctor hurried to reassure them both. "She is an exceptionally bright child, with a world of potential."

"I can't do this again," Dad choked out, dropping his head in his hands. "Not again."

"Michael, I know you have concerns, but your daughter, with the correct medication, will live a *full* and *healthy* life."

"What can we do?" Reaching for my hand, my mother held it tightly in hers. "How can we make life easier for our daughter?"

"Take your daughter home and love her," the doctor replied simply. "Never underestimate the healing power of a mother's love."

YOU'LL ALWAYS BE MY LADY, MILADY

Hugh

OCTOBER 31, 1996

TODAY WAS MY NINTH BIRTHDAY AND, AS USUAL, MY HOUSE WAS PACKED WITH friends. The lads were happily plowing their way through my house like a wrecking ball with a game of tip the can, but I didn't join in. I couldn't enjoy my party until *she* arrived.

When Mam came into my room and told me the good news—that Lizzie was finally home from the hospital—I'd lost it. I had no clue what came over me in that moment, but I broke down and bawled before proceeding to rant like a deranged lunatic at my mother for keeping something so important from me.

When I finally calmed down enough to listen, Mam sat me down and gave me a similar speech about my friend—minus the derogatory slurs Caoimhe had injected—before warning me that, under no circumstances, was I to *ever* breathe a word of Lizzie's private business to my sister, Gibs, Feely, or a single other living soul.

Mam told me that she knew I was bright, but there were some things a mind as young as mine just couldn't comprehend, no matter how many books I read.

She also told me that I shouldn't believe what Caoimhe said about Liz being crazy and dangerous because *her* mind was also too young to grasp the situation.

When Catherine called this morning to let Mam know that Liz was feeling better and would be coming to my party, it was the best birthday present ever. I didn't care about the unopened parcels waiting inside for me.

All I wanted was Liz.

I was sitting on the porch steps when her dad's car finally pulled up in front of my driveway. Excitement thundered to life inside of me when Mike climbed out of the driver's seat and opened the back passenger door. The moment she stepped out of the car and my eyes landed on her, I felt the strange sensation in my chest return. It felt like my heart had been caught up in a fishing hook and I was being reeled back to her.

Liz was wearing red dungarees and an oversized, cream, knitted cardigan, with frilly white ankle socks and patent black shoes. It was a strange combination, but she made it look so fucking cool. But when she started to walk up the driveway, panic rose up in my chest because she moved like she had cement blocks attached to her feet.

"Liz!" Hurrying down the porch steps, I quickly closed the space between us, not stopping until I had her wrapped up in my arms. "I've missed you so much."

Two months.

It had taken *two* long months to see my friend again, and now that I had my arms around her, I was afraid to let go.

"Hugh!" Liz didn't hesitate to wrap her arms around my waist, trembling all over, as she buried her face in my neck. "I promise I've missed you more."

"I wanted to come see you, I promise," I told her, tightening my arms. "I would have come if they'd let me."

"I know." She gripped my shirt tightly. "I believe you."

My attention momentarily shifted to her father, who was still standing near his car talking to my mother. It looked serious. Mike's brow was creased, and he was talking in a hushed voice, while Mam nodded repeatedly.

Something about the way they both flicked their eyes to Lizzie as they spoke caused me to pull her to my side and wrap an arm around her protectively.

He was *not* taking her away again.

Over my dead body.

"Do you want to play tip the can with the lads?" I asked, quickly guiding her into the house before her dad changed his mind and snatched her back. "Or we could go to the treehouse?" I closed the front door behind us and gave her a reassuring smile. "Whatever you want to do is fine with me."

"It's okay, Hugh. You should go enjoy your party," she replied, voice low and quiet. "I'll just sit down for a bit."

No, I wasn't about to plop her on a chair and leave her alone for the entire party, not when I just got her back.

"I don't give a shit about my party," I told her, and it was the truth. The only thing I cared about in this moment was her. "Come on." Taking her hand in mine, I pulled her toward the staircase. "We can hang out in my room." I kept a firm hold of her while I led her up the staircase. "It'll be quiet up here."

"Oooh," Danny Call teased when we walked into my room. Of course, he was being a nosy bastard, as usual, and going through all my stuff like he always did when he came over. "Biggsie's *girlfriend* is here."

"Get out of my room, Danny," I ordered, pointing to my door. "Now."

"Hughie and Lizzie up a tree, K-I-S-S-I-N-G," he snickered, while obliging me by moving for the door. "First comes love, second comes marriage, third comes a baby Biggsie in a golden car—"

I closed the door on his face before he could finish. "Do you want to know a secret?" I asked, walking Liz over to my bed. "I can't *stand* that guy."

Climbing onto my bed, she curled up in a ball on her side, facing me. "Then why do you always invite him to your parties?"

"Because he's still one of the lads, I suppose," I replied, flopping down on the mattress beside her. "It would be lousy to invite everyone and leave him out."

"Even though you can't stand him?"

I rolled onto my side, facing her. "Manners cost nothing." I smirked. "At least, that's what my mother constantly tells me."

A smile ghosted her lips. "You're like her."

"My mam?"

Nodding, she reached up and covered my cheek with her small hand. "You're good on the inside."

"So are you, Liz."

"No, Hugh." She shook her head sadly. "I'm not."

Frowning, I draped an arm around her and pulled her close. "Why would you say that, Liz?"

Shivering, she rested her forehead against mine and whispered, "Because it's the truth."

"Nope." Shifting closer, I rested my hand on her cheek. "It's not even close to being the truth."

"I'm sorry I was late to your party," she whispered, changing the subject, as another shiver racked through her. "Happy birthday."

"It's okay." I stroked her cheekbone with my thumb. "I'm just glad you're here."

"You are?"

I nodded.

"Caoimhe said she told you. About me scratching her. About the hospital." A tear trickled down her cheek when she whispered, "Do you hate me now?"

"I could never hate you," I replied, feeling my heart crack. "I love you, remember?"

She clenched her eyes shut. "Everyone thinks I'm crazy."

"I don't," I countered, rubbing my nose against hers. "I *know* you're not crazy."

Sniffling, she peeked an eye open, and then, in a small, hopeful voice, she asked, "You do?"

"Yep." Tucking her hair behind her ear, I resumed stroking her cheek. "Trust me, I know these things."

"I do." Her eyes widened, giving me a small glimpse of the girl I knew. "I *do* trust you, Hugh."

"You get sad sometimes, and that's okay," I told her, feeling the strongest urge to pull her close and protect her from the world. "And you get angry, but who doesn't?"

"What about the scary lady?" she whispered, sounding uncertain. "And the monster?" Her eyes filled with tears. "Nobody else can see them, but I swear I see them, Hugh." A pained sob escaped her lips. "They hurt me."

"Are they here now?"

"No." She shook her head. "They never hurt me when you're around." Sniffling, she moved so close that her body was pressed tightly to mine. "They're scared of the brave knight."

"I'm the brave knight?"

Tearful, she nodded. "Am I still your lady?"

"You'll always be my lady," I promised. "Milady."

YOU'RE A BIG GIRL NOW

Lizzie

DECEMBER 31, 1996

I KNEW I WAS DREAMING WHEN THE MONSTER CAME INTO MY ROOM TONIGHT BECAUSE the doctors told me he wasn't real. I'd made him all up. The scary lady, too. They were a figment of my imagination, delusions I invented inside my own head, and I think that made me feel better because it meant I wasn't really being hurt.

The scary lady wasn't pushing me under the water in the real world, and the monster wasn't putting things inside of my body, either. I didn't have to fight back and scream and warn the monster that my best friend told me about the bad touch because it wasn't happening.

That made me feel so much better.

I didn't have to scratch and bite and push the monster off me. I could just lay there and be quiet because he couldn't hurt me. The doctors said so. It was all in my head.

When the monster turned me over and pushed my head into the pillow, I didn't need to beg to die because this was a dream. When he put the bad thing inside my body, I didn't hope he would push me into the darkness and leave me there because he lived in the dark and I lived in the light. When he put the bad thing in my mouth, called me bad names, and told me to do what he taught me, I just did it. Whatever the monster wanted, the monster took, and I didn't flinch. I didn't have to wish to be a ghost without a body he could violate because in the real world, he couldn't reach me.

In the real world, I was free.

"Come on, Liz! It's the middle of the afternoon!"

Feeling sleepy, I blinked awake to find my sister standing over me. "What?" I groaned, snuggling deeper into my mattress. "I'm tired."

"You're always tired these days," she replied, rolling her eyes. "Dad said you need to get up and help get the house ready for tonight."

"Why?" I mumbled, eyelids drooping. "What's tonight?"

"Uh, *hello*? Our annual house party." My sister looked at me like I'd grown an extra head overnight. "It's New Year's Eve, Liz."

"Oh." Yawning sleepily, I rolled onto my back and mumbled, "Okay."

"Come on," she continued to say, reaching for my covers. "Dad said you have to help." When she ripped the covers off me, her brows shot up in surprise, and she called out, "Mam! Come here, quick! Lizzie's after getting her period!"

I was?

Confused, I pulled myself up on my elbows and glanced down at my blood-stained thighs. "I'm bleeding." I looked back to my sister. "Am I dying?"

"No, no, you're not dying, Liz, and I promise this is totally normal," Caoimhe was quick to explain. "It's called a period."

"A period?" Numb, I continued to stare at my bloodstained sheets. "What's that?"

"A period is when a girl bleeds from her vagina for a few days every month." She helped me out of bed and quickly set to work on stripping the mattress. "It's totally normal and happens to all of us."

"Does it happen to you?"

"Yeah, Liz," she replied. "Every month."

I shivered in revulsion. "Oh."

"Oh, my poor baby," I heard my mother croon from my bedroom doorway. "It's okay, sweetheart." Using her cane, she limped over to us and pulled me against her chest. She was skin and bones, and when she held me to her flat chest, it caused my heart to pound and my thoughts to race. "We knew this might happen a little earlier for you."

I didn't know what she was talking about, and I didn't have the energy to care. The only thing that was troubling me was *her*.

The medicine the doctors gave me in hospital slowed my thoughts down, and my angry feelings didn't bounce around like they used to. I also realized, after spending nearly two months in hospital and away from my mother, that I felt *better* when I wasn't around her. Because I was afraid of what would happen if she didn't get better the next time. Because there was *always* a next time. Mam got sick and then better, and then sick again, while every time seemed worse than the last one.

It was a strange feeling, to not want my mother to hold me, while not wanting her to let me go all at once. But that's what I felt when she held me.

"Come on, sweetheart," Mam said, leading me into the bathroom. "I'll run you a bath." Sitting down on the closed toilet lid, I watched her draw a bath, not taking in a word of what she was saying. I knew she was trying to explain what was happening to my body, but I didn't care. Because I didn't like having a body. Then Caoimhe walked in and explained all about tampons. I didn't care about that, either. It was fine. Whatever I needed to do, I would do.

"What if the bath water turns red?" I asked them, when I lowered myself into the water.

"It won't," Mam assured me before leaving the bathroom to give me privacy and taking my sister with her. The moment they were gone, I reached up with my foot and twisted the hot water tap with my big toe.

When the piping hot water started to bubble and the steam started to rise, I held my foot under the flow.

I was good with pain, and pain was good for me.

It made me feel better.

It helped me to concentrate.

To stop my thoughts from running rampant in my head.

The pain made all my thoughts float out of my head, and I sighed in relief.

Eyelids fluttering shut, I remained perfectly still as the water blistered and scorched my flesh.

Later that night, when my parents party was in full swing, I stayed upstairs in my room, too tired to talk to grown-ups whose names I never remembered.

I got a brand-new hi-fi stereo system for Christmas this year, with my very own copy of Fleetwood Mac's *Rumours*, the deluxe edition. Tonight, I had Stevie and Lindsey playing on a loop, using their voices to block out the noise coming from the party. My belly ached and I was nervous to walk around in case my insides fell out. Periods were scary.

When my friends arrived, they came upstairs to me, but Claire and Gibsie eventually scampered off in search of snacks. Not Hugh, though. Instead, he flopped down beside me on my bed and stayed with me.

Keeping me company all night, he told me stories about his adventures with Gibsie over Christmas break, the new computer games Santa had brought him, and the new books he had read.

"I fucking hate him, Liz," he admitted when I asked if he was happy that his dad had come to the party tonight. With his arms resting behind his head, Hugh stared up at my bedroom ceiling and sighed. "He might as well have just stopped swimming that day because he hasn't lived a day since."

The pain in his words was one I was all too familiar with. It hurt my best friend to watch his dad retreat from life. Unlike Claire, who never seemed to notice, Hugh took it hard. I thought it might have something to do with his big brain. It made it harder for him to ignore the problems at home. He saw it all, watched it happen, and it broke him daily.

Rolling onto my side to face him, I tucked my hands under my cheek and whispered, "You'll always have me, Hugh."

He shifted onto his side to face me and smiled at me. "You really love this band, don't you?" By changing the subject, he was letting me know that he was finished talking about his dad. That was okay. I didn't mind. I was happy to listen to him talk about anything, just as long as he stayed with me.

"What's wrong?"

My brows scrunched up. "What do you mean?"

He touched my hand that I was using to cradle my stomach, looking concerned. "Do you feel sick?"

"No, not sick," I replied. "Just sore."

His brown eyes locked on mine. "Why are you sore, Liz?"

My cheeks flushed. "I got my period."

"Is that the thing that happens to women?" He frowned. "With the bleeding."

I nodded.

"But you're not a woman yet."

"I know."

When he reached over and cupped my cheek, I felt that familiar swell of excitement rise up inside of me, causing my heart to buck wildly. "Are you okay?"

"I'm okay." Nodding, I forced a small smile. "I just...I don't like all the changes."

Several seconds ticked by in companionable silence. He shifted closer and moved his hand from my cheek, draping his arm around my body instead. "Don't worry, Liz." He wrapped me up in the warmest, safest hug I'd ever felt. "You'll always have me, too."

IF IT KEPT HER SAFE

Hugh

DECEMBER 31, 1996

THE PARTY WAS IN FULL SWING DOWNSTAIRS, BUT LIZ WASN'T IN THE MOOD TO JOIN in the celebrations, so I remained by her side the whole night. There would be a million more parties, but there would only ever be one Lizzie Young.

I knew she was doing better since coming home from hospital, but she wasn't the same. There was something different about her. I didn't understand what that something was or why it had happened, but I knew it *had.*

Liz was always tired now, and she didn't spin around in circles on the grass like she used to. Her eyes didn't twinkle with mischief anymore, and she was a lot quieter these days. It took her longer than usual to answer questions or toss out a smart-ass comeback—something she had always been the queen of doing.

Now, grown-up things were happening to her body and there was nothing I could do to stop it from happening or make her feel better.

All I could do was stay.

So that's what I did.

Because I knew deep down inside that I would sit with Lizzie Young for the rest of my life if it kept the sadness out of her eyes.

If it kept her safe.

"Hey, Hugh?" Liz said a little while later, when we were reading on her bed.

"Yeah, Liz."

She pointed to the clock on her nightstand. "Happy New Year."

I checked the time and saw it was indeed gone midnight, which meant one thing. Leaning in close, I pressed a kiss to her cheek, finding it a little more difficult to pull away this year. "Happy New Year, Liz."

WAKE ME UP WHEN TOMORROW ENDS

JANUARY 5, 1997

"What's wrong?" Crying on my bed in the darkness, I hooked my arms around my knees and rocked. "Why are you angry?"

"Because you got your fucking period," the monster snarled, appearing from darkness in a cloud of smoke. "You're nine!" His eyes were glowing red. "Why are you getting your fucking period when you're nine?"

Wake up, Lizzie.

Wake yourself up.

Do it now!

"I'm sorry," I cried, burying my face in my knees, too afraid to look at his sharp teeth. "I didn't mean to."

"It's because you're bad. God is punishing you for being a filthy, little whore." Stalking toward me, he gripped my face between his hands and glared down at me. "You need to be punished for doing this to me." He reached for his belt buckle with his other hand. "Tonight, you're going to learn about how rough it can get, but first, I need you to take this."

"What is it?" I strangled out, chest heaving, as I tried to remind myself that it was just a dream. I would wake up soon and everything would be better.

"Good girls take their medicine, or they get swollen bellies," the monster hissed, forcing a small pill into the back of my throat. "You don't want a swollen belly, do you?"

I shook my head.

"You're going to take one of these pills every night," he continued to threaten. "I'll make sure of it."

"I don't want to," I cried, hating the sensation of the pill sliding down the back of my throat. "Please don't make me take more medicine."

TWO WEEKS TOO MANY

Hugh

JANUARY 17, 1997

SINCE STARTING FIRST CLASS LAST SEPTEMBER, LIZ TOOK THE THREE O'CLOCK BUS home from school with me. However, two weeks had passed since we'd returned to school after Christmas break, and Lizzie still hadn't returned.

I knew what that meant.

She was sick again.

After tormenting my mother for days to call Lizzie's mother, Mam finally gave in last night. After spending half an hour on the phone with Catherine, Mam returned to my room to assure me that Lizzie hadn't gone back to hospital, but that she was at home in bed with the flu.

Maybe she was, but none of it sat well with me, and I was losing patience fast.

By the time Mam left for work on Saturday morning, I had reached my limit. Sneaking into the kitchen was a doddle when Caoimhe was in charge because she spent most of her time with her tongue down the cretin's throat.

Thankfully, she didn't bring him inside too often when she babysat during the daytime, choosing to hang out in the garden instead.

Dialing the phone number that I learned off by heart at the age of seven, I held the receiver to my ear and listened to the shrill ringing sound.

"Hello?" a familiar voice came down the line.

"Hi, Mike, it's me," I replied, keeping my tone even. "Can I speak to Lizzie please?"

"Elizabeth's still under the weather, Hugh," her father replied in a friendly tone. Mike liked me a lot, and while the feeling wasn't entirely reciprocated on my end, I always made an effort to be polite. "She's upstairs resting."

"Yeah, I know she's sick," I replied, careful not to let my emotions get the better of me when all I wanted to do was scream *put her on the fucking phone*. "But it's really important that I speak to her. I wouldn't ask you otherwise, Mike."

"Hold on, son," he said, giving in way quicker than I had anticipated. "I'll go and see if she's up for a chat."

"Thanks, Mike."

Several nail-biting minutes ticked in silence by before Lizzie came on the phone. "Hello?"

"Liz." Gripping the phone like my life depended on it, I sagged against the wall and exhaled a relieved breath. "It's me."

It took her longer than usual to respond. "Hugh?"

"Yeah, Liz, it's me."

"Hi."

"Are you okay?" I managed to ask, while my heart thundered in my chest. "I heard you have the flu?"

"The flu?" There was another long, exaggerated pause, before she mumbled, "Oh yeah."

"You don't sound good, Liz."

"I'm okay…just…tired." Several seconds ticked by before she added, "I have to go now, Hugh."

"Liz, wait—"

The line went dead.

"Fuck!" Slamming the phone down on the receiver, I picked it back up and slammed it down another three times. "Goddammit to hell!"

"Hey!" Caoimhe snapped, coming through the front hall and into the kitchen. "What did the phone ever do to you?"

"Is your sister really okay?" I came right out and asked—demanded, truth be told. "I already know everything about her, Caoimhe, so bear that in mind before you lie to my face."

"If you already know everything about Liz, then why are you asking me?" I narrowed my eyes. "She doesn't have the flu, does she?"

"No, she does," my babysitter replied. "She genuinely does have the flu." Stepping around me, she moved for the stove, where mam had left lunch on the hob. "But she's having one of her episodes, too."

"Oh." My heart sank into my ass. "Is it a bad one?"

"No, not like before," she replied quietly. "But she's had her medication readjusted, so she's super out of it at the moment." She shrugged before offering me a reassuring smile. "She'll come around again. Lizzie's like a boomerang. She always comes back to herself."

Yeah, but what if she didn't?

I wanted to know more about her illness, but nobody would explain it to me in any great detail, and Lizzie seemed as in the dark about it as I was.

I decided to lie, while mentally plotting my next move. "I'm going over to Gibsie's for a few hours."

"Uh, hello?" Caoimhe pointed to the ceiling. "Gibsie's upstairs with Claire."

Dammit. "Then I'm heading to Robbie's."

"Do I look like I came down in the last shower, Hugh Biggs?" Caoimhe planted her hands on her hips and gave me a hard look. "Where are you really going?"

"To Robbie's," I doubled down and told her before heading outside to the garage. "Hand on my heart."

"Hmm." Caoimhe followed after me, looking wary. "And your Mam agreed to this?"

Well, she never *disagreed*, and I planned on capitalizing on the lack of parental warning.

"Yep." Pushing my bike out of the garage, I hopped on and pedaled down the driveway. "I'll see ya later."

"Be safe on the roads, Hugh!" she called after me.

Pedaling like a demon through town, I cycled on the footpaths until they were replaced with country roads.

I wasn't worried about the traffic whizzing past me or the potential of taking a wrong turn. I was a confident cyclist and had an excellent memory. I would find my way to her. If it was the last thing I did.

———————————

Forty-five minutes later, when I cycled past the signpost for Robin Hill Road, I felt a surge of pride that I had managed to find my way without any help. When I reached the gates of Old Hall House a few minutes later, the property looked just as impressive as I remembered.

There was a little pedestrian gate to the side of the driveway that her family never bothered to lock up, so I slipped through there with my bike before biking up the graveled driveway to the house.

Mike was coming out of the house when I reached the courtyard. "Hugh?" His brows shot up in surprise. "I didn't know you were calling, son."

"Yeah," was all I decided to say, while I hopped off my bike and pushed it up the rest of the way. "I'll head right in, if that's okay?"

"Suit yourself, lad," he replied with a shrug before heading off in the direction of the stables. "Elizabeth's in her room."

Letting myself inside, I made a beeline for the imposing staircase, feeling my heart race with every step I took. When I reached her bedroom door, I slipped inside without knocking.

"Liz?" When I saw her curled up in a ball on the middle of her bed, I swear I felt my heart crack. Moving straight for her, I didn't stop until I was sitting on the mattress next to her. "Liz, are you awake?"

Nothing.

"Hey." Reaching for her arm, I tried to rouse her as gently as I could. "It's me."

However, the moment I touched Liz, she went berserk, lashing out wildly with her arms and legs. She didn't say a word throughout the whole ordeal. On the contrary, she was deathly silent in her hysteria, thrashing and kicking like her life depended on it.

"Jesus!" Startled, I staggered away from the bed and held my hands up. "Lizzie, it's me, Hugh."

When I spoke my name, something shifted inside her and she stopped moving altogether. "Hugh?"

"Yeah, Liz, I'm here," I replied, wanting to go to her but unsure if that was what she wanted. "Roll over and look at me."

With great effort, she did, and when her eyes met mine, I felt a stab in my chest. Because they didn't look like her eyes. They weren't pale blue anymore. They were almost black.

"Sorry," she whispered, tucking her hands under her cheek. "I thought I was still in my dream."

"That's okay," I replied, standing at the side of her bed. "Was it a bad dream?"

She shrugged. "They're all bad."

"Do you want to talk about it?"

She shook her head. "Too tired."

"Can I sit?"

She nodded.

Feeling relieved, I slowly lowered myself onto the mattress. "I've been worried about you."

"Hmm." Her eyelids fluttered. "I'm okay."

She wasn't.

She absolutely was *not* okay.

"What happened?"

"I was bad," she mumbled.

"Bad?"

She nodded.

"I don't understand."

"Me either." Her tongue poked out to wet her cracked lips. "I'm sick, Hugh."

My heart sank. "You are?"

She tapped her temple. "In here."

"No, you're not." Unable to stop myself, I reached down and stroked her cheek. "You're perfect."

"I'm sick." Her hand shot out from under the covers and covered mine. "I'm not right in the head."

"Don't say that," I pleaded, feeling panicked. "You're my Lizzie. Same as you've always been."

"The doctor gave me new medicine," she whispered, keeping my hand on her cheek with her own hand. "I'm so tired all the time."

"Did you tell them that?"

She nodded wearily. "It's for the best."

"Can I do anything to help you?"

"Stay," she replied with a whimper. "Don't leave me."

"I won't leave you, Liz," I promised, resisting the urge to pull her into my arms. "I'm staying with you."

"No matter what?"

"Yeah, Liz." Stroking her cheek, I leaned down and kissed the top of her head. "No matter what."

"Will I be okay, Hugh?" she asked then, looking up at me like I had the answers. "Will I ever be normal like the other girls?"

Her words tore strips out of my heart and I felt an intense urge to soothe her fears. "Listen to me, because I'm going to let you in on a little secret."

"You are?"

"Mm-hmm." Reaching for her arms, I gently pulled her into a sitting position before smoothing her matted hair over her shoulders. "There's no such thing as normal, Liz. It doesn't exist. It's just a word someone invented to make everyone behave the exact same way so they can tick the exact same boxes."

"Really?"

Hell if I knew, but that was my theory on the matter. "It's just a word," I repeated, wiping a tear from her cheek. "And you are *way* too special to tick the 'normal' box."

"I am?"

"Yep." Nodding, I smiled at her. "You could never be described by a word, Liz, and especially not a boring one like *normal*. You know what else? I wouldn't change a single thing about you. I love that you don't tick that boring box."

Sniffling, she reached for my hand. "You wouldn't change me if you could?"

"Nope." Her tongue poked out to wet her cracked lips. "I'm sick."

"How come?"

"Because then you wouldn't be *you*," I explained, wiping away another one of her tears. "And a world without Lizzie Young would be a travesty."

"Travesty," she repeated slowly, mulling over the word.

"Listen, I know you're feeling tired, and it's totally grand if you don't want to, but would you like to take a walk outside with me?"

She stared at me for a long time before nodding her head. "Yeah, Hugh, I'd like that."

YEAH, ELIZABETH

Lizzie

JANUARY 17, 1997

FEELING DAZED AND OFF BALANCE, I TRUDGED THROUGH THE FIELDS AT THE BACK OF our property with Hugh by my side. Stumbling over uneven surfaces and potholes, I tried to get my bearings, while Hugh remained patient the entire time.

I felt like I was emerging from hibernation. Like a bear waking up after a long winter's sleep. The watery sunshine felt strange on my face, but the feel of his hand in mine felt *right*.

I knew Hugh could walk a lot faster than this, and I was slowing him down, but he seemed content to keep pace with me, while I felt more alive than I had in weeks.

We walked for hours through the fields and country lanes, while Hugh filled me in on everything that had happened since our last meetup. I couldn't retain much of what he was telling me, but the sound of his voice was so soothing that I never wanted him to stop talking to me. I could spend the rest of my life listening to his voice and never grow tired.

It was hard to explain the comfort Hugh's presence gave me.

He made it easy to be alive.

I knew that was a strange thing to think, but it was how I felt.

Living was a lot easier when Hugh was nearby.

When I was doing my living with him.

By the time we made it back to my house, after spending an eternity rambling through the countryside, it was dark outside. I wasn't afraid, though. Not when I had the brave knight to protect me. I had faith in his ability to keep the monsters away. I trusted him to never let go of my hand.

No matter what.

"Aw, crap," Hugh groaned, when we rounded the side of my house and locked eyes on his mother's car. "I'm a dead man walking, Liz."

I opened my mouth to ask him why, but his mother got there first.

"Hugh Andrew Biggs!" Sinead called out. "That better be you skulking behind the house!"

Hiding behind the side of my house, Hugh released an audible groan. "Jesus, she sounds really pissed."

"Why?" I asked, turning to look at him.

"So, I sort of didn't tell her I was coming over," he explained sheepishly. "And I sort of didn't ask for permission to cycle to your house, either."

"Oh." I felt myself laugh for the first time in weeks. "You are *so* dead."

"Elizabeth Eleanor Young!" That was *my* mother. "Return the boy to his mother right this instant."

"Yeah, *Elizabeth*." Hugh waggled his brows playfully. "Return me to my mother right this instant."

This time my smile morphed into a full-on grin.

PART 5

Friendship Lifelines

BUILDING BIKES AND FRIENDSHIPS

Hugh

MARCH 17, 1997

AFTER THE ST. PATRICK'S DAY PARADE IN TOWN THIS AFTERNOON, CATHERINE YOUNG invited us to Old Hall House to play. The weather was too good to stay inside, so the five of us decided on building a treehouse.

While Gibs, Feely, and Claire snooped through the stables for potential materials we could use, Liz and I combed through the storage sheds on the other side of the property.

However, all plans of building a treehouse went clean out the window when we spied a cobweb-infested bicycle at the back of one of the sheds.

"Can you hold that?"

"Yep."

"You got it, Liz?"

"I've got it, Hugh."

"Good job."

Nodding my approval, I greased up the chain links on the rust bucket of a bike we'd found. Pulling the chain into line, I readjusted the links until I was certain the chain would stay on. "I think we're all set."

"It's as easy as that?" Liz asked, sounding fascinated.

"Yep." Kicking the stand up, I held the handlebars while she climbed onto the saddle. "Give it a test ride to see if the chain holds."

Pushing off on the pedals, she flew down the gravelly driveway, pedaling like a demon to pick up speed.

"Switch up the gears!" I called out with a laugh, attention glued to the blond-haired girl whizzing off on the bike. "See if it holds?"

"It's holding," she called back, voice laced with excitement. "You did it."

Smiling with satisfaction, I wiped the oil from my hands with a cloth and watched my best friend cycle. "Careful, Liz, the brakes are seized to shit."

"I don't care," she called back, laughing as she whizzed past me. "I don't want to brake, Hugh. I want to go faster!"

"She looks happy," I heard someone say, and I turned to see Lizzie's mother at the front door. Her smile was almost as wide as her daughter's. "Look at her go."

"Yeah," I chuckled, walking over to her. "She's a daredevil, that one."

"You're a good friend to her, Hugh." She turned her attention to me. "Thank you."

"She's a good friend to me, too," I replied with a shrug, eyeing the frail woman. "How are you feeling, Catherine?"

"Aren't you a sweetheart," she chuckled, eyes filled with emotion. "I'm feeling much better these days."

I smiled back at her, feeling relieved, because I liked Catherine Young a lot. She was a really nice lady, and it sucked that she spent so much time in the hospital. I understood why—my own mother had explained her illness to me—and I was rooting for her to get better. I even said a prayer for her before I went to bed at night. Every night. I made sure to never skip. Just to be safe.

"Liz is feeling a lot better these days, too," I decided to tell her, because I knew she wanted to ask me but never would. The relief in her blue eyes when I told her that had me quickly continuing, "She's laughing more, and she's cracking jokes like she used to." It was the truth. Liz was doing so much better since the New Year, and while she never spoke about her *actual* diagnosis, she didn't try to hide it from me anymore.

Trusting me to keep her secrets, she told me all about the medicine she had to take every day, the one that made her feel *steady*, and how it didn't make her feel as tired anymore. I knew all about her therapy sessions and the doctor who looked like Santa, that she had to visit every second month.

She still had her quiet days, and when she was sad, she wasn't just sad, she was devastated, but it didn't happen as often these days. Everything about my best friend seemed more balanced.

"You're a good boy, Hugh Biggs." Catherine patted my hand. "Your mother is very blessed to have a son like you."

Several hours after repairing the old bike we christened *Rust Bucket* and after a pains-taking trek through the meadow with planks of timber, the treehouse we originally planned on making was starting to take shape.

We found the perfect oak tree in the meadow and had the floor laid down on the strongest branch. We would have had the walls erected, too, but Gibsie decided to throw a fit when Feely accidentally smacked his thumb instead of the nail and *launch* our *only* hammer into the field below. All five of us had searched through the knee-high grass to no avail. It was like trying to find a needle in a haystack.

"Gerard said he was sorry, Hugh," Claire said, defending him for the hundredth time. "He'll find another hammer. You'll see."

"Where?" I shot back, still annoyed. "In his ass?"

"Hugh!" Claire scolded, while Lizzie snickered beside her. "Don't curse."

"It'll be dark in an hour, Claire," Feely offered calmly.

"Exactly," I snapped. The evening was setting in and we were losing light. "Even if he finds another hammer, we won't have enough time to put the walls up."

"Let alone the roof," Feely chimed in, in agreement.

"Oh my God, guys, look!" Liz laughed, pointing toward something in the distance.

Claire and I turned our heads in unison to see Gibsie dragging a sledgehammer toward the treehouse. "I found one, lads!"

"Ahh," Liz continued to howl laughing. "He looks like Thor with his hammer!"

"Did you hear that, Gibs?" Feely called out with a chuckle. "Lizzie thinks you look like a superhero!"

Grinning wolfishly up at us, Gibsie winked and immediately starting flexing his nonexistent biceps.

"Oh yeah," Liz encouraged, cheering him on. "Show us those guns, Thor."

THE FEIS, THE FEELS, AND THE FAMILY DAY OUT

Hugh

JUNE 8, 1997

"This is the best birthday weekend ever," Lizzie declared excitedly as we wandered through the crowds at the county fair on Sunday afternoon.

She was turning nine tomorrow, and we couldn't have asked for a better day to celebrate. The sun was splitting the stones, her mother was looking healthier than she had in months, and the girl holding my hand was glowing. I meant that in the literal sense. Lizzie was *glowing*.

Keeping a firm hold on her hand, I weaved through the crowd at the ice-cream van, with our two 99 ice-cream cones secured. Our families were at the other side of the fairground, waiting on the feis to start.

"You should have asked for the mint syrup on yours," she said, licking the green slime trickling down her cone. "It's so good."

"No thanks. I'll stick to plain old vanilla," I tossed back, looking over my shoulder to smile at her.

Liz looked nothing like the other girls at the fair. She wasn't wearing a poufy dress or pink Boyzone shorts—which, apparently, were all the style considering the number of girls wearing them—and she didn't wear fancy bows in her hair.

Clad in her statement oversized denim dungarees, white T-shirt, and high-tops, she looked better than every other girl at the fair. She had her hair pulled back in a single plait that fell to the middle of her back. Her blond hair was a lot darker now, streaked with flecks of honey and golden brown. I'd never seen hair like hers, with so many different shades going through it, and thought it suited her better than the white it used to be.

My sister labeled the color as *dirty blond* once, and while I had no clue about hair shades, I was sure Lizzie's one was my favorite.

But the very best thing about Lizzie had to be her fearlessness. She didn't scream when we got stuck at the top on the Ferris wheel or bawl like a baby when someone crashed into her on the bumper cars. Instead, she laughed and went hell for leather right back at whoever bumped her. She had zero fear of heights, just like me, and that made her the ultimate companion at the fun fair.

We'd spent most of the afternoon running back and forth to our parents to scavenge money and went on every single ride at the fair.

"What time are Gibs and Claire onstage?" Liz asked, dragging me from my thoughts. "It has to be soon, right?"

"Yeah, it should be any minute now," I replied, craning my neck to get a better look at where the feis was being held.

The feis was an Irish-dancing competition, and they held one every year at the county fair on the bed of an articulated lorry. I'd been dragged along to countless feis competitions over the years and wasn't that excited, but this was Lizzie's first time attending. She was buzzing with excitement to see Gibs and Claire take the stage, while I was just happy to see her smile.

Pushing through the crowds, we skipped past the fairground rides and stall sellers until we reached the stage. Weaving through the rows of chairs and picnic blankets, we found our families near the front.

They were sitting near each other on a few blankets strewn over the recently harvested ground. All too familiar with how those prickly straw spikes the farmers left in the fields after baling felt on bare skin, I quickly scoped out room on her sister's blanket. While I detested the asshole sitting next to my babysitter, I was wearing shorts today and had no intention of spending the rest of the day itching and tearing my skin raw.

Ignoring Mark and Caoimhe, who were eating the faces off each other, I settled down on the blanket with Liz and steered her attention to the stage and pointed. "Look, Liz, they're coming onstage."

"Woo!" Lizzie cheered, clapping and squealing in delight when Gibsie took to the outdoor stage with my baby sister in tow. "Yes, guys!"

I felt a surge of pride when the people around us started to whisper and point them out. It always happened when Claire and Gibs took to the stage, and I often wondered why the other dancers bothered competing against them.

"They're all older than them," Liz noted, pointing to the other competing couples lined up beside them, with all the male dancers standing behind their female counterparts. "They look so small next to them."

"Yeah," I agreed, eyeing the older teenagers onstage. "Don't worry, though," I added, knowing that none of them could take the shine off our guys. "It's in the bag."

Claire's curls were pinned to the top of her head, and she wore a green velvet, traditional Irish-dancing dress. Standing behind her, Gibs wore black trousers with suspender straps and a white shirt. His hair was combed smartly to the side, and his shoes were black and shiny with a clicky heel, while Claire had the black ones with the laces that went up her shins.

Even though she was smiling, I could tell my sister was nervous. Not Gibs, though. Nope, he looked as proud as punch as he stood slightly behind my sister, hands in position with hers.

When the Ceili band on site kicked off with their own lively, traditional version of "Glasgow Reel," the couples onstage started to move.

"Whoa," Liz breathed, attention glued to Gibsie and Claire. "They dance like they're floating."

"I know," I agreed. Floating was the only way to describe the way these two moved their bodies around the stage.

My sister looked like a swan, with her limbs in perfect symmetrical poise, while Gibsie danced like he was born to dance this very dance with her.

Usually, the girls were the stars onstage and the boys danced awkwardly in the background, but not this boy.

Not our Gibs.

He took ahold of that stage like he was the headlining show. He could move his body like nothing I'd ever seen. His coordination was phenomenal, and he seemed to feel the rhythm in his bones.

He didn't put a foot wrong throughout, and even when Claire faltered on her solo, he was right there to spin her back into the rhythm, taking on the lead in a dance that would see them win the entire tournament.

It was a complicated pattern, one way more advanced than their age, but they nailed it. Not only did they nail it but they nailed it with smiles on their faces.

Ignoring their much older competition, Gibs and Claire glided across the floor, taking on the complicated dance routine like it was second nature to them. They kept their eyes on each other the whole time, dancing for each other and not the judges. I thought their dedication to one another on the stage might be why the cabinets at home were bursting to the seams with trophies and medals.

When the song ended and the dancers froze in their final positions, the cheers from the crowd were deafening. Everyone was on their feet, clapping and whistling their approval, and as I predicted, Claire and Gibsie were quickly crowned the winners.

"Yes, Thor!" Lizzie screamed at the top of her lungs when one of the judges placed a medal around Gibsie's neck, while another thrust an enormous trophy into his hands. "You're the champion!" Hooting and hollering like a maniac for her friend, she bounced on her feet before flicking her attention to my sister, who was receiving her matching silverware and screamed, "You're the best, Claire!"

When they finally left the stage and Liz flopped back down on the blanket, she had a smile on her face as big as the moon. "I'm so proud of them." Her eyes were sparkling with excitement. "That was the best thing I've ever seen." With her legs sprawled out in front of her, Liz planted her hands on the blanket behind her to support her weight as she continued to speak to me.

I tried to listen, but I couldn't concentrate on anything except the way Mark kept playing with her braid.

Lizzie didn't seem to notice, she was too engrossed in whatever she was saying, but I did.

I noticed, and I didn't like it.

Not one bit.

I tried to keep smiling and ignore it, because he'd been in Lizzie's life so long that he was practically her brother, and I, myself, often ruffled my sister's curls with playful affection. But I *couldn't* seem to shake off the protective feeling roaring to life inside of me. Maybe it was because I knew just how badly Mark bullied Gibsie and seeing him near Liz made me feel protective, or maybe it was something else, but I couldn't shake off the bad feeling.

When he pushed her braid aside and placed his hand at the nape of her neck, I felt myself snap. "What are you doing to my friend?"

My voice was loud enough to startle both Caoimhe and Liz, who looked at me like I'd lost my mind. Meanwhile, Mark arched a brow at me. "What?"

"With your hand," I argued, voice rising right along with my temper. "You're touching her."

"What are you talking about?" Mark shot back, looking taken aback. His gaze flicked to Liz who had a blank expression on her face before returning to me. "I'm not doing anything."

"I'm not blind, asshole," I instructed, gesturing to where he was still gripping Lizzie's neck. "Take your hand off my friend *now*."

His brows shot up in surprise and he quickly dropped his hand. "Relax, Biggs. I was only playing with her." He nudged Lizzie's shoulder before adding, "Isn't that right, munchkin?"

"Yep," Liz replied, looking at me like she didn't understand why I was annoyed. "Mark always plays games with me."

"Aw, look at you, getting all protective and jealous over my baby sister," Caoimhe cooed, clearly thinking this was hilarious. "Don't worry, Hugo Boss-Man, the whole of Ballylaggin knows Lizzie's heart belongs to you."

Ignoring them both, I looked at Lizzie. "Are you okay?"

"I'm fine," she replied, looking up at me with confusion. "Are you?"

"Yeah," I muttered, attention flicking back to Caoimhe and Mark, who were both laughing at me like I was a stupid child.

I wasn't.

I knew all about Mark Allen and how he liked to hit kids. Kids younger and weaker than him. I also knew if he even *thought* about pushing Liz around like he did Gibs, I was going to lose my mind.

I saw the bruises he'd left on my friend when he beat him up. He might have had everyone else tricked into thinking he was the golden boy of Ballylaggin, but he couldn't fool me. And unlike Gibsie, I had no problem calling him out on his bullshit. I had done just that on countless occasions but to no avail, because he was a clever bastard who had managed to pull the wool over his stepmother's eyes.

Thing was, I didn't care if anyone believed me; I was more than willing to keep screaming his indiscretions from the rooftops.

Narrowing my eyes, I glared at Mark, while mentally promising, *One of these days, the grown-ups are going to see your true colors, and when that day comes, I'll be right there to watch your fall from grace.*

SACRED VOWS, SCARY LADIES, AND SECRETIVE SISTERS

AUGUST 23, 1997

"LIZ, COME HERE, QUICK," HUGH CALLED OUT FROM THE OTHER SIDE OF HIS STREET. "The sun is so strong, it's melting the tarmac on the road."

"It is?" Springing up from my perch on the footpath outside, I dropped the chalk I'd been playing with and hurried over to him.

"See?" Hugh poked the black tarmac with the stick he was holding. "It's squishy."

"That is so *cool*." Intrigued, I knelt down and poked the tarmac with my finger, thrilled when it moved. "I know the sun is hot today, but I didn't realize it could melt the *road*."

"Tarmac is a lot like chocolate," Hugh explained, crouching down beside me to investigate. "When it's hot, it softens, and when it's cold, it hardens."

"How come?"

He shrugged. "It has a lot to do with its physical components and the effect on the tar when it absorbs the sun's heat energy."

Fascinated, I listened carefully to every word as he explained another one of earth's mysteries to me. Hugh was good like that. He always knew the answers to all our questions. Not only did he know the answers, he explained them in a way that wasn't boring. Even Gibsie, who hated school, enjoyed listening to Hugh break stuff down.

Out of the corner of my eye, I spotted a familiar, dark figure lurking in the distance, and my stomach sank.

The scary lady.

She was *back*.

I hadn't seen her during the daytime in a very long time. The medicine I took helped me with keeping her out of my head. But she was here now. She had followed me all the way to Hugh's house.

Blinking rapidly, I looked away before casting another glance in her direction, and this time she was gone.

Sadness bloomed inside of me because I didn't want to start seeing the scary lady again. Not like the way I used to see her before the tablets. If that happened, my father would send me away again, and I didn't want to get sick again.

"We should write our names," Hugh declared, dragging me from my thoughts.

"Huh?"

"Our names," he explained, smiling warmly. "We should write them in the tarmac."

"Oh." Shaking my head to clear my thoughts, I offered him a bright smile and focused all my attention on him. "Okay."

Using the pointy end of the stick he'd found, Hugh scraped the letter H into the tarmac. "Here." He passed me the stick and pointed to the + symbol next to his letter H. "Make sure you dig your L deep. Otherwise, it'll fade."

Grabbing the stick, I set to work on carving the letter L into the tarmac next to his, while pushing my worries to the back of my mind.

"There." Sitting back on the curb, I admired our handywork. "H plus L." I grinned at him. "Together forever."

"Yep," he agreed, draping his arm over my shoulders. "And in twenty years' time, when we come back here to visit, we can show this to our kids."

"So you *are* going to marry me," I teased, elbowing his side.

"I thought I already told you I would," he replied, sounding confused.

"*No*, you asked me would I say yes," I corrected, shifting closer. "But you never actually said you *would* ask me."

"Oh." His cheeks turned pink. "Well, consider this conversation my confirmation on that matter."

I choked out a laugh. "You talk so funny sometimes."

"In what way?"

"Like a grown-up," I snickered, thoroughly enjoying him. "Or a nerd."

He shrugged his shoulders and grinned. "Maybe, but I bet I can kick a drop goal from the ten-meter line better than any nerd you know."

"I don't know about rugby kicks, but you're prettier than any other nerd," I replied. "Any other rugby player, too." My words caused Hugh to full-on blush this time and I cackled. "You look even prettier when you blush."

"You're not supposed to call me pretty, Liz," he muttered, looking embarrassed. "I'm supposed to call *you* pretty."

"Then call me pretty."

He rolled his eyes. "You know you're pretty."

"Come on, I want to hear you say it." Turning my body sideways, I reached up and grabbed his face between my hands, forcing him to look at me. "Don't be shy."

"You're pretty," he said, eyes locked on mine. "The prettiest girl in Ballylaggin."

"Thank you." I beamed back at him. "And what else?"

"What do you mean?"

"Wasn't there something you were going to ask me?"

He rolled his eyes again. "Yeah, Liz, when we're nineteen, not nine."

"Nineteen is too far away." I laughed, feeling mischievous. "Ask me now."

"This is so embarrassing," Hugh groaned, and then, because he knew I wouldn't let it go, he cleared his throat before asking, "Elizabeth Eleanor Young, would you do me the great honor of becoming Elizabeth Eleanor Biggs?"

"Why yes, Hugh Andrew Biggs," I gushed through fits of laughter. "I would be delighted to."

"Milady is too kind," he replied in his playful, brave-knight accent, before climbing to his feet and bowing dramatically. "From this day forth, dear Wife, this sword shall be sworn to you." He placed his stick at my feet and bowed again. "I shall slay all your enemies, shield you from dragons, and protect you with my life."

"And I shall protect you with mine, dear Husband." Snatching the stick, I jumped to my feet and swished it around. "Have no fear, brave knight, for I shall be your secret weapon in every battle."

Hugh opened his mouth to respond but quickly clamped it shut when his attention shifted to something behind me.

"Are you okay?" I asked, watching his expression carefully.

He didn't look okay. In fact, his eyes were narrowed, and his face was set in a deep frown.

"Hugh?"

"Liz." He kept his eyes trained on something over my shoulder and pointed. "Do you see that?"

Curious, I swung around to look, only to freeze on the spot when my eyes took in the familiar figure.

"Oh my God." I turned back to gape at Hugh. "You see her, too?"

"Yeah." He nodded. "I see her, Liz."

My heart slammed so hard in my chest I thought it might burst.

Hugh could see her.

He could see the crazy lady.

It wasn't all in my head.

"Come here, Liz," he instructed in a stern voice, holding out his hand to me. "Right now."

I didn't argue, moving straight to his side without hesitation. "That's her, Hugh."

I took his outstretched hand in both of mine and burrowed into his side. "That's the scary lady."

"I see her," he replied, attention trained to the stranger watching us through the tree line at the end of the cul-de-sac. Snatching the stick out of my hand, he pulled me close and wielded it in front of us. "Don't worry. I'm here."

"I think she's a monster," I admitted with a shiver. "She has sharp claws and everything."

"She's not a monster," he replied, slowly walking me backwards toward his driveway. "She's a weirdo."

"But you can really see her, right?" I continued to probe, needing his validation, as he backed us up his porch steps. "I'm not dreaming, am I?" Feeling panicked, I clung to his hand. "This is real, isn't it? We're really here?"

"Yeah, Liz," he confirmed, sounding so steady and sure of himself that I felt better. "I'm right here with you, I promise."

When we reached the front door, Hugh pushed me inside before following in after me and slamming the door shut. "Caoimhe!" he roared, still holding the stick. "Come here fast!"

My sister was babysitting for Sinead today, and when she poked her head around the living room door, she looked annoyed. "What?"

"The scary lady's back!" I choked out. "She found me."

My sister rolled her eyes. "Liz, we've talked about this a million times. There is no scary lady."

I opened my mouth to protest, but Hugh got there first. "I don't know about scary ladies, but there's a creepy woman at the end of the street," he said, once again tucking me into his side. "I saw her myself, Caoimhe. She's been watching us."

Caoimhe stared at Hugh for a long beat before laughing. "Yeah, okay, guys, pull the other leg."

"Do you see me laughing?" Hugh snapped, pointing to the door. "She's right down the street, Caoimhe. At the end of the cul-de-sac. In the woods."

"You're serious?"

Hugh nodded. "Deadly."

"Oh my God." My sister's smile fell. "Where's Claire?"

"Upstairs with Gibs."

"Okay. Okay." Nodding to herself, she moved for the door, looking like she might puke. "Both of you stay in the house," she instructed before swinging the door open. "Do not follow me."

The moment she charged out the driveway and bolted toward the end of the street, we, of course, rushed outside to see.

"Where did you see her?" Caoimhe demanded when she returned a few minutes later.

Standing at the end of the driveway, we pointed toward the tree line at the end of the cul-de-sac. "Right over there."

"There's no one over there," she snapped, sounding frustrated. "If you two are playing some pathetic prank on me, I'm going to be seriously—"

"She was right over there, Caoimhe," Hugh interrupted, sounding equally frustrated. "This is not a prank."

"Yeah, well, it sure looks like one because there is nobody in the wood, Hugh."

"Then she must've disappeared again," I offered, trembling. "The scary lady is good at doing that. She can just go poof and disappear into—"

"Oh my God, give it a rest with the scary-lady bullshit," Caoimhe roared, glaring at me. "It's bad enough you've warped your own mind with crazy bullshit, but you're warping his now, too."

"Hey!" Hugh snapped, stepping in front of me. "Your sister didn't warp my mind, Caoimhe. I saw the woman with my own eyes."

"Sure you did, right along with Saint Patrick himself and the Easter Bunny," she shot back sarcastically, stomping back to the house. "Pull a stunt like that again, Hugh Biggs, and I'm telling your parents."

"She doesn't believe me, Hugh," I said when my sister slammed the front door behind her.

"It doesn't matter what she believes," he growled, tucking my hand in his as he glowered at his closed front door. "You're telling the truth."

"I am?"

"Yeah, Liz." When his eyes flicked to mine, I could see the sympathy pouring out of them. "You are."

"Okay." I blew out a shaky breath, and Hugh gave my hand a reassuring squeeze. "Okay."

185

THIS IS BRIAN

Hugh

SEPTEMBER 5, 1997

"DO YOU WANT TO COME OVER FOR A KICKABOUT?" I ASKED GIBS WHEN WE STEPPED off the school bus on Thursday afternoon.

"Yeah, just let me get this prison uniform off," he replied, trudging up the driveway to his front door. "What's your mam making for dinner tonight?"

"Bacon and cabbage," I replied, following him inside his house. "With roast spuds."

"Woohoo," Gibs cheered, looking delighted. "My all-time favorite."

"Boys!" Sadhbh called out from the living room. "Come and see the wedding gift Keith got me."

Gibsie turned to stone in the hallway, and I knew his head was about to spin, so I placed a reassuring hand on his shoulder and whispered, "Keep the head."

"Keep the *head*?" Looking mutinous, Gibs glared back at me. "It's bad enough she forced me to attend their stupid fucking wedding in Paris—they ruined the most magical place on earth for me, by the way—but now she expects me to admire her stupid wedding presents."

"I know, I know," I coaxed, steering him toward the living room door. "But she's still your mam, lad." However, all attempts to play peacemaker flew clean out of my head when I locked eyes on the creature scaling the curtains in their living room.

"What the fuck is that?" Gibsie voiced my thoughts aloud, as he pointed to the gigantic moving ball of white fluff.

"This is Brian," Sadhbh declared proudly, gesturing to the demented-looking fur-ball tearing strips out of her good room curtains. "Isn't he beautiful?"

Frowning, Gibsie took an uncertain step into the room. "Is that a *cat*?"

Was it? "No, clue, lad," I muttered, following him inside. "Looks a bit big for a cat."

"Of course he's a cat," Sadhbh chuckled. "Brian's half–Maine Coon, half-Persian."

"Main Coon?" Gibsie's eyes widened in horror. "What the fuck is *that*?"

"Language, bubba," his mother scolded, as she walked over to the window and retrieved the oversized feline. "Now, don't let his size put you off. Brian is a sweet, little kitten at heart."

"Why does its paws look like they belong to a labrador, Hugh?"

"I've never seen a labrador with claws like those, Gibs."

"Don't be silly, boys." Sadhbh carted the beast over to where we were standing and smiled. "Come on and give him a little rub."

No fucking thank you, I thought to myself, taking a safe step back, while simultaneously pushing Gibsie forward. "You can pet him first, lad."

"Why do his ears stick up like horns?" Gibs asked, eyeing the yellow-eyed creature. "Why does he look like he wants to kill me?"

"Don't be daft, bubba," Sadhbh laughed, cuddling the enormous ball of white fur. "Brian's just curious."

Yeah, about what my friend tastes like.

Looking uncertain, Gibs raised a hand to pet Brian's head, and that's when all hell broke loose.

Spitting and hissing like the beast it resembled, Brian lunged for my friend, and I swear I thought I saw his eyes turn red when he locked on to Gibsie and started to attack.

"Ahhhh!" Gibsie's high-pitched scream would have been comical if he wasn't being mauled. "He's killing me, Mam!" Dropping to the carpet, Gibs rolled around on the living room floor, desperately trying to wrestle the feral beast off him.

"No, no, no, Brian!" Sadhbh half scolded, half cooed as she hurried to intervene. "Gerard is your brother, my little puss-puss. You can't bite your brother."

Yeah, fuck that.

Turning on my heels, I booked it out of their house as fast as my legs could carry me, all the while shouting, "Not today, Satan, not today!"

THE BIG, BAD WOLF

Lizzie

OCTOBER 31, 1997

"THANKS FOR HAVING ME OVER, LIZ," CLAIRE SAID ON FRIDAY MORNING, DURING AN epic coloring session in my living room. "I had the bestest sleepover ever with you."

Last night, Claire slept over at my house for the very first time. I invited Shannon too, but she didn't come. I wasn't surprised about that. She never came to Claire's sleepovers either. Her parents were strict about that sort of thing.

"Me, too," I replied, although I didn't do too much sleeping. Claire made the strangest snoring noises in her sleep, which usually kept me awake, but I never cared about that. I was just happy to be with her. Claire was always happy and when I spent time with her, I felt happy, too. Like right now, for instance. We were coloring in my front room, while we waited to be picked up for Hugh's party, and I felt *happy*. I wasn't scared or sad or angry. All I felt was peace and contentment. Claire gave that to me without even realizing.

"You make the best duck ever," I added, eyeing her Halloween costume. She was wearing a fluffy, yellow duck costume, with yellow tights and gigantic, webbed feet.

"I'm a chicken," she corrected, tongue poking out, as she concentrated on her coloring. "Gerard's an egg."

"Oh." Covering my mouth to stifle my laughter, I retrained my attention on the picture I was working on. I liked to design covers for all my stories, and this was going to be the cover for my latest one. It made me so proud when my dad printed them out on his computer and stapled them together.

Today's story was titled *The Adventures of Dorothy Tickle and Samson Strong*.

With the contents of my pencil case strewn on top the coffee table, I worked hard on staying between the lines like Hugh had shown me. I knew what to do, of course, but I didn't seem to have handwriting as neat as his. My coloring wasn't as tidy, either.

"How are my favorite girls?" a familiar voice said from the doorway, causing me to tense and Claire to groan. "Ugh." Scrunching her nose up in disapproval, she narrowed her eyes at Mark. "You are so annoying."

Chuckling, Mark strode into the room and settled on the couch behind us. "You make a cute chick, Baby Biggs," he mused, flicking through channels on our television.

"And you make a bad smell, Stinky Mark," Claire replied, coloring extra hard on her page.

"What about you, munchkin?" He nudged my hip with his sock-clad foot. "What's with the black wig and creepy dress. You going as a witch or something?"

"Lizzie is *not* a witch," Claire corrected, sounding outraged. "She is Morticia Addams."

"And let me guess; your brother is Gomez."

"That's right, and we already have a friend going as Lurch, so you should stop making your face look so stupid."

"You're a cheeky, little witch, aren't you?"

"I'm a chicken, not a witch, dummy."

They continued to argue, while I tried to make myself as small as possible, wishing I could snap my fingers and go *poof* like the scary lady.

Feeling sick, I retrained my attention to my picture of Dorothy and Samson. Dorothy looked just like me, and I was going to give Samson a beautiful golden cape, I decided. Golden to match his skin. And he was going to have pretty, whiskey-colored eyes and wavy, blond hair.

"Turn that off," Claire ordered loudly, dragging my attention to where she was pointing at the television. "That's not 'propriate for my eyes."

"It's *Baywatch*."

"So? It's still not 'propriate for my eyes."

"Says who?"

"My mam."

I glanced at the television screen to where two lifeguards were kissing and touching each other in the shower.

I knew all about that.

And it came after the touching.

The monster showed me.

"What about you, Baby Biggs?" Mark continued to taunt my friend. "Ever kissed my brother like that?"

"Are you stupid?" Claire scrunched her nose up in disgust. "I'm eight."

"What about you, munchkin?" He poked me with his foot again. "I bet you've been kissing her brother like that."

"Hugh's her friend, you weirdo, and Liz is only nine," Claire defended, slapping his foot away. "Quit annoying us or I'm telling Catherine on you!"

"You've got fire in you, don't ya, Baby Biggs?" Mark laughed, clearly unbothered by her warning. "That's good."

The sound of the front door slamming shut filled my ears then, followed by my sister's voice when she called out, "Look who I found outside, girls." My sister appeared in the doorway with a familiar, curly-haired boy beside her.

"Gibs!" I exclaimed at the same time Claire cried out, "Gerard."

"Look at the state of you," Mark snapped, glowering at my friend. "What the fuck kind of costume is that?"

"He's an egg," Claire defended, making a beeline for Gerard. "And I'm a chicken."

"He's a dickhead is what he is," Mark muttered.

"Leave him alone," Caoimhe admonished, elbowing his side when she joined him on the couch. "He's only a child."

Gibsie's eyes flicked to Mark before focusing on Claire. "Are you okay?"

"Of course," she replied happily, throwing her arms around him. "I missed you, Gerard."

"I missed you, too," he replied, attention shifting from his stepbrother to Claire. "Your mam's outside talking to Catherine," he added, turning them around so that he was the one with his back to the couch. "I wanted to come with her to make sure you were okay." He shrugged. "You're sure you're okay?"

"I'm fine, Gerard," Claire laughed, bouncing from foot to foot from the sheer excitement she clearly felt from being reunited with him. "Mam's outside?"

"Yeah, she's talking to Catherine."

"I'm going to go hug her," she announced before bolting for the door. "Will you grab my bag from your room, Liz?"

"Yeah," I replied, watching her disappear from sight.

"Gibs!" Mark barked, causing both of us to jump. "Come over here, fucker. I want a word with you."

Gibsie reached for my hand at the same time I reached for his, and I asked, "Do you want to come upstairs with me to get Claire's bag instead?"

Nodding eagerly, he fell into step with me as we bolted into the hallway, heading straight for the staircase at top speed.

Not stopping until we were inside my room, Gibsie stood with his back to my door and exhaled several shaky breaths.

"Are you okay?" I asked, feeling worried.

"Yeah, I'm…" Breathing hard, he held a hand up and momentarily focused on his breathing until it evened out. "I just hate that guy."

"You do?"

He offered me a clipped nod. "I've never hated anyone before, but I truly hate him."

"Can you keep a secret?" I whispered, feeling nervous.

Gibsie's eyes were wary, but his head was nodding slowly, as he walked over to my bed and sat down next to me. "I'll keep your secret, Lizzie."

"You swear?"

Another noble nod. "Pinky promise."

Hooking my pinky finger through his, I turned and gave him my full attention. "I think I hate him, too."

The moment the words were out of my mouth, I started to shake. "I'm sorry," I was quick to blurt. "I shouldn't have said that."

Not out loud at least.

"It's okay," he replied, reaching for my hand. "It's okay, Liz."

It wasn't okay.

Because if he found out…

Breathing hard and fast, I tried to concentrate on Gibsie's face and not the voices growing louder in my head.

I didn't want the monster to come out now.

Not during the daytime.

My friend sat with me for a long time, eyes locked on mine, before he finally spoke. "Has he hurt you?"

"Who?"

"Mark."

I thought about it for a long time before shaking my head.

"Are you sure?"

Was I?

I used to think so, but not anymore. It was the monster in my dreams all along, not Mark. The monster got me at night when I was sleeping, but the doctors said he wasn't real. But my sister? He definitely got her.

Leaning close, I whispered in his ear, "He hurts Caoimhe." And then I pointed to my bed for good measure to emphasize what I was trying to tell him. "He does things to her."

His entire body stiffened. "What kind of things?"

"Bad things," I whispered, remembering it vividly. What I'd seen. In the dark of the night when I was supposed to be sleeping. Her cries. The sadness. The pain in my heart. "He takes off all her clothes, and then he makes growling sounds when he holds her down on the bed. He pushes the hard thing inside her and she cries, Gibs. She cries so hard, but he always covers her mouth with his hand and keeps poking her until she stops crying. And then, when he stops wrestling her, when the white stuff comes out, he gets out of her bed and goes back to…he goes downstairs for a drink."

Gibsie reached up and wiped a tear from his cheek. "He's bad, Liz. He does it at my house, too."

My eyes widened in horror. "To Caoimhe when she sleeps over?"

Gibsie paused for a moment before closing his eyes and nodding.

"I want him to go away," I admitted, scurrying closer to him, as I admitted my thoughts for the first time out loud. "I don't like when he's in my house." Shivering, I added, "I want him to go away and *never* come back."

"Me, too," he whispered, turning his shiny, gray eyes back on me.

"I haven't told anyone else," I whispered. "Not even Hugh."

"Me either," he whispered. "Not even Claire."

"Promise you won't tell?" I held up my pinky finger. "I can't get in trouble again." They'll send me away.

"I promise if you promise," he vowed, hooking my pinky with his. "I'll take it to the grave."

"Me, too." I breathed out a huge sigh of relief before asking, "Do you think we should try to break them up?" I shrugged before adding, "At least that way he would have to stop hurting my sister at nighttime."

"Your sister won't break up with him," Gibsie replied, eyes laced with sadness. "She wants to marry him."

"I don't want Caoimhe to marry Mark." Sadness bloomed in my belly at the thought. "He'll be here forever then."

"Don't worry." Gibsie tried to soothe me, wiping a tear from my cheek now. "We'll be grown-ups by the time that happens, with our own houses, and *he* won't be invited inside."

"Like the three little pigs and the big, bad wolf?"

"Exactly," he agreed with a small smile. "Mark Allen can huff and puff all he wants when I'm a grown-up, but I'll be strong enough to keep him out."

"Me too," I agreed, balling my small hand into a fist. "And the brave knight will stop him with his sword if he tries to come down my chimney."

"Hey, Lizzie?"

"Yeah, Gibs?"

"You sure you're okay?"

"Yep." Smiling, I reached up and brushed a tear from his cheek. "I'm always okay, Gibs."

PART 6

Growing Pains

CREATURES AND CREATURE COMFORTS

Lizzie

FEBRUARY 22, 1998

I ALWAYS FELT AT MY BEST WHEN I SPENT TIME AT CLAIRE AND HUGH'S PLACE. IT didn't matter what games we played or what delicious meal Sinead served for dinner. Their home felt like a *real* home, and it was the only place I could go to escape the bad dreams. When I stayed at their house, I could relax.

I could breathe.

Today was no different, except for the fact that I was *supposed* to be across the street attending Gibsie's tenth birthday party. Instead, I had crept back to number four and was currently curled up in a ball on Hugh's bed.

Everything about Hugh's bedroom was comforting—his bed, his desk, the pictures hanging on the walls, the books he read that were piled on top of his nightstand, and even the scent of the washing powder his mother used on his sheets.

I loved Gibsie, he was one of my greatest friends in the world, but sometimes his house reminded me of mine, and I didn't want to be there, either.

"So this is where you've been hiding." Hugh stood in his bedroom doorway with a smile etched on his face. "You just missed the funniest thing ever, Liz," he told me, eyes dancing with excitement. "Danny Call just got a whole chunk taken out of his ankle, courtesy of Brian." Snickering to himself, Hugh padded over to his bed and flopped down next to me. "You should've heard him scream."

"That feral feline belongs in a zoo," I mused. "I don't care what Sadhbh says about him being part Persian, because I swear, he's part albino tiger."

"He's part demon is what he is," Hugh corrected with a chuckle. "He escaped out the back door and terrorized all the lads. Everyone's scratched to shit from trying to catch him." Another hearty laugh escaped him. "Gibs and Claire are outside now trying to attach a leash to his collar to coax him back into the house."

"Then I'm glad I missed it," I replied. "Because if that beast bit me, I'd bite him back."

"Don't you mean to say you'd bite him *again*?" Hugh teased, nudging my shoulder.

"Hey! I only did that because he bit *my* ear first and wouldn't let go until I returned the favor," I defended, unable to stop my smile from spreading or my heart from fluttering when he took my hand in his. "You know how the saying goes, Hugh." Grinning, I shrugged. "Play stupid games."

"And win stupid prizes," Hugh finished for me, still chuckling as he entwined his fingers with mine. "Yeah, well, I reckon Brian will think twice before he takes you on again."

"As he should," I laughed. "Did he get you?"

"Nah." Hugh smiled at me. "I'm too fast."

"You mean you're too clever to go anywhere near him."

"That, too," Hugh replied, sighing in amusement before his smile quickly morphed into a frown. "Oh shit." Untangling our joined hands, Hugh turned my hand over and stared at my wrist. His eyes darkened when he trailed his finger over the recently scabbed-over jagged line. "Did Brian get you again?" His concerned, brown eyes flicked to mine. "Is that why you left the party?"

No. "Yeah." Repressing a shiver, I slid my hand from his and pushed my sleeve down. Pulling myself into a sitting position, I clasped my hands together and shrugged. "Sorry."

"Don't be sorry, Liz," he replied, turning his body to face me. He had a smile on his face, but his eyes still held the world of concern in them. "Do you want my mam to have a look at that scratch? It looks fairly deep."

"Nah, I'll be grand." Anxious, I reached up and tucked my hair behind my ears. "I can't even feel it."

Hugh stared at me for a long time before recapturing my hand in his. "What's wrong?"

"What do you mean?"

"You look scared." His eyes searched mine. "You're not telling me something."

"I'm fine." Smiling, I forced a laugh, but it was a weak attempt. "Honestly, I'm grand, Hugh."

He didn't look convinced. "Talk to me."

I couldn't.

Oh God, I wanted to.

But I just *couldn't.*

"Did one of the lads say something to you?" he asked then, shoulders tensing. "At the party? Was someone being a dick?"

"No."

"Then why do you look like you're two seconds away from crying?"

"I don't." Tears filled my eyes. "I'm not."

"Liz, come on." He gave me a disbelieving look. "It's *me*."

"I'm just…" Shaking my head, I blew out a pained breath before muttering, "It doesn't matter."

"If something is upsetting you, then it matters," he replied, keeping his whiskey-brown eyes locked on mine. "It matters a *lot* to me."

"I…" I opened my mouth to answer him but all that came out was a shaky breath, because what could I tell him?

That I was plagued by the monsters my own imagination had conjured up to terrorize me?

That I was tormented by sickening images and horrendous thoughts that made me want to die?

Or how about telling him that I was filthy, impure, and defective?

Which one was I supposed to tell him about?

Which sin would be the one that drove him away?

"I'm just having a bad day," I finally settled on.

Hugh looked at me like he didn't believe me, but he didn't push. Instead, he squeezed my hand and whispered, "I love you, Lizzie Young."

Guilt and hope bloomed in my chest, making me feel both excited and devastated all at once. "No matter what?"

"Yeah, Liz." He leaned in close and pressed his forehead to mine. "No matter what."

THE EDGE OF SEVENTEEN

Hugh

MAY 2, 1998

MY SISTER AND GIBS HAD A DANCE COMPETITION UP THE COUNTRY THIS WEEKEND, and my mother had organized for me to stay at Lizzie's house until they got back.

It should have been the greatest weekend of my life, and it probably would have been if it hadn't been for Caoimhe and I still being on the outs.

I'd barely spoken more than ten words to her since last summer, when she point-blank refused to believe Liz and I didn't invent the woman in the woods.

Worse than not believing us, she convinced our *parents* to take *her* side, which left everyone thinking we made the whole thing up. Even my own *mother* was swayed to the dark side, believing I had conjured up the woman in the woods.

I hadn't.

I knew what I saw that day.

I had a feeling that, deep down inside, Caoimhe knew, too.

The fact that she continued to label me a liar only intensified my thirst for vindication.

And the stronger my grudge grew.

She turned seventeen last Thursday and had a big bash planned at the house for Saturday. I didn't even wish her a happy birthday when I came downstairs to the party tonight with Liz. Yeah, my so-called babysitter could have one of those when she started telling the truth.

As for her asshole boyfriend who pranced around the house like he owned it, well, he could take a long walk off a short beach. Seriously. I really hoped he would, because the mere sight of his smug face had my teeth on edge and my upchuck reflex locked, loaded, and ready to blow.

Gobshite.

Sticking to each other like glue throughout the party, Liz and I rotated between watching movies in her room and sneaking downstairs to swipe snacks.

She seemed a lot more relaxed this weekend and had slept like a baby last night. She credited this to having me in her room, having told me numerous times that I was her own personal dream catcher. Apparently, my presence in her room, with my makeshift bed on the floor next to hers, kept the monsters at bay.

I didn't like to think too much about it because whenever I did, I was crippled by wave upon wave of devastation. It was a reminder that she was different. That she had a problem that I couldn't fix for her. I couldn't fight what I couldn't see, and it made me feel helpless.

None of it scared me off being with her, though. Because, even if I didn't have the emotional capacity to truly appreciate the battles she fought, I had the wherewithal to acknowledge the gifted mind hidden beneath the fractured particles.

Her family didn't seem to understand her—well, her father and sister certainly didn't—but I did.

My best friend had a beautiful, complicated, and brilliant mind, and I knew I had enough love in my heart for her to remain right by her side.

No matter what.

"It's your sister's birthday," Mark stated, walking into Lizzie's room for the third time tonight.

Without knocking.

For the third time.

"The next time you walk in here without knocking on the door, I'm going to rip your fucking head off," I warned, glaring up at him from my perch on her bedroom floor. Shaking the dice in my hand, I dropped them on the Monopoly board before adding, "Fair warning."

"Two sixes takes you past my hotel," Lizzie groaned, looking thoroughly devastated when I moved my boot figurine across the board. "Damn you, Hugh Biggs. I was depending on that money to get me out of jail."

"Did you not hear me, munchkin?"

Ignoring him completely, Lizzie picked up the dice for her turn, but her hand was shaking in a way that made me know she was stressed.

Beyond irritated by his presence, and angered further by that horrible fucking pet name, I climbed to my feet and stalked toward him. "Are you honestly this devoid of intellect?" I demanded, having had more than my regular quota of Mark Allen for one weekend. "If you're too thick to take the hint, then let me spell it out for you. Liz doesn't care about your girlfriend's party. Not even a little bit, and neither do I. So why don't you do all of us a favor and fuck right off."

The asshole looked so taken aback that someone younger than him had the nerve to stand up to him that he was distracted when I made my next move.

Shoving at his chest as hard as I could, I felt a surge of satisfaction when he staggered backwards, giving me ample opportunity to close and lock the door.

"You cheeky, little shit," he snarled from the other side of the door. "You'll get yours, Biggs. Just you wait."

"Looking forward to it," I called back, rolling my eyes. "Dick brain."

"That was epic!" Looking up at me with a wide-eyed expression, Liz beamed at me. "But aren't you afraid of him retaliating?"

"No, because it's all talk," I replied, entirely unafraid of the bully I was quickly gaining on in the height department. Returning to her side, I snatched the dice up to roll my turn. "Bullies feed on fear." Shrugging, I added, "And Mark can't feed on me."

"Why not?"

"Because I *don't* fear him."

"You don't?"

"No, Liz, and you shouldn't either," I replied. "Because I would kill him before I *ever* let him hurt you."

"You would?"

"Without a doubt."

"Why, though?"

I shrugged. "Because you're my best friend, and there isn't anything I wouldn't do to protect you."

Her blue eyes softened when she whispered, "I love you so much, Hugh Biggs." Reaching out, she covered my hand with hers and smiled. "I wish you could stay with me forever."

BIRTHDAY WISHES AND HAND KISSES

Hugh

JUNE 9, 1998

"Happy birthday to you, happy birthday to you, happy birthday to Milady, happy birthday to you." Crooning like a defective crow, I wandered through the tall grass in the Young family's meadow after school on Tuesday, armed with birthday presents, a picnic blanket, and a cake in the shape of the number ten.

Releasing a hearty laugh, Lizzie jumped off one of the wooden swings attached to a tree and ran toward me. "Why thank you, brave knight." When she reached me, she stretched up on her tiptoes and pressed a kiss to my cheek. "My hero."

As usual, she was rocking dungarees, but these ones stopped at the knee. Another staple item she wore was a flannel shirt and today was no different. She had the plaid fabric tied around her waist. Her grass-stained knees complemented her unbrushed, grass-specked hair, and the mud smeared across her cheek.

"Thanks for coming over," she said, dragging me from my thoughts.

"Always, Liz."

Grinning, she playfully tipped her imaginary hat at me before adopting a southern drawl to say, "Looks like you're not the only ten-year-old in town, cowboy."

"Now, slow down there, Miss Dolly," I replied, feigning a southern drawl of my own. "I'll be your elder again in four full moons."

"You're so weird," she snickered, tucking her hair behind her ears. "Thank you for my cake." A laugh escaped her when she eyed the bite-sized chunk taken out of the number one. "Gibsie?"

"Do you even need to ask?" Handing Liz the cake Sadhbh had baked her, I laid the picnic blanket out on the grass and sank down on it. "You're lucky I caught him in the act, or you'd be celebrating with a zero instead of ten."

"It's grand," she replied, lowering herself down to sit cross-legged, facing me. "You're all I want for my birthday."

The way she said it in such a blasé tone, like it was a given that she would only want me, made me feel like a million quid. Even though her words were like an electric shock to my chest, I played it cool and didn't react.

Liz looked so relaxed and content that I thought better of it than to toss a nuke into the mix by listing all the complicated feelings I had developed for her.

"Did your mam say yes to you sleeping over tonight?" She swiped a dollop of icing up with her finger and popped it into her mouth. "And taking the bus to school from here in the morning?"

"It was a tricky negotiation." I sighed dramatically. "But I managed to get it over the line."

Her blue eyes lit up. "You did?"

"Yep." I smiled. "She's handing over my uniform and schoolbag to your mother as we speak."

"Oh my God, yes!" Squealing with delight, Liz lunged forward and threw her arms around me. "You're the best."

Later that night when we were back in her room, after eating dinner and watching a film with her family, we combed through her impressive book collection.

I knew the lads at school would call me an egghead for admitting it, but I fucking *loved* reading. Thrillers, murder mystery, true crime, autobiographies—it didn't matter. I devoured every genre like crack. For me, books trumped rugby, soccer, and pretty much every other extracurricular activity I found myself lumped into.

One of my favorite things about Liz was that she matched my enthusiasm for reading. We could easily sit for hours in each other's company reading, without feeling an ounce of pressure to make awkward conversation because there was never any awkwardness between us.

I knew Liz was gorgeous, but her appearance could never hold a flame to her mind. The fact of the matter was she both challenged and intrigued me to the point where I was wholly invested in her.

When Liz set her paperback down a little later and proposed we play a new game, I found myself more confused and thrilled than usual.

"Come on," she coaxed, extending her arm to me. "Show me how you plan to do it."

Sitting cross-legged on her bed, facing her, I stared down at her hand in confusion. "You can't be serious."

"Please, Hugh," she begged, shifting closer until our knees were touching. "I want to know."

Nervous, I glanced down at her wrist before flicking my gaze back to her face. "Why?"

She smirked. "Because I'm nosy."

I arched a brow. "You're weird is what you are."

"That, too," she snickered, still holding her hand up to my face. "Please, Hugh. Just kiss it."

"Okay, I'll do it." Repressing a shiver, I caught ahold of her arm and pulled her closer. "But if you tell the lads, I'll never talk to you again."

"Your secret's safe with me," she promised, eyes twinkling with mischief. "Now, pucker up."

Leaning in close, I kept my eyes trained on hers when I pressed my lips to her wrist. I had no clue what to do once my lips were there, so I just stared at her for a long beat before asking, "Is that okay?"

"Perfect." Liz slowly withdrew her hand from mine and exhaled a shaky breath. She then proceeded to blow my mind when she kissed her own wrist in the *exact* spot I kissed her.

"What are you doing?" My heart thundered so violently that I thought it might explode. "Why'd you do that, Liz?"

She kept her eyes on mine when she cradled her wrist to her chest and whispered, "Because I wanted to know what it felt like to kiss you."

PADDLING POOLS AND KNICKERBOCKER GLORIES
Lizzie

JULY 10, 1998

RESTING A SET OF LARGE STEREO SPEAKERS ON THE KITCHEN WINDOWSILL, HUGH disappeared from sight, only to reappear a few seconds later when the sound of KC and the Sunshine Band's "Give It Up" blasted from the speakers. "Is this the song you wanted, Gibs?"

"That's the one, Hugo," Gibsie crooned from his perch on one of the sun loungers in Hugh's back garden. "Good man yourself. You can slap that song on repeat. It tickles my fancy." In Gibsie's hand was a tall glass containing an impressive ice cream float, complete with both a straw and a cherry on top. "This is the life, lads." Bopping along to the music playing, he took an exaggerated slurp from his straw and released a contented *ahh* sigh. "And this is the greatest knickerbocker glory I've ever tasted."

"Can't argue with you there, Gibs," Patrick replied. He was sprawled out on an inflatable float bed in their gigantic, fourteen-foot paddling pool, basking in the sunshine with his own knickerbocker glory in hand, while a mischievous Claire steered the inflatable unicorn she was riding like a horse into the side of him. "Keep it up, Baby Biggs," he warned when she crashed into him for the millionth time. "Because if I'm going under, you're coming with me."

Sighing in contentment, I sat cross-legged on their conservatory roof and took in my surroundings.

The sky was crystal-clear, the sun was shining, and I was surrounded by my favorite people in the world. Hugh was right this morning when he told me today would be a good one.

In fact, I couldn't remember the last time I had felt so carefree.

"I'm warning you, Baby Biggs." Laughing, Patrick reached out and pushed her float away. "If I go under, I'm taking you with me."

"Careful with the hair, Patrick," Claire groaned, narrowly avoiding getting dunked. "It takes forever to tame these curls."

"How's the coast, Liz?" Hugh asked, leaning out the window on the second floor of his house.

"Clear as a whistle," I called back, taking another sweep of his parent-free garden. "Sadhbh called your mam over for coffee."

He grinned down at me before disappearing from my line of sight only to reappear a few seconds later when he climbed out onto the windowsill.

"Wait, wait," Patrick warned, falling off the inflatable bed he was lounging on and scrambling out of the pool, taking Claire with him. "Okay," he added when he was out of dodge. "As you were."

"Are you mental?" Gibs demanded, removing his sunglasses to glare. "There's four and a half feet of water in there, lad."

"I know," Hugh laughed, and then he catapulted fearlessly from the windowsill.

Completely awestruck, I watched him execute the perfect landing in the water before jumping to his feet. "Piece of cake."

"You're a raving lunatic," Gibsie muttered, putting his glasses back on. "I can't be dealing with your antics."

"Are you ready?" Hugh asked, giving me an expectant grin. "You've got this, Liz."

"I really don't," I replied with a snicker.

The conservatory roof was a shorter jump than the window Hugh had leapt from, and I wasn't nearly as graceful in water as he was, but I was going to give it my best shot.

"Okay, okay." Grinning mischievously, I climbed to my feet and backed up a few feet before making a run for the edge. "Here I come...ahhh!"

There was only a space of two or three seconds between jumping from the roof and hitting the water below, but the adrenaline those seconds in midair sent rushing through my veins was *so* worth it.

"You're such a badass," Hugh praised when I jumped to my feet, coughing and spluttering, because, of course, I forgot to hold my breath. "That was epic, Liz."

"Looks like you've met your match in the crazy stakes, Hugo," Gibsie offered drolly. "You should put a ring on it, lad. Maybe on your honeymoon, you can take her diving off Niagara Falls."

YOUR SON IS MY SUN

Lizzie

OCTOBER 3, 1998

The monster was furious tonight. I was glad I was dreaming because I didn't think I could survive the pain if it were real. He kept snarling and hissing at me, blaming me for revealing his secrets.

I hadn't.

All I did was fall asleep tonight and meet him in my dreams.

Someone had made him angry, though.

Cruel enough to choke and punch me.

Rough enough to break me from the inside out.

"I didn't say anything, I swear," I tried to plead, but it was no use. The monster wasn't listening to me.

"What did he tell her?" he continued to demand, scratching and tearing at my clothes. "You know something, don't you?"

"I don't, I swear," I strangled out, not bothering to fight back.

It didn't matter because it wasn't real.

I would be okay.

Everything would be better when the sun came up.

In the darkness, the monster pinned me down and hissed all his commands in my ears...

"On your knees."

"Bend over."

"Don't make me hurt you."

"Quiet, or I'll snap your fucking neck."

Over and over again.

Until I wanted to die.

"What's wrong?" Caoimhe asked from the driver's seat of Dad's Jeep on our way to Avoca Greystones. "You're doing that weird, spaced-out thing again."

"I'm grand," I lied, clearing my throat.

I wasn't grand.

I was the opposite.

I had an anxious energy building up inside of me and felt like I was two seconds away from snapping.

But I would never tell Caoimhe that.

Not when she was our father's eyes and ears.

"What time are you supposed to be at Sinead's house?" I asked instead, steering the conversation to safer waters.

"Ten minutes ago," she muttered under her breath, weaving through the country roads. "I don't know what happened this morning. I never usually oversleep." Groaning, she shifted gears and tightened her grip on the wheel. "I feel like I've been hit by a lorry."

Welcome to my world, I thought but decided to keep to myself. "There's a bad bend up here," I warned, gesturing to the winding part of road ahead of us. "Take it handy."

"I know how to drive, Lizzie!"

Maybe, but she wasn't very good at it. Since getting her license back in April, my sister had racked up an impressive number of scratches and dents on our father's Range Rover.

"Ugh!" She complained loudly again. "Why do I feel like I'm doped off my head?"

"Were you drinking last night?" I knew she drank alcohol with her friends on the weekends. She smoked, too. Not in front of our parents, of course, but I often spied her in the stables with a cigarette in her mouth. "Maybe you're just tired from a hangover or something."

"I was home all night," she replied, sounding frustrated. "We had a takeaway and watched movies in my room."

We.

Meaning her and Mark.

"Oh." Clasping my hands together tightly, I stared out the window. "Then I don't know."

Caoimhe continued to complain all the way to Sinead's, while my anxiety continued to intensify. When we finally pulled up outside the familiar house, I bolted up the driveway and into the house without giving my sister a backwards glance.

I couldn't have if I'd wanted to.

Because I was about to burst.

Moving on instinct, I barreled up the staircase, not stopping until I reached his bedroom door.

"Jesus Christ, Liz!" Hugh exclaimed when I practically blew his bedroom door off its hinges in my rush to get to him. "What's wrong?" His tone was panicked. "What happened?"

I didn't answer him.

Because I *couldn't*.

Instead, I walked straight to him, not stopping until I had clambered over the books strewn across his bed and was nestled on his lap.

The tears I had managed to hold in all the way over here had reached their breaking point and my emotions exploded out of me in a flurry of heaving sobs.

Hugh tossed the book he was holding aside and quickly wrapped me up in that familiar cocoon of safety and warmth. "It's okay," he coaxed, tightening his arms around me. "I'm right here." He smoothed my hair over my shoulder and rocked gently. "Shh, Liz, I'm right here with you."

Hearing his voice only made me cry harder and cling tighter. "It happened again."

"You had another nightmare?"

"It felt so real this time." Nodding, I trembled violently. "Please don't leave me."

A tremor racked through his big body, and I slowly felt him relax on my mattress. "I'm not leaving, Liz." His arm came around me, and then his lips were on my ear. "I'm staying."

Two words that meant more coming from him than any declarations of love or promises of forever.

Just to *stay*—that's all I needed.

And he was giving it to me.

I was making so much of a racket that Claire barreled into the room, demanding to know what was wrong, but Hugh didn't have the answers, and I couldn't tell.

Eventually she gave up and left, only to return with her mother and my sister.

"Oh my God," I heard Caoimhe groan from somewhere behind me. "I am so sorry about her, Sinead. I'll call my dad to come pick her up."

"No!" That was Hugh. "She can stay, can't she, Mam?"

"Of course she can," I heard Sinead reply. "Lizzie, sweetheart, what's upsetting you?"

I couldn't explain it.

Because it *wasn't* real.

Because Sinead would think I was crazy.

Just like everyone else.

"Why don't you come and have a little chat with me before I leave for work. Hmm?" She gently squeezed my shoulder, and her touch felt like Hugh's. "Would you like that?"

I shook my head, unable to release my hold on her son.

Because her son was my *sun*.

"I just want Hugh," I strangled out, voice shaking almost as much as my body. "Just…just Hugh, okay?"

PART 7

The Dangerous Art
of Dissociation

HOLDING ROPES AND HERO BROTHERS

Lizzie

OCTOBER 15, 1998

AFTER THE DOCTORS CHANGED MY MEDICINE AGAIN, I DIDN'T FEEL PANICKED ANY-more. In fact, I didn't feel anything at all. I went through the motions at school and home, content in a hazed numbness.

No scary lady.

No monster under my bed.

Nothing at all.

Focusing was difficult because all I wanted to do was sleep, and I found myself zoning out a lot during class.

Mam told me that the fog would soon wear off and I would go back to normal again, but I wasn't sure what that looked like. Not when I couldn't remember a point in time when I had been me.

The only time I truly felt anything was when I was with Hugh. He seemed to be the only person capable of kick-starting my emotions, and boy did they kick-start when he was around.

The me without chemicals, that was.

Exhausted by the time Thursday came around, I offered to hold the skipping rope for my friends at big lunch. I didn't have the energy to engage further. Right now, holding the rope was the best I could do.

"Cinderella dressed in yellow went upstairs to kiss her fella, by mistake she kissed a snake, how many doctors will it take," the girls around me all chanted, while I held one end of the jump rope and Marybeth held the other. Between us, Claire jumped over every loop like a superstar. *"One, two, three, four, five, six, seven, eight, nine, ten…"*

Claire was the best jumper at school, even better than the older girls, and I knew she could go all lunch break without missing a skip. She reminded me of the bunny rabbit on the television commercial for batteries, except Claire didn't need batteries to charge her up, just sunshine.

"England, Ireland, Scotland, Wales, inside, outside, puppy-dog tails!" another group

chanted across the schoolyard, while two girls stretched the elastic with their legs and another jumped and weaved between it as fast as she could without touching the elastic.

They were loud.

Everyone was so *loud*.

Behind me, I could hear another game taking placing.

"Orange balls, orange balls, here we go again, the last one to touch the ground has a boyfriend!"

Hands trembling, I closed my eyes and took a steadying breath.

"A sailor went to sea, sea, sea, to see what he could see, see, see, but all that he could see, see, see was the bottom of the big blue sea, sea, sea."

It was too much.

All of it.

"You're messing up," someone declared before snatching the rope out of my hand. "Move, Lizzie, I'll swing the rope."

Feeling overly stimulated, I backed away from the skipping rope, only to be intercepted by another girl from my class.

"Come on, Lizzie," Cadence encouraged, holding her palms up expectantly. "Play the clapping game with me. You know the pattern."

I *did* know the pattern, or at least I was *supposed* to know, but right now I couldn't remember. Everything was blurry in my head.

"Backwards, forwards, clap right, clap left, clap, clap," Cadence chanted, clapping her hands against mine. "Come on, Lizzie, you're not even trying."

"Sorry, I need to use the bathroom," I mumbled, hurrying away from the yard.

I didn't.

I just needed some *quiet*.

The louder the noise grew, the more disorientated I became.

I already knew that.

I'd learned it a long time ago.

Find Shannon, the kind voice in my mind instructed, *she makes it go quiet for you*.

She didn't want to play in the yard at lunch today, so I thought she might be still in class, but when I checked our classroom, it was empty.

Returning to the schoolyard, I searched the playground for my friend before heading down to the big field, a.k.a. the pitch.

As usual, the fifth and sixth class boys were on the pitch, kicking the living daylights out of each other under the pretense of hurling.

I didn't care about them.

My whole focus was on the small girl crying on the sidelines.

Shannon.

She was holding her school jumper in her hands and sobbing inconsolably, while her big brother comforted her.

I felt something then, a lurching sensation in my chest, as I took in the sight of her torn jumper.

Anger. That's what I was feeling, and it was bubbling inside of my stomach, growing hotter with every tear that spilled from her eyes.

When Joey whipped his own jumper off and placed it over her head, I felt another wave of emotion hit me.

Sadness.

Because his jumper wasn't in much better condition than hers. But at least it hadn't been torn to ribbons by bullies. The move left my friend swamped in an oversized jumper that fell to her knees, while her brother perished in his creased, white school shirt that had seen better days.

In fact, the cuffs seemed so old, they were practically worn off and barely reached his forearms. Oblivious to the fact that his shirt was about three sizes too small for him, Joey Lynch rolled what was left of the sleeves up to his elbows before ruffling his sister's hair and offering her a warm smile.

It wasn't raining today, but the cold October breeze was skinning, and I knew he had to be freezing.

So why did he do it?

Why did he give her something he didn't have to spare?

I didn't have the answer, but his selfless gesture sparked something inside of me, and I made a mental note to sneak my spare jumper into school for Shannon tomorrow.

At least that way, her brother wouldn't be cold.

When I got to school on Friday, I waited for the perfect opportunity to catch Joey Lynch on his own.

It wasn't easy because, unlike Shannon, everyone seemed to flock to him. It didn't matter that they feared him. They still wanted to be around him.

I understood that he had something mysterious about him that made people want to get closer, but I thought his sister was even more mysterious.

To me, at least.

My opportunity arrived near the end of the day, when Ciara Maloney hit Shannon on the back with a blackboard duster, and I, in turn, hit Ciara in the face with my fist.

Of course, I was told to pack up my belongings and sit on the bench in the hall until school was over. This was nothing out of the ordinary for me. I spent a lot of time on the bench, but today, I had a companion, and just by happenstance, that companion was Joey Lynch.

Again, this wasn't out of the ordinary because he spent even more time than I did on the bench. But it *was* good fortune.

Shannon's brother didn't speak to me when I slumped down beside him. In fact, he didn't even look in my direction. It didn't bother me because, aside from Claire and Shannon, I never wanted anyone at school to talk to me, either.

Like yesterday, he was wearing a shirt that looked small enough to belong to Shannon, and he didn't have a jumper. He didn't even have a coat resting on his schoolbag to wear when school ended. No scarf, gloves, or hat either. His left runner had a tear on the side that revealed the color of his sock. *Gray.*

Settling my schoolbag between my legs, I unzipped it and rummaged under my books until I found what I was looking for.

Withdrawing the plastic carrier bag that contained my sister's Sacred Heart uniform, I tossed it on his lap.

"Do I look like a bin, blondie?" he drawled in a deep, sarcastic tone.

Ignoring him, I zipped my schoolbag back up and leaned against the wall at my back, arms folded across my chest. Just like him.

"You're Shan's buddy, aren't ya?" he asked then, voice not nearly as mean as before.

I turned to face him and nodded once. "Yep."

He stared back at me with his big, green eyes. "What's in the bag?"

"Just some spare stuff I had lying around the place."

Frowning, he slowly opened the bag, took a glance at the contents inside, and then quickly deposited the bag onto my lap. "No thanks."

"Take it," I argued, grabbing the bag and tossing it back to him.

"*No.*"

"Why not?"

He sounded furious when he hissed, "Because I don't want your charity."

"It doesn't matter if you don't want it," I argued back, unwilling to back down. "Because you still *need* it."

He looked at me like I had slapped him. "Fuck you, kid."

"Fuck me?" I grumbled, feeling just as outraged. "Fuck you, *fucker.*"

"Wow." Joey arched a brow. "Is that the best you've got?"

"Not even close, *fucker.*" I narrowed my eyes. "Do you want to hear some more, *fucker?*"

He continued to glare at me for several seconds before his lips twitched. "Jesus." Releasing a growl, he shook his head and looked away, while muttering, "Where did my sister find you?"

I kept my frown in place when he unzipped his schoolbag and shoved the carrier bag inside, but on the inside, I was smiling.

And I think he was, too.

YOU CAN CALL ME PADDY SPICE

Hugh

OCTOBER 31, 1998

"This is beyond degrading," Feely declared, appearing from my downstairs bathroom dressed in a pair of shiny blue tracksuit bottoms, an orange belly top, a ponytail wig, and a full face of makeup. "I feel like a tool."

"You look like one, too," I choked out through fits of laughter.

"Says the fella head to toe in leopard print," he shot back. "Nice wig, Hughie. You're certainly living up to the label, ya scary bastard."

"People in glass houses, Feely," I shot back. "And give it a rest with the moaning." Grimacing, I glanced down at the skintight, leopard-print catsuit I had been forcefully wedged into and then to the horrific platform boots that were cutting off all circulation in my feet. I could hardly stand in them, so I wasn't holding out much hope for walking. "At least you get to wear trackies and runners."

"And toilet-roll tits," he reminded me, gesturing to his padded chest. "Don't forget the toilet-roll tits, Hugh."

"What do you call these?" I demanded, grabbing my own pair. "And mine are bigger than yours!"

"Don't touch your boobs, Hughie," my sister cried, rushing toward me. "You'll ruin the shape."

"At least you fuckers get to wear pants," Gibs huffed, wobbling into the living room in knee-high, red-leather platform boots and a ginger wig. "And if you think toilet-roll tits are bad, try having balloon tits!"

"Because Ginger Spice has the biggest boobs," my sister called over her shoulder as she readjusted my tits. "And I already explained the dress situation. Hugh's and Patrick's legs are too hairy."

"I'm not sure if that's a compliment or an insult," Gibs mused, scratching his chin.

"It's a compliment," she assured him, turning her attention to Feely's chesticles. "You have the best legs, Gerard."

"No, *she* has the best legs," Feely whispered in my ear.

Following his line of sight, I locked eyes on the lanky blond on the other side of the room, attempting to hide her long hair beneath a dark wig.

Feeling irrationally irritated by Feely's observation, I strived for calm when all I wanted to do was take off this shitty platformed boot and clatter him with it.

Liz had on the tiniest black dress I'd ever seen. The fabric was so tight, it was practically sewn to her milky cream skin. Her legs looked long on a normal day, but when she wore those sky-high stilettos, they looked like *ladders*.

Knowing that my friend was looking at her the way *I* looked at her made me want to break up the band before we even started.

"No, no, no!" my sister screamed then, claiming everyone's immediate attention. "You are supposed to be wearing red, white, and blue, Gerard," she wailed in dismay as she circled Gibs. "Not green, white, and gold!"

"Not too shabby, huh?" Twirling around to show off his makeshift mini-dress, which clearly consisted of a couple tricolor flags hastily sewn together, Gibs draped an arm around my sister's shoulders and winked. "You can call me Paddy Spice."

"The lads are going to give us hell for this when they get here," Feely announced, looking thoroughly disgusted with himself. "I can hear Danny's smart-ass remarks already."

"Danny's a dick," Liz chimed in, moving to stand beside me. "And if he gives you guys shit for this, I'll take off my shoe and stab him with it." She looked at me and winked. "Especially you, birthday boy."

Oh fuck.

My poor, poor heart.

My birthday party went ahead without a hitch. As Feely predicted, Danny Call went to town on our costumes the moment he arrived but quickly shut his mouth when Posh Spice threatened to relocate the hole he pissed from. After that, he was exceptionally quiet.

Overall, it was a good party, but I'd be a liar if I said I wasn't counting down the minutes until my school friends went home. Because I wanted to be with my gang, the people who knew me better than everyone else. The friends I could be myself with and not have to worry about being perfectly polished or diplomatic because they accepted the raw, uncensored version of me in the same way I wholly accepted them.

Because Feely and I were both eleven this Halloween, we were allowed to head out trick-or-treating without a grown-up. Of course, Mam and Sadhbh had given us the speech about being responsible and looking out for the younger ones in our group. What they really meant to say was *Gibs and Claire are liabilities and, if at all possible, could we please prevent the two eejits from getting knocked down by a car or taken away in the back of a stranger's van.*

They didn't need to worry; I'd been keeping them alive for as long as I'd been here. Yeah, they were an absolute headache for me at times, but I knew I'd miss them if a stranger lured them away with sweets.

Toward the end of the night, when we were laden down with enough sweets to stack the shelves in the local shop, I purposefully fell back. Slowing my pace until my friends were a few houses ahead, I used my shoes as my excuse, but I had an ulterior motive.

I wanted to be alone with *her.*

"Can I talk to you about something, Liz?"

"Of course," she replied, automatically falling back to walk with me. "What's up?"

I didn't know how to phrase the thoughts that had been plaguing me all day, so I just blurted it right out. "He likes you."

"Who?"

Feeling another surge of intense jealousy, I pointed up the street to where Feely was wrestling with Gibs.

Liz looked to where I was pointing and nodded. "Yeah." She sighed heavily. "I know."

"You do?"

She sighed again. "He told me."

Okay, this was new information to me.

New information that I didn't like.

Nope, I didn't like it one fucking bit.

"You never said anything."

She shrugged. "I totally forgot about it until you brought it up."

"Oh." Trying to steady my emotions, I looked at her when I asked, "When did he tell you?"

"A while back," came her quiet response.

Another wave of jealousy surged through me, and this time it was more intense.

Feely liked Liz.

And Liz knew Feely liked her because he *told* her.

A while ago.

What the actual fuck?

When was anyone planning on telling *me?*

Jesus Christ, I wanted to kill him.

I'd never felt such an irrational surge of fury.

I wanted to ask her a dozen more questions, but I didn't.

Because I had no right to.

I didn't own her.

She was my best friend.

That's it.

I didn't have the right to interrogate her.

What the hell, though?

Seriously.

What the actual fuck!

"I didn't say it back, Hugh." Grabbing my hand, Liz pulled me to an abrupt stop on the middle of the footpath. "It was back in the summer when we all went bowling for his birthday. We were getting slushies at the counter, and he just blurted it out."

"What did he say exactly?" I managed to ask, sounding surprisingly calm given the fact that my entire world was crashing down around me. "Did Feely say he had a crush on you?"

"Patrick just told me that he liked me before asking if I wanted to go out with him." Her eyes were full of sincerity when she looked up at me. "I said no, Hugh. When he asked me to be his girlfriend, I said no."

She said no.

She turned him down.

Breathe, Hugh, breathe.

My chest rose and fell rapidly, and I exhaled a ragged breath, desperately trying to manage the emotions battering through my heart. She continued to hold my hand with both of hers and the way my pulse skyrocketed from the contact made it hard to form a coherent sentence.

Dread.

Fury.

Panic.

Hope.

I was drowning in *all* of them.

"You, ah…" My voice cracked and I roughly cleared my throat before casting a glance at her. Liz looked so composed, while I was losing my shit on the inside. Because the prospect of her being with someone else had suddenly hit me like a fucking wrecking ball.

My breathing was hard and uneven when I finally asked, "You really turned him down?"

I needed her to tell me one more time.

I needed the reassurance, dammit.

I needed a lifeline.

When Liz nodded in confirmation, the panic and dread that was suffocating me was purged from my lungs in an audible whoosh.

Jesus Christ.

"What did you say?" I managed to get out relatively unjumbled. "When he, uh, when Feely asked you?"

"I told him that I really liked him, too." Still gripping my hand with both of hers, she added, "But I couldn't be his girlfriend."

"Did he ask you why not?"

"Yeah, he did."

"What did you say?"

"I told him the same thing I tell any boy who asks."

So there were other lads.

What was I thinking; *of course* there were others.

Fuck.

"Which is?"

"That there's only one boy I want as my boyfriend." She kept her eyes on mine when she stepped closer, so close that I could feel her heart thundering in her chest. "And he's the only boy I'll ever say yes to."

DEAL OR NO DEAL

Hugh

NOVEMBER 2, 1998

"COME ON, HUGHIE," FEELY LEANED OVER OUR SHARED DESK AND WHISPERED ON Monday morning. "You can't honestly still be mad about the Lizzie thing."

"Oh, you better believe I am," I hissed back, roughly digging him in the side with my elbow. "Now fuck off back to your own side of the desk."

"Fine," he spat back, returning my elbow with an equally painful one of his own. "Go right ahead and sulk about it." Shaking his head, he retreated to his side of the desk but continued to scowl at me. "But you're pissed about nothing because I asked her months ago and she—"

"That makes it even *worse*," I interrupted, attention flicking between our teacher with his back to us and my traitorous friend. "Now, stop talking to me."

"No."

"Fine. Stop looking at me."

"No."

I narrowed my eyes in warning. "Feely—"

"She said no, Hugh," he continued to say in a hushed whisper. "Lizzie doesn't like me, lad. Not like that, so I don't know why you're so upset."

"I'm upset because you should have *told* me," I seethed. "Because you went behind my back."

"Why should I?" he demanded right back. "She's not your girlfriend." Narrowing his eyes, he tossed out, "Because you're too chicken to ask her."

"Who's a chicken?" Gibsie asked, turning around from the desk in front of us to join the fray.

"Hughie," Feely replied. "He's pissed off because I had the balls to ask Lizzie to be my girlfriend and he doesn't."

"No," I corrected hotly. "I'm pissed off with you because you did it behind my back."

"I didn't realize I needed your permission, Hugh."

"It's basic manners, Patrick."

"Well, I'm telling you now."

"Yeah," I snapped. "Four months after the event."

Feely shrugged. "Better late than never."

"Better *never* than never, more like."

"Oh, no, no, no." Gibs tutted and shook his head in disapproval. "You shouldn't have done that, Pa."

"Why the hell not?" Feely demanded, looking outraged.

"Because Hugo Boss-man loves our little viper," he replied solemnly, gray eyes wide and unblinking. "You know that."

"Yeah, well, you might want to tell *Hugo Boss-man* to stop being such a chicken," Feely grumbled. "Besides, I asked Liz out because I *like* her, not because I wanted to hurt him."

"He's not a chicken," Gibs defended. "He's a gentleman—at least, that's what my mam says."

"*Thank you*, Gibs," I replied, feeling vindicated.

"You *would* take his side." Feely rolled his eyes. "Especially since you're obsessed with his sister."

"That I am," Gibsie replied with a smile, only to frown a second later. "Hold up." Narrowing his eyes, he gave Feely a wary look. "You didn't ask Claire out when you were scampering around looking for a girlfriend, did you?"

"No, Gibs," Feely chuckled. "I wouldn't dream of it."

"Good. You go right ahead and keep on *not* dreaming about it," Gibsie replied in a warning tone. "Because I'm not as in control of my actions as he is." He pointed to me while keeping his eyes trained on Feely. "And I'll kill ya dead, Patrick Desmond Feely." Gibs made a throat slashing sign with his finger. "Don't let this angel face fool you," he continued, pointing to himself. "There's a killer lurking beneath. One that'll kill ya stone dead if you try to take my Claire-Bear, ya hear?"

"I hear you, Gibs," Feely replied, trying not to snicker, while I made no such effort. Slapping a hand over my mouth, I tried to stifle my laughter. "I promise you faithfully that I will never try to take your Claire-Bear," he continued, tone laced with amusement.

"Good," Gibsie replied, looking mollified. "Because I would miss you an awful lot if I had to kill you." Smiling again, Gibsie waved a finger back and forth between us. "Now, kiss and make up."

Repressing a groan, Feely turned to look at me. "I'm sorry for not telling you about Lizzie." He blew out another pained breath before adding, "I got my answer, though, and I won't ask her again. Not if she means that much to you."

"She does," I replied, still annoyed but willing to put it behind me if he was. "And

I'm not a chicken," I added, feeling the need to defend myself. "I'm just…I'm working up to it."

"Fair enough. You keep on working up to it, and I'll keep out of it." Smiling ruefully, Feely extended his hand to me. "Does that sound like a fair deal?"

"Yeah, lad," I replied, shaking his hand. "It's a deal."

I'm not a chicken," I added, feeling the need to defend myself. "I'm just... I'm working up to it."

"Yeah, lad," I replied, shaking his hand... deal. "

DEEPENING FEELINGS AND COPING MECHANISMS

Lizzie

NOVEMBER 15, 1998

THE FIRST TIME I TOOK A KNIFE TO MY SKIN WAS LAST SPRING, AND IT WAS THE RESULT of an accident peeling an apple. The slice of the knife through my fingertip brought an instant onslaught of pain and blood. But it also brought a strange sense of *clarity*. I remembered because that was a bad day and afterwards it was bearable.

The next time I hurt myself it was an almost accident with a bowl of piping hot porridge. I remembered it like it was yesterday. Sitting on the couch with the steaming hot bowl on my lap. Staring into the bowl, I slowly tipped it sideways to taste the lick of burn on my legs. Watching the thick, burning gruel seep through my tights, searing my flesh like a thousand needles.

The pain was instant, and it was *glorious*.

The third time was no accident, even though it was the most plausible. Intentionally sitting on the fire hearth in my nightdress, with my toes directly in front of the roaring fire, lying in wait, I remained motionless every time a spark landed on my bare legs. It wasn't until a larger knob of reddened coal landed on the hem of my nightdress that any of my family took notice of what I was doing. Even then, as my nightdress caught on fire and they quickly whipped it over my head, they didn't question my motives, putting my carelessness down to a reckless child getting too close to the fire.

Before then, I used to scratch and tear at my skin or burn myself in the bath when the pressure in my head got too much, but *nothing* I'd ever tried before compared to the peace I found from the sharp edge of a blade.

After that, I was a slave to the pain.

To the temporary relief from my pain.

The pain nobody could see.

The pain in my mind.

I was careful to conceal my scars from the outside world with stacks of bracelets on my wrists and oversized clothing. I protected my secret solace like my life depended on it, because in all honesty, on my really bad days, it *did*.

My weapon of choice became the blade, and my flesh became the battlefield, where I waged an internal war on the parts of me that couldn't be healed. The battle began on the inner side of my fleshy thighs, until there wasn't any room left to fight, and by that stage, the battlefield transferred to my stomach, and then to my breasts, until settling on my wrists.

The temporary relief from mental torture led me to playing with knives while other girls my age played with dolls. I was clever to conceal, to cut just deep enough to find relief but not bring attention to myself. After all, it was attention that had started the war in my head.

I didn't feel bad about it, either.

I was doing this for me.

I was trying to *survive* and had finally found a way to make it through the days without wanting to die.

"What's wrong?" Hugh asked for the tenth time since I'd arrived at his house. "I know something's wrong." We were sitting in his treehouse, where we were *supposed* to be reading, except instead he was worrying. *About me.*

"Hugh, I'm *grand*," I replied for the tenth time. "Stop worrying."

"I can't." He reached over and traced his finger over the part of my brow between my eyebrows. "You get a dimple right here when you're worried."

"I do?"

"Yeah, it's a tiny one, but it's there," he explained, brown eyes flicking to mine. "So I *know* something's bothering you."

Knowing that he wouldn't give in until he got his answer, I sighed heavily before admitting, "It's the nightmares."

Concern filled his eyes. "They're happening a lot again?"

I nodded.

"What about the lady?" He didn't laugh or smirk when he asked. He looked genuinely concerned. "Have you been seeing her, too?"

"I'm not supposed to talk about it." It pissed my father off and I couldn't risk getting on his bad side. "You know that."

"You can tell me anything," Hugh pushed, unwilling to let it go. "And I want to hear about it, Liz."

I arched a disbelieving brow. "You want to hear about *my* mental delusions?"

"You're not mental, Liz." Reaching for my hand, he pulled me onto his lap. "And you're not delusional, either." Wrapping his arms around me, he snuggled me tightly. "But you may be guilty of being a little weirdo."

"You dick," I snickered, elbowing his stomach. "You know what they say about weirdos, don't you?"

"They're drawn to fellow weirdos?" Hugh mused with a knowing smile. "That must be why I'm so obsessed with you."

My heart skipped a solid three beats in my chest when he said that.

Feeling irrationally excited, I burrowed in closer, wishing I could weld my body to his and never be parted. "Hugh?"

"Hmm?"

"Do you think she's real?"

"The scary lady?"

I nodded. "The one in my dreams."

"I've never seen the one in your head," he replied, sounding sincere. "But I know what we saw that day, Liz, and if you say that's her, then I believe you."

"You do?"

"Yeah." He leaned back to look at me. "I do."

"I think you might be the first person who ever has," I whispered, fingers knotting in his hoodie. "Thanks."

"Don't thank me for believing you," he replied, sounding pained. "Thank me when I catch her and prove to everyone else that we were telling the truth all along."

My eyes widened. "You want to catch her?"

He nodded. "Oh, you better believe that I'm *going* to catch her." Smirking, he added, "She's the kind of weirdo *not* welcome in our club."

I shuddered in revulsion. "Definitely not."

"When I catch her, our first pit stop will be the car wash," he continued to say, lips twitching with amusement. "We'll probably have to put her through the platinum wash twice to get the filth off her—and borrow an angle grinder to tame those claws."

I couldn't help but laugh because Hugh had somehow made something so traumatizing funny instead.

ARE WE GETTING A NEW MILLENNIUM OR NOT?

Hugh

DECEMBER 31, 1998

"WHO'S READY TO WELCOME THE NEW MILLENNIUM?" GIBSIE ASKED WHEN HE SAUN-tered into my room on New Year's Eve with a party streamer balanced between his lips. Laden down with a stack of leftover selection boxes containing his favorite chocolate bars and with a party hat perched on his head, he nestled down on my beanbag, armed and ready to ring in the New Year.

"You're a year early, Gibs," Feely replied, focusing on the game we were playing.

"Yeah, Feely, I know," Gibsie huffed, sounding annoyed. "That's what I meant when I asked who's ready to *welcome* it."

"He means the new millennium begins in 2000, Gibs," I explained calmly, as I continued to kick Feely's ass on *FIFA*. "We're still in 1998, lad."

"The how come *he* said it's next year?" he argued in a disbelieving tone.

"Because *he's* right," Feely shot back dryly. "It *is* next year."

"But how is it next year when you said it's *not* next year?" Gibsie complained, sounding skeptical. "Are we getting a new millennium or not?"

Feely shook his head and muttered, "You'll have to take this one, Hugh."

"It's eight o'clock in the evening on the very last day of 1998. When the clock strikes midnight, it'll be 1999." Pausing the game, I turned to our friend and continued to explain. "So tonight, as in right now, it's 1998, and in four hours' time, it'll be 1999. The new millennium comes at the *end* of 1999, not at the start."

"So *next* year?" Gibsie asked, brows furrowed.

"Yes, Gibs." I nodded eagerly. "*Exactly.*"

"Okay, that makes sense." He looked thoughtful for a moment before turning to scowl at Feely. "Why didn't you just say that at the *beginning,* Patrick."

Feely opened his mouth to protest, only to think better of it and mutter the words "give me strength" under his breath instead.

It was at that exact moment my bedroom door opened inwards, and my father's head appeared. Of course, he didn't look like the father I used to have, with a full, untamed beard and sunken eyes. The parts of his face that weren't covered in hair were gaunt and hollow. He looked like the definition of a shell of a man. "Are you all settled in for the night, lads?"

"Pete!" Gibsie cheered, looking as thrilled to see my father as Claire did when he made one of his sporadic appearances. "That's a fancy shirt."

"I thought I best make an effort given the night."

Make an effort.

What a fucking joke.

"Are you and Sinead going to Old Hall House for the night?"

"We are, Gibs." Dad smiled before turning his attention to me. "Are you all set for ringing in the New Year with your friends, son?"

Choosing to ignore him like he did me, I resumed playing *FIFA*, while my eyes burned holes in the television screen. Feely, sensing my discomfort, nudged my shoulder with his in silent solidarity.

Because he got it.

"Pete! The taxi's here, love!" I heard my mother call from downstairs, followed by, "Claire! Lizzie's here with Caoimhe."

My heart started to gallop almost as loudly as my sister's heavy footfalls as she thundered out of her room and down the stairs, screaming "Lizzie, Lizzie, Lizzie!"

Yeah, Baby Sister.

Me, too.

——————

"You know what I just thought?" Feely announced several hours later. "If Caoimhe marries Mark, then Liz and Gibs will be family."

"Shit, you're right," I muttered, brows creasing. "They'd be in-laws."

"No, we wouldn't," Gibs protested, sounding horrified. "Because he is *not* my brother."

"Definitely not," Claire agreed from her perch on my bed, where she was painting her toenails. "Ew, Patrick. Don't insult the Gibson genes."

"*Thank you*, Claire-Bear," Gibsie replied, stretching a hand up to high-five my sister. She paused mid-toe to pat his hand. "That shite-hawk will never be my family."

"His father *did* marry your mam, lad," Feely reminded him with a good-natured chuckle. "That makes him your stepbrother."

"Don't fucking remind me," Gibsie groaned, retraining his focus on the game of *FIFA 98* we were playing. "Keith Allen." He sniffed the air like the name offended him.

"He should be called Keith Alien because that's what he is." He tapped furiously on the PlayStation controller. "A fucking parasitic intruder."

"What did I miss?" Lizzie asked, returning with an armful of snacks from the kitchen. Dressed in a long-sleeved, flannel shirt and baggy jeans, she looked beautiful. Dropping a packet of Minstrels on my lap, she eyed the beanbag I was sharing with Feely before deciding against it. She then moved for my bed before hilariously recoiling in horror when she eyed the unfolding pampering session.

Backing away from my sister as inconspicuously as she could, Liz found sanctuary with Gibs on a purple, inflatable *Groovy Chick* armchair. The armchair said sister had traipsed into my room with earlier.

Claire had insisted that we all stay in the same room and have a slumber party. She had grander notions of pillow fights, gossip, and girl talk and was insistent that we stay in her room. However, my room possessed the PlayStation, and the boys held the majority, hence the current setup.

"Who's a parasitic intruder, Thor?" Liz asked, butting his hip with hers to scoot over. "Who do I need to hurt?"

"You would, wouldn't ya?" Gibs chuckled, shoving over to let her slide onto the seat next to him. "Little viper."

"Keith Allen," Claire chimed in, toenail painting resumed. "And I wholeheartedly agree."

Oh, here we go.

Stifling a groan, I flopped back on the beanbag and braced myself for trouble.

"I was just saying that if your sister marries Mark, then you and Gibs will be family," Feely explained, clearly out of the loop when it came to our friend and his feelings toward his stepfamily.

It wasn't Feely's fault. He didn't live on the street, and Gibsie was a master concealer. The worse shit got at home, the more outrageously funny he became. "According to Gibs, that's not a good thing."

"It's not," Liz agreed, sharing a packet of Tayto with Gibs. "Besides, we don't need them to get married to be family."

"Exactly," he said, wholeheartedly agreeing with her.

"Can we not talk about that creep?" Claire asked, looking almost as disgusted as she sounded. "It's bad enough he's in our lounge, sucking face with Caoimhe." A shudder rolled through her. "Ew."

"Agreed," I chimed in, grinning when I scored another goal against Feely's team. "It's Christmas, lads, not Halloween."

"Speaking of Christmas..." With a hearty chuckle, Gibsie hooked a playful arm around Liz's neck and pulled her close. "I have a present for you."

"Don't you dare," the rest of us started to protest, but it was too late for that when a painfully long and painfully foul-smelling trump ripped through the air.

"Oh my God, Gibs, did you just *fart*?" Liz choked out through fits of laughter, as she tried to wrestle her way out of Gibsie's headlock. "Ah, ah, I think I can taste it."

"Breathe it in," Gibsie encouraged, using his foot to fan the air toward her. "That's my special recipe."

"Jesus Christ, what did you eat?" Feely demanded, using his T-shirt to cover his nose. "It smells like something *died* inside of you, lad."

"You know I like baked beans with my spuds," Gibs laughed before breaking into song. "*Beans, beans, are good for your heart, the more you eat, the more you fart, the more you fart, the more you eat—*"

"*The more you sit on the toilet seat,*" Claire chimed in, pegging her nose with her fingers. "How many tins of beans did you *eat*, Gerard?"

"Hey, at least it wasn't spinach," he laughed back before crooning, "*Popeye the sailor man, he lives in a caravan, he lives with his mammy, she tickles her fanny, he's Popeye the sailor man...*"

"You are *sick*," Feely snickered, shaking his head. "Absolutely vile, lad."

"I have more," Gibsie offered, still laughing. "Do ye want to hear them?"

"No!" all four of us chorused.

"Fine," he huffed before retraining his attention on Liz, who was trying to break free of his hold. "Come here, Liz. Santa forgot to deliver your present, so he asked me to give it to you."

"If you fart on me again, I will kill you dead," she squealed, trying and failing to scramble to safety. "Fair warning, Gibs."

"Too late," he chuckled, wrestling her onto the floor. "It's on the way."

"Gibsie, no!" Laughing hysterically, Liz pushed at his chest when he started making engine noises. "Don't you dare—ahh!"

"Brmm, brmm, brmm," he snickered, making engine noises as he slowly lowered his ass onto her face and let out the vilest ripper of a fart. "Merry Christmas!"

"Ahh! I can taste it," Liz screamed. "I can taste beans on my tongue!"

I wanted to help her, but I was too busy laughing uncontrollably.

Heaving and gagging, Liz scrambled out from beneath him and dove for my bedroom window.

Pushing the window open, she leaned over the sill, gulping for air through fits of laughter. "If I get conjunctivitis from you, I swear to God, Thor, I will make it my life's mission to torment you."

"Ooh, fighting words, viper." Jumping to his feet, Gibs banged on his chest like a gorilla. "I'm ready for ya."

"Oh yeah?" Challenge accepted, Liz climbed onto the windowsill and took aim at Gibs. "You think you're hard enough to take me on, do ya?"

"Oh, you better believe it, viper. I'm Matt and Jeff combined," Gibs goaded, beckoning her with his fingers to go for it. "I'm the third brother of the Hardy Boyz."

"Yeah, well, get ready for Lita's moonsault, bitch," Liz warned and then proceeded to turn her back to him and crouch.

"Liz, no, no, no, there's no padding!" Gibs tried to protest, hurrying to intercept her. "Wait! You're going to break your—ahhhh!"

"No fucking way!" I cheered completely mesmerized by the girl who executed the perfect backflip off my bedroom window. Not only that but she managed to flatten Gibs like a pancake.

"I'm dead," he wailed from beneath her, while my sister squealed from behind a pillow. "I'm dead, I tell ya!"

"Smell that, Thor," Liz cackled, pinning him to the carpet, wrestling style. "*Victory*."

"You are a strange and terrifying female," he mused. "But an unforgettable one."

Cackling, she helped him up. "Are you hurt?"

"Only my pride."

PART 8

Monsters Everywhere

I'LL BE SEEING YA, KID

Lizzie

IT HAPPENED AGAIN LAST NIGHT.

The monster attacked me in my sleep again, hurting me so severely that I brought my injuries back to reality with me.

It hurt to sit on my chair in class, and by the time big lunch rolled around, I was close to losing my mind. Every part of my body ached, but it was my mind that was truly shaken up. Because it was getting harder and harder to tell the difference between what was real and what was my imagination.

Reaching my breaking point, I avoided my friends at break, escaping from the classroom as soon as the lunch bell rang. Praying for an escape and seeking out solace, I hid behind the wall at the back of the pitch, knowing Shannon and Claire wouldn't find me here.

Sitting cross-legged on the grass, I slumped against the wall behind me and tried to breathe through the pain. I wasn't sure which was worse: the pain in my mind or the one between my legs.

The scalding-hot tears trickling down my cheeks were my only assurance that I was, in fact, awake and in school. I could feel, touch, taste, and see my tears. Those were *real*, which meant I was, too.

Sniffling, I placed my trembling hands on my thighs and forced myself to look. My body tensed when I saw the claw marks the monster had left on my skin.

Dark purplish fingerprints were imprinted into my flesh. They looked bad, but I knew they paled in comparison to the damage the monster inflicted inside of me. On the parts I couldn't see in the mirror.

The scariest part of it all was that I thought a small part of me might be starting to like it, which didn't make any sense because I *knew* I didn't. I hated the monster, and I never wanted to go to sleep at night because I dreaded him crawling into my body. But lately, something strange was happening inside of me—a horrendous pulsing feeling that made me feel sick.

It was growing deep down inside of me and got worse when *boys* looked at me. Especially Hugh. When he looked at me, it grew so strong, it felt like I had another heartbeat in my belly. The worst part of it all was I thought I might *like* it.

I was *not* a good person.

Crying harder now, I balled my hands into fists and hit myself in the head repeatedly, hoping and praying I could somehow erase the bad thoughts.

I'm bad.

I'm bad.

I'm bad.

My fists continued to flail until I grew exhausted from the effort it was taking to bludgeon myself. Still trembling, I clenched my eyes shut and dragged in several deep breaths, desperate to steady myself before the bell rang.

"This seat taken?" Startled from the sudden intrusion, I turned to see Joey Lynch take a seat on the grassy embankment beside me. "Why are you crying, kid?"

Sniffling, I quickly batted the tears from my cheeks and cleared my throat. "I'm not."

He arched a disbelieving brow but made no further comment. In his hands, he held a battered-looking Discman.

Instantly distracted by his presence, I turned my attention to the sound of music drifting from the tiny earbuds in his ears. "What are you listening to?"

He didn't respond; instead, he took his right earbud out and handed it to me. When I pressed it to my ear, it took me a few seconds to register the song blasting as Michael Jackson's "They Don't Care About Us."

"Found it at work," he explained, holding the Discman up. "Boss was chucking it." He shrugged before adding, "Just in case ya assumed I lifted it."

"Why would I think you stole it?"

He shrugged but didn't respond. Instead, he took a quick glance around us, scoping out the area, before retrieving a rolled-up cigarette and lighter from the pocket of his school trousers.

Intrigued, I watched as he wet his bottom lip before placing the cigarette in his mouth and lighting the other end.

"So." Joey took a deep drag of the cigarette and then seemed to hold the smoke in his lungs for an extra-long beat before slowly exhaling. "Feel like naming the culprit yet?"

"The culprit of what?"

"Your tears."

"No, because I *wasn't* crying," I snapped, attention riveted to the strange circles of smoke he exhaled from his mouth. "You know, you'll get expelled if the teachers catch you with a cigarette in your mouth."

His lips twitched. "Is that so?"

"Yeah," I replied, scrunching my nose up when the sickly sweet smell invaded my senses. "That doesn't smell like a normal cigarette."

"Because it's not," he mused, sounding like he didn't have a care in the world. He took another deep drag and exhaled slowly before adding, "We all have our ways of getting through the day, don't we, kid?"

"Yeah, but you're only in sixth class." I frowned, feeling confused. "You won't get into secondary school in September if they catch you taking drugs, Joey."

His green eyes flicked to mine in challenge. "Are you going to rat me out?"

"No." I shook my head. "I know how to keep a secret."

"Yeah." He exhaled another cloud of smoke. "Me, too, kid."

Sighing heavily, I hooked my arms around my legs and rested my chin on my knees. "I bet I'm better at it than you are."

"Hmm." His lips twitched, and he turned his attention back to staring straight ahead. "So let's have it." Flicking a trail of ash onto the grass, Joey took another drag of his self-made cigarette. "Who made you cry?"

"Why?" I arched a brow. "Are you going to beat them up?"

"I might," he replied with a lazy shrug. "If you need me to."

"I don't need anyone."

Now he *did* smile. "I figured."

"What's so funny?"

"You," he replied. "You remind me of someone I used to know."

"Who?"

"My younger self," he surprised me by saying, before turning to face me. "Listen," he said, all business now, scowl firmly back in place. "We can do this the easy way or the hard way, but either way, we're still going to end up at the same conclusion."

"Which is?"

"You telling me who made ya cry, and me fixing it for ya."

"Why?" I narrowed my eyes. "Why would you help me?"

"Why would *you* help me?" Joey shot back, fisting the jumper he was wearing. I knew it came from the bag I had given him because I remembered the green thread mam had used to fix the sleeve.

"I did that for *Shannon*," I explained. "Besides, you don't even like me."

"I don't have to like you in order to help you," he explained calmly, taking another drag of cigarette. "I just have to help."

"Just like that."

"Just like that, kid." Letting his head fall back, he exhaled heavily and let his shoulders relax for what I thought might have been the first time ever. "Besides, I don't like owing people."

I didn't know how to answer that, so I kept quiet, dutifully studying the scary boy sitting beside me.

The one I knew wasn't like the others.

He remained beside me, smoking his strange cigarette until there was nothing left. It wasn't until his cigarette was quenched and the tiny stub was tucked in his pocket that Joey spoke again. "I *will* return the favor, kid."

"Oh yeah?" I replied, tracking his every move as he stood up and dusted himself off. "How?"

"That's up to you," was all Joey replied before he turned around and walked away. "I'll be seeing ya, kid."

RECTUS ABDOMINUS

Hugh

GIBS DIDN'T COME TO SCHOOL TODAY, WHICH WAS BEYOND STRANGE CONSIDERING WE got cake from the teacher on our birthdays.

In all the years I'd known him, which was literally *all* the years of my life, he'd never once refused cake on his birthday. Hell, he even demolished the cake given out on *my* birthday.

That could only mean one of two things: either he was at death's door or had passed through it.

When I reached his front porch after school and tried to let myself inside like I'd done every day since I'd learned how to walk, I was met with resistance.

The door was locked.

Since when did we use locks?

It felt strange to ring the doorbell of a house I knew the alarm codes to, but I did it and waited impatiently.

After about twenty-five rings of the doorbell, it finally opened.

When my eyes locked on the asshole in front of me, I felt my blood run cold.

Mark Allen.

I swear, this prick set my teeth on edge.

"Where's Gibs?" I asked, not bothering with formalities. I knew he didn't like me, and the feeling was mutual.

Mark Allen had a god complex and couldn't stand that someone younger than him could trump him intellectually. That someone was me, and I took great pleasure in kicking the shit out of him with my mind.

"How the fuck am I supposed to know?" Mark seethed, standing in the doorway in a pair of low hung sweats and nothing else. "What's with ringing the doorbell a hundred fucking times. I was trying to work out, asshole!"

"Hopefully your brain," I shot back dryly, trying not to heave at the sight of the creature. "Because, evidently, your rectus abdominus are a lost cause."

"Hold up." He narrowed his eyes. "What did you say about rectum?"

I smirked, feeling amused. "Case in point."

"Biggs, you better tell me what you want right now or get the fuck off my doorstep," he snarled, taking a menacing step toward me. "Because I am in no mood for your hotshot lingo."

Instead of flinching, I laughed. "You really are thick as shit, aren't you?"

"Just you wait." He pointed at my face and nodded grimly. "Another couple of years and I'm going to kick the living shit out of your smart ass."

"I'm right here," I laughed back. "Give it your best shot."

"Oh, you'd like that, wouldn't ya?" he sneered. "Clever little bastard like you would probably have a camera filming."

I grinned. "Why don't you try it and see if you're right?"

"Why don't you climb back up the hole you came out of," he roared before unceremoniously slamming the door in my face.

"Actually, I'm the product of a caesarean section, asshole," I goaded. "So your attempt to insult me is a futile one."

The sound of the lock clicking filled my ears.

The fucker.

"I hate that guy," I muttered to myself, glaring at the closed door.

Well, he couldn't keep me out that easily.

Skulking around the side of the house, I scaled the old oak tree outside Mark's open window, the room that used to be Beth's, before launching myself at the window.

Easy peasy.

Climbing through the window, I landed lightly on my feet, only to scowl at the absolute pigsty that was his room.

Graphically explicit posters of naked girls adorned the walls, and he had a bunch of instant photos littered on his nightstand. I didn't bother investigating those because whatever piqued Mark's interest would be of zero interest to me.

He clearly used the floor as his waste bin because there was more rubbish scattered over it than inside our wheelie bin. He didn't even have a sheet on his mattress, and there was an obvious—and very large—urine stain in the middle.

This asshole was feral.

Abandoning his room before the fumes altered the chemicals in my brain, I headed straight for Gibsie's room and let myself inside.

I didn't bother to knock because we didn't do that kind of thing. I strolled over to his bed and inspected his limp body, huddled under the duvet. "Are ya dead, Gibs?"

Startled by the sound of my voice, Gibs shot straight up, only to hiss out a pained breath and gingerly settle back down on his side. "I am, lad."

"Is it catching?" I asked, sitting down beside him. "You do look like you're halfway dead all right." I reached out a hand and touched his clammy forehead. "Jesus, you're burning up, lad." Concern roared to life inside of me. "You're drenched in sweat, Gibs."

"I'm okay, Hugh," he whispered, trembling beneath the covers, as he curled up in the fetal position. "I'm always okay."

"Where's your mam?"

"Work."

"Keith?"

"Work."

"Mark's babysitting you?"

He nodded stiffly.

Frowning in concern, I touched his brow again, feeling unhappy about leaving him here. "Can you get up?"

"Why?"

"Because it's your birthday and I'm not going to leave you here on your own," I explained, standing up. "Come over to our house, and we'll look after you until your mam gets home from work." Smiling, I added, "Claire's baking you a cake—although, fair warning, I caught her drooling all over the spoon."

"But I'm supposed to stay here with him."

"Yeah, fat lot of good Mark is," I grumbled. "He's too busy 'working out' to bother checking on you. You should have heard the way he roared at me when I knocked on the door. He was raging that I disturbed him." Shaking my head, I reached for his hand and helped him into a sitting position. "Nah, you're coming home with me." Draping his duvet over his shoulders, I wrapped an arm around my oldest friend and led him out of his room.

"And where the fuck do you think you're going?" Mark demanded when we reached the landing. He stepped in front of the staircase and folded his arms across his chest. "Your mother left me in charge of you." He turned his attention to Gibs and said, "Get back into bed now."

A shiver racked through Gibs, and he reached for my hand, squeezing it almost as tightly as Lizzie did when this creep was around. "He's coming with me," I warned, taking a protective stance in front of my friend.

"I'm in charge of where he goes." Mark's nostrils flared with temper. "He's my brother."

"No, you fucking cretin," I seethed, whacking his hand away when he tried to grab my friend. "He's *my* brother. Now get out of our way."

He smiled darkly. "Make me, egghead."

Now, I rarely lost my temper; in fact, I was praised on my ability to keep the head, but this bully drew the worst out of me.

Mark Allen was a mean bastard. He was always goading, mocking, and tormenting Gibs, and when he wasn't making my friend cry, he was making my babysitter cry.

Difference was, I wasn't Gibsie or Caoimhe. I wasn't Claire or Liz, either. I wouldn't stand for it. Yeah, I was younger than him, but I was tall for my age, and I wasn't afraid to throw down, even if the probability of getting my ass handed to me was high.

I had no doubt Mark could hammer the living daylights out of me, but the fact that I wasn't afraid to go head-to-head with him, with the knowledge that I would surely get in a few shots of my own, caused him to pause a moment.

Yeah, because it wouldn't be a good look for Mark to get caught battering kids. He had a reputation to uphold—one he had sold to every adult in our community.

Everyone loved this guy.

Everyone.

I tried to tell Sadhbh about the bullying, but she wouldn't hear a word said against her precious stepson. I tried to tell Caoimhe, and she believed me even less.

"Do you really want to do this with me?" I asked him, unwilling to back down. "Right here and now?"

Mark must have realized how serious I was because he shook his head and sneered, "You're not worth going to jail over," before shoving past us.

Taking that as my cue to haul ass, I carted my friend down the staircase and out the front door before his bully had a change of heart.

"Thanks for that," Gibs said when we were in my driveway.

"No bother, lad," I replied, guiding him up the porch steps. "Anytime."

"I might hold you to that," he chuckled, still clutching my hand.

For some strange reason, I didn't pull my hand from his, not even when we got inside. Instead, I let him hold my hand for a solid five minutes before he finally let go.

CINEMA TRIPS AND GOBSTOPPER LICKS

Hugh

FEBRUARY 20, 1999

I DIDN'T EXPECT TO RUN INTO THE CRETIN SO SOON AFTER OUR PREVIOUS ALTERCA-
tion, but that's what happened when I opened the door the following day and found
him on my doorstep.

Like a bad smell the street couldn't shake, Mark Allen stood in front of me. He had
his arms resting on either side of the doorframe in his obvious attempt to make himself
look as imposing as possible. If he was expecting me to cower in fear, then he hadn't
learned a damn thing. Because, like I'd say a thousand times, he could kick me up and
down the street and I'd still come back swinging at the fucker.

The only reason I hadn't returned the favor and slammed the door in his face was
the fact that Gibs was there, too.

"What?" I asked in a flat tone.

"I was sent over to ask if you and your sister wanted to go to the cinema with us,"
the cretin surprised me by saying.

"The cinema." I arched a disbelieving brow. "With *you*?"

"Do you want to go or not?" Mark snapped, sounding impatient.

"Do I want to *go*?" My eyes bulged in their sockets. "Asshole, you must be off your
rocker if you think or imagine I would *ever* willingly breathe the same air as—"

"Please come, Hugh," Gibsie cut in, looking up at me with a pleading expression.
"Please."

"Come where?" Claire asked, slipping under my arm. "Oh, hi, Gerard." The beaming smile she had for our friend quickly morphed into a scowl when her eyes landed
on Mark. "Ew."

"Caoimhe's meeting us at the cinema," Gibsie continued to say, eyes locked on
mine. "The old one in town. It's her present to me." He shrugged helplessly. "You know,
for my birthday."

Dammit, Gibs!

He had to play the birthday card there.

"I'll come." Claire was quick to accept the invitation. "Hold on," she added, quickly backpedaling through the hallway. "I'll go ask Mam for money."

Dammit, Claire!

Now I had to go because there was no way on God's green earth that I would allow *my* baby sister to get in that asshole's car without me.

My bad mood quickly lifted when I walked into the cinema foyer thirty minutes later and locked eyes on Lizzie, standing off to the side, while her sister paid for tickets at the counter. Claire and Gibs made a beeline for the refreshments, but I couldn't move.

Momentarily struck dumb at the sight of her, I could do nothing but stare like a dope and soak the image of her into my mind.

Liz was wearing an oversized, green babydoll dress, an even bigger white cardigan, frilly white ankle socks, and black army boots. Her hair was loose and flowing over her shoulders, and she had a plaster on her knee. The clothes she was wearing swamped her and clearly belonged to Caoimhe, but somehow, Liz made it look so fucking cool. She oozed a lazy sort of confidence that wasn't common in girls our age.

She was staring off blankly, but when I caught her attention, her eyes literally sparked to life, and then she was moving, weaving through the crowded foyer like a woman on a mission.

When Liz reached me, she didn't hesitate to wrap her arms around my neck, nor did she think twice about burying her face in my neck. "Good," was all she said, inhaling deeply and displaying yet another strange quirk that I found adorable.

Not hi, hey, or hello.

Just *good*.

Somehow that was better than any other mundane greeting.

I could feel the tension leave her body when I wrapped my arms around her waist and pulled her close. She grew even more pliant when I took her hand in mine.

I didn't give a shit if any of our friends saw me holding her hand. I'd long since left the embarrassed-boy phase behind me.

All I felt when I held her hand these days was privilege and pride.

Because Liz picked *me* to hold her hand.

"Thank God you're here," I told her. "I thought I'd be stuck between Dumb and Dumber, and Barbie and Ken."

"I thought the same thing," she laughed, holding on to my hand with both of hers. "I've missed you."

"You saw me two days ago, Liz."

"I know."

Not only did her response tug at my heart but it made all kinds of *other* things happen inside of me, but I managed to distract myself by asking, "So what film are we watching?"

"*Varsity Blues*," she replied with a shrug. "At least I think that's what Caoimhe said it was called."

Liz looked about as interested in being here as I sounded on the front porch when the cretin suggested it. While I had little to no interest in being here, I was thoroughly invested in the company.

"Come on, guys!" Claire called out, waving like a blinged-up unicorn at the other end of the foyer. That wasn't an exaggeration, either. My sister was literally wearing her My Little Pony hairband—the one with sparkles and a pink, glittery horn. Claire pointed to where the others were heading into screen one before adding, "I'm going to lick your gobstopper if you don't hurry up, Hugh."

Liz grinned. "You know what that means, don't you?"

"Of course I do," I grumbled, guiding her toward the door labeled screen one. "It means the curly-haired demon has *already* licked my gobstopper."

"Yep." My best friend threw her head back and laughed. "Exactly."

Everything seemed to be going fine until about three-quarters of the way into the movie when Lizzie started to twitch uncontrollably in her chair. With her knees and shoulders bopping restless, Liz pulled at every thread on the sleeve of her cardigan until it started to unravel. She then proceeded to remove every one of the many bracelets and bangles on her wrists before putting them back on, only to remove them right away.

Leaning over, I placed my hand on hers and whispered, "Are you okay?"

Nodding, she readjusted her cardigan when it slipped off her shoulder. "Yeah, I'm just..." She looked around before retraining her attention on the screen in front of us. "I think I need to use the bathroom."

"Do you want me to walk you..." I started to say, but she was already out of her seat and bolting off in the direction of the exit.

Beyond confused by her sudden shift in mood, I looked to Gibsie and Claire to see if they had noticed what I had, but they were engrossed in the movie. I glanced over at Mark and Caoimhe, only to instantly regret it when I spotted them eating the faces off each other.

Fucking disgusting.

When ten minutes passed and Liz still hadn't returned, I slid out of my seat and handed Gibs my popcorn before heading outside to search for her.

Checking all the toilet cubicles and coming up empty, a nervous energy started to rise up inside of me. My Spidey-Senses were on high alert.

Where'd she go?

Something was off.

Something wasn't right.

Wandering through the foyer, I checked out front before making my way back through the corridor, checking behind every unlocked door as I went.

It wasn't until I pushed through the exit doors at the back of the building and locked eyes on the back of her blond head that I felt any ounce of relief, and even then, it was thwarted by the sight of her tearstained face.

"What happened?" I demanded, feeling my heart rate spike. "Liz."

Sniffling, she turned around and looked at me, giving me a front-row view to the heartbreak in her eyes.

She didn't even try to conceal it.

Not from me.

No, I was given a private audience to her devastation as it played out in her stormy, blue eyes.

"I don't know," she finally strangled out, walking right into my arms. "I think I might be going a bit mad again, Hugh."

"Everyone's a bit mad," I replied, wrapping my arms around her. "Look at my dad, Liz. He's a lot more than a bit mad."

"Yeah, but at least your dad knows the difference between real life and his imagination," she whispered, clinging onto me for dear life. "I don't."

"That doesn't mean you're mad, Liz," I reassured her, pulling her close. "It's okay. It's just how you think sometimes."

"But it's all wrong, Hugh," she cried harder now. "I don't want to think this way."

I knew that, and I wanted to have the answer to all her problems, but I was only eleven and trying to learn on the job. I had never encountered these problems with Claire. Her biggest concern was the safest method to capture butterflies and ladybirds.

But *this* girl?

This girl felt sadness in her *bones*.

Liz felt things deeper than other people our age and she always had. Some days were better than others, and some days were worse. Today was one of her harder ones but telling her that wouldn't help.

"Today is a *good* day," I told her instead, giving her the words she needed to hear. "You are having a *good* day, Lizzie Young." I pulled her closer to me, wanting to envelope her body with mine and protect her from the world. "You're happy and safe because you're with me, and you know I won't let anything bad happen to you."

"I am?"

"Yes, you are," I coaxed, being the reassurance she needed when her mind played tricks on her. "You are right here with me, happy and smiling, and having the *best* day."

"With you."

"With me," I promised. "And you're healthy, and brave, and smart. Just like me."

"Just like you?"

I nodded in confirmation. "And you know what else you are?"

"What?"

"You're my best friend."

Her breath hitched. "What about Patrick?"

"What about him?" I replied, keeping my eyes on hers. "You're the only one who really knows me, Liz."

"Same," she replied, looking up at me with lonesome, blue eyes. "Nobody gets me like you do."

"I'm going to keep you safe," I promised, tucking her hair behind her ear. "Always."

"No matter what?"

"Yeah, Liz," I confirmed, not truly comprehending the vow I had taken upon my young shoulders. "No matter what."

MOODS SHIFT AND THUNDER ROLLS

FEBRUARY 26, 1999

MY MIND WAS SLIPPING AGAIN.

I could feel the shift in mood coming down the tracks like a freight train, aimed and poised to annihilate every ounce of progress I'd made.

"Get down on your knees and beg me to stay…"

"Stop fighting me and I won't hurt you next time…"

"Be a good girl and take your pill…"

"You crazy, little whore, I can feel you getting off on this…"

"Bend over, slut, and remember, if you scream, I'll kill her…"

Plagued by nightmares and memories of a life that never existed for me, I relied heavily on the scissors hidden under my mattress to get me through the days.

Stars and scars, gaping and hollow, cut, cut, cut, slice, slice, slice.

The bloodier the mess, the longer the peace of mind.

Imprints on my skin that mirrored the pain imposed on my heart.

"Elizabeth, come out, come out, wherever you are…"

"You can't hide from me…"

"I can feel you inside me…"

"I can find you anywhere, little, busy Lizzie bee…"

My thoughts raced so wildly that not even the medication put in the back of my throat could tame the beast awakening inside of me.

I wanted to take off all my clothes and feel the sun on my skin.

I wanted to peel the skin from my bones, strip by strip, until everyone could see how impure I was on the inside.

I wanted to throw myself out of my bedroom window and impale my torso on the window bars below.

I craved to know how it would feel to sever my carotid artery and watch the blood drain from my body.

Would there be enough to drown the monster?

Maybe I could sharpen my nails into daggers like the scary lady and kill him in my dreams.

Losing grip on reality wasn't something unfamiliar to me, but every time it happened, I was consumed by the fear that I might not make it back this time.

Please don't let me make it back this time.

THINK TWICE BEFORE YOU TOUCH MY GIRL

Hugh

MARCH 17, 1999

I KNEW LIZ WAS STRUGGLING.

I just didn't know how to help her.

For weeks she had been withdrawing from life, barely speaking to her friends, and losing track of time.

I hadn't seen her this sad in a long time, and it scared the shit out of me. Because I could see the pain in her eyes and had no way of taking it away for her. I couldn't fix this problem for her.

Even as kids, when Liz was sad, she wasn't just sad. She was *devastated*. She always seemed to feel things deeper than the rest of us and then soaked up all the pain around her like a sponge. Excellent at masking, she had learned how to hide her turmoil from her friends.

Not me, though.

I saw right through her armor, which was how I knew she was struggling lately.

She still came over to my house as often as always, but a lot of the time it felt like she was only here physically. It was as if her mind was somewhere else entirely, and I wasn't the only one to notice. I knew my mam saw it, too, because she often took Liz to one side for chats the rest of us weren't privy to.

I wanted to help her, but whenever I asked her what was happening, Liz just shrugged and told me that it didn't matter.

Of course it mattered.

Anything that made her feel *this* sad mattered.

I knew she had mental health issues. My mother had explained that much to me, but I still felt like I was being kept in the dark. I wasn't stupid, and I wasn't naive like Claire and Gibs. I could handle whatever was happening to my best friend, if the grown-ups in our lives gave me the chance to.

I understood why the grown-ups used kid gloves when handling delicate issues, but I was the wrong target to wrap up in cotton wool. Because whether Mam wanted to admit it or not, I wasn't unaccustomed to depression—or whatever the hell my best friend was suffering from.

After all, I'd been exposed to my father's mental decline for years.

When almost a month had passed by with no improvement in Lizzie's mood, I found myself growing increasingly protective of her. If there were a way for me to travel into her mind and bring her back, I would have, but there wasn't, so I had to settle with shielding her from what I *could* control.

From the monsters I could see.

My opportunity to do just that arrived on St. Patrick's Day, during a friendly game of rugby, of all things. We were at the local park with our friends after the parade in town. Claire, Gibs, and Liz were sprawled out on the grass at the edge of the field, while myself and Feely were pushing at the back of a maul, along with twenty or so lads from town, when it all kicked off.

"Head's up, Fatty," Pierce O'Neill called out about two seconds before the ball went whizzing past all of us and smacked Gibsie directly in his face.

The moment it happened, the lads on the pitch erupted with laughter, while Gibs climbed to his feet, holding his face with his hand. When he pulled his hand back and saw the blood on his fingers, he was out like a light and faceplanting into the ground.

"Gerard!" Claire cried out, dropping to her knees to comfort our friend. It wasn't the first time either one of us had witnessed Gibs faint from the sight of his own blood. It was a common occurrence but never usually happened in such a public setting. I was horrified for my friend, and the sound of laughter around us was doing nothing to lower my spiking blood pressure.

"Did he just faint?"

"Lads, Fatty just fainted."

"Is he all right?"

"This is priceless, lads. Billy Elliot's afraid of blood!"

"Shut the fuck up, Danny," Feely snarled, targeting the loudmouthed prick laughing, while I stalked over to the main culprit.

"You did that on purpose, didn't ya?" The smirk on Pierce's face assured me that I was right. "Why don't ya throw something at me instead?" I demanded, shoving his chest hard enough to topple the little prick onto his ass. "Yeah, that's what I thought," I sneered, as I stood over him and glared. "Not so fucking tough now, are ya?"

"I was only messing, Biggsie," Pierce choked out, holding his hands up in retreat like the coward he was. "Relax, will ya?" Shrugging, he added, "It was just for shits and giggles."

"You consider that humorous?" I narrowed my eyes in disgust. "If wit was shit, you'd be constipated."

"Hey! Someone stop that little bitch!" one of the other lads roared, dragging my attention back over to the side of the field once more, just in time to see Lizzie kick the ball we were playing with over the wall that separated the park from the river.

"You fucking idiot!" Danny roared, stalking toward her. "That was *my* ball!"

"Oh yeah?" I heard Lizzie shout back at him, while moving to stand in front of Gibsie. "Well, now it belongs to the fish."

"If you know what's good for ya, you'll get my ball now."

"And if you know what's good for *you*, you and your asshole friends will leave *my* friend alone!" Looking furious, she pointed to Gibs, who was sitting up again, while my sister held the sleeve of her jumper to his nose. "You have the nerve to call Gibs 'Fatty'? At least when he bleeds actual blood comes out. If we poked a hole in your fat ass, tomato sauce would come out!"

Now, everyone was laughing again, but at *Danny's* expense this time.

"Do you want to say that to my face?"

"I thought I already had," Lizzie shot back sarcastically. "But do you want to turn around for me to tell your other side, you two-faced prick?"

"Enough of your lip," Danny seethed, closing the space between them, as he pointed toward the river. "You better climb in there and get it back."

Liz stood her ground and glared up at him in defiance. "I would rather shit in my hand and clap."

"Get my ball, bitch," Danny threatened, pushing his chest against her. "Now."

"Get it yourself, *bitch*," Lizzie hissed, shoving him backwards. "And get out of my face."

I was already moving toward them to break up the fight, but when Danny pushed Liz hard enough to knock her over, I saw red.

"Hey!" Bolting toward them, I fisted the back of Danny's jersey and dragged him away from Liz. "Back the fuck off!"

"She kicked my ball into the fucking river," Danny argued, trying and failing to step around me in his bid to get to Liz. "She's getting my goddamn ball back, Hughie!"

"Fuck your ball," I roared, slapping down the fist he had reared back that I *knew* was intended for Liz. "And fuck you for even thinking about it."

"What the hell is wrong with you, Biggs?" he demanded, turning his fury on me now. He pushed his chest against mine and hissed, "We've been friends since we were four and you're taking *that* bitch's side?"

"Call her a bitch one more time and you're going to find out how much on her side I am," I warned, squaring up right back at him. "And if you ever think about putting your hands on her again, I'll take the head clean off ya."

"Whoa, lads." That was Robbie Mac as he and Feely pushed between us. "Settle down, Dan," he coaxed, trying to steer his asshole best friend out of harm's way. "It's just a ball, lad. It's not that deep."

"He's a pussy-whipped prick," Danny shouted, louder now that Robbie had moved him out of punching range. "Do ya hear me, Biggsie? That little bitch has you whipped big-time, lad."

"Keep the head, Hughie," Feely instructed, keeping a firm grip on my shoulders. "Keep the head, lad."

"Hey, Danny!" Lizzie stalked across the pitch to where he was being held back by Robbie. "Wait, I forgot to give you something."

"Bitch, the only thing I want from you is my ba-alllllllll!" Danny's words broke off into a high-pitched scream when Liz kicked him right in the gonads.

"That's for laughing at my friend," she hissed, planting her hands on her hips. "And for calling him fat."

Folding like a pancake, Danny rolled around on the grass, whimpering and cupping his junk.

"And if you think you're in pain now, just wait, asshole, because if you even *think* about calling him names again"—she paused to jab a thumb in *my* direction, before continuing—"I'll do a hell of a lot more than kick you in the balls." Crouching down so he would hear her, she spat, "I will cut them out of your *gooch* and feed them to your bitch-ass friend."

Having said all that, Lizzie kicked him once more before turning and shoving Robbie out of her way.

"Lad," Feely chuckled, nudging my shoulder with his as we watched Liz walk toward us. "I don't know if I'm in love or in fear for my life."

I could only hope it was the latter for Feely because I was fairly sure I was stuck on the former.

AT LEAST YOU DIDN'T BITE HIM
Lizzie

MARCH 17, 1999

BECAUSE THE FIVE OF US HAD CYCLED INTO TOWN FROM HUGH'S PLACE TO WATCH THE parade—something we were only allowed to do because Caoimhe was in charge—and Feely and I didn't have our bikes with us, we had to double up on the back, too. Claire cycled her pink unicorn bike, while Gibsie gave Feely a saddler on the back of his bike, and Hugh gave me one on the back of his.

Even though he'd been on the receiving end of a bloody nose, Gibsie was in flying form and spent the entire ride home praising me for being a *badass*.

I wasn't a badass.

Far from it.

I'd messed up again.

Really bad this time.

I knew when I was fighting with Danny that I needed to *stop*, but I couldn't seem to restrain myself.

If word got back to my dad, I would be in a world of trouble. Worse, I embarrassed Hugh. Those guys were his friends, and I screwed it all up for him.

I tried so hard to keep my cool, but when they targeted Gibsie, I lost it. He was so sweet and gentle, and he didn't deserve to be picked on all because he didn't want to play their stupid game.

Feely and Claire joined in with Gibsie as they laughed and joked about the fight at the park. Not Hugh, though. He was quiet the entire way home.

Panic-stricken, I balanced on the saddle behind him, while I held on to his waist for dear life and prayed he wouldn't start hating me now.

Abandoning their bikes on the footpath once we got back to Hugh's place, everyone went inside, with the fight still the hot topic.

I knew I was screwed the minute Claire burst into the lounge and began to regale my sister with the events. She looked so proud of me as she told Caoimhe all about how I defended *Gerard's* honor, while my heart sank further. Because while Claire might consider my actions justified, my father would see them in a very different light.

He would hear all about it now.

It was inevitable.

Caoimhe knew, which meant it would only be a matter of time before Dad did, too. The moment my sister's eyes locked on mine, I sighed in defeat.

I'm so screwed.

———————————————————

"Are you okay?" Hugh asked, settling down beside me on the couch in the front room, remote in hand. "You've been really quiet since we got home."

I was too afraid to speak in case I said something stupid again. We'd been home from town for about three hours now, and I felt like I was on borrowed time. Because I just *knew* that when I saw my dad later, all hell would break loose. To be honest, I was surprised he hadn't driven over here by now to take me home. Clearly, Caoimhe hadn't phoned him yet.

"Liz." Shaking my knee, Hugh drew my attention back to his face. "Are you okay?" Concern filled his eyes. "Talk to me."

"Sorry, I was just watching the film," I mumbled, offering him a watery smile. "I'm grand."

"What film?" Hugh asked, brows furrowed deeply, as he gestured to the blank television screen. "What's on your mind?"

"Do you hate me?" I blurted out, and then sucked in a sharp breath, fearful of his answer.

"Hate you?" He shook his head, looking bewildered. "Why would I ever hate you?"

"For making a scene," I mumbled, feeling my body tremble. "And for kicking your friend in the balls."

"Danny's not my friend, Liz." He rubbed his jaw, looking thoughtful. "He's just… Danny." A smile ghosted his lips then. "I think he pissed himself a little bit when you threatened to cut off his gooch."

"Ugh." Groaning, I dropped my head in my hands. "I'm such a freak."

"You're brilliant," he chuckled, peeling my hands away from my face. "And hey, at least you didn't bite him."

"Ha-ha," I grumbled, cheeks flaming. "Very funny. Let's all laugh at the headcase."

"I don't see any headcases," he shot back, tone serious now. "From my viewpoint, the only thing you're guilty of is being a good friend."

Maybe, but that wasn't going to cut it with my family.

"You're loyal, Liz," he continued, draping an arm over my shoulders, brown eyes warm and full of sincerity. "And brave and so epically strong."

"I don't feel so strong lately, Hugh," I admitted, sidling closer to him. "I feel tired and…"

"And what, Liz?"

"Scared," I whispered, burying my face in his chest. "I'm always so scared."

"Of what?"

I clenched my eyes shut and whispered, "Me."

PART 9

Joining the Dots

CHECKING OUT AND STEPPING UP

Hugh

MARCH 18, 1999

"HUGH, I THINK THERE'S SOMETHING WRONG WITH LIZZIE," CLAIRE ANNOUNCED after school the following evening when she got home from dance practice. "She was being really strange at school today."

"Huh?" My head snapped up from the homework I was doing at the kitchen table. "How?" Immediately on alert, I flicked my attention to my sister, who was hovering at the kitchen island, wearing a rare frown. "What happened?"

"She took off her shoes and tights in class and ran outside." My sister squirmed in obvious discomfort. "She said she wanted to feel the sun on her legs, but it was raining, Hugh."

Fuck.

"I thought she wasn't at school today," I muttered, rubbing my jaw. "She wasn't on the bus."

"Because she was late to school this morning, and then her dad came and took her home early."

Double fuck.

Shoving my chair back, I moved for the door. "Where's Mam?"

"Still at the hairdresser," Claire replied, worrying her lip. "Do you think Liz is okay?"

"Yeah, she's grand," I lied through my teeth and said in my desperate attempt to protect my friend. "I dared her to do it."

Claire's eyes widened. "You did?"

"Yep." I forced a laugh. "I can't believe she went through with it."

Clearly, I was a better liar than I used to be because my sister bought it. "You big dummy!" Scowling, she marched toward me and slapped the back of my head. "You could have gotten her in big trouble, Hugh. She got sent to the principal's office and everything!" Hands planted on her hips, my little sister glared up at me. "Don't ever do that to Lizzie again, okay? That was a really mean thing to do, and you made her look super silly. Everyone was laughing and pointing at her."

Feeling shredded inside, I forced myself to say, "Okay, Claire," even though I was having a hard time trying to catch my breath. "I won't."

Stepping around her, I moved for the staircase, taking two at a time until I reached the attic door, a.k.a. my father's office. I debated knocking but decided if he was going to ignore me, he could do it to my face.

Yanking the door open, I climbed the narrow staircase and marched straight into my father's lair of isolation. As expected, he was slumped over his desk, the one that held the computer he'd taken to writing murder mystery novels on.

"Dad." I walked over to where I knew he was sleeping and slammed my hand on the desk. "Dad!"

Like I predicted, he jerked awake with a startle, looking around with wide eyes.

Jesus Christ.

When was the last time the man shaved?

He was beginning to resemble Al Pacino in *Serpico.*

When I finally had his attention, I locked my eyes on his and said, "I need your help."

"Where's your mother?"

"Unavailable," I bit out, trying to keep the head. "Which is why I need *your* help."

Eyes that looked exactly like mine stared back at me. But there was no fire in my father's eyes anymore. It had been snuffed out four years ago. "What do you need, son?"

"I need you to drive me to Lizzie's house," I said in as even a tone as I could muster. "It's really important."

His brows furrowed in confusion. "Lizzie?"

"Yeah, Dad, *Lizzie,*" I snapped, unable to conceal the bite in my voice. "My best friend. The girl who has stayed at our house nearly every weekend for the past four and a half *years.*"

My father looked at me with regret in his eyes. "I'm sorry, Hugh." He shook his head, shoulders slumping in defeat. "I'm not doing too... I mean, ah...today's not a good day for me, son."

"No day is a good day for you anymore, Dad," I replied, tone laced with disappointment as I turned to leave. "Don't worry. I won't ask for your help again." *Hell will freeze over first.*

"Hugh," he called after me, sounding broken. "Wait, son!"

I didn't wait.

And I didn't look back, either.

UP, UP, AND AWAY

MARCH 18, 1999

"I USED TO LIVE ON ANOTHER PLANET," I MUMBLED, TRYING AND FAILING TO MAKE EYE contact with the stranger in front of me. "Under the water." Mashing my lips together, I traced my lip with my tongue but couldn't feel a thing. "She has claws." Yep, I was really gone this time. "And the monster scratches me." I could see four of the stranger now. "They flew me here on an airplane."

"Is she okay?" That was my mam. She was crying. I could hear her. I knew that made me sad, but I just couldn't *feel* it. "What's happening to her?"

"Don't worry, that's the Midazolam sedating her system," I heard the lady in the white coat tell Mam. "She'll be extremely drowsy for a day or two until it works its way out of her body."

"What do we tell the school? How do we explain what she did today?"

"I'll write a letter for you to take to the principal explaining this morning's incident. Please try not to worry, Mrs. Young. Schools are highly sympathetic to children with complex medical issues, and this in no way will affect Lizzie's opportunity to learn with her peers."

"And what about all the school she's been missing?"

"The Board of Education have already been informed of Lizzie's condition and an exemption has been granted in her favor, so you won't have any trouble regarding truancy claims. Regarding her education, all correspondence from her teacher has confirmed that despite her bipolar disorder, your daughter continues to thrive academically. I'd even go so far as to wager Lizzie is scoring in the top five percent."

"At least that."

"Yes, it's not all doom and gloom."

Slumped in the chair between my parents, it took everything inside of me to hold my head up. I could hear the doctor talking about bipolar episodes and something else called rapid cycling.

I didn't care, though.

Not anymore.

"Can you help me die?" I slurred, turning my head to see the shadow of a man. "Hey, mister man, can you help me find my friend?"

"Jesus Christ," the man cried. "How can we keep living like this?"

"Michael, please," I heard my mother wail. "Not in front of her."

"Hey, mister doctor?" My head bobbed and weaved like an apple on a string. Was I bobbing for apples? "Can you stop the monster?"

"Elizabeth, it's me, Dad."

"Dad," I repeated, letting the word roll off my tongue. "Hey, mister dad? Can you make it stop hurting?"

The man cried again, louder this time, and I didn't understand why.

I couldn't figure any of this out.

"It's all right, Elizabeth." Someone picked up my hand and held it. "You'll be okay." Would I?

Did I even care?

The injection the doctor gave me made me feel numb inside.

I couldn't feel a thing.

RAISE A MAN, EXPECT A MAN

Hugh

MARCH 18, 1999

Two hours later, I found myself sitting in the passenger seat of my mother's car as she pulled up outside Old Hall House. "Before we go inside, I want to talk to you about something," Mam said when she parked the car in her usual spot. "And I need you to hear me out." She jacked the handbrake before turning in her seat to give me her full attention. "Can you do that for me, Hugh?"

I wanted to say no, because I knew Mam was going to plead my father's case, but how could I do that when she'd literally dropped everything to drive me over here? I couldn't, so I nodded stiffly. "Yeah, Mam, I can do that."

"I know you're struggling with your feelings about Dad right now and how you feel like he's been absent in your life."

No, Mam, I'm not the one struggling with my feelings. Dad is, and I don't feel like Dad has been absent in our lives. I know he has.

"But I need you to know that Dad loves you so much, Hugh, and he's heartbroken to think he upset you this evening."

Yeah, but not enough to actually help me, though.

"Dad's devastated, Hugh," she continued. "I know that's hard for you to accept at this stage in your life, but I need you to show him some grace." She reached across the console and ruffled my hair. "A good man shows compassion, and I'm raising you to be a good man."

I waited a beat to see if she planned on adding anything else. When she didn't, I nodded and unfastened my seat belt. "Gotcha."

"Hold up." Mam reached for my arm. "Gotcha? That's all you have to say?"

"What do you want me to say, Mam?" I replied, shrugging. "You asked me to hear you out and I did."

"Hugh." I could hear her disappointment when she said my name like that. "Please try to put yourself in your father's shoes for a moment—"

"I did what you asked, Mam," I cut in and told her, reaching for the door handle.

"I heard you out. I listened to you cover for him for the millionth time, but that's all I have, okay? When it comes showing grace to Dad, I'm fresh out of it."

"Hugh, you can't say things like that," Mam argued, tone hurt and weary. "Not about your father."

"You're my father, Mam. *You!*" I snapped back, turning to glare at her. "You're the only parent either of us have had since the accident."

Her breath hitched. *"Hugh!"*

"Listen…" Blowing out a frustrated breath, I pressed my fingers to my temples, trying to soothe the tension rising up inside of me. "I know he's my father, and I know you don't want me to have these feelings, but I've never tried to force you or Claire to feel the way I do about him, so please don't try to force me."

Mam looked like she was about to argue for a moment, but then her shoulders slumped in defeat. "I'm sorry." Slumping against her seat, she pressed a hand to her brow and whispered, "I'm just so sorry that I haven't been able to protect you from this."

"Mam, you have *nothing* to be sorry about." Reaching across the console, I snatched up her hand in mine. "You've gone over and above for us every day of our lives." I gave her hand a reassuring squeeze. "Claire and I couldn't ask for a better mother."

Her eyes were glassy from the tears I knew she would never spill in front of me or my sister. Because she saved those up for when she was in the bath and thought no one could hear her.

I heard her, though.

Every night.

"How did you grow up so fast?" Smiling sadly, she reached up and cupped my cheek. "My baby boy isn't a baby anymore."

"I don't know what to say, Mam," I replied with a shrug. "Raise a man, expect a man." A smile ghosted my lips before adding, "But if you need a baby boy, I reckon you have another three years with Gibs before he cops on."

That made her laugh, and I was glad, because I didn't want to see my mother upset. This was the woman who gave me life. I would rather be raked over hot coals than cause her distress.

"What would I do without you, hmm?" Mam reached over and stroked my cheek. "Love you."

"Love you, too, Mam, and thanks for the spin." Reaching for the door handle, I cleared my throat before adding, "For everything."

I'M BIPOLAR

Hugh

MARCH 18, 1999

Leaving my mam in the kitchen with Catherine and Mike, I headed straight upstairs, anxious to see my friend. When I walked into her bedroom, Liz was where I thought she might be: curled up in a ball on her bed. The small lamp on her bedside locker illuminated her motionless frame.

Kicking off my shoes, I moved straight for her bed, not stopping until I was lying on my side, facing her. Her eyes were open, but they were dull and lifeless. "Hey." Smoothing her hair back, I rested my palm on her cheek and whispered, "I'm here, Liz."

Her hand shot out to fist my shirt, but she made no move to speak. She didn't even blink. She just continued to stare right through me. It was like a part of Liz *knew* I was here, but that part was trapped inside a frozen cage.

"It's okay." Shifting closer, I nuzzled her nose with mine before resting my brow against hers. "I hear you, Liz."

She was breathing—I could see her chest rise and fall—but she wasn't here. Every now and then, a single tear would trickle down her cheek. I made it my personal mission to wipe each one.

"You can sleep," I whispered, stroking her cheek. "I'll stay right here and keep the monsters away." She had to be exhausted. I knew I was. But she didn't close her eyes.

Reaching up, I brushed another rogue tear from her cheek before quickly swiping one from mine. "I won't let anything hurt you." Whether it was the right thing to say or not, I said it. "Because you're my best friend in the whole wide world." Sniffling, I cupped her cheek again and leaned in close. "And I'm always going to love you, Lizzie Young." I pressed a kiss to the tip of her nose. "No matter what."

When I moved to pull back, I felt her tug on my shirt, pulling me closer, bringing me back to her.

Calling me home.

"Hugh," she managed to say, though her voice seemed slurred.

"Yeah, Liz." I wiped another tear from her cheek. "It's me."

"Hugh." Finally blinking, she opened her eyes and tried to locate my face. "I love you, too."

"I know you do." My heart seemed to soar and break all at once. "Did they give you medicine to make you sleepy, Liz?" I knew they had. She was completely spaced out. "Hmm?"

"Yeah," she replied groggily. "I was…uh, bad at school."

"You weren't bad, Liz," I told her, fucking hating when she said that about herself. "You've never been bad."

"I'm sorry."

"For what?"

"Not sure." Liz tried to shake her head. "Just am."

"Well, I *am* sure, Liz," I told her, feeling my heart shattering into a thousand pieces. "I'm sure that you're good and kind and the most amazing girl I've ever met." Swallowing down my emotions, I smoothed a hand over her hair and leaned in close to whisper, "You are all of the *good* things in the world and none of the bad. You won't feel this way forever. Okay? You're going to feel better again."

"No, I'm not, Hugh," she mumbled drowsily, eyelids fluttering shut. "I'm bipolar."

"Bipolar?" I croaked back. "What do you mean you're bipolar, Liz?"

"Mm-hmm."

"Is that what they diagnosed you with?" I asked, feeling beyond concerned for my friend, while I worked frantically to register the word *bipolar* and bring what information I had on the matter to the forefront of my mind.

"Liz?" Sitting straight up, I took her hand in mine, feeling a million complicated emotions crash through me all at once. "Did the doctors say you're bipolar?"

"Mm-hmm."

"Liz." At a complete loss, I stared down at the girl I'd spent most of my childhood adoring and croaked out, "Why didn't you tell me?"

"Too scared," she mumbled, squeezing my hand. "You'd leave."

"I wouldn't leave," I strangled, chest heaving, as I tried to make sense of all I'd learned in such a short space of time. "I *won't* leave," I quickly clarified, heart thundering violently. "I'm *not* leaving."

Bewildered by the complex emotions I had for this girl, I took her hand in mine and kissed the back of it. I had no idea why I did it, only that I needed to. "I'm staying, okay?" I kissed her hand again. "No matter what."

"I need you."

"I know." Nodding, I cradled her hand to my cheek, needing to feel her touch. "I need you, too."

"So tired." With her eyes still closed, she nodded sluggishly before mumbling, "Please stay."

"I am staying," I promised, attention flicking to her hand I was still holding. "Right here." Turning it over, I stared in horror at the deep welts on her wrist. "Brian didn't do that to your wrist, did he, Liz?"

Nothing.

"Liz," I said, a little sterner now, attention still riveted to her wrist. Beneath the fresh cuts were older scars. Deep scars. Ones I'd never noticed before because she always wore dozens of bracelets. "Where did these scars come from?"

"Don't go," was all she replied, and it was a barely coherent mumbled slur. "He gets me when you're not here."

"It's okay, Liz. You can sleep," I whispered, resigned to the fact that I wasn't getting answers tonight. She was too out of it. "I won't let the monster get you." Trembling, I blinked back the tears filling my eyes because I knew this was bad. "Or the scary lady."

"No matter what?"

"Yeah, Liz." Sniffling, I used my shoulder to wipe the tear on my cheek. "No matter what."

I waited until I was sure Lizzie was asleep before sneaking out of her room and straight into their family bathroom. I spent enough time at this house to know where everything was kept. Including the prescription Liz took daily.

Stalking over to the cabinet above the sink, where they kept the medicine, I swung it open and started rummaging through the countless bottles until I found one with her name on it.

Elizabeth Young.

Clonazepam.

Quickly pocketing the bottle, I kept searching through the bottles until I found another one with Lizzie's name on the label along with the word *Olanzapine* and shoved that in my pocket, too.

Beyond pissed off, I stormed down the spiraling staircase, moving straight for the kitchen, with only one thing on my mind.

Answers.

When I walked into the kitchen, Catherine and Mike were sitting opposite my mother at the kitchen table, drinking coffee.

"Hugh," Mike acknowledged, while Catherine offered me a watery smile and asked, "Did Lizzie speak to you, love?"

"Yeah, she spoke to me," I replied, moving straight for the table and pulling out a chair next to Mam. "She spoke a lot, actually." Taking a seat, I retrieved both bottles from my pocket and set them down on the table in front of me. "As a matter of fact, she had a lot to say about *this*." I took my time glaring at each of them individually before asking, "Why didn't any of you tell me that my *best friend* is bipolar?"

Mind reeling, I sat at the table in the Young family's kitchen, listening as the grown-ups around me spoke to me like they were communicating with a toddler.

In the past forty minutes, I'd lost count of how many times I'd heard the words, *"Lizzie just gets a bit down in herself from time to time"* or *"she has her up and down days, but it's nothing for you to worry about"* or, my personal favorite, *"she'll pull herself together in no time."*

Yeah fucking right.

Did they honestly think I was buying any of this?

Their daughter wasn't just down. Liz had bottomed out to the point where she couldn't lift her head off the pillow. This wasn't the first time it had happened, either. I knew because I'd witnessed similar episodes in sporadic fashion all the way back to the first day we met.

I knew that when she got sad, she couldn't be coaxed out of it.

Nothing worked.

The grown-ups told me that when her mood dropped this low, it was called a dark episode, and I thought that might have been the most sensible comment I'd heard all night. At least the word *dark* accurately portrayed how lifeless she became. How, when she went dark, she reminded me of a corpse with a beating heart.

"She has a very complicated mind."

"The best people do."

"Elizabeth has struggled since she was a toddler."

"But those were mostly tantrums."

"She hit puberty far earlier than we hoped, and because of that, her hormones are causing her some problems."

"But that's nothing for you to be concerned about."

"Once her body gets used to the new medication, Lizzie will be back to herself," Catherine said, offering reassurance instead of *actual* facts. "Please try not to worry, Hugh."

Drumming my fingers on the table, I strived for calm when all I wanted to do was scream. Why were they doing this to me? Why were they so insistent on puking out this watered-down, kid-gloved explanation?

"Is it my turn?" I asked when all three of them looked like they were fresh out of bullshit to spew. "Can I speak now?"

Lizzie's parents nodded, while my own mother pressed a hand to her forehead.

"Can you please not talk to me like I'm dull of comprehension?" I asked them, unable to conceal the bite in my tone. "I'm young, I accept that, but I happen to possess the ability to grasp sensitive topics."

Sighing wearily, Mam pressed her thumbs to her temples. "Oh, Hugh."

"I'm serious, Mam," I shot back, unwilling to climb back into the infant-labeled box they put me in. "I've been friends with Liz for going on five years, and I've always known she has mental health issues. Contrary to our friends, I'm not blind, dense, or oblivious to what's happening to Liz. She's my best friend, for God's sake. I *want* to help her, but I can't do that if you guys don't *let* me."

"I know you mean well, Hugh, but you're a child," Mike interjected, sounding even wearier than my mother. "You don't have the slightest understanding of what's happening here, son."

"I have a better grasp on this than you...think," I replied, forcing myself to add *think* at the end of my sentence.

Because regardless of how I felt about Mike, falling out of favor with him might jeopardize the time I got to spend with his daughter.

"I know she's cutting herself," I decided to throw out. Their reactions assured me they weren't expecting me to know. "I know she's been doing it for at least a year," I added, mentally retracing my memories to the first time I'd seen unexplained marks on her body. "I can *help*," I reiterated, imploring her parents to let me in. "You can *trust* me. I swear you can. All you have to do is *just* let me in!"

CONCEAL, DON'T FEEL, AND NEVER REVEAL

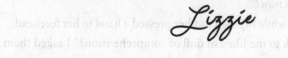

MARCH 22, 1999

"HOW ARE YOU FEELING NOW, LIZZIE?"

"Fine."

"That's not what your mother told me."

I didn't respond.

What was there to say?

"Your mother told me that you've been cutting again."

Shrugging, I pulled at the sleeve of my jumper and stared at my jean-clad thighs.

What could they do about it?

Not a damn thing.

Of all the things in life I could depend on, it was the doctors' inability to fix me.

Because they didn't listen.

They didn't ask the right questions.

They didn't believe me.

So I stopped believing in them.

I knew what would happen next.

It was the same thing as last time.

They would either up the dosage of my current medication, or they would try a brand of chemical-dependent poison.

It wouldn't work.

Because broken minds like mine were immune.

"Can you tell me what you're thinking right now?" the doctor asked, wheeling her chair over so that she was facing me. "And I want you to be completely honest." Taking my hands in hers, she offered me a warm smile. "Just let it all out."

Inhaling deeply, I stared into her brown eyes and said, "I'm feeling a lot better now, Doctor. Thank you for fixing me."

Disappointment filled her eyes.

Nothing new there.

"All right, Lizzie." She sighed heavily. "We'll try again at your next appointment."

WHEN IN DOUBT, HIT THE BOOKS

Hugh

MARCH 31, 1999

I HAD LEFT OLD HALL HOUSE THAT NIGHT WITH MORE QUESTIONS THAN ANSWERS. Despite my pleading, Catherine, Mike, and Mam continued to wrap me up in cotton wool, unwilling to consider the prospect that a "kid" might be capable of helping. Yeah, I didn't take that lying down and decided there and then if they wouldn't explain what was happening to Liz, I would figure it out myself.

Taking matters into my own hands, I hit the public library after school the following day. Scouring the nonfiction section, I combed through every medical textbook I could get my hands on. Because my membership stated I was under sixteen, I wasn't permitted to take any of the medical textbooks home. Therefore, I returned to the library after swim practice and rugby training the following weekend, where I photocopied every passage correlating to early-onset bipolar.

The book that served my interest best was the one labeled *Diagnostic and Statistical Manual of Mental Disorders*. Within the pages of that particular dust-ridden hardback, I learned more about the human mind than I ever had in Mr. Coulson's classroom at Scoil Eoin and quickly developed my own theories about the problems in my best friend's mind.

Determined to prove to my best friend that I had no intention of disappearing from her life, I got off the school bus at her stop every day to visit with her. This small act won me brownie points with her parents, but I didn't care about that. While it was nice that Catherine and Mike were warming up to the idea that Liz could have friends who knew about her illness and didn't bolt, my visits weren't for their benefit.

I was solely focused on their daughter.

The first three visits consisted of just hugging my friend and whispering words of reassurance in her ear, as she cried on my shoulder.

On the fourth visit, she smiled.

During the fifth and sixth visits, we played cards.

She slept through visits seven and eight.

By the ninth visit, she was out of bed and dressed.

Visits ten, eleven, and twelve were spent outside, rambling through the fields and holding down a one-way conversation.

Today marked visit thirteen, and when I climbed off the bus, I was surprised to find her waiting for me at the gates of her family's estate.

"Are my eyes deceiving me, or is that Lizzie Young I see?" I called out when I spied her leaning against the metal gates.

Lizzie laughed and I swear, it was the best sound I'd ever heard. She raised her hand to wave and called out "hey," while I jogged the rest of the way.

"Well, shit, it *is* Lizzie Young," I teased, slipping through the pedestrian gate. Letting my schoolbag fall from my shoulder, I fisted the front of her flannel shirt and pulled her in for a hug. "There's my girl."

"Yep." Her arms came around my waist and she pressed her body to mine tightly. "Here I am." And then she did something so incredibly Lizzie-like that I knew I had my friend back.

She *sniffed* me.

FIGHT FOR IT
Lizzie

APRIL 9, 1999

"YOU NEED TO START OPENING UP TO THOSE DOCTORS, LIZ," CAOIMHE REPEATED WHEN we got home from my latest appointment. I'd listened to this exact same spiel all the way home from the clinic. Usually, Mam took me to all my appointments, but she wasn't feeling good today, and since we were on our Easter holidays from school, Caoimhe had taken her place.

"I sat outside that door for forty-five minutes and heard your voice a grand total of six times."

"You're not supposed to eavesdrop," I replied, flopping onto a chair at the kitchen table. "It's breach of privacy."

"Pssh. You're my baby sister," she replied, batting the air as if that was reason enough for her to invade my privacy—not that it bothered me.

On the contrary, I couldn't have cared less.

I kept my mouth shut most of the time.

"Come on, Liz," she continued to ramble as she whizzed around our kitchen, searching for snacks. "How are they supposed to fix you if you don't tell them what's wrong?"

They can't fix me.

"I don't know what's wrong," I reminded her, resting my chin in my hand. "That's the whole problem, Caoimhe."

"Well, at least you're human again," my sister replied, using her hip to close the fridge. "You freaked the hell out of us the last time you spiraled."

Yeah, I already knew that.

Caoimhe had told me countless times.

Problem was, I had no memory of it.

Apparently, the new medication the doctors were trialing me on was the cause of my lethargy and I would feel better soon. I wasn't sure about feeling better, but I definitely didn't feel as hollow as before.

I could get of bed again, which was something I'd been struggling with for a while. I wasn't screaming and raving, either—another bonus. I was back attending school regularly, and my parents were watching me with hawk eyes.

I wasn't sure if I was out of the woods yet; I was afraid to get my hopes up on stability when my mind could snatch it away in an instant, but I wanted to be okay again.

When there was a knock on the front door, followed a few moments later by the sound of my sister calling out, "Liz, lover boy's here for your daily visit," I bit my lip and smiled.

Because if I had a hope of being normal, then I had to fight for it.

And I would.

For him.

I could get out of bed again, which was something I'd been struggling with for a while.

I wasn't screaming and raving either—another bonus. I was back attending school regularly, and my parents were watching me with hawk eyes.

I wasn't sure if I was out of the woods yet. I was afraid to get my hopes up on stability when my mind could snatch it away in an instant, but I wanted to be okay again. When there was a knock on the front door, followed a few moments later by the sound of my sister calling out, "Liz, lover boy's here for your daily visit," I bit my lip and smiled.

Because if I had a hope of being normal, then I had to fight for it.

And I would.

I began.

PART 10

Igniting Flames and Embers

BIRTHDAY WISHES AND TRUANT SISTERS

Hugh

JUNE 9, 1999

WHEN I CLIMBED ON THE BUS AFTER SCHOOL ON WEDNESDAY, I DIDN'T BOTHER TRYING to conceal the way my eyes sought her out. The minute I found Liz halfway down the aisle, on the right-hand side, I made a beeline for her.

Tossing my bag on the floor between the seats, I dropped into the seat beside her and draped an arm over her shoulders. "Happy birthday, Liz." Feeling brave, I pressed a kiss to her cheek and then dutifully ignored the wolf whistles and teasing from my classmates.

"Thanks, Hugh," she chuckled, shifting closer until she was snuggled under my arm. "I missed you."

"Missed you, too," I replied, relaxing into my seat. "Your present's in my bag. I'll give it to you when we get to your place."

"You know I don't want presents."

"And *you* know I'm still going to give you presents."

She smiled. "How long do you get to stay at my house for?"

"Half nine," I replied, fucking delighted at the thought. "Mam said she'll pick me up after her shift."

The beamer of a smile that spread across her face assured me that Liz was as delighted as I was about the late pickup.

She was doing so much better since March. The new combination of medication she was taking seemed to be really working for her, and I found myself encouraging her every day to keep going. I knew she hated the pills, but I also knew, without them, she wouldn't be able to function.

"How are you eleven already?" I mused, shaking my head. "Feels like it was only yesterday that you were six years old and sitting on this bus, sniffing my neck like a little puppy."

"Oh my God," she snickered, resting her cheek in the crook of my arm. "I *did* sniff your neck."

"At least you only sniffed me," I shot back, chuckling. "I was a lot luckier than the other kids you decided to bite chunks out of."

"To be fair, the puppy reference is a lot kinder than I deserve." She laughed again before adding, "I was feral back then."

"You're *still* feral," I countered, laughing. "It's grand, though. I've grown fond of your wild streak."

"Jesus," I exclaimed when we stepped foot inside Old Hall House and were greeted by the sound of loud screaming. "What's that about?"

Mike's voice thundered through the air, joined by Caoimhe's hysterical wailing, and then the sound of Catherine, who was clearly trying to calm everyone down.

"No clue," Liz replied with a sigh, edging closer to the closed kitchen door. "But I'm sure we're about to find out."

"How could you do this?" Mike demanded from the other side of the door. "You've ruined your whole future, Caoimhe!"

"Michael, please calm down."

"Calm down? How the fuck do you propose I do that, Catherine, when our daughter swanned off to England with her boyfriend instead of sitting her leaving cert exams?"

Holy crap.

Caoimhe skipped her leaving cert exams?

I turned to look at Liz, but she seemed as bewildered as I was, with a wide-eyed expression etched on her face.

"It was one exam, Dad," Caoimhe tried to plead, though it was muffled from the sheer height of her crying. "I'm sorry, okay? I'm sorry, Daddy. I swear I'll sit the rest of my exams. It'll be fine, I promise. I'll ace the rest of my subjects."

"No, it won't be fine, Caoimhe," Catherine chimed in, sounding pissed now. "English is a core subject, and you skipped the exam. Without English, you automatically fail the leaving cert, regardless of how well you do in your other exams!"

"I didn't know that!" Her screams and wails grew louder. "I didn't know, I swear!"

"You knew you were supposed to be at Tommen this morning at nine o'clock sharp," Mike interjected. "You *knew* that much, Caoimhe, but oh no, you couldn't do that one simple thing, could ya? No, because instead, you decided to flush your future down the drain for a dirty weekend with that prick Mark Allen!"

Well, shit...

Go Mike.

"I said I'm sorry!" Caoimhe screamed, and the sound of a chair scraping on tiles filled my ears. "But I had to go, Dad, I was running out of time—"

"Don't you dare say it!" her father roared. "I'm already fully aware why he took you over on the boat to England. I don't need you verbalizing my worst fucking nightmare out loud!"

"Why, Caoimhe?" Catherine sobbed. "Why didn't you come to me, love?"

"Because of him!" Caoimhe screamed. "Look at his reaction, Mam. How could I talk to you about what was happening when all he ever does is lose the head and pass judgment? I did the right thing for *me*, and I thought I was doing what was best for the—"

"Don't fucking say it!"

"Michael, please try to calm down."

"How are we going to show our faces at mass, Catherine? She's brought shame down on the whole family."

"Nobody knows, Dad, I promise."

"God knows, Caoimhe!"

"Are you fucking serious, Dad?" Caoimhe screamed. "You're worried about your God in the sky when your flesh and blood is standing right in front of you, begging for help?"

"No daughter of mine would do what you did," Mike shouted back. "Don't you ever bring that prick around here again. Do ya hear me? He's not to step foot through the front door of this house ever again!"

"Dad, please!"

"No, don't try to hug me! I can't stand to look at you right now."

"Dad, I'm begging you to understand—"

"Just get out of my sight, Caoimhe," Mike roared. "Please. Go now, before I do something I'll regret."

"Quick," Lizzie whisper-hissed when the sound of footsteps came closer. "Run."

She didn't need to tell me twice.

Grabbing her outstretched hand, we bolted for the staircase, quickly retreating upstairs to the safety of her bedroom.

"Holy fuck," I strangled out, with my back to her closed bedroom door. "Your sister's in some serious shit."

"I've never heard my father shout at her like that," Liz agreed, eyes as wide as saucers. "Usually, he saves that up for me."

Yeah, I knew he did, and that was a huge reason why I disliked her father.

"Even Mam sounded cross," she continued, moving for her bed. "And she has the patience of a saint."

"Did you know she was going to England?" I asked, following her over to her bed. "Did she say anything to you about it?"

"No, not me, but I heard her mention something about it when she was talking on the phone to one of her friends," Liz replied, sitting cross-legged on her bed. "I didn't take any notice because, honestly, I don't really care what she does. And when she was gone all weekend, I just presumed she was at a friend's house studying." Shrugging, she added, "Her leaving cert exams started today. She was supposed to have English Paper I."

"Do you think she might have taken the boat over to England because she was pregnant"—pausing, I lowered my voice to a whisper before saying—"and now she's not?"

While it wasn't something anyone dared to speak about out loud, everyone in Ireland knew why girls took unexpected boat trips to England, and it wasn't to take in the sights.

"I don't know," Liz replied, chewing on her lip anxiously. "Maybe."

SOLO TRIPS AND SOBBING SISTERS

Lizzie

JUNE 25, 1999

"Elizabeth," Dad said, standing in my bedroom doorway. "We'll leave in five minutes, okay?"

"Okay, Dad," I called back, climbing on top of my suitcase in a last-ditch effort to close it. "I'm almost ready."

"Have you packed everything you need?"

"I think so."

"Are you sure?" he pushed. "You'll be away from home for three nights."

"I know, Dad." And I couldn't *wait*. Sinead Biggs had invited me to join her family on their annual trip to her father's holiday home on the West Cork coast. I'd never been on holiday without my family, and my dad had *agreed* to let me go. Better again, Claire and Hugh told me all their aunts, uncles, and cousins on their mam's side of the family would be there and that the kids got to camp out in their grandfather's backyard every year. According to the siblings, Grandad Healy was fond of the drink, even more fond of mischief, and always let his grandkids get away with murder, which only increased my excitement.

I knew I had Caoimhe to thank for Dad letting me go, because if my sister hadn't messed up so bad, our father wouldn't be giving me this chance to prove myself. It didn't hurt my cause that Sinead Biggs was an experienced senior-level nurse. My parents trusted her to know what to do if my mood shifted unexpectedly.

I felt bad for Caoimhe, I really did, and I knew the past three weeks had been hard on her, but the truth was I'd never felt *better*.

For the first time in eleven years, I wasn't the sole cause of our family dysfunction. My sister had screwed up so colossally that she managed to make *me* look like the good one, something I'd never been accused of before.

Her unexpected fall from grace had given me a reprieve from our parents' worried looks and disapproving scowls. I'd quickly realized that my parents' approval was something I liked a *lot* and found myself wanting to do better to impress them more to keep them happy. It was much easier to do now that I was actually sleeping at night. I hadn't been plagued by nightmares in weeks and was managing to get a solid eight hours each night.

"Did you pack your meds?" Dad asked, dragging my attention back to him.

"Yep." I smiled and patted the front pocket of my duffel bag. "And I took today's dose already."

"Good girl." Dad smiled at me then, and it was a real, genuine smile. "I'll be downstairs when you're ready."

Grinning like I'd won an Olympic gold medal, I watched my dad walk away, and then I listened to the sound of his footsteps as he descended the staircase.

Today is a good day.

And I'm not bad.

Because my dad loves me.

I can be lovable.

Finally managing to close my suitcase, I heaved it off the bed, slid my shoulders through the straps of my duffel bag, and then hurried out of my room. When I passed Caoimhe's bedroom door on the landing, I froze. Setting my suitcase down, I listened to the low, keening sobs coming from the other side of the door.

It had been weeks, and she was *still* crying.

Deciding to check on her before I left for the camping trip, I slipped inside her room and padded over to where she was curled up in a ball on her bed.

"Caoimhe?"

"Wh-what?" she choked out through racking sobs. The only part of her I could see was her blond hair splayed over her pillow. The rest of her was hidden under her purple duvet.

"Are you okay?"

"Wh-what the f-fuck do you th-think?" she strangled out, crying harder now.

"No," I muttered, forcing down the sharp retort on the tip on my tongue because I hated it when she talked to me like that. "I just wanted to say bye," I added. "Before I leave for the trip."

"Bye," she snapped. "You c-can go n-now."

I sighed heavily. "Do you want to talk about it—"

"If I did, you'd be the l-last person on earth I'd w-want to t-talk to!" she screamed, sitting up and shoving the covers off her body. "So just g-get the fuck out of my r-room, Lizzie!" When I didn't leave immediately, she lunged forward and pushed me hard enough to knock me backwards. "I said g-get the f-fuck out, you f-fucking l-lunatic!"

"Fine!" I snapped, climbing to my feet. "Enjoy wallowing in bed." Balling my hands into fists at my sides, I backed away from her bed before I lost my cool and ruined my chance at going camping. "I'm going camping with my friends."

"Go!" Caoimhe screamed, throwing her pillow at me as I went. "And do us all a f-favor and d-don't come back!"

DEEP, DEEPER, DEEPEST

Lizzie

JUNE 27, 1999

"HUGH ANDREW BIGGS, CLIMB DOWN OFF THOSE ROCKS RIGHT THIS INSTANT!" SINEAD screamed, but it was too late for warnings. Especially when her firstborn was in the process of attempting an impressive backwards flip from a terrifying height. "Oh my Jesus, Lizzie, he's doing it, isn't he?"

"Yep," I laughed, clapping and cheering from the beach when Hugh executed the most perfectly timed backflip off the cliff's edge. "He sure is!"

"Is he okay?" Clamping her hands over her eyes, his mother let out a pained groan. "Please tell me he made it."

"He made it," I assured, patting her shoulder, while my eyes tracked the boy swimming back toward the boat.

"Calm down, woman," her father, a.k.a. Grandad Healy, admonished, while cheering on his grandson. "Good man, Hughie!" he called out, beaming with pride. "That's the job, boyo!"

Grandad Healy was a tall man with snow-white hair and a thick, matching white beard. He sort of reminded me of Captain Smith from the movie *Titanic*, and I liked him a lot. He was a jolly-looking man, with a cracking sense of humor. He also appeared to heavily favor his eldest grandson, who had been named after him—something we both had in common.

"He doesn't even have a life jacket on," she continued to wail. "Sweet Jesus, I told that boy to keep it on."

"He's grand, Sinead," Grandad Healy laughed, not sounding one bit concerned. "The boy wins gold in the county meets three times on the trot, and you're worrying about a bloody jacket."

"I don't care." Sinead released a ragged breath and pressed a hand to her chest. "I'm going to kill him."

"Don't be getting on the young fella's back, Sinead," Grandad Healy warned, while snapping pictures of his grandson with an ancient-looking camera. "If a bit of cliff diving is the worst he does, you'll be doing grand." He turned, giving her a knowing look, before adding, "Yourself and Pete certainly did worse when ye were the boy's age."

"Why do you think I'm so concerned?" she groaned, sinking down on the bench.

"You know, I think it's really great that you took us out on the boat," I decided to tell her. "I know it's probably really scary for you after what happened to Gibsie's family, but Hugh really loves the water."

"I know he does, sweetheart," she replied with a sad smile. "He's always been my water baby."

I didn't doubt it. My best friend loved the water more than anyone I'd ever known. Hugh had a lot of hobbies and played a wide range of sports, all of which he excelled at, but I knew his true passions were books and swimming. He was never more alive than when he was in the water, and it made me sad that he didn't get to take these kinds of trips with his family as often as they used to.

I completely understood why Gibsie had remained back at the holiday home with Claire and her cousins, but I also thought Sinead Biggs was one hell of a strong woman to take her son back out on the water.

"Breathe, Sinead," Aunty Sarah mused from where she was sprawled out on her father's deck, trying to catch a tan. "You'll get wrinkles."

"Are you mental?" Sinead screamed when Hugh reached the boat. "Of all the irresponsible, stupid, reckless things to do, you decide to throw yourself off a bloody cliff." Towel in hand, she leaned over the edge of the boat and continued to rant. "And worse, you take your life jacket off to do it. You could've killed yourself, you bloody eejit!"

"Did you see that?" Hugh asked excitedly, heaving himself back onto the boat. Ignoring his mother's rant, he looked at his grandfather and laughed. "Did you see my flip?"

"I did, boyo," Grandad Healy chuckled, giving his shoulder a proud squeeze. "That was something else."

"That was fucking epic," Hugh chuckled, spraying everyone near him when he shook his head. "What an adrenaline rush."

"Language," his mother snapped, slapping him upside the head before draping a large, navy towel around his shoulders. Not an easy feat nowadays considering her son towered over her. "And for the love of all that is holy, put your life jacket on, will you?"

"It slows me down, Mam."

"It keeps you floating, that's what it does."

"Liz." His whiskey eyes landed on me, and he grinned before making a beeline for me. "What did you think?"

"That was amazing!" I blurted, still thrumming with excitement. "You have to take me up there." Reaching up, I grabbed the sides of his towel and readjusted it to cover his broad shoulders. "I want to feel that rush, too."

"Over my dead body," Sinead interrupted. "Hugh, don't you dare take that girl up the cliffs. Do you hear me?"

"I hear ya, Mam," Hugh replied, while offering me a sneaky wink. Entwining his hand with mine, he nudged me toward the other side of the deck, while whispering, "Come on, I want to show you something."

My heart fluttered with excitement. "You're going to take me up there?"

"I'm going to take you somewhere even better," he replied with a cheeky smile, as he swung one leg over the side of the boat and discarded his towel. "But we've got to be quick." He gestured to the water and gave me a knowing look. "Okay?"

I nodded eagerly, knowing exactly what I needed to do. "Okay."

"Hugh," Sinead said in a warning tone, eyeing us warily. "No funny business, ya hear?"

Too late.

Her son was already in the water with his arms outstretched toward me.

I didn't hesitate.

Not for a second.

Releasing a squeal of excitement, I clambered over the side of the boat and dropped into the water.

"Oh my God," I yelped, momentarily startled when my body registered the frigid temperature. "It's so cold."

Hugh's arms came around me instantly. "I've got you."

"Oh, for the love of God," Sinead groaned, leaning over the side of the boat to glare down at us. "At least this one has the good sense to wear a life jacket."

"Mam, I've got this," Hugh laughed, swimming us away from the boat. "We're just going to go for a swim," he explained. "Over to the fairies' sea cave and back. Just to show Liz the caves."

"Hugh, you know how dangerous the water can be," Sinead called back. "And Lizzie's not as strong a swimmer as you."

"I know," he replied, as we drifted farther away. "And you know I won't let anything happen to her."

"I can't touch the ground, Hugh." I knew I was floating, my life jacket assured me of that, but I had never been out of my depth like this before. "What if I float away?"

"I've got you," he coaxed, keeping ahold of the strap of my life jacket, while using his free arm to swim. "You're safe with me."

"Keep her safe," Sinead called out, looking mildly terrified as she leaned over the edge and watched us slowly drift away from her line of sight. "I'm warning you, Hugh."

After a good ten minutes of Hugh swimming and me bobbing along after him, we finally reached what he referred to as the fairies' sea cave.

"Whoa," I breathed, taking in the sight of an impressive cave entrance hidden deep in the rocks.

"It's completely unreachable by land," he explained, guiding me inside by the strap of my life jacket. "It's only explorable when the tide is out."

"Is the water still deep inside here?"

"You better believe it," he replied, carefully maneuvering us through the narrow stream of seawater that flowed through the cave, while avoiding the sharp rocks on either side of us. "It's like a bottomless pit, Liz."

"That is so cool," I replied, fascinated by how my words seemed to bounce off the cave walls and echo back at me.

The sound of loud dripping came from all directions, but it still felt incredibly quiet. Sunlight poured through the cave opening, lighting the way through the darker tunnels. I'd never seen anything so beautiful in my life and told Hugh just that.

"Told you this was better," Hugh chuckled, using his body to protect mine from a particularly narrow part of the cave. He pulled me around another tight corner and then, suddenly, we weren't squashed between narrow walls of jagged rocks. Instead, we entered what I could only describe as heaven on earth.

"Welcome to the fairies' sea cave," Hugh chuckled, waving a hand around. "Pretty cool, huh?"

It was more than cool.

It was breathtaking.

I had thought the narrow trail we swam through was the point of interest, but clearly not, because that narrow, rocky channel of water led to paradise.

In complete awe, I looked around the glistening cavern walls that seemed to sparkle almost as much as the underwater pool we were floating in. Even better, the water in here felt *warm*. Tiny fragments of sunlight had clearly bore their way into the cave, illuminating it in a mystical, glowing hue.

"No wonder they call this place the fairies' cave," I breathed, taking it all in. "It looks magical."

"I know," Hugh agreed, swimming us over to a nearby rock. "But we can't stay long."

"We can't?"

"Nope." Heaving himself onto it, he turned back and held out his hand for me.

Trusting him entirely, I grabbed his hand and went willingly when he pulled me out of the water and onto the rock with him. *Onto his lap.* "In a couple of hours this place will be underwater," he explained, readjusting my life jacket, as he tried and failed to make more room on the rock for me. "Sorry about the seating." He offered me a sheepish smile. "I guess I didn't think this through."

I was thrilled he hadn't because I couldn't think of a better place to sit than on his lap. "It's like Aladdin's cave," I breathed, hooking an arm around his neck. "We're completely isolated from the rest of the world in here."

"Don't worry, you're safe," he was quick to promise. "I would never let anything happen to you."

"I'm not worried, Hugh." Our bodies were so close now that I knew I would rather die here in this cave and never be recovered than to leave his side. "I'm *happy.*"

"Good." My response seemed to relieve his tension and he visibly relaxed beneath me. "Because I *want* you to be happy, Liz."

"I'm always happy when I'm with you."

"Yeah," he replied, voice sounding a little deeper than usual. "It's the same for me."

"Thanks for picking me by the way," I said, shifting closer. "I know you and Claire got to pick one friend each to come on this trip, and I *also* know that Claire picked Gibs." I smiled before adding, "Which means you picked me."

"I'll always pick you, Liz." Hugh's arm came around my waist and he pulled me closer to his chest. "You'll always be first choice."

"For trips?"

"For everything."

His response sent a shiver of pleasure rippling through my entire body. "I love you, Hugh Biggs." Exhaling a sigh of contentment, I wrapped my other arm around his neck and smiled. "I'd stay here forever with you, if we could."

Brown eyes full of warmth locked on mine. "Yeah?"

I nodded slowly. "I don't want to ever leave."

"Neither do I." His voice was gruff and thick, and his breath fanned my face when he spoke. "Liz." The way he said my name caused a shiver to roll down my spine.

Like he knew me.

Like I was *his.*

Like I belonged entirely to him.

Hooking an arm around my waist, he pulled me close until our chests were pressed together. With my arms wrapped around his neck, I clasped my hands together tightly in anticipation.

Hugh's movements were slow and purposeful, like he had thought about what this day would look like a thousand times before. So had I, but my imagination had *nothing* on the real thing.

I couldn't take another second of anticipation and clearly neither could Hugh because he lowered his face to mine at the same time I tilted my chin up.

And there it is.

Finally!

The moment our lips touched, a crackling surge of electricity ricocheted through every part of me. Instinctively, my eyelids fluttered shut, and I clung to his body, feeling a blast of adrenaline so powerful that no amount of cliff diving could compete with it.

Nope, it was clear to my poor, fickle heart that only one person could pull the strings of my heart like this.

Hugh Biggs.

His kiss was a featherlight touch.

A soft, sweet brush of his lips.

Once.

Twice.

On the third brush of his lips against mine, Hugh lingered, keeping his lips there, pressing just a little deeper, pulling my heartstrings just that little bit tighter until I felt I was so highly strung, I might burst apart in his arms.

They were sweet, innocent pecks that caused my body to explode in an uncontrollable tremor. Hugh's lips were surprisingly soft. I wasn't sure what I had been expecting, but his kiss exceeded any expectations I had conjured up these past few years, and it *definitely* beat practicing on my hand.

My arms were wrapped far too tightly around his neck, and a part of me worried about cutting off his air supply, but I couldn't let go.

Nothing in this world could trick me into releasing this boy.

Not my thoughts.

Not my mind.

Not my broken pieces.

Nothing.

When Hugh pulled back and his whiskey-colored eyes searched mine, I felt myself nod, desperate to reassure him that I wanted him to keep going.

This time when he pressed his lips to mine, he didn't pull away. Instead, they lingered on mine, and then, achingly slowly, he moved his lips against mine. I wasn't sure which one of us was shaking more—I could only assume we were on equal measures of nervousness because, when he cupped my face with his hand, deepening our kiss, I felt like I had been electrocuted directly from the power grid.

No, scratch that. It felt like he had hooked me directly up to it and I was powerless to stop it.

Hugh kissed carefully, like he knew exactly the kind of way I liked it, which was surprising because I didn't even know how I liked it until he put his mouth on mine. It was the *best* first kiss ever.

PART 11

Limbo

INKLINGS OF DOUBT

JULY 31, 1999

"I HEARD HE'S SOME HOTSHOT FROM DUBLIN."

"His dad's one of the Kavanaghs from town."

"And he's joining our class after summer?"

"Yeah, he joined sixth class for a couple of weeks before we broke up for the holidays."

"He did?"

"Yeah, and apparently, he was supposed to be starting first year but has to repeat sixth class because of the move."

"What's his name?"

"Jonathan, I think? At least that's what I think Cormac said."

"He's meant to be unreal at rugby."

"Where does he play?"

"Outside center, I think."

"What part of Dublin is he from?"

"The rich part."

"No shit?"

"For real. My father used to go to school with his father, so I know for a fact his parents bought Wild Rose Manor over on upper west, so the lad has to be minted."

"How minted are we talking?"

Sprawled out on the sidelines of the pitch at the rugby club, surrounded by a few of my classmates at Sacred Heart, the boys from Scoil Eoin, and a few girls from St. Bernadette's Convent, I listened to the conversation happening around me and sighed.

Danny Call and Patrick had come to blows yesterday, while Pierce O'Neill and Hugh had come close. Yet here they were, laughing and tossing a rugby ball back and forth like they didn't have a care in the world.

Boys were so strange.

When they had an issue with each other, they resolved it by kicking the living daylights out of one another and then went right back to being friends.

I wasn't nearly as forgiving and still harbored a Gibsie-sized chip on my shoulder when it came to some of those boys. Thankfully, he and Claire had scampered off behind the clubhouse, so I didn't have to worry about holding my tongue if they decided to pick on him today.

"We should play spin the bottle." One of the convent girls giggled, sidling up to Patrick. "With two-minute kisses."

"*With* tongue," another one of the girls from St. Bernadette's chimed in. This one took a seat next to Hugh and dusted a piece of imaginary fluff from his T-shirt. "Who's up for it?"

I didn't know about spin the bottle, but I knew with absolute certainty that I was up for ripping her hand off if she kept touching *my* best friend.

Fury rose up inside of me at a rapid rate, and I balled my hands into fists at my sides to stop myself from grabbing her stupid red hair.

That was a problem I had: obsessing over things I loved the most. It wasn't something I had control over. When I felt things, I felt them with every part of my heart. When I was sad or cross, it was the same. I couldn't be steady or still in myself. I felt the full wrath of my emotions at any given chance. And right now, I was feeling incensed because *she* was touching the person *I* loved most in the world.

I wanted to stand up, march over to where they were sitting, and shove her away from him. I wanted to scream *he's mine* at the top of my lungs, but I *couldn't* because he *wasn't*.

Hugh kissed me that day in the cave, but a month had gone by since the trip to the coast, and he hadn't brought it up once.

In fact, a small part of me wondered if the kiss in the fairy cave really happened or if it was just another figment of my disastrous imagination.

Anxious, I sat cross-legged on the grass and pressed my fingers to my temples. I was doing well this summer, and I'd been taking my medication every day without fail, but I could never be sure of myself. I always had an inkling of doubt.

I was so deep in my thoughts, I hadn't noticed the circle everyone had formed on the grass.

A circle that I found myself in, sitting opposite Hugh.

"You okay, Lizzie?" Marybeth asked in a gentle voice while she and her twin sister sat on either side of me. "Do you have a headache?"

"No, I'm fine." Forcing a smile, I clasped my hands together. "It's all good."

FINISH YOUR TANORA AND SPIN THE BLOODY BOTTLE

Hugh

JULY 31, 1999

"Hughie!" Robbie Mac shouted. "Finish your Tanora and spin the bloody bottle, lad."

Feeling uncomfortable, I chugged the last fizzy drop in my bottle, re-screwed the cap, and tossed the bottle in his direction.

No way in hell was I taking the first turn.

Dammit, I should have asked Liz to be my girlfriend when we were on holidays. If I had, then I wouldn't be sitting in a circle with my friends, trying to mask a panic attack.

Because I *was* fucking panicking.

Every time one of the lads spun that damn bottle, I thought I might die. I wasn't sure how I would react if it landed on her. Would I be able to sit still and watch someone else kiss her?

I doubted it.

Fourteen spins of the bottle around the circle, and I found myself with the bottle in hand, ready to take my first turn.

Please Jesus, don't let it land on the touchy-feely redhead.

Please, God, save me from this mess.

I'll do anything if you just make that bottle stop on...

"Lizzie!" the girls cheered, and my pulse skyrocketed when I saw that my spin had landed on *her*.

Thank you, thank you, thank you, Jesus!

"There's no way you haven't kissed her before anyway," Danny challenged, sounding peeved.

I didn't answer him about whether Liz and I had kissed before because it wasn't his business. To be fair, though, I would be pissed too if he got to kiss Liz while I had to kiss *Bernadette Brady*.

Ugh.

When I locked eyes on Liz, who was moving into the position in the middle of the circle, I could hear my pulse thundering in my ears.

Exhaling shakily, I joined her in the middle of the circle, while everyone around us cheered and wolf whistled.

"Two full minutes, Biggsie," Lukey called out, laughing. "We'll be timing ya."

"With tongues," another one chimed in.

Ignoring our friends, I focused my attention on the girl kneeling in front of me, trying to gauge her reaction.

Liz didn't look nervous.

On the contrary, her eyes twinkled with what I thought was excitement. Offering me an encouraging nod, Liz placed her hands on my shoulders and smiled. "Hi."

"Hi," I croaked out, settling my hands on her waist.

"Do it!" they all chanted. "Do it, do it, do it!"

My brain went into overdrive, while my heart freewheeled into her pocket.

I had to do it.

It was now or never.

I had to kiss her.

I wanted to kiss her.

I *would* kiss her.

Still, I couldn't stop the uncertainty growing inside at the prospect of being wrong. *You're not wrong, asshole. Now stop overthinking and just do it!*

With every nerve in my body shot to hell and my breathing uneven, I lowered my face to hers. I moved slowly. Achingly fucking slowly, but I couldn't afford to mess this up.

When her eyelids fluttered shut and she tilted her chin up to meet mine in anticipation, something relaxed inside of me. Inhaling a steadying breath, I closed my eyes and the space between us.

The moment our lips touched, I felt that familiar blast of white-hot electricity surge through me. I knew Liz felt it too, because she tightened her arms around my neck and pulled me closer.

I had no fucking clue what I was doing and somehow managed to know *exactly* what to do. I was taking the lead in a game I'd only sampled once and didn't know the rules of. I could only put it down to my enthusiasm trumping my inexperience.

The pressure, the consequences, and the never-ending feelings.

This girl and these lips would haunt me for a lifetime.

K-I-S-S-I-N-G

Lizzie

JULY 31, 1999

Hugh Biggs was kissing me again.

My heart was racing so hard, I was sure everyone around us could hear it, but I didn't care. Because this was the best day of my life.

His lips brushed against mine once, twice, and then on the third brush, he kissed me deeper, tightening his hold on my waist.

My body felt like it was being shocked by an electric fence. Everything inside of me twitched and jolted with excitement.

And then I felt it—the tip of his tongue gently swiped against mine. It didn't feel bad, like the other girls had complained when they kissed their dares.

This felt *amazing*.

Somehow, I knew what to do, like I didn't know but did know all at once.

It was confusing and exciting and not enough all at once.

His tongue was in my mouth, gently brushing against mine in slow, drugging swipes that felt nothing like what I had witnessed earlier.

Unable to stop myself, I pulled him closer so our chests were touching and wrapped my arms around his neck as tight as I could.

Because I wanted to keep him right here forever.

I wanted to feel this for the rest of my life.

The longer we kissed, the more familiar we became with each other.

Hugh wasn't forceful, and he didn't shove his tongue down my throat. He wasn't slobbery or, worse, a biter like Danny Call was when he slurped around in Bernadette's mouth.

When we finally broke apart, his cheeks were flushed, while I knew mine were scarlet.

Scrambling back to where the girls were sitting, I resumed my perch on the grass and willed my heart to steady up, while the girls gushed and gossiped.

The boys on the other side of the invisible line were all cheering and clapping Hugh on the shoulders.

He caught my eye then, brown on blue, and I felt a rush of heat flood my body.

The way he was looking at me was different to how he looked at everyone else.

A faint smile ghosted his lips, and he blew out a shaky breath before offering me an adorable shrug.

Mirroring his smile, I shrugged back and clasped my hands together tightly.

I wanted to do that again.

Every day.

For the rest of forever.

And I think he did, too.

A CRAZY LITTLE THING CALLED HORMONES

Hugh

AUGUST 28, 1999

EVERYTHING CHANGED FOR ME AFTER THE TRIP TO THE COAST. I KNEW THE EXACT moment it happened. Deep inside the fairies' sea cave, when she wrapped her arms around my neck and I pressed my lips to hers, it hit me like a wrecking ball that I *loved* the girl sitting on my lap and wanted to *be* with her in *none* of the ways I used to.

That realization was solidified even further when we kissed again during spin the bottle.

Yeah, that kiss wrecked me.

I never tried to hide the fact that I held a flame for Lizzie Young, but said innocent flame exploded that day, igniting into a blazing fire that hadn't stopped spreading through me since.

With the fire came feelings—deep, powerful, fervid feelings, all directed toward Lizzie, that were as intense as they were complicated.

Even more confusing were the dreams that accompanied these newfound feelings. Dreams I was *not* supposed to have about my best friend.

The most embarrassing part of the whole ordeal was my body's sudden reaction to her, which made it even harder to spend time with my best friend.

Meanwhile, Liz had no such problems and continued to be as cuddly and affectionate with me as she always was, which wouldn't have been a problem if I'd had a single iota of a clue about how to make it *stop*.

I didn't know how to act around her now, because every time she was near me, all I could think about was grabbing her and doing it all over again.

I couldn't stop thinking about her.

How her lips felt on mine.

How her tongue tasted.

How *good* it felt.

How she did crazy things to my body.

I wanted to kiss her so fucking bad again, but I didn't have the balls. I wanted to ask her to be my girlfriend, but every time I tried to broach the subject, I panicked.

So I kept it to myself and waited, promising myself that I would do it the next time I saw her. Problem was, I'd been putting it off all summer and I felt beyond agitated.

I just wanted her to be *mine*. More than I ever wanted anything in my life. Including my PlayStation. Honestly, if I could put her on my Christmas list this year, I'd retire from asking for gifts for the rest of my life. If I could just have *Liz*.

Just her.

Plenty of other lads liked her, too, and it made me feel fucking sick thinking about what would happen if one of them worked up the courage to ask her out before I did.

Would she say yes?

If she did, how would I handle it?

Would I die?

I thought I might die.

I truly felt like my heart would stop beating if that happened.

"Did you hear a word I said?" Feely's voice infiltrated my thoughts, and I blinked in confusion. "Hugh," he continued, smirking at me from the other side of the tent we were attempting to erect in my back garden for our upcoming sleepover later tonight. "You completely dazed out there, lad."

"Yeah," I muttered, refocusing on the pole I was supposed to be threading through the tent loops. "Hey, Feely?"

"Yes, Hugh?"

"Can I ask ya something?"

"Fire away, lad."

"I was just wondering," I mumbled, feeling my face redden as I tried to broach the subject. "Are you still a frigit?"

"Unfortunately not," Feely replied, attention trained on the peg he was hammering into the grass. "Maura McGuinness saw to that back during a game of spin the bottle while you were on holiday."

"No shit." I cocked a brow. "You never said."

"Not exactly something I wanted to publicize, lad."

"Fair enough," I mused, giving him my full attention. "How was it?"

"It was like putting my tongue in a washing machine," he replied, reaching up to adjust the collar of his T-shirt. "With teeth."

"Jesus." Swallowing down a gag, I covered my mouth with a hand. Lizzie didn't have

304

a tongue like a washing machine. While we had only kissed twice and used tongues during one of those kisses, I was quietly confident that no one could kiss as well as Lizzie Young. "Unlucky, lad."

"Yep." Feely finished hammering the peg into place before craning his head back to look at me. "What's on your mind, Hugh?"

"You don't want to know."

He smirked. "Try me."

"Seriously, lad." I shook my head in warning. "The only place the thoughts in my head should be spoken about is in a confession box at mass."

"Okay, now you *have* to tell me," Feely chuckled, abandoning the tent. "Come on, lad." He stretched out on the lawn and grinned. "Out with it."

Knowing I had only two potential candidates to talk about this with—Feely or Gibs—had me thinking *fuck it.*

Sitting my ass down on the lawn, I spilled my guts to my friend, all the while renewing my resentment toward the man I once called Dad.

I was three months shy of twelve and puberty had kicked in with a vengeance, bringing with it body hair, hormones, a voice that deepened daily, and a momentous growth spurt. *Everywhere.*

I was far from uninformed when it came to the birds and the bees. I knew how everything worked like sex, periods, puberty, ejaculation, masturbation. You name it, I knew it. But there was a monumental gap between *knowing* what to expect from your body and *understanding* that something when it arrived.

I couldn't go to my mother for reassurance about the things happening to my body, and I shouldn't have had to go to my friends, either.

I *should* have been able to go to my father.

Twenty minutes into our conversation, it became blatantly evident that, while Feely was the oldest of us and the resident expert on farm animal reproduction methods, he didn't have a bull's clue about his own species. This resulted in *me* explaining *his* reproductive organs to *him.*

To be fair, I thought Feely had even less luck than I had in the paternal department. He had Paddy Feely to turn to, the poor, misfortunate bastard. Even the closed door my father hid behind was more understanding than Feely's dad.

By happenstance, it turned out that erecting the tent in my back garden became an invaluable teaching tool, and by the end of our talk, I was quietly confident that, should Feely be given a surprise test on the matter, he would pass with flying colors. Meanwhile, I found myself just as emotionally ill-equipped to handle my raging hormones as I had been when I woke up that morning.

THE BANSHEE OF BALLYLAGGIN

Lizzie

AUGUST 28, 1999

"THAT'S NOT HOW IT GOES," GIBSIE PROTESTED WHEN PATRICK FINISHED HIS RETELL-ing of a local ghost story. "What utter bullshit."

We were camping out in the back garden of No. 4 Avoca Greystones and the boys were attempting to terrorize us with spooky stories and ghoulish tales.

Meanwhile, I was quietly confident that nothing they conjured up could rattle me half as much as my sister's behavior this summer had.

For the longest time, I thought I was the only one with problems in our family, but since returning from her trip to Liverpool, Caoimhe had continuously proved me wrong. She spent most of the summer crying in her room, and when she wasn't crying, she was screaming at our parents about the unfairness of her life.

According to Caoimhe, she was over eighteen and deserved to have her boyfriend stay over whenever she wanted. However, since falling out of favor with our father, she was quickly realizing the life of privilege she'd enjoyed since birth was exactly that: a *privilege*. The fact that privileges could be revoked at any time was another cold, hard lesson she was facing.

Not only was my sister's boyfriend forbidden from stepping foot on our property, but she would have to repeat sixth year in the local public school while Mark got to repeat his final year at their old school. Dad refused to pay another year of tuition for Caoimhe to attend Tommen College. His decision had caused eruptions at home, and I was glad to be away from the house for a night.

"Feely has his facts all wrong," Gibs declared, drawing my attention back to the present. Wrestling the torch away from Patrick, he shone it on himself before announcing, "I know the *true* story of Grainne Ní hÓigáin, otherwise known as *the banshee of Ballylaggin*."

"Tell us, Gerard," Claire encouraged, all the while sidling up to her big brother for protection.

"Legend has it Grainne was a witch," he began, making his voice sound extra creepy for special effect. "The townspeople knew Grainne dabbled in the occults, but back in those days, a lot of people in Ireland practiced paganism and worshipped priestesses, druids, spirits, and deities, so Grainne was left alone by her neighbors. They were happy to live alongside her, providing she didn't practice her sorcery on them."

"But she did, right?" Claire interrupted, hooking arms with Hugh. "She did something bad, didn't she?"

"Worse than bad," Gibsie confirmed solemnly. "On the night of the full moon, on the sixth day of the sixth month, Grainne took six children from their homes and drowned them in the Ballylaggin river."

"Why?" I asked, intrigued because this version of events was way freakier than Patrick's version. "Why drown the kids?"

"Because she wanted the gift of eternal life and made a deal with the devil in order to get it," Gibsie replied in an eerie tone. "And the blood of six innocents was the devil's price."

"Yeah, you're right," Patrick mused, looking as invested as the rest of us. "Your version's way better, Gibs."

With a smug look on his face, Gibs continued with his tale. "When the parents of the six children awoke in the morning to find their children missing from their beds, all hell broke loose in the town. Search parties were formed, and everyone went out looking for the missing children."

"Shit," Hugh muttered, rubbing his jaw. "This is actually class, Gibs."

"When the lifeless children were eventually discovered on the edge of the riverbank, all six of their bodies were missing their hearts!"

"Holy crap!" Claire choked out, wide-eyed and terrified. "The witch ate their hearts?"

"Worse," Gibsie replied. "She took their hearts back to her house and placed them on her unholy alter."

"That's how the townspeople found out who killed the kids?" I asked, shifting closer to Hugh's other side. "Because they found their hearts in Grainne's house?"

"Exactly," Gibsie agreed, shining the torch at me before retraining the light on his chin. "When the townspeople of Ballylaggin caught up with Grainne, they were enraged."

"What did they do?"

"They sought the help of another witch," Gibsie continued, enthralling the rest of us with his tale. "A powerful priestess from a nearby village."

"To do what?"

"The parents of the dead children, along with the rest of the townspeople, decided the punishment should fit the crime and convinced the priestess to do their bidding. Determined to inflict an eternity of torment upon Grainne, they persuaded the priestess to cast a curse so vile, so despicably unmoral that it had never been heard of before then."

"What was it?"

"They didn't think death was enough of a punishment for Grainne's crimes, no matter how painful or slow that death came, so along with the priestess, the townspeople conjured up a curse that would chain her for eternity in limbo."

"Limbo?" Claire arched a brow. "What's that?"

"Limbo is where ghosts live," I explained. "They're not in our physical world, but they're not gone, either."

"Exactly. It's like the in-between after you die," Hugh added, while he draped a reassuring arm around each of us. "You're not on earth, and you're not in heaven or hell. You're in limbo."

"So that night, as the sun set in the west and the priestess summoned the powers of her deities to enforce the curse upon the evil witch, the townspeople of Ballylaggin tied Grainne Ní hÓigáin to a stake on the hill outside her house and burned her alive."

"Holy shit, Gibs," Patrick breathed, shaking his head. "Please tell me there's more."

"After her death, the townspeople thought they had seen the last of the witch, and they had, for a time…"

"Until?"

"Until six years later, when another six children disappeared from their beds, only to be found the following morning in the exact same spot on the riverbank and with their hearts removed from their lifeless bodies."

"Okay, what the hell?" Claire squealed, looking panicked. "This is too much."

"Legend has it the priestess made a fatal error when casting the curse," Gibsie explained in a deathly cold voice. "One that—on the sixth day, of the sixth month, every six years—allowed the witch to return. Free to roam the townland of Ballylaggin, in search of six more children."

"Oh my God, I have the heebie-jeebies so bad," I snickered, burrowing into Hugh's side.

"Because she drowned the original children in the river, she was forbidden by nature to cross water, trapping her wandering spirit to the town land she died in, and legend has it that, late at night, when the sound of wailing screams fill the darkness, it's Grainne screaming in the afterlife, as she relives the pain of being burned alive."

"Holy crap, Gibs," Hugh exclaimed, sounding impressed. "That was epic."

"So there you have it," Gibsie chuckled, finally breaking character and resuming his playful mood. "The *true* story of the Banshee of Ballylaggin."

Meanwhile, the only thing the rest of us could do in that moment was give him a round of applause.

"Oh, oh, oh!" Gibsie yelped, holding a hand up. "I almost forgot!"

"What?" we all demanded in unison.

"There's something else. Something even worse," he whispered in an eerie tone. "Because, according to town records, one of the five of us is a direct descendant of Grainne Ní hÓigáin." He flashed the torch on and off for spook factor. "In fact, one of our houses is built on the very spot the witch's house used to sit."

"Who?" Claire demanded. "Oh no! Am I related to a witch?"

"No, Claire, we're not related to any witches," Hugh drawled. "Although, Aunt Sarah is questionable."

"Shut up, Hughie," Claire whimpered. "I'm really freaked out."

"It's me, isn't it?" Patrick laughed. "I'm a descendant of the fucking banshee."

"Actually," Gibsie mused, shining the torch on all of us until settling it on me. "It's the resident viper."

"Omigod!" Claire screeched, trying and failing to pull her brother to safety. "She's a witch, Hughie."

Meanwhile, I bent over snickering. "That is so cool. I've always wanted to be a witch."

"Because of Stevie?" Hugh mused, offering me a wolfish smile. "Fleetwood Mac, right?"

"Right," I agreed, still laughing. "I love her witchy vibes."

"'Silver Springs'?"

Grinning, I nodded. "You remembered."

Hugh winked. "I remember everything about you, Liz."

"Why are you guys laughing?" Claire demanded, sounding genuinely petrified. "This is *terrible* news."

"Relax, Claire," Hugh chuckled. "It's complete bullshit."

"And if it's not?" his sister demanded.

"Then I promise not to hex you," I teased.

"Oh God," Claire groaned, making the sign of the cross on her chest. "I need to take mass in the morning."

"Guys, I'm scared," Claire declared several hours later when she sprang up in her sleeping bag. "I want to go inside."

"Quit being a baby," Hugh groaned, draping an arm over his face. "You're perfectly safe."

"But what if the Banshee of Ballylaggin gets us?"

"She can't," Gibsie soothed. "She's not due around for another four years."

"You swear?"

"Hand on my heart, Claire-Bear."

"Okay, but what if Lizzie gets us?"

"I won't," I laughed.

"You promise?"

"Cross my heart, hope to die."

"Okay." Claire was quiet for all of twelve seconds before asking, "What if a bear gets us?"

"In Ballylaggin?" Patrick groaned loudly. "We don't have any bears in Ireland. The worst you're going to see around this neck of the woods is a fox."

"Or a squirrel."

"Or a badger."

"Or a frog."

"Or a hedgehog."

"Or a field mouse."

"Or maybe a rogue bullock."

"Highly doubtful considering we're on the outskirts of town."

"Aw, crackers, I don't like cows."

"You like all animals, Claire."

"Normally, but not cows."

"Don't worry. I'll protect you from the cows, Baby Biggs."

"What about me? I don't like cows, either."

"I'll protect you from the cows, too, Gibs."

"You promise, Pa? You super swear you'll save us?"

"Oh, for fuck's sake, just pack it in, will ye?" Hugh snapped. "You're creeping yourselves out."

"Don't get cross with me, Hughie! I'm younger than you, okay!"

"I know, Claire. That's why you should listen to me, your elder, when I tell you to shut up and go to sleep."

"You know what, lads, if Claire-Bear's not staying, neither am I."

"Shut up, Gibsie." That was Patrick. "Everything's fine. Just close your eyes and go to sleep."

"Fuck, what if there's a rat out here?" Gibsie groaned. "I don't cope well with rats."

"It's the tails, huh, Gerard?"

"Yep, that and the impending Weil's disease, Claire-Bear."

"Super spooky."

"I don't want to get a disease."

"Nope, me either."

"Oh my Jesus," Hugh groaned. "I am begging the two of you to just stop talking."

"Baby Biggs, get out of my sleeping bag!"

"Oops, sorry Patrick. I can't see in the dark. I thought it was Gerard's sleeping bag."

"Claire! Stay out of Gibsie's sleeping bag."

"But we don't sleep apart, Hugh. You know that."

"I can't cope with this." Huffing and puffing like a grumpy bear, Hugh climbed out of his sleeping bag and flicked on a torch, bathing the tent in a dull yellow hue. "I'm out of here."

"No, Hughie, don't go," Claire called after her brother, while I rummaged around for my own torch and switched it on. "You're closest to the door," she called after him. "We need you to stay so the rats have to go through you to get to us."

Too late.

Her brother had disappeared into the darkness of the garden, armed with his sleeping bag. A few moments later, the sound of the treehouse ladder creaking filled the air.

"At least he's not going inside," Gibsie offered. "Because our mams definitely won't let us sleep outside without Hugo Boss-man."

"I'm older than Hugh," Patrick huffed, sounding insulted.

"Ah, you see, but Hugh is the *sensible* one," Claire explained, mimicking her mother's voice, while nestling into the sleeping bag with Gibsie. "Mam says Hughie got all the wisdom, and I got all the wildness."

"Happy now?" I asked dryly, when Gibsie and Claire were snuggled up like litter-mates in one sleeping bag. "You two are ridiculous."

"I told you before I can't sleep without her," Gibs explained, curling up like a cat around our friend. "It's not my fault."

"And he keeps me warm," Claire added with a sleepy yawn. "'Night, Gerard, love you."

"Love you more, Claire-Bear."

"You better not fart," Patrick warned, pointing a finger at Gibs before turning his attention to Claire, "and you better not snore." With that, he settled into his sleeping bag and covered his head with the pillow he was supposed to be using beneath him.

I waited for the others to fall asleep before carefully climbing out of the tent and making a beeline for the treehouse.

I didn't want to sleep in a tent with boys if that tent didn't contain Hugh Biggs. Excitement thrummed inside of me at the thought of spending time alone with him.

When I reached the top of the ladder and crawled through the doorway of the treehouse, I found Hugh reclining in a sleeping bag, using the light from his torch to read a weathered paperback copy of *Angela's Ashes*.

The minute my eyes landed on him, a surge of heat attacked my skin, and my heart galloped wildly. "Hey. Can I stay up here with you?"

"Hey." His attention immediately shifted to me. "Uh, yeah, of course." Setting his book down, Hugh lifted the side of his sleeping bag and gestured for me to climb inside.

Without hesitation I did just that, thrilled when my cold feet were instantly warmed by the heat emanating from his legs.

"You're getting hairy," I told him, feeling the coarseness of his leg hair brush against the smoothness of mine. "It's strange."

"Nothing I can do about that, I'm afraid," he replied, twisting around to drape a warm arm around my shoulders as I turned with my back against his chest. "Warm enough?"

"Mm-hmm." Nodding, I reached up and grasped his forearm with both of my hands and snuggled in close. "Toasty."

"You feeling okay, Liz?"

"Yeah, Hugh." Sighing in contentment, I snuggled in deeper. "I'm having the best summer of my life."

"Yeah." His arm tightened around me. "Me, too."

Unable to repress the shiver of pleasure that rolled through me when he held me close, I turned my head and nuzzled his chest with my cheek. "You make me feel happy." Inhaling deeply, I whispered, "You make me feel safe."

"Yeah?"

"Mm-hmm."

"So I should probably tell you something."

"Oh?"

"It's about us."

"What about us?"

He was quiet for a long time before he said, "I'm having a bit of trouble being around you lately."

My heart sank. "Do you want me to go?"

"What? No, Liz!" He tightened his arm around me. "I would never want that." I felt his nose brush against the back of my head before he whispered, "You know I love you, right?"

"Right."

"I'm just…I'm having a bit of a problem with loving you *too* much."

My heart skipped. "Too much?"

I felt him nod behind me. "It's okay, I'll figure it out, but I just wanted to let you know if I seem a bit off, it's nothing you've done, okay? I'm just, uh, it's just a bit confusing for me right now."

"You know I love you, too, right?" came my whispered reply as I clenched my eyes shut and forced myself to be brave. "Too much."

He was quiet for the longest time, so long that I was beginning to think the conversation, at least for him, was over, but then his trembling hand moved to cover mine.

Excitement sparked to life inside of me and I was certain I had never grabbed a hand as quickly as I grabbed this particular boy's hand.

In fact, not only was I holding on to Hugh's hand for dear life, but I was also squeezing the hell out of it.

With *both* hands.

"Okay then." A low, nervous chuckle escaped him. "I'm glad I'm not alone in this."

"You're definitely not alone in this," I replied, shivering all over.

"Hey, Liz?"

"Yeah, Hugh?"

"Can I ask you a question?"

"Of course."

"Do you think it would be all right"—his voice was low and full of uncertainty—"if I held your hand?"

"You always hold my hand, silly."

"Yeah, but do you think it would be okay if I was the *only* boy who got to hold your hand?"

"Yeah." A delicious ripple of excitement racked through me. "That would be more than okay."

"Okay." I felt his chest move behind me when he exhaled a relieved breath. "That's good to know."

There was a long stretch of silence before I worked up the courage to whisper, "Remember that time in my room when you kissed me on the wrist?"

"I remember."

"I liked it."

"Yeah." He sighed. "Me, too."

"I liked it even more that day in the fairy cave when you kissed me on the lips," I forced myself to admit, my words barely more than a breathy whisper.

"You did?"

"Yeah, Hugh."

Anxiety was gnawing at my gut because I wasn't sure which way this would go, but I *had* to try. I *had* to make the first move if Hugh wasn't going to. And he clearly *wasn't*. September was closing in on us, and I had waited the entire summer for him to make a move, to kiss me again, but he hadn't.

Exhaling shakily, I twisted onto my belly to face him and whispered, "And I really think you should do it again."

"Liz..."

"Unless you don't want to," I hurried to add when I saw the uncertainty in his eyes. Suddenly, a wave of uncertainty of my own washed through me and I tried to backpedal. "You know what? I'm being silly—"

"Liz—"

"No, no, it's okay." Throwing the covers off, I scrambled away, feeling my face burn with embarrassment. "I'm sorry, Hugh, just forget I said anything, okay? I shouldn't have said that to—"

"Liz, stop, don't go—"

"This was silly. I'm being silly. Don't worry about it—"

"Liz!" Hugh snapped, and this time he caught my attention. "Come back."

Exhaling shakily, I stepped back to his side and sank down on my knees.

Without saying a word, Hugh reached for my hand and raised it to his lips. Keeping his eyes on me, he turned it over and pressed a kiss to the scars covering my wrist.

My breath caught in my throat, and I thought my heart might burst. Shivering violently, I watched him kiss my shame away. Because those scars on my wrists depicted the ugliest parts of my mind. But Hugh kissed each one like they were beautiful. Like *I* was beautiful. Like I was still *me*.

Unable to stop myself, I shifted closer, wanting to fold my body into his, wanting to give him all my broken pieces and see if he could work miracles and put me back together again. Because on nights like this, when my mind quieted and my heart beat strong, he made me feel like he could.

"I want to kiss you," Hugh said, eyes locked on mine. "But I need to ask you a question first."

"Uh, okay?" I breathed, chest rising and falling quickly.

"You're my best friend, Liz, and I never want that to stop," he said carefully, looking nervous. "But I don't just love you like a friend anymore." He flicked his attention to our joined hands and roughly cleared his throat. "I love you like a boyfriend loves his girlfriend."

"You do?"

"Yeah." He nodded slowly. "So I was wondering if you might consider loving me like a girlfriend loves her boyfriend?"

"I already do," I strangled out, unable to stop the smile from spreading across my face. "I always have."

His eyes searched mine hopefully. "Yeah?"

I nodded eagerly. "Always."

"Oh, thank God," Hugh replied, heaving out a huge, audible breath. "Because I've been wanting to ask you to be my girlfriend since 1994, and I don't think I can hold it in another day."

"I've been waiting to say yes since 1994," I laughed, bursting with excitement. "Are you asking now, so I can finally say yes?"

"Yeah, Liz," Hugh chuckled with a nod. "I'm asking now." Shaking his head, he looked me in the eyes and asked, "Will you be my girlfriend?"

Finally.

"Yes!" I beamed at him. "I will."

Hugh grinned. "Thank you."

"You're welcome."

"Okay then."

"Yep."

"So you're my girlfriend."

"Yep, and you're my boyfriend."

"I sure am."

"Whoa."

"I know."

"Do you want to…maybe kiss me now?"

"I definitely want to kiss you, Liz. If you want me to kiss you?"

"I definitely want that, Hugh."

"Okay." Heart racing violently, I held my breath when my best friend guided my arms around his neck before slowly drawing my body close to his. "I will."

PART 12

New Millenniums

PARTY LIKE IT'S 1999

Hugh

DECEMBER 31, 1999

"STOP CHEATING."

"I'm not cheating."

"Yes, you are. You can't hide in the mansion, Claire. You have to complete *actual* missions."

"I told you not to give her a turn," I grumbled from my perch on my bed. I tossed a rugby ball into the air and then snatched it back up, while my sister and Gibsie battled it out for dominion over my PlayStation controller. "Claire plays with the butler instead of doing missions."

Tonight was New Year's Eve, and my parents, along with Sadhbh and Keith, were heading to Catherine and Mike's annual bash at Old Hall House. Clearly, all our parents had chipped in to pay Caoimhe a pretty penny to babysit all of us because there was no other way she would've agreed to give up the last night out of an entire millennium.

Christ, even my father had somehow managed to resurrect himself from the pits of despair to go out with Mam. I had no doubt it was temporary, of course. If I'd learned anything over the past four years, it was that my father had developed a "ready, steady, stop" attitude toward life. Sometimes he tried; more times he gave up. It was a pattern my mother and sister had grown accustomed to—and even accepted. Not me. I knew the man he once was would never stand for his broken promises. The father I knew would kick the father I have's ass.

"It's called *Tomb Raider II* for a reason," Gibsie growled, bringing me back to the present, while failing to win back the controller. "Because she raids tombs, Claire. Not kitchens cupboards."

"I'm exploring, Gerard," she defended with a huff, tongue poking out from the corner of her mouth as she concentrated on locking the butler in the freezer. "Besides, it's my turn, guys. I can do what I want."

"I told you," I mused, feeling validated. "It's worse than when we give her a turn on *GTA*, and she stops in traffic at the red light."

"Because the red light means stop, Hugh Andrew Biggs."

"Not in an alternate universe, Claire Bridget Biggs."

"Ah, lad, look at Lara Croft's boobs," Gibsie chuckled around a mouthful of popcorn, as he pointed at the screen of my portable television. "Make her jump again, Claire-Bear."

"Gerard! Don't say *boobs*."

"Can you zoom in?" he asked, hooking an arm around her to tap on the controller. "Make it go closer."

"What—hey, no! Stop looking at Lara's boobs."

"Why?"

"Because it's not nice."

"Hugh looks at her boobs."

"I don't care what Hugh looks at—"

The shrill sound of our doorbell chiming echoed through the air, bringing with it a sudden jolt of electricity straight to the heart.

Tossing the rugby ball down on my bed, I sprang to my feet and dove for the bedroom door, ignoring Gibsie's request for more sweets from the kitchen.

He had two perfectly good feet.

When I reached the top of the landing and heard her familiar voice, the electric jolts in my chest morphed into full-on shocks throughout my entire body.

Finally.

I'd been checking the time all evening. Thankfully, I managed to the take the stairs two at a time without cracking my neck. Slip-sliding off the second-to-last step, I slid across the hallway tiles in my socks, not stopping until I had my hand pressed to the glass frosting of our front door.

"Nice moves, lover boy," Caoimhe snickered, grinning down at me. "That was some *Risky Business*–style sliding you had going on there."

My brows furrowed in confusion. "Huh?"

"Eighties' reference, kid. Never mind," she replied with a chuckle, stepping aside to reveal the only girl who could conjure electricity in her mind and shoot it into me. Because that's what she did.

Liz grinned up at me, eyes twinkling with mischief, and I had to stifle a groan. Looking at her was getting more and more complicated because with age came beauty, and with beauty came hormones, and with hormones came urges. While I tried to conceal it as best as I could, I had some seriously strong urges directed solely toward this girl.

My girl.

"Hey, Hugh." Snatching up my hand, she quickly moved to my side. My body burned with heat when her skin touched mine, and I had to repress the urge to shiver. "Thanks for inviting me to your sleepover."

"You can always sleep with me, Liz," I replied, feeling flustered. "I mean, you're always welcome to my sleepovers."

Normally, I would wait around to see my mother off, but tonight, I bolted upstairs with my girlfriend instead.

Call me petty, but I had no intention of patting my father's head and telling him what a good boy he was for making the effort. Not when I knew in my heart that it would be months before any such effort would be repeated.

"Wait," Liz whisper-hissed, yanking me away from my door before I opened it. "Do you have your phone?"

"Yeah." I slid my hand into my pocket to retrieve the Nokia 3210 mobile phone I got for Christmas. "Do you have yours?"

"Yep," she replied, grabbing my phone while handing me hers.

"You know, our mams probably went shopping for these together," I mused, while I stored my number in her contacts and Liz stored hers in mine. "Claire and Gibs got the exact same make and model as us."

"Probably," she laughed, swapping phones again.

We both grinned at each other before tucking our phones away. "I'll call you tomorrow."

"Not if I call you first," she shot back with a wink.

"Fair enough." Chuckling, I shook my head and moved for my room. "But you better be fast because the early bird catches the worm."

"Wait," she called out, grabbing my sleeve and pulling me back to her. "I have something for you."

"But you already gave me your phone numb—" My words broke off when her lips crushed against mine. Her arms went around my neck, pulling my body closer to hers, and I went willingly.

Because I felt *everything* for this girl.

She only had to put her lips on mine and every nerve in my body was shot to hell. She had an uncanny talent for throwing my nerves into absolute disarray, while simultaneously seizing my ability to form a coherent thought.

When Liz finally tore her lips from mine, she left me with a horrendous problem in my jocks and her chewing gum in my mouth.

Her pupils were so dilated, they were almost black. I could only assume that they mirrored mine.

"Your sister won't let me kiss you later," she explained, still breathless from destroying me for any other girl. "So I thought I'd get my kiss now."

She was right about that.

My sister had thrown the mother of all meltdowns when she found out about me and Liz. She even stopped speaking to us, though her silent treatment had only lasted a few weeks.

Liz had been devastated by the cold shoulder, while I'd been fucking elated with the peace and quiet.

The girls had managed to patch things up, but our relationship was still a sore spot for my sister, and because of this, Liz went out of her way to not touch me when Claire was around. We kept our relationship on the down-low, and Liz wouldn't even hold my hand these days if my sister was looking.

It pissed me off to no end, but I couldn't deny how much I enjoyed our stolen kisses when no one was around.

Reaching up, Liz trailed her finger and thumb over my bottom lip before retrieving her chewing gum from my mouth and popping it back into hers. "Tastes like you." She winked. "My favorite flavor."

Fuck.

Grinning, Liz patted my cheek before stepping around me with a definite hop in her step.

"Hey, guys," she called out, opening my bedroom door and joining our friends.

Meanwhile, I remained frozen in my spot for a solid ten minutes, desperately trying to calm the hell down.

"Why do you have to go?" Claire whined an hour later, holding on to Gibsie's hand with both of hers. "Don't leave me on the millennium, Gerard," she continued, digging her heels in when he tried to leave. "What if the world ends?"

"Claire-Bear, you have to let me go," Gibsie chuckled, holding on to the doorframe with his free hand. "Johnny's outside in the car waiting for me."

"So?" she huffed, narrowing her eyes. "I'm your Claire-Bear."

"I know you are," he tried to coax, "and I'll be home to my Claire-Bear in the morning."

"Noooo," she wailed. "If you go, I'll be alone with the lovebirds." She paused to shoot a glaring look in my direction before continuing her whining. "I'll be all alone."

"Uh, hello?" Feely, who had arrived shortly after Liz, interjected from his perch on the beanbag. "What am I? Dog shit?"

"Oops, sorry, Patrick," Claire replied, reddening. "I forgot you were here."

"Lovely." Feely rolled his eyes. "Just lovely."

"I will call you as soon as the clock strikes midnight," Gibsie vowed, breaking free from her hold. "I love you." He blew her a kiss before bolting from the room. "You're still my best friend, Claire-Bear."

"Yeah right." Huffing out a dramatic breath, she flopped onto Feely's lap and folded her arms across her chest. "I'm sulking."

Her theatrics evoked an eye roll from me and a chuckle from my girlfriend. "Claire, he's allowed to have other friends."

"No, he's not."

"Aw, what's wrong, Baby Biggs?" Feely asked, coddling her and feeding the drama queen. "Missing your playmate already?"

"Yes, because he's always at Johnny's house now," Claire erupted, curls splaying wildly. "Going on trips with Johnny's family, and sleepovers, and going to matches, and discos, and…and *training*." She rolled her eyes to the heavens and fake gagged. "It makes me sick, Patrick. Like super sick."

"Don't tell me that you're jealous of Johnny Kavanagh."

"I'm not jealous of him," Claire defended, cheeks turning bright pink. "I'm mad at him. He stole my best friend."

"Would you relax?" I chimed in, too fucking weary to deal with her drama. "Gibs slept here every night since Christmas, and he spent all morning, afternoon, and evening with you."

"And where is Gerard now, huh?" she demanded. "At a disco with Johnny Kavanagh, that's where. And do you know what Johnny Kavanagh does at discos? He kisses girls, that's what he does. Lots of girls. With tongues."

"They're not at a disco," Feely said, attempting to calm her. "They're at Cap's house."

"Exactly," I agreed.

"Cap?" Claire narrowed her eyes. "Why do you call him that?" She looked around innocently. "Does he wear a lot of hats or something?"

"Yeah, Sis," I laughed. "That's why."

"No, he doesn't wear a lot of caps, Baby Biggs," Feely explained, clearly taking pity on my baby sister. "We call him cap because he's our captain."

"Of what? Your imaginary ship?" Lizzie chimed in with a snicker. "I can see it now: Captain Fantastic and his flock of fanboys."

"The rugby team, actually," Feely shot back. "But good one, viper."

"Well, I bet he's making him practice rugby, which is silly because Gerard only likes rugby because *Johnny* likes rugby." Claire huffed before asking, "Hey, are you guys sure they haven't gone to a disco?"

"If Cap and Gibs were at a disco, we would be there." Feely consoled her, patting her head.

"Yes, we would." I nodded in agreement. "And far away from your tantrums."

"Yeah, well, maybe if Johnny Kavanagh found a best friend of his own, I wouldn't be so upset," she doubled down and said, looking comically wounded. "Why did he have to pick *my* one?"

That was a question that continued to confound our class. Back in September, when Johnny Kavanagh sauntered in on the first day of sixth class, he'd taken an immediate shine to Gibsie, and they'd been inseparable at school ever since.

None of the lads in our class could understand why someone like Johnny would want to hang out with Gibsie.

I could.

Gibsie was the greatest friend a person could have. He was loyal, trustworthy, had the best personality in the whole school, and really fucking cared about the people he loved. Feely and I both knew that friends like Gerard Gibson didn't come around too often, and I was glad Johnny realized it, too.

I would never say it out loud, because I didn't want to embarrass the lad, but I was thrilled he had finally found his wings. He would always have me in his corner, no matter what, but seeing him making his way at school, and making friends for himself, made me so fucking proud. Because Johnny Kavanagh was *his* friend. Yeah, the four of us all hung out at lunch together, and Feely and I considered Johnny our friend, too, but everyone knew where Cap's loyalties rested.

With our Gibs.

"What are you thinking about?" Liz asked, grinning at me. "You've got the biggest smile on your face."

"Nothing," I replied, still smiling. "I'm just happy."

TOO GOOD TO BE TRUE

JANUARY 1, 2000

FOR THE LONGEST TIME I HAD PROGRAMMED MY HEART TO EXPECT SADNESS. I PUT IT down to the fact that I had an unsettled mind and had learned from a young age that everything was temporary.

Good or bad.

No matter how long something lasted, it would never be permanent.

I knew this, and *still* I let myself slip into a false sense of security.

I allowed my heart to trick my mind.

For months, I allowed myself to believe that I had turned a corner, that life wouldn't be so hard for me anymore.

I had the greatest boyfriend on planet earth.

I had the best friends.

I had a healthy mother.

I had a father who looked happy to see me now.

I was healthy.

I was stable.

I didn't want to die anymore.

The bubble shattered this morning when Sinead woke me up before the others. Taking me by the hand, she led me downstairs to the kitchen. From there, she proceeded to tell me that, during the New Year's Eve party at my house last night, my mother had taken a turn.

For a moment, I just sat there, frozen in place, as I listened to the woman who I'd come to love like a second mother explain how my *real* mother had suffered a confirmed heart attack.

Sinead promised that Mam was holding her own after the heart attack, but when they ran some tests on her at the hospital, one of the scans picked up a shadow.

She didn't need to say anything else after that.

I already knew what a shadow meant.

It's back.

"You mustn't think like that, sweetheart." Sinead tried to console me when I voiced my thoughts aloud. "Nothing has been confirmed yet—not until the biopsy results come back."

"They think it's back, though," I pushed, using the sleeve of my pajama top to wipe my eyes. "They wouldn't be taking a biopsy if they didn't."

With a sympathetic expression, she reached for my hand. "They're not sure, Lizzie."

"If it's back, it's going to kill her," I whispered, squeezing her hand. "It won't stop until it kills her."

"Your mother is the strongest woman I've ever met," Sinead countered, sounding so confident that I almost believed her. *Almost.* "If—and that's a very big *if*—the cancer has come back, then she will fight tooth and nail to defeat it." She used her free hand to wipe a tear from my cheek. "And I will do whatever I can to help *you* through it."

"Me?" I croaked out, unable to stop myself from leaning my cheek into her touch. "Why?"

"Because I love you, sweetheart," Sinead replied, giving me a warm smile. "As a matter of fact, this entire family adores you, Lizzie Young, and you won't be alone in this." She wiped another tear from my cheek. "Not while there's a Biggs in this town."

"Okay," I squeezed out, feeling a blanket of dread settle over me. Sniffling, I added, "Can I go and talk to Hugh now?"

"Of course you can." Sinead pulled me in for a tight hug and pressed a kiss to the top of my head before pulling back to offer me a watery smile. "Go on upstairs to my son, sweetheart."

On wobbly legs, I bolted for the staircase, barely making it to the top without falling. I couldn't breathe. I couldn't walk straight. Everything was spinning. Everything falling apart again.

Holding my breath to stop my screams escaping, I barged into Hugh's room with one hand clamped over my mouth. Falling over Patrick, who was asleep on the bedroom floor, I scrambled toward the bed, not stopping until I got to Hugh.

"Liz?" Hugh's raspy voice filled my ears as he blinked awake. "What's up?" Noticing my expression, he sat up straight on the mattress and reached for me. "What happened, Liz?"

"Hugh!" Unable to hold it in another second, I flung my body at his and fell apart in his arms.

Because *these* arms were the *only* arms that never left.

SHE HAS HIM, BUT YOU HAVE ME

Hugh

JANUARY 1, 2000

THE FIRST THING I NOTED WHEN WE PULLED UP AT OLD HALL HOUSE WAS A FAMILIAR car that *shouldn't* have been there.

The way Lizzie squeezed my hand when she noticed the car assured me that we were thinking the same thing.

What the fuck is he doing here?

Mark Allen had been prohibited from stepping foot on this property since last summer. Ever since Mike realized that Mark had impregnated his teenage daughter and then taken her to England to get an abortion—but Mike also considered Mark to be the driving force behind Caoimhe's failed Leaving Cert to boot.

I knew for a fact the cretin knocked up Lizzie's sister, because I had heard it from the horse's mouth. I hadn't been intentionally eavesdropping, but when I slipped downstairs to grab a drink during a sleepover, I'd heard Catherine and Mike talking about it. *In graphic detail.* Returning to my makeshift bed on Lizzie's bedroom floor, I'd laid back down in bed and never once breathed a word about what I heard that night.

Not even to Liz.

So why now, after half a year of giving Mark the cold shoulder, was Mike standing on his front porch hugging *him*?

"He's back," Lizzie whispered, tightening her hold on my hand. Sniffling, she turned to look at me with wide, glassy eyes. "Why is he back, Hugh?"

"I don't know, Liz," I admitted, pulling her hand onto my lap. While I fully accepted that grief evoked strange reactions from people, this took the biscuit.

"Best behavior, Hugh," Mam instructed from the driver's seat. Unfastening her seat belt, she turned back to give me a warning look. "I mean it."

Jaw ticking, I swallowed my frustration and watched as Mam climbed out and walked up to the house to join Caoimhe, Mike, and the cretin.

"Look at me," I instructed, turning my attention to my girlfriend. "Liz, look at me."

Reluctantly, she did.

"Tell them I'm staying with you," I instructed, squeezing her hand. "When we go over there, tell them you want me to stay."

"I *do* want you to stay," she strangled out, unfastening her seat belt to crawl onto my lap. "I don't want to be here without you."

"I know you do," I coaxed, wrapping my arms around her. "I just need my mam to hear you say it because otherwise she'll think I'm overstepping."

"I *want* you to overstep," she pleaded, wrapping her arms around my neck so tightly, I felt slightly dizzy. "Whenever Mam gets sick, Caoimhe *always* gets to have him over." She choked out a pained sob. "It'll happen again this time. Dad will leave and I'll be left alone."

"No, it won't because I won't let that happen," I promised, holding her close. "She has him, but you have me."

———————————————

According to Mike, things weren't great at the hospital, and one of the nurses had suggested letting the girls visit their mother—just in case.

Mam had dropped all three of them back to the hospital and had agreed with Mike that I could stay the night, to be there for Lizzie when she got home.

This was how I found myself in my current position, sitting opposite Mark Allen in the front room of Old Hall House, waiting for the sisters to get home.

He sat in the armchair on the left side of the open fire, while I sat in the one opposite him on the righthand side.

Drumming my fingers on the armrests, I continued to stare at the asshole across from me, silently daring him to say something. I'd never thought much about eye color before tonight, but after staring at his soulless eyes for over an hour, I was glad my eyes were brown and Lizzie's were blue because this prick had ruined green eyes for me.

There was a fire poker within reaching distance of my right hand, and I wouldn't think twice about shoving it up his hole if he started his shit.

Just one word.

That's all I needed.

Like usual, he wasn't nearly as brave in my presence as he was around Gibs. It was like I'd told our parents a thousand times: Mark was a fucking bully, and bullies were nothing if not cowards.

He knew I had taken his measure. I could see it in the nervous way he turned away whenever he dared to look in my direction and found me staring right back at him. I could smell the uncertainty rolling off him in waves.

It also didn't hurt that I was closing in on him in the height department. He was eighteen, while I wasn't even thirteen yet, and he barely had an inch on me.

"Do you mind?" he finally broke the strained silence we'd been stewing in. "Can you stop fucking staring at me like that?"

"If you don't like it, you could always leave," I deadpanned, purposefully keeping my eyes trained on his. "You know where the door is."

"Oh, you'd like that, wouldn't ya?" he sneered. "You and your sister can't wait to see the back of me."

"Because we have good judgment," I shot back dryly. "Unlike others."

"Meaning?"

"Do you need me to spell it out for you?"

"What the fuck is your problem with me, Biggs?" he demanded then, losing his cool. "I've never bothered ya, but you're hell-bent on making trouble for me every chance you get."

"I don't like you," I replied simply. "I can't stand you, truth be told. The way you look, the way you speak, the way you think, the way you drive, the way you conduct yourself. Everything about you disgusts me." Leaning back in my chair, I gave him a harsh appraisal. "And that's not taking into account that you're a sadistic, not to mention pathetic, bully who gets off on tormenting a child who had to watch his father and sister drown in front of him." I narrowed my eyes at him. "I was there that day on the boat, asshole, and I was at the funeral, too. I remember *everything*. I especially remember the *smirk* you had on your face when my friend was saying goodbye to his father, who, just so happens to be *my* godfather."

"*Was* your godfather," Mark shot back with a cruel smirk. "Joe Gibson is past tense."

Instead of losing the head, I smiled in response, and it seemed to throw him off-kilter.

"Is that how you do it?" I asked with a low chuckle. "How you get under people's skin? You target their deceased loved ones?" I laughed again, thoroughly enjoying how his face reddened. "Jesus, you're even more pathetic than I realized."

"Oh yeah?" Sitting forward, he rested his elbows on his thighs and narrowed his green eyes in challenge. "Well, I could tell you a thing or two that would wipe that smug look off your face."

Grinning, I mirrored his actions by sitting forward and resting my arms on my thighs. "Go for it."

Mark opened his mouth to respond, only to think better of it at the final second and shake his head instead. "Nah. You're not worth the effort."

I laughed harder. "You are such a coward."

"You do realize I'm in sixth year, and you're in sixth class, don't ya?" he growled, glowering at me. "I could snap you in half if I wanted to."

"Don't worry about what class I'm in," I mused, still chuckling. "I'm sure by the time I reach sixth year, you'll be ready to graduate."

"You think you're so fucking smart." He seethed, balling his hands into fists. "You mark my words, Biggs, one day in the future, when you're all grown-up, I'm going to hunt you down, and I'm going to put a bullet in your head."

"Oh yeah?" Still smiling, I locked eyes on him and warned, "Or maybe, one day in the future, when I'm all grown-up, I'll hunt you down and put a bullet in yours."

PART 13

Unchartered Turbulence

BACK WITH A VENGEANCE

EVERYTHING WAS BACK.

My mother's cancer.

My sister's boyfriend.

My father's bad mood.

The scary lady's voice in my head.

The monster in my nightmares.

The urge to slit my wrists.

Everything.

Mam came home from hospital two weeks after her heart attack with another surgery under her belt and a new battle to fight.

My parents sat both me and Caoimhe down and explained where the cancer was this time and how the doctors were optimistic that she would beat it again, but I tuned it out.

I didn't want to know.

I couldn't hear another word about it.

The word alone made my skin crawl.

Home didn't feel like it used to. There was a sadness in the air that hadn't been there last summer. I knew my parents were trying to do their best to ease the pressure on me and Caoimhe. They had let Mark practically move in to support my sister, who wasn't taking Mam's latest diagnosis well, and they never stopped me from having my friends over or spending my weekends at Avoca Greystones.

None of that helped.

I wanted to be anywhere but home, and that made me feel even worse because I knew I should want to spend as much time with my mother as I could—because if the cancer overtook her this time, I wouldn't have another chance.

I wouldn't have a mother.

I wouldn't have a home.

My one light in the darkness was the boy with whiskey eyes and a smile that healed parts of me the medicine couldn't.

Unlike me, Hugh wasn't afraid to spend time at my house or be around my mother. Instead, he threw himself into the mix, on hand to help and unfazed by Mam's skeletal frame as she went through treatment.

On the days I couldn't go to his house, he came to mine and always brought a present for my mother. Be it a book he took out on loan from the library or a flower he stole from Old Murphy's garden, he never came empty-handed.

After a while, I thought Mam looked forward to his visits almost as much as I did. Especially on the days she couldn't get out of bed. Hugh would coax me into her room, where we would both sit at the end of her bed and fill Mam in on everything going on in our lives.

When they discovered Mam had developed diabetes, Hugh was the one who sat with her as the home health nurse showed her how to inject herself with insulin.

When Hugh was around, everything in my life stabilized. It was as if he held my world in his hands and forced it to stop spinning, giving me time to catch my breath and get back up on my feet.

School nights were the worst, when I had to sleep in my own bed, without him there to keep the darkness away. *To stop the nightmares.*

Every weeknight, I prayed for the weekend to come, so I could have a temporary reprieve from the relentless torture I suffered in my dreams.

"You're very quiet today," Hugh told me on the bus home from school on Friday. "What's on your mind?"

"Hmm?" I turned to look at his pretty face and smiled. "You're handsome."

My words caused his cheeks to flush bright red.

It was so adorable.

Smiling, I reached up and traced his cheek with my thumb. "I'm so glad it's the weekend."

"Me too," he replied, brown eyes locked on mine. "What were you thinking about earlier?"

"When?"

"Liz, you spaced out for like twenty minutes," he chuckled, capturing my hand from his cheek and placing it on his lap. "What's on your mind?"

334

"America," I filled in with a sigh, thinking back to the conversation I'd had with my family last night. "We have to go."

"Go?" Confusion filled his eyes, and he frowned. "To America? When?"

"April," I replied, shivering when he entwined his fingers with mine. "They're trialing a new drug or treatment that Mam's a candidate for," I told him, trying to remember what I'd been told. "Caoimhe said it's crazy expensive, but Mam has more than enough money to cover the cost a thousand times over." Shrugging, I added, "The success rates are decent, too."

"That's fantastic," Hugh replied, looking genuinely thrilled at the prospect of my mother recovering. Meanwhile, I was terrified to get my hopes up.

"They want Mam to start treatment right away, so she's flying out with Dad next week," I continued to tell him. "I'll stay home with Caoimhe, and we'll fly out the next month. On April sixth."

"How long are you going to be gone?"

"Three and a half weeks, I think," I told him, feeling a wave of devastation at the thought of being away from him for that long. "Because of Easter break, we'll only miss two weeks of school instead of four. I'll be back on the first of May."

"Will Catherine be finished with her treatment by then?"

I shrugged. "Who knows?"

"I'm going to miss you," Hugh told me, and hearing him say those words made my heart crack.

Because I didn't want to go.

If I had the choice, I'd remain right here in Ballylaggin with Hugh. Not go halfway around the world with Caoimhe and Mark. I knew that's exactly what would happen. Dad would spend all his time at the hospital with Mam, and I would be left with *them*.

SHE'S JUST A FRIEND, I SWEAR

Hugh

MARCH 17, 2000

"Make her stop," Feely groaned, covering his head with a pillow. "Please, Hugh, I can't take another loop of that fucking song."

Neither could I.

We'd been playing PS1 for just under an hour, and already, I'd counted fifteen loops of NSYNC's "Bye Bye Bye."

"Claire saw the music video playing on MTV and hasn't stopped trying to master the dance routine since," I explained, tapping on the controller in my hand. "You know how she fixates on things, lad. Look at Gibs."

"Well, if she doesn't hurry the hell up and master it, I'm going to Van Gogh myself."

"Don't be so dramatic," I chuckled, shaking my head. "Eejit."

"You'll see drama when I chop my fucking ears off," Feely warned, tossing his controller aside. "There's no point. I can't concentrate on the game."

"It's not that bad," I replied, tossing my controller aside now that he had given up. I couldn't play two-player without him. "It's better than her 'My Heart Will Go On' phase."

"Jesus, don't remind me." Feely shuddered. "Your sister ruined that film for me. I couldn't even enjoy Rose's tits in peace."

"Lad." I threw my head back and laughed. "She wasn't that special."

"You're mental," he argued, narrowing his eyes. "That woman was pure perfection in the film. Every part of her. Especially her hair."

I snorted. "Especially her tits, you mean."

Feely grinned. "Those, too."

"You know who has great tits?" I mused. "Sharon Stone."

"True," he replied in a thoughtful tone, clearly weighing up both options. "But you can't beat a redhead with a perky rack."

"Now *you're* being mental," I argued back, eyeballing him. "Sharon Stone, lad. Sharon fucking *Stone*." I held my hands up for emphasis. "Come on, Feely, you have to admit the blond wins every time."

"Like hell she does," he grumbled. "Kate Winslet as a redhead is unquestionably stunning."

"Fine, you take Kate, and I'll take Sharon."

"Fine." He nodded in acceptance. "I will."

"Good." I returned his nod with one of my own. "Glad that's cleared up."

It was at the precise moment that "Bye Bye Bye" started up again on the other side of my bedroom wall.

"I'm sorry, Hugh," Feely grumbled, stalking toward the door. "I really am, but I'm going to throttle that curly-haired menace!"

Snickering, I followed him, knowing full well he would do the complete opposite.

Claire had all the lads wrapped around her baby finger.

Of course, they'd all rather swallow glass than admit it, but they were kittens when it came to my sister.

"What did you *do* to him!" Feely demanded, clearly outraged, as he stood in Claire's bedroom doorway with his mouth hanging open. "Gibs! Stop that right now, ya hear!"

Dare I look?

Like, honestly?

Is it going to leave a permanent scar?

Primed for pain, I joined my best friend in my sister's doorway and quickly repeated his previous sentiments. "What did you *do* to him?"

Gaping in horror at the scene unfolding before my eyes, I watched as Gibs, Claire, and Liz performed that bloody dance routine in perfect sync with each other.

Both girls were caked in makeup, sprouting pigtails and wearing matching pink vests.

Worse, they had groomed *Gibsie* to within an inch of his life.

His blond curls?

Yeah, they were bunched together in two stumpy pigtails on either side of his head, while the pink vest he was sewn into stretched at the seams in protest.

"Guys, look!" Squealing with excitement, Claire gestured to their dance routine. "We finally nailed it."

"You are in Ireland," I reminded them, lips twitching. "Not Hollywood."

"And *you* are in sixth class," Feely added, speaking directly to our classmate, who clearly couldn't give two shits that we'd caught him dancing with the girls.

That's when the big ape pushed past the girls and took front and center to mime the high notes of the song.

Fisting the air with enthusiasm, Gibs *sang* his heart out, while executing the dance routine better than all of them.

When they finished their performance, Claire and Gibs both took dramatic bows, while Liz flopped down on the bed in a fit of laughter.

Unable to hide my amusement, I gave in and clapped for the three stooges, while Feely hauled ass toward the Barbie stereo system and swiftly yanked the plug out of the wall.

"Hey," Claire huffed. "Who said you could touch my stereo!"

"Yeah," Gibs chimed in defensively. "Who said you could touch her stereo?"

"God told me," Feely replied drolly.

"No, he didn't."

"And he also told me to remind you that you are too fucking old to be playing dress up with girls!"

"No, I'm not."

"Gibs, you're twelve!"

Ignoring their exchange, I made a beeline for the girl sitting on my sister's bed.

Christ, it was so damn good to see her laughing. She hadn't been doing a whole lot of it lately.

The new millennium had hit my girlfriend's family like a wrecking ball, but unlike my father, who buried his head in the sand, Lizzie climbed out of bed every day and kept fighting. I couldn't have been prouder of her. Most grown-ups didn't possess a tenth of the tenacity and resilience Liz displayed on the daily.

"I can't believe they roped me into that," Liz cackled, still thoroughly amused. "When have you ever seen me wear pink?"

"When have you ever worn these?" I mused, playfully tugging on one of her pigtails.

"Oh my God, stop." Her cheeks flushed bright pink. "I look like a dope."

My lips twitched. "You look adorable."

"Fine, I'm an adorable dope," she shot back with a grin.

"No, those two right there are adorable dopes." Resting on my elbow, I inclined my head to where Gibs and Claire were arguing with a flustered Feely. "*You* are adorable." I retrained my focus on her face. "Minus the dope part."

Her blue eyes blazed with warmth. "I love that you think that about me."

I just plain love you. "Stop looking at me like that, Liz."

Clambering onto her knees, she shifted closer until there wasn't an inch of space between us. "Like what?"

I bit back a groan. "You know what."

Eyes twinkling with mischief, she cupped my ear and whispered, "You want to kiss me again, don't you?"

Nodding my head, I clenched my eyes shut and strived for calm.

Be calm. Be calm. Be fucking calm, Hugh.

"Like you kissed me in the garden last week." She continued to torment me with whispers. "Or like how you kissed me in the cupboard under the stairs." Grinning mischievously, she pulled back to gauge my reaction. "Do you like kissing me, Hugh?"

I cast a nervous glance to our friends before nodding. "You know I do."

"Hmm." She discretely reached for my hand. "Then do it again."

"When?" I croaked out, feeling way too much all at once.

She squeezed my hand and grinned. "Right now."

Fuck.

"We can't," I muttered, feeling everything inside of my body coil tight. Jaw clenched, I gestured to my sister. While I had no problem telling Claire to go fuck herself, I knew Liz couldn't take another blow out. "She's right *here.*"

"Oh crap!" Liz gasped, loud enough for everyone to hear. "I left my phone in the treehouse!" She offered me a knowing wink before climbing off the bed and bolting for the door. "I'll be right back, guys."

She was so damn convincing, I almost believed her.

Almost.

Our friends didn't bat an eyelid, too invested in their conversation to care about missing phones.

I managed to make it to the count of ten in my head before I sheepishly stood up, stretched my arms over my head, and then slowly walked out of the room.

Once I had the bedroom door closed behind me, I booked it down the staircase at lightning speed, not stopping until I reached the kitchen patio door, when my mother's hand shot out and fisted the back of my T-shirt.

"Where are you off to in such a hurry, mister?"

"I, uh, I, uh…I, uh…"

"You, uh, uh, uh, what?" Mam mocked, hands on her hips. "You were sneaking off to the treehouse with your girlfriend, that's what you were uh, uh, uh doing."

Sadhbh, who was sitting at the kitchen table, burst out laughing, and my face flooded with heat. "I don't know what you're talking about."

Mam rolled her eyes. "Lie better, son."

"I was going to help her find her phone," I huffed, defensive. "Jesus, is that a crime now or something?"

"Ah, Sinead, go easy on him," Gibsie's mam chuckled. "Can't you see the poor boy's in the throes of puppy love?"

"She's my *friend*," I lied through my teeth and argued, casting a mutinous glare in Sadhbh's direction. "*Just* a friend."

Mam arched a brow. "Do you think I came down in the last shower?"

"Just a friend," Sadhbh chuckled, thoroughly amused. "The lines never change over the years, do they, Sinead?"

"I swear," I bit out, glowing red now. "I'm being a friend and helping her find her phone."

"Hmm." Mam clicked her tongue, eyes laced with suspicion. "Make sure that's *all* you're doing, young man."

"It is," I called over my shoulder, lying through my fucking teeth, as I yanked the sliding door open and bolted outside.

"What took you so long?" Liz asked when I reached the top step of the ladder. "I thought you weren't coming."

"It's my mam." Red-faced, I climbed up the rest of the way and then quickly slipped inside, slamming the rickety door shut behind me. "She's a menace." Blowing out a frustrated breath, I sagged against the door at my back and groaned. "I think she knows."

Liz arched a brow. "Knows?"

"Yeah." Exhaling another breath, I nodded wearily. "About us."

Her eyes twinkled with excitement. "What about us?"

"Come on, Liz," I muttered, feeling another wave of heat attack my neck. I could hear my heart beating in my ears. It was thundering so loud, it was deafening. "You know."

Snickering, she crawled toward me, not stopping until she was kneeling between my legs. "Now who's the adorable-looking one?" Grinning, she reached up and stroked my cheek with her finger. "You're blushing."

Yeah, and it tended to happen when I was around her.

I reached up to move her hand but somehow my fingers ended up entwining with hers. Holding her hand always sent an electric shock through me and today was no different.

I flicked my eyes back to her face and found her already watching me with that familiar heated stare. "Liz."

Her pupils got bigger when she whispered my name. "Hugh."

"Do you want to talk for a bit?" I offered, trying to be supportive but already knowing her answer. "About how you're feeling about your Mam being away at treatment?"

She shook her head. "Talking is the last thing I want to do."

"Are you sure?" I probed, not taking it to heart because I knew her better than I knew myself, and when things got rough, she preferred to soldier on, instead of exploring her feelings.

Liz shifted closer. "One hundred percent."

Jesus, the anticipation was killing me because I knew it would happen, I *knew* she would kiss me, and when she did, it wouldn't be enough.

The kiss would end and then I would drive myself crazy with thoughts of her until it happened again. And then again. And then again and *again*.

I knew deep down that I was never going to be able to get enough of this girl, and that was a terrifying concept. Knowing she held so much power over me made it hard to breathe.

When she leaned in close and her familiar scent infiltrated my senses, I made peace with the knowledge that I was a lost cause. That I couldn't be cured of my addiction to this girl. That I would forever seek her out.

When she said, "Kiss me," I didn't hesitate.

Closing the space between our mouths, I pressed my lips to hers.

It was just a kiss.

An innocent kiss.

Nothing more.

But it meant so much *more*.

Because it felt like I was signing off on a permanent decision.

MISTER RESPONSIBLE

Lizzie

APRIL 4, 2000

"...SHUT THE FUCK UP AND LET ME FIX THIS."

"No, no, no, please!" I screamed at the top of my lungs, thrashing violently as I tried to fight him off. *"Please! Please, stop! It hurts!"*

"Stop fighting me on this!" he snarled, ramming the coat hanger deep inside of my body. *"Relax, okay? I know what I'm doing. I watched a video."*

"It hurts!" I screamed, ripping and tearing at my hair as the pain threatened to take me under. *"I'm dying!"*

"Yeah, and I'll be dead if that belly of yours gets any bigger." He shoved a pillow over my face. *"Scream into that if you have to..."*

"Liz!" Hugh's frantic voice penetrated my thoughts, and I watched through bleary eyes as he cleared the back of the couch in his rush to get to me. "What happened?"

Dazed and disorientated, I glanced around in confusion. I was in the living room. How was I in the living room? I was sleeping only a moment ago. "Hugh?" I blinked around, searching for him. "What are you doing here?"

"You weren't on the school bus. I was worried." Dropping to his knees beside me, Hugh grabbed my face. "What happened, Liz?" His eyes were wild and frantic as they searched mine for answers I couldn't give him. "Where are your clothes?"

"My clothes?"

"Yeah, Liz, your clothes," Hugh strangled out before proceeding to whip off his Scoil Eoin jumper and push it over my head before feeding my arms through the sleeves. "Did something happen to you?"

I stared blankly at him. "Like what?"

"I don't know, but you don't show up at school today, and when I come to check in, you're curled up on your living room floor with no clothes on!" His eyes were wild with panic, matching his voice, when he gripped my shoulders and pulled me close to him. "So I'm kind of freaking the fuck out right now!"

"I, uh, Caoimhe gave me the day off school to pack for Texas." Shaking my head, I tried to make sense of the thoughts whizzing around in my head. "I think I fell asleep and had a nightmare."

"A nightmare?"

"Yeah." Trembling violently, I clutched the fabric of his jumper I was wearing. "I think he got me, Hugh."

"Who?" he demanded, looking around the room. "Was someone here, Liz?" He jerked to his feet. "Was someone in this house?"

"No, not here," I tried to explain, pressing a hand to my brow as pain consumed me. "In my nightmare."

"I still think I should call your parents," Hugh declared twenty minutes later. "Or maybe your doctor."

Sitting on the couch, wearing fresh pajamas, I curled up on his lap and buried my face in his neck. "Hugh, I'm grand, I promise."

"What about Caoimhe?" he argued, arms tightening around my body. "It's half past five. Why the hell isn't she home from school by now?"

"She never comes home until at least eight or nine o'clock," I reminded him. "You know that."

"Well, she damn well should be," he snapped, sounding pissed. "She's supposed to be looking after you, Liz."

"Please don't be cross with me," I pleaded, burrowing in deeper. "I'm sorry for scaring you."

"I'm not cross with you, Liz, I'm worried." He was quick to clarify, dropping a kiss to my hair. "I'm furious with your sister, though. This is bullshit and I'm going to be having a word with her about leaving you alone like this."

"There's nothing she can do for me," I sighed. "It happens."

"Yeah, well, I'm not leaving your side until she gets home."

True to his word, Hugh remained glued to my side for the rest of the afternoon and late into the evening. We ended up ordering pizza for dinner, using the money my dad left in the cup on top of the fridge to pay for it, before gorging on my sister's favorite ice cream.

It was gone nine o'clock when Caoimhe finally got home, and by that stage, Hugh

343

was close to having a conniption fit. When she strolled into the living room, armed with a dozen shopping bags, my boyfriend exploded on her.

"What time do you call this?" Hugh demanded, jerking off the couch. "School finishes at four, Caoimhe, not half past fucking nine at night!"

"Whoa, okay, Mr. Responsible," my sister responded, looking confused. "How about you cool your jets and tell me what's got you on edge?"

"How about I cool my jets when you act your fucking age!" Hugh seethed, pacing the floor like a madman. "You left your little sister alone in the house all goddamn day, Caoimhe. The same little sister you are *supposed* to be looking after while your parents are abroad."

"Is *that* it?" Caoimhe demanded, arching a disbelieving brow. "You're really getting yourself all worked up because I left Liz at home?"

"Yes!" Hugh hissed, nodding eagerly. "Because she had a *nightmare*, Caoimhe."

"She always has nightmares, Hugo," she remained him. "And in case it passed your attention, my sister's more than capable of looking after herself."

"Maybe, but this was a bad one."

"They're all bad, bud," my sister replied. "I should know. I'm the one she keeps awake at night with her screaming."

"This is not on, Caoimhe," Hugh continued to rant, unwilling to back down or give an inch. "This is seriously not fucking on. You can't just leave her on her own like this!"

"Okay, hold up a sec," Caoimhe interrupted, holding up a hand as she turned her attention to me. "Are you okay, busy Lizzie bee?"

"Yeah, I'm grand," I croaked out, feeling mortified. "I had a nightmare and must have sleepwalked downstairs." I turned to look at my boyfriend. "I'm really sorry for upsetting you, Hugh."

"You didn't do anything wrong, Liz," he was quick to say in a far softer tone than the one he used with my sister. "I'm just concerned, okay?"

Shivering, I nodded. "Yeah, okay." *But I'm still sorry.*

"Ooh, pizza," Caoimhe exclaimed then, reaching for the empty box on the coffee table. "You greedy, little pigs ate an entire sixteen-inch by yourselves?"

"Yeah, and we cleared out your stash of mint-chocolate-chip ice cream in the freezer, too," Hugh said, goading her unapologetically. Narrowing his eyes, he added, "*Both* tubs."

PERVERSE PERIODS AND STOLEN INNOCENCE

Lizzie

APRIL 5, 2000

BECAUSE WE WERE FLYING OUT TO MEET OUR PARENTS FIRST THING IN THE MORNING and Caoimhe had one final babysitting job tonight, she decided to give us both the day off school to finishing packing our suitcases and cleaning the house.

I was glad of the day off because when I woke up this morning, it was to horrendous stomach and back pain. When I told Caoimhe about it, she put it down to period cramps and asked me if I was due on.

When I told her I had no idea and didn't keep track of those things, she gave me paracetamol for the pain and told me to "suck it up, buttercup."

It didn't help.

By the time three o'clock rolled around and Hugh was due to arrive to spend the evening with me, I was in agony and could hardly stand.

Of course, when I dragged myself to her room to tell my sister this, I found a note to say she'd gone to the shops and would be home for dinner.

Great.

"Holy fuck," Hugh exclaimed when he walked into my room and took one look at my face. "Jesus, Liz." Dropping his schoolbag at my bedroom door, he rushed to my side. "Are you okay?"

"Sorry," I squeezed out, devastated that I was buckled over in pain on the last day I would see him for a whole month. "I'm just…" Hissing out a breath when a sharp pain ricocheted through my pelvis, I grabbed his arm and whimpered. "I need to go to the bathroom."

"Here, just hold on to my arm, and I'll take you." Wrapping an arm around my waist, Hugh helped me into the bathroom before asking, "Should I call a doctor?" His voice was laced with concern. "Because you don't look too good, Liz."

"No, I'll be grand," I strangled out, pushing him out of the bathroom. "Just give me a sec, okay?"

"Yeah, okay," he replied, looking panicked when I closed the door in his face.

"Liz? Are you okay in there? It's been twenty minutes."

Hugh continued to knock on the closed bathroom door, but I couldn't answer him. I was too scared of the blood running down my legs.

"Liz, if you don't answer me, I'm coming in there."

"No, no, don't come in," I called back, biting down on my fist when the pain threatened to overtake me. "I'll be out in a minute."

There was a pause and then his voice filled my ears. "Are you sure?"

"Yep," I squeezed out, attention riveted to the plum-sized glob of blood that had fallen out of my body and onto my bathroom floor.

I wasn't sure what it was, but it wasn't my period.

It looked like a clump of veins.

It looked like a monster.

Terrified, I reached for another towel from the rack and shoved it between my legs.

BLOOD-DRENCHED TOWELS AND BROKEN GOODBYES

Hugh

"HOLY FUCK," I CHOKED OUT, FALLING OFF THE COUCH WHEN LIZ FINALLY EMERGED from the bathroom looking deathly pale and carting several bloodstained towels. "What happened?"

"Nosebleed," she replied quietly, moving for the utility room. "I'll be fine."

"No, you're not." Rushing to intercept her, I grabbed her shoulders to steady her. "What happened?"

"I told you," she snapped, sounding emotional. "I had a nosebleed."

"Liz, you were holding your stomach when you went into that bathroom, so I *know* you didn't have a nosebleed. Besides, a nosebleed wouldn't cause this much…" My words trailed off and I stared at the towels in horror. "Did you do something to yourself?"

"No, I had a fucking nosebleed, Hugh!" she screamed, shoving past me and moving for the washing machine. "Why are you always doubting me!"

"I'm not doubting you, Liz," I tried to coax, thrown off-kilter by both the blood and her sudden shift in mood. "But that's a lot of blood."

"I don't want to fight with you," she choked out, pressing the heel of her hand to her forehead. "I'm just…" Liz shook her head and burst into tears. "I don't know what happened to me." She threw the towels on the ground and shuddered violently. "What's happening to me, Hugh?"

The fear in her eyes made my chest hurt, and I quickly closed the space between us. "Come here."

Liz came willingly, barreling into my arms.

"It came out of me," she cried, shaking violently. "There was so much of it."

"The blood?"

Nodding, she buried her face in my neck.

Fuck.

It was her period.

Mam gave me the talk years ago. She told me that some girls had really heavy ones. I knew Liz got hers, but I didn't know it could be so fucking bad.

Unsure whether I should ask Liz about her cycle or if that would only make her feel worse, I decided to do something productive instead.

"Come on," I coaxed, hooking an arm around her waist and leading her out of the utility room. "Let me take care of you."

"I'm sorry," she mumbled, leaning heavily against me on the staircase. "I ruined our last day together."

"Today isn't our last day together," I replied, taking all her weight as I led her back to her room. "We have eighty years' worth of tomorrows to spend together." When I pulled back the covers and helped her into bed, I locked eyes on a large bloodstain on her pajama bottoms.

Christ, I was so glad that I would never have to deal with a period.

Females get the raw end of the deal.

"Can I get you anything?" I asked, sitting down beside her. "Hmm?" Reaching over, I stroked her cheek with my thumb. "What usually helps with the pain?"

"You." Tears filled her eyes, and she gripped my forearm. "You help."

"I was thinking more along the lines of a hot water bottle," I mused, leaning in to kiss her forehead. "Do you want some painkillers?"

"You," she repeated, clinging onto my arm. "Just you."

"You have me," I whispered, feeling too much for this girl. "You'll always have me."

"I don't want to go tomorrow," she choked out, crying hard now. "I don't want to be away from you."

I didn't want her to go, either. "It's only for a little while," I coaxed, heart breaking. "I'll message you every day." Smiling, I added, "And think of all that Texan sunshine."

"Sunshine means nothing to me if you're not in it."

"Liz—" My voice cracked. "I'll be here when you get home."

"I know." She tightened her grip on my arm. "That's the only thing keeping me going."

"What does that mean?"

"I don't want to be alive without you."

"Don't say that, Liz," I warned, feeling my heart crack clean open in my chest. "Don't you ever say that again."

Tears streamed down her cheeks. "It's the truth."

"If anything ever happened to you, it would destroy me," I admitted, unable to make the tremble in my voice. "You are my whole world, Lizzie Young, so don't you dare talk about not being alive."

"I love you so much," she sobbed, chest heaving violently. "I love you, Hugh. I do, I swear I do."

"I know you do, and you know I love you back," I croaked out, hating the way my eyes were starting to water. "Listen, Caoimhe's babysitting Gibs tonight. Why don't you come home with me? Your sister can pick you up after she's finished."

"No." Sniffling, she wiped her eyes. "I don't want your sister to see me like this. Claire hasn't started her period yet, and this'll just scare her."

"Claire lives on cloud nine," I tried to persuade her. "She won't notice a thing, I promise."

"I think I'll stay home." She sniffled again, but this time she forced a watery smile. "Just to be safe."

"You okay, bud?" Caoimhe asked on the drive home later that evening. "You're awfully quiet."

"I'm worried about Liz."

"Why?"

"She was bleeding a lot."

"What do you mean?"

"Her period." I shifted in discomfort. "It was a bad one."

"Ah, the joys of womanhood," Caoimhe mused. "I thought she was due on. She was complaining of cramps all day."

"Yeah, except that she's not a woman, Caoimhe," I shot back, still peeved with how dismissive she was of her sister's nightmares. "And she's been going through this crap since she was nine." I sighed heavily. "It's not fucking fair."

"Well, aren't you a walking green flag," Caoimhe teased with a chuckle. "Listen, relax. By this time tomorrow, we'll be basking in the sun and Liz won't have time to think about period cramps."

"Will you look after her?"

"Duh, she's my sister."

"No, I'm serious." I stared hard at her side profile. "I *need* you to look after her, Caoimhe."

"Yeah, Hugh, okay." She gave me a puzzled look. "I always do."

"Will you check on her when you get home tonight?" I added, shifting in discomfort from the knot building in my stomach. "Even if she's asleep, can you just go in and make sure?"

"Don't worry, Romeo," she teased. "I promise to check on your little lovebird when I get home."

DON'T DO ANYTHING STUPID

Lizzie

APRIL 5, 2000

THE SOUND OF A CAR REVVING STARTLED ME AWAKE LATE THAT NIGHT, FOLLOWED BY a second car screeching to a stop.

Confused, I remained motionless in my bed, listening in the darkness to the sound of two people screaming outside the house.

I knew from past experience that the screaming was coming from my sister and her boyfriend.

This was nothing new to me.

Throughout their relationship, Caoimhe and Mark had always argued, but since January, when Dad allowed Mark back in the house, their fights had become more frequent and vicious than ever.

Moments later, the front door slammed, and the screaming grew louder, following by heavy footsteps on the stairs.

"Let's just go on the holiday and we can talk about it when we get back," I heard Mark say.

"Are you completely mental?" That was Caoimhe. "I'm not going anywhere with you, you fucking pedophile!"

"Don't call me that."

"You raped your stepbrother," Caoimhe screamed at the top of her lungs. "You're an adult. Gibsie's a child. You defiled his body. I saw you with my own eyes. That's called being a pedophile!"

The sound of a nearby door slamming filled the air, followed by fists pounding against wood. "Open the fucking door, Caoimhe!"

"Go to hell!"

"Don't do anything stupid." The pounding grew louder and louder. "I'm warning you!"

"Get out of my fucking house," Caoimhe screamed. "I'm calling the Gards right now, and when they get their hands on you, you'll never see the light of day again, you sick, twisted bastard!"

A loud crashing ricocheted through the air, followed by my sister screaming, "What the hell are you—no, stop! Give that back. No, Mark, don't—ahhh! Get your hands off me!"

"No, you're not going anywhere until we talk about this!"

"There's nothing to talk about because I see you, Mark. I finally see what you are. You're a monster in disguise!"

"...I finally see what you are..."

"...You're a monster in disguise..."

"...You're a monster..."

Eyes widening in horror, I gripped my duvet and pulled it over my head.

Monster.

He was a monster.

The monster was real.

Mark was the monster.

MY FAMILY IS YOUR FAMILY

Hugh

APRIL 5, 2000

WHEN I GOT HOME AND CONFIDED IN MAM ABOUT LIZ'S SUDDEN DROP IN MOOD, SHE gave me a sad smile and told me low moods came hand in hand with bipolar and the only thing I could do to help was to be there for her.

Sleep didn't come easy that night. My mind was set on panic mode, and I couldn't shake the horrible, unsettling feeling in the pit of my stomach.

Liz was slipping again.

I saw it on her face today.

I heard it in her voice.

The light in her eyes was dimming, and I didn't know how to reverse it.

I was still tossing and turning when my bedroom door creaked open in the middle of the night, followed by the sound of sniffling.

"No, Claire, the Banshee of Ballylaggin isn't coming to get us," I called out in the darkness. The sobbing sounds grew louder, and I sighed in defeat. "Fine." Holding up my duvet, I patted the mattress beside me and grumbled, "You can sleep with me tonight, but this is the last time."

The sound of her footsteps filled the air moments before she clambered into bed with me. However, the trembling body that welded itself to mine didn't belong to my sister. It belonged to...

"Gibs?" Confused, I tried to sit up to switch on my lamp, but the way he was clinging to me made that impossible. "What happened, lad?"

"Hughie." Sobbing uncontrollably, my oldest friend in the world locked his arms and legs around me. "Hughie."

"I'm here, lad," I tried to coax, wrapping an arm around him. "Where's Caoimhe? Does she know you're over here?"

Heaving out a choked sob, he shook his head. "N-no."

"Did you sneak out?"

Nodding his head, Gibs squeezed me tighter. "I want my d-dad."

My heart sank.

Fuck.

"I know you do, Gibs," I replied, patting his back. "I know, lad. It's not fair."

"I j-just want my d-dad to c-come back," he continued to cry, burying his face in my chest. "I d-don't want to g-go home."

"Did you have another nightmare?" I coaxed, while silently thanking Jesus for sparing me from the horrendous affliction. "Hmm? About our communion day?"

He nodded slowly. "It's m-my f-fault they died—"

"No, it's not," I cut in, heart shredding in my chest. "None of what happened that day was your fault, Gibs. Do you hear me? It was an accident." Swallowing down my emotion, I steadied my voice before adding, "It was a horrible, awful, terrible thing that happened, Gibs, but it was an *accident.*" I tightened my arms around his trembling frame. "I know you feel alone in that house since your mam married him, but I promise you that you're not. You have us. My family is your family, too." Clenching my eyes shut, I squeezed the shit out of my friend, desperate to soothe his pain. "And you have me, Gibs. You will *always* have me."

"Brothers f-forever?" he croaked out.

"Yeah, Gibs," I promised. "And then some."

PART 14

The Dissolution of Life as We Know It

A HUGE MISUNDERSTANDING

Hugh

APRIL 24, 2000

"Hugh, love," Mam said in a hushed voice, as she shook me awake in the middle of the night. "I need you to get up and throw some clothes on."

"Hmm?" Blinking my eyes open, it took me a few seconds to get my bearings. "What's wrong?" Locating my mother's face, I pulled up on my elbows and frowned at her tearstained face. "Mam?" An immediate surge of panic set in. "What's wrong?"

"Mark called," Mam choked out, using the back of her hand to wipe the tears streaming down her face. "Keith's already on the way over. Sadhbh's downstairs."

"On the way over where?" Heart racing, I glanced at the alarm clock on my nightstand and felt even more confused. "Why is Sadhbh in our house at four o'clock in the morning?"

"She's going to watch Gibsie and Claire," she strangled out, pressing a hand to her chest. "They're still asleep in her room, but I need you come with me and Dad."

"Come where?" I demanded, instantly on edge. "Where are we going, Mam? What's going on?"

"Oh, love, I'm so sorry," she choked out a gut-wrenching sob. "Caoimhe Young passed away tonight."

My whole world bottomed out the moment those words came out of my mother's mouth.

"What are you *talking* about?" Throwing off my covers, I jumped out of bed and reached for my sweatpants. "What do you mean Caoimhe *passed away*?" I waited for her to explain, and when she just continued to cry, I started to panic. "Mam! What the fuck are you talking about?"

"Come here, love." Dad strode into my room, moving straight for my mother. "I'm here."

Mam folded into his arms, sobbing uncontrollably. "Pete!"

"I know," he replied in a soothing tone, wrapping her up in his arms. "I've got you."

Meanwhile, I scrambled to throw my clothes on as quickly as I could, while demanding, "What the hell is happening?"

"Caoimhe had an accident tonight, son," Dad explained in that steady, soothing tone that made everything feel better. The tone I hadn't heard him use for years. "It's serious, and we need to go," he continued, holding on to my mother, who looked like she had lost all ability to stand on her own feet. In fact, if Dad let go of her now, I had no doubt Mam would hit the floor like a sack of spuds. "Mark's over at Old Hall House with Lizzie, talking to the Gardaí."

"At the *house*?" I gaped at my father, feeling like I was two seconds away from having a stroke. "What are you *talking* about?"

"Just go downstairs and get in my car," Dad instructed, moving for the door with my mother. "We'll talk on the way."

"Okay, okay," I strangled out, hurrying after them, even though I knew they were mistaken.

Whatever was happening, my parents had gotten it wrong.

Lizzie and Caoimhe were in *Texas* with their parents.

Christ, even *Mark* was in Texas with their family.

This was a huge misunderstanding.

It had to be.

NO MATTER WHAT

Lizzie

APRIL 25, 2000

"What the fuck did you do to my sister…"

　　"Liz?"

"You can't keep us locked in here forever…"

　　"It's me, Hugh."

"She's a child, you monster. She's a fucking baby and you put a baby inside her…"

　　"Can you hear me, Liz?"

"He's a monster, Lizzie. You need to get out…"

　　"I'm right here, okay?"

"I'm so sorry I didn't protect you both…"

　　"I won't leave you on your own, Liz, I promise."

"Run, Lizzie, and don't look back…"

　　"No matter what."

　　No matter what.

　　No matter what.

　　No matter what.

　　Hugh!

DEAD GIRLFRIENDS AND SILENT SISTERS

Hugh

ON THE NIGHT OF APRIL 24, 2000, CAOIMHE YOUNG LEFT HER FAMILY HOME IN THE middle of the night, drove to the Ballylaggin footbridge, and took her own life.

None of it made sense.

Why Caoimhe threw herself into that river.

Why she was in Ballylaggin in the first place and *not* in Texas like she was supposed to be.

Why she left her sister alone at the house that night.

Why her boyfriend, who was sleeping over that night, didn't stop her.

Why the letter she left for Catherine didn't sound like her.

Why Liz hadn't reached out to me once in those three weeks.

Why all my text messages had gone unanswered.

I had a whole heap of questions that I feared would remain unanswered forever because all Caoimhe had left behind was a broken trail of puzzle pieces that led to nowhere.

Because of this, the Gardaí and her family could only rely on what her boyfriend told them.

According to Mark, Caoimhe's mood had plummeted over the previous three weeks because she couldn't visit her parents as planned. Mark told the Gards that Lizzie was diagnosed bipolar and suffered a psychotic break on the morning they were due to fly out.

Caoimhe then called her parents to tell them about her sister's state of mind, which was when her father told her they were to stay home and *not* travel. He said that he had noticed over the past several months that Caoimhe had been abusing her sister's prescription medication.

When Catherine and Mike flew home two days later, they verified to the detective on the case that their daughter had indeed called them that morning, relaying the same information to them. They also confirmed that they had spoken to their eldest daughter in the three weeks that followed and noted a dip in mood, as well as being aware of her consuming illicit substances since failing her leaving cert last year.

The night she died, Mark told the detectives that when he woke up and found her gone, he had a *bad* feeling. That's when he woke up Liz, who, at their father's request, Caoimhe had been keeping heavily sedated, and loaded her into his car, before heading out to search for his girlfriend.

When he was questioned as to why a doctor or a family friend hadn't been called for Lizzie at any time during those three weeks, Mark told the detective that Caoimhe was ashamed of her sister's disorder, that Liz was prone to frequent, violent outbursts and had learned from her parents how to handle it in private.

Mark told the detectives that it was while he was driving around town searching for Caoimhe that he first noticed the sirens and flashing lights coming from the river. He said he felt instantly panicked and went straight to the bridge, thinking it might have something to do with Caoimhe, which was when he saw members of the Gardaí and fire brigade pulling his girlfriend from the river.

After that, Mark shut down, saying that was all he could remember about the night and had become unwilling to speak about it since.

There were so many unanswered questions, and Mark's version of events was all anyone had to go on because his girlfriend was dead and my girlfriend wasn't talking.

Lizzie hadn't spoken since the night Caoimhe died.

Not when the Gardaí asked for her statement.

Not when I arrived at the house.

Not when the doctors were called.

Not when her parents flew in from the States.

Not a single word had passed her lips since the night the Gardaí dredged her sister's lifeless body from the river.

Depositing a slice of pizza onto a paper plate, I weaved through the throngs of sympathizers in my girlfriend's kitchen and made my way upstairs to her bedroom.

She was exactly where I'd left her.

Buried beneath her duvet.

"Come on, Liz, I have food."

Nothing.

Not so much as a twitch.

"I know you can hear me." Setting my plate down on my makeshift mattress, the one I had slept on every night since her sister died, I climbed over a mountain of blankets and sat on the edge of her bed, plate in hand.

"So here are your two choices," I stated calmly, breaking off a piece. "You can sit up and eat this yourself, or I'll feed it to you. The method is optional. The eating is not."

I didn't want to come off like an insensitive asshole, but Liz couldn't survive without food, and her parents were too consumed in grief to take the reins.

Enter Hugh.

"Helicopter dinner it is." Moving the plate to her nightstand, I tore off a tiny piece of pizza and brought it to her mouth. "Come on, Liz." Stroking her cheek with my free hand, I tried to coax her back to life. "One bite for me?"

A noticeable shudder rolled through her body, and she opened her mouth.

Thank God.

"That's it," I praised when she accepted the tiny morsel of food. "Now, I need you to chew, Liz." I stroked her cheek again, wiping the fresh stream of tears trickling from her bloodshot eyes. "Can you do that for me?"

Obliging without protest, she chewed the piece of food and then seemed to wait for my next instruction.

"You can swallow it, Liz," I said, feeling my heart break for the millionth time since this nightmare began. When she did just that, I tore off another piece and repeated the ritual until I had managed to hand-feed her the entire slice, minus the crust because she was lying down and I didn't want her to choke.

When she had eaten enough to sustain her for another day, I cleaned her face before settling down on her bed, facing her.

Her pale blue eyes stared right back at me, swollen and bloodshot.

"I love you," I whispered, resting my hand on her cheek. "I'm always going to be here for you."

Liz didn't respond with words, but when she placed her trembling hand on my cheek, I knew she was listening.

She could hear me.

She was *still* in there.

YOU'LL NEVER FORGET ME, MUNCHKIN

Lizzie

APRIL 30, 2000

"WHY DIDN'T YOU DO SOMETHING…"

"Michael, she's only a child…"

"Why didn't you help her? She was your family! You should have done something…"

Numb, I clutched the ropes of the swing on either side of my body and kicked at the dirt every time I swung low enough to reach the ground.

Even from here, I could still hear them back at the house.

Pouring tea.

Eating sandwiches.

Making conversation.

Acting like the world was still spinning.

Shut up.

Shut up.

Shut the fuck up!

Betrayal filled the empty shell in my chest, fueled with a level of hatred that made me want to scream.

Tears burned at my eyes.

Coldness spread throughout my body, turning my heart to ice.

Anger settled deep inside of my bones.

It wasn't fair.

"I've been trying to work up the courage to speak to you all day, but I don't have the right words," a familiar voice said, and I turned to see Gibsie sit on the swing next to mine. "So I'm just going to sit here with you, okay?"

Help me, I wanted to scream, *you're the only one who can.*

My voice betrayed me like it had when I was a child.

Nothing came out.

All I could do was stare at Gibsie's big, gray eyes and *will* him to hear the words I couldn't say out loud.

"I want to leave," I begged, feeling drowsy and disorientated, as I stumbled toward my sister. "Please, Caoimhe." Falling on my hands and knees on her bedroom floor, I reached for her hand and squeezed. "Make him let us go…"

"It's going to be okay." Sniffling, she tucked me under her arm, while she continued to scribble furiously into her notebook. "We'll get out of here, and when we do, he'll pay for everything, Liz. I promise."

"I don't care if he pays," I sobbed, clinging to her body. "I just want to leave."

Tearing out a page from her journal, my sister folded the page in half and then folded it again and again until it was the size of a matchbox. "Here." She shoved the note into my sock and grabbed my hands. "You're going to be okay, I promise." Her blue eyes watered as she spoke. "But if anything happens to me, and he doesn't let me out of this room—"

"Caoimhe, no!" I cried, throwing my arms around her neck. "Don't say that."

"I have to," she choked out, holding me tightly. "If anything happens to me, Liz, and I don't get out, I want you to get this note to Gibsie. Can you do that for me?" Sniffling, she pulled back to look in my eyes. "I want you to tell him everything you told me tonight, and then I want you both to go to the police…"

I couldn't be sure if these recurring hallucinations were memories or delusions.

I had many of them, but I couldn't be sure, and I couldn't speak.

I couldn't *breathe*.

Fear gripped me to the point where I prayed for my mind to break apart and let me drift away.

Like it had drifted away that night.

I floated out of my body, up, up, and away from the pain.

Away from the image of her lifeless body.

From her dead-eyed stare as she looked straight through me.

I still had it, though.

The folded-up note.

It was in my pocket right now.

It teleported from my mind to my pocket.

I knew what I was supposed to do.

What *she* told me to do.

But I was afraid of what would happen.

I was afraid that I was in the throes of a delusion and speaking out would only cause more heartbreak for my mother.

I didn't want her to suffer any more than she already was.

The sound of her constant wailing haunted me.

But I was even more afraid that I *wasn't* hallucinating, because if I wasn't and this was real, then it was even more important that I made myself forget.

Because if I had to remember, then I had to acknowledge, and if I did that, if I told someone, like he did, then I would lose the person I loved most.

I would lose *Hugh*.

He promised he would do it.

But Caoimhe promised the opposite.

She promised if I told Gibsie, if I just gave him the note, we would be safe.

He wouldn't be able to get me again.

But she wasn't here anymore.

She couldn't help me.

What if Gibsie told him?

What would happen to Hugh?

But what if none of this was real?

What if my mind was playing tricks on me again and I was going to wake up and find Caoimhe eating cereal in the kitchen?

What if I was the one who died that night?

What if I killed her?

Maybe she didn't jump?

Maybe I pushed her?

Or maybe I pushed myself?

What if the scary lady was putting bad thoughts in my head?

"Can I give you a hug?" I heard Gibsie ask, distracting me from my frazzled thoughts. "Would that be okay?"

Sniffling, I nodded and watched him climb off his swing and walk over to me.

"I'm so sorry, Liz," he croaked out, wrapping his arms around me. Numb, I rested my cheek on Gibsie's shoulder. "I'm so, so fucking sorry."

As I listened to him whisper the word *sorry* over and over, I reached into my pocket and fisted the note.

Please help, I mentally begged, and then, whether it was real or not, I placed my last shred of hope in my friend's coat pocket. *Please save me.*

"What are you two doing out here on your own?" a familiar voice said, causing every muscle in my body to lock tight.

The monster.

Clenching my eyes shut, I clung to the boy hugging me and prayed he wouldn't let go.

Don't let go, Gibs.

Please don't let go.

Don't leave me on my own with him.

"I'm hugging my friend," Gibsie replied, tightening his arms around me. "Her sister just died. I *know* what that feels like."

He was close.

I could smell his cologne.

I could feel words crawling out of my mind and onto my skin.

"Go back to the house, Gibson," *he* instructed. "I need to talk to my girlfriend's sister."

No, Gibs!

Don't go.

Please don't leave me.

"I, ah, I want to stay with her," I heard my friend protest, but his voice shook almost as much as his body when he spoke. "Hugh had to go home for an hour, and he told me to *stay* with Liz. He told me *not* to leave her."

"Go inside. I'll stay with her."

No, no, no, no, no!

"But Hugh said—"

"Get your fucking hole back in the house or I'll kick you in there."

For a brief moment, when Gibsie squeezed me tighter, I felt a flicker of hope inside my chest, but then he released me and stepped back, causing that hope to snuff out.

He let go.

Fresh tears streamed down my cheeks as I watched him leave.

"You know you were holding your sister's killer, don't ya?" *he* mused, taking the seat on the swing next to mine. "It's his fault this happened."

I didn't dare look at him, keeping my attention trained on Gibsie's back as he disappeared from my line of sight.

"If Caoimhe were here, she'd be so disappointed in you." He sighed heavily. "Hugging the person responsible for her death."

Come back, I wanted to scream, but all I could do was tighten my hold on the ropes of the swing and pray he could somehow hear me. *Please come back.*

"He filled your sister's head with poison," he continued to say, tormenting my mind with self-doubt. "It's her birthday today and she's not here to celebrate it because of that little prick, so don't you ever forget who's truly responsible for her death."

"This is his fault!" Grabbing the back of my neck, he forced me to look. To lean over the edge and see. "She's dead because of him. Because he got in her head. My brother's big mouth killed your sister."

"Help her! Please do something!"

"Say it, munchkin." His hand tightened on the back of my neck, and he pushed me so far over the rail that I couldn't touch the ground anymore. "Tell me you understand."

"Please," I wailed, shaking violently as my eyes tracked my sister being swept up in the current. "You have to help her!"

"There's nothing I can do to help her. Gibsie saw to that when he filled her head with lies." He set me back down only to turn me around to face him. "Say it, munchkin." He gripped my throat and pushed me against the barrier. "Tell me you understand what happens when you lie." He slammed me against the rail again. "Tell me who's responsible for this? Who told lies and killed your sister?"

"I..." Tears trickled down my cheeks. "...he did."

"And who's he?"

Another tear rolled down my cheek. "Gibsie."

"And what'll happen to your little boyfriend if you even think about telling lies about me like Gibsie did?"

"No!" I clenched my eyes shut. "Please don't hurt him."

"Say it!" He squeezed my throat tighter. "Where will lover boy end up?"

"In there," I strangled out, body growing limp against the railing at my back. "With her..."

Shaking my head, I clenched my eyes shut and tried to force the images from my mind.

"You know you're unstable, don't you?" he said then in a sad tone. "Your mother can't escape death forever. One of these days, it's going to catch up with her," he told me. "And when she dies, you'll be alone, with no sister or mother to love you."

A pained sob escaped my lips, but he just kept talking.

"Catherine's on borrowed time, and we both know she's the only thing standing between you and that mental hospital Mike has planned for you."

His words caused fear to rise up inside of me and sent my mind spiraling.

"If I were you, I would keep on *not* talking," he continued in a soft, gentle voice that made my skin crawl. "Everyone already thinks you're insane, so no need to fuel the fire with crazy ramblings—*not* that anyone would believe you, either way."

I knew *he* was looking at me.

I could feel his eyes burning the side of my face, but I didn't dare turn my head.

Instead, I focused on the dirt trail my shoes made in the grass under the swing.

"I'll be leaving town soon, munchkin," he told me. "Once I finish my leaving cert next month, I'm leaving Ireland. I'm going to do a bit of traveling before college." Another sigh escaped him. "I'm going to miss our special visits."

My skin crawled, while my stomach heaved and my mind screamed in protest.

No!

Don't think about it.

"I wish we could have another night together, but I'm afraid the last one will have to do."

Don't let yourself remember.

"I'll take you with me, though. Wherever I end up, I'll always have your pictures."

Protect yourself and don't ever go back there.

Never again.

"And I'll aways be with you, too. You'll never forget me, munchkin."

Just block it out.

"A girl never forgets her first."

Let yourself go.

Just drift off.

"And I'll always be your first everything, munchkin."

Up, up, and away.

TARGET ON THE BACK

Hugh

APRIL 30, 2000

It took six days for Caoimhe's body to be released back to the family, and even then, her parents were told it would take time for the autopsy report to be finalized.

When my babysitter returned to Old Hall House, it was in a brown coffin that had to remain closed because of the damage caused to her body while in the river.

The whole town showed up to the wake to pay their respects to the family, and there had been a steady flow of traffic coming and going from the house all day. She would spend her last night in her family's home, surrounded by the people who loved her most.

When tomorrow came, on what should have been her nineteenth birthday, Caoimhe Young would be laid to rest after twelve o'clock mass, in the adjoining grave-yard of St. Patrick's Church.

Forever eighteen.

I hadn't left Liz's side for a moment until today, when I had to go to town with Mam to get measured for a suit for the funeral. When I got back to Lizzie's house a couple of hours later, I found her exactly where I left her. But it wasn't Gibsie keeping her company, like I had implicitly instructed him to do.

It was Mark.

Lizzie was sitting on the tree swing, with her feet trailing in the mud, while that prick sat on the second swing we had added a few years back.

The minute I saw him, I was incensed.

"Hey!" I roared, climbing over the wooden fence and bolting toward them. "What the fuck are you doing?"

"What does it look like?" Mark narrowed his eyes as I approached. "I'm talking to her."

"No, you're not," I countered, moving to stand between them. "You have nothing to say that she needs to hear."

I didn't want him anywhere near Liz. It had taken me six days to get her out of that bed, and I wasn't about to let that prick upset her with talk of her sister.

Besides, the time for talking was weeks ago.

The fact that he and Caoimhe hadn't reached out *once* to my family or his in those three weeks didn't sit well with me.

If he was telling the truth about Liz having a mental breakdown—and I couldn't prove he wasn't—it meant they had kept her in that house for three fucking weeks without seeking medical intervention.

I knew my girlfriend. I knew how low her moods could plummet, but she wasn't dangerous like Mark had portrayed her to be.

He told her parents that Liz attacked both him and Caoimhe on multiple occasions throughout the course of those weeks, which had led to them having no choice but to keep her sedated with her prescription of clonazepam. He even accused her of holding a knife to his throat.

Now, if he had said she tried to bite him, it would have been a lot more plausible, but oh no, he had to go with a knife.

I didn't believe a word of it.

Not one fucking word.

"Actually, I'm the only one that *should* be speaking to her," Mark replied, glaring at me. "Because I understand her. Because *I* was with her that night, *not* you. I hate to tell ya, Biggs, but *I'm* the one she needs right now."

My girlfriend proved him a liar when she sprang off the swing and dove for me. Trembling, Liz fisted my T-shirt and buried her face in my neck.

"Oh, yeah? Well, I find that really hard to believe given the circumstances," I shot back, wrapping a protective arm around Liz. "I mean, it's not like you have a good track record of being there when you're *needed*."

"How *dare* you speak to me like that," Mark seethed, jerking off the swing. "You have some fucking nerve to say that to my face."

"Yeah, well, someone needed to," I shot back, unwilling to show empathy to an asshole who didn't deserve it. "The truth hurts, asshole, but it's still the truth."

"My girlfriend is inside that house laid out in a fucking coffin," he snarled, stalking toward me with a bull-head expression. "You have no idea how much pain I'm in."

"Yeah, and maybe if you had spent a little less time thinking about *your* pain and a little more time thinking about your girlfriend's pain, she might not *be* in that coffin," I snapped back, keeping a firm hold on Liz, while I stood my ground. "Caoimhe's death doesn't give you a clean sheet, asshole. It doesn't erase the shitty way you mistreated her for years, and no amount of lies you tell yourself will purge the hand you had in her decision to end her life."

"I never mistreated Caoimhe—"

"That shit might float with Catherine and Mike, but don't waste your time trying it on me," I cut in, unwilling to listen to him feed me another one of his lines. "You mentioned earlier something about understanding what *my* girlfriend is going through because you were with her that night. Am I right? Hmm? Is that what you said?" I waited for him to nod before I continued. "Well, I was with *your* girlfriend on multiple occasions down through the years when you messed her around and fucked with her head." Wholly enraged and unable to contain myself, I fired from all cylinders and let him have it. "You are incapable of understanding anyone because in order to do that, you would have to possess a conscience and that's something we both know you *don't* have."

"Shut your mouth, Biggs." He narrowed his eyes in warning. "You have no idea what you're talking about."

"You treated your girlfriend like she was a piece of meat. Like she was a subpar human, whose sole purpose on earth was to please you. Instead of taking care of her like a man is supposed to, you impregnated her and ruined her future!"

"I took care of that," he seethed, looking truly rattled that I knew his dirty little secret. "I looked after my girlfriend."

"Yeah, you did a great job of looking after your girlfriend when you ferried her off in the middle of her leaving cert." I narrowed my eyes in disgust. "Boyfriend of the year in the making."

"That was *her* decision," he roared, getting in my face, oblivious to the trembling girl clinging to me. "Or am I to blame for Caoimhe not wanting to keep it?"

"No. It was her body and her choice to make," I replied, twisting sideways to keep Liz out of the firing line. "But you're sure as hell to blame for putting her in that situation in the first place. I haven't even turned thirteen yet and I know that. You were *supposed* to protect her, and you *didn't*."

"You are stepping over a dangerous line, Biggs," he said in a deathly cold tone. "Don't push me."

"Kind of like how you walked over Caoimhe?" I shot back. "You trampled all over that girl like she was a fucking doormat, and you didn't think twice about it. So don't you stand here and tell me that *my* girlfriend needs *anything* from a piece of shit like you when you both know you are the *worst* type of cancer that *ever* entered her family."

"You're going to regret this," Mark hissed, but I had already turned to walk away, deciding that I had already wasted too much of my energy on him.

Fucking cretin.

"You'll get what's coming to ya, Biggs," he continued to call after me, as I led my girlfriend as far away from him as I could. "You better watch your back!"

"Ignore him," I told Liz, who was trembling violently beside me. "Remember what I told you about bullies?" I added in a gentler tone, as I helped her climb over the fence, before jumping over it myself. "Bullies feed on fear, and if you don't feed them, they starve."

"And die."

My head snapped in her direction.

Two words.

She spoke two words.

Finally.

Be normal with her, my brain commanded, *don't bombard her with questions that'll put her back in her shell.*

"That's right," I agreed, draping an arm around her shoulders, while mentally instructing myself to *not* react. "They die."

"Hugh?" Liz stopped walking and turned to look at me. "Don't die, okay?"

"I'm not dying, Liz."

"Please." Tears filled her eyes as she stared into my eyes and begged, "Don't ever leave me."

"I won't." My heart cracked in my chest. "I'm not going anywhere, Liz."

"No matter what?"

"Yeah, Liz." I pressed a kiss to her forehead. "No matter what."

"Do you believe in heaven, Hugh?" she asked a little while later, when I had taken her far away from the house that contained her sister's dead body and the meadow that contained the cretin.

We were still on their property, but I'd put about forty acres between us and the rest of the world. Because I needed to keep her calm and *talking.*

"That's a hard question," I replied thoughtfully, scratching my chin. "The scientist in me says no, but the Catholic in me says yes." Sprawled out on the grass, I leaned back on my elbows and looked at her. "Do you believe in heaven, Liz?"

"No." She shook her head. "Not anymore."

"How come?"

"Because I don't believe in anything anymore," she replied, never taking her eyes off the daisy chain she was making. "I used to, I think, but not anymore." She shook her head again. "Maybe I'm just broken inside."

"There's nothing broken in you, Liz," I replied gruffly. "You're just sad. It's okay to be sad."

"But I'm not just sad," she whispered, crushing the daisy chain in her small fist. "I'm angry."

"That's okay, too."

"Is it?" Sniffling, she turned to look at me, making my stomach twist up in knots, when her sad, blue eyes locked on mine. "Am I okay?"

"Maybe not right now." My heart cracked when I heard her pain. "But you'll be okay one day."

"What if I'm not?" She reached up and batted another tear away. "What if I'm never okay again?"

"You *will* be, Liz."

"But what if I'm *not*, Hugh?" she choked out, crawling onto my lap. "What happens then?"

"Then that'll be okay, too." Sitting up, I wrapped her up in my arms and whispered, "Because no matter how happy or sad you feel, I'll be right here with you."

"You will?"

"Every step of the way."

HE DID IT, DADDY!

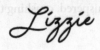

MAY 1, 2000

IN MEMORY OF

CAOIMHE CATHERINE YOUNG

LOVING DAUGHTER, SISTER & FRIEND

April 30, 1981–April 24, 2000

FOREVER EIGHTEEN

IGNORING THE LADY STANDING AT MY SISTER'S GRAVESIDE, PLAYING FLEETWOOD Mac's "Landslide" on her guitar, I strained to hear the sound of scratching, so I could tell the men to stop lowering her coffin into the hole and bring her back up instead.

So I could tell the priest that my sister was in a deep sleep, one that had lasted seven days, but she was awake now, and they needed to let her out of the box.

Come on, Caoimhe, we're running out of time.

Hurry up and scream, cry, shout...

Anything!

Numb to the bone, I watched as someone produced a chair for my mother to sit on, while my father dropped to his knees at her graveside, crying and begging a God that couldn't hear us to bring his daughter back to him.

Meanwhile, I stood alone and watched the men in black suits lower my sister's coffin into the ground.

Caoimhe was in there.

Inside that wooden box.

Clasping my hands together tightly, I willed my sister to make a noise to prove to all these people in black clothes that they were mistaken.

Her voice.

Her eyes.

Her smile.

Her last moments.

No, this *couldn't* be it.

She didn't belong in here.

My big sister.

My only sibling.

She was never coming back.

No.

No.

No!

Someone reached for my hands and gently peeled them apart before entwining their fingers with mine.

I didn't need to look to know whose hand was holding mine.

I could *feel* his presence: strong, dependable, and safe.

He was the *only* thing I could feel nowadays.

Tightening my hold on Hugh's hand, I looked on wordlessly as my sister's burial slowly came to a close.

She was in the ground now.

The were throwing fistfuls of dirt on top of her, cementing that she wasn't coming back.

This was no mistake.

Caoimhe was gone.

Forever.

The priest told my parents that God had taken my sister's soul to heaven, but he forgot to mention that Caoimhe had taken my soul with her.

I knew she had.

There was a piece of me in the ground with her.

I could feel it.

A hollow, gaping ridge in my chest where she used to be.

Where I used to *feel.*

Towering over me by several inches, Hugh stood by my side, holding my hand throughout the rest of the service. Even long after it ended, when the mourners lined up to offer my family their condolences, he remained right beside me.

I didn't accept a single one of the countless handshakes I was offered, choosing instead to hold Hugh's hand with both of mine.

I didn't want their touch.

I didn't want to feel another hand on my skin ever again.

Only *this* boy.

Hugh.

375

After a while, Claire and Patrick came to stand with us.

"Liz." With tears streaming down her face, she hooked her arm through mine and gave me an awkward hug. "I'm so sorry."

"Thank you, Claire," I replied, feeling as lifeless as my sister.

"I don't know what to say, Liz," Patrick added, stepping forward to rub my shoulder. "I'm just so sorry for your loss."

"Thank you, Patrick," I repeated back, feeling dead inside.

Sniffling, Claire adjusted my cardigan, placing it back on my shoulder, though I hadn't noticed it falling off in the first place.

"She's grand, Claire," Hugh interjected, shooing his sister away from the buttons on my cardigan. "Leave her be."

"I'm just trying to help," my friend sobbed, looking up at me with lonesome, brown eyes. "I want to help you, Liz." Sniffling, she added, "But I don't know what I'm supposed to do."

"Hugh," I breathed, feeling my body grow weak when my eyes tracked a shadow looming on the other side of the graveyard. "Look."

"Look at what, Liz?" Claire asked, looking around us. "What do you see?"

"The scary lady," I whispered. "She's here."

"What scary lady?" she strangled out, looking panicked. "Who is she?"

"A ghost," I mumbled, feeling slightly delirious as I continued to watch her bob and weave around the headstones. "She has sharp claws and watches us when nobody's looking."

"Wh-what?" Claire choked out, gripping Patrick's arm. "Is it the banshee?"

"No, it's not, and there's no banshee," Patrick reassured Claire, wrapping an arm around her. "Liz is going through a lot right now. She probably hasn't slept in days. It's normal for a person's eyes to play tricks on them when they're going through something like this."

"There's nothing wrong with her eyes," Hugh cut in, attention riveted to the headstone I last noticed her hiding behind. "I see her, too."

"She's here, isn't she?" I choked out, turning to look at him. "It's her, right? The one we saw in the woods by your house that day?"

"Yeah." He nodded slowly, eyes narrowed as he stared off in the distance. "I think it is."

"Hugh, stop it!" Claire cried out. "You're scaring me."

"They're both sleep deprived, Baby-Biggs," Patrick said, consoling her. "He's been with her every day since the accident. Don't worry about it."

"Can you still see her?" Hugh asked, ignoring our friends, as he craned his neck to scope out the area.

"No." I shook my head. "Can you?"

He shook his head. "No."

"Well, that's one bit of good news," Patrick chimed in, still soothing Claire who looked like she was about to jump out of her skin.

It was at that exact moment I noticed the family that had come to stand beside my parents.

My blood ran cold immediately.

His father was holding my father up, while his stepmother consoled my mother.

Betrayal more potent than anything I'd ever felt overcame me when I locked eyes on the boy standing beside *him*.

He stared back at me with gray eyes.

Guilty eyes.

How could he do that?

How could he stand with him?

Didn't he know?

He *had* to know.

I did what she'd asked.

She promised he would help.

He hadn't.

Tears filled his eyes, matching the ones burning mine.

Narrowing my eyes, I flicked my attention back to *him*. He was standing at my sister's grave, taking their condolences and wearing his false grief like a badge of honor.

And that's when it happened.

That's when the first scream escaped me.

It was a shrill, piercing sound that caused everyone to turn and look at me.

My friends included.

"Elizabeth, stop it!" my father cried, leaning heavily against Keith Allen for support. "Show some respect for your sister."

I couldn't stop.

I couldn't hold it in another second.

Seeing him standing at my sister's grave, consoling my parents had flicked a switch inside of me.

"He did it, Daddy." With tears streaming down my face, I screamed at the top of my lungs and pointed to *him*. "He killed Caoimhe!"

DON'T EVER SPEAK TO ME AGAIN

Hugh

I WAS IN THE TWILIGHT ZONE.

I had to be.

It was the only explanation for this crazy fucking day.

One minute I had convinced myself that I could see the creepy woman from the woods lurking behind a headstone a few rows back from where I was standing, and the next, Lizzie had accused Mark Allen of killing her sister.

The moment those words came out of her mouth, all hell broke loose.

Momentarily stunned into silence, all I could do was watch on, while the worst kind of accusations were thrown about.

"He did it, I swear," Lizzie was screaming and pointing at Mark on one side of the graveside. "He made her go in the river. He hurt her. He made her die!"

"Dad, I don't know what she's talking about," Mark protested from the other side. "I never laid a hand on Caoimhe!"

"Why are you doing this?" Keith strangled out, looking horrified. "Why are you saying these things about my son?"

"Stop telling lies, Lizzie," Sadhbh screamed, while *my* mother grabbed her shoulders and gave her a stern look before ordering her to *calm down.*

Meanwhile, Gibsie was crying so hard, he could hardly breathe, Claire rushing to his side to comfort him.

"You're a liar," Lizzie screamed at the top of her lungs as she tugged and pulled on her hair. "I *saw* you! I know what he did, Dad." She swung her gaze back to her father. "He's a monster. Caoimhe said so! He does bad things. With his thing." She swung her glare back to Mark and screamed, "I saw you take her clothes off and make her do that!"

"Do what?" Mike demanded, grabbing his daughter's shoulders. "What did he make her do?"

"He put his *thing* inside," Lizzie sobbed, clinging to her father, while her mother slumped in the chair, clutching her arm and struggling to breathe. "He wasn't supposed to."

"His *thing*? His penis?" Mike demanded, shaking Lizzie. "Elizabeth, are you telling me that he raped your sister?"

"He made her die, Daddy." Crying hard and ugly, Lizzie nodded. "I know he did. You *have* to believe me."

"She's a fucking liar," Mark roared, pointing his finger right back at her. "She's insane, Dad. Yeah, I had sex with Caoimhe, but she was my girlfriend." He shook his head and glared at Mike. "Your daughter's a fucking lunatic, and you need to get her sectioned!"

"Did you rape my daughter?" Mike demanded, body vibrating with anger. "Did you force yourself on *my* daughter?"

"No!" Mark bellowed, looking outraged. "I never once forced your daughter into anything she didn't want to do!"

"Then why is my daughter in the ground, Mark?" Mike roared back at him. "Why is my other daughter blaming you?"

"Because she's a fucking nutjob, that's why!" Mark tossed back cruelly, still pointing at Liz. "And you ruined Caoimhe's life the day you decided to bring that vicious little bitch into—"

"Hey!" I roared, jumping into the mix. "Don't even think about calling her names, you fucking asshole!"

"Hugh!" My father grabbed the back of my jacket and yanked me away from the fray. "That's enough."

Meanwhile, my mother rushed to tend to Catherine, who was slumped over on the chair.

"She's fucking nuts, Hugh," Mark continued to roar, turning his attention to me. "Even *you* know that."

"What I know is you're a sanctimonious bully who lies through his teeth," I roared back. "And if you call her crazy one more time, I'm going to show you the true meaning of the word."

"Hugh!" I felt my father place his hand on my shoulder and I roughly shrugged him off. He could fuck right off. I didn't need his support. I didn't need a damn thing from him.

"Tell them, please tell them," Lizzie cried out, staggering toward Gibsie of all people. "You know." She dropped to her knees in front of him and grabbed his hands. "I know you know, Gibs. I helped you. I did. I helped you, and now you have to help *me*."

"I…" Looking deathly pale, Gibsie shook his head. "I *can't*."

"Yes, you can!" Lizzie screamed, banging her fist on his chest. "You know! You do, you do!"

I moved to go to Liz, but my dad dragged me back, and this time, he wouldn't let go.

"Leave my son out of your lies," Sadhbh screamed, grabbing ahold of her son and dragging him away from both Lizzie and my sister. "Don't you dare try to fill his head with your poison, you wicked, evil, little girl."

"Don't cry." Dropping to her knees, Claire threw her arms around Lizzie and hugged her tight. "Shh, please stop screaming."

I didn't think Liz *could* stop.

The feral screams escaping her were the result of seven days of grief, pain, and anger finally bursting to the surface.

"What's going on here?" a Garda demanded, while three more arrived on the scene, along with the paramedics. The grown-ups immediately jumped into action, fighting and arguing to have the first word.

"I thought you were my friend," Lizzie cried, looking more broken in this moment than I'd ever seen her as she stared at Gibsie, who was standing with his family. "You're supposed to be my *friend*."

"I *am* your friend." Gibsie was crying as his mother ushered him back to where Mark and Keith were standing. "I am, Liz, I promise."

"Then *tell* them what you told my sister," she begged, still on her hands and knees while *my* sister held her. "Tell them he killed my sister!"

"He can't because I *didn't* do anything to your sister!" Mark roared, clamping a hand down on Gibsie's shoulder. "I'm innocent and my brother knows that. Don't you, Gibs?"

"I don't know what you want me to say," Gibsie sobbed, crying as hard as Lizzie now. "I'm sorry, Liz, I wasn't there."

Lizzie released one more gut-wrenching sob before looking Gibs right in the eyes and saying, "Don't *ever* speak to me again."

It was at that exact moment I came to the sudden realization that nothing would ever be the same.

PART 15

The Great Divide

FLASHBACKS AND FLEETING MEMORIES

Lizzie

MAY 2, 2000

"GET AWAY FROM ME!"

"You're not leaving!"

"No, because you're the one leaving. Get out of my house!"

"This is one huge misunderstanding, Caoimhe, I swear."

"Mark, I saw you with my own fucking eyes!" my sister was screaming. "How could you do that to a child!"

I froze in the doorway. The hairs on the back of my neck began to prickle. My entire body broke into a cold sweat. It almost felt like my stomach had bottomed out.

Gripping the duvet, I felt a little lightheaded, almost like I was about to faint.

"Elizabeth! Come here right now." She sounded like she wanted to kill me, so I did the only thing I could in this moment. I bolted. "I need to talk to you!"

Holding my breath, I climbed into my wardrobe and quietly closed the door behind me. Covering my mouth with my hand, I froze and waited.

"Gibsie knows what you are!" Caoimhe was threatening him. "And so do I!"

What did they know?

What was happening?

"Don't fucking threaten me, Caoimhe!"

And why was my skin crawling?

Why did I want to peel my ears off to stop myself from hearing his voice?

"Oh my God!" Caoimhe continued to scream. "I brought a pervert around those kids. I brought you around my sister—"

"What did she say?" he demanded. "What did that little bitch tell you? Because you know she lies, Caoimhe. You can't believe a word that lunatic says."

"What do mean what did she tell me?"

"Nothing, forget I said that."

"What did you mean, Mark?" Caoimhe demanded. "What did you do to my sister?"

"Can you stop screaming for one fucking second!" he roared back at her. *"I'm trying to think."*

"No, no, no, no!" Caoimhe released an earth-shattering scream. *"Tell me you didn't! Not Lizzie!"*

"Caoimhe, stop screaming and let me explain..."

I tried to tell them.

To make them all understand.

About the monster in my nightmares, the scary lady watching me in the shadows, and my sister's dead eyes.

My thoughts were muddled, and I tried so hard to make it all make sense, but all my efforts of explaining came out as a jumbled mess of frantic pleas and frenzied accusations that nobody seemed to take seriously.

I BELIEVE YOUR DAUGHTER

Hugh

MAY 3, 2000

"You have a lot of nerve showing up here, Hughie," were the first words Michael Young said when he opened his front door and found me on his doorstep on Wednesday morning.

I couldn't blame the man for his hostility. Not when I had witnessed the showdown at his eldest daughter's funeral two days ago. My oldest friend's stepbrother had been accused of raping my girlfriend's sister. My parents had taken the side of said oldest friend's mother, which meant, to this man, that I belonged to the enemy camp. But I also couldn't be held accountable for the actions of others.

When everything went to shit at the graveside and Liz and I were ushered away in opposite directions, I didn't have a choice in the matter. I *had* to leave with my family. I also wasn't given the chance to speak my mind at the graveside, either—although, that was something I had made up for later.

When we returned to our street and were shooed upstairs to Gibsie's bedroom so the grown-ups could talk in private, I'd lost my shit and stormed downstairs.

Aside from blowing a head gasket when I heard Sadhbh talking about my girlfriend in a less-than-favorable light, I'd lunged for Mark the moment he returned from the Garda station with his father.

My momentary slip in sanity cost me a broken nose—courtesy of Mark—and a lifelong ban from number nine—courtesy of his father.

It was worth it, though, and I would gladly take a dozen broken bones if it meant that I got to hit that prick again.

Better still, Dad had taken leave of his senses when he saw the condition of my face and had beaten seven kinds of shite out of Mark for putting his hands on "his child." I wasn't too happy about being referred to as a child, but I couldn't deny the solid my father had done for me. After all, Dad had been given a lifelong ban from number nine right along with me.

Everything had gone to hell on my street, and I knew I was taking a gamble cycling over here, but how the hell could I not?

I refused to abandon her.

No matter what.

"Why don't ya go back to Avoca Greystones?" Mike continued to seethe, looking more broken than he had at his daughter's funeral. "Hmm? Run on back to the Allens and defend their rapist, bastard son like your parents have decided to."

"I'm not my parents," I said calmly, steeling my resolve. "And I'm not that rapist bastard, either."

My words seemed to throw Lizzie's father and give him pause for thought. "What are you saying, Hugh?"

"I'm saying I believe my girlfriend," I replied, pouncing on the temporary crack in his resolve. "I *believe* your daughter, Mike," I told him, straightening my shoulders to make myself look as grown-up as I could. "And I came here to tell her exactly that."

Mike blew out a breath and I watched as the tension slowly left his rigid shoulders. "Well then." Stepping aside, he held the door open. "You best come inside, son."

The first thing that greeted me when I reached the landing was the high-pitched, wailing noises coming from behind Caoimhe's closed bedroom door.

Instantly, I recognized the disturbingly unnatural sobs as those of a grieving mother. Only once before had I heard keening like that, and it had come from Sadhbh Allen when Bethany died. The excruciating keening sound that came out of a bereaved mother when her child died was hauntingly distinctive and something I hoped like hell I would never have to endure for a third time.

Repressing a shudder, I moved straight for Lizzie's room, trying to block out her mother's pained cries. When I slipped inside, I didn't bother to knock because I knew there was no point. My girlfriend was lifeless on her bed, dosed to the high heavens with God knows whatever the doctors had prescribed to numb the pain.

Moving straight for her, I kicked off my shoes and climbed under the covers next to her. "Hi, baby, it's me," I heard myself whisper and then quickly frowned when I realized the endearment that had escaped my lips. Whoa. I'd never called Liz *that* before. Even stranger was the fact that it felt *right*. Like I was supposed to call her that.

"Hi," Liz whispered, still staring lifelessly at the ceiling above her, as tears trickled down her cheeks. "I can't turn my head."

"That's okay," I replied, reaching for her. "I can do it for you."

"They gave me an injection," she croaked out when I rolled her onto her side to face me. "Another one." Puffy blue eyes greeted me. "I can't feel a thing."

"Maybe that's a good thing," I offered, resting my hand on her cheek. "You've felt enough pain, Liz."

"I want to feel you," she whispered, eyes locked on mine. "And I can't."

"You can't feel me now?" I asked, stroking her cheek.

"No," she replied as another tear fell from her long lashes.

"That's okay," I replied gently. "I can feel you."

"You can?"

"Yeah, I can, Liz."

"How do I feel?"

"Honestly?"

"Always."

"You burn me," I admitted, stroking her cheek. "In the best possible way imaginable."

She seemed to think about that for a moment before asking, "Does anyone else burn you?"

"No," I replied, wholly fixated on her face. "Only you."

"Really?"

"I swear on my life."

"Oh God." Her chest heaved. "I've missed you so much, Hugh."

"I've missed you more, Liz," I replied, battling down the tsunami of emotions rising up inside of me.

"I've made everything a million times worse," she confessed then, chest rising and falling quickly. "I broke my parents."

"No, you didn't," I coaxed, shifting closer so I could press my brow to hers. "You didn't break anyone, Liz. That was all him."

Her breath hitched in her throat. "You *believe* me?"

"Of course I do," I replied thickly. "And I am so damn sorry for how everything went down at the funeral." A pained breath escaped my parted lips. "I wanted to go with you after the fight, I promise I did, but my parents forced me home."

"Nobody else believes me, Hugh," she strangled out, blue eyes widening. "But I'm telling the truth, I swear."

"I know you are," I replied gruffly, hating the tremor in my hand when I smoothed her hair off her face. "And that's not true, Liz. Your parents believe you, too."

"Only because they're my parents," she whispered, expression falling. "Only because it's easier to blame him than me."

"Why would they blame you?"

"Because I'm me," she strangled out. "Because I was there and didn't stop her."

"How were you supposed to stop her?" I pushed in as gentle a tone as I could muster.

Lizzie blinked in confusion. "I stopped her?"

My heart cracked and I did the only thing I could in this moment; I leaned in and pressed a kiss to her cheek before whispering the words, "I love you," in her ear.

The events of that night were still a mystery, and I knew Liz held a lot more information inside her complicated mind than that lying bastard had given the authorities. The only problem was Lizzie's memories were fractured, fragments that needed to be carefully pieced together, and only time could restore them. How much time, I had no idea, but if I pushed her now for more than she was capable of divulging, she would slip back inside her mind, and I would lose her again. I refused to do that because, selfishly, I wanted to keep her healthy more than I wanted to know the truth.

"Your nose," she whispered then, focusing on my face. "Your eyes." Her breath hitched. "You're bruised all over."

"I'm grand." I dismissed her words with a smile. "You should see the other fella."

"Who hurt you?"

"No one, Liz."

"Was it me?"

"You?" My brows furrowed in confusion. "No, Liz, of course it wasn't."

"Oh." She seemed to heave a sigh of relief. "I'm sorry."

"Don't be sorry for something you didn't do," I told her, capturing a rogue tear with my thumb. "Besides, I'm the one who should be sorry."

"Why are you sorry?"

"For leaving you after the funeral."

"But you came back."

"Two days later, Liz."

"But you still came back, Hugh."

"I'll always come back to you," I offered, wanting to fold her into my body and keep her safe. "No matter how often I have to leave, just know that I will *always* come back for you."

"To me or for me?"

"Both."

"Good, because you're the only reason I'm here."

"Don't, Liz." My heart cracked. "Please don't say that."

"It's the truth." Her expression caved and she clenched her eyes shut to stem her tears. "I think fate got it wrong."

My brows furrowed in confusion. "What do you mean?"

"I'm the one supposed to drown, not her," she explained. "I'm going to die in water, Hugh."

"Liz." My entire body tensed. "Why would you say that?"

"Because of my dream."

"What dream?"

"The one where I'm trying to swim to the surface and someone is pushing my head under."

"Holy shit, Liz." I couldn't hide my horror. "How long have you been having that dream?"

"Since as far back as I can remember," she whispered. "The person holding me under screams at me to stop fighting, to just give up and breathe." A full-body shudder racked through her. "When I do, I die, and that's when I wake up."

"That's horrendous."

"I think it's an omen," she admitted, sounding broken. "That I was never meant to be here...that I'm supposed to die under water."

"No." The word came out a lot harder than I meant, but I couldn't stop it because my heart was gunning in my chest. "No, Liz, that's not true, so don't you dare believe it."

"It's kind of hard not to when I really want to *not* be here, Hugh."

"I need you here, Liz," I croaked out. "I *need* you."

"You don't need me, Hugh," she replied sadly. "You want me, but you won't always feel that way."

"That's bullshit and you know it," I argued back, pulling her body closer to mine. "Aside from the fact that you're my girlfriend and I adore you, you've been my best friend since I was seven. You're the keeper of all my secrets and the only girl on this planet I would willingly spend my time with. I absolutely *do* need you, Liz."

"I'm so broken, Hugh."

"You're not broken," I replied gently. "You're grieving."

"I *am* broken," she strangled out, looking devastated. "I'm not *good*, Hugh. I'm not the girl you think I am, and one of these days, you'll figure that out and leave."

"I won't," I shot back insistently, feeling fucking crippled that she had so little faith in my ability to stay with her. "I won't leave you, Liz."

"Caoimhe left," she whispered, eyelids fluttering shut to conceal her pain from me. "You'll leave, too."

"That's not me," I argued back, reaching for her hand. "I'm not that person." I placed her hand on my cheek. "I won't *ever* leave you on your own."

"Maybe you should," she mumbled. "Before you get hurt."

"Are you going to hurt me, Liz?" I asked, covering her hand with mine.

"No, but he might."

"Mark?"

"Maybe." Her fingers twitched beneath mine. "Or maybe the monster will get you first, or the scary lady."

"The monster's not going to get me," I promised her for what felt like the millionth time over the course of our relationship. "And neither will the scary lady. As for Mark fucking Allen, he should be afraid of *me* getting him."

Her eyes snapped open. "No, Hugh! Don't!" Fearful, blue eyes locked on mine. "Don't go anywhere near him."

"I'm not afraid of him, Liz," I said, trying to console her. "And he's going to get what's coming to him." *One way or another.*

"Promise me, Hugh." Her hand jerked to fist my shirt. "Promise me that you'll stay away from him."

"Well," I sighed heavily. "At this present moment in time, I'm forbidden from stepping foot inside his house, so you really don't have a whole pile to worry about."

"Why?"

"It's no big deal, Liz."

Her fingers tightened around the fabric of my shirt. "*Why*, Hugh?"

I debated lying to protect her fragile emotions, but I *couldn't*. Not when she was looking at me with complete trust in her eyes. "I got in a fight with Mark." Sighing in defeat, I quickly continued, "I smacked the shit out of him for all of three minutes before he broke my nose—oh, and then my dad broke his nose." Shrugging, I admitted, "Dad's banned from the house, too."

"Why would you do that?" she strangled out, fingers shakily tracing my cuts and bruises. "He's a lot older and a lot bigger than you."

"Maybe right now," I begrudgingly agreed. "But he won't always be." Snatching up her hand in mine, I pressed a kiss to her scarred wrist. "I'm going to grow up, Liz. One day, I'll be a man, and if that prick even looks in your direction, I'll put him in the ground."

Her eyes widened to saucers. "You w-would kill him?"

"If he touched you? Absolutely," I confirmed grimly. "And I wouldn't feel bad about it, either."

"You would do that for me?" A deep shudder rolled through her body. "But *why*?"

"Because I *love* you," I urged, kissing her wrist again. "And because I *believe* you, Liz." I entwined her fingers with mine before adding, "I *believe* he raped Caoimhe." Shifting closer, I pressed my forehead to hers once more and whispered, "And I will *never* let that animal do to you, Claire, or any other girl what he did to your sister. But mostly you."

"Why mostly me?"

"Because I love you most of all."

I'M GOING UNDER AGAIN

Lizzie

MAY 10, 2000

Screaming my name at the top of her lungs, Caoimhe barged into my room. *"Elizabeth, come out right this instant. I need to talk to you!"*

Fumbling with the wardrobe door, I gingerly climbed out, feeling panicked. "I'm sorry, Caoimhe."

"Did he touch you, Lizzie?" my sister demanded, shoving Mark away when he tried to hug her. "Did Mark force you to have sex with him?"

My body turned to stone, and I looked up at my sister with tears streaming down my cheeks. "Am I in trouble?"

"She's lying," Mark snarled, pushing my sister so hard, she fell to the floor. "Tell her I never forced you, munchkin!" He grabbed my arm and forced me to stand. "Fucking tell her, you little cunt!"

"Don't touch her!" Screaming and snarling, Caoimhe flung herself at him, scratching and tearing at him. "You fucking monster."

"I'm broken," he sobbed, trying to pull her body close to his. "I need help, baby, I'm sick."

"What did you do to her?" she continued to scream, knocking him to the floor. "How long has this been going on?"

"She wanted it, I swear," he tried to plead, pinning my sister down. "She was always jealous of us. What I have with you. She's a fucking whore, baby. Your sister led me on. You have no idea what she's capable of."

"She's a child!" Caoimhe snarled, bucking her hips to knock him off her chest. "What the fuck is wrong with you?"

"You can't tell anyone, Caoimhe," he cried, pinning her hands above her head. "Please, baby, please. I'll kill myself. You don't want that, do you? Do you want me to die, baby? Because that's what'll happen…"

The Gardaí didn't believe me.

Neither did the grown-ups.

Nobody believed me.

Except Hugh, my mind encouraged, *the brave knight believes his lady.*

Everyone else thought I was disturbed.

Maybe I was.

They were so sure that I was mistaken that it jarred me.

It shook my resolve.

It made me doubt myself.

DON'T BE HIS FRIEND ANYMORE
Lizzie

MAY 24, 2000

AS THE DAYS TURNED INTO WEEKS, MY SISTER'S MEMORY BEGAN TO SLOWLY DWINDLE. The steady flow of trays of baked goods and home-cooked casseroles that had been delivered daily by our neighbors had come to a stop. As had the arrival of well-wishers at the front door.

Today was her one-month anniversary and nobody had bothered to turn up to the house. In a way, I was relieved because I didn't think I could shake another stranger's hand without losing what was left of my sanity—and I really didn't have much to spare at this point in time.

The only consistent figure that continued to visit was the boy whose hand was holding mine.

Hugh was the only person who kept coming, and to me, his presence meant more than the entire community of Ballylaggin. The whole town could stay away forever if it meant I got to keep him.

If it meant this boy stayed.

"Where's your dad?" Hugh asked, distracting me from my thoughts. "I didn't see his car outside."

"Oh, I think he went to work," I mumbled, tucking my hair behind my ears as I watched him move around my bedroom, folding clothes and tidying up. "Yeah, I think that's what he told me."

"When did he leave?"

"This morning." *I think.* "Mam's in her room." Like he needed me to tell him that. We could both hear the crying coming from downstairs.

"Can I take you out today?"

I shook my head, recoiling against the pillows at my back at the thought. "Not today."

He turned to look at me, brown eyes warm and full of understanding. "Don't panic, Liz. I'm never going to force you to do anything you don't want to do."

I breathed a sigh of relief. "Okay."

"But one of these days, I'm going to *persuade* you to come out of this room," Hugh added in a playful tone, as he closed the space between us. "We'll start with going downstairs." Climbing onto my bed, he waggled his brows and reached for my hand. "And then we'll shoot for the garden." Pulling me onto his lap with minimal effort, he draped an arm around my back and nuzzled his cheek against mine. "Maybe then, we'll aim for my house."

"No." My body turned to stone in his arms. "I can't."

"Don't be so hasty," he continued to tease, lips brushing against my bare shoulder. "This skin needs sunshine." He pressed an affectionate kiss to the curve of my neck. "Think of the vitamin D."

"No, I mean I can't go there," I squeezed out, shivering when his lips touched me. Oh yeah, I could definitely *feel* his lips. His kiss was innocent but it made my body respond in a not-so-innocent way.

Bad girl.

Evil girl.

Filthy whore.

"I can't go anywhere near that street," I blurted out, desperately trying to focus on the present and block *him* out. "I can't go to your house, Hugh. Not when he's there." *And he's always there.* "I'm sorry."

Hugh was quiet for a long moment before releasing a heavy sigh. Instead of arguing with me, like I half expected him to, he turned me on his lap to face him. "I love you," he said, whiskey-brown eyes searing mine. "I love you so much." Reaching up, he cupped my face between his hands and pressed a kiss to my forehead. "Tell me you know that, Liz."

"I know you love me, Hugh," I whispered brokenly, as I straddled his lap. "But you love him more."

"No. I don't." Looking sad, Hugh slowly shook his head. "Not even close."

Yeah, he did.

Whether he wanted to admit it or not, Hugh loved Gerard Gibson like a brother. They had a bond that ran far deeper than friendship. Their lives were entangled in a way that was deeper than anything I'd ever known. There had been many occasions throughout the years when I had wished my own sister had loved me like Hugh loved *him.*

I understood why, of course. I once loved him like a brother, too.

Until he protected the monster responsible for my sister's death.

Until he betrayed me.

Until he broke my heart.

He did this to her.

He killed your sister.

Don't ever forget that, munchkin.

He's responsible for all of this.

You'll never see your sister again and it's all his fault.

"Then don't be his friend anymore, Hugh," I begged, already knowing what his answer would be. No. Just like the last time I asked him and the time before that. "Please." *It hurts too much.* "Just…" *Just pick me.*

"Liz, please." Hugh pinched the bridge of his nose and released a pained groan. "I can't just abandon him. He didn't do anything wrong. Gibsie is as innocent in all of this as you are."

I wasn't surprised by his response.

Just deflated.

And a little more dead inside.

Because Hugh would never choose between us, which meant that he chose *him*. Just like Claire and Patrick had chosen him, too. I was the disposable person in our friendship group. They would never leave him behind because to the Biggs family, Gerard Gibson was indispensable. He was more their family than I ever would be, and it hurt.

"He's his brother," I whispered, even though I knew there was no point. I could never make my boyfriend understand something I didn't understand myself. I couldn't explain why I wanted to peel the skin from my bones when I heard Gibsie's name, but it was a very real, very physical reaction for me. One my mind assured me that I was right to feel.

Because he's bad.

Like him.

Because they hurt me.

Because they killed my sister.

"Not by choice," Hugh stated calmly. "Gibsie's mother married Mark's father. That doesn't make them biological brothers."

A shudder of revulsion rolled through me. "They're still family."

"Gibs is my family, too. *By choice*," Hugh countered in a frustrated tone. "Does that mean I'm guilty by association, too?"

"Forget it," I mumbled, blinking away my tears. "Forget I said anything." Sniffling, I climbed off his lap and retreated to the opposite side of my bed. "He's your family and I'm just a girl."

"That's not true, and you know it, Liz," Hugh snapped, voice thick and gruff. "You have never been just a girl to me, but I can't keep having this same fight with you."

"Then stop coming over and you won't need to," I hissed, feeling defensive. "You should leave."

"Like hell I'm leaving," he countered, twisting around to glare at me. "Don't you even think about pulling that stunt on me. It won't work."

"What stunt?"

"Pushing me away?" He shook his head. "I'm not leaving, Liz, so quit it."

"I can't be with you if you're with him," I heard myself shout, tears flowing freely down my cheeks now. "I don't want anything to do with his family and you have *everything* to do with them."

"You don't need to have a damn thing to do with any of them in order to be with me!" Hugh shouted back, pushing a hand through his hair in obvious frustration. "So just be with *me*, Liz!"

"I don't want to be anywhere, Hugh!" I lost all control and screamed. "And I especially don't want to be in this fucking house!" Pulling up on my knees, I dragged my hands through my hair in frustration and choked out a furious scream.

"No, Liz, stop!"

"My sister's dead, and my mother's dying!" Pulling so hard on my hair, a clump came away in my hand, I tossed it away and quickly reached for my shorts-clad thighs.

"Lizzie, please—"

"My father hates me, and I've lost all my friends!" Digging my nails into my skin, I tore at my flesh deep enough to draw blood. "I wish I could switch places with Caoimhe!" Ignoring his protests, I continued to scream and claw at my skin. "I wish I fucking died that night!"

"No, baby, no!" I felt Hugh's arms come around me like a vise, rendering me helpless. "Please, Liz, don't hurt yourself."

"It's not fair!" I screamed at the top of my lungs. "Why did she have to die, Hugh? Why Caoimhe? Why like *that*? Why *my* sister?"

"I don't know, Liz," he replied, keeping a firm hold of me. "I wish I had the answers for you, but I don't. The only thing I can tell you with absolute certainty is that I am glad it wasn't you."

"Don't say that!"

"I'm *glad* you didn't die that night, and I would *never* wish for you to switch places with Caoimhe. Not in a hundred thousand lifetimes! I pick you every single time, Lizzie Young, because I love you!"

"No, you don't!" I screamed, trying and failing to escape his relentless hold. "You don't love me because you can't!" He was so much stronger than me that I couldn't break free no matter how hard I tried. "Do you hear me? You fucking can't!"

"I do, I do," Hugh continued to whisper over and over, while he fused my back to his chest, my arms pinned to my sides. "I love you, and you can't make me stop."

"You're his friend, not mine!" I lashed out, desperate to prove myself right. Because he would leave me, too. That's all I knew for sure in this life. Nobody stayed. "You're *his*!"

"I'm yours," he soothed, voice steady and unwavering while I sounded feral. "I'm all yours."

"Don't lie to me," I warned, feeling my chest heave from the sheer height of panic clawing at my chest. "I can't take it."

"I'm yours," Hugh continued to promise, lips brushing against my ear as he spoke softly. "I've only ever been yours."

"But I'm not a good person," I cried out, feeling broken. "I'm a bad girl."

"That's not true," Hugh replied, voice thick with emotion. "Every single thing about you is *good*, Lizzie Young, and I'm your best friend, so I should know."

"But I'm bipolar," I croaked out, feeling my body grow limp against his.

He kissed my temple. "I know."

"That's *not* good."

"Says who?"

Sniffling, I choked out a pained sob. "Everyone."

"Not me." He kissed my temple again. "I happen to adore that complicated mind of yours."

"It's not complicated—it's crazy."

"You couldn't be more wrong if you tried," he replied in a confident tone. "You're going to live a *great* life, Liz. A little complicated, sure, and maybe challenging at times, but it'll be a fucking great one."

"I am?"

"Yeah, Liz, you are."

"How can you know that?"

"Because I'm going to make sure of it."

THE OPPRESSION OF DEPRESSION

Hugh

MAY 25, 2000

AFTER CAOIMHE'S FUNERAL, THE ALLEN AND YOUNG FAMILIES HAD QUICKLY BECOME the talk of the town. Rumors were rampant, and Caoimhe's cause of death became the focal point of every gossip-filled conversation within a ten-mile radius.

Mark was steadfast in his assertion of innocence, while his parents were determined to defend him with unwavering resolve.

Keith and Sadhbh wouldn't even entertain the notion that there might be truth to what Lizzie said. Instead, they not only discredited her, but they defamed her entire family—including her dead sister.

Meanwhile, Gibsie was so inconsolable over the whole ordeal that he could barely function.

Beyond devastated at the realization of losing one of his best friends, Gibs had spent most nights since the funeral in floods of tears, finding comfort in Claire, who, aside from school, remained faithfully by his side.

Despite my father's intense dislike of the Allens, he was determined to stand by his best friend's surviving son, which meant he, too, was—albeit reluctantly—on the side of Mark.

Meanwhile, my mother and sister continued to feign neutrality, but it was clear they were of the same opinion as Dad.

Keith and Sadhbh's haughty dismissal of Lizzie's disclosure only seemed to fuel the flames when it came to Catherine and Mike, who were staunch in their quest for a thorough inquest into their daughter's death.

For weeks, Gardaí came and went from number nine Avoca Greystones, asking questions and looking for statements, but nothing had seemed to come from it.

No arrests had been made so far, and Mark continued to reside at the house across the street from mine and attend his classes at Tommen, but he didn't get off scot-free with the people of Ballylaggin because, despite the lack of evidence, the whispers continued to spread like wildfire.

While nobody outwardly accused Mark of being a rapist, and the preliminary results of the autopsy stated no foul play, the seed of doubt had been planted, and he quickly became the town leper. People avoided him in the streets, and steered clear of him at school, which only served to cause more division between the families.

While my father's injunction at number nine had been quickly rescinded by Sadhbh, mine would remain in force until Mark left for college at the end of June.

On top of that, I had been instructed to avoid all contact with the rapist bastard himself and to not even cross the street when his car was in the driveway.

Like I gave a damn.

I wouldn't have pissed on the prick if he was on fire.

Not when he was the instigator behind this living, breathing nightmare.

Because of his actions, a line had been drawn straight down the middle of my world, with my oldest friend on one side and my girlfriend on the other.

The whole thing made me sick to my stomach, and I honestly didn't think another human could feel as torn in half as I did.

Because I *believed* her.

The authorities doubted her recounting of the night, and the grown-ups labeled her mentally ill, but I knew Lizzie Young better than anyone else, and if they could just be patient with her and look beyond their own fucking stigma, they would see what I saw.

A girl who was telling the *truth*.

I knew her story had changed and shifted many times since the funeral, ranging from Mark pushing Caoimhe into the water himself to him being the reason she jumped in, but that *wasn't* because Liz was lying. It was because she was *traumatized*. All she needed was time to piece her thoughts together, but apparently, that wasn't how the law interpreted the holes in her story.

Unlike the others, I didn't doubt my girlfriend for a minute.

If Lizzie said Mark raped her sister, then that's what happened.

What I found myself torn over was her sudden and intense hatred of Gibsie. She blamed him for Caoimhe's death as much as she blamed Mark. Maybe even more. I saw it in her eyes that day at the graveside when she fell to her knees in front of him. It was like a switch had been flicked in her mind, and he had become her mortal enemy. I knew she wasn't thinking rationally, and I didn't blame her one bit, but it broke my heart to watch her turn her anguish on Gibs.

Because while I wholeheartedly believed my girlfriend when it came to Mark's role in Caoimhe's demise, I also knew with absolute certainty that Gibsie had no hand in it.

He was as innocent as she was.

Something died inside of her that day, though. There was a part of my girlfriend that went into the ground with her sister, and I couldn't stop it from happening.

It was as if her sister's death had broken a pivotal part of her mind, and I couldn't reach her like I used to. The light in her eyes was gone and the change in her personality was as swift as it was contrasting.

Liz was a lot more closed off and aggressive now, with rapid shifts in her mood that could give a person whiplash. Her highs were nerve-wracking, and her lows were even more terrifying. At any given moment, she could switch between distant and aloof to affectionate and handsy.

Through trial and error, I learned on the job, finding ways to maneuver around and navigate through my girlfriend's mood swings, but it was clear she wasn't the person she used to be. Worse, nothing I did seemed to revive the part of her spirit that had been snuffed out that night.

All I could do now was try to hold on to the parts of her I could still reach.

Hold on for dear life and pray she didn't slip from my fingers.

Readjusting the sleeping girl on my lap, I leaned against the stack of pillows at my back and forced my heart to keep a steady rhythm. I could feel her tears seeping through the fabric of my school shirt, but I didn't move. Even in sleep, she cried for all she had lost, and it broke my fucking heart.

With her cheek pressed to my chest and her hands fisting my shirt, Liz clung to me like I was her last lingering lifeline, and sometimes, I thought I might be.

I had certainly become the on-call man when she took leave of her senses. Probably because I was the only one with balls enough to root around in her head and bring her back to me.

Her father certainly didn't put in any effort. On the contrary, Mike had emotionally checked out after the funeral and Catherine, while she was here in the flesh, didn't have the strength to get out of bed. Claire had all the sense of a springer spaniel puppy, full of wagging tails and kisses but no substance, while Gibsie was her self-proclaimed enemy. Patrick was at a loss for how to help, and because of the rift between our families, my mother *couldn't* help.

That left me.

"Hugh?" she mumbled drowsily. "Hugh?"

"Yeah, Liz," I replied gently. "I'm here."

"Am *I* here?"

"We both are."

"Am I awake?"

"Yeah, Liz, we're both awake," I whispered, stroking her cheek with more affection than was sensible. "You're awake and you're right here in your room."

"With you?"

"With me," I whispered, reaching for her hand. "Feel me?"

Her breath hitched. "I *feel* you."

"Hear me?"

"I hear you."

"Good girl," I praised, craning my neck down to press a kiss to the top of her hair. "I love you so much."

"No matter what?" She hiccupped, fisting my shirt for dear life.

"Yeah, Liz." My heart slammed against my chest bone, and I kissed her hair again. "No matter what."

NEVER HAD AND NEVER WOULD

Lizzie

MAY 29, 2000

"CAOIMHE?" I WHISPERED IN THE DARKNESS, KNOWING THAT EVEN THOUGH SHE WAS on the opposite side of the room, she could still hear me. "Are we going to die here?"

It took a long time for her to answer me, and when she finally did, her voice didn't sound like how it used to. "No, Liz." Her words were slurred and stretched. "I won't let that happen to you."

Sniffling, I hooked my arms around my knees and rocked back and forth. "What about you?"

Silence.

Panic rose up inside of me.

"I hate your bedroom," I bit out, burying my face in my knees. "I don't want to be here anymore."

"Me, too," she replied, voice cracking. "I want Dad."

"I don't," I sobbed, feeling my body tremble from the cold. "I just want Hugh..."

After her funeral, the Gardaí carried out a half-hearted investigation that was immediately closed when the coroner's report came back ruling my sister's cause of death as suicide.

Everyone took his side.

Because Mark's story added up and mine didn't.

Because he was sane, and I was labeled a sick child.

Because *Gerard Gibson* wouldn't help me.

I couldn't be sure of a lot in life — I always had trouble distinguishing dreams from reality — but I knew one thing for absolute certain.

It wouldn't matter what I did or said about that night.

Nobody was going to take *my* side.

Nobody was going to believe *me*.

They never had and never would.

So why bother trying?

Why bother caring?

Why bother breathing?

WHEN GIRLFRIENDS CRY AND PIGS FLY

Hugh

JUNE 1, 2000

"Why can't you just let me die!" Lizzie screamed, launching her porcelain piggy bank at the wall. "I don't want to be here anymore!" The porcelain pig shattered into a dozen jagged pieces, and coins and paper money exploded from his belly. "Nobody understands me!"

The rest of the world might not understand her, but I sure as shit did, which was how I knew *exactly* what she was plotting when she sank to her knees.

"Give it to me," I commanded, vibrating with tension, as I closed the space between us. "Give it to me *now*, Liz."

"Wh-what?" she sobbed, curling up in the fetal position, while she cradled her hands to her stomach.

"You know exactly what," I strangled out, kneeling to pry the bloody shard of porcelain from her hands. "And you better not even *think* about it."

"I'm a bad person, Hugh," she said, continuing to break my heart. "You should just let me go."

I knew Liz didn't mean the things she said, it was the grief talking, but it wasn't easy to hear.

I hadn't been swimming or gone to rugby training since the funeral, choosing to spend every free moment outside of school with my girlfriend, but nothing I said or did made a blind bit of difference. The hostility I faced from my coaches and teammates over my absence was a hard pill to swallow, but I would gladly shoulder their disdain if it meant I eased her pain.

Problem was, I was beginning to think that I was doing more harm than good by visiting.

But how could I leave her alone in this?

I *couldn't*.

Walking away from Lizzie Young wasn't something I had the capacity to do.

"No, no, no!" Liz cried out when she noticed me move for the waste bin in her room. "Don't go, Hugh!" Scrambling onto her hands and knees, she crawled across the floor to get to me. "Please—please! I didn't mean it, I swear. I'll be good, I promise!"

Tossing the bloodstained shard of porcelain in the bin, I crouched in front of her. Returning to her side was like the habit of a lifetime for me, but I did it without a hint of reservation, because regardless of how far she had fallen into the dark abyss of depression, there was no other girl on this planet I wanted to be with. "Look at me."

"Please, please, please," she cried, clinging to whatever part of my body she could grab. "Don't leave me."

"*Look* at me, Liz." Cupping her face between my hands, I pulled her close. "Open your eyes and *look* at me."

Reluctantly, she did.

Pale, sunken eyes that seemed to be void of life stared back at me.

"Where am I?" I asked in a steady tone, keeping my eyes trained on her. "Right here and now. Where am I?"

"You're here," she strangled out through heaving sobs.

"And who am I here with?" I continued, keeping a firm hold of her face. "Hmm?"

"You're here with m-me."

"I'm here with *you*," I confirmed, stroking her tearstained cheek with my thumb. "And what am I not going to do?"

She hiccupped a sob before whispering, "L-leave?"

"That's right. I'm *not* going to leave you," I agreed, keeping eye contact with her. "And why am I not going to leave you?"

Sniffling, she squeezed out, "Because you're my b-best f-friend?"

"I *am* your best friend," I confirmed with another nod. "And what else?"

"My b-boyfriend?"

"I *am* your boyfriend," I agreed in a gentle but firm tone. "But you've forgotten the most important reason I'm not leaving you."

She looked so small and fragile when she looked up at me and whispered, "Because y-you love m-me?"

"Exactly." My heart squeezed so tight in my chest, it was hard to get the words out. "I love you more than I have ever loved anyone or anything."

"I'm sorry." Her expression caved and she barreled into my arms. "I'm so, so sorry, Hugh."

"It's going to be okay," I whispered, sinking onto my ass and wrapping my arms around her. "We'll get through this."

I'LL NEVER LET YOU GO UNDER

Lizzie

JUNE 9, 2000

"CAOIMHE?" I SCREAMED OUT HER NAME, BUT SHE DIDN'T ANSWER ME. SHE DIDN'T OPEN her eyes. "Caoimhe, please—"

"She's fine." He fastened the seat belt around my sister's limp body. "She's just sleeping."

"What's wrong with her?" I wailed, reaching for my sister. "Why does she look like that?"

"Because of him," he told me, bundling me into the back seat. "He wanted to hurt her. This is his fault, munchkin, and don't you ever forget it!"

"No, no, no," I croaked out, feeling my eyes roll as the world spun madly around me. "He wouldn't hurt her. He's my friend…"

"He's not your friend, you stupid, little cunt!" Rounding the car to the back seat, he leaned inside and gripped my face. "He's a vicious, spiteful, little prick who ruined everything."

"Stop," I pleaded, trying to break free of his hold, but it was no use. "Please…"

"He's your enemy, munchkin, and a dangerous one at that." Gripping my face so tight, I thought the bones in my jaw might shatter, he leaned in close and hissed, "He's going to take everything from you."

"Why?" I cried, reaching between the seats for my sister, desperate to make her wake up. "Caoimhe, please open your eyes."

"Because he hates your guts." Pulling a lighter out of his pocket, he began to burn the pages of her journal one by one. "He did this to your sister, he made all this happen with his lies, and he'll do it again to everyone you love."

"No!"

"Yes," he spat, tossing away a singed piece of paper. "Mark my words, munchkin. His lies will take your friends from you like his lies have taken your sister."

"What are you doing?" I choked out, feeling woozy and disorientated. "Stop burning her journal…"

"Happy birthday."

The sound of Hugh's familiar voice startled me, and I blinked myself back to reality to find him sitting on the edge of my bed, holding a small parcel in his hands.

"Hi," I croaked out, feeling my heart spike at the sight of him. "Thanks."

"You're welcome." His brown eyes were full of warmth and affection when he reached for my hand. "How are you feeling?"

Like I want to die. "Not too bad."

His thumb grazed my knuckles. "Did you sleep last night?"

No, I haven't been able to sleep since I watched them fish my sister's lifeless body from the river. "A bit."

He tucked several strands of matted hair over my shoulder and smiled sadly. "I've missed you."

I knew he did. It was the same for me. "I've missed you, too."

"Here." He thrust the small parcel into my hand. "For you."

"You didn't have to get me a gift."

"Yeah, yeah." He rolled his eyes. "Just open the box."

I did and my breath caught in my throat when my eyes landed on the shiny silver inside. "What's this?"

His cheeks turned red. "It's an ankle bracelet."

It wasn't just an ankle bracelet. It was the most beautiful ankle bracelet I'd ever seen.

I felt my body grow hot as I registered how each individual charm had been carefully selected by my boyfriend.

"The Gemini zodiac sign for your birthday, and the heart represents, well, you know." He blushed a deeper shade of red. "The book represents the one I know you're going to write one day, and the pill is so you remember to take yours."

"The witch's broomstick?"

His lips twitched. "Because you're my little witch."

I smiled. "And the life buoy?"

"I couldn't stop thinking about what you told me, about how you've always felt like you were supposed to drown," he explained, carefully clasping the anklet around my left ankle. "Well, I put that there to remind you that as long as I have air in my lungs, I'll never let you go under."

"Hugh." My eyes filled with tears. "Thank you."

"You're welcome, and I know you feel alone right now, but I need you to know I'm here, Liz." His eyes burned with sincerity when he gently squeezed my hand. "I'm *still* here."

I sucked in a trembling breath and squeezed his hand back. "I know you are."

Keeping his brown eyes locked on mine, Hugh tenderly stroked my cheeks, and then my chin, and then my neck, before finally resting his hand on my shoulder. "You're beautiful."

I wasn't.

I was filthy.

Inside and out.

I wanted to tell him just that, but when I opened my mouth, all that came out was a broken sob.

I tried again, but another cry tore out.

And then his arms were around my body, pulling me close. "Let it out." Wrapping me up as tight as he could, he rocked me in his arms. "I'm here and I'm not leaving you, okay? No matter what."

Feeling weak from exhaustion, I folded myself into his arms and cried.

It wouldn't help.

Nothing could bring her back.

Nothing would stop the nightmares.

But I didn't let go.

A little while later, after Hugh convinced me to take a shower, I stood in the kitchen, holding his hand.

It had been so long since I came downstairs that I felt unsteady.

My legs were wobblish, like a newborn foal, and I was depending far too much on the boy standing beside me to keep me upright.

I could hear my mother wailing in a nearby room, and the sound made me want to scramble back to my bed and never come out again.

"Take a walk with me," Hugh said, as aware of my mother's crying as I was. He cleared his throat and quickly walked us to the back door. "It's gorgeous outside."

I didn't want to take a walk.

I didn't want to take a breath.

But I *did* want to be near Hugh, so I followed him outside without a fight.

BACK TO HER GRAVESIDE

Hugh

"HUGH? IS THAT YOU, LOVE?" I HEARD MY MOTHER CALL OUT THE SECOND I STEPPED through the front door after school on Tuesday.

"Yeah," I called back, dropping my bag down in the hallway before joining her in the kitchen. "Sorry I'm late. The school bus broke down. We had to switch onto another bus. It took forever to arrive."

"No, Catherine, the school bus broke down," Mam relayed into the landline, visibly concerned. "Try not to panic." Mam gave me the usual once-over with her eyes before adding, "I'm sure Lizzie hasn't gone far."

Hasn't gone far?

My stomach bottomed out when I heard that.

Jesus Christ!

"Mam," I tried to interrupt, but she had her back to me now, coaxing Catherine Young into not worrying about her daughter when she absolutely *should* be worrying.

It had to be bad for Catherine to call my mother.

They weren't exactly on speaking terms.

My next decision was one rooted in instinct, and turning on my heels, I bolted outside to grab my bike.

Pedaling like a demon, I rounded the familiar narrow path in the graveyard and almost fell off my bike in relief when I spotted her blond head up ahead.

Hopping off the saddle, I let the bike go and moved straight for her, ignoring the sound of metal clanking onto the ground when it crashed behind me.

"Goddammit, Liz," I strangled out, breathing ragged, when I found her fast asleep on top of her sister's grave. "Your mam is looking for you."

She wasn't even dozing—no, she was in a deep sleep because she didn't even twitch when I spoke.

All she had on was a pair of denim jean shorts, a plain white T-shirt, and an old pair of scuffed, red high-tops.

With her hands tucked under her left cheek and her long, blond hair splayed over her shoulders like a golden blanket, it physically hurt to look at her.

Because I didn't know how to ease the pain she was drowning in.

I couldn't pull her to safety.

I couldn't save her from this.

Feeling pissed off and irritated, I pulled my phone out of my pocket and sent two quick texts that contained the same information to both her mother and mine.

* I have her. *

Sweating buckets from my excursion, I sank down on the grass beside her and loosened my school tie before ripping it off altogether and tossing it aside.

Un-popping a couple of buttons on my school shirt, I blew out a pained breath and rested my elbows on my knees and then my head in hands, wondering what the fuck I was supposed to do next.

Filled with unspoken resentment for the girl in the ground and fucking shattered for the girl asleep on the grass beside me, I wondered if there would ever come a day when the torture of Caoimhe's suicide subsided for my girlfriend.

I had so much I wanted to say, so many angry words I wanted to scream, but I never would. Instead, I kept my mouth shut like the good boyfriend I vowed to be and did my best to love her back to life.

I could feel the darkness was settling over her, threatening to overtake her, and I was determined to keep her heart in the sunshine.

No matter what.

LET'S STEAL AWAY

Lizzie

JUNE 17, 2000

"ARE YOU GOING BACK TO SCHOOL BEFORE THE SUMMER HOLIDAYS?" HUGH ASKED ON Saturday evening, as we sat in the tall grass in the meadow on my parents' property. "I suppose there isn't much point," he added in a thoughtful tone when I shook my head. "Not when there's two weeks left of term."

"How is school going for you?" I managed to ask him, forcing myself to come back to the real world and *be* with him. "When is your sixth-class graduation?"

"School is as underwhelming as always," he replied with a coy smile. "And I graduate the Thursday after next."

"You do?"

"Yeah." A slow smile crept across his face. "It's still surreal."

"Do you know if you're getting it yet?" I asked, feeling a flicker of excitement inside of me. "The student of the year award?"

"Yeah, Liz," he replied, scrubbing his face to hide his smile. "I'm getting it."

"I knew you would," I replied, feeling proud. "I'm so proud of you."

He was quick to interject, "Enough about me," giving me his full attention. "Talk to me, Liz."

"About what?"

"About you." He reached up and stroked my chin. "I want to hear about you."

I don't.

"Uh, what about rugby?" I blurted out. "How's that going for you?"

"Really?" Smirking, Hugh arched a disbelieving brow. "You want to talk about rugby?"

"I want to talk about anything that isn't me," I admitted, exhaling shakily. "I want you to distract me, Hugh. Please."

His brown eyes burned holes in mine for a long beat, and I thought he was going to go deep, but then he shook his head and cleared his throat.

"Rugby." He tilted his head to one side, clearly thinking about the subject. "It's been a lot better since the Dub joined the team. I think we have a real shot at snagging some silverware next season."

"Do you *want* the silverware?" I asked, focusing all my attention on our conversation. "Is it important to you?"

"I couldn't give less of a fuck if I tried," he admitted with a chuckle. "But it's good craic and I have an excellent kicking game, which keeps me out of the ruck—and the hospital." Grinning, he added, "You know I don't care about that kind of thing, Liz."

Yeah, I did.

Hugh had the physique of a natural-born athlete, and he was a gifted rugby player, but his heart belonged to the water, not the rugby pitch. "And swimming?"

"I came third at nationals last weekend."

"You did?" Swallowing deeply, I reached for his hand and squeezed. "Congratulations."

"Thanks." He smiled. "Which I still don't understand how, considering I'd been out of the pool for so long." Hugh smiled again, but this time his cheeks flushed an adorable pink color. Because he was proud. Because swimming was his passion. "But it's really not a big deal."

"Yeah, it is," I replied, shivering when he turned his hand over and entwined our fingers. "I'm really proud of you."

"I got my acceptance letter for Tommen College in September," he offered then, tracing my thumb with his. "The entrance examination results came in the post, too."

"And?"

He blushed. "My results were the highest in all three participating schools in town. Mam got a handwritten letter about it and everything."

"I knew you would." I smiled and it was the first genuine one since, well, before. "Because you're a genius, Hugh Andrew Biggs."

"I don't know about that," he replied, looking a little uncertain. "Johnny is a fair bit of a genius himself."

"The Dub?"

"Yeah. Aside from you, I've never encountered anyone with a brain like mine," he said with a nod. "Maybe the transition to secondary school won't come as easily to me as…"

"Everything else?" I filled in for him.

"Yeah." Nodding, he blew out a shaky breath. "Everyone always harps on about the extreme contrast between primary and secondary-level education." He shrugged again, looking uneasy. "It could be difficult."

"Not for you," I promised, attention shifting to our joined hands. Hugh's hand was so much larger than mine now, with tanned skin and prominent, masculine veins. Jesus, he had beautiful hands. "First, you'll take Tommen College by storm, and then Trinity College, and then the whole world."

"I hope so, Liz."

"I know so, Hugh." I sighed heavily. "And then, when you're a world-renowned heart surgeon, you can come back home and fix mine."

Pain flashed in his eyes. "Liz."

"It was a joke," I mumbled weakly.

"I *will* fix your heart," he said gruffly, pulling me onto his lap. "But I won't need to come back home to do it."

"You won't?"

"No," he replied, nuzzling my neck. "Because I won't be leaving you behind in the first place."

Shivering, I folded into his arms. "You're going to take me with you?"

"First to Trinity," he confirmed, tightening his arms around me. "And then around the world."

"What about school?" I teased, burrowing into his chest. "I know there's only four months between us, but I'm two classes below you."

"You can skip fourth year," he filled in quickly—too quickly. "That way you'll turn eighteen the summer I leave for university and can legally come with me."

"And if my parents say no?"

"Then we'll get married, and they won't have a choice in the matter."

"Just like that?" I laughed.

"Yep." He snapped his finger for emphasis. "Just like that."

"So we get married when I turn eighteen and you steal me away to Dublin," I mused, playing along now. "What happens then, huh? When you're at university. Where do I finish secondary school?"

"Easy," Hugh filled in breezily when I rested my head on his shoulder. "You'll attend Royce College, whose head of enrollment, by the way, will be so impressed by your impressive transcript, they will practically snap your hand off to enroll you."

"Hmm." Releasing a sigh of contentment, I gripped his forearms, forcing him to tighten his hold on me. "You sound like you've put a lot of thought into this."

"That's because I have."

"Since when?"

"Since the day you told me you would say yes if I asked you to marry me," he replied without a hint of hesitation. "So you better keep that heart beating, ya hear?" He pressed a kiss to my shoulder. "Because I need you, Lizzie Young. More than you realize."

"I will," I whispered. "I promise."

BREAKING BREAD AND MENDING BRIDGES

Hugh

JUNE 24, 2000

SPRAWLED OUT ON A MOUNTAIN OF CUSHIONS ON MY GIRLFRIEND'S BEDROOM FLOOR, I tapped on the controller in my hands and stared at the screen in front of me, only half-interested in the game I was playing.

I'd brought my old gaming console over to Lizzie's place last weekend and had set it up on the fourteen-inch portable in her bedroom. The graphics were dog shit compared to the top-of-the-range PS1 back at my own house, but it came in useful on days like this, when she couldn't lift her head off the pillow and I couldn't quite get myself to leave her bedside.

She was sleeping now, and I wasn't sure if her catatonic state was from sedatives or exhaustion. I suspected both. The doctor had made an out-of-hours house visit today, and I knew she'd been given an injection of some sort.

I had faith Liz would get through this, that she would eventually come back to me, but her lows were intensifying in both length and frequency, and I couldn't be sure if her grief was the driving force behind it or her bipolar disorder.

It was heartbreaking to watch her fade away in front of my eyes and know that there was nothing I could do to stop the depression from consuming her. My only solace when she was like this was the fact that she was too exhausted to hurt herself. At least when she was experiencing a depressive episode, I could stand guard over her.

I can keep her safe.

A low knock sounded on her bedroom door, followed by Mike popping his head around the door. His eyes went to his daughter first before settling on me. When he was satisfied that I was a safe distance from her bed, he nodded in approval. "Any movement?"

"Not since the doctor knocked her out," I replied, pressing pause on my game to give him my full attention. "How's Catherine?"

Mike shook his head, and that was enough to tell me that his wife *wasn't* good. "Come downstairs for a bite to eat, son." His gaze flicked to his daughter once more and he sighed. "She'll be out for the night."

"I was unfair to you, Hughie," Mike announced as we sat across the kitchen table from each other. "After the funeral, I let my grief blind me. You've always been a good lad, and I shouldn't have taken my anger out on you."

"You were under a lot of pressure," I offered, shoveling a forkful of pasta into my mouth. "Still are."

"True," he replied, clearing his throat. "But I'm not too proud to admit that my wife and I couldn't have gotten through the past couple of months without your help."

Unsure of what to say, I simply nodded my head and continued eating.

"It's her anniversary," he added after a long beat. "Two months today."

"Yeah." Releasing a pained sigh, I set my cutlery down and leaned back in my chair, giving the man my full attention. "I know."

"Caoimhe Catherine Young," he whispered, staring lifelessly across the table at me. "My beautiful, blue-eyed baby girl."

I wanted to tell him that he had another blue-eyed baby girl upstairs in bed, but I didn't have the heart to kick the man when he was down, especially since he made the effort to cook a meal for me. The fact that I was the only one eating while he nursed a tumbler of whiskey was proof to that pudding.

"You're keeping the head, Mike," I decided to tell him. "You're doing *okay*."

Lonesome, pale-blue eyes, so similar to my girlfriend's, stared back at me. "I'm hanging on by a thread here, son."

"That's okay," I replied carefully. "Just as long as you *keep* hanging on."

"Yeah, well, maybe it'll be easier now that bastard Mark Allen is gone."

"Yeah," I agreed quietly, knowing that I had a whole heap I wanted to say about the prick but having the good sense to keep it in my head. "I heard they took him to the airport this morning."

"Good fucking riddance." Mike's eyes narrowed and his voice took on a menacing tone when he added, "Although, how he gets to swan off traveling the world while my daughter rots in the ground is something I'll never come to terms with." The hand he was using to grip his tumbler of whiskey started to tremble. "And to think I welcomed him into my home with open arms." He cleared his throat again, but it sounded like a snarl. "Meanwhile, you were seven years old when you came bounding up the lane." He paused to drain the contents of his glass, before adding, "And even then, you were more of a man than he'll ever be."

Jesus.

Mike's admission confounded me because, while I'd never been on his bad side, my girlfriend's father certainly hadn't taken much of an interest in me. Sure, he was polite and friendly in passing, but nothing like *this*.

"I suppose I backed the wrong horse, didn't I?" Mike choked out a humorless laugh, while discretely wiping a tear from his eye. "Well, I'm not afraid to admit my mistakes." He gave me a meaningful look when he said, "I have my differences with your parents, and we don't need to go into why, but there's no denying they raised a fine young man."

"I'm not *him*," I blurted out, tone urgent. "I swear it, Mike." Resting my elbows on the table, I leaned forward and implored him with my eyes to *believe* me. "I will *never* hurt your daughter."

OH YEAH? WATCH ME

Hugh

JUNE 29, 2000

"Ignore them," I tried to coax, but it was no use. The smart-ass remark tossed at Gibsie's expense, in the school car park after our graduation tonight, had sent him on a downward spiral. "You know Danny Call's a mouthy gobshite."

"He called me a pervert." Gibsie cried harder, dropping onto my sister's bed. "He said I was like *him*."

"He was talking out of his hole," I reiterated, feeling my temper rise. Jesus Christ, one of these days, I was going to break that asshole's nose. "Did anyone hear him?"

"Me," Claire chimed in from her perch underneath the sprawled-out flanker, who was still clad in his graduation gown and using my sister as his personal cushion. "He said it, Hughie," she confirmed, with Gibsie's graduation cap perched on top of her wild curls. "I heard him with my own ears."

"Anyone else?" I pressed, flinging my cap and gown onto the foot of her bed. "What about Cap?"

"As if," Claire snorted. "He wouldn't dare open his mouth to Gerard with Johnny Kavanagh around."

Yeah, I knew that and couldn't have been more grateful for his recent implantation into our lives. Kav was worshipped by our peers, and because Kav had deemed Gibsie his right-hand man, Gibsie's popularity had soared. While he continued his polite-but-distant approach with me and Feely, Cap's peculiar emotional attachment to Gibsie had worked wonders for him, and Gibs had become untouchable at school *and* on the pitch.

In fact, this was the first time I'd even caught wind of anyone giving Gibsie hassle in months.

Of course, the culprit *had* to be Danny Callaghan.

"I'll sort it out, Gibs," I told him, feeling a surge of protectiveness shoot through my veins. "I promise Danny won't say anything about it again." *Not if he wants to keep his ability to walk.* "I'll make it right, lad."

"Don't tell Johnny," he strangled out, chest heaving. "Please. I don't want him to know anything about it."

"I won't," I promised, already knowing that Gibs didn't want anyone outside of the family to know. "I haven't told him anything before, have I?"

"No," he croaked out, sniffling. "But I haven't told him about it, and I don't want him to think badly of me."

"Gibs, nobody could think badly of you," I replied with a sigh. "You're a good egg, lad, and Cap knows that."

"Liz does," he sobbed. "She thinks badly of me."

"Liz is just sad," Claire interjected, stroking his hair. "She's not thinking clearly right now. Isn't that right, Hugh?"

"Uh, yeah, that's right," I replied, watching my sister cradle his blond head to her chest. "Speaking of Liz," I decided to add, knowing this could blow up in my face like it had on several previous occasions. "Have you thought any further about what she meant that day at the grave?"

"Hughie, no!" Claire snapped, wrapping a protective arm around his broad shoulders as he sprawled on top of her. "Can't you see he's upset?"

"I know he's upset, Claire," I replied evenly. "I'm trying to help."

"Then stop pushing him," she shot back, using her free hand to drape her pink duvet over his shoulders. "Gerard already told you everything he knows."

"I know he did," I bit out, unable to smother my frustration. "But Liz's reaction doesn't make sense—"

"Because her sister just died!" Claire countered with a warning glare. "She's grieving, Hughie. You *know* what that does to people." Her gaze momentarily flicked to Gibs before she gave me a meaningful look. *You remember what it did to Gibsie,* her eyes told me. "Nothing she's been saying makes any sense. It's been three days since I last visited her and I'm *still* trying to make sense of her ramblings."

"I don't know what she wanted me to say at the grave," Gibsie strangled out through heaving sobs, as he clung to my sister. "I wanted to help her, I still do, but I didn't see what happened to Caoimhe that night, guys!"

"We know you didn't, Gerard." Claire tried to console him, trailing her fingers through his curls, while he soaked her T-shirt with his tears. "You were here with us."

"I thought they were in America," he continued to sob, holding on to my sister like she was the only thing anchoring him to earth in this moment. "I didn't know they were still in Ballylaggin. I didn't, I didn't, I swear–"

"I think he did it," I blurted out, finally addressing the elephant in the room. "I think Mark raped Caoimhe."

You could have heard a pin drop.

"Hughie!" Claire gasped, looking horrified. "You can't say that out loud."

"Why not?"

"Because Sadhbh said we're not supposed to."

"Yeah, well, no offense to Sadhbh, or you, Gibs, but I don't give a damn what she said," I snapped, feeling my emotions roar to the surface. "Because I believe my girlfriend."

"Hughie!" Claire squealed again, mouth hanging open.

"I mean it, Claire." Pushing off the windowsill, I paced my sister's room like a man on a mission. "Not about the whole Gibs thing—obviously. But Mark?" I shook my head in disgust. "Liz wouldn't say it if there wasn't some truth to it. That prick definitely did something to Caoimhe that night."

"The Gardaí said he didn't," Claire squeezed out, looking fearful. I knew why. She thought my admission would wreak havoc on Gibsie's frazzled nerves, and maybe it would, but I had to say something, dammit. "They deemed her death as suicide, and Mam said Lizzie is very traumatized over seeing Caoimhe being pulled out of the river—"

"I believe her, Claire!" I cut her off by shouting, beyond agitated now. "And the whole fucking town can twist it whatever way they want, but it won't change my feelings on the matter." Turning my attention to my friend, I said, "Gibs, I want you to look at me when I say this."

Reluctantly, he did.

"I will *always* protect you," I promised, locking eyes on his tearful, gray ones. "Do you hear me? I will always be here to look after you. And I *know* you haven't done anything wrong, okay? So, don't for one second think that I'm ever going to turn my back on you. Blood or not, you're my baby brother and you always will be."

"But?" Gibs interjected with a sniffle.

"But she needs me," I forced myself to say, feeling my heart boom like a drum in my chest. "Do you understand?"

Gibs shook his head, looking up at me like a lost puppy. "No."

"I'm going to be spending a lot of time at Lizzie's place this summer," I explained in a steady tone. "Which means I won't be around much…"

"To hang out with me." He finally tweaked, which only made him look even more lonesome. "But you're still my friend, right?"

"Always," I vowed, crossing my heart. "But she's my girlfriend, and she doesn't have anyone else." *You have Claire.* "I can't leave her on her own in this."

"I don't want you to turn your back on Liz," he croaked out weakly. "I don't want her to not be my friend."

"Maybe Liz will come around," Claire offered in a hopeful tone. "When she's not so sad anymore."

"She's never not going to be sad," Gibsie replied, sniffling again. "Trust me, that kind of sadness never goes away. The world just stops seeing it."

"We graduated tonight, and sports are out for the summer," I offered up, focusing my attention on my friend. "So when I head over to Lizzie's tomorrow, I plan on staying awhile."

"For how long?"

I shrugged. "As long as Catherine and Mike will have me."

"Hold your horses!" Claire spluttered, raising a hand. "Who said you could stay with your girlfriend for the summer?"

"I said," I replied evenly.

"Yeah, that's not happening," my sister was quick to dismiss. "Mam is *never* going to allow you to do that."

"Why not?" I countered. "She let Gibs stay with us when Joe and Beth died."

"But that was different."

"Why?"

"Because we live across the street from each other," Claire filled in. "And Lizzie isn't just your *friend*, if you know what I mean."

"Get real," I snapped, tone laced with disgust. "Her sister just died."

"True, but you guys do a lot of kissing," Claire muttered, worrying on her lip.

"We've kissed a handful of times," I challenged. "It's not a big deal."

"Except that it *is*," my sister stressed. "You can't sleep in her house if you're kissing her, Hugh. It's ew."

"Oh, yeah?" I arched a brow in challenge. "Watch me."

LATE-NIGHT PHONE CALLS

JUNE 29, 2000

"Keep talking," Hugh purred down the line late Friday night. "I love your voice."

"You're so weird," I mused, cradling my phone to my ear as I lay in bed and stared at the ceiling. "How was your graduation?"

"Uneventful," he replied. "How was your dinner?"

"I didn't have dinner," I replied with a frown and then quickly grimaced. "Dammit, you're a slick one, Biggs."

"And you're a little promise breaker, Young," he shot back. "You promised you would eat dinner every night."

"I genuinely forgot this time," I offered sincerely. "Honestly, I did."

"I could never be a girl," he mused down the line. "I've never forgotten to eat a meal in my entire life."

"Are you in bed?" I asked, plucking at a thread on my duvet.

"Just climbing in," he replied, followed by the sound of ruffling sheets. "Are you?"

"Yeah." I rolled my eyes. "No surprises there, huh?"

"Maybe not tonight." There was a teasing lilt to his voice. "But that'll change from tomorrow on."

"Yeah, *okay*."

"Don't believe me?" Okay, he was *definitely* teasing me now. "Go downstairs and ask your dad what's happening tomorrow."

"What?" Dread filled me at a rapid rate. "Oh my God, Hugh, please tell me."

"Your parents have a lodger arriving."

I frowned in confusion. "They do?"

"Yep. And I have it on good authority that he's a total hard-ass, with a penchant for dragging girls named Lizzie out of bed at the crack of dawn."

"Oh?" I narrowed my eyes in suspicion. "Keep talking."

"I think you'll be pleased to see this visitor," Hugh continued. "In fact, I know you will. He is your boyfriend, after all."

"Shut up." My eyes widened to saucers. "You're lying."

Hugh chuckled down the line. "So, what do you say, milady. Will you house a brave knight for the summer?"

"You know I will," I choked out, feeling my heart rate spike from the sudden rush of excitement thrashing around inside of me. "Are you really coming to stay?"

"Your parents agreed immediately," he confirmed. "To be honest, I thought your old man would put up a fight, but he seemed even more enthusiastic than your mam."

"He did?"

"I know, right?"

"And your parents?" I asked, thrumming with excitement now. "Your mam said yes?"

"I managed to talk my mother into it," he confirmed, sounding smug. "Well, I managed to emotionally blackmail her into it, but a win's a win."

"And your dad?"

He snorted down the line. "He'd agree to me flying to the moon if it meant he was left alone."

"You really want to stay?" I asked, clutching my phone tighter than necessary. "You're not just doing it out of pity? Because you really don't have to do that."

"Are you joking? I get to look at my girlfriend all summer. My reasons are entirely selfish."

Exhaling a relieved breath, I smiled down the phone. "I love you."

"I love you more," he replied without missing a beat. "I'm going to be with you, Liz," he added, voice taking on a gruff tone. "When you open your eyes in the morning, my face is the first thing you're going to see. All day, every day, and every fucking night if I get my way, until school starts in September. Because you are more important to me than anything else in my life. And because there's nowhere else that I would rather be than right there with you."

I knew I was crying by the time he finished speaking.

My throat wasn't making any noise, but I could feel the tears landing on my cheeks.

I wasn't sure if I felt relief or devastation swell up inside of me.

Probably both.

Because I felt so alone and desperately wanted to have him close, but I was also terrified of him seeing me at my worst—really seeing me...and walking away.

Because there was something wrong with me, something broken inside of my head, and while I used to have some control over it before, that control had been eradicated that day at my sister's graveside.

When I realized no one would ever believe me.

When I decided I didn't believe myself, either.

Since that day, I didn't have it in me to mask and conceal.

I barely had it in me to breathe.

As for friends and family, the bustle of coddling was a short-lived experience. After a while they stopped coming around.

Not the boy on the other line, though.

That boy came every day without fail.

"Thanks, Hugh," I finally managed to squeeze out when my voice found me once more. "For everything."

LUSTFUL LOOKS AND HOVERING MOTHERS

Hugh

IT TOOK A HERCULEAN EFFORT ON MY PART TO PERSUADE MAM TO LET ME STAY AT Old Hall House for the summer. I went into negotiations armed and ready with receipts in the form of countless awards for athletics, academics, and good behavior. The proof was in the paperwork, and I pulled out every dirty trick in the book to bend her will.

The fact that I was, by far, her most responsible child and had never given her so much as a whisper of trouble in almost thirteen years—unlike a certain curly-haired, demon wild child and her equally wild, equally curly-haired sidekick—didn't hurt my cause either.

The killer blow to her argument came when I reminded her that she had no qualms about allowing Gibsie to stay with Claire for *months* after Joe and Beth died.

The moment those words came out of my mouth, I knew I had her over a barrel. Mam couldn't deny the truth, and she couldn't forbid me from offering the *exact* same comfort to Lizzie without displaying favoritism. I knew no such favoritism existed in my mother's heart, but I wasn't above emotional blackmail. Not if it got me back to her.

In the end, and after a *strained* phone call with Catherine, Mam agreed—albeit reluctantly—to a two-week stay, with strict stipulations that included me sleeping in the guest room and coming home every second day for dinner. While I had zero intentions of following through on Mam's terms, I accepted the deal because it was a start, and asking for forgiveness was a lot more favorable than asking for permission in this instance.

The following morning, when I was finishing up packing, with my mother hovering anxiously in my bedroom doorway, she decided to try a manipulation tactic of her own.

"Hugh, do you think it's sensible to spend this much time alone together?" Mam asked, worrying her lip. "Surely this cocoon you've built around yourselves isn't healthy."

"Funny, because I didn't hear that argument when Gibsie practically lived in Claire's room for six months after Joe and Beth died," I replied, glancing over my shoulder. "Or when Dad holed himself up in the fucking attic five years ago and forgot to come out."

"Hugh!"

"Sorry," I forced myself to say, even though I wasn't.

The truth hurts, Mam.

"Listen, all I'm trying to make you see is that staying at Old Hall House isn't something I'm comfortable with."

"Why not?"

"Because of the feelings involved," she explained with a sigh. "Because of the way you look at Lizzie."

"How do I look at her, Mam?" I tossed back, busying myself filling my bag with enough clothes to last the summer.

"With *lust*, Hugh."

"Lust," I scoffed, rolling my eyes. "Yeah, okay, Mam."

"I'm serious, son," Mam argued sternly. "I'm not blind and I'm far from stupid. Don't you think I know what's happening to your body at this age? It's frighteningly obvious that puberty has set in, and you'll be heading off to secondary school in a couple of months, which will only exacerbate matters." She blew out another pained breath. "Things are changing, Hugh, and rules need to change, too."

"How is the way I look at Liz any different to the way Gibs looks at Claire?" I protested, spinning around to glare at my mother. "Well? The whole world knows those two are obsessed with each other and yet you have no problem allowing him to sleep over."

"Oh please." Now Mam was the one to roll her eyes. "Those two are children, Hugh."

"And what am I?" I demanded, pointing to myself. "A geriatric?"

"You were born old," Mam quipped, lips tipping upward. "Even as a toddler, your dad used to say there was a cranky, old pensioner trapped inside of you."

"Wow," I deadpanned. "How flattering."

"Listen, how would you feel about Lizzie coming to stay with us instead?" Walking over to my bed, Mam sat down and plucked a T-shirt from the pile. "I'm sure a change in environment would do her the world of good," Mam hedged, as she folded my shirt. "It can't be easy for her all alone in that big house with only her parents for company. Especially with her mother still undergoing treatment." Handing me the folded T-shirt, Mam plucked another from my haphazard pile. "If Lizzie was to come to *our* house for the summer, I could look after her." Another neatly folded T-shirt came my way. "I would feel a lot better about this if you were both under my roof, where I could keep an eye on you."

"I would love that," I replied evenly, shoving another T-shirt into my bag. "But it won't work."

"Why not?" Mam probed, unwilling to give in. "I've told you that she's always welcome at our house."

"Yeah," I agreed, closing the zip of my duffel bag. "And I've told *you* why she can't come here."

"Mark's gone," Mam urged. "You know that, Hugh. He won't be back for a very long time."

"Yeah, I know," I replied. "He's not the problem."

Mam was quiet for a while before the penny finally dropped. "Gibs."

Bingo.

"Oh, Hugh, love. You know Gibsie has nothing to do with that mess."

"Yeah," I agreed, jaw clenching. "*I* know that."

"Lizzie must know that, too," she pushed. "Gerard is her friend. They've been thick as thieves for years."

"I *know*, Mam," I bit out, feeling the pang of anguish in my chest. "You're not telling me anything I'm not aware of."

"Then surely she has to know he's not at fault," Mam urged. "She has to believe he's innocent."

"Oh, *she* has to believe." My tone was hard and laced with sarcasm. "Well, maybe Liz is a little short on belief these days, Mam, especially considering nobody has shown *her* the same grace."

"Hugh." A deep sigh escaped her. "Please don't bring that up again."

"I *believe* her, Mam." I went right ahead and brought it up. *Again.* "I *believe* Mark raped Caoimhe, and I don't blame Liz one bit for wanting to stay as far away from this street as possible. It kills me that she's projecting her pain onto Gibs, but I can't honestly blame her. Because if the shoe were on the other foot and something happened to Claire, I would lose my mind, too."

"You know what the Gardaí said. Mark was cleared of those accusations."

"Yeah, and I know what my girlfriend said, too."

"Hugh, you know I adore Lizzie. She's like one of my own. But you also know that she's a very troubled—"

"Don't say it," I warned, instantly on edge, as I held a hand up in warning. "Don't use her bipolar disorder against her. Don't be like the others."

"It's not like that, and you know it," Mam countered, voice thick with emotion. "I love Lizzie like she's my own flesh and blood. I always have."

"But?"

"I'm *concerned*, Hugh!"

"You *should* be concerned," I wholeheartedly agreed. "Her sister killed herself, Mam." Had everyone forgotten that tidbit of information? "Liz was there when they pulled Caoimhe's body out of the river. She *saw* that."

"I know." Tears filled my mother's eyes. "That poor girl."

"Her dad's a walking zombie since the funeral," I continued, unyielding. "And her mam's a weeping corpse. My girlfriend is completely alone in that house, and I won't let that stand." Steeling my resolve, I looked my mother dead in the eyes and said, "And I won't allow everyone to label her a liar, either."

"I don't I think she's lying," Mam hurried to defend. "I believe that Lizzie believes every word."

"That's the same fucking thing," I snapped back. "Jesus, why do you insist on speaking to me like a child? I have a firm grasp on semantics, Mam, and that's exactly that you're doing right now."

"Hugh, this isn't helping anyone," Mam urged, looking devastated. "Two families are in ruins right now, and instead of fanning the flames of resentment, we should be supporting them and encouraging *healing*."

"Then why don't you do that, Mam?" I countered, giving her a hard look. "Why don't you practice what you preach and visit Catherine? I mean, she's your friend, too, after all. Or does Sadhbh Allen hold the deciding factor on who you can offer *support* to?"

"That's not fair, and you know it," Mam shot back, looking wounded. "Sadhbh is family, Hugh."

"No, Mam, *Gibs* is our family," I argued, finally allowing myself to say what I had been holding in for half a decade. "The *Gibsons* are our family and Sadhbh is not a Gibson anymore. She's an Allen."

"Hugh!"

"I *told* you about him," I hissed, losing my cool and visibly trembling with tension. "I told *all* of you, but ye wouldn't hear a word of it." Furious, I stalked over to my television and started unplugging my PlayStation. "That prick tormented Gibs for years, and we all saw how he mistreated Caoimhe." Wrapping the cables around my console, I shoved it into another bag as I continued to rant. "Caoimhe was miserable with him, so why is it so implausible to even consider that Liz might be right about him?"

"Because the authorities said she is *wrong*."

"Yeah, and maybe the authorities are *wrong*," I snapped back. "Jesus, why can't you try to see it from the other side, Mam? Why can't you be unbiased?"

"I *am* trying, sweetheart," Mam offered with a sigh. "But as you well know, it's not so easy when you're stuck in the middle of friends."

"Yeah, I do, and I have a hell of lot more to lose than anyone else," I snapped back, verbalizing my deepest fears to my mother. "Gibsie is my oldest friend in the world, and Lizzie is the *only* girl I'll ever love."

"Oh, stop it," Mam sighed, rolling her eyes. "You have a crush on the girl. A little less of the dramatics please, son."

"*No*, I don't have a crush on *the girl*," I countered evenly. "I'm in *love* with *the girl*, and contrary to your dismissal of my feelings, I assure you that not only are they very real but very permanent." I scowled back at her amused expression. "But it's good to know where you stand on my relationship, Mam. Let's rehash this conversation in twenty years when I swing by the house with my wife—previously known as *the girl*—and our children." Narrowing my eyes, I added, "I look forward to your apology—although I can't promise I won't gloat."

"Is that supposed to *reassure* me?" Mam demanded, turning pale. "Because I am two seconds away from locking you in this bedroom for the summer, young man."

"You can try," I mused, standing my ground. "But I'll still find a way to be with her."

"See, this is *exactly* why you *shouldn't* go," Mam erupted, jerking to her feet. "And on top of that, the son I raised would never speak to his mother like this."

"Maybe because the son you raised knows the difference between right and wrong," I countered angrily.

"And I don't?"

"Not recently," I shot back. "No."

Mam looked up at my face like she didn't quite understand what she was seeing. "Why are you being so disrespectful to me?"

"Because you are the *only* parent I have, and you're not *listening* to me."

"I *always* listen to you."

"Not about Mark Allen, you didn't."

"Hugh, I am not having this fight with you again."

"And I'm not letting it go," I argued back. "I will *never* let it go, Mam."

"It's *not* our business."

"*She's* my business."

"And you're *my* son," Mam shouted, losing her cool with me. "A child. A minor in *my* care. Remember your place in this family, Hugh."

"Maybe that wouldn't be so difficult if I actually knew what that role was," I tossed back.

"Excuse me?"

"You heard me."

"You know what, you can forget about going to Lizzie's house," Mam snapped, looking both hurt and furious. "You've clearly forgotten your manners, and until you find them, you can stay home," she continued, prodding my chest with her index finger. "In fact, you are officially grounded until I say otherwise, young man," she added, folding her arms across her chest and glaring up at me. "Is that clear?"

"The only thing that's clear, Mam, is that in *this* family, good behavior is punished," I countered, mirroring her actions by folding my arms across my chest. "I get straight A's at school. I achieve countless academic merits. I make the team in every sport I play. I never bring trouble to your door. I follow all the rules. I look after Claire and Gibs. I cook the meals and iron the uniforms when you get called into work. I clean my room. I do my laundry. I mow the lawn. I take out the rubbish. I change the light bulbs. I don't break curfew. I don't drink. I don't smoke. I don't take drugs. I don't mess around with girls." Chest heaving, I blew out a breath and hissed, "I do the right thing, Mam." Reaching for my duffel bag, I slung it over my shoulder and moved for my other bags. "Every single time and you are *punishing* me for it!"

"That's not what I'm trying to do, Hugh!" Mam cried out, throwing her hands up. "Why can't you see that I'm trying to protect you? You are too young to handle the sadness in that house!"

"And you think this place is any better?" I demanded, chest rising and falling quickly. "When Dad's depression blankets every room in this house!"

"Hugh!"

"I'm not Claire," I strangled out, feeling too damn much in this moment. "I see. I hear. I observe. So don't try to keep me from her when you would never leave him!" *No matter how badly he drags the rest of us down.* "I guess the apple doesn't fall too far from the tree, does it?"

"Hugh, wait!" Mam started to say, but I'd had enough.

Ignoring my mother's pleas, I stormed out of my room, bags in hand, and moved for the staircase at top speed.

"Whoa—where are you going in such a rush?" Gibs asked, hovering on the top step of the stairs, clad in a dinosaur onesie and balancing two bowls of cereal. "Hugo?"

"Get out of my way, lad" was all I could reply, too consumed in my anger to think clearly. The hypocrisy in this house was stifling and I'd had enough.

Beyond furious, I stalked out the front door without a backwards glance and moved for my bike.

"Wait!" Mam called out, running out of the house after me. "Hugh, please just wait a minute!"

"Don't bother," I warned, balancing the saddle between my legs, while I adjusted my bags over both shoulders. "I'm going."

"Yeah, I gathered that." Sighing in defeat, my mother plucked her car keys from her pocket. "I'll drive you."

I looked at her, feeling uncertain. "You will?"

"It doesn't look like I have much of a choice, now, does it?" Another weary sigh escaped her and she moved for her car. "Pop the boot and load your bike in—and for the love of God, call me if you need anything. I mean anything, Hugh. Just pick up the phone and I *will* come to you."

THE BOY WHO STAYED

Lizzie

AUGUST 4, 2000

WHEN HUGH ARRIVED AT MY HOUSE THE MORNING AFTER OUR PHONE CALL ARMED with a duffel bag and his beloved PlayStation, he proceeded to set up camp on a blow-up mattress on my bedroom floor.

My nightmares didn't scare my boyfriend off, nor did my rapidly altering mood swings or my inability to get out of bed most days.

Hugh quickly adapted to the dysfunctional dynamic of my home life, and instead of shying away, he threw himself into the mix, learning from my father about the different kinds of meds I needed to take and when.

He didn't buckle under the weight of my mother's illness, like I did, or my father's increasingly bad mood. The revolving door of nurses to the house didn't seem to faze him, nor did the horrendous side effects of Mam's chemo, and he waited patiently outside every door of every psychiatrist I was deposited in front of.

Deep down inside, I had always known I didn't deserve a friend like Hugh Biggs, but that knowledge was only vindicated further by his actions this summer. Anyone else would have turned on their heels and bolted, but not Hugh. He stayed despite the tears, trauma, and tantrums.

He stayed.

For me.

Five weeks had quickly ticked by, and Hugh had remained faithfully by my side throughout, proving, once again, that *this* boy kept his word. Aside from the two nights each week that he had to be home for dinner, we had spent every single second of summer together.

I'd always known I loved Hugh, but my feelings for him had deepened over the summer. Like the roots of the tall oak tree in the meadow that sprawled deep beneath the surface of the earth, the love I felt for this boy had taken ahold of my heart to the point where I honestly thought I might die without him.

Even on my darkest nights, when I truly felt like death was my only option, I held firm in the knowledge that I could endure the agony that was my fucked-up mind if it meant I got to stay with *him*. If I died, he wouldn't be there, and I couldn't bear it.

So I *had* to keep going.

I had to *fight*.

"Mam called," Hugh announced on Friday evening when we were washing the dishes after dinner. "She collected my uniform today."

"For Tommen?" I asked, setting a sudsy mug on the draining board.

"Yeah," he replied, snatching up the mug to dry it with his tea towel. "I'm starting on the thirtieth of August."

"Oh." My heart plummeted. "I wish I were going with you."

"Not half as much I wish you were," he replied, opening a cupboard door and depositing the mug inside. "When are you back to Sacred Heart?"

"August thirtieth. Same as you." I shook my head in disappointment. "It's so unfair, Hugh. I should be going into first year with you."

"I know, Liz," he replied, sounding just as frustrated. "I agree."

"I'm too old to be stuck in primary school for two more years."

"You're too smart to be stuck in primary school for two more years."

"I'll be fourteen by the time I get to secondary school." Reaching into the kitchen sink, I pulled the plug and watched as the water swirled down the drain. "Everyone's going to think there's something wrong with me."

"No, they won't." Hugh was quick to rebuff my argument, neatly folding the tea towel before setting it down on the draining board. "Because there is *nothing* wrong with you. Besides, it'll even out after your junior cert." Reaching for my hand, he pulled me into his arms. "You can skip fourth year, and then we'll only be one year apart."

"I know." Shivering, I rested my cheek in the curve of his neck and wrapped my arms around his waist. "But I just want to be with you now."

"You *are* with me now." Hooking an arm around my waist, he cupped the back of my head with the other and whispered, "And I'm with you."

Exhaling a shaky breath, I allowed my eyelids to flutter shut and my body to fold into his. "You make me feel so much."

"In a good or bad kind of way?"

"In the *best* kind of way."

"That's a relief," he mused, quite content to hold on to me. "It's the same for me, Liz."

It wasn't.

It couldn't be.

He couldn't possibly understand the feelings he evoked from deep inside of me or the reaction my *body* had to his touch. I knew I wasn't supposed to feel that way, so I didn't dare tell him, but it was growing stronger by the day.

What had started out as a pleasurable flutter in my chest whenever Hugh touched me had grown into a more urgent itch that needed to be scratched, before evolving into a full-blown hunger.

Holding my hand helped eased the hunger pains and hugging me like this took the edge off a little more, but I was still *starving* and had no idea how to make it stop.

In the forefront of my mind was the conversation we once had about the bad touch, and I was acutely aware that I had to keep my hands to myself.

That I had to *not* touch him.

Kissing only seemed to make the ache grow stronger, which resulted in my body moving in strange ways against his. Even worse was the frantic urge I had to move my hands over his skin in ways I knew were *bad*.

It made me feel so confused because all the scary things the monster forced me to do, all the awful things that hurt me inside and made me cry, were the very things I wanted *this* boy to do to me.

The monster's gone, a voice that sounded awfully like my sister echoed in my mind. *You're free now.*

No, I wasn't.

Because the monster might have been gone, but I would never be free of him.

Of the things he did to me.

Of the things that made me want to peel the skin off my bones for *craving.*

"What's wrong?" Hugh's voice penetrated my thoughts, and he pulled back to inspect my face with concerned, brown eyes. "Your body just went completely rigid."

"Nothing," I replied, looking up at him. "I was just daydreaming."

"About me?" he teased with a playing wink.

"Yeah, Hugh." I forced myself to smile. "About you."

"What's this?" he asked then, snatching up my hand.

"What's what?"

"This." Rolling up my sleeve, he pointed to my wrist. "What the fuck is *this*, Liz?"

"Nothing," I muttered, pulling my hand out of his and yanking my sleeve back down. "Just forget about it, okay?"

"How am I supposed to do that?" he bit out, snatching my hand back up. "You promised."

It wasn't the betrayal in his eyes that made my heart ache.

It was the concern.

It was the fear.

"I'm okay again, Hugh." I forced myself to keep eye contact with him. "See." I pointed to my smiling face. "It's all good."

SUMMER AT OLD HALL HOUSE

Hugh

AUGUST 28, 2000

AFTER SPENDING THE ENTIRE SUMMER CRASHING ON A BLOW-UP MATTRESS IN LIZZIE'S room, I felt secure in the knowledge that if I didn't make it as a cardiothoracic surgeon, I could easily turn my hand to oncology or psychiatry.

I was certainly prepared for it.

I was quite aware that my calm approach in a medical crisis was in direct contrast to most lads my age, but then again, most lads my age weren't fascinated by aortic root surgery.

The only thing that seemed to get in my way was my heart and how it seemed to beat solely for the girl whose room I was crashing in. Because when she was in pain, holy fuck did I feel it, too.

Every night without fail, Liz would wake in a panicked state, and every night without fail, nobody would come to check on her. It didn't matter how loud she screamed or how frantic she became; she was left alone with her demons.

The first night it happened, I remained rigid on my mattress, too afraid to go to her in case her father came into the room and thought I was getting notions—something he made implicitly clear I was *not* to get.

I understood that Catherine was too frail right now and physically incapable of coming to her daughter's aid, but Mike had two perfectly good legs—and two perfectly good ears.

When no one showed up that night, and Liz continued to cry, I had taken matters into my own hands and climbed into bed with her. When she realized I was there, she had scrambled on top of me and clung to my body tighter than Gibsie did when he had a bad dream.

After that night, it had become a habit. Liz would wake in the middle of the night, and I would climb out of my bed and into hers. From there, she would wrap her limbs around me and hold on for dear life, while I whispered words of comfort in her ear. The crying would stop, but the violent shaking would continue until the sun came back up. She never let go until the room was bright enough to cast the shadows out, and neither did I.

Some nights she would ramble fervently about the monsters in her room, scary ladies in her head, and the nightmares that plagued her. While her late-night whispers were rarely coherent, I listened carefully to every word because I knew she was trying to tell me something important. Something her mind refused to make sense of.

Every night, I waited for my girlfriend to beckon me to her bedside, and then I listened intently, willing that brilliant mind of hers to throw me a bone to work with. Just one tiny scrap of a coherent memory so I could help her.

I knew the evidence was nonexistent, and my mother thought I was doing more harm than good by indulging her, but my heart assured me I was onto something. I'd known Liz for most of my life, and something deep inside assured me that I should trust her instincts on this. Hell, even my own gut instinct, the one that never steered me wrong, demanded I *believe* her.

Therefore, I would continue to back her up one hundred and fifty percent both in public and in private until I took my last breath. The only thing I couldn't support her with was her insistence on punishing Gibs for a potential crime he had no part in, and while my girlfriend was determined to condemn every member of the Allen family, blood related or not, I reserved my condemnation solely for Mark.

I couldn't say the past few months hadn't been a challenge, and I'd always thought I understood my girlfriend's mental health better than most, but I couldn't have been more naive.

Clearly, Liz had saved up every ounce of energy and joy for our daily visits, because seeing what she went through in a standard twenty-four hours broke my fucking heart.

Because her mind wasn't just complicated; it *tortured* her to the point where I found myself understanding her sudden and drastic shifts in mood.

The worst was the self-harming—something that I learned she did daily. That really took the air out of my lungs. Knowing that if I turned my back at any given moment, she could and *would* take a razor to her flesh. I'd caught her on three occasions, and those three fights were the only time I had ever raised my voice to her.

Because I needed her to *hear* me.

Because I needed her to know what when she cut herself, she cut me, too.

"Hugh?" Liz whispered in the silence, and the sudden intrusion of her voice, not to mention the hand she stretched over the side of her bed to trail her fingers in my hair, all but gave me a damn heart attack. "Are you awake?"

"Yeah, Liz." I blew out a breath, chest heaving. "I'm awake." When her fingers continued to tousle my hair, I reached an arm up and rested my hand on the edge of her mattress. "Did you have another nightmare?"

"I think so," she replied softly, snatching up my hand in hers. "But I don't know if I was asleep when it happened."

"Do you want to talk about..." My words quickly trailed off when my girlfriend rolled off the side of her bed and onto the mattress beside me.

"Hi," she breathed, settling on her side, facing me.

"Hi," I replied, swallowing deeply. "Did you just fall out of your bed?"

Liz shook her head, and the intense way she was looking at me caused every hair on my body to stand to attention. "You're leaving tomorrow."

"Yeah, I sort of have to." A dull ache settled in my chest. "School starts the day after."

"I don't want to sleep without you tonight," she whispered, reaching up to stroke my jaw. "Not when it's our last night."

Careful to not read this wrong, I slowly raised my arm and waited for her reaction. When she immediately burrowed her head into the crook of my arm, I relaxed and wrapped my arm around her. "It's not our last night," I promised, voice thick and gruff. "We'll have thousands of more nights together."

Inhaling deeply, Liz draped one long leg over my hips and flattened her palm over my bare stomach. "You always smell so good."

"Well, I sort of have to, now don't I?" I teased, striving to keep my mind off the way my body was steadily burning up. "When my girlfriend spends most of her days sniffing me."

"True," she mused, fingers moving to my navel. "Hey, did you know you have hair under your belly button now?"

That wasn't the only place I had hair, but I sure as hell wasn't about to tell her that. Not when I was doing everything I could to mentally counsel my body into calming the hell down.

"Hugh?"

"Hm?"

"Did you hear me?"

"Yeah, Liz." I cleared my throat and snatched her hand up in mine. "I heard you."

"I'm sorry," she whispered, sounding guilty. "Was that a bad touch?"

"No." I shook my head and repressed a shiver. "Not bad. Just unexpected."

"Oh." She moved closer, wreaking havoc on my poor fucking heart. "Hugh?"

"Yeah, Liz?" I replied, clenching my eyes shut when her inner thigh settled on top of me.

"When do we get to touch?"

Forget swallowing; I damn near choked on my spit when she asked me that. *"Touch?"*

"Yeah," she breathed, nuzzling my shoulder with her cheek. "Like how girlfriends and boyfriends touch each other."

Fuck, I couldn't hide it anymore.

"What's that?" she asked then, clearly noticing my problem.

Jesus Christ, my mother was *right*.

My heart loved this girl, but my body was definitely *lusting* for her.

Aw, crap.

"We can touch when we're a lot older than this," I strangled out, desperately seeking out common sense and self-restraint in the haze of lust settling over me. "When we're both in secondary school."

"But you'll be in secondary school for two years before I get there," she protested. "What if you find some other girl to touch?"

"I won't."

"But what if you do?"

"I *won't*, Liz," I repeated, feeling my legs tremble. "I won't."

"How can you be so sure?"

"Because I know it won't happen."

"But how do you know?"

"Because I only want to touch you."

Her breath hitched. "You do?"

"Yeah," I replied before quickly adding, "when we're *older*."

"How much older?"

"I already told you when we're in secondary school," I replied, recapturing up her hand when it started to trail down my stomach again. "There's no rush, Liz, and I'm not going to go off looking or touching any other girls when I start secondary school, okay?"

"Or kissing?"

"Or kissing," I confirmed. "I won't do any of those things, so all you need to do is have patience and trust me, because I'm not going to do anything that could hurt you."

"I *do* trust you, Hugh."

"Good." Rolling onto my side to face her, I pressed a hand to her cheek and smiled. "Because we have all the time in the world for that kind of thing."

Sunken, pale-blue eyes peered back at me. "Okay."

"I love you," I whispered then, needing her to know. "No matter what."

"I love you, too." My words caused the light in her eyes to reappear. "No matter what."

"Do you want to tell me about your nightmare?" I asked then, needing to steer the conversation back to something I could handle. "The one you thought you weren't asleep in?"

Her body tensed up immediately. "I was in a room."

"This room?"

She shook her head. "A different room."

"Okay." Keeping my tone gentle, I continued to stroke her cheek with my thumb. "What else was in the room?"

"A bed."

"Were you in the bed?"

"No." Liz shook her head. "She was."

"Caoimhe?"

She offered me a stiff nod. "She was crying."

"That sounds scary." My heart started to gallop in my chest, but I didn't dare let her know that. Instead, I kept my voice as soothing and relaxed as I could when I asked, "Was there anyone else in the room?"

She shook her head frantically before nodding.

"There was?"

She shook her head again and then nodded.

"There wasn't?"

"I don't know." Clenching her eyes shut, Liz expelled a shaky breath. "I don't want to think about it anymore."

"Okay," I replied when all I wanted to scream was *no, don't stop now*. I couldn't do that to her, though. Not when I was going home tomorrow and wouldn't be here to pick up the pieces. "We don't have to talk about it tonight." Draping an arm around her narrow waist, I pulled her close so that our chests were flush. "Try and get some sleep, okay?"

"What if the monster crawls out of my dreams?"

"I'll be right here," I promised, tightening my hold on her. "Watching over you."

"And keeping me safe?"

"Yeah, Liz," I croaked out, feeling my heart crack. "Keeping you safe."

PART 16

New Horizons

THE BOYS OF TOMMEN

Hugh

"OH, MY JAYSUS, WHO LET YA OUT OF THE HOUSE LOOKING LIKE THAT?" JOHNNY Kavanagh demanded in his thick Dublin accent, as he circled Gibsie in the car park of Tommen College on our first morning of secondary school. "There's no bleeding way I'm letting you walk into school with that thing on ya, Gibs." He turned his accusing, steel-blue eyes on me. "How could you *allow* this to happen, Hughie?"

"I'm not his keeper, Cap," I laughed, holding my hands up.

"No, but apparently he is," Feely interjected with a chuckle.

"I beg all of your pardons," Gibsie huffed, grabbing the lapels of his ultra-posh, navy blazer. "My mam said I look smart."

"Yeah, and my ma said the same thing when she tried to wrestle me into one, but I wasn't thick enough to believe her," Kav countered, grimacing. "Take the bleeding thing off, will ya? Or you'll be the laughingstock before first bell."

"But all the other first years are wearing blazers," Gibs complained, pointing to a group of fresh-faced first years hurrying past us before smoothing the sleeves of his tailored blazer. He then cast a disparaging glance at all three of us before huffing out a breath. "Don't be jealous because I look beautiful while the three of ye look like dog shit in jumpers."

"Yeah, well, I'll take dog shit any day over Carlton bleeding Banks," Kav grumbled before he proceeded to physically wrestle the blazer off our friend. "No best friend of mine is walking around with a target on his back."

"You just called me your best friend."

"No, I didn't."

"Yeah, you did."

"No, I bleeding didn't."

"Yes, you did!"

"Yes, you did, *Jonathan*, admit it."

"It was a minor slip of the tongue, *Gerard*. Don't read into it."

"Say it."

"No."

"Say it or I'm putting the blazer back on," Gibs warned, snatching the blazer back. Kav narrowed his eyes in challenge. "You wouldn't dare."

"Oh no," Gibs said loud enough to draw attention to us as he made an exhibition of feeding his arm through one of the sleeves. "If only I had a best friend to show me the way."

"Fine—fine!" Kav snapped, snatching the blazer back. "You're my best friend," he grumbled, balling the fabric up and stuffing it into his bag. "Are ya happy now?"

"Ecstatic!" Gibsie exclaimed, and I swear if he had a tail in this moment, it would have been wagging. He turned back to us and grinned. "Johnny called me his best friend."

"He sure did, Gibs," Feely and I laughed in unison, thoroughly amused by the horrified expression on Cap's face. "He must love ya, lad."

"Yeah, well, it's a coercive relationship status at best," Kav grumbled, closing his bag and tossing it over his shoulder. "And loosen that tie, will ya?" he added, giving his *best friend* a final once-over. "You're heading into a classroom, Gibs, not a courtroom."

"Anything for you, bestie," Gibsie replied, quickly falling into step with him.

"If you call me that again, I'll throttle ya," Kav grumbled, while planting a hand on Gibsie's shoulder and steering him away from a puddle of rainwater.

"Aye-aye, Captain."

"This place is a zoo," Feely declared when we finally found each other at big lunch. Meanwhile, Gibs and Kav were nowhere to be found. "I've never felt so intimidated in my life." Sinking into the chair beside mine in the lunch hall, he unscrewed the cap on a bottle of Tanora and took a deep swig. "I'm not sure about this school, Hughie, I'm really not." He took another gulp of his drink before whispering, "The girls here are fucking terrifying."

He didn't have to tell me twice.

After spending the last eight years in an all-boys school, Tommen College felt like we had been transported to an entirely new planet, and I felt acutely grateful to my sister for preparing me for this alternate universe.

"See the blond over there, the one with the ponytail?" Feely gestured toward a group of girls sitting at the table opposite ours. "She full on grabbed my ass at the lockers this morning, and when I turned around, she didn't even look away. She just stood there and winked at me."

"No shit," I laughed. "What did you say to her?"

"I didn't have a fucking chance," he replied, pulling at the collar of his shirt. "She laid it on me before I could get a word out."

"What do you mean she laid it on you?"

"I mean *she* stuck her tongue in *my* mouth!"

"Who stuck their tongue in your mouth?" Pierce O'Neill asked, joining us. "Well, Biggsie?" He turned his attention to me. "Don't tell me you got the shift already, you jammy bastard."

"I have a girlfriend, asshole," I snapped back defensively. "I'm hardly going around shifting randomers."

"You're still knocking around with your sister's friend?" Pierce asked in an incredulous tone.

My entire frame stiffened. "And?"

"Isn't she still at primary?"

I narrowed my eyes in challenge. *"And?"*

"And nothing," he muttered, looking uncomfortable "I thought you would've binned her off by now."

"Why would I do something as absurd as that?"

"Look around ya, Biggsie," Pierce replied, sounding genuinely confused by my reaction. "Why would you want to be tied down to the same girl you've been with since primary school when you could get with a hundred girls here?"

"Because I *don't* want any of these girls."

"How can you say that?"

"Because I already *have* the girl I want."

"But how can you know for sure if you don't at least test the waters?" he continued to push. "You're a shoo-in for the number ten jersey, lad. You're going to have girls falling at your feet, and you're telling me you're going to give that all up for—"

"The blond at the next table," Feely swiftly interjected, only too aware of how this asshole rubbed me up the wrong way. "She kissed me."

"No fucking way," Pierce cheered, attention immediately shifting to Feely. "You're a legend, lad."

Several of the lads from Scoil Eoin joined our table then and quickly set to work on ranking, rating, and eyeing up the girls around us like the desperate dogs they were.

Meanwhile, I pulled my phone out of my pocket, while I tried to calm myself down. *Fucking Pierce.* There wasn't a girl at this school who could hold a candle to Liz, and even if there were, I still wouldn't be swayed because Lizzie's looks weren't what had me locked down. It was *her*.

Scrolling through my phone, I noticed I had one unread text message and quickly tapped into it. My pulse quickened when I saw it was from Liz, with the time marked 08:39.

You can look but don't touch. x

Keeping my chin ducked low to hide my smile, I tapped out a response and pressed send.

The only girl I'm looking at is **my** girl, and she's the only girl I'll be touching. x

Knowing I wouldn't get a response from Liz until she finished school, I slid my phone back in my pocket and retrained my attention on the mind-numbingly dull conversation happening around me which consisted of girls, girls, and more girls.

Blonds.

Brunettes.

Redheads.

Tall girls.

Short girls.

Girls with small tits.

Girls with big tits.

Girls that looked like grown women.

Girls that were off limits.

Jesus Christ, it was exhausting listening to them.

"But you would if you could get away with it, wouldn't you?" Lukey asked, directing his question at me.

Shaking my head to clear my thoughts, I gave him my attention. "Would I what?"

"Score with another girl?"

"No."

"You have to answer honestly, Biggsie."

"I did," I deadpanned. "And it's still no."

"I saw that girl in Irish trying to talk to ya."

"Yeah, I saw her, too."

"Jesus, she was a bit of all right that one."

"She was hanging off his every word."

"She asked me for a pen."

"And your number. I heard her."

"Did ya give it to her, lad?"

"That would be another no."

"Aw, come on, Biggsie," several of the lads chorused. "She was hanging off ya in class."

"Lad, that girl was stunning."

"Too right."

"Jesus, she can have my number if she wants it."

"Don't bother with Biggsie, lads. He's sworn off all the talent at school," Pierce guffawed. "Because he's in *love*."

"Why don't you shoot your shot with her," I challenged, locking eyes on the dopey bollocks in front of me. "Or are you too much of a pussy to actually walk up to a girl and speak to her?"

"I'm not interested in your sloppy seconds, lad," Pierce laughed. "Although, I would absolutely make an exception for that girlfriend of yours." Waggling his brows, he teased, "Be sure to pass her over when you're done."

"Oh my Jesus, you shouldn't have said that," Feely groaned, dropping his head in his hands.

"You *really* shouldn't have said that, lad," Robbie Mac added grimly. "Bad form."

"Yeah." Roughly shoving my chair back, I jerked to my feet and moved for him. "You really shouldn't have said that, asshole."

LATE-NIGHT PHONE CALLS

Lizzie

AUGUST 30, 2000

I WAS BITTER ABOUT A LOT OF THINGS IN LIFE, BUT TODAY'S BIGGEST REASON WAS THE fact that I should've been starting first year with my boyfriend and *not* fifth class with his sister.

I felt left behind as a child when I had been held back in specialist schools, instead of getting to attend mainstream with peers my own age. I felt it even more when my sister left this world and, now I was feeling it all over again.

Because Hugh was going on and I was staying behind.

It pissed me off so bad because some of the sixth-class students that had graduated from Sacred Heart last summer were even younger than me. Now, they got to head off to secondary school, while I remained in primary for two more years.

It was so fucking embarrassing because not only was I going to turn fourteen in sixth class, but I would be *fifteen* by the end of first year, while everyone else in my class would only be entering their teens.

Twelve and a half starting fifth class.

What a fucking joke.

I was older than all the sixth class, who were either eleven or had *just* turned twelve, and the difference was even more disparaging in my actual class.

Claire and Shannon were eleven, along with a few other boys in fifth class, while most of the other girls were still ten.

What the hell did I have in common with ten-year-olds?

I had to shave my legs and armpits regularly, while they shared no such ordeals. I had breasts, a boyfriend, and menstrual cycles, while they still played with Barbies and talked to boys on Dream Phone.

Aside from Claire and Shan, I didn't know how to blend in with the other girls because I never felt I'd *been* one. I had no memories of my life before the age of three, and all my memories since were filled with doctor appointments, hospitalizations, tears, tablets, tantrums, and trauma.

In fact, I had never even owned a doll. I could remember receiving plenty of them at birthdays and Christmas, but I had either passed them on to my friends or used them for target practice when I went pellet-gun shooting with Hugh and the boys.

I couldn't relate to the pleasure other girls got from playing dress up, and I despised the thought of twirling around in frills and bows. I wasn't opposed to wearing dresses occasionally, but my style was worlds apart from what the stores promoted for girls my age or what my friends wore.

On top of my advanced age and physical maturity and inability to relate to my peers, the curriculum at primary school level was too easy for me. Most days, I grew more and more depressed at school because my mind was unstimulated, and I needed the stimulation to stay on track. I needed a challenge to distract me from the never-ending storm brewing inside of me.

When Hugh finally called after his first day at Tommen, I felt an immediate flush of heat.

"Hey, Liz." When I heard his familiar voice down the line, a blanket of warmth washed over me. "Sorry I'm late calling. I had practice after school."

"It's fine." I blew out a contented sigh and laid back on my pillows. All day, I hadn't been able to concentrate, too wrapped up in thoughts of his adventures at secondary school. "How was your day?"

"Hectic," my boyfriend chuckled. "The place is like a zoo."

"Really?"

"Yeah, it's fairly wild, but I managed" came his easygoing response. "Coach held rugby trials after school, and the lads and I got called up for the school team."

"Which lads?"

"Kav, Feely, and, uh, Gibs."

I couldn't describe the stabbing sensation that pierced through my breastbone when Hugh said his name. For a moment, I wasn't sure I could breathe, but I finally managed to squeeze out the word *congratulations*, even though it almost killed me to do it.

"Liz." There was a long pause down the line before he spoke. "I'm sorry, baby, but you know he's my friend."

Don't be his friend, I wanted to scream, but I held back, too afraid to push away the only person I had felt was truly in my corner. "Tell me about Tommen," I said instead, needing to change the subject before I exploded. "Who are your teachers?"

Sounding relieved, Hugh gave me a detailed rundown of his day from start to finish, while leaving out any mentions of *him*, which I was deeply glad of.

"Are their girls in your class?" I asked a little while later, feeling more related.

"A few," he replied evenly.

I smirked. "Any one nice?"

"No one with the name Lizzie Young" came his teasing response. "I'm not looking at them, Liz."

"I wouldn't be mad if you were," I admitted with a sigh. "I'm not exactly the easiest girlfriend."

"I'm not looking, Liz," he repeated, tone serious now. "You're the only girl I've ever wanted, and I have zero plans of doing anything to mess that up."

450

DATE NIGHTS AT THE POOL

Lizzie

NOVEMBER 23, 2000

"I'm going to get a job here when I'm old enough," Hugh announced on Thursday evening as we splashed around in the water.

Back in September, when he suggested we take up swimming on weeknights after school, I thought it was only a fleeting notion rolling around in his head because he loved to swim.

But when he continued to bring it up, I quickly realized he was deadly serious. After convincing my parents of all the ways exercise could benefit my mental health, they'd practically kicked me out the door.

Every weekday evening for the past two months, at 7 p.m. on the dot, Hugh arrived at my house on his faithful yellow slingshot, with his swimming bag slung over his shoulder.

From there, we would cycle to the hotel and private leisure center in town, where both our families were members, and swim until they kicked us out at closing time.

For two whole hours, I got him all to myself, after which he cycled me home, before heading home himself.

Maybe it was the endorphins from swimming or maybe it was Hugh, but I felt a stillness in the water that I didn't feel anywhere else.

"Seriously." Hugh gestured to the empty lifeguard chair. "That's going to be my seat."

"I believe you," I replied, wrapping my arms and legs around him. "You've accomplished everything you've ever set your heart on."

"Not everything," he shot back with a flirty wink. "Some things I've set my heart on can't be rushed."

My heart fluttered in my chest. "Is that so?"

"Uh-huh." He gripped my thighs and hoisted me closer. "I can't stop thinking about you."

"I'm right here," I laughed, reaching up to push his drenched hair out of his eyes.

"You look adorable with wet hair." Grinning, I leaned in close and pressed a kiss to his nose. "Like a big, brown-eyed puppy."

"What every lad wants his girlfriend to say."

"That's not what I mean—"

My words were swallowed up by his lips when they crashed against mine. His tongue swiped tentatively against mine, probing a reaction, waiting for approval. Shivering in pleasure, I kissed him back greedily, wanting nothing more than to fuse my mouth to his forever.

When Hugh kissed me, it wasn't like anything I'd experienced before or since. He was loving me with his mouth. Expressing his feelings with every flick of his tongue. It was deep. It was all-consuming. Like I was the sole recipient of his time, focus, heart, and affection.

The number of kisses we shared had increased drastically since he started secondary school, and even more so since his birthday last month. It was almost like his body had caught up with mine, and we were *finally* on the same frequency. Hugh was always careful to make sure we *only* kissed, and I was perfectly content to follow his lead because *holy crap* could he make me feel things with his kisses.

A part of me had feared Hugh would drift away from me once he started at Tommen and was around other girls, but he seemed more determined than ever to carve out alone time with me.

My boyfriend kept his word and his eyes on me, even though plenty of girls at his new school were determined to turn his head. While Hugh never breathed a word about it, his sister, on the other hand, sang like a canary the second she got the dirty details from his friends.

Apparently, the boy who'd been my best friend since junior infants had become quite the heartbreak prince at Tommen, with an impressive line of admirers vying for his affection. According to Patrick, and to Hugh's utmost credit, he was mostly oblivious to the attention, keeping his head in the books during class and his eyes on his phone at lunch break. And even when the really bold ones outright propositioned him, he politely *and* firmly declined.

"Okay, we need to stop," Hugh announced in a panicked tone as he tore his lips from mine.

"Why?" I moaned, peppering his neck with kisses. "I wasn't finished kissing you."

"I'm really sorry about this." With his breathing hard and uneven, he grabbed my waist and tossed me out of his arms. "But I need a minute."

"Oh, that's a real nice way to treat your girlfriend," I cackled, spurting out a mouthful of water as I paddled back to him. "Tossing me away like that."

"Please stay back," Hugh warned, holding up one hand while he used the other to swim away from me. "I mean it, Liz."

"Oh, stop trying to swim away, you big baby," I laughed, rolling my eyes. "I already know what's happening in your shorts. It's been poking me in the back all summer."

"Thanks, Liz. Say it louder, why don't ya?" Hugh groaned before disappearing under the water, only to reemerge a full minute later at the opposite end of the pool.

Pulling himself out of the water with effortless ease, he rested on the edge of the pool, with his feet still dangling in the water. "Okay," he called out, giving me two thumbs up. "I think I have it under control."

"Have I told you lately how proud I am of you?" Hugh declared after swimming, when we were making the trek through the unlit car park to where we parked our bikes.

"Proud of me for what?" I asked, enjoying the feel of his hand on mine, and how he always tucked my hand behind his. I wasn't sure why I noticed that or why it even mattered, but it was just one more box he ticked for me. Another was the way he always made sure he was on the outside when we walked near roads.

"For getting back in the water," he explained, and then, with an uncomfortable shrug, he mumbled, "after, well, you know."

Yeah, I *did*. "I'm not afraid of drowning, Hugh," I told him, moving closer to him for body warmth. *Because I'm not afraid to die.* "Water doesn't scare me—"

"Holy shit!"

Startled, I opened my mouth, ready to demand to know what the hell was the matter when Hugh spun me around and slammed my chest to his. "Don't panic," he whispered in my ear, while he tucked my face into his chest. "You're with me, and I won't let anything happen to you, but I think I see her."

I didn't need to ask who he was referring to.

I already knew.

"Where?" I squeezed out, keeping my face buried in his jacket.

"Across the road, under the streetlamp," he replied calmly. "It's really dark, and I can't be sure, but I think it's her."

"Is she looking at me?" I cried, feeling my body shake. "Can she see us?"

"I don't think so," he replied, while he slowly backed us up behind a parked truck. "The car park's pitch-dark."

"What do we do?"

"We go back inside the hotel and call the Gards."

"They won't believe us, Hugh."

"They will, Liz," he vowed, as he slowly retraced our steps through the car park. "I'll make them."

_____

"Why would I make it up?" my boyfriend demanded forty minutes later, as we sat side by side in the hotel lobby, with two stern-looking Gardaí scowling at us. Meanwhile, I remained silent beside him. Because I knew how this would go.

"I'm telling you that's the third time I've seen that woman skulking around," Hugh continued to plead our case. "Surely that has to constitute stalking!"

"Has she approached you any of those times?" one of them asked, notebook in hand.

"Well, *no*." Clearly aggravated by their lack of concern, Hugh pushed a hand through his hair and sighed. "But she *looks* at us."

"There's no law against looking at fellow pedestrians."

It doesn't matter what you say. They're not going to believe us, I wanted to tell him, but I settled for placing my hand on his forearm instead. Because whatever hope he had of getting through to these people would go clean out the window if I opened my mouth.

"Where is he?" Sinead Biggs barged into the lobby, looking around frantically for her son. "Where's my son?"

"Mam!" Hugh exclaimed, relief written all over his face. "Thank *God*." Springing to his feet, he barreled toward his mother and quickly filled her in on the night's events.

Meanwhile, I didn't move a muscle, too mistrustful of the men in navy uniforms towering over me.

"Do you have anything you would like to add, miss?" one of them asked.

I shook my head.

"Is that a no?"

I nodded.

They looked at each other and shook their heads in silent unison before retreating to where Hugh was speaking animatedly to his mother.

Expelling a shaky breath, I gripped the armrests of the chair and stared out the floor-to-ceiling window that led out to the car park.

She was out there.

I could feel it.

The monster had disappeared.

But the scary lady was always watching.

OUT WITH THE OLD, IN WITH THE NEW

Hugh

DECEMBER 31, 2000

AFTER THE INCIDENT AT THE POOL, LIZZIE'S MOOD HAD TANKED, AND NOTHING I seemed to do brought it back up.

I couldn't pull her out of the darkness that had settled over her, and because I was swamped with school, swim meets, and rugby, we weren't able to spend as much time together as before.

It broke my heart because I *knew* why this was happening. The Gardaí's underwhelming response to our statement about seeing the woman from the woods had triggered memories of her sister's death. Personally, I felt incredibly irked by not only the authorities' lack of belief in my statement but our parents' also. I was still salty as hell over what went down and couldn't imagine how it felt for Liz to be failed *twice*.

They could try to blame it on my girlfriend's mental health until the cows came home, but I knew what I saw that night, and I absolutely *saw* the woman from the woods.

What really rubbed me up the wrong way was when our parents decided to immediately pull the plug on our weeknight swims. They took precautions to prevent what they said *didn't happen* from happening again. A lot like how my parents *didn't believe* Mark was a rapist, while simultaneously *prohibiting* my sister from going across the street until he moved away.

Better safe than sorry.

The events at the pool seemed to fuel my outrage of my girlfriend's treatment this past year, bringing with it a roaring surge of protectiveness.

I did my best to be there for her, skipping as many rugby practices as I could get away with to steal a few extra hours with my girl, but Liz was fading fast on me.

Christmas had been a bust, with all the plans we made to hang out evaporating when she took to the bed the second the school holidays arrived.

I slept over at Old Hall House as often as I could swing it during Christmas break, but Mam was on my back over our relationship and didn't want to leave us in any potential scenarios where *temptation* might arise.

Still, I managed to persuade her to let me stay with Liz tonight, but I thought that might have a lot more to do with the New Year's Eve disco being held at the rugby club than Mam having a change of heart.

All the lads from school were heading to the disco and had been blowing up my phone all week, trying to sway me into attending. When they got wind of why I wasn't going, I took a healthy dollop of teasing for choosing a girl over a night out with the lads.

I didn't give a shit, and their taunting ran off me like water off a duck's back, because I was the one curled up in bed with Liz, while they were off getting shit-faced in bushes and swapping spit with randomers.

"What time is it?" Liz asked then, stirring me from my reverie. Draping one long leg over mine, she burrowed deeper into my side, cheek resting on my chest. "Is it midnight yet?"

"Hang on, I'll check." Reaching for my phone on her nightstand, I quickly unlocked the screen and read the time out to her. "One minute to midnight."

"That's good." Her voice was barely more than a whisper. "I thought I slept through it."

It wouldn't have bothered me if she had. I was relieved to see her get some decent sleep. I knew she suffered bad from insomnia when her mood was low and spent days lifeless in bed with her eyes staring off into nothing.

"Okay, now it's midnight," I stated, stroking her hair. "Happy New Year, Liz."

"Happy New Year, Hugh." With great effort, she lifted her face to mine and pressed a soft kiss to my lips before dropping back down. "Thanks for staying with me tonight. It means everything to me."

"And you mean everything to me," I reminded her, stroking her arm with the one I had draped over her. "Besides, we've rang in every new year together since 1994, and I have no plans for breaking the tradition."

"Is this our tradition?"

"Of course," I replied, reaching for the remote balancing on my stomach to pause the television running in the corner of her room. I had no clue what I'd been watching all night, but the white noise was oddly comforting. "I'm going to ring in every new year by kissing you until my lips fall off."

"No matter what?"

"Yeah, Liz." I pressed a kiss to her hair. "No matter what."

She was quiet for a long pause before whispering, "I remember now."

"You remember what, Liz?" I asked, feeling my body grow tense.

"Him."

My heart rate quickened. "Mark?"

I felt her nod. "Hurting her."

Holy shit.

Holy fucking shit.

"That night?" I asked, forcing myself to remain calm.

Another nod. "Lots of nights."

Jesus Christ.

"Holding her down," she whispered, and then, after another long pause, she croaked out, "putting things inside her." A huge shiver racked through her. "She tried to tell him no...but he never listened."

"He hurt her more than once?"

She stiffened before squeezing out, "Every night."

"Since when?"

Another shiver rolled through her, but this one was far more violent, making her entire frame jerk uncontrollably. "The start."

"The start of their relationship?"

Her breath hitched and she nodded. "All the time," she choked out a sob. "He said she would die if anyone found out, but she died anyway, Hugh, even when she didn't tell! She did what he wanted, and she still died."

It took every ounce of self-control I had inside of me to *not* react, but I somehow managed. "Did Caoimhe tell you this, Liz?"

Trembling uncontrollably, she nodded.

"When, baby?"

"That night." Her body grew rigid, and she clenched her eyes shut. "I'm not lying. I swear it. I'm telling the truth."

"I know." I tightened my arm around her, feeling faint. "I believe you."

"Nobody believes me." Tears trickled onto my chest. "I don't even think my parents believe me anymore."

"I believe you," I declared hoarsely, mind completely fucking reeling. "I believe every word, Liz."

"Don't leave." Sniffling, she clutched me tighter. "Please stay with me."

"I'm not going anywhere," I vowed, tightening my hold on her. "And I'm going to do something about this, Liz. I promise."

"There's no point," she whispered sadly. "They won't listen."

SOUND THE ALARM

Lizzie

JANUARY 4, 2001

TELLING HUGH ABOUT MY MEMORIES WAS A MISTAKE.

Not because he didn't believe me, but because I didn't believe myself.

My memories continued to fuse with my imagination until I couldn't tell the difference.

I couldn't be sure of anything anymore, which didn't help matters when Hugh called a meeting with my parents on New Year's Day and demanded we file another statement with the Gardaí, providing them with the details I had given him the night before.

I tried to remain stable, I truly did, but when I was taken to the station and faced with more officers, I lost it.

Unable to retain any coherent detail of the night my sister died, I had rambled on deliriously until they called in a doctor.

After that, everything went dark.

When my parents brought me back to the station three days later, I was questioned intrusively on the state of my home life by another officer. This one didn't a wear a uniform, but she spoke like one and bombarded me with questions she had no business asking.

"Is there any history of abuse in the home?"

"No."

"Are you sure? This is a safe space, where you can be truthful."

"No."

"Has anyone ever touched you inappropriately?"

"No."

"What about when you were little?"

"No."

"Are you sure about that, Lizzie?"

"Yes."

"How is your relationship with your mother."

"Good."

"And your father?"

"Fine."

"Has either one of your parents ever harmed you?"

"No."

"No physical reprimands or spanking?"

"Never."

"And your sister?"

"No, they never touched her, either."

"Did your sister ever harm you?"

"My sister's dead."

"I'm aware of that," the woman replied coldly. "Before she died, did your sister harm you?"

I narrowed my eyes. "No."

"You were violent to her, though." She watched me carefully as she spoke. "My records say you left a permanent scar on your sister's right cheekbone after an altercation."

Shame filled me. "I don't remember doing that."

"You have a clinical diagnosis of bipolar disorder, is that correct?"

"Yes."

"You were diagnosed in early childhood with the condition?"

"Yes."

"Which type?"

"What does that matter?"

"Delusions and hallucinations are more common in those with type 1." She eyed me for a long moment before saying, "Is it safe to assume type 1?"

Instantly despising this woman, I gripped the armrests of the chair I was sitting on and hissed. "I'm not delusional."

"But you do hear voices."

"No, I *don't*."

She arched a disbelieving brow. "Your parents gave us permission to speak with one of your doctors, and it was confirmed to us that you have been hearing voices since early childhood." She gave me a hard look. "The scary lady, for instance."

My face flamed with heat. "The doctor shouldn't have told you that."

"The doctor had your parents' written permission to release any information that pertains to your latest accusations," she countered evenly. "I presume this 'scary lady' is the same one you convinced your friend was stalking you?"

Hugh.

She was talking about Hugh.

"I didn't *convince* him of anything," I strangled out, feeling my body vibrate with tension. "We *both* saw her."

"You've been making very serious accusations with no evidence to back them up." Resting her elbows on the table between us, she clasped her hands together as she spoke. "These accusations are both time-consuming to the officers in question and costly to the state. Do you understand?"

My nostrils flared. "*Yes.*"

"I *am* sympathetic to your position," she offered in a gentler tone. "You've been through a terrible ordeal, which I have no doubt has exacerbated your bipolar symptoms."

But...

"But this constant stream of accusations cannot continue," she filled in. "We have received formal complaints from Mr. Allen's stepmother and while we *are* sympathetic to what you're going through, if this behavior doesn't stop, there will be legal consequences."

"Sadhbh filed complaints against me?" I managed to squeeze out, breathing hard and fast. "Accusing me of *what?*"

She shuffled through her notes before saying, "Defaming her sons."

"Sons," I whispered, feeling weak. "Plural?"

"Yes. Both Mrs. Allen's stepson and biological son are listed as victims in her complaint."

Victims.

Did I hear that right?

They were victims?

"Nobody wants to see you in trouble, Miss Young," the officer continued to say. "Certainly not any member of my team, but you are pushing it to the point where we are going to *have* to intervene if this behavior doesn't stop." She paused for a long beat before adding, "None of us want to see a grieving child in a Garda station, so can I have assurance that you will stop slandering the Allen family?"

"Don't worry," I mumbled, feeling my heart turn cold. "You'll never see me back here again."

GET OVER IT

Hugh

"What's with the face?" Feely asked when Claire stomped into my room on Saturday night, looking like someone pissed in her cornflakes.

"I've been ditched," she declared dramatically before flopping down on my bed. *"Again."*

"Ignore her," I said, rolling my eyes. "She's throwing her toys out of the pram because Gibs went to Dublin with Cap for Easter."

"Dublin," Claire huffed, folding her arms across her chest. "What possible reason would they have for going to *Dublin.*"

"Uh, maybe because that's where the Kavanaghs are from?" I offered dryly. "And Johnny's parents still own property and businesses in Dublin they might like to check in on?"

"Aren't Cap and Gibs attending an event while they're up there?" Feely asked.

"An event?" Springing up on my bed, Claire's eyes bulged. "What *kind* of event?"

"The rugby youth's annual award ceremony."

"For what?"

"Cap won half a dozen trophies," Feely explained. "Gibs is his plus one."

"You don't own the lad, Claire," I reminded her. "Gibs is allowed to have other friends, you know." I shrugged. "Besides, it might do you some good to have a little space from him."

"Are you serious, Hughie?" My sister gaped at me like I had just told her the world was flat. "Why would I *ever* want space from Gerard?"

"Maybe so you spend time with your other friends," Feely offered. "Like Lizzie?"

"Exactly," I agreed, pausing the movie playing on my TV. "You do remember her, don't you?"

"You mean my friend who likes to suck face with my brother?"

"She's got you there, lad," Feely chuckled.

"She's still your friend, Claire."

"She likes you more than me."

"Most people generally do," I agreed. "But that's no reason to not put yourself out there."

"You're an ass," Claire snickered, tossing a pillow at my head.

"Seriously," I added. "You should call her, Claire."

"I would if she spoke more than four words to me," my sister replied with a sad sigh. "She's just so sad."

"Fuck," Feely muttered with a flinch. "She's not getting over it, is she?"

"Nope." Claire shook her head. "She just keeps getting sadder."

"Get *over* it?" I snapped, instantly pissed off. "It hasn't been a year since she watched her sister being fished out of the fucking river, lad. How do you propose she gets over something like that?"

"Sorry, lad," my friend replied, looking embarrassed. "I didn't mean it like that."

"She only wants to talk to you," Claire chimed in then. "Seriously, Hughie. She barely talks to anyone at school anymore, and she never answers my text messages." Sighing sadly, Claire flopped back down on my bed. "I want to help her, really I do, but she gets so mad at me over Gerard, and we always end up fighting."

I understood where my sister was coming from. Gibs was a thorny subject to my girlfriend, but it wasn't fun to hear she was becoming more and more isolated.

"I don't know what to do," I admitted with a sigh. "Or how to help her."

"Clearly you do because you're the only one she speaks to," my sister replied, giving me a supportive smile. "You really are going to be a great doctor, Hughie, because you've been working miracles on Lizzie for months."

On the contrary, I had messed things up spectacularly for my girlfriend. Insisting on her making a statement to the Gardaí after New Year's not only traumatized Liz but it had broken her. Like *seriously* broken her.

The Gards didn't do anything about her mental breakthrough, which knocked Liz back ten damn steps.

She had retreated into her shell and refused point-blank to talk about what they said to her or how she was feeling.

She was cutting more and missing more school, had had her meds changed several times, and it was entirely my fault.

If I'd kept my mouth shut, she wouldn't be spiraling.

SO THIS IS THIRTEEN?

Lizzie

JUNE 9, 2001

"I LOVE HOW YOU NEVER TAKE THIS OFF," HUGH SAID, FINGERS PLAYING WITH THE charms of my ankle bracelet while we lazed on my bed in a top-and-tail position. "It feels like I'm branded on you."

"You are," I replied, sliding my other foot under his T-shirt. "And I'll never stop wearing it."

"Never?"

"I'll be buried in this thing," I vowed, dangling my foot in front of his face and making the charms jingle. "Thank you for my new charm." I eyed the latest addition—an infinity charm—and smiled. "I love it."

Propped up against my headboard, Hugh smiled back at me. "You're welcome."

Resting my bracelet-clad foot on his shoulder, I exhaled a contented sigh. "So this is thirteen."

"Yep," he mused, while stroking my calf absentmindedly. "Fairly underwhelming, isn't it?"

Everything about life was underwhelming. Hugh was the only exception to the rule, and I was pleased to level up with him once again. "Hey, Hugh?"

"Yeah, Liz?"

"Can we kiss?"

His hand stilled on my leg, and he gave me a strange look. "Yeah." His tone was gruff. "Of course we can."

"Good," I breathed, flopping onto my back and letting my legs fall on either side of his body. "Because you haven't kissed me in a while."

"Not because I haven't wanted to." Pulling up on his knees, Hugh moved into position, hovering above me. "I *always* want to." Heated, brown eyes locked on mine. "But you've had a hard few months." Resting his weight on one elbow, Hugh leaned in close and stroked my nose with his. "And I didn't want to make it worse."

"You're the only thing that makes it better." Reaching up, I cupped his jaw and pulled his face to mine.

His lips touched mine, slowly at first, before the growing ache thrummed and pushed us forward.

Kissing him with a desperation I couldn't explain, I pulled and tugged and yanked at every spare inch of his skin, desperate to feel more.

More.

More.

More!

The moment his fingers grazed my shoulder, a prickling sensation spread all over my skin.

Grabbing his hand, I tried to move it lower, but he kept returning to my waist.

Didn't he understand what I wanted?

How badly I *needed* to feel his body on mine?

When I grabbed his hand and pressed it to my chest once more, Hugh groaned into my mouth, and it was the best noise I'd ever heard in my life.

"Liz," he moaned into my mouth, moving his hand from my chest to my hip. "We should slow down."

"No." Too lost in my feelings, I continued to pull and tug his back, needing to feel him all over. Needing his touch to force out the bad ones. "I want you."

"No, Liz." Breaking our kiss, he pulled back to look at me, breathing uneven. "We can't do things like that yet."

"Why not?"

"Because we're not ready."

Tears filled my eyes, and I choked out a pained sob. "I wish I could get you to understand."

"Then tell me," he urged. "I'm here, Liz. I'm always listening."

I knew he was, and that broke my heart a little bit more because I didn't want him to see and run.

To turn away from me.

To think I was dirty and tainted.

Because I was supposed to be his.

I *belonged* to him, but a part of me had been stolen.

And I needed him to put it back for me.

PART 17

Fresh Starts

ONE STEP FORWARD, TWO STEPS BACK

Hugh

AUGUST 7, 2002

"Jesus Christ!" I strangled out when I strolled into Liz's room on the morning of my sister's thirteenth birthday. "I am so fucking sorry for not knocking." Because not only was my girlfriend standing in front of her full-length mirror but she was fully *naked*. Like *fully* naked. "I thought you'd be in bed." In fact, I had been so sure of it that I had arrived an hour earlier than agreed for the sole purpose of peeling her off the mattress. "But you're up…and naked."

"Wow, nothing gets past you, does it?" Liz teased, completely unfazed while I was freaking the fuck out. "Relax," she laughed, glancing over her shoulder at me. "It's not like you haven't seen my body before."

I had.

But not all of it.

And definitely not when she looked like *that*.

"So," she said in a playful tone. "Do you plan on standing around ogling my ass all morning, or are you waiting for a tit shot?"

"Oh shit, yeah!" I strangled out, slapping a hand over my eyes and giving her my back. "Once again, I am *so* sorry."

Wardrobe doors clanking open and shut filled the air followed by the distinct sound of clothes hangers rattling. "Okay, the coast is clear," she announced a few minutes later. "You can look at me."

I turned around to find her standing directly in front of me with her top pulled up.

"Goddammit, Liz," I groaned, unable to stop my eyes from roaming over her glorious tits. "*Why* would you do this to me?"

"Because I can." She cackled mischievously before pushing her vest back down into place. "Look at that blush." Reaching up, she squeezed my cheek. "You are *so* adorable."

Hooking an arm around her waist, I pulled her flush against me. "And *you* are a troublemaker," I growled before dipping my head to kiss her, unable to resist the temptation of her pouty lips. The deeper I kissed her, the harder she dug her nails into my hips and the move drove me wild. Hormones were invading me like the plague, and I was burning the hell up for this girl. Because she was as reckless as a person came, *I* had to be the sensible one in the relationship. I had to be the guard for both of us, even when it went against every primal urge I had inside of me.

"Oh my God," Liz breathed against my lips. "You are *such* a good kisser."

I couldn't answer her. I was too busy claiming her lips once more, while I kissed her with everything I had inside of me.

Fisting her hair with one hand, I grabbed her hip with the other, reveling in the feel of her body crushed to mine. All I wanted to do was lay her down on the bed and show her how much I loved her. How much I wanted her. Repeatedly. Until I finally calmed the fire inside of me. Until I satisfied this overwhelming urge to get naked with her.

When I felt her hands slide under my shirt and then her fingers sneaking into the waistband of my shorts, I knew it was time to stop.

With enormous effort, I ended our kiss and took a safe step back. "Don't give me that look," I warned, breathing hard and uneven when I caught her scowling at me. "You know the rule."

"Kiss, don't touch." She rolled her eyes. "It's a stupid rule."

"It's a *safe* rule," I corrected, trailing my thumb over my bottom lip. "You bit me."

"And?" Liz planted her hands on her hips and smirked. "Did you like it?"

I fucking loved it.

"Come on, my little biter." Repressing a hungered groan, I shook my head and moved for the door. "Let's get out of this room before we start breaking rules."

"It'll be okay, won't it?" Liz asked when she joined me on the landing. "I mean, your mam doesn't mind me coming over?"

"Liz, my mam loves you," I coaxed, taking her hand in mine. "She's thrilled that you're coming."

"And, uh, um…" She swallowed deeply before expelling a shaky breath. "He won't come near me, right?"

"Right." I gave her trembling hand a reassuring squeeze. "Gibs will be there, but he's going to be with Claire." I tipped her chin up with my free hand and pressed a soft kiss to her lips. "And you'll be with me."

"I'm scared," she blurted out, eyes wild and full of fear. "What if I mess up?"

It had been over two and half years since she'd stepped foot inside my house, and a huge part of me wanted to tell her that she didn't have to do this. But if I did that, if I gave her an out, I knew she would never do it.

"I'll be right beside you the entire time," I promised, desperate to reassure her while my heart split clean down the center. "I won't let anything bad happen to you."

468

"You swear?"

"Cross my heart."

"Okay."

"Yeah?"

Liz nodded. "Yeah."

I exhaled a sigh of relief.

"I know it's Claire's birthday, but I'm doing this for you, not her," she squeezed out and then pushed up on her tiptoes to kiss me hard, while her entire frame trembled violently.

I knew she was, and it meant so damn much to me.

Several hours later, we were all lazing around in our back garden, with a dozen or so school friends and a game of spin the bottle in full swing.

Liz was strewn out on the grass beside me, with her feet crossed at the ankles, and a pair of sunglasses perched on her nose. She had her head perched against my thigh, which caused her blond hair to spill onto my lap and tickle my skin. She was wearing a white vest, a pair of khaki combats, and army boots, and I was having a hard time not staring at the way her nipples were poking out.

Apparently, so were the lads, which pissed me off to the point where I couldn't hear a word of the conversation happening around me.

Why was Feely staring like that?

What the fuck was Robbie Mac's issue?

Did Danny Call honestly think he was being discreet?

As for Pierce O'Neill? Well, Pierce was going to get another smack in the mouth if he didn't stop openly ogling her.

There were plenty of other girls sitting around to gawk at. Christine Grundy from our year was one, and Bernadette Brady was another. Pierce's twin sisters, Marybeth and Cadence, were another two. Why couldn't they avert their beady little eyes to any of them?

My only reprieve was the fact that Gibs *wasn't* staring at my girlfriend's tits, but even that was a double-edged sword, because I knew if I followed *his* line of sight, it would lead to my *sister's* tits.

Out of the corner of my eye, I spotted him scampering off with my sister toward the treehouse, and I narrowed my eyes, instantly suspicious.

Jesus Christ.

I couldn't catch a break.

The fact that Liz hadn't completely lost her shit when Gibsie arrived earlier and was still here with us without picking fights was reason enough for me to swallow my feelings. Because I *wanted* her to spend time with her friends. I wanted her to remember that she wasn't alone. That she still had us. Even Gibs.

"Ah, unlucky, Biggs," Pierce snickered when the bottle he was spinning landed on Liz. Meanwhile, I turned to stone. "Don't worry, lad, it's only a shift."

"I'm not playing," Lizzie replied breezily, plucking at a blade of grass. "Spin again."

"Bullshit," Pierce argued, growing red-faced. "You know the rules. If you're in the circle, and it lands on you, you have to kiss."

"You heard her," I cut in, bristling. "*Spin again.*"

"Fine, it doesn't have to be a shift," he conceded with a huff. "A kiss will be grand. No tongue."

"What part of *I'm not playing* did you not understand?" Liz asked coolly, pulling up on her elbows to glare at him. "Are you so dull of comprehension that I have to repeat myself, or did you catch it this time?"

Her retort caused several of the lads to roll around on the grass, laughing their asses off.

"Ah, she's got you there, lad."

"Burn, Piercy boy!"

"Yeah, whatever, at least I'm not a frigid bitch who chickens out," Pierce muttered, burning with embarrassment, throwing daggers at my girlfriend with his eyes. "I bet you're a terrible fucking shift anyway, viper."

"You better watch your fucking mouth, asshole," I warned, moving to stand, only for Liz to put a swift stop to that when she clambered onto my lap.

"Too bad you'll never find out, asshole." Kneeling on either side of my hips, Liz grabbed my face in her hands and forced my chin up to hers. Snaring me with her blue eyes, she lowered her face to mine and purred, "Because I only kiss *this* boy."

I wasn't expecting it when her lips crashed against mine. I was even less expecting the hot swipe of her tongue when it entered my mouth. Or the way she crushed her chest against mine. *Holy fuck* was she pulling out the moves.

I knew everyone around us was watching, I could hear their loud cheers and wolf whistles, but in this moment I didn't care. All logic and reason flew clean out of my ears. I grabbed her hips, roughly pulling her down on my lap, partially to hide my raging hard-on from the lads, but mostly because I wanted to feel *her* against me.

My girlfriend came willingly, sinking down hard on my lap, while never once breaking our kiss as her tongue devoured mine.

Her hands were in my hair. Her tongue was in my mouth. Her ass was on my lap. Her hips were rocking against mine. I was in utter sensory overload. I had no fucking clue how I was going to stop this. I only knew that I didn't *ever* want to.

"All right, all right, you've made your point."

"Jesus Christ, lads."

It was only the sound of my sister screaming, "Ew! Lizzie Young, get off my brother right this instant!" at the top of her lungs from the treehouse that managed to break us apart.

Tearing her mouth from mine, and with her chest rising and falling rapidly, Liz stared at me with a hungry expression before releasing a frustrated groan.

"Jesus fucking Christ, Claire!" I snapped, feeling just as frustrated and hungry. "What's the matter with you?"

"It's me," Liz whispered with a resigned sigh. "I'm the matter with her."

"Don't get up yet," I half whispered, half pleaded when she moved to climb off my lap and reveal to our friends just how frustrated I felt.

Her cheeks flushed, and she gave me a subtle wink. Twisting around to sit sideways on my lap, she watched, right along with me, as Claire climbed down the treehouse ladder and thundered toward us.

The look on her face had the rest of our friends all scrambling out of the line of fire. Because a publicly pissed-off Claire Biggs was a rare sight. Even Feely scooted away. Meanwhile, I narrowed my eyes in challenge, only too willing to face her down.

The little, curly-haired demon.

"What's the matter with *me*?" Coming to stand directly in front of us, my sister planted her hands on her hips and glared down at me. "What's the matter with you, Hugh?" Her attention shifted to the girl on my lap. "And you!" She narrowed her eyes in disgust. "That's my brother you're sitting on." Her cheeks turned bright pink. "And that's also my brother's mouth I just saw you ramming your tongue down!" Another furious shriek escaped the curly-haired menace, and she stomped her foot. "You're supposed to be my best friend."

"I am, Claire," Lizzie replied with a defeated sigh, because this wasn't a new battle for her. My sister and my girlfriend had been hashing out this exact same argument since we started going out. "You know I am."

"Then act like it, Liz!" The hurt in Claire's brown eyes was as clear as the hurt in her voice when she strangled out, "It's *my* birthday party, not my brother's. You're supposed to be hanging out with me."

"Grow the hell up, Claire," I cut in, having had my fill of the bullshit. She didn't see me throwing tantrums every time Gibsie came over and they disappeared together for hours on end. The hypocrisy was real, and I opened my mouth to tell her just that, but Liz placed a hand on my arm in warning.

"I'm sorry," Liz interjected, pandering to her bullshit, and I was instantly pissed. "In future, I promise not to kiss your brother when we're supposed to be hanging out." The fact that she continued to give into my sister's tantrums only proved to me how much she valued their friendship.

"I would prefer if you don't kiss my brother at all," Claire replied, sniffing the air. "It's nauseating."

"You're nauseating," I couldn't stop myself from tossing back.

"*Hugh.*"

"What?" I replied, not bothering to protect myself from the rogue elbow that came my way—courtesy of my coconspirator. "She's being a child about this. She needs to grow the hell up."

"Claire-Bear." Gibs arrived on the scene then. "It's grand. Let the lovebirds be." He slung an arm around my sister's shoulders and smiled. "No need to get cranky. We're all friends here."

The mere presence of Gibs in her personal space was all it took to send my girlfriend spiraling.

Scrambling out of my lap like she had just been scalded, Liz sprang up, eyes wild and feral.

"Shit." Blowing out a pained breath, I cupped the back of my head in defeated resignation before climbing to my feet.

With none of the grace and patience she had shown my sister, Liz pointed a trembling finger at Gibsie. "We are not now nor will we *ever* be friends. Do you hear me? I will *never* be friends with you." Shaking all over, she glared up at Gibs and shook her head. "And I will *never* forgive you or your family."

Gibsie didn't say a word in response. Instead, he turned around and walked away.

"Lizzie." Claire placed her hand on Liz's shoulder and sighed sadly. "It's not Gerard's fault."

"*Don't!*" Roughly shaking her hand off, my girlfriend spun around to glare at my sister. "Don't defend what you don't know." Tears streamed down her cheeks. "You *don't* know what I know." She sucked in a shuddering breath. "You *didn't* see what I saw."

Claire looked to me, eyes pleading, and I subtly shook my head. There was no point in arguing. Not about this. Not when they were in the same vicinity as each other. We'd tried that before, and it didn't go down well.

With a torn expression etched on her face, Claire backed away slowly before turning around and heading in search of Gibsie.

"Breathe," I instructed, stepping in front of Liz to shield her from everyone's view. "It's okay." Placing my hands on her trembling shoulders, I forced her to look at me. "Just *breathe*."

"I need to leave." Swallowing down a hysterical sob, she reached up and swatted the tears from her cheeks, while her entire body shook violently. "I need to go *now*." The frantic look in her eyes assured me that she was moments away from losing it in front of everyone.

"Come on." Wrapping my arm around her, I drew her into my side and quickly walked us into the house. Claire could deal with everyone else. "I've got you."

"I kn-know he d-did it!" she choked out, barely able to breathe from the force of her cries. "I kn-know he r-raped my s-sister!"

"It's okay," I coaxed, leading her through the kitchen and into the hall. "I've got you." Bringing her here was a mistake.

It was cruel.

"I r-remember the s-sounds, H-Hugh. And h-his sm-smell. I w-was th-there!" Her fingers knotted in my shirt. "I k-know the t-truth and n-nobody b-believes me!"

"I do, Liz." Guiding her up the staircase, I kept a tight hold of her waist, knowing that this could go south quickly. "I believe you."

"I s-swear I'm t-telling the t-truth," she strangled out, clinging to my body as I led her into my room. "I j-just c-can't pr-prove it."

"Where's your bag, Liz?" Setting her down on my bed, I crouched down in front of her and gently peeled my shirt from her fingers. "Hmm." Reaching up, I tucked a strand of hair behind her ear before wiping a tear from her cheek. "Where's your bag, baby?"

"O-over t-there," she heaved out, chest rising and falling in a frantic pattern as she pointed toward the door. "B-but I'm n-not c-crazy, H-Hugh."

"I know you're not." Rising to my feet, I made a beeline to retrieve the bag. "You know I don't think that, Liz." Unzipping her rucksack, I rummaged through the contents until my hand closed around the familiar bottle labeled *Clonazepam*. "I would never think that about you." Unscrewing the cap, I poured the lone pill into my palm. She only carried around one at a time because her mother was a smart woman. "Open your mouth, baby."

"No, n-no, n-no!" The sight of the pill caused Lizzie's entire expression to cave, and she dropped her head in her hands, crying even more hysterically than before. "I am s-so f-fucking s-ick of t-tablets!"

"Me too," I replied, and that wasn't a lie. I didn't want to fill her up with medication. I fucking hated it. But I also remembered last summer and knew what would happen if this wasn't stamped out fast. After last time, her mother had given me explicit instructions on what to do. I *had* to calm her down.

"Please, Liz," I begged, loathing the words as they came out of my mouth. "Please do this for me."

Sniffling, she snatched the pill out of my hand with her trembling one and shoved it in her mouth.

Any relief I felt from her complying was eclipsed by devastation when she looked at me with betrayal in her eyes.

"I love you." Crouching back down in front of her, I held her tearstained face between my hands and tried to explain myself. "Do you hear me? I love you so much that it *kills* me to see you hurting like this." Swallowing down a lump in my throat, I continued to look at her as I spoke. "I'm not trying to hurt you, Liz." *I would die first.* "I only want to help you."

She clenched her eyes shut, blocking me out.

Still, I persevered. "I know you hate the medication." A tear dropped from her lashes, landing on my thumb. "And I know you hate all the doctor visits." Another tear dropped. "But I also know that you're *not* crazy."

Her breath audibly hitched, and she leaned into my touch as a pained sob tore from what sounded like her soul.

"You're going to get through this." Using my shoulder, I quickly wiped the tears from my own cheek, voice cracking with emotion. "And I'm going to be right here with you for all of it."

Sniffling, she reached a hand up and covered my hand with hers.

"I'm not leaving," I vowed hoarsely. "I'm staying right here with you."

Exhaling a ragged breath, she sagged forward and rested her forehead against mine. "N-no m-matter w-what?"

"Yeah, Liz." I clenched my eyes shut and exhaled a ragged breath. "No matter what."

THAT'S MY GIRL

AUGUST 7, 2002

"I KNOW YOU'RE HURTING, SWEETHEART," SINEAD SAID, AS SHE DROVE ME HOME FROM the party. "If there were anything I could do to take this weight from your shoulders, I would do it in a heartbeat."

I didn't have anything left inside of me to answer.

Instead, I slumped against the window and stared lifelessly.

At what, I had no idea.

My head was spinning, and the meds were kicking in, making my body grow warm and my head light.

"I want you to know that you are *always* welcome in our home," she continued, reaching across the console to take my hand in hers. "I love you like a daughter, and I always will." She squeezed my hand. "You have a place in my heart and that will never change."

Tears trickled down my cheeks.

Sniffling, I squeezed her hand back.

"That's my girl."

PROTECTIVE BOYFRIENDS

Hugh

AUGUST 7, 2002

AN HOUR LATER, WHEN I FOLDED MY GIRLFRIEND INTO THE BACK SEAT OF MY MOTHer's car and watched them drive off, I stormed back into the house like a madman.

"You just couldn't leave it alone, could you?" I seethed when I found Gibsie and Claire skulking in her room. "You had to fucking stir up drama."

"I didn't mean to upset her," Gibs was quick to declare, holding his hands up. "I swear, lad."

"Not you," I snapped, turning my attention to my sister. "You." Narrowing my eyes in disgust, I hissed, "You have no clue how much it took for Liz to come today. How much it meant to me to have her here and you fucked it."

"Back off, Hugh." Gibs was quick to defend Claire, wrapping a protective arm around my sister. "She said she was sorry. We both are."

"Yeah?" I spat, chest heaving. "Well, sometimes sorry isn't fucking good enough!"

"I'm so sorry, Hugh!" Claire blurted out, covering her face with her hands. "You were kissing my best friend, and I lost my mind for a moment."

"Yeah, well get fucking used to it," I snapped back. "Because your *friend* is *my* girlfriend and she can kiss me whenever the hell she wants, and she sure as shit doesn't need my baby sister's permission to do it."

"I know, I know, I'm sorry," she strangled out, looking genuinely guilty. "I knew I was wrong the moment the words came out. I just…I just… I wasn't thinking."

"Well, *start* thinking!" I hissed, beyond furious. "And don't ever put her in a position like that again. She can't fucking take it, Claire. That girl you call your friend is hanging on by a fucking thread!"

"What's wrong with her, Hugh?" Gibsie asked, giving me a strange look.

"Nothing!" I snapped, pushing a hand through my hair. "She's grieving her sister, that's all."

"Yeah, but I know grief, Hugh," Gibs replied slowly, brows furrowed. "And that wasn't it."

I stared hard at him for the longest time before blowing out a weary breath. "Just leave her alone, all right?" *And let it go.*

"All right," he replied, nodding slowly. "I will."

EVERYTHING'S JUST PEACHY

Lizzie

AUGUST 31, 2002

PISSED OFF, I SAT IN THE DOCTOR'S OFFICE ON THURSDAY AFTERNOON, WITH MY ARMS folded across my chest and my heart sealed off.

"Are you in the mood to talk today?" the woman behind the desk asked in a pleasant tone.

"Depends on the topic," I answered flatly. This doctor was new, a younger-looking woman I had never met before. I didn't bother to learn her name because after half a dozen sessions, we would never meet again. That's how it was. How it had always been. There was no regularity to these appointments. No familiarity. I could spin a new yarn each time, and they would never know.

The impressive stack of notes on her desk led them to believe this stranger knew all about me.

She didn't and never would.

The shiny MD credentials attached to her name were what assured my parents that she was the latest in a long line of saviors that could fix their broken daughter.

She couldn't.

Little Red Riding Hood was devoured in whole by the Big, Bad Wolf.

The doctor decided to start with, "I see you've celebrated a birthday this summer," while flicking through my notes. "Your fourteenth." Her eyes returned to my face. "Did you do anything special for it?"

Okay, this was a slightly different approach to the standard *how are you feeling*, but nothing I couldn't handle.

"Yeah, I did," I replied. "And no, I didn't."

"Really?" She arched a disbelieving brow. "Nothing?"

Like I'm going to tell you shit. I shrugged in response.

Her lips tipped up. "You're not going to make this easy, are you?"

Not a chance in hell.

When I didn't take the bait, she returned to scouring my notes, while I waited impatiently for the clock to run down. Thirty-seven more minutes and I was out of here.

"It says here that your mother has battled cancer throughout your childhood." Her eyes brightened as she read through my notes. "And she's made a miraculous recovery back to full health."

"Yeah," I bit out. *Until the next time.*

"You don't sound happy about that."

"I'm ecstatic," I deadpanned, eyes boring holes in hers. "Can't you tell?"

Concern flickered in her eyes. "How have things been going at home?"

"Peachy."

"And your relationship with your parents?" She continued to probe. "How is that going?"

"Picture perfect."

"And your mood? How are you feeling, Lizzie?"

There it was. "Splendid."

The doctor released a frustrated sigh. "You know I can't help you if you don't talk to me."

"Isn't that the whole point of your job?" I arched a brow. "Figuring out ways to *get* me to talk?"

"Yes," she replied evenly. "But you could make my job a lot easier if you opened up."

"You're getting paid to be here." I shrugged. "I'm not."

"Do you have somewhere else you would rather be?"

Yes. "I see what you're doing."

"A friend's house, perhaps?" She continued to challenge. "Or maybe a boyfriend?"

"You're the one with the notes," I countered. "You tell me."

"Have you always been this mistrustful?"

No.

There were moments in time, back when I was a little girl, that I thought I could be happy. Back then, contentment felt attainable. But darkness had a way of sweeping innocence up in the riptide.

That's what happened to my innocence.

To me.

Everything went dark once the monster crawled into my bed. There were only glimmers of hope, fleeting flecks of sunshine that teased my soul. Until she died and took my last flicker of trust to the grave with her.

It had been two years, four months, and six days since they pulled my sister's body from the water, and it had been two years, two months, and eight days since *he* left town. Eight hundred and fifty-three days of being *not* believed and this doctor was questioning my ability to *trust*?

What a fucking joke.

"Like I said," I deadpanned, "you're the one with the notes."

"How did your session go?" Mam asked on the drive back home. "Did you like your new doctor?"

"It went well," I replied as I stared lifelessly out the car window. "She was nice."

"And she's happy with your progress?" She continued to probe while she navigated through the lunchtime traffic. "No adjustments to your meds?"

"Nope." I repressed the urge to scream. "Everything's fine."

"Oh, sweetheart." Mam reached across the console and squeezed my knee. "I'm so glad to hear that."

"Yeah, Mam," I whispered. *I know you are.*

"Did she give you any pointers on how to handle secondary school next week? Or coping techniques if you get overwhelmed?"

"I won't get overwhelmed, Mam," I replied with a sigh. "I'm not nervous about it."

"I know that, sweetheart," she conceded in a gentle tone. "But it's going to be a big change for you, and you know how *change* can unsettle your mood."

Yeah, I knew that, but there wasn't a whole pile I could do about that. I couldn't cut the bipolar out of my mind like her doctors could her cancer. It was a *part* of me. "I'll be grand."

"I'm so proud of you, Lizzie. I hope you know that."

Yeah, and I didn't deserve it. Her pride was misplaced because if she knew the real me, she wouldn't feel that way. If she knew about my bad thoughts or the things I *craved*, she would be repulsed. "I'm proud of you, too, Mam."

"So, what else did you talk about in your session?"

"The usual," I replied with another defeated sigh. "How am I sleeping? How am I feeling? Do I feel like the new meds are working? Oh, and she asked me about my nightmares."

Mam winced. "They're still happening?"

Every night. "They aren't as bad as before."

"That's a relief to know, love."

"I keep having this one dream lately, though," I said, deciding to tell her. "About, uh, well, about her."

My mother's expression fell. "Oh?"

"Yeah." Swallowing deeply, I asked, "Did we live somewhere else before here?"

"You know we did, love. We lived in Tipperary."

"No, not Tipperary," I muttered, feeling confused. "Somewhere farther away. Somewhere we would need to fly to."

Mam frowned. "What are you talking about?"

"In my dreams, I'm on an airplane." I expelled a frustrated breath. "We all are. The whole family. We're flying somewhere and Caoimhe looks really happy about it, and I think I am, too." Frowning, I added, "But the moment the plane lands, I wake up."

"Maybe you're reminiscing about a holiday we took?"

"No." I shook my head, brows creased. "I don't think so."

"Well, you can stop worrying, love." She smiled cheerfully. "Because it's just a dream."

"Yeah," I mumbled, discretely digging my fingers into my flesh to soothe the anxiety rising up inside.

My phone pinged then, and I quickly snatched it out of my pocket and clicked on the unopened text message. The moment I read his name on the screen, excitement roared to life inside of me. *I roared to life.*

Four more days. x

A sudden flush of heat washed over my body because I knew exactly what that cryptic message meant. Feeling my heart thump erratically in my chest, I fumbled over the keypad of my phone, desperate to get a message back to him.

Come home from swim camp early. ☺ We can get a head start. x

Holding my breath, I stared at the screen and waited for his response, only to visibly tremble with excitement when my phone pinged a few moments later.

I'm stuck in Kerry until Sunday. ☹ x

Stifling a groan, I typed out another message and pressed send.

That means we won't see each other until school on Monday. ☹ x

His reply came instantly.

Don't worry. I'll make it up to you. ;) x

Smirking, I replied.

How? 😊 x

My phone pinged ten seconds later.

Lots of touching ;) x

My heart jackknifed in my chest, and I grinned devilishly before texting him back.

😊😊😊 FINALLY. x

"Well, there's only one person who can put a smile that wide on your face," Mam laughed. "So I'm not going to ask who's texting."

"Hmm?" Blushing, I quickly pocketed my phone and exhaled a shaky breath. "Oh, it's Hugh."

"Yes, sweetheart," Mam mused. "I gathered that."

"He won't be home from camp until Sunday," I told her, heart still thumping wildly. "So we won't get to see each other until school."

"Oh no!" Mam feign-gasped. "How will the two of you ever survive?"

"He's been gone for a week," I reminded her with a huff. "Seven days, Mam."

"Then I'm sure you'll survive another four days without lover boy," Mam laughed unsympathetically. "I have to say, I've missed seeing him around the house, too— although not nearly as much as your father has."

Yeah, I was quietly confident that my father loved my boyfriend more than he loved me.

Things were tense at home, with my parents' relationship on the rocks since the funeral, but Dad really seemed to snap out of his bad mood whenever Hugh came around.

Mam said it was because he enjoyed having another male around, but I knew better.

Dad loved Hugh because he picked up the slack for him. When he bounced, which happened frequently, Dad knew he could rely on my boyfriend to take on the role of "man of the house" in his stead.

The more my parents fought, the more my father left, and the more my father left, the more my boyfriend stepped up.

It wasn't right how much both of my parents had relied on Hugh in the past two and a half years, but he never complained. Worse was my inability to function without him, but again, my boyfriend never faltered or shied away, and I knew with absolute certainty that the salvageable parts of my body, heart, and mind would forever belong to him.

Despite the meltdowns and mania, Hugh continued to wade into my world, like a brave knight, and shield me from the emotional shrapnel hell-bent on tearing me to shreds.

I was nowhere near good enough for this boy, nor did I deserve the patience he extended to me, but I desperately tried to be.

My mind drifted back to the shitstorm that was the summer of 2001, and I flinched when I thought about how close I had come to losing Hugh.

My sister's first anniversary had brought with it my first truly severe manic episode, most of which I had very little memory of. I could, however, remember the shame that had engulfed me when I woke up in a hospital bed in the depths of depression. I couldn't remember stopping taking my meds, but that's what the doctors said happened. I couldn't remember destroying my room, ripping Caoimhe's pictures off the walls, or running naked through the fields at the back of our house. But that's what they told me happened. The worst thing by far was hearing that not only did I tie a horse rein around my neck and throw myself off the upper loft in the haybarn, but *Hugh* broke his elbow when he fell over the ledge trying to cut me down.

He *did* end up cutting me down and saving my life that day, and he never once held it against me, but I did. *I* held it against me and would *never* forgive myself for putting him in harm's way.

Afterward, the drop was so severe that I would spend weeks of my summer holidays in bed, barely eating, rarely showering, and generally rotting beneath the covers.

After that, I came back to life, but I was tortured by the mistakes I had made when I was high. Worst of all, I only had myself to blame for my actions and my dad was more than willing to tell me just that.

That dark period in my life wasn't something I liked to think about because I was terrified that, if I thought about it too long, I would jinx myself.

Claire's birthday a few weeks back had been another stark reminder of how quickly my world could come crashing down around me.

"Listen, I know we've had a hard few years, but how about we draw a line in the sand and consider you starting Tommen College our fresh start?" Mam cast a hopeful glance in my direction, and I had to force myself not to flinch at the sight of her weathered face. "Hmm? What do you say, baby girl?"

"Sounds like a plan," I offered, willing myself to be the daughter she needed me to be.

GIRLS OF TOMMEN

Lizzie

SEPTEMBER 2, 2002

"IT'S LIKE A CASTLE," CLAIRE EXCLAIMED, CLUTCHING HER BOOKS TO HER CHEST, AS she twirled around in the courtyard, clearly awestruck by the medieval-looking building that would be our academic home for the next six years. "Isn't it beautiful, Liz?"

"Yeah," I replied, squeezing the straps of my schoolbag as I took in my surroundings of ivy-clad walls of ancient, church-like brick. "It's something all right."

"Mrs. Lowney said Tommen College was built in 1667," she gushed, reeling off the stats our primary school teacher had doled out about the prestigious boarding school. "Admission acceptance is highly competitive, not to mention pricey tuition fees, and the school only offers six academic scholarships annually."

"Yeah, Claire, I know," I said with a sigh. "I was in class the day Mrs. Lowney gave the presentation."

"Sorry," she replied with a sheepish smile. "I forgot."

I had been absent a lot in the past two years, so I couldn't blame her for forgetting. "It's okay." I indulged her with an encouraging smile. "As you were."

"Really?" She looked at me with big, hopeful doe eyes. "Can I give the full synopsis? I remember it off by heart."

Of course she did. I smiled. "Go for it."

Bustling with barely contained excitement, my friend cleared her throat before throwing herself into the role of expert tour guide. "Tommen College is a prestigious, private post-primary boarding school located in the idyllic countryside of County Cork, fifteen miles from the bustling town of Ballylaggin. Sprawled over three hundred acres of woodland and greenery, Tommen College offers admission for day and boarding, sporting separate male and female student accommodation buildings with a total capacity of two hundred and fifty."

"Whoa," I laughed, genuinely impressed by her ability to memorize the pamphlet. "That was ridiculously professional."

"Ooh, ooh, I have more," she exclaimed happily, bouncing from foot to foot. "At

Tommen, we offer state-of-the-art facilities to support our students' academic careers as well as a nationally recognized athletic department of excellence."

"Sounds like an athlete's dream school."

"It sure does," she mused, whipping out the pamphlet we'd been given and proceeding to read aloud. "Facilities within Tommen College include a dedicated music room, six spacious common rooms, a weights gym, a sports hall, a flood-lit astro turf pitch, a twenty-five-meter indoor heated swimming pool, nine-hole golfing facilities, a running track, three individual science buildings, a horticultural garden, two libraries, a pottery room, state-of-the-art home economics classrooms, *three* dedicated rugby pitches, a sports recovery room—"

"Okay, okay, I get the picture," I cut in before she morphed into the human form of Tigger and bounced off. Hooking my arm through hers, I led her toward the gigantic double doors that led into the main building. "Let's just go inside and find our lockers."

"Do you think Shannon will be okay at BCS, Liz?"

No. "Yeah, Claire, I do."

"Really?"

"Absolutely," I replied, even though my heart plummeted at the thought of Shannon alone in a new school. "She has her brother."

"Yeah, and he won't let those mean bullies hurt her."

"Exactly."

"I'm so glad you're here with me, Liz," Claire mumbled when we stepped inside, where she was clearly overwhelmed by both the size of the gigantic entrance hall and the several hundred students bustling around inside. "I think I might be scared without you."

"You've got this, Claire Biggs," I promised, pulling her closer. "Give it a month, and you'll be the school's sunshine sweetheart."

"You really think so?"

"I know so."

"What about you?"

"Me?"

"Yeah, what will you be?"

"You can't have sunshine without rain," I offered with a shrug. "I'll be the school raincloud."

That made her laugh, and I was glad because it was important to me that this girl never lost her shine. *Like I did.* Claire had a unique kind of innocence about her. She saw the world through untainted eyes. Her heart was pure, and her mind was uncorrupted. Whether that was down to her mother's parenting or the invisible bubble of protection her big brother projected around her, I couldn't be sure, but she was a special girl who, despite her stark differences to me, I couldn't have loved more.

"Omigod, yay!" Claire squealed then, releasing her hold on my arm. "Gerard!"

My body turned to stone as I watched her bolt off in the direction of a crowd of older boys kitted out in rugby attire. Well, older than Claire, at least. I was about the same age as all those assholes.

When she threw her arms around him, I honestly thought I might vomit.

"Claire-Bear!" he exclaimed just as excitedly before lifting her into the air. "Lads, this here is my intended, so keep your eyes and hands off, ya hear?"

Beyond nauseous and unable to mask my scowl, I stormed off in the opposite direction, needing to put as much distance between my hands and his throat as possible.

Body trembling, I tried to step around a group of older girls who were blocking the entire corridor as they yapped.

Trying to be calm, I stood in front of them like a dummy waiting for them to move, before giving up on being polite and shoving my way through them.

When you're walking through hell and all that jazz.

"Uh, excuse me! You can't just barge your way through us," one of them called out, catching ahold of my arm when I tried to get past. "Who the hell do you think you are, baby first year?"

"Your worst fucking nightmare if you don't let go," I spat, swinging around to glare at the dark-haired girl. "Seriously," I warned when she didn't let go of my arm. "You have five seconds to take your hand off me or I'll cut your fingers off."

"What a bitch," one of them muttered, taking a safe step back from me, while the one still holding me seemed to ponder whether I was serious or not.

"Oh, you have no fucking idea how serious I am," I told her, stepping closer.

"Let it go, Bella. She's not worth it."

"Yeah, Bells, let's just leave."

"Five, four, three, two, one—"

"In future, ask nicely when you want someone to move out of your way," the girl they called Bella sneered, while still having the good sense to remove her hand before I finished counting. "I'm a fourth year, you know, which makes me your superior around here."

"In future, don't block the entire corridor," I shot back, unwilling to give an inch. "And, bitch, I wouldn't care if you were Mother Teresa herself."

"Fiery *and* bitchy." She arched a finely plucked brow, looking strangely impressed. "I think I could use a little firecracker like you in our gang." She turned back to her posse and said, "What do you think, girls?"

The girls around her immediately agreed like a flock of obedient sheep.

"What do you say, little firecracker?" She turned back to smile at me. "Fancy a spot at the big girl's table?"

"I think you should go to hell," I deadpanned.

Her eyes narrowed in outrage. "Excuse me?"

"And maybe get a hearing test," I added before storming off, flipping them the bird when one of the sheep shouted the word *bitch* after me.

I managed to find the first-year locker area without asking for directions, but just before I reached my locker zone, I was hauled inside an emergency exit stairwell by a boy donning Tommen's number-ten rugby jersey.

"Finally," my boyfriend growled when the emergency door slammed shut, cloaking us in darkness. "I've been waiting here all morning for you."

Instantly bombarded by a sudden flood of emotion, I lunged for him, needing his touch more than I needed air.

"Hugh," I breathed, climbing his body like a drainpipe to seal my mouth to his.

With his lips on mine and his hands gripping the fleshy part of my thighs, he walked forward until my back hit the wall. The move caused the growing ache between my thighs to intensify, and I greedily tightened my arms and legs around him.

"Just so you know, I would gladly kiss you in front of everyone." His lips moved against mine as he spoke. "This shitty stairwell is for your benefit—should I say the curly-haired demon's benefit?"

"You know it upsets your sister when she sees us together."

"I don't give two shits if seeing us together upsets my sister," he argued back, lips trailing up my neck. "I care that my sister reacts in a way that upsets *my* girlfriend." Everything inside of me clenched tight when he called me that. "Anyway, I wanted to wish you luck on your first day before the bus leaves," he continued to say, while his hips gyrated against mine in a way I was certain could make me unravel. "I have an away game in Clonamore."

"Skip it," I begged, shivering when his tongue collided with mine. "Stay here with me instead."

"I would if I could," he whispered, kissing me with more love and affection than I'd ever been given from another human being. "But I'm already on Cap's shitlist for missing preseason conditioning...fuck, Liz!"

"It's D-day, Hugh." Smiling against his neck, I continued to trace my tongue over his fluttering pulse. "You smell so good." Closing my lips around him, I sucked and stroked his flesh with my lips and tongue. "Mm."

"You should stop," he protested weakly, only to lean in closer and bare his throat to me. "Christ, don't ever stop."

I didn't plan to.

Not until I left my mark on him, at least.

HYPOTHETICAL SCENARIOS AND THE TOP 1 PERCENT

Hugh

"About fucking time, Biggs," Coach Mulcahy barked when I finally joined him and the rest of the team on the bus. "Jesus Christ, I thought I would have to send a search party out for my fly half."

"Sorry for being late, Coach," I mumbled, climbing the steps of the bus. "It won't happen again."

"Yes, well, considering you're usually always on time, I'll let it slide," he grumbled, hands planted on his hips. "But don't make a habit of this."

"Thanks, Coach," I replied, making a beeline for the aisle.

"Hold up." Clamping a hand on my shoulder, he pulled me back to face him. "You're all right, aren't ya, Biggs?" Concern filled his tone. "You're not feeling sick or anything?"

"I'm grand, sir."

His eyes studied mine for a long beat before he shook his head and released me. "All right then, Biggs. Go take your seat."

"Did someone skip breakfast this morning?" Feely snickered when I collapsed onto the seat beside him "Holy fuck, lad, she ate the neck off ya."

You have no idea. Knees bopping restlessly, I exhaled a shaky breath and strived to calm my nerves. "I'm in so much trouble, lad."

"With Coach?"

"No, not Coach," I spat, turning to gape at him. "With her, Pa, with *her.*"

Instead of offering support to a friend in need, *my* friend decided to laugh into my face. "I thought you'd be delighted to finally have your girlfriend join Tommen."

"I *am* delighted," I choked out, eyeballing him. "I'm *too* delighted."

"There's no such thing as being too delighted, lad."

"There is when you have a girlfriend that looks like *mine.*" Feeling panicked, I bit down on my fist and whispered, "Did you see her in that uniform?"

"Is that a trick question?" my best friend replied, instantly wary. "If I say yes, are you going to rage at me for looking?"

"You *did* see her in that uniform," I strangled out, burying my head in my hands. "How in the name of Jesus does she walk with those stilts for legs?"

"No clue, Hugh, but they are, by far, the sexiest stilts for legs I've ever seen."

"Not fucking helping, lad."

"My apologies."

"She wants me."

"Yeah, Hugh, that's generally how it goes when you're in a relationship."

"No." I turned to look at him again. "I mean she *wants me* wants me."

"Relax, will ya?" Feely laughed, patting my shoulder. "You have the self-control of a eunuch monk."

I shook my head. "Not with her, I don't."

Feely grinned back at me. "And that's a problem because?"

"Because I haven't, I mean we haven't, and I don't...ugh!" Groaning in pain, I dropped my head in my hands once more. "It's like the more I try to be respectful, the more she encourages me *not* to."

Feely snorted. "Talk about first-world problems."

My head snapped up. "Excuse me?"

"You are sickening, do you know that?"

"*How?*"

"Can you hear yourself right now?" he asked, looking thoroughly amused. "You're practically in tears because your girlfriend *wants* you. That's a top 1 percent problem, Hugh." Chuckling, he added, "Have you any idea how the other 99 percent of lads struggle?"

"Says the fella sticking his dick in anything with a pulse since his fifteenth birthday."

"Hey! I never said I was part of the 99 percent, asshole," he shot back with a laugh. "Besides, someone has to fly the solo flag."

"Yeah, and you do more than enough flag waving for the rest of us," I grumbled, giving him the side-eye.

Feely shrugged unapologetically. "It's my hands." He raised one for emphasis and wiggled his fingers. "Guitar fingers, lad."

"Get that thing out of my face before I puke on you," I warned, slapping his hand away.

"I'm so glad I don't live at Avoca Greystones," he mused thoughtfully, scratching his jaw. "There's clearly something in the water that makes lads lose their heads. I mean, Gibs can act the player as much as he wants, but we both saw him rocking in a corner from the sheer height of guilt over shifting Bernadette Brady at the disco last year. At least you had the balls to put a label on you and Liz—even if you're too pussy to *be* a real boyfriend to her."

"I beg your fucking pardon!" I spluttered, feeling extremely offended. "I'll have you know that I'm a damn good boyfriend."

"Have you felt her tits yet?"

"*Yes.*"

"Under her bra?"

I opened my mouth to respond but nothing came out.

Feely laughed. "Thought not."

"How does feeling her tits make me a better boyfriend?"

"Because if you touch her tits, you might actually make her feel good," he replied drolly.

"I always make her feel good."

"Sexually, Hugh."

I narrowed my eyes. "I can make her feel good sexually."

"Not by holding her hand, you can't," he laughed.

"Like you're an expert on the matter."

"Oh, you want an expert?" Grinning, he stretched up in his seat and called out, "Cap, come over here a sec, will ya?"

"Are you *mental*?" I strangled out. "I'm not talking to him about this."

"You don't have to," he replied. "I'll do the talking."

"What's the story, lads?" Kav said, dropping in the seat in front of ours.

"You've had a lot of sex, haven't ya?" Feely came right out and asked, while I mentally dug myself a hole to die in.

"Whether I have or haven't is irrelevant." Kav was quick to shut down the conversation. "Because I don't discuss my sex life with anyone."

"Yeah." Feely rolled his eyes. "Which means he's had a lot of sex with a lot of different girls."

"What's this about, Feely?" Kav snapped, sounding irritated.

"If sex was off the cards, would you use fingers or tongue to get her off?"

"Jesus Christ, Pa," I choked out, appalled.

"Hypothetically?" Kav offered, sounding mildly interested now.

"Of course."

"In what context?"

"You and a random girl."

"Fingers," Kav replied without hesitation. "No tongue." Grimacing, he stroked his chin before adding, "Never use tongue on randomers." A shudder racked through his enormous frame. "That's way too intimate."

"And if you were in a committed, long-term relationship with her?"

Johnny frowned like he didn't understand the question. "If we were in a committed, long-term relationship, then why *wouldn't* we be having sex?"

Feely cracked up laughing.

"I'm confused," Kav admitted, brows furrowed.

"Don't worry about it," I replied, digging into the ribs of the asshole beside me. "Feely's having a moment."

Johnny stared at us for a long beat before shaking his head and rising to his feet. "I'm not sure what either one of you bright sparks is up to, and I honestly don't have the headspace to worry about it, but make sure you roll *hypothetical* condoms on your *hypothetical* dicks before you start fucking around." He started to walk back to his seat before stopping in the middle of the aisle to turn around and say, "And save the oral for your *hypothetical* committed relationships."

"Nice one, Feely. Now he thinks we're deranged."

"Don't worry about it, Hugh. He probably thinks we're fucking each other."

"No offense, lad, but I'm way too far out of your league for him to think that."

"Whatever you say, *virgin*."

"Right back at ya, *whore*."

HEAVEN ON EARTH

Lizzie

SEPTEMBER 27, 2002

"WHERE ARE WE GOING?" HUGH ASKED, FOLLOWING ME UP THE ANCIENT BRICK STAIR-well at the back of the main building at school. "Liz, we only have five minutes left of lunch break."

"Trust me," I coaxed, racing up all four flights of cobbled staircase until I reached heaven on earth—well, at Tommen, at least.

"Holy shit," Hugh breathed, joining me in the impressive stone archway that led to the school's original library. It took up the entire fourth floor of the building and was the only part of the school that had been spared of modernization. The architecture resembled the late 1600s, when the school had first been built, and it was a treasure trove for book enthusiasts—sprawling aisles of stacked books from floor to ceiling, with antique furniture, and glorious drawback, velvet curtains ordaining the Victorian windowpanes. Best of all, there were aisles of books in here that were as old as the building itself.

"How did you find this place, Liz?"

"I have contacts," I teased, deciding not to mention Mrs. Reidy, the elderly school librarian who had taken a shine to me. "This place is open to students, but nobody ever comes here," I explained, taking his hand and leading him through the aisles. "Everyone uses that modernized library. You know, the one in the basement level?"

"Yeah, I know it," Hugh replied, wide-eyed as he took in our surroundings. "I pass it every day on the way to the swimming pool."

"Come on." Dragging him down the sprawling aisles, I took a left at the end of the central area. "Wait until you see this." Weaving through aisles of floor-to-ceiling bookcases in the left wing, I led my boyfriend to the original stone wall that housed the true wonder of this room.

"What the hell is that?" Hugh asked, attention locking on the narrow, rectangular-shaped hole in the bricks.

"Follow me." Heaving myself onto the ledge, I squeezed myself through the narrow opening until I reached the secret room.

"Holy shit," Hugh breathed, climbing in after me and then standing up to take in the sight of the small ten-by-ten-foot stone room. "What was this place used for?"

"I've been researching, and from what I can tell, it was used as a safe room by students in the flying columns, during the War of Independence."

Hugh's eyes widened to saucers. "No fucking way."

It was a small stone room without any windows or natural light, though electricity had been wired through in the form of an ancient-looking, rusty lamp attached to the wall nearest the opening. Carved into the brick were the initials of who I presumed used this very room during the war. The only pieces of furniture in the room were a desk with a matching chair and an even older-looking army cot. Like the ones they used for soldiers in the war.

"Welcome to my crib," I laughed, waving a hand around. "Pretty cool, huh?"

"I'll say," Hugh replied, looking at me with a peculiar expression etched on his face. "You never stop surprising me, Liz."

"Oh really?" I purred, closing the space between us. "Well, how about I surprise you with something even better." Hooking my arms around his neck, I pushed up on my tiptoes and pressed a kiss to the curve of his jaw. "Hmm?"

"I'm not going back to class, am I?" my boyfriend asked gruffly, hands clamping down on my hips.

"Not if I have my way," I whispered before covering his mouth with mine.

Roughly pulling me flush against his chest, Hugh knotted his hand in my hair and angled my face up to deepen our kiss.

The moment his tongue entered my mouth, I felt a surge of electricity surge through me and moaned. "Mm."

He was just so beautiful, and I wanted to have him more than I wanted anything else for the rest of my life.

Just this boy.

Forever.

Groaning into my mouth when he felt my fingers hooking into the waistband of his school trousers, Hugh walked me backwards until my back hit the wall. "Fuck, baby."

A delicious shiver rolled through me when he called me *baby*, and I tugged on his belt buckle, mentally willing it to disappear.

Grabbing his right hand, I moved it to my thigh and encouraged him to hitch it around his waist. When he obliged and I felt our bodies align just right, the throbbing ache between my legs grew stronger.

"You are so beautiful," he whispered between kisses, while he ground his hips against mine. "I can't take it."

"More," I begged, arching into his touch, while my hips gyrated furiously against his. "Please."

"You're going to fuck me up, Liz," Hugh groaned, gripping my thigh tighter as he continued to thrust himself against me. "You're all I can think of."

"Then have me," I encouraged, reaching between us to touch the front of his school trousers. "Whoa."

"Don't," he begged, hips losing their rhythm when he felt me feel *him*. "I won't be able to handle it." Reaching between us, he snatched my hand up in his and moved it away from his crotch. "I want to, really fucking badly, but we can't." Another pained groan escaped his lips. "Not yet."

"Then me," I breathed, lips moving against his as I guided his hand under my school shirt. "Touch me." I felt his hesitation and the way his body tensed, but I didn't relent, guiding his hand up my stomach until he was palming one of my breasts. "Like this."

"You're not wearing a bra," he said in a gruff tone. "Fuck, Liz."

"I hate bras," I replied, arching my hips forward while my hand remained on top of his, encouraging him to keep going.

"We've never done this before," he whispered, sounding achingly vulnerable. "Are you sure this is okay?" He pulled back to look at me, brown eyes full of heat and longing. "To touch you like this?"

"More than okay," I breathed, slowly removing my hand from his. "What about you?" I asked, pressing my body into his touch. "Do you like it? Do I feel okay?"

He nodded slowly, while his thumb grazed my pebbled nipple. "You feel perfect." Gently palming me, he leaned in close and recaptured my lips. "You feel like mine."

Because I am.

PICKING OUTFITS AND PUSHING LIMITS

Hugh

OCTOBER 5, 2002

STRETCHED OUT ON MY GIRLFRIEND'S BED, WITH MY HEAD PROPPED AGAINST A STACK of plush pillows, I forced myself to keep my eyes trained on the pages of the book I was attempting to read and *not* the girl who was prancing around half-naked.

Unfortunately for me, *Ulysses* didn't hold a spark to Lizzie Young.

"How's this one?" she asked, and I watched from my peripheral vision as she prowled toward me.

Liz didn't need makeup and dresses to look feminine, and I didn't need the bullshit aesthetics to stroke my ego. Because I knew what she was, what she had, and it was everything and more. She was all I would ever want, ever crave, and ever desire. She was it for me.

Those kinds of girls bored me to tears because I *lived* with one of those girls. No, I didn't want the girlie girl, with the stuffed animals and pink everything. I wanted the feisty girl with the sharp edges and the tomboy attitude. I wanted the girl who glowered at me when I held the door open, instead of blushing. The one who responded to "ladies first" with "age before beauty."

That girl lit me up.

That girl floated my entire fucking boat.

"Very nice," I replied, quickly retraining my attention on my book before she could pounce.

"Liar, you haven't even looked."

"Don't need to," I replied, turning over to the next page. "You look good in everything."

There was a disco at the town's rugby club tonight for the fourth years to celebrate their junior cert results. Instead of getting shit-faced with the lads beforehand, I was being held captive by a blond in a thong.

Apparently, my girlfriend needed my help to choose an *outfit* for tonight, and it was a matter of life or death.

This was a crock of shit for two reasons.

First, I had spent virtually every day with the girl since I was seven and never once had I heard her ask anyone's opinion on fashion. Liz couldn't care less about clothes if she tried. She wore what she wore when she wanted to wear it and that was the grand total of effort that went into her outfit picking.

Second, we had a momentary slip in the library last month, where I lost my head and spent the last three classes of the school day dry humping my girlfriend. Ever since that day Liz had been hell-bent on finding another hole in my moral chain-link fence.

It wasn't like I wanted to hold back. I was weeks away from turning fifteen. *Of course* I wanted to have sex with my girlfriend. Christ, I thought of little else, and I knew most of my friends were happily cracking on with different girls every weekend, but I couldn't do that. Because this was *Liz*, and I was determined to do the right thing by *her*.

We talked about it often and had agreed on her sixteenth birthday as the date. So when she pulled stunts like this one, it made being good a hell of a lot harder.

"So this dress is fine for tonight?" she challenged. "You'll be perfectly fine with me wearing *only* this to the disco?"

"Perfectly."

Her tone hardened. "So you'll be okay with your friends seeing your girlfriend completely *naked*."

I rolled my eyes. "You're not naked, Liz."

"Ha, so you *are* looking," she challenged, sounding gleeful.

"I may or may not have briefly glanced," I mused, pushing the glorious visual of Liz in a bra and thong to the back of my mind, but not before leaving a mental note to return to said visual when I was alone tonight. "Accidentally, of course."

"And?" she pushed. "What do you *accidently* think?"

That you're the most beautiful thing my eyes have ever seen.

"It's your body, Liz," I said instead, not giving her an inch. "You decide what you wear."

"And if I decide to wear nothing?"

"I'll bring a spare coat in case you get cold."

"Dammit, Hugh, just look at me so I can seduce you already!"

"So you admit it!" I exclaimed, snapping my book shut and pointing an accusing finger at her. "You sneaky, little, would-be virginity stealer!"

She feigned innocence. "I have no idea what you're talking about."

"Your underhanded tactics won't work on me, witch," I laughed. "I know every dirty trick in your sneaky, little handbook. Hell, I'm the muse for most of them!"

"I didn't invite you over to seduce you, asshole," she said, doubling down, this time in a much softer voice. Her breath hitched, and she looked up at me with a lonesome, puppy-eyed expression, bottom lip wobbling and everything. "I really needed your help with an outfit."

"Nice try," I replied, laughing into her face. "But you already pulled that trick on me one time too many. A plus for effort, though."

Her expression shifted in an instant, switching from angelic and frail to pissed off and frustrated. "You're such a killjoy, Hugh."

"Hmm." Thoroughly amused by her antics, I returned my attention to my book and exhaled a contented sigh. "Whatever keeps your clothes on, Liz."

"Oh yeah?" Unwilling to take the *L* like a champ, the little demon pounced on top of me, not stopping until she was straddling my hips. "We'll see about that, won't we?"

"Liz, stop." Choking out a laugh, I attempted to protect my sides from her ticklish onslaught with my book, but she was merciless. "You know I can't take it."

"Take my clothes off."

"Nope."

"Fine, take your clothes off."

"Ah, mercy, mercy…ah…ah…mercy, baby. Mercy!"

Using one hand to torment me with tickles, she pried the book from my hands with the other and tossed it over her shoulder.

Wrapping her hands around my wrists, she attempted to pin my hands to the mattress above my head.

I indulged her, allowing her to pin me down, because she was too fucking cute when she was playful.

"Ha." Grinning victoriously above me, she leaned in close and purred, "Joyce can't save you now, Biggs."

I smiled in amusement back at her. "You didn't save my page."

Her eyes narrowed to slits, and I choked on a laugh.

"Oh my God, you are *infuriating*!" Wiggling her hips, she rocked on top of my obvious hard-on. "I can *feel* you, Hugh. I *know* you want this as much as I do."

"I'm hard because I love you." Another laugh escaped me that seemed to only aggravate her more, which resulted in more laughter on my end. "Because you make me happy."

"Oh please." She rolled her eyes. "You're hard because you want to have sex with me." She threw her hands up in frustration. "And every part of your anatomy knows it *except* your brain!"

"What's the obsession with us having sex?"

"What's the obsession with abstaining from having sex?"

"We agreed to wait until your sixteenth birthday."

"I thought we agreed on *your* fifteenth."

"No, we definitely agreed on *your* sixteenth."

"Ugh." She released a despondent sigh. "But it's too far away."

"It's only a year and a half away." Settling my hands on her hips, I stroked her bare skin with my thumbs to soothe her. "What's another year and a half, huh?"

"A lifetime when you feel the way I do," she groaned, collapsing onto my chest with a loud huff. "You have no idea how frustrated I am, Hugh. You laugh about it and make a big joke out of it, but it's not funny to me. It actually hurts me. Like I feel physical pain because the urge is so strong. It's like an itch I can't scratch. All the time. Constantly. And I'm trying so hard...and you aren't interested, and I just...ugh, forget it."

"Liz." Sighing heavily, I wrapped an arm around her. "You know I'm interested." I reached up with one hand to stroke her cheek. "I want you so fucking bad it's all I can think about most days." I contemplated my next admission before blowing out a breath and saying to hell with it. "In the last two years, I can't think of a single night when I *haven't* gotten myself off to the mental image of being inside you."

"Really?" She sprang back up, lap-straddling resumed, and looked down at me with an excited glint in her eyes. "You're not bullshitting me?"

No, I wasn't bullshitting her.

I was being honest.

Painfully, embarrassingly honest.

"Would you take one look at yourself?" I replied and then made the mistake of taking my own advice. The sight of her straddling me in nothing but a frilly white bra and matching knickers caused a groan to escape. "Jesus Christ, you're so beautiful, it hurts to look at you. There's not another girl in my world that can hold a candle to you, and that's not an exaggeration because I haven't taken my eyes off you since I saw you on the school bus in first class."

Her breath hitched and she asked, "You really think that about me?"

"Yeah, Liz, I really do," I confirmed gruffly. "I always have."

"It's only the exterior," she whispered, gesturing to her body. "It's wallpaper, Hugh." An audible breath escaped her parted lips, and she cast her gaze downward. "I promise what's on the inside doesn't look like this."

"There's nothing ugly about you, Liz." When she didn't respond, I sat up and reached for her. "Hey...hey, look at me." Holding her face in my hands, I forced her to look at me. "There is *nothing* ugly *inside* of you."

"You don't know that." She clenched her eyes shut, blocking me out. "You don't know about the things I think about."

"I don't have to know about them." I smoothed her hair off her face and pulled her face closer to mine. "Because I know you."

"It's not just the thoughts." Her voice was small and broken. "It's the slips and the gaps and the urges."

Hearing her admit this out loud broke my fucking heart, because she was voicing both of our fears out loud. We'd had an amazing summer. Months of stability and calm. But we both knew that, at any moment in time, the shift could happen. "If you slip again, I'll be there to pull you back." Stroking her cheek with my thumb, I nuzzled her nose with mine. "And if you lose track of time, I'll be there to ground you." Unable to stop myself, I leaned in and pressed a kiss to her lips. "And if you feel the urges, I'll be there to protect you."

"I don't want to slip again," she choked out, fisting my T-shirt with a death grip. "I'm so afraid."

I couldn't tell her that it wouldn't happen, because we both knew that would be a lie.

All I could do was promise her that if it happened, I would be there on the other side.

"I'll be here." I kissed her again. "Always."

"No matter what?"

"Yeah, Liz." I kissed her softly. "No matter what."

WHEN THE CAT'S AWAY, THE KITTENS PLAY

Lizzie

OCTOBER 31, 2002

SINEAD BIGGS HAD ALWAYS THROWN THE SPLASHIEST, NO-EXPENSE-SPARED BIRTHDAY parties for her children. Because her son was born on Halloween, their house had always been the place to be on the spookiest night of the year.

The only difference this year was Pete's cousin's wedding fell on the same day. The wedding was up the country and would be a weekend event, so instead of canceling her son's party, Sinead enlisted the help of her father to hold the fort in her stead.

Leaving Grandad Healy in charge for the weekend was her first mistake.

Leaving the liquor cabinet in the good room unlocked was her second.

What was intended to be a sensible gathering of friends to celebrate her son's fifteenth birthday had quickly veered into the mother of all house parties—with Grandad Healy at the helm of the chaos.

After spending a solid hour and a half locked in a battle of wills with Claire over Halloween costumes—and my lack of desire to wear one—we had finally joined the others downstairs.

The moment we stepped off the last step of the staircase, we were instantly swallowed up by a crowd of drunk teenagers. Not only was the entire ground level of the house heaving with costume-clad peers from school but the music blasting from one of the sixth-year boy's decks was deafeningly loud.

"This is amazing!" Claire exclaimed as she bopped around to "Whoomp! (There It Is)."

She looked ridiculously cute in blue, spandex dungaree shorts, thigh-high white socks, matching white gloves, and a cropped, skintight red shirt. Perched on top of her straightened, blond hair was a matching red hat with the letter *M*.

"I have a camel toe in these damn dungarees," I grumbled, readjusting the skintight fabric at my crotch. Because *of course* we were in matching costumes. "Okay, and *now* I have a wedgie."

"That's because you have a long back," Claire offered in a supportive tone, as she straightened my green hat. "You are the hottest Luigi I have ever seen."

"Yeah, yeah." I rolled my eyes. "Right back at ya, Mario."

She smiled approvingly at the outfit she had managed to emotionally blackmail me into wearing only to frown when she noticed my well-worn high-tops.

"*Converse*, Liz?" Claire expelled a frustrated growl. "You are *supposed* to wear the green heels to match my red ones."

"Don't push your luck, Biggs," I laughed, holding a hand up. "Just be glad I'm wearing everything else."

"Holy fuck!" some random lad dressed as Batman exclaimed, coming to stand in front of us. "I think I've died and gone to heaven, girls."

"Keep holding your breath and maybe you will," I shot back, instantly on edge.

"Well, Luigi's clearly on the rag," the asshole laughed before turning his attention to Claire. "What about you, Mario?" He stepped closer and stroked her chin. The alcohol wafting from his breath was stifling. "Fancy taking a trip to Mushroom Mountain with me?"

"Fancy eating through a feeding tube?" I cut in, smacking his lingering hand away. "Touch my friend again and it's a done deal, *Batman*."

"Christ," he growled, planting his hands on his hips. "You're a real bitch, aren't ya?"

"Better a bitch than a prick," I shot back before catching ahold of Claire's hand and walking away.

"That was really mean, Liz," Claire scolded, hooking her arm through mine as we maneuvered through the mob—a mob that included her grandfather dancing on the kitchen island top. "He was just being friendly."

"He was being a dog," I corrected, keeping a protective eye on the gorgeous picture of innocence next to me. "And *you* need to keep your guard up."

"How come?"

"Because girls like you look like juicy bones to dogs like him."

Her eyes widened to saucers. "Why would he think I'm a bone?"

"Never mind," I sighed, knowing in my heart that she wasn't quite grasping my meaning. I was fourteen months older than her and acutely aware that I knew things no one her age should. "Just be careful, okay?"

"Okay, Liz." Big, brown eyes full of innocence stared back at me. "I will."

"Good." Nodding, I smiled back at her. "Because I only want to keep you safe."

Claire's gaze flicked to something behind me then, and her entire face lit up before a surge of panic filled her eyes. "Liz." Her eyes flicked to mine, and she pointed over my shoulder. "Are you going to be okay if I go and talk to Gerard?"

Attending the same school, on top of the forced proximity of sharing the same friendship circle, had helped build my tolerance levels up, but I wasn't naive enough to believe I would be okay if *he* came over to speak to me.

"I'll be fine," I squeezed out, using every ounce of strength I had inside of me to *not* overreact. To *not* blow a fuse and scream. Because I wanted to. I *really* fucking wanted to.

Christ, I couldn't even *think* his name in my head, let alone speak it. On the rare occasion I had to address him by name, I used the only word that seemed to come out: the childhood pet name I had given him.

It hurt a little less that way, and I could manipulate my mind to separate the two. *Because the monster never said the name Thor.*

"It's okay if you want to hang out with Thor for a bit, Claire." I tried to smile then, truly I did, but from her reaction, I knew it had to look like a pained grimace. "I'm fine with it."

Claire didn't look convinced. "Really?"

"Really." I nodded. "I'll be fine, I promise."

"Okay, now I feel even worse about how I reacted on my birthday," she declared before snatching my hands up and going on a full-blown tangent. "I'm so sorry for making you feel bad for being with my brother. I didn't mean to, I swear. I was just afraid you were going to stop hanging out with me and spend all your time with Hugh. And I think I might have been a little jealous, too. But I'm over it, okay? I swear it, and I won't try to block you guys anymore. I know how important you are to my brother, and I don't want to be that mean girl."

"You have *never* been a mean girl, Claire, and I'm never going to stop hanging out with you," I promised, squeezing her hand. "You're the Mario to my Luigi, after all."

"I know, I know," she hurried to concede. "But I think it had more to do with Hugh asking you to be his girlfriend and Gerard *not* asking me—which I know you probably don't want to hear me say," she added with a wince. "Sorry."

"It's okay," I forced myself to say because I couldn't project my pain on her. "I *can't* be the friend you confide in about Thor, but I will *always* be the friend in your corner."

Her eyes lit up with excitement. "And I can't be the friend you talk to about my brother—because that's just ew—but I will *always* be the friend in your corner, too."

"Okay then." I smiled. "It's a deal."

"It's a double deal," Claire squealed, bouncing from foot to foot excitedly. "But not a double date."

"No," I confirmed, shaking my head. "*Never* a double date."

After briefly hugging it out, Claire scampered off in search of Thor, while I went in the opposite direction, in search of her brother. When I found him in the lounge, necking shots in front of the fireplace with his grandfather, a warm flush of heat swept through me.

Sighing in contentment, I leaned against the archway and took a moment to just *look* at him.

Unlike almost everyone else at the party, Hugh wasn't dressed up in a costume. Standing apart from the crowd, my boyfriend wore dark jeans and a tightly fitting white shirt, with the sleeves rolled up to his elbows, revealing his ridiculously sexy, corded forearms. His hair was styled in that sickeningly sexy way he always wore it: tight around the sides and back, with a mop of sexily tousled curls on top, held in place by a dollop of gel.

Clocking in at an impressive six feet in height and still growing, Hugh couldn't have looked more different to the boy I lost my heart to at the age of six. The softness of his face had become more sharply defined, while his once-lean stomach now sported an impressive ripple of finely carved abdominal muscles to go with the generous dusting of hair that began at his navel and trailed beneath the waistband of his boxers. His back was broader, his biceps more prominent, and he possessed a pair of gloriously strong legs, with rock-hard thigh and calf muscles.

And this is the boy I am supposed to not touch!

"Back in my day, you were a man at fifteen," Grandad Healy exclaimed, dragging me back to the present. Thick as thieves with his favorite grandchild—and a bottle of Jameson—he filled two glasses with amber liquid before handing one to Hugh.

"I can't drink another one, Granda. It tastes like shit," Hugh groaned, staring into the amber-filled tumbler in his hands. "Maybe I should stick to cans."

"Leave the cans for the boys and the whiskey for the men." Draping an arm around his grandson, the old man clinked their glasses together before knocking his drink back in one impressive gulp. "This will put hair on your chest, my cherished namesake."

"Aw, fuck it," Hugh groaned before quickly tossing the drink back, only to splutter and cough violently afterward. "It's worse than shit," he strangled out, sounding hoarse. Setting his glass down on the mantelpiece they were leaning against, Hugh looked at his grandfather and said, "You know what? I think I'll live without the hairy chest." He wiped his mouth with the back of his hand before adding, "I've enough of it everywhere else." He glanced in my direction then, only to do a quick double take when he registered me standing there. His eyes widened to saucers in surprise. "Holy fuck."

Now *that* "holy fuck" reaction was one I was more than happy to hear. Grinning, I pushed off the wall and walked over, loving the way his eyes never once left my body.

"Happy birthday," I announced with a smile when I reached his side. Hugh automatically raised his arm for me to take my place at his side, which I did without hesitation. "Having fun?"

"I am now." His arm came around my shoulders, pulling me closer, while his eyes continued to rake over me. "You look incredible."

Maybe Claire was onto something with this whole costume thing...

"Hey, Granda Healy," I said, turning my attention to the old man grinning at Hugh. "It's been a while."

"Too long, Elizabeth," the mischievous old man replied, shaking my hand while smirking at Hugh. "And a relief to know my grandson had the good sense to hold on to you." He winked again at Hugh. "Good lad, yourself."

"Like I'd be thick enough to let her go," Hugh chuckled, tucking me into his side. He dropped a kiss to my head before adding, "Liz is the one, Granda."

Oh God.

My entire body burned with heat. The way he so openly claimed me as his, even to his grandfather, made me feel like I might be actually *worth* something.

———————————————

Several hours and several alcoholic beverages later, I found myself getting a piggyback from the sexiest fly half in Ballylaggin.. *Maybe even the whole wide world.*

"I think we might be a small bit drunk, Hugh," I snickered on our fourth attempt to reach the top of the stairs. Well, Hugh's fourth attempt. I was hitching a ride on his back. "And I think"—I paused to hiccup—"it's from Granda Healy's whiskey."

"Oh, I *know* it is," my boyfriend grumbled, fighting hard with his feet to go in the same direction. He had lost his coordination, right along with his shirt. "My grandfather is a demon."

"Your grandfather is a legend," I cackled and then quickly cheered when we reached the landing. "Yay! My hero!"

"Do you need to pee?" he asked when he crashed against the bathroom door. "Go now if you do because your carriage is making a beeline for his bed."

I thought about it for a moment and shook my head. "Nope."

"You sure?"

"Yep."

"All right then." Staggering toward his bedroom door, he pushed it open with his head and slurred, "Prepare for a soft landing, baby."

"Uh, a little privacy!" some random girl squealed, as she rolled around on my boyfriend's bed with a vaguely familiar-looking boy on top of her.

"Goddammit, Feely!"

"My apologies, Hughie."

"Out!" Hugh ordered, leaning heavily against the door to support both our weights. "Now!"

"Yeah, *Feely*," I snickered, watching through bleary eyes as our friend grabbed a pile of clothes and hurried out of the room, with a semi-naked girl hot on his heels.

"Prick," Hugh grumbled, kicking the door shut behind them before stumbling toward the bed. "Timber!" he warned moments before faceplanting into the mattress with me still on his back. "Feely better not have fucked her in my bed."

"He still had his jocks on," I offered, flopping onto my back beside him. "But the blond he was dry-humping didn't have a stitch on her."

"See, that's some horseshit right there," my boyfriend slurred, dragging a pillow under his head. "He knows you're the only blond allowed to get naked in my bed."

"Yeah right," I snorted, reaching over to pat his shoulder. "If I were naked in your bed, you'd throw holy water on me and cart me off to confession."

"Not tonight, I wouldn't."

Snickering, I turned to look at his face and grinned. "Are you saying you want me naked in your bed?"

"I never *not* want you naked in my bed." Lying on his stomach, with his arms wrapped around the pillow and his head angled toward me, Hugh whispered, "Thanks for coming home, baby."

"Home?" My heart skipped four solid beats, and a violent shiver racked through me. "How am I home, Hugh?"

With a heated expression, he pulled up on one elbow and reached for me with his free hand. "Because you belong in this house." Cupping the back of my head, he drew me closer. "You belong in this bed." Fisting my hair, Hugh angled my chin up to his and traced his tongue over my bottom lip before pulling back to look in my eyes. "You belong with me."

And then he crushed his lips to mine.

The moment his tongue entered my mouth, I knew I was a goner. The familiar feeling of filth and unease was replaced with a desperate yearning. His hands were on my body, pulling me closer, and the feel of him, so strong and warm and real, breathed life into my fractured soul. I was broken inside, truly rotten to the core, but I felt my redemption in his kiss.

Desperate to taste him back, my lips opened of their own accord, accepting his offering like my body had been programmed to receive this boy. His tongue coaxed mine almost lovingly, with soft, drugging swipes that caused my nipples to harden painfully in their bid to snatch his attention.

Overcome by the sensations thrashing through my body, I tugged on his shoulders until he rolled on top of me. Welcoming his weight, I let my thighs fall open to bring him closer, shivering in delight when his metal buckle rubbed against me. "Mm."

Layers of horrible clothes separated our flesh, and it made me so fucking mad. Beyond agitated, I dug my fingers into his back, shivering in pleasure when he strained against me. I wanted him so much, I wanted to cry.

"Are you okay?" he asked, lips moving to my neck as he pushed me deeper into the mattress, hips rocking in perfect synchrony with mine. "Is this okay?"

"You know it is," I breathed, fisting his hair while I rubbed myself against him. "Start touching me."

"Where?"

"Everywhere."

DRUNKEN FUMBLES

Hugh

ROLLING ME ONTO MY BACK, LIZ STRADDLED MY HIPS AND KISSED ME WITH A DESPER-
ation that matched mine. Too drunk to care about my erection I *knew* was digging into
her, I threw caution to the wind and *enjoyed* the moment.

I didn't slam the brakes as she peeled the straps of her dungarees down her arms,
and I didn't protest when she whipped her green shirt off, either.

When she momentarily climbed off my lap to remove her dungarees, I reveled in
the glorious view, and when she took my hands in hers and pressed them to her glorious
tits, I died and went to heaven.

Because she was perfect.

Honest to God, this girl was heaven on earth to me.

Unable to stop myself, I let my eyes rake over her full, perky tits and gorgeous rose-
tipped nipples that seemed to strain toward me. Releasing a groan of arousal, I gently
traced the swell of her breasts before moving to her nipples. "You're so fucking sexy."

"I want you so bad," my girlfriend moaned, hips bucking wildly on top of me, while
she pushed at my hands. "Touch me everywhere."

Happy to oblige, I flipped her onto her back and moved between her thighs. "We're
not having sex," I declared, words slurred as I hitched her thigh around my waist. The
move caused our bodies to align in the most primal of ways and both of us to moan in
pleasure. "Just touching."

"Fine, fine, whatever you want," Liz moaned, digging her nails into my back. "Just
don't stop."

"Feel me?"

"I feel you, Hugh."

"That's how much I want you."

"Really?"

The alcohol flowing through my bloodstream allowed me to be achingly vulnerable with her. "I want to be inside you."

"I want that, too."

"I'm just waiting," I admitted, straining against her. "We agreed your sixteenth."

"I don't think I can wait that long, Hugh."

Neither do I.

Shivering, I covered her breasts with my hands at the same time I covered her lips with mine. Jesus, she was perfect.

Drunk or not, I had the mental capacity to know this girl was my entire world and if I ever did something she wasn't ready for, I honestly wouldn't be able to live with myself.

What that prick did to her sister was always in the back of my mind, and I think Grandad's whiskey had finally forced me to acknowledge it was the driving factor behind my standoffish approach to intimacy.

"It's okay," Liz encouraged, seeming to hear my thoughts aloud as she pushed my head downward. "I *want* your touch."

Kissing a trail from her lips to her neck and then her collarbone, I slowly made the descent down her body until my tongue circled one of her pebbled nipples.

"Yes." Her breath hitched and her hands shot out to fist my hair. "Don't stop."

Obliging, I used my lips, fingers, and tongue to make myself acquainted with this once-forbidden part of her anatomy.

"I think it might happen," she moaned, pushing herself into my face. "I think it might, Hugh."

"Are you okay with that?"

Nodding eagerly, she clenched her eyes shut and writhed beneath me. "I need more." And then, grabbing my hand in hers, she pushed it between her thighs. "More here."

Holy fuck, I was learning on the job tonight.

Pulling up on one elbow, I glanced down at her flushed expression, while my fingers traced the lacy fabric between her legs. "Are you sure it's okay for me to touch you here?"

"If you don't, I think I'll scream," she moaned, rocking her hips against my hand. "Please touch me."

Before I could talk myself out of it, I slid my hand under the scrap of lace and lightly traced one finger up and down her slit before gently pushing one finger inside her.

"Move inside me," she instructed, breathing hard and uneven. "Crook your finger...mm, yeah, just like that."

"Is that okay?"

"Yeah, yeah, please," Liz cried out, frantically bucking her hips into my touch. "Keep going, Hugh. Please, please! Make me better."

Make her better?

It was a strange comment to make in the throes of passion, but I was too drunk and too fucking lost in the moment to care. Overcome by lust, I relished how tight and hot and wet she felt.

"Tell me what to do now," I whispered, feeling uncertain, because this was her body, and I had no fucking clue what I was doing. "What should I do?"

"More," she commanded with a shudder. "More."

"Fingers?"

"Yes." Flush faced and frantic, she rubbed herself against me while I gently eased another finger inside her.

"Is that okay?" I asked a few seconds later when she started to tighten around my fingers. "Liz, are you okay?"

She didn't answer me with words, only breathy moans, and she jerked violently and her eyes rolled back.

This continued for several seconds before her entire body went completely lax.

"Whoa," she breathed as a smile began to spread across her face. "That was amazing."

Feeling proud of myself, I gently withdrew my fingers and smiled.

"Look at that grin," she teased, reaching up to squeeze my cheek. "You look like the cat that got the cream."

"Uh, *Liz*."

"Sorry. Bad analogy."

LIKE A SHARK SMELLING BLOOD

Hugh

DECEMBER 21, 2002

MY GRANDFATHER WAS A LOT OF THINGS, BUT A SQUEALER WASN'T ONE OF THEM. NOT only did he manage to sway Old Murphy into keeping his mouth shut about the antics on my birthday, but he took the rap for a large wine stain on Mam's white carpet in the good room that no amount of scrubbing could remove. And God knows we scrubbed that fucking carpet.

All in all, my first dabble into underage debauchery had been a roaring success for all but one glaring snag. In my drunken haze, I'd taken my girlfriend into my bed that night and touched her in places I had no business touching.

When I woke up the following morning and found her in my bed, I damn near had a heart attack. The only thing that had stopped me from having a full-blown panic attack was the fact that we *still* had our underwear on.

Liz, on the other hand, had a much more positive reaction to our drunken shenanigans and had been ramping up the heat on our relationship ever since.

Clearly, my girlfriend had caught the scent of my rapidly depleting willpower and was circling me like a shark.

"You better swim for your life, Biggs," Liz teased as we splashed around in the pool on the first Saturday of Christmas break. "Because I'm going to pants you."

"No, no, no," I warned through fits of laughter, as I threw myself backwards in my futile attempt to avoid the little witch that had disappeared under the water. "Don't you dare, Lizzie Young," I started to shout but it was too late. With a firm grip of my shorts, Liz yanked them down around my knees.

When her head reemerged from the water, she grinned devilishly. "Told ya."

"You're such a menace," I laughed, quickly yanking them back up and swimming off before she could catch me again.

"Dammit, Hugh," Liz complained, trying and failing to keep up with me. "I swear half of your genetics were switched with a mermaid."

"More like a shark," I called over my shoulder.

"Nah, you're too pretty to be a shark," she grumbled back. "You're definitely half-mermaid."

"Don't be so sure about that," I warned before diving under the water and making a beeline for her legs.

Pushing my head between her thighs, I stood up and took her with me on my shoulders.

Squealing with delight, Liz balanced awkwardly on my shoulders before letting herself flop backwards, taking me with her.

When we emerged again, our limbs were a tangled mess.

"You look like Simba in the film when he fell in the water," I laughed, pointing at the clumps of blond hair hanging over her face.

Smirking, she cupped the back of my head and yanked me close before spurting a mouthful of water at me.

"Lovely," I sighed, while Liz cracked up laughing. "My girlfriend's spit." I wiped my mouth. "Just what I wanted for Christmas."

"Why don't we sneak into the sauna room, and I can give you your real present," Liz purred, hooking an arm around my neck. "It's a one-of-a-kind gift," she continued to tease, wrapping her legs around my waist. "And we'll both enjoy the unwrapping part."

"You keep those sneaky, little fingers away," I warned when I felt her hand slide under the waistband of my swimming trunks. "Liz, *please*," I grunted when she gripped my ass hard. "You're killing me here."

"Not nearly as much as you're killing me," she whispered, lips moving against mine before her tongue snaked out to taste mine.

Fuck me, this girl was something else.

"I know what you're trying to do," I growled, feeling myself turn to rock. "And it won't work."

"Yeah, it will," she replied breathily. "Because it's like you said: I belong with you." She gripped my ass hard again before whispering, "And you belong in me."

"Jesus, Liz," I groaned, unable to take the pressure in both my heart and shorts. "You can't say things like that."

"Why not?" she purred, hips rocking against mine as I held her up in the water. "And don't call me Liz. Call me baby."

"Okay."

"Say it now."

"Baby."

"Call me baby again."

"Baby."

512

"Mm," she moaned in approval before resuming teasing my tongue with hers.

Could people get arrested for kissing in swimming pools? It was something I was going to have to search up. Because the way her tongue was skillfully massaging mine in such an erotic manner, yet in such a public setting, made it feel illegal.

Just when I felt like I was drowning in her kiss, she ripped her mouth from mine and whispered, "I have dirty thoughts, Hugh." Pressing her lips to my ear, she traced my earlobe with her tongue before saying, "Filthy urges."

"Don't worry about it." I hissed out a breath when I felt her teeth on my neck. "I have plenty of those, too."

"Do you touch yourself and think about me?" she stunned me by whispering in my ear. "Because I do." Her tongue was on my ear again. "I push my fingers inside my underwear and pretend it's you inside me again."

"Fuck me."

"That's what I pretend you're doing to me," she continued to torment me by whispering. "Is that bad?" I felt her shiver in my arms. "Am I bad person for craving those things?"

"You're not bad," I replied, forcing her to look at me and instantly recognizing the look in her pale-blue eyes as one of uncertainty. "You're just horny." *And so am I.*

"The doctors keep asking me about it," she offered then. "Whenever I have an appointment, they bring it up."

"What?" I frowned. "They bring up *horniness*?"

She nodded slowly. "Apparently, it can be a sign."

"Of what?"

"An incoming episode." She swallowed deeply. "It can be common for teens with bipolar."

"I think feeling horny is common for all teens, Liz," I said, trying to soothe her. "Bipolar or not."

"I don't want it to happen again, Hugh," she admitted quietly while her gaze dropped. "What happened last summer." Another shiver racked through her body, and she sighed heavily. "I just want to be normal."

"What did I tell you about normal?" I asked her, determined to put on a brave face while my heart broke inside. "Hmm?"

"It doesn't exist."

"Exactly." Stroking her nose with mine, I pressed a kiss to each of her cheeks before pecking her lips. "And whatever this is"—I pulled back to look in her eyes—"whatever we've built, with your mind and mine, is *everything* I want."

THE DARK DAYS AREN'T OVER

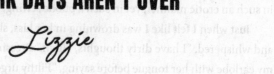

Lizzie

DECEMBER 25, 2002

THE SOUND OF MY PARENTS SCREAMING HAD INTENSIFIED TO THE POINT WHERE I WAS glad that we lived on such a sprawling property. If we had neighbors living closer, the Gardaí would have been at the door.

Numb, I sat with my back to my bedroom door, listening to the accusations being thrown back and forth on the landing.

Nothing they were accusing each other of was new to me. I'd heard these fights a hundred times before, but the holidays always brought out the worst in my parents. Because it brought out the pain.

Sitting around the table for Christmas dinner with my sister's empty chair was a stark reminder of how we would never be a family again.

It didn't matter how well things went or how hard I tried.

I would never be enough for them to be happy.

I would never be enough for my father.

PLUCKING UP COURAGE

Lizzie

JANUARY 14, 2003

"Well, if it isn't the famous five assembled in my kitchen," Sinead called out in a cheerful tone when she sauntered into the kitchen on Friday evening. "Not that I don't love all your bright, little faces, but isn't there another mother's kitchen you would like to descend on for a change?"

We all stared blankly at her.

"No? Okay then." Setting a couple of carrier bags full of groceries on the counter, she turned her attention to the kitchen table. "Do we have to have the talk, people?"

"No, we don't," Hugh groaned, burying his face in my neck.

"Tables are for glasses not for asses, Gibs, love" came Sinead's first instruction, followed swiftly by, "Dear daughter of mine, please refrain from licking spilled honey from the tablecloth—and no, that doesn't mean you can stick your finger in the jar, either, my feral, little offspring."

"Will do, Sinead." Hopping down from the table, Thor sauntered toward where Sinead was standing and unashamedly began to raid her shopping bags for snacks. Meanwhile, Patrick, the sneak, was already righting his wrong by hiding his drumsticks under the table.

"Why thank you, Patrick, pet," Sinead said approvingly. "In future, though, please refrain from using my solid oak table as a soundboard for your rhythm sticks."

"My apologies, Sinead," Patrick replied, red-faced, while Claire grumbled something about a five-second rule.

Turning her attention to the opposite side of the table, her warm, brown eyes locked on mine and her brow arched.

"Lizzie, sweetheart, while I'm sure my hormone-ridden, teenage son has a comfortable lap, what's left of my good nerves will be much more comfortable with your backside on a chair."

"Sorry, Sinead," I muttered, quickly sliding onto the seat next to Hugh, while he grumbled something unintelligible under his breath.

"So what's the plan of action for tonight, kids?" Using her hip to butt Thor out of her way, Sinead set to work on putting the shopping away, expertly snatching packets of crips and chocolate bars out of his greedy, little hands as she moved. "Anything exciting planned?"

The others quickly descended into a conversation with Sinead Biggs, while I remained quiet, observing my surroundings.

Smothering my frustration at *his* presence with personal aggression, I discretely settled my hands on my lap under the table and used my long nails to scratch at an itch I was sure I could never fully sate.

Feeling restless, I bit down on the inside of my cheek until I tasted the familiar tang of copper.

Relief flooded me.

It was almost euphoric.

Because the pain weakened my mind's grasp on its rage.

It was how I had learned to function.

To bury it all down.

It was at that moment that a larger hand came to rest on top of mine.

My boyfriend's touch was gentle but unyielding, and when he parted my hands, separating my nails from the flesh they were tearing, I could do nothing but let him.

Taking one of my hands in his, Hugh entwined our fingers and settled our joined hands on his lap.

Heart racing, I held my breath for a long beat, both reveling in the sensation of having his skin on mine and dreading his reaction to my mistake.

When I plucked up the courage to look at him, his attention was cast downward, to his lap. A deep frown was set on his face as he methodically studied every spare inch of skin on my hand.

My eyes drank in the sight of him and made the rest of the world seem to fade and quieten. His tanned fingers, so much longer than mine, trailed over my flesh, sending sparks of life back into my body. His thumb traced over each one of my knuckles before moving to the inside of my wrist.

Startled, I moved to pull my hand away, but he was unyielding. Turning my hand over, Hugh continued his mission of killing me with his touch, thumb tracing the jagged edges of every self-borne scar I had inflicted on my flesh. He didn't falter and he didn't recoil. He touched my skin with a reverence that could never be matched. Not in a hundred thousand lifetimes.

That's how I knew that I would never get over this boy.

For the rest of this life and whatever followed—be it heaven, hell, purgatory, or a thousand reincarnated lifetimes—my heart would eternally beat for Hugh Biggs.

That was also how I found the strength to be here, in his home, enduring the discomforting company of a boy who made both my skin crawl and the voices in my head grow louder.

I was doing this for *Hugh*.

YOU'RE MY BABY
Lizzie

APRIL 15, 2003

"Okay, I'm finished," Hugh declared three hours deep into a revision session during Easter break. Closing the textbook on his lap, he tossed it onto his bed with all the others and leaned back on his pillow. "I have officially retained every word of the course syllabus."

"Not so fast, buddy." Swiveling around on his desk chair to face him, I arched a brow in challenge. "Name a gas the earthworm produces during respiration."

He rolled his eyes. "Carbon dioxide."

"What's the chemical name for marble chips?"

Another eye roll. "Calcium carbonate."

"Give me the name of the two products formed when sodium reacts with water."

"Sodium hydroxide." He rolled a piece of paper into a ball and tossed it at me. "And hydrogen gas."

"Now explain refraction of light," I laughed, dodging the airborne missile.

"The bending of light when it passes from one medium into another," he reeled off, sounding bored. "Can we do something else now?"

"Nope." I shook my head. "Not until you list the first thirty elements on the periodic table."

"Seriously?" Hugh grumbled, sounding impatient. "I could do that in my sleep."

Yeah, I knew he could, but his ability to retain and recite fascinated me. "Hey, you're the one sitting his junior cert exams in June," I laughed, holding my hands up. "I'm just trying to be a supportive girlfriend."

"If that's the case, then feel free to support me," he replied with a smirk, patting the mattress. "I could always use a refresher course in human biology."

My body burned with heat when he said that because I knew he meant it. Clearly, something had changed between us that day in the library, because not only was Hugh not slamming the brakes on touching, but he was starting to *initiate* it.

"Do you have any idea how attractive you are?" I mused, enchanted by this boy. "Seriously, you are the sexiest nerd alive."

"You're calling *me* a nerd?" Rolling off his bed, my boyfriend prowled toward me, shirtless and in a pair of low-slung shorts. "You're a bigger bookworm than I am."

"True," I mused, eyes raking over his glorious six-pack. "But I don't care about school like you do."

"Because you're a little rebel." A shiver racked through me when Hugh placed his hands on the armrests of my chair and leaned in close, caging me in. "Aren't ya?"

"Maybe," I breathed, heart bucking wildly, when my legs opened of their own accord, and he slid between them. "But I'm your rebel."

"No." His lips brushed against mine as he spoke. "You're my baby."

RAISED TO BE A GENTLEMAN

Hugh

MAY 31, 2003

My junior cert exams were kicking off next week, and instead of revising like I *should've* been, I found myself entertaining two blond terrors.

"Use the cheat," Liz instructed from her perch on my bed, while she inhaled more than her fair share of our bag of microwavable popcorn.

"Come on, Hugh," she complained, pointing at the television screen, where I was attempting to dominate a game of *GTA*. "You'll never outrun the cops with three stars."

"Wanna bet?" I muttered under my breath, tapping furiously on the controller in my hands, while I drove through the streets of Vice City like a maniac. "Watch me." The words were no sooner out of my mouth than three sneaky cop cars crashed into my car.

"Hah! Told you so." Looking smug, Liz tossed a piece of popcorn in her mouth. "Should've listened to me, Biggs."

This playful side of Liz was a rare and glorious sight, because life had hardened my baby, but tonight she was basking in her youth. In this moment, she looked *happy*.

"How are you so perfect?" Claire groaned, poking at my girlfriend's stomach. "You eat like a full-grown man, and you get to keep that washboard stomach."

"What are you talking about?" Liz laughed, tossing a piece of popcorn at her head only for it to get stuck in her mop of curls. "You're the perfect one, with your Shakira hips."

"I dance every day to keep these hips at bay. Meanwhile, you can eat whatever you want and still roll up looking like a bloody runway prodigy."

"Oh, cop on," my girlfriend tossed back, entirely uninterested in having the insecure-girl talk. "That's the biggest load of bollocks I've ever heard."

I grinned to myself and continued to tap on the controller.

That's my baby.

"You know you're a complete ride, Claire, so stop fishing for compliments."

"No, *I'm* the cute and endearing one," my sister argued. "*You're* the complete ride."

"You've got that right," I chimed in, causing Liz to snicker and Claire to groan.

"Ew, Hugh," she snapped. "I'm legit right here."

I shrugged unapologetically, retraining my attention on the game. It was bad enough that I couldn't hold my girlfriend's hand when my sister was around without sending her into a meltdown; I'd be damned if I couldn't pay her a compliment. Because even though Claire had relaxed about our relationship in recent months, Liz still refused to participate in public displays of affection. Seriously, it was so bad, she wouldn't even hold my hand at school, let alone kiss me. We didn't eat lunch together, either, but that had a lot more to do with the company I kept at the rugby table than my sister.

Claire was accurate in her assessment of Liz, though.

She *was* a complete and utter ride of a girl.

"Okay, enough of the stinky *boy's* room," Claire declared. Bouncing to her feet, she grabbed my girlfriend's hand and pulled her up. "We have a movie night to prepare for."

"Okay, okay," Liz laughed. "I'm coming."

"Have fun," I said, stretching up for a kiss from my girlfriend, only to receive a platonic pat on the head instead.

Thanks, Claire.

Later that night, when my mother lured me down to the lounge with the prospect of watching the movie adaption of her favorite book together, I should have known it was a trap. Instead of pressing play on *Falling for a Dancer*, when I joined her on the couch, Mam turned to look at me and said, "We need to talk."

"About what?"

"You and Lizzie," Mam confirmed, setting her reading glasses on her lap. "Are you doing things with her?"

Aw, fuck.

Here we go.

"Yeah, Mam, I'm doing things with her," I replied, not even bothering trying to deny it. What was the point? A blind man could see that I was head over heels for the girl. "I'm with her."

"And when you say 'with her,' what exactly does that entail?" Mam asked.

"It means I'm hers and she's mine."

"In what context, Hugh?"

"In every context, Mam."

"I'm looking for more information on the physical, son."

Yeah, I knew she was, and I was desperately trying to steer the conversation *away* from that information.

"She's younger than you, Hugh," Mam pushed. "You're *both* very *young*."

"By eight months," I reminded her, feeling my back go up. "And I'm aware of how old we are, Mam."

"Then you're also aware that you're far too young to have an intimate relationship."

"Define intimate."

"Sexual intimacy, Hugh."

"We're not doing anything like *that*," I offered, shifting in discomfort. "We kiss, Mam. That's it."

She arched a disbelieving brow. "Don't lie to me."

Aw, crap.

Aw, crap.

"We're both virgins," I tossed out, feeling my palms sweat. "And I intend to keep it that way for a long time."

Her brown eyes locked on mine, clearly taking my measure, before she let out a shaky breath. "I'm relieved to hear that, son, because I raised you to be a gentleman."

"Yeah," I croaked out. "And I'm being one, Mam."

BIRTHDAY TRIPS TO THE BEACH

Lizzie

JUNE 8, 2003

WE DIDN'T LIVE FAR FROM THE COAST, A TWENTY-MINUTE DRIVE, WHICH MADE ORGA-nizing transport a breeze on sunny days. When Mam dropped us off at the beach this morning, Hugh and I spent the whole day splashing around in the ocean, exploring rock pools, and lazing about on the sand.

Because my boyfriend was knee-deep in exams, with another stacked week ahead, including my fifteenth birthday tomorrow, we decided to celebrate today, instead.

"Don't even think about it," he warned later that afternoon when we decided to take a stroll up the cliffs.

"Oh, come on," I coaxed, taking a step closer to the edge. "It'll be fun."

"True, but you're not a strong enough swimmer." Catching ahold of my hand, Hugh pulled me back to him. "And you're fully dressed."

"Clothes can be removed, Hugh," I teased, wrapping my arms around his waist. "Come on." I pressed a kiss to his cheek. "Live a little."

"And if you drown?"

"How can I drown if I have a life buoy?" I shot back with a wink, wiggling my foot to jingle my ankle bracelet. "And a merman for a boyfriend."

"Shark, not merman," he corrected, a smile creeping across his face. "You really want to do this?"

I nodded eagerly. "It can be my birthday present."

"You already got your birthday present," he replied, gesturing to the shiny new semicolon charm attached to my bracelet.

"And I love it," I agreed, pecking his lips. "Almost as much as I love you."

"All right, all right, you win," he chuckled, hands moving to my waist. "Let's do this."

"Yay!"

Lifting me up with freakish ease, my boyfriend instructed me to wrap my arms and legs around him, while melding my chest to his. "Don't let go," he instructed, hooking one arm around my waist and taking several steps back. "You ready?"

"I won't," I squealed excitedly, burying my face in his neck. "And yeah, I'm ready."

Hugh ran at full speed toward the edge of the cliff and then launched our joined bodies over the edge.

Screaming with delight, I clenched my eyes shut as the wind whipped at my face. The exhilarating feeling was nothing like I had expected. It was so much more, and I quickly realized that I had been missing out all these years, sitting on the shoreline, watching my boyfriend participating in this thrilling pastime.

When we crashed into the ocean, the water sucked us down, and I instinctively kicked my legs. Instantly, I felt a hand grab mine and I was surging toward the surface.

"Holy shit!" Hugh screeched when we broke the surface. "This is freezing."

He was right. The water was perishing, but my adrenaline was pumping on full throttle, and my body was thrumming with a reckless sort of energy.

"That was amazing!" I shrieked, hooking an arm around my boyfriend's broad shoulders as he treaded water. "Can we do it again?"

Hugh grinned. "Oh yeah."

"Holy shit, I'm freezing," Hugh announced when we made it back to the block of changing rooms opposite the beach. Peeling off his soaked T-shirt, he bounced around from foot to foot. "I can't feel my nuts."

"Hah!" Grinning, I unbuttoned the front of my equally drenched dress and let the fabric fall from my shoulders. "How do you think I feel with razors for nipples?"

"No clue, but you look amazing." Turning his back to me, Hugh pushed his shorts and boxers down and gave me a glorious view of his bare ass. "You would think the water would be warmer than that," he continued to say, stepping out of his shorts. "It *is* summer."

"It *is* Ireland," I scoffed, reaching up to unhook my bra. "Never expect anything to be warm or dry."

"True," he mused, draping a towel around his hips. "Are you decent if I turn around?"

"Yep."

Hugh swung around, only to groan when his whiskey-brown eyes locked on me. "Liz."

Cackling shamelessly, I kicked off the rest of my underwear and walked into the shower stall.

"What if someone else comes in?" Releasing a pained groan, my boyfriend grabbed an extra towel from our bag and held it out in front of the stall like he was my personal bodyguard. "You know these changing rooms are unisex."

Snickering, I glanced over my shoulder at him. "I don't care."

"Well, I do."

"Why?"

"Because you're mine to look at." My heart slammed in my chest. "Not anyone else's."

I turned around to face my towel-wielding bodyguard and grinned. "Then look."

"Don't fucking tempt me."

Snickering, I lathered my hair with shampoo from the dispenser attached to the wall. "Saint Hugh."

"You'd get some fright if I came in there," Hugh grumbled, concealing my nonexistent virtue with a towel while averting his eyes like a gentleman.

"Actually, I'd be thrilled," I called back. "There's room in here for two, you know."

"Behave yourself."

"Never."

———————————————

Later, when we were decent once more and gorging on ice cream at the pier, Hugh looked at me and smiled. He was sitting on the wall of the pier with his legs dangling over both sides, while I sat cross-legged on the wall, facing him.

"What?" I asked, mid-lick of my cone. "What's funny?"

"Nothing." He shook his head and took a lick of his cone, still smiling.

"Clearly, there's something." I pushed, mirroring his smile. "Tell me."

"I'm just happy, that's all." He took another lick of his ice cream and turned his attention to the water. "Today was a good day." He rested his hand on my knee and sighed in contentment. "A good day, baby."

Yeah, it was. "I love being here," I told him, feeling my body soften right along with my heart. "With you."

"Me too, Liz." He gave my knee a reassuring squeeze. "Me too."

SCHOOL'S OUT FOR SUMMER

Hugh

JUNE 19, 2003

"That's it," Gibs declared, drop-kicking his schoolbag across Tommen's central courtyard. "These hands won't be touching another book for the rest of summer."

"Jaysus." Rolling his eyes, Johnny stomped across the cobblestone courtyard and retrieved the bag from where it had landed in a flower bed. "What did I tell ya about damaging property, Gibs?"

"That wasn't damaging property, Johnny," Gibs shot back with a grin. "That was *returning* school property."

"By lobbing it into the gardener's petunias?"

"I'll catch up with ye," I told my friend before veering over to one of the picnic tables. Tossing my schoolbag on the table, I sank down before quickly powering my phone back on. The moment it lit up, I dialed the number I knew off by heart, too impatient to wait for the contacts to load, and pressed it to my ear. When my girlfriend's familiar voice came down the line, the hairs on the back of my neck shot to attention. "Well?"

Jesus Christ, even her voice turns me on.

I smiled down the line. "Done and dusted."

"Yay!" I heard her cheer. "What's the plan? Where are you now?"

"Still at school with the lads." Reaching up, I loosened my tie. "We're meeting up with a few more lads this evening before heading to the disco."

"Well, don't get too off your tits beforehand," Liz laughed. "Because I'm not going to all this effort for nothing, buddy."

"Effort?" Now, I was intrigued. "Is my baby getting dolled up for tonight?"

"Your *baby* is contemplating sneaking a clonazepam into your sister's drink," she grumbled. "Maybe that would slow her down."

"Claire's being hyper?"

"Hyper is putting it mildly, Hugh."

"Is she bouncing?"

"Like Tigger."

"Oh shit," I chuckled. "Well, don't let her anywhere near you with a razor. I walked in on her trying to shave her legs in the bathroom sink the other day and it was a bloodbath."

"No fear of that, because she's too invested in breaking my will one pedicured toe at a time," she replied in a dry tone. "So you better be clearheaded enough to appreciate it."

"Are you wearing your anklet?"

"Always."

"Are you doing to dance with me?"

"Never."

I laughed down the line. "I better get back to the lads."

"If you must," she replied, sighing dramatically. "Meanwhile, I'll be sure to protect myself from your sister's penchant for hair removal."

"You do that," I chuckled. "See you tonight."

"Love you."

"Love you, too, Hugh."

Hanging up the call, I returned to the lads, only to find Gibs and Kav fighting like an old married couple.

"They caged me in a cell for two weeks, Johnny!" he declared, hands flailing wildly. "Like a fucking lab rat. So *excuse* me for not giving two shits about the groundskeeper's precious petunias."

"Would you give it a bleeding rest?" Kav shot back as walked down the footpath toward the school's exit. "You're like a broken record, Gibs."

"And we weren't caged in a cell," Feely chimed in, adding his two cents. "We were sitting our junior cert, lad."

"No, *you* weren't caged in a cell to do your exams," Gibs corrected with a bite to his tone. "Meanwhile, *I* was in a special little room all by my lonesome, with a man, who I can only describe as the reincarnation of Smithers, to write down my answers, and that freaky fucking guidance counselor Miss Moore chaperoning." His gray eyes widened right along with his outrage. "And she's *pregnant*, Patrick. You know how stressed pregnant bellies make me get."

"I do, Gibs, and I'm sorry you were forced into proximity with one," Feely replied, giving our friend a supportive clap on the back.

"But the whole separate-room gig was for your benefit," I filled in.

"Exactly," Kav agreed. "The scribe was there to help with your dyslexia, lad."

"True, and Smithers the scribe *did* write all the answers," Gibs agreed in a thoughtful tone before grinning deviously. "Hm. Looks like I know who's getting the blame when the results come back in September and my mam has a conniption fit over me failing."

"Don't be hasty, Gibs," Feely offered. "You might surprise yourself."

"Lad," Gibs snorted. "You wouldn't say that if you'd seen the look on Smithers's face when I told him what to write." A hearty chuckle escaped him. "The poor bastard was begging me with his eyes to *stop* talking."

The rest of us laughed at that before I asked, "All right, lads, whose house are we getting ready at?"

"Yours," Gibs and Feely said in union.

Meanwhile, Johnny's brows furrowed in confusion. "Getting ready for what?"

"Tonight's disco in town."

"And before you even start the bullshit *I can't, I have training tomorrow* protests, just know that you *are* coming," Gibsie interjected. "It's happening, Cap, get with the program."

"Because I *can't*," Kav urged. "I *do* have training tomorrow."

"Then clear your schedule," Gibs replied, draping an arm over his shoulder. "Because tonight, you're out with the lads."

DIBS, HE'S MINE

Lizzie

FOR THE FIRST TIME IN FOREVER, I HAD MADE A GENUINE EFFORT WITH MY APPEAR-ance. I figured I owed it to my boyfriend for suffering through countless months of feral-Liz. He deserved girlie-Liz for at least one night.

Dolled up to the nines in a skintight, lemon, mesh-lace boob-tube dress that left little to the imagination, I found myself queuing up outside the rugby clubhouse. Donning a full face of makeup—courtesy of Claire—and with my hair falling to the middle of my back in loose hanging curls, I consoled myself with the knowledge that my feet would be comfortable even if the rest of me *wasn't*. My faithful high-tops, my one nonnegotiable, were securely on my feet.

Ballylaggin RFC was the venue for tonight's disco. The event was being fully funded by both our school and the rugby club, offering an open bar of nonalcoholic refreshments and a line of security to keep order.

I knew BCS had a separate disco happening across town at the local GAA pavilion, but we didn't go there. Warned by our teachers and parents to steer clear of "those kinds of boys," we were segregated to be with the boys we went to school with. The *good* boys, the *promising* ones, with fat wallets and even fatter egos.

It was a fucking joke.

I wasn't sure how I had managed to drag myself out of bed this morning, let alone had the strength to sit through a four-hour pampering session with Claire, but as we stood here now, surrounded by hundreds of other teenage girls, I had to admit, we looked fierce.

"I can't wait to get inside," Claire squealed, bouncing around in excitement in her pink leather dress that concealed just enough of her body to stop her brother from having a conniption fit when he arrived. "I'm so excited!"

"Yeah, Claire, I can tell."

"Do you think the boys will be here soon?"

"Who knows?" I replied with a shrug. "They've been drinking all evening. I wouldn't be surprised if they're passed out in a bush somewhere."

"Well, Gerard will definitely be here," she replied confidently. "He promised me the first dance."

Holding back for the sake of the night that was in it, I swallowed down my retort and my pain, and forced a small smile. "Whatever you say."

"I'm scoring with Danny Callaghan tonight," Shelly, one of the girls from our year, declared. "He texted me last night." Shimmying toward us in skyscraper heels, a black rara skirt, and a pink halter neck, Shelly grinned like the cat that got the cream. "He's so fine, girls."

"Ew," Claire said quietly, scrunching her nose up, while I, not so quietly, fake heaved at the thought.

"I think Robbie Mac wants to score with me," Helen, another girl in our year and Shelly's faithful sidekick, said, sidling up to her bestie. "He texted me an hour ago."

"I wouldn't if I were you," Claire warned. "Those boys are on the rugby team with Hughie, and they're total players."

"We know," they both cackled in unison.

"Ew."

"Oh my God, that's them!" Shelly shrieked, elbowing Helen while gesturing to the group of teenage boys strolling up the pathway of the club grounds.

Swinging around, I studied the dozen or more giant-looking boys and quickly homed in on the one that belonged to *me*. As soon as I locked eyes on Hugh, laughing and messing around with his friends, it felt like my entire body had caught on fire. Clad in jeans and a tight, fitted shirt, with his hair styled in his usual sexily tousled way, my boyfriend looked fucking edible.

"How is it that boys only need to throw on a shirt and jeans and gel their hair to look so dreamy?" Helen groaned, speaking my thoughts aloud. "It's not fair."

"Okay, now I'm scared," Shelly chimed in, looking nervous.

"You don't have to kiss anyone," Claire reminded her. "I'm not." Smiling, she added, "I came to dance."

"Dammit," one of the third-year girl's standing in front of us in the line complained. "Johnny Kavanagh isn't with them."

"Why are you so surprised?" said another girl. "He never comes to these things."

"Well, I don't know about Captain Fantastic coming, but his sexy sidekick will be coming for me later tonight," laughed another.

"Gibsie?" the first one exclaimed.

"Yes, Gibsie," the dark-haired girl confirmed. "Have you seen that boy without his shirt on? He's fire."

One look at Claire's heartbroken expression, and I knew she could hear the conversation unfolding beside us.

"Ew," Claire whispered, innocent, brown eyes looking to me for help.

"Ignore her, Claire," I said loud enough for the girls to hear me. "The only thing she'll be coming on tonight is her hand."

"Oh God," Shelly and Helen groaned in unison, taking a safe step behind Claire.

The third-year girls' laughter quietened and one of them swung around to toss me a dirty look.

The moment we locked eyes on each other, recognition filled her blue eyes.

Oh *yeah*, she remembered me.

Our previous encounter at school, when I caught wind of her trying to sit on my boyfriend's lap during Irish, had been a memorable one.

"Ugh," the brunette sneered, glaring at me. "Of course it's *you*."

I grinned. "Hi."

"How does it feel to be the biggest bitch in school?"

"Trust me, you haven't met my version of bitch yet," I shot back without missing a beat. "But put your hands on that boy and you'll quickly find out."

"You girls don't own those boys, you know."

"See, that's where you're wrong," I argued back at her, half hoping she'd go it a little further and do something stupid like push me. I only needed one excuse. Just one. "Because you claim what you lick and Claire called dibs on that boy a long time ago, so why don't you hurry along and find some other misfortunate asshole to sink your teeth in?"

"Fuck you, bitch."

"I'd rather be a bitch than a whore. Now, off you go, *whore*."

"Yeah," Claire added, finding her voice with a little backup. "You heard her. Skedaddle."

A few more insults were tossed back and forth before the lads joined us.

"How are the ladies?" Robbie Mac acknowledged, while he and the rest of his teammates cut in line and joined us near the front. Of course, because they were the rugby gods of Tommen, nobody said a word about it. *Assholes*.

"Claire-Bear!" Making a beeline for my friend, Thor draped an arm around her shoulders and pulled her to his side. "Christ, you're a sight for sore eyes."

My usual discomfort at his presence was replaced by smugness when I watched the girls we were arguing with turn green with jealousy.

Hah!

"There's my baby," a familiar voice whispered in my ear, and a deep, illicit shiver rippled through my body when his chest brushed against my back.

Glancing over my shoulder, I looked up at my boyfriend and exhaled a contented breath. "Hi."

God, he was so much taller now. For a while when we were younger, we were almost the same height. He was always an inch or so taller, but I thought I might catch up. Not anymore, though. No, because his hormones had taken puberty seriously and he was now towering above me.

When his hand came around my middle, palm flattening against my lower belly, I couldn't stop myself from sagging against him, absorbing the heat of his body against mine. My hand moved to cover his instinctively, like I had been programed to respond to his touch.

Because his touch was good.

It was safe.

It was so fucking right.

When he was with me, I finally felt like I was okay again. Like the world was back on its axis. Normality had resumed and I would survive. I had another night of living left in me, but only if I got to live it with him.

Hugh continued chatting to our friends, while I lost track of everything that was happening around us, too engrossed to focus on a word of it. Every now and then, he would press a kiss to my bare shoulder, and that only complicated things further.

Because I was *starving* for this boy.

TAKE ME TO THE CLOUDS ABOVE

Lizzie

JUNE 19, 2003

THE HEAT WAS STIFLING INSIDE THE CLUBHOUSE, AND THE DJ WAS TOP-NOTCH, SPIN-
ning gold from his decks, while the strobe lights shone down on us. The crowd was
insane with nearly everyone from first year to fourth in full attendance. There wasn't
a spare inch of space on the dance floor as the third years celebrated the completion of
their exams and the rest of us celebrated the start of summer.

When Annina, DJ Chucky, and XTM's "Fly on the Wings Of Love" started to play
and a large crowd formed on the dance floor, I rolled my eyes when I realized *who* had
captured their attention.

With his shirt cast to one side, Thor danced like no one was watching, mouthing
every word of the song to Claire as he seduced her with those snake hips. The pair were
so impressive when they moved together that I honestly couldn't blame the crowd for
forming, although I would never admit that out loud.

Their chemistry was undeniable, and it caused a familiar swell of sadness to grow
inside of me because I knew there would come a day when I would lose her entirely
from my life. Right now, I was managing to somewhat cope with his presence in my life,
but my best friend truly loved him, and when they finally made it official, I would lose
her. While I knew Claire cared about me, her feelings for him far outweighed anyone
else in her world, and it was only a matter of time before the scales weighed in his favor.

Because this was excruciating for me.

Walking the line.

Keeping my thoughts to myself.

Burying my pain.

It was bubbling inside of me.

One of these days, I was going to go off like a bomb.

I only prayed I could hold on.

"So this is where you've been hiding." Hugh's voice infiltrated my thoughts, and I
felt his hands come around my waist, crushing my back to his chest. "Where'd you go?"

I slipped away from his group of friends earlier in the night. While I wanted to be with my boyfriend every second of the day, I was uncomfortable around the team—namely Thor—and needed a breather. Besides, the boys were all drunk, while the unattached ones were on the prowl and bringing back girls I couldn't stand to be around. "Just needed some air," I replied, shivering when his lips grazed my ear.

The urge to fold myself into him was overwhelming. There was no explaining what he did to me and the sheer adoration I felt for him was incomprehensible. Hugh somehow seemed to stimulate me and soothe me all at once. He wasn't uptight and he wasn't reckless. He was the perfect medium, letting his merits and achievements shine organically, rather than shoving them down everyone's throats.

"Here, Hughie!" Luke Casey called out, pushing through the crowd to get to us. "You might want to have a word with Gibs, lad, because he's got your sister riding his thigh like a fucking horse."

I expected my boyfriend to charge into the circle formed around Thor and his sister, to put an abrupt end to their handsy shenanigans, but that's not what he did.

"I don't care," Hugh told his teammate, while he turned me in his arms and fisted my curls. "I'm dancing with my girl."

"Oh, no, no, no," I warned, staring up at his adorably flushed face. "You know I hate dancing." Grinning, I reached up and stroked his cheek with my finger. "You look so cute when you're drunk."

And drunk, he most certainly was. The alcohol wafting from his breath was strong enough to make *me* tipsy.

"If you knew what you do to me, Liz." His eyes were darker than usual, with large, dilated pupils and a hungry glint. Palming my ass, he gripped me tightly and roughly pulled my body flush against his. "If you only knew."

And then we were kissing.

Clumsily pulling and groping at every part of one another we could get a hold of. His tongue was in my mouth, his hands were on my body, and I was drowning in sensation. Wonderful, elicit, glorious feelings that only this boy could draw from me.

LMC and U2's "Take Me to the Clouds Above" had taken over from the previous song, and I thought it was so fitting in this moment, because Hugh Biggs could take me anywhere and I would go with him gladly.

This boy was a hot commodity at Tommen, he was a high-valued rugby boy, our school's star fly half, and I reveled in the knowledge that his eyes spent their days on *me*.

I was the girl on his mind.

In this moment, I didn't care if Claire saw us or not.

Right now, I wasn't concerned about her feelings or her disdain.

I was too in love.

His tongue snaked out, teasing mine, as he slowly walked me backwards. He didn't even try to conceal what we were doing. He was giving everyone around us a free viewing. The raw, uncensored version of what he felt for me. He was too lost in the moment and it fucking thrilled me.

Step-stumbling to the notorious *wall*, the one where all the serious couples got off with each other, I felt my back hit the cool concrete moments before his big body crushed against me. If I could have taken all our clothes off right here in this dance hall, I would have. That was how desperate I felt.

Thrilled and aching, I moved against him, hips gyrating against his, breasts straining against his chest, needing to feel the hardness of him against the softness of me.

It was madness.

It was ecstasy.

And I had never felt *more*.

THE SUMMER OF LOVE

Hugh

AUGUST 23, 2003

FROM THE MOMENT I LOCKED EYES ON LIZZIE YOUNG ALL THE WAY BACK IN FIRST class, I felt connected to her in a way I had never experienced with anyone else.

At the time, I didn't understand the infatuation, nor had I any inkling of how deep the roots of my feelings for this girl would go. Young and green, I went into it blindly, falling hard and fast for the girl with the lonesome, pale eyes.

Throughout the years, we had become closer than close and forged a bond that time only seemed to deepen and intensify. When Liz agreed to be mine the summer before sixth class, I thought I had peaked in life.

When her sister died and Liz's bipolar symptoms worsened right along with the grief she was drowning in, it didn't break us. Instead of us drifting apart like she did with everyone else, we grew closer. Because despite withdrawing from life and locking everyone out of her world, she left a key out for me.

When puberty hit us both like a wrecking ball and I was thrown into the world of Tommen two years before she could join me, we didn't let it separate us. Despite most of the lads at school insisting I would grow bored of Liz and move on, the opposite occurred.

Because the older we got, the more drastically our bodies changed, and our hormones raged. My infatuation with the girl only strengthened to the point where I was scarcely holding on to my self-control. I wanted her *badly*, and with the feeling reciprocated by Liz, I was running out of steam when it came to slamming on the brakes during intimacy.

I knew once I turned sixteen in October, I would be taking on a job as a part-time lifeguard, a role I had already been headhunted for by Kim, the manager of the hotel's leisure center, and wouldn't have as much free time as before. Because of this, I'd made sure to spend every spare second of summer break with Liz.

The phrase "summer of love" had taken on a whole new meaning this summer, and Liz and I were teetering dangerously close to the point of no return.

I'd learned more about the female anatomy this summer than I had in almost six-teen years, and holy fuck, did I have an amazing teacher. I had eight months on Liz in the age department, but she took the lead under the covers and checkmated me every single time.

Because of my competitive streak and intense desire to succeed at all things in life, whenever Liz and I messed around, I committed to memory every one of her lust-filled commands and breathy instructions, determined to not only accomplish competency in the art of seduction but to thoroughly master and excel in it.

Liz wasn't shy about telling me what did and didn't work for her, and I was grateful for her honesty because who the hell else was going to show me? Liz was the only girl I'd been with or intended to be with, and it was important to me that I *knew* how to please her.

Feely always complained about my unquenchable thirst for knowledge, method-ical attention to detail, and desire to attain a level of excellency in all areas of my life that bordered on obsession—Feely's words not mine—but my girlfriend made no such complaints.

Instead of razzing me over my perfectionist tendencies like Feely and the lads did, Liz wholeheartedly encouraged this quality and showered me with praise whenever I stepped it up another notch and ticked a new box.

If Mam knew a tenth of what Liz and I had gotten up to this summer, she would have locked me up until I turned eighteen, and if Mike ever got wind of all the places I'd kissed and touched his daughter, well, I might as well start digging my own grave.

Honest to God, we were holding on to our virginities by a thread, and Liz's master idea of us trying "everything but sex" only made the ten months to her sixteenth birth-day feel like sixteen *years*.

Tonight's end-of-summer bash had been organized by the upcoming sixth years and held at fellow teammate and sixth year Terrance Crean's house. His parents ran an equestrian center from their property and *holy shit* was his home fancy. It didn't come close to being in the same league as Old Hall House—nowhere did—but it *was* impres-sive and reeked of wealth.

Even though we were only going into fourth year and tonight's party was strictly for fifth and sixth years only, our positions on the senior rugby panel secured us an invite.

Because of bullshit school politics and hierarchy, the lads on the rugby team's senior panel were almost always invited to attend house parties and events, along with their better halves.

Because Johnny was still holidaying in the South of France with his parents and Feely was balls-deep in harvest season on the farm, Gibs and I were left to fly the flag tonight. Unfortunately, he had decided to bring the curly-haired demon as his date, which did nothing to help me relax. Because a hyper Claire and a hyper *and* drunk Gibsie made for trouble.

"I can't believe school is right around the corner," Gibs complained. Sprawled out on a sun lounger in Crean's back garden, my old pal chugged on his beverage of choice—tequila. "Where the hell did the summer go?"

"Don't worry about where the summer went, lad," I mused from my perch on a matching sun lounger, while I sipped on what might have been my seventh pint glass of the weird, green shit the sixth-year girls called Fat Frog. Aside from vodka, I had no idea what they used to brew the snot-green concoction, but it tasted delicious—and went straight to the head. "Worry about leaving Claire unsupervised with a dozen or so horses nearby."

"Ah, Christ on a bike," Gibsie groaned, rolling off the sun lounger and racing off. "I told your sister to steer clear of the stables."

"Giddy up like your Shergar, lad," I called over my shoulder, words slurring from the alcohol that was hitting the spot.

Chuckling to myself, I drained what was left in my glass, leaned over, and set it down on the patio. Knowing Claire and Gibs, I was about to witness an even greater escape than Tito and Ossie's in the film *Into the West*.

"I need you," a familiar voice whispered in my ear then. "Right now." Dropping onto my lap, Liz hooked an arm around my neck and tongued my ear. "Badly."

"Christ, Liz," I groaned, instantly hardening when she rocked her ass on my lap. "I'll lose it right here."

"That's what I want." Her lips trailed over my jaw, peck after seductive peck, until her tongue traced my bottom lip. "So, lose it, baby." The scent of alcohol on her breath was almost as strong as mine. "In me."

Jesus.

This girl was hellbent on killing me.

"We're drunk."

"I don't care."

"I do," I slurred—or at least the sober version of me did. Meanwhile the drunk version of me, a.k.a. the current version, wanted to bury myself inside this girl and never come out. "Baby, don't tempt me."

"Be tempted," she encouraged, sliding her fingers inside the buttons of my shirt. "Fuck me."

Fuck her?

Christ.

"You want me to fuck you here?" I strangled out, expecting her to realize how crazy that sounded and come to her senses. "You want our first time to be at a house party?"

Of *course*, Liz had to nod. Worse, she hitched a leg over me and straddled my lap. "I can feel you," she moaned against my lips. "You're hard for me." Her tongue snaked out and licked mine, while she arched her hips against me and rocked. "Have me."

"We're not having sex," I protested, lips colliding with hers while my dick wept in protest. "Not until your birthday."

"We'll see," she replied, fisting my hair in challenge and sealing her mouth to mine.

CLOSE ENCOUNTERS AND EVEN CLOSER CALLS

Lizzie

AUGUST 23, 2003

Fueled by a lethal concoction of alcohol and lust, we stumbled into the house and found the first available room. Too drunk to care that it was a closet-sized washroom, I quickly turned the lock before pushing my boyfriend down on the closed toilet seat.

"Liz, baby—"

"Shh." Straddling Hugh's lap again, I greedily accepted his lips when they crashed against mine.

Shamelessly rocking my body against his, I ripped and tore at his shirt, desperate to feel his skin on mine. The pulsing shocks in my core when I rubbed myself on the hard bulge of his jeans sent me spiraling.

When Hugh reached behind me and loosened the knot holding my halter neck up, I moaned in approval and quickly tore at the buttons on his shirt to get him naked.

When the fabric of my halter pooled at my waist, his hands moved expertly to my breasts, caressing my flesh exactly how I liked. "Mm," I encouraged when he rolled one of my nipples between his forefinger and thumb, while continuing to caress the other. It was too much. The sensations he drew from my body exceeded every one of the dirty dreams he starred in.

When he applied more pressure, squeezing me harder, I moaned into his mouth, encouraging him to keep touching me. "Don't stop."

My boyfriend obeyed my wishes, working my mouth and breasts over with his fingers and tongue, while he rocked his jean-clad erection into my crotch.

My breath caught when one of his hands trailed south and disappeared between my thighs. Thrilled I had taken Claire's advice, I quickly reached for the skirt she'd convinced me to wear and hitched it up to pool at my waist. Desperate to give my boyfriend unfettered access to my body, I moved to push my thong aside, but he got there first.

"Fuck," I cried out when I felt his fingers tracing my slit, teasing and probing me like he'd perfected this summer. "Please—"

"Shh." Crushing his lips against mine once more, he gently pushed two fingers deep inside me and started to move. Giving my body time to acclimate to his welcome invasion, Hugh moved slowly at first, taking his time to work up to a wicked rhythm that threatened to send me over the edge.

Desperate to make him feel good, I clumsily reached for his jeans, ripping and tugging at the button and zip until he was free.

Holy shit.

He was big and thick and hard.

Lustful and in love, I fisted his thick length and tugged.

The move caused his fingers to falter and a delicious growl vibrated from his lips into mine.

Every flick of his wrist caused my body to jerk and shudder in pleasure as I rocked relentlessly into his hand, desperate to reach my breaking point.

"That's it, baby," he encouraged, lips still on mine as he crooked his fingers and pushed deeper, faster, harder, and I worked him over with equal speed and intensity.

"Oh God," I cried out, tearing my lips from his when my body got dangerously close to the edge. "Ugh…omigod…Hugh! Oh, holy fu—"

Hugh swallowed my cries with his mouth once more, wrapping his free arm around my waist to hold me in place while he finger-fucked me into oblivion.

I was going to come on his hand. I knew it. I could feel the familiar ripples of pleasure building up inside, threatening to crest and crash over me. He clearly knew this, he could obviously feel my body clenching him, and he upped the ante to a blistering level.

"I'm coming," I cried against his lips. "I'm coming." Eyelids fluttering, I kept my eyes locked on his as the wave of pleasure eclipsed life itself.

"Good," he encouraged, growling against my lips.

"Jesus." Bucking and jerking restlessly, I rode the wave shamelessly, taking from him what I needed—what he had so effortlessly given me.

"Please," I begged, resuming my orgasm-disrupted hand job, while hitching myself up so that I was hovering over him. "Put it inside me."

"This is so bad," Hugh groaned, burying his face in my neck as he reached for his jeans and boxers and pushed them down his hips.

Breathing hard and ragged, I cast a glance downward and moaned when my eyes took in the glistening head of his thick length. His erection was long and thick and rigidly hard, and all I could think of was sitting on it, needing to feel him stretch my body to make him fit. Because I needed this boy to finally claim my body as his. That was the only way I could make it all go away. His touch was the only thing that could erase the monster's.

"Condom," Hugh whispered, against my mouth. "Need a condom."

"No." Shaking my head, I gripped him hard and lowered myself down, probing my lips with his thick head. "You don't."

Chest heaving, Hugh leaned back and released the sexiest male groan I'd ever heard. "Not without a condom."

"Yeah, fine. Whatever." Excited, I looked around wildly, drowning in anticipation. "Is there one in your wallet?"

"No," he admitted, looking genuinely tortured. "I don't have one."

"It's okay." I was quick to soothe him, pumping his shaft with my fist. "You don't need to wear one."

"Liz, no." A vein bulged in his neck, and he released another guttural groan, like his refusal caused him physical pain. "We *can't.*"

"Hugh, no!" I practically cried, needing to feel him inside my body more than I needed to wake up in the morning. Because I would happily die right now if it meant that I died with him deep inside me. *"Please!"*

"I want to," he groaned right back at me, still rocking into my touch. "But not without protecting you." He slowly pulled his fingers out of me and looked up at me with a remorseful expression. "I'm sorry."

Feeling equal parts devastated and aroused, I swallowed down my frustration, knowing that however bad it was for me, he was feeling it a million times more. Because he'd already scratched my itch, but I hadn't thoroughly scratched his.

"It's okay," I soothed, leaning in close to press a kiss to the curve of his jaw. The move caused my bare breast to graze his chest, and he hissed out a moan.

Incentivized by the primal noises he made, I slid my fist up and down his length. He moaned softly and it caused everything inside of me to tighten back up.

He was in such a vulnerable position beneath me that I felt oddly powerful. Knowing that I was stirring this reaction from him was empowering.

Hugh had the capacity to physically dominate me at any given moment if he wanted to, like the monster had, and there would be nothing I could do to fight him off, just like there hadn't been with the monster. This boy could take whatever he wanted from my body with force, and I felt secure in the knowledge he never would.

Hugh filled my cup up with the very things I had been drained of in my nightmares. Instead of inflicting pain, fear, and harm like the monster had, my boyfriend instilled power, trust, and respect inside of me.

"You like that, baby?" I asked softly, fisting the base of his thick shaft. "You like it when I touch you like this?"

His response was to close his eyes and nod weakly, while straining his hips into my touch. His tongue snaked out to trace his bottom lip and he gripped my ass as I worked him over. "Have me, baby."

His words ignited a pulsing ache between my legs, and I quickened my pace, working him over at a merciless pace and reveling in every sexy, primal, male groan that escaped him.

When Hugh's entire frame tensed beneath me, I knew he was on the edge. "It's okay," I praised, upping my pace when he tried to push my hand away. "Don't be shy." When he clenched his eyes shut, I licked and nuzzled his neck. "Let go for me."

"Liz," he strangled out, hips thrusting wildly. "I can't hold it…"

"Don't hold it," I commanded, attention riveted to his impressive length. "Let go."

And then I watched in fascination as the glistening head of his thick shaft twitched a couple of times before releasing a thick trail of cloudy, white liquid.

"Christ, I'm so sorry, Liz," Hugh groaned, chest heaving, while his powerful body trembled beneath me. "I tried to hold it."

I didn't want him to stop it.

I wanted to watch him do it again.

Breathing hard, his gaze raked over me, and when he reached my midsection, he stifled a groan. "Fuck, I didn't mean to get you with it."

"There's a lot of it," I mused, glancing down at the mess between us. "You must have really wanted in me."

"Jesus, Liz, please don't say that," he begged, and I looked down and quickly realized why. Mesmerized, I took in the sight of his now semi-hard shaft as it began to thicken and grow.

"Wow."

"Ignore it."

"You want more?" I rocked on his lap. "Me, too."

"No." Hugh sat straight up. His cheeks were flushed, and his hair was tousled from the force I'd been pulling on it with. "We can't. Not here. Not when we're both…" He paused to wave a hand between us. "We both know what'll happen, and that is not how I want our first time to go."

"How do you want it go?"

"In a bed, for a start," he replied, pushing his hand through his thoroughly fucked hair. "You deserve a bed, not a bathroom." And then, as if he just realized what he said, he looked around us and groaned. "I am never drinking those Frogs again." Glum, he reached for the toilet paper hooked to the wall and ripped off a big heap. "I am so

543

fucking sorry," he continued to say, quickly setting to work on cleaning us up. "Shit, I got your top, too." He shook his head and dabbed at the fabric between my legs. "I'm a disgrace, I tell ya. Honest to God, I shouldn't be left outside the front door."

"I had the best night," I told him with a huge smile. "I don't remember feeling this happy." *Ever.* "I love you, Hugh."

"I love you, too, Liz."

"No, I mean I *really* love you," I said, gripping his broad shoulders. "Heart and soul." I smiled. "Body and mind."

His head snapped up from where he had been focusing on cleaning the aftermath of his cum shot, and he looked me right in the eyes. "If anything was ever to happen to you, I wouldn't be able to go on."

His words were sobering and hit me like a sucker punch to the heart.

It was such an unexpected thing for him to say.

He was usually so logical and sensible.

"I'm fine," I replied weakly, feeling a sudden rush of emotion wash over me. "Nothing's going to happen to me."

"What I feel for you exceeds anything the realm of love could conjure up," he told me, eyes full of something I couldn't quite decipher in my drunken state.

"You have the best lines," I purred, hooking an arm around his neck and smacking a playful, smooching kiss to his lips.

"It's good to know my intolerance to vodka stimulates you," he slurred. "However, I need you to climb off my lap, so I can put *this* overstimulated bastard back in his place."

"Between my legs?"

"Not helping, Liz. Not helping."

Breathing hard, he dropped his head to rest on my chest. "What was I thinking?"

"You weren't, and I loved it."

"No, Liz." He shook his head and groaned. "I was two seconds away from fucking you in a toilet." He looked full of drunken remorse. "I am so sorry."

I wanted to cry.

I wanted to scream at him to not be sorry and to just keep going, but the look in his eyes assured me that, for tonight, our fun was over. His body was sending a direct message to mine, and his conscience needed to catch the hell on. This was good. This was *exactly* what we both wanted. I could feel myself slipping; I could feel my impatience taking over.

"Don't regret me, Hugh," I said quietly.

"Never," he vowed, embracing me with tenderness. "You're the only part of my life I can't plan for." He pressed a kiss to my lips. "And the only part I can't live without."

RENEGOTIATING THE DATE

Hugh

AUGUST 24, 2003

IT ALMOST HAPPENED AGAIN LAST NIGHT.

It *would* have happened if I'd had the foresight to carry protection.

I'd never bought condoms before, and a part of me wanted to delay the transaction because if condoms weren't on hand, then we couldn't go further. But an even bigger part of me demanded I haul my ass to the nearest chemist because if Liz had taken it further last night, I wouldn't have stopped her.

My lack of self-control when it came to my girlfriend was both a terrifying realization and a glaring chink in my armor.

Throughout the course of my life, I had taken great care to plan, prepare, and act in a responsible manner in all aspects of my life, so to know that I was willing to throw caution to the wind on such a serious matter rattled me.

I was cresting sixteen, and I didn't know how much longer I had it in me to be a gentleman. I knew I was supposed to be, but every time she put her mouth on me, I felt my resolve slip another inch.

"Do you think it would be smart if I bought condoms?" I asked Liz the following afternoon when we were hanging out in my room. Setting the book I was *trying* to read aside, I glanced at the gorgeous creature sprawled out on her stomach, with her arms and head resting on my lap. "Just to be safe?"

Liz's attention snapped up from her own book, and she turned to look at me. "I think that's the smartest idea you've had all summer." Her smile widened. "If we leave now and take our bikes, we'll make Sully's Chemist before it closes."

"Settle down," I chuckled, smoothing a hand down her spine. "I wasn't suggesting we do the deed right here and now." To be honest, I'd come to terms with the very huge possibility that we weren't going to hold out until next summer, and my focus had shifted to making it to *my* birthday. "What are your thoughts on renegotiating the date?"

"If it brings me closer to what I want, then I'm thinking hell yes," Liz replied, quickly pulling up on her knees.

With her knees on either side of my legs, my girlfriend crawled up my bed, not stopping until she was hovering above my lap.

"What do you have in mind?" she asked, staring down at me with that familiar glint in her eyes.

I knew *exactly* what that twinkle in her eyes and those flushed cheeks meant.

My willpower was about to be tested.

"My birthday," I replied in a gruff tone, instantly hard. There wasn't a damn thing I could do about the way my body reacted to hers, and I'd long since stopped worrying about it. My body responded to hers. It was basic human biology.

My girlfriend's eyes blazed with heat as she slowly lowered herself onto my lap. "Really?"

Nodding slowly, I watched her carefully. "Only if you're ready. I don't want to do anything you don't want or aren't ready for."

"Hugh." Liz gave me a pointed look. "I've been ready, waiting, and wanting you for a long time now." She rolled her hips and slid her hands under the hem of my T-shirt. "You can have me now if you want," she teased. "Hmm?"

"My birthday," I replied in a thick voice, hands moving to her hips of their own accord. "We can hold on until then."

"Can we?" she breathed.

I knew she was going to kiss me; I'd felt her mouth on mine a million times before tonight, but when she covered my lips with hers, my heart still reacted like it was the very first time.

She was on top, grinding her hips against mine, and for a moment, I panicked because I was too excited. My body was overreacting to the point where I was losing control.

Christ, I couldn't explain what happened to my body when the words *you can have me* escaped her lips. It wasn't the first time Liz had told me that, but every time, it seemed to awaken an intense, virile part of my subconscious.

Relaxing against the pillows at my back, I welcomed the feel of her mouth on mine, her hands on my skin, and her tight, little body rocking on top of me. It was a feeling like no other, and for the first time in my life, I could relate to the lads that ended up as teen fathers.

Because I couldn't deny the primal urge inside of me to claim her, body and soul. The raw desire I had to put a ring on her finger and fill her up with babies was potent. It wasn't rational and I wouldn't act on it—not until we were much older—but fuck was it there.

There wasn't another person on this planet I could give myself to like I had given myself to her. She could do whatever she wanted to me, and I would lie down and take it.

Because I was stuck on her like glue.

SUMMER, SAUNAS, AND SHIVERS

Lizzie

AUGUST 30, 2003

I WAS IN A PICKLE.

Torn between wanting summer 2003 to stretch on forever, while wishing the new school year would hurry up and arrive.

On the one hand, I didn't want the summer to end because I was having the time of my life with Hugh. On the other, returning to school meant we would see each other almost every day.

I was drowning so deep in my feelings for this boy that I wanted to press the fast-forward button on my life and skip five years into the future.

We had a detailed plan carved out, one that consisted of us both attending Trinity, with Hugh studying medicine, while I worked on an undergrad in English Studies.

We would rent a small apartment on the outskirts of the city and survive on beans on toast until we established ourselves in our chosen careers.

Money would be tight for the first few years, with me taking on the role of primary breadwinner until my boyfriend attained residency and the real money started to roll in. From there, Hugh would take on the role of provider, while I concentrated on writing my first novel.

While I wasn't privy to when Hugh would ask me to marry him, we both agreed to have the first of two children before thirty. Because we both wanted to be homeowners before we had a family, and with Hugh's insistence on being married beforehand, I predicted the ring would arrive somewhere between my twenty-third and twenty-fifth birthday.

"Are you coming?" Hugh called out, and I quickly dragged myself from my daydream to see him lingering near the door of the sauna with a smirk on his face.

Hell yeah I was coming.

Climbing out of the swimming pool in record time, slip-sliding across the tiles in my rush to get to him.

Grinning, Hugh opened the door of the sauna and pulled me inside. The moment I stepped inside, the smell of eucalyptus filled my nose. "Oh God, this smells amazing."

"You know what smells even more amazing?" He sank down on the wooden bench and pulled me onto his lap. "My girlfriend."

My smile widened. "Is that so?"

"Mm-hmm." Nodding, his lips brushed my neck. "I could eat you up."

Hooking an arm around his neck, I squeezed my thighs together, feeling too much in this moment for him. "I wish you would."

His lips still against my fluttering pulse. "Hmm?"

Blowing out a shaky breath, I repeated my words. "I wish you would."

He adjusted me on his lap so that I was straddling him. "I want to."

Excitement flooded me. "You do?"

"Yeah." He nodded slowly, brown eyes locked on mine. "I do."

"You can," I breathed, shivering when I felt him harden beneath me. "Whenever you want."

"I want to *be* everywhere, Liz," he admitted in a pained groan. "Badly."

"You want me badly?" I rocked my hips against him, enjoying the way his hands clamped on my hips and his nostrils flared. "You want to be inside me?"

"So fucking much," he groaned, pulling me down on his lap, while he thrust upward.

"You're hard."

"I know."

"I'm wet."

"I know."

"Have me."

"Soon."

"I can't wait anymore."

"We can still touch," he whispered, trailing his fingers over my belly and thigh. "We can still taste."

"Can I taste?"

He thickened beneath me. "Do you want to taste?"

I nodded. "Badly."

"Fuck."

I leaned in and kissed him.

"You're going to ruin me, aren't you?"

"You're already ruined," I teased. "I'm just going to make it worth your while."

"I'm in."

"I don't want fingers," I protested, reaching a hand between our bodies. "I want this." Dipping my fingers under the waistband of his boxers, I gripped *him*. "In me."

A sharp hiss escaped his lips, and his hips thrust into my touch of their own accord. "Don't do that, baby. I'll come."

"That's what I want." Moving in a slow rhythm, I glided my hand up and down his shaft, reveling in the way he strained beneath me. "Give it up, Biggs."

"You're so fucking…good at that," he bit out, cheeks flushed as his eyelids fluttered. "God, please don't stop."

"I won't," I promised, working doubly hard on getting him to the point of no return.

PART 18

The Downward Spiral

RUN, AS FAST AS YOU CAN

SEPTEMBER 1, 2003

TODAY WAS MONDAY, THE FIRST DAY OF A NEW SCHOOL YEAR, AND I WAS SLIPPING.

I had to be.

The meds I took to help me live a relatively productive life for two years were clearly waning in effectiveness. It was either that, or my body had built up a tolerance to them. That was the only explanation I had for the situation I found myself in.

All summer, I had basked in my brand-new and wonderful ability to sleep a solid eight hours at night *without* dreaming. I thought I was finally turning a corner. I was out of bed more often than in it, and I shed tears less than I laughed.

My relationship with Hugh had gone from strength to strength, I socialized more often, and I even shook my head when Thor offered me a cookie back in July. Politely, I may add, without the menacing scowl or balled-up fists.

The ship that was my life felt like it had finally reached calmer waters.

When I woke up for school this morning, I felt both rested and relaxed. I brushed my teeth and hair, washed my face, and threw on my fresh, new uniform. I ate breakfast, took my meds, and then caught the bus to school. I took my regular seat on the bus, next to my boyfriend, where we kissed until we arrived at school with swollen lips and plans to sneak off to the library at lunch.

From there, I sailed through my first six classes, hooked up with my boyfriend for a sneaky make-out session at big lunch, attended my *last* three classes with a Hugh-shaped smile on my face, before reuniting with him on the bus ride home.

All in all, my first day back to school had been as close to perfect as I'd ever experienced.

So why, when I stepped through the gates of my property, after feeling the best I had in years, was I hallucinating?

Why, when I *finally* seemed to have things going for me, did I experience the scariest, out of body experience in living memory.

The nightmare started after I kissed my boyfriend goodbye before stepping off the bus. From there, I had stood at the gated entrance of my home and waved him off on the bus before skipping through the open gates.

Yeah, I *distinctly* remembered skipping.

I felt *that* much joy.

My memories turned hazy after that.

I remembered hearing rustling in the nearby tree line, and I remembered walking over to the trees that lined our driveway on the right-hand side to investigate.

That's when it happened.

That's when my mind slipped.

One minute, I was tiptoeing from tree to tree in the hope of catching an up-close glimpse of one of the many wild deer that roamed freely on my mother's estate, and the next, I was cloaked in darkness.

There was something on my head, covering my face and cutting off my air supply to the point where it was difficult to drag enough air into my lungs. I tried to reach up to rip the scratchy sack-like fabric away, but the unbearable weight on top of my body, pressing me into the dirt, rendered me helpless.

It wasn't until I heard *his* voice in my ear and my blood ran cold that I realized I was dreaming.

No, not dreaming.

I had clearly tripped, bumped my head, and landed slap bang into my scariest nightmare to date...

"Did you miss me?" the monster snarled, gripping my throat with one hand, while pushing my thighs apart with the other. *"I'm afraid it's only a flying visit to tie up some loose ends. But I couldn't resist paying my little munchkin a visit."*

I tried to respond, but I couldn't see or speak or breathe or move.

Helpless, I flailed on the ground, as the sound of a zipper opening and leaves crunching beneath me filled my ears.

"Have you been a good girl, munchkin?"

I could feel his claws tearing at my underwear.

"Goddammit, why'd you have to be on the rag!"

Oh no, no, no, no, no!

"Fuck it; we can pretend like it's our first time."

My body braced itself for the pain I remembered would come next.

"Let's see if your tight, little body remembers me."

When it did come, and the monster impaled me, it hurt almost as bad as the first time.

"Pity you've grown up so much."

When I was five.

"I miss how you used to look."

Grunting and groaning, the monster punished me over and over until my body grew weak.

"Cry, bitch. You know it makes me hard."

His hand left my throat, and I heaved out a pained cry.

"I said cry, you little whore."

I cried harder, desperately trying to gather the strength and breath to scream. "Hu... gh..."

"Does Saint Hugh know what a dirty, little whore you are?" the monster snarled, destroying me from the inside out. "Does he know all the ways I've had you, munchkin?"

"Hugh," I screamed, louder now, as I fought to push him off me and wake up. "Hugh!"

"He'll never have your firsts, munchkin. All of those belong to me," the monster taunted, gripping my throat tighter than before. "My seed will always be the first to have grown inside you." He laughed cruelly then. "Does your precious Hugh know that? Huh? Have you been a bad girl while I've been gone and told your hero boyfriend about our little arrangement?" He impaled my body so hard I bit my tongue. "Do I need to take care of him like I took care of Caoimhe?"

Shuddering violently, I shook my head over and over while blood filled my mouth and tears fell from my eyes.

"You better hope he never finds out." Hissing out a sharp breath, the monster grunted loudly and then collapsed on top of me, finally growing still.

My body grew limp beneath his, and I quietly prayed for one of two things to happen: either to die right then or wake up, because I honestly couldn't take another second of this.

"I have a present for you, a little keepsake to remind you of the filthy whore you are. I'll leave them right here," he whispered in my ear, shoving something into the waistband of my skirt. "If you think about screwing me over, I'll make sure Biggs knows just how big of a whore his little girlfriend is." The monster laughed cruelly and used both hands to squeeze my throat. "And then I'll kill him..."

Even in my dream, I lost consciousness. When I finally woke up, I remained perfectly still, not daring to move a muscle out of fear of jinxing myself and passing out again.

Numb, I just laid on my back for a long time, staring at the late-evening sky. How long I'd been asleep, I couldn't say, but it had to have been several hours because the sun was much lower in the sky.

Turning my head to the side, I stared into the woods and felt a tear trickle down my cheek when a red deer took a tentative step out from behind a tree less than ten feet from where I was lying.

The deer watched me with me with wide, unblinking, brown eyes.

I didn't move a muscle, momentarily captivated by the raw beauty of this ethereal creature, while a swell of sympathy washed over me.

We were so very similar, this deer and me.

We were both prey.

An owl hooting high in the trees broke our trancelike stare down and the deer quickly skittered away.

"Run," I whispered, watching it disappear from my view. "As fast as you can."

CLOSE YOUR EYES AND JUST LET GO

SEPTEMBER 3, 2003

Fear had taken hold of my body to the point where I couldn't leave my bed. With my arms hooked around my knees, I rocked back and forth, feeling overwhelmed and numb all at once.

My body ached all over, and the stabbing sensation between my thighs sent my mind into a deep spiral.

How long I had been here, I had no idea.

Why this had happened again was another unanswered question.

I only knew this was worse.

I felt worse.

I was trapped, and there was no escape.

I had been captured once more by the monster in my mind and caged inside of my body.

I wanted to purge my soul of this poison.

I wanted to slit my wrists to the bone and bleed the pain away.

At least that way, it would be over.

It would stop.

Because I needed it to all just *stop*.

Swept up in my sudden emotional turmoil, I tried to make sense of my thoughts, but everything was cloudy.

Confusion had swallowed me whole, while echoes of *his* voice tipped me over the edge.

Teeth chattering, I continued to rock back and forth, while glancing at the instant photos I had found in the waistband of my skirt.

A little girl that looked just like me.

No!

Lying on her bed.

Stop it!

Without any clothes on.

It's not real!

Taking her medicine.

It was never real!

Being a good girl for the monster.

No, no, no! It's not real! Don't you ever think about that again!

A hoarse sob ripped from my throat, and I quickly smacked the photos away from my body, desperate to get clean.

You know you're a bad person.

You were a bad child, too.

Filthy little girl.

All those urges.

You are bad.

You shouldn't be here.

You are a mistake.

You are a liar!

I knew the monster was swallowing me up in his belly again, but I couldn't chase him off this time. Unraveling, I lost my grip, too weary to hold on.

Let go, busy Lizzie bee.

Close your eyes and just let go.

When I did, when I finally stopped fighting against it and let the voices swallow me up, I felt nothing at all.

And it was wonderful.

A STORM IS COMING

Hugh

THERE WAS SOMETHING VERY WRONG WITH LIZ.

I couldn't pinpoint the trigger for the sudden and drastic shift in her mood. Every time I tried to bring it up, she either flew off the handle or her clothes flew off. She was deep in the throes of rapid cycling, and I was petrified of one of those highs sticking because a manic Liz was terrifying.

The last time I'd seen her this out of control, she'd tried to hang herself with a fucking horse rein. That wasn't a period in my life I cared to think about because I was still traumatized by it. I had vivid memories of her wild, black eyes staring through me as she balanced on the edge of the loft in one of her family's barns and asked me to watch her fly.

She jumped that day, even when I begged her not to, even when I bawled like a fucking baby. She just *let go* of life, and I ended up breaking my elbow when I climbed up the bales to cut her down.

There was a storm brewing inside of my girlfriend, and I was desperate to find a way to *stop* history repeating itself.

I couldn't make sense of why this was happening now, after having the best year of our lives since her sister passed away. For the first time in years, there was an air of stability and contentment to Liz that hadn't been there before. Things had been going steady for over a year, her mood had stabilized after her hospitalization in 2001, and aside from the odd hiccup or bad week, she was thriving.

That all changed the moment we returned to school. Within twenty-four hours, her entire personality had shifted. Liz didn't return to school after her first day back, and when I tried to get in contact with her, all my calls and texts went unanswered.

When I biked over to her house the following evening to check in, every single window and door that offered access to the home had been locked and bolted.

This wasn't overly concerning to me because I knew Mike and Catherine were in Tipperary for the week, attending a family funeral. On the contrary, I was relieved my girlfriend was taking her personal security seriously.

What bothered me was the fact that, for the first time ever, I found myself on the outside looking in.

The only contact I received from my girlfriend came that evening, when I was pounding on the front door, and it came in the form of a text message.

Really sick. Can't let you in. Might be contagious.

When I replied to her message, letting her know that I didn't care if I caught it, she sent one final message before going dark.

I care. Don't worry. I'll be fine in a day or two. Go home. x

That was it, the grand total of communication I had with my girlfriend until she returned to school yesterday. The moment I locked eyes on Liz in the corridor between classes, all my concerns were vindicated. Because she certainly wasn't the Liz I'd waved off the bus the previous week.

My girlfriend's entire frame was coiled tight with tension, her eyes wild and dark, and she was radiating a bone-chilling air of hostility. Because she rarely interacted with me at school—*thanks, Claire*—I had to wait until big lunch to get her alone. When I playfully snuck up on Liz in the library, something we often did to each other, and pulled her back to my chest, she *lost* it. Releasing a feral scream, Liz thrashed, kicked, and scratched the shit out of my arms.

When my girlfriend swung around and realized it was me, she lunged at me in an entirely different way.

Releasing a breathy moan, Liz literally jumped into my arms, wrapping her arms and legs around my body as she sealed her mouth to mine.

Completely thrown off-kilter by the sudden shift in her mood, I didn't stop her like I should have and ended up getting dangerously close to giving her my virginity while taking hers.

I understood my girlfriend had a complicated, ongoing battle with mental health, and I had spent my life supporting her throughout her ups and downs, but this time felt different. A part of me worried this was more than exacerbated symptoms of her bipolar disorder.

Because this felt darker.

"Where's your head at, Hugo?" Gibs asked, pulling me from my thoughts. "You look like a broken man."

"Not broken," I replied in a lighthearted tone. "Just worried."

"About?"

I inclined my head to where my girlfriend was throwing shapes on the dance floor and sighed.

Tonight's disco was to celebrate our junior cert results, but I couldn't concentrate on anything other than the out-of-character behavior my girlfriend was displaying.

I had no problem with Liz having fun with friends. On the contrary, I wholeheartedly encouraged her to get out in the world and enjoy herself. My concern stemmed from the fact that I *knew* Liz despised dancing and would rather chew off her hand than be caught shaking her ass to generic bubblegum pop music with a gaggle of girls.

"Oh," Gibs replied, following my line of sight to where Liz was rubbing herself all over Claire and a few girls from their year. "Well, at least she's enjoying herself."

Liz wasn't *enjoying* herself, she was spiraling, and my sister was too innocent to notice the difference.

"Well, if it isn't the genius himself." Robbie Mac, thankfully, interrupted us. Relief flooded me when he threw himself down on the bench next to us. "What'd 'ya get again, Hughie?" he asked, slurring from the sheer height of vodka he'd necked, right along with the rest of our year. "A fucking bazillion honors?"

"He got eleven honor-level A's," Gibsie informed him proudly. "All higher level." Grinning, he leaned over and patted my head. "They'll be no manual labor in this fella's future. Fucker's going to be a heart surgeon."

"Jaysus." Robbie released a low whistle. "Are ya, Hugh?"

"That's the plan," I replied, catching a glimpse of Feely scampering off with a tiny redhead.

"Well, fair play to ya," Robbie replied and then pointed a finger at himself. "I'm as thick as the ditch, me. I barely scraped a pass on most of my exams—failed three of them. I'll be shoveling shite on the aul fella's farm for the rest of my days."

"Join the club," Gibs said, offering his two cents. "The only university I'll be seeing is when I visit the lads."

I tried to keep up with the conversation, truly I did, but no matter how hard I tried, my attention returned to Liz.

A horrible sinking feeling settled in my stomach, while a voice in the back of my mind warned, *A storm is coming.*

I'VE NEVER FELT BETTER

SEPTEMBER 22, 2003

"How are you feeling, Lizzie?"

Like I want to ram that pen you're twiddling in your eye. "Fine."

"Any recent nightmares?"

Like you give a shit. "No."

"How are you testing at school?"

Higher than you ever did. "Straight A's."

"Do you have any questions?"

Yeah. "No."

I could see the concern in the doctor's eyes.

I could register that much, but nothing else was coming through.

The poor fool was out of his depth with me, which suited me fine because nothing made sense anymore.

Except the colors.

Holy fuck, the colors were mesmerizing.

My senses had heightened to the point where I felt I had spiritually leveled up.

I could feel the air touching my skin.

I thought I might be the first person to see oxygen.

It was blanketing my skin like ecstasy.

Breathing made me ache for Hugh, and I couldn't stay still.

I was restless and full of unbearable urges and desires.

Fuck, I loved this life.

I wanted to climb onto a cloud with Hugh Biggs and take him away from all our so-called friends.

Keep him forever and never give him back.

Perhaps this was what it felt like to spiral.

I had no clue and I cared even less.

Everything was a trigger, spurring me into an agitated state of needing to move.

Unease thrummed inside of my veins like a drum, pushing me to move and laugh and run and do anything I could to get the feeling out of me.

To push *him* out.

Push him away.

Far, far away.

Think of Hugh.

Think of how good his fingers make you feel.

Stifling a groan, I clenched my thighs shut and resisted the urge to rock on the hard seat beneath me and pretend it was his face.

My body was burning.

Flames igniting from my fingertips.

I'm hungry.

I'm so fucking hungry.

I needed the physical.

I needed it like I needed to breathe.

Like I needed my veins to keep distributing blood to my black heart.

All I wanted was Hugh.

"Okay, Lizzie," the doctor said, clearing his throat. "Why don't you take a seat in the waiting room while I speak to your mother."

I didn't want to take a seat in the waiting room.

I wanted to *touch*.

"How long have you been experiencing these symptoms?" Mam asked on the car ride home.

"Hmm?" I mused, captivated by how the houses looked so blurry as we whizzed past. "Faster, Mam."

"I'm going the speed limit, Lizzie."

Pressing the button on my door, I shivered in delight when a sudden blast of air attacked my senses.

The smell.

The taste.

The sight.

Holy fuck, I'd never felt more alive.

Like I could take on the world.

Like I could take down my enemies.

"Lizzie!" Mam shouted, demanding my attention.

"What?" I snapped, suddenly furious. "I was doing something!"

Mam glanced over at me, and her eyes were full of concern. "Dr. Priestly thinks you're experiencing rapid cycling."

"He's talking shit," I laughed, reaching over to pat her knee. "I've never felt better, Mam."

SLIPPING GIRLS AND SEETHING CENTERS

Hugh

OCTOBER 9, 2003

"You need to get your head in the game," Kav instructed when I walked onto the pitch ten minutes later than the rest of the team. "This is the fourth time this month you've been late to training, and you skipped last Thursday's game." He gave me a hard look. "Which would be annoying if you were a mediocre player, but you're not. You're a damn good fly half and the best ten we have. The team needs you, so get your bleeding priorities in order, lad."

"I've a girlfriend, Cap." *A sick one at that.* "Sorry I'm late, but she needed me." Shrugging, I added, "She comes first."

My captain looked at me like I had grown two heads in front of his eyes. "Are you mental?"

"No," I replied slowly. "But if you're expecting rugby to be my top priority, then I'll tell you now that it's never going to happen," I replied, unwilling to take his bad mood. *Not when I've already taken hers.*

While I appreciated the physicality of rugby and the adrenaline rush it provided, it wasn't my entire world like it was Johnny's. I enjoyed all sports because I was naturally athletic, but that's as deep as it went for me. I planned to continue playing until I finished secondary school and then hang up my boots for university. Because if I got the course I wanted at Trinity, and I *would* get it, there would be little time for sleeping, let alone extracurriculars.

Shaking my head, I jogged off in the direction of the rest of the team before our exchange got heated.

Unlike the one he had with Gibs, Johnny and I didn't have the kind of friendship where I could confide in him about the true reason behind my absenteeism.

When he first moved to Ballylaggin, he was extremely standoffish to anyone without the name Gibsie. Back then, he was so pissed off over the move that he didn't want to entertain the notion of putting down roots with friends. He was so hell-bent on going back to Dublin that he point-blank refused to engage with anyone but Gibs. He sat with the three of us at lunch, and we forged a somewhat square, but I swear back in the early days, Feely and I could have discussed building a bomb in front of him, and he wouldn't have flinched. He was completely unattached from us. By the time we hit second year and Johnny finally started to accept that his new home was his permanent one, he began to warm up to the rest of us.

That wasn't to say that Johnny wasn't a good friend of mine. He *was*. He was the first one to step in to defend the three of us and *always* kept his word. If Cap told you he would do something, it got done, and if he told you he'd be somewhere, you didn't have to worry about him not showing up. His word was good, his heart was gold, his love life was private, his lips were sealed, and his devotion to rugby was unmatched.

Johnny lived his life on a rigid schedule and saw the world through a black-and-white lens. Even if we were close enough to discuss deep and meaningful topics, my relationship with Liz wasn't one he was well-versed in.

Because Johnny arrived on the scene only a handful of months before her sister died and he had a jam-packed schedule that left little to no free time, I never had a chance to introduce Liz to him.

After the funeral, any chance of them interacting was blown to smithereens when Liz removed herself entirely from our friendship group in a bid to distance herself from Johnny's closest friend.

When Liz joined Tommen two years later, she kept a wide berth of Gibs. At school, my girlfriend kept her distance from anyone and anything even remotely involved with Gibs, which just so happened to include her boyfriend. *Me*.

My sister's initial reaction to our relationship had deeply affected my girlfriend to the point where she continued to go out of her way to keep our relationship out of Claire's face, even though Claire had long since stopped caring. Therefore, on the rare occasion we met during school somewhere other than the old library, she was never openly affectionate with me.

In fact, Liz kept to herself so much at school that I couldn't remember a time she had ever spoken to Johnny.

On the other hand, Johnny had zero interest in learning a single detail of our personal lives that didn't pertain to nutrition, sleep quality, and precision on the pitch. The only time he spoke about girlfriends was to warn us not to get distracted. Never once in the three years I'd known him had he even asked me what my girlfriend's name was.

Which begged the question, how could Johnny relate to what I was going through with Liz? How could he understand that a girl came before rugby for me?

He couldn't.

Maybe one day, a girl would walk into his world and bring him to his knees, like Liz did to me, but until that day came, it was easier to say nothing.

"Everything okay, Hughie?" Feely asked when I joined him stretching. Concern filled his blue eyes. "You've been late an awful lot lately."

"Not you, too," I grumbled, stretching out my glutes. "I just got it in the neck from Cap, lad. I don't need another lecture from you."

"No lecture," he replied calmly. "Just concerned."

"Yeah, well, me too," I muttered under my breath.

Feely winced. "Is she okay?"

No. Not even close.

The call I'd received from her mother after Liz's last appointment had confirmed that I was dead on the money.

My girlfriend was spiraling again.

The doctors had upped the dose of her current medication and had added another pill to the long list, with the hope of veering her away from the edge of full-blown mania, but so far it had been ineffective.

"She'll be fine," I said instead.

Feely wasn't dense and knew something was up, but had the good sense not to ask questions. He knew, when it came to Liz, I was extremely protective. *And even more private.*

"All right, lad," he replied, giving my shoulder a supportive squeeze. "I'm here when you need me."

HUGS, KISSES, AND HYPERSEXUAL MANIA

MEDICINE DIDN'T WORK ON ME ANYMORE.

Therapy worked even less.

When I told Hugh just that, after my latest sit-down with the white coats, he went off on a tangent.

"If you opened up and told them what's going on inside that brain of yours, then maybe they could find the correct form of treatment." Leaning against my kitchen counter, he continued to peel an apple. "I know you're not speaking up in your sessions," he continued to grumble. "And I know your bipolar symptoms are wreaking havoc on you, baby, so please do me a favor and start talking to the doctors." He implored me with his eyes to listen. "They can help you if you just open up."

Yeah fucking right.

"All they do is prescribe more tablets," I reminded him from my perch on said island. "I don't need any more fucking tablets, Hugh."

"You absolutely do if that's what they think will help," he argued, placing the neatly peeled skin into my waiting hand. "This is *serious*, and we need to get a handle on this now, baby."

"Look at me, Hugh." I beamed at him. "I'm fine."

"Presently," he replied. "But you're not okay, Liz. You know your moods are shifting way too fucking fast to be okay."

"I'm *not* manic," I argued back, hating that he was killing my buzz. "I won't *become* manic."

"You know how it starts," he continued, ignoring my pleas of sanity and serenity. "Just like this. You're up and down for a few weeks, while the roller coaster ascends higher and higher, until you peak and get sucked up in another crushing episode."

I arched a brow, amused by his analogy. "I'm a roller coaster?"

"You're a roller coaster of mood swings," he quipped. "It starts with the climb, a.k.a. the joy, and then you go higher to the kissing part, and then higher again to the sleepless nights and get more fucking reckless with your life, until you peak, do something that almost gets you killed, and drop into the depression." Scratching his jaw, he took a bite of his apple before adding, "Don't forget I've been a passenger on said roller coaster since I was seven."

"If you hate it so much, why do you keep riding it with me?"

"Because I love you," he replied simply. "And life's never boring with you."

I watched as his teeth sank into the apple and a shock of awareness hit me deep in my core.

Unable to stop myself, I raked my gaze over him greedily.

He had the best forearms. His shirt was pulled up to the elbows and he had gorgeous, corded forearms. Veiny and strong with a dusting of dark hair.

Fucking beautiful.

"Get naked," I purred, flicking open the buttons of my school shirt. "Now."

"Oh, no, no, no," my boyfriend warned, holding a hand up. "Cover those tits, witch. We're not going there right now."

"Why not?" I said, backing him up against the counter. I dropped to my knees and reached for the button on his school trousers. "You know I have a free house until tonight."

"See, this is exactly what I meant about your moods shifting," Hugh argued, trying and failing to wrestle my hands away. "Baby, we're in the middle of a conversation and you're trying to...fuck!" A sharp hiss escaped him when my mouth came around his length.

"Mm," I moaned, frantically working him over with lips, teeth, and tongue.

"Wait, wait, wait," he groaned, hips thrusting of their own accord. "You don't need to do this..."

His words broke off when I locked eyes with him and traced his length with my tongue.

"Baby," he whispered, and then one of his hands was in my hair, while the other cradled the back of my head. "I can't think straight when you put your mouth on me."

Good.

That was exactly what I wanted.

SMILING FRIENDS AND SNEAKY GIRLFRIENDS

Hugh

OCTOBER 17, 2003

"WHO PUT THAT SMILE ON YOUR FACE?" I ASKED FEELY WHEN HE JOINED ME AT THE bus stop after school on Friday. "Lad." I laughed when I took in his flushed expression. "You're blushing."

"I'm not blushing, Hughie," he replied, attempting to conceal his blush by rubbing his jaw. "I got out of last class later than expected." He shrugged dismissively. "I'm flushed from the run."

"You're flushed from a girl," I challenged with a laugh. "Who is she?"

"No one, because there's no girl," he said quickly—too quickly.

"Come on," I teased, elbowing his side. "Out with it."

"All right, fine!" Pushing a hand through his dark hair, he looked anywhere but me before saying, "There might be a girl."

"Hah." I laughed. "And who might this girl be?"

"Just someone I met in the school music club."

"Oh really." I grinned. "Do I know her?"

"Don't think so," he replied. "She's new."

"And does this girl have a name?"

"She does," he replied slowly. "But it's early days, and I don't want to say more until I know more." He blew out a breath. "Does that make sense?"

"Yeah, lad," I replied, clapping his shoulder. "It does."

"But, ah, if I happen to know more by the time your birthday rolls around, do you think it would be all right if I, ah…" His words broke off and he shifted in discomfort.

"You can bring anyone you want, lad," I filled in, taking pity on my friend because I knew this wasn't easy for him.

Feely's communication skills had always been lukewarm at best. From as far back as I could remember, he'd never been one to express himself or demand attention from people. It wasn't that he was particularly shy or lacking in confidence. He just seemed to withdraw socially. He played his cards close to his chest and was almost as allergic as Johnny was to the thought of being tied down.

While Feely had more than his fair share of random hookups, he never introduced a girl to us. When we were younger, I used to think it had something to do with his childhood crush on Liz, but once he leveled up in secondary school, I realized that he was just emotionally closed off. So this mystery girl had to have a special something about her to pluck one of Feely's highly guarded heartstrings.

The school bus rolled up a moment later and we took our usual seats. I didn't have to wait long for my bus buddy to arrive because she came barreling onto the bus a moment later, dragged behind my rambunctious sister.

"Sorry, we're late, sir," Claire told Micky, our elderly bus driver. "There was a boy." Heaving out a huge breath, my sister blocked the traffic to talk to the driver. "His name is Jamie Kelleher." She pointed to her chest. "And he asked me out, sir. *Me!*"

"Claire, how many times do I have to tell you not to call me sir?" Mickey replied. "I'm a driver, not a teacher, love." He chuckled before adding, "Off you go now, that's a good girl."

"Okay, sir," my sister chirped, thankfully releasing her grip on my girlfriend's hand when she moved for her seat. "Uh, I mean Mickey, sir."

"She ate a bag of Skittles in double maths," Liz explained, when she reached our seats and hitched her skirt up to clamber over my lap. "Which is the equivalent of hooking her up to an electricity pole."

"Sounds like you're going to have an eventful sleepover in her room tonight," I mused, gaze shamelessly moving to the up-close and X-rated view of her thighs.

"Who said anything about me sleeping in *her* room," she teased.

I opened my mouth to flirt back, but my words got stuck in my throat and my entire frame stiffened.

Goddammit to hell!

"Expect a late-night visitor in your bed," Liz purred, flopping down on the window seat.

Jaw clenched, I forced myself to nod.

Because here was *not* the place for what I had to say to her.

DOUBLING DOWN AND DIGGING IN HEELS

OCTOBER 17, 2003

"WE NEED TO TALK" WERE THE FIRST WORDS HUGH SAID WHEN HE FOLLOWED ME INTO his downstairs bathroom as soon as we got off the bus.

"Uh, I'm literally peeing," I reminded him from my perch on the toilet seat. "Can it wait?"

"No, it can't," he snapped, giving me his back. "So, hurry up."

Jesus.

He sounded furious.

Hurrying up my business, I quickly readjusted my clothes and flushed the toilet before moving to wash my hands in the sink.

"Okay, I'm finished," I announced. "What do we need to talk about?"

"Not here," he replied, turning around to look at me. "My room." And then, before I had a chance to respond, he grabbed my hand and practically dragged me upstairs with him.

"Okay, now can you tell me what's wrong?" I demanded when he slammed his bedroom door shut behind us. "Hugh?"

"I knew it," he spat, pacing his bedroom floor like a madman. "I fucking knew it, Liz."

"Would you care to inform me what you know?" I snapped back, hands planted on my hips. "And why you're so pissed with me?"

"You're cutting again," he bit out. "When you fucking *promised* me, you had stopped."

"I *have* stopped," I shouted back. "The scars on my wrists are old, Hugh."

"Do you think I'm stupid?" My boyfriend swung around to glare at me. "Do you think I can't tell when you're hiding something from me?"

"I'm not!" I hissed, feeling my temper rise right along with his. "I'm not doing anything wrong."

"Come here," he said then, moving for his bed and taking a seat on the edge. "Come here, Liz." He patted the mattress beside him, still looking furious. "I want to show you something."

Begrudgingly, I stomped over to where he was sitting and plopped down beside him. "What?"

He grabbed the hem of my school skirt and asked, "May I?"

"Yeah, fine," I tossed back angrily. "Do whatever."

Inhaling a deep breath, he peeled the fabric of my skirt up to reveal the apex of my thighs. To reveal the recently healed lesions on my skin. The ones I inflicted on myself in the bath last night.

Aw, crap.

Hugh expelled a frustrated breath and readjusted my skirt back into place. "I noticed when you got on the bus." He turned to glare at me. "*Now* tell me you aren't cutting again."

My mind went completely blank, and I couldn't think of a single thing to say in response.

Because I forgot.

Because I lied.

Because I broke my promise.

"But that's not all you've been hiding from me, is it?" Standing up, he strode over to his desk and grabbed my schoolbag. Returning to my side, he thrust my bag on my lap before instructing me to "take them out."

Panic filled me.

I was staying at his place for the weekend, and he knew that meant Mam packed my entire prescription. "Hugh."

"Take them out, Liz," he repeated sternly. "Take them out right now, or I'm taking you home and we're talking to your parents."

"No, no, no, please don't do that."

"Then *take* them out."

A deep shudder of revulsion washed over me, and I quietly did as he asked.

"I'm sorry," I whispered when I handed over the bottle. "I thought it would be okay."

Hugh didn't respond.

Instead, he unscrewed the lid on my pill bottle and tipped the entire contents into one hand.

Full of shame, I waited in silence as he counted every pill before popping them back into the bottle. "How long have you been off your meds?"

"Just a few weeks," I squeezed out, feeling my eyes water. "When they changed the dose, it made my brain feel foggy and sluggish, so I just—"

"You just decided to come off them without medical observation *again* and to hell with the consequences *again*," Hugh deadpanned.

My tears spilled over, and I tried to plead my case. "You don't understand how they make me feel."

"I understand what happens when you don't take them," he snapped, emotions rising right along with his voice. "I understand the last time you did this, you almost *died*." His eyes filled with tears and his chest heaved as he continued to shout, "I had to cut you down from a makeshift noose, Liz! You spent six weeks in a goddamn hospital bed. Why would you even *think* about coming off your meds again?"

"I'm sorry, I'm sorry," I strangled out, quickly moving for him. "I don't know what I was thinking or if I was even thinking to begin with. I just…I just…"

"You just *what*, Liz?" he demanded, looking broken. "What did you think was going to happen?"

"I didn't think," I choked out, feeling too much right now. "That's the point."

"I'm not going through this with you every time you decide you're cured," he warned, shaking his head. "There's no cure, Liz, but there *is* treatment, so let yourself be fucking treated!"

"I just wanted to be normal, okay!" I screamed, tears flowing freely down my face. "I just wanted a fucking shot at being like every other person our age who doesn't have to ram pill after fucking pill down their throat in order to function!" Feeling myself slip, I fisted my hair and tugged, needing the physical anguish to distract my mind from the very real meltdown brewing. "I don't want to live my life like this. A fucking guinea pig for psychiatrists to try different treatments on."

"Liz, come here." Hugh tried to coax me, moving for me with his arms extended. "It's okay, baby, we'll handle this."

"No, no, no—don't do that." I shook my head and backed away from him. "Don't hold me when you're mad at me, Hugh, because I know it'll be out of pity!"

"Well, that's too fucking bad," he snapped, closing the space between us and roughly pulling me into his arms. "Because I'm never not going to hold you, Liz."

I'M GOING DOWN SWINGING

Lizzie

THE MOMENT I STEPPED THROUGH THE FRONT DOOR OF HOME ON SUNDAY EVENING, having spent the last forty-eight hours at the hospital, I went straight to my room despite my mother's protests to come downstairs and *talk* to her.

Yeah, she could go to hell—right along with my asshole dad and my traitor boyfriend.

Screw every last one of those assholes.

Slamming my bedroom door shut, I paced the room like a crazed person, earning every letter of my diagnosis.

Early-onset bipolar disorder was a term that had been thrown around since as far back as I could remember and the reason doctors had given for my catastrophic mind.

When the illness began in early childhood, like it had for me, it was extremely difficult to treat and often considered more severe, with a worse prognosis, than bipolar disorder that was not early onset.

Because the treatments available to those with adult-onset bipolar weren't available to children, it became a matter of trial and error from the medical professionals until they found a treatment that stuck.

This was the explanation I had been given every time I found myself in front of a new doctor or was prescribed a random new drug to "cure" me.

While my mood seemed to stabilize with the last concoction of drugs they cooked up during my last hospitalization, the effectiveness had waned to the point where I was rapid cycling.

The psychiatrist on call at the hospital this weekend told my parents the extreme highs and lows I was going through, shifting quickly between manic and depressive episodes, was a result of experiencing "mixed episodes"—something common in children and teens with my illness.

I understood that.

It was *my* lived experience, not theirs.

I was the one who got swept up in mania before being spat back down to the hellish depths of depression.

I was the one who lost track of time and memories.

I was the one whose will weakened with every passing day.

I was the one without faith or hope for the future.

I was the one whose mind chipped away at my soul.

And *I* was the one who had to live like this until the day I died.

None of these assholes had a single clue of how life was for me, and no number of books, research, or college credentials could teach them, either.

Of course, Mam's first instinct was to cry, while Dad's was to try to admit me for inpatient treatment.

Thankfully, he didn't get his way, and I was allowed to return home this evening, dosed to the high heavens with antipsychotics and sedatives, and a new script my father vowed to physically force into me if I even thought about fucking around.

Like I give a shit what he does.

He could try to lock me up all he wanted, but I would go down swinging.

"Liz." Hugh's familiar voice came from the other side of my bedroom door. "Can I come in?"

"So you can do some more spying for my parents?" I called back, halting mid-pace to glare at the closed door. "No thanks, Judas."

I heard my boyfriend release a frustrated growl before pushing the door open and stalking into my room. "I know you're pissed, but I need you to talk this out with me."

"Why? Have you spent your thirty pieces of silver already?" I countered angrily, planting my hands on my hips. "Need to siphon some more of my secrets?"

"I *didn't* betray you," he snapped back, mirroring my actions. "And you're going to see that when you're—"

"When I'm what, Hugh?" I screamed, body blistering from anger. "Huh? When I'm *what*!"

"When you're *you* again!" he roared, losing his cool with me. "When you're *you*, Liz."

"News flash, asshole, this is me!" I screamed back, throwing my hands in the air. "This is me, and you can take it or leave it."

"Liz." Hugh's voice was calmer when he walked over and placed his hands on my shoulders. "*Look* at me."

"No, no, no," I strangled out, shaking my head. "Don't even think about pulling that stunt on me."

"I'm not pulling any stunts," he replied, voice achingly gentle when I was screaming like a banshee. "And I'm not leaving you, either." His hands drifted up to cup my face. "Just look at me, baby." His thumbs caressed my cheeks tenderly. "Hmm?" He stepped closer. "Come back to me…"

"Does he know all the ways I've had you, munchkin?"

"He'll never have your firsts, munchkin…"

"All of those belong to me…"

"I'll make sure Biggs knows just how big of a whore his little girlfriend is…"

"And then I'll kill him…"

A lone tear trickled down my cheek and I leaned into his touch. "I can't."

LUNCHTIME LIAISONS IN LIBRARIES

Hugh

OCTOBER 24, 2003

"DID YOU ASK LISA DONOVAN FROM SIXTH YEAR TO BE YOUR GIRLFRIEND AT THE weekend?" Feely asked Johnny at big lunch on Friday.

We were breaking up from school today for the Halloween midterm and instead of being thrilled about my upcoming birthday and a week off school, I'd never felt more stressed.

"Because she's telling the entire school she's with you."

"Did I fuck?" Kav spluttered, looking thoroughly offended at the notion. "What do ye take me for? A bleeding eejit?" Craning his neck up, he squinted across the lunch hall. "Which one is she?"

Feely pointed across the lunch hall to the girl in question. "The blond with the huge ass."

I watched as our captain strained to get a better look at the blond before shaking his head. "Nope," he confirmed before resuming his lunch. "Never happened."

"Well, according to her, you did."

"Well, according to me, I didn't," Kav snapped back, sounding irritated by the inquisition. "Lad, I've never spoken to that girl, let alone asked her to be my bleeding girlfriend."

"You could do a lot worse, Johnny," Gibsie snickered. "She's a sixth year, you know."

"Then why don't you go ask her out, Gibs?" Kav shot back, smacking Gibs upside the head with a rolled-up ball of tinfoil. "Since you're so fond of older women." Shrugging, he added, "Besides, I don't like blonds."

"You don't?" Feely asked, eyebrows raised in surprised.

"What can I say?" Kav replied with another shrug of his shoulders. "I'm more of a brunette man."

"*I don't like blonds,*" Gibsie mimicked before sticking his middle finger up at him. "What do you call me, asshole?"

"Am I fucking you, Gerard?"

"I sincerely hope not, Jonathan."

"Well then, there you go."

"Say you like blonds."

"I will not."

"Say it."

"It's a preference. I'm *allowed* to have a preference, asshole."

"You most certainly are not," Gibsie huffed. "Not when it leaves me out."

"Oh my Jesus, Gibs, it's nothing personal, lad," Kav groaned. "It's just my ma's blond."

"So?" Gibsie glared across the table at him. "I'm not asking you to fuck your mother." Grinning, he added, "I'll save you the trouble and do it for ya."

"You keep your beady, little eyes off my ma, ya hear?"

"I don't have beady eyes. I have bed-me eyes."

"Someone take him away from me before I throttle him."

"No can do, Cap," Feely laughed. "You took permanent custody of him in sixth class. He's yours to handle."

"To be fair, I think we'd all fuck your mam, Johnny," Robbie Mac tossed out.

The rest of us cracked up around him, while our captain glowered in silence, staring into his shitty chicken-filled lunchbox like he was *so misunderstood.* "I hate the lot of ye."

"Did you fill Hughie in on your genius plan yet?" Feely asked then, eyes laced with amusement, as he looked at Gibs. "You probably should, considering it's taking place at his house."

"What?" Stifling a groan, I looked between the two of them. "What did you do, Gibs?"

"It was supposed to be a surprise, Patrick," Gibsie huffed, eyeballing our friend. "Can you keep nothing to yourself?"

"*Me?*" Feely laughed. "You're one to talk, lad. Besides, I'm fairly sure Hughie would've twigged on when you started smuggling slabs of beer into his kitchen."

He didn't need to say another word.

I had already clicked on.

My sister had received a phone call from the school's hockey coach last week. The senior team had an important blitz in Kildare the day after my birthday, and a member of the team had broken her ankle. When the coach asked Claire if she would be willing to temporarily jump ships from the junior team to the senior one, she'd instantly agreed.

Mam being Mam had immediately agreed to take her, and had swapped out shifts at work to make it happen. It would entail an overnight stay, with Mam and Claire leaving at the crack of dawn the day after my birthday.

The most shocking part of the plan was when *Dad* told them to book adjoining rooms at the hotel because *he* was going with them.

"Tell me you haven't," I said flatly, staring across the lunch table at Gibs. "Tell me you haven't planned a party at *my* fucking house."

He grinned sheepishly. "I'm afraid I can't, Hugo."

I knew it.

That sneaky, little, pierced-nippled fucker had been acting sketchy ever since the call came in from my sister's coach. "Mam's already throwing me a party on Halloween night."

"And *I'm* throwing you an even better one on *Saturday* night," he chimed back, grinning like a dope. "Minus the Irish mammy."

"Cancel it," I bit out, glaring at him.

"Can't do that either I'm afraid." He chuckled nervously. "The invites went out days ago."

"Why don't you move it to your house, Gibs?" Feely asked, while I repressed the urge to throttle the pain in my hole that was Gerard Gibson. "Your parents are in Spain until Sunday, aren't they?"

"*Parent*," Gibs corrected before quickly rambling on. "And I would if I could, but you know how Brian freaks everyone out, and Mam gives him free rein of the house."

"Just lock him in the garden for the night," Feely suggested. "A bit of fresh air won't harm him."

"Brian's not the one I'm afraid of coming to harm," Gibsie muttered under his breath, looking comically terrified. "He's the size of a goat, Feely. A very mean, very evil goat, I tell ya!"

Deciding to excuse myself before I lost what precious patience I had left, I went in search of the girl who had been carefully avoiding me all week.

I knew I was on her shit list for telling her parents she came off her meds, and Liz knew she was on mine for coming off said meds.

A huge part of me regretted opening my mouth because Mike had instantly resorted to threatening his daughter with hospital. That particular threat was one that usually scared my girlfriend into a panic, but instead of submitting, she laughed in his face.

Her mood swings were off the charts, and I had whiplash trying to keep up. We both felt betrayed, but instead of hashing it out like we usually did, my girlfriend had taken to avoiding me, which, I had to admit, was a first for us.

When she wasn't with Claire at their table, I knew exactly where she would be. The same place she'd been sneaking off to since she walked through the doors in first year.

Because I could read her better than any number of the books she surrounded herself with. She was my chosen field, my strongest subject, and I was sure no other heart could be a specialist in the field of Elizabeth Eleanor Young.

When I reached the old library, I headed straight for the left wing, knowing she would be lurking there.

At the very end, sprawled out on her belly with her schoolbag propping her chest up, Liz flicked through the pages of a book, while she swung her feet around aimlessly.

With her chin propped up in one hand, she hummed softly, shoulders and legs swaying along to the beat in her head, thoroughly engrossed in whatever she was reading.

"'Silver Springs'?" I broke the moment by asking, taking a seat on the floor.

Liz looked over her shoulder, giving me a glimpse of those soul-sucking blue eyes before turning back to her book. "Why break the habit of a lifetime?"

"What are you reading?"

"*Lady Chatterley's Lover.*"

My brows shot up. "Where'd you find a copy of that?"

She pointed toward a particular dusty shelf and smirked. "Who knew Tommen had such interesting reading material."

"Clearly you," I mused. "Have you taken your meds today?"

She responded by giving me the finger.

Lovely.

"Have you been here all day?"

"Yep."

"Are you ready to hash this out with me?"

"Nope."

Lips twitching, I hooked my arms around my knees and asked, "Are you planning on going to the rest of your classes?"

"Nope."

"Why not?"

"Because there isn't a member of faculty nearly as stimulating as D.H. Lawrence."

I forced back the smile that was attempting to spread across my face. "You know, if you keep skipping your classes, you're going to fall behind."

Liz snorted in response, like it was the most ridiculous thing she'd ever heard, and when it came to her freakishly gifted mind, it probably was.

"Okay then, maybe you won't fall behind, but you'll get in trouble."

"What can they say, Hugh?" she drawled, entirely unperturbed by the notion. "*Stop going to the library?*"

The bell sounded then, signaling the end of lunch break.

"You better get going," Liz muttered, flicking over another page of her book. "Don't you have rugby training after big lunch on Fridays?"

"I do," I replied slowly. "Don't you have your weekly session with the school counselor after big lunch on Fridays?"

"I do," she replied, not giving an inch.

"And are you planning on attending?"

Her response was to flip to the next page.

I sighed heavily. "Liz."

"I'm not going today, Hugh."

"Why not?"

"Because, thanks to you, I spent all weekend holed up in the hospital being grilled by a revolving door of medical professionals that don't know me and can't fix me. So excuse me if I'm tired of *talking*," she strangled out, voice thick with emotion. "And even if I weren't sick to death of having people poke holes in my sanity, there's no goddamn way I would let that nosy bitch of a guidance counselor root around in my head like I'm her special project." Reaching up, she swiped a tear off her cheek before adding, "But I don't expect you to understand that, considering you're pro-counseling, pro-medication, pro-fucking-everything-that-makes-me-feel-dead-inside!"

WE'RE LIKE BIRDS, HUGH

OCTOBER 27, 2003

TODAY WAS THE *BEST* DAY.

I didn't feel an ounce of anger.

Not one little bit.

Instead, I felt *enchanted*.

Like the world was glowing with sunbeams.

Everything was blissful and glorious.

No fear.

No sorrow.

Just *everything*.

"This is where it happened," I declared, stopping midpoint on the bridge. "Over here." Gripping the metal bars of the railing, I leaned over the side to glance at the river below. "This exact spot."

Loud swishing.

Lustrous water.

Absolute revelry.

"This is where she went over." Glancing over my shoulder at my boyfriend, I inclined my head to him. "Come see."

Reluctantly, he did.

Closing the space between us, Hugh pressed his chest to my back and looked over my shoulder. "You think this is where she fell in?"

"I know it is," I mused, reveling in the feel of his big, strong body pressed to mine. Desire instantly roared to life inside of me when his arm came around my waist, and my body pulsed with need. "Mm. You make me feel so good."

"How do you know that?" he asked softly, nuzzling the side of my head with his cheek. "Hm?"

"Because I was there, silly."

"What do you mean you were there?"

"I mean I was there." Pushing my hands through my hair, I inhaled deeply, while my body absorbed the cold autumn breeze attacking my senses. "I see her every night." Releasing a breathy moan when my nipples hardened from the stinging wind, I leaned back and felt enveloped in his love. "She comes to see me in my dreams, you know."

"You've had dreams about her falling in?" Hugh's voice was gentle and probing. "In your dreams, this is where she goes in?"

"Mm-hmm." Nodding lazily, I turned around to face him. "You're so pretty."

Whiskey-brown eyes stared down at me. "You feeling okay, baby?"

"Mm-hmm." Reaching up to cradle his face with both hands, I pulled his mouth down to mine. "You're going to make me better soon," I breathed, lips brushing against his tenderly. "You're my medicine, aren't you?"

"I'll be anything you need me to be," he replied against my lips, while slowly backing away from the railing and taking me with him. "Why don't we go back to my place, and I'll cook dinner for you?"

"But I don't want dinner," I complained against his lips, desperately trying to deepen our kiss. "I want your special medicine."

"I don't have special medicine, Liz," he said, trying to coax me, while he reached up and covered my hands with this. "But I have your favorite ice cream in the freezer and a couple of movies rented from Xtra Vision." He leaned in and kissed me softly. "Hmm?" Another gentle kiss. "We can bring a duvet downstairs and have a movie day on the couch?"

"Mm-hmm." Nodding, I pressed a kiss to his lips before pushing his hands away and returning to the railing. "Bye, Caoimhe."

"Liz." Hugh sounded sad. "Let's just go home, okay?"

"Yeah, okay," I mused, stepping onto the bottom bar of the rail and then the next one up before turning around to face him. "Hey, Hugh?"

"Yeah, Liz?"

"Would you come with me if I jumped?"

"Liz." Fear flashed in his eyes, and somewhere in the back of my mind, I could tell that he wasn't enjoying this nearly as much as I was. "Climb down. Now."

I could hear the panic in his voice, see it in his eyes, but I pushed for more.

For the breaking point, without feeling, without care for the consequences.

"We're like birds, Hugh," I continued to tell him, as my mind spiraled and my body was engulfed in a hundred thousand sensations. All at once. "We could soar if you just give it a chance." Inhaling a deep breath, I raised my hands to the sky. It was magical. "Just close your eyes and fly."

"I'm not going to do that, Liz, and neither are you, okay?"

"God, I feel so much, Hugh." Smiling, I closed my eyes, stretching my arms out as far as they could go. "It's like the sun is kissing my skin. Can't you feel it, Hugh? Is it kissing you, too?"

"Yeah, baby, I can feel it. Just come down, please."

"I love you so much, Hugh."

"Liz!"

Inhaling the deepest breath I could, I let myself fall backwards and waited for the water to embrace me.

It didn't come.

The only thing I felt was a pair of strong arms around my body as he pulled me to safety.

As he pulled me back to him.

Back to the here and now.

Back to life.

I'M KEEPING MY BABY

Hugh

OCTOBER 28, 2003

WHEN I COAXED LIZ BACK TO MY HOUSE YESTERDAY AFTERNOON, AFTER THE INCIDENT on the bridge, I had immediately called her mother for help.

Unfortunately, I could only reach Mike, who proceeded to tell me that he was waiting on a doctor to visit Catherine, who had fallen ill from the stress of trying to raise—and I quote—"the biggest misfortune to ever happen to them."

As you can imagine, that comment went down like the *Titanic* with me, and after an extremely heated exchange, I was told to have my mother drop Liz off at the nearest hospital because he had washed his hands of her.

He had washed his hands of his mentally ill teenage daughter.

My girlfriend's father actually *said* those words *out loud.*

Prick.

Whether it was the right thing to do or not, it wasn't something I was capable of doing to my best friend.

Lying down on the road outside my house and having the neighbors drive over me with their cars would hurt less than abandoning my girlfriend at a hospital.

Confiding in my mother wasn't an option, either, because I knew in my heart that Mam would do what *I* couldn't.

So instead of doing any of those things, I spun a yarn to my mother about Liz needing to stay over for a few days while her folks were away, and did everything I could to protect my girlfriend's dignity.

Holed up in my room, I used every tool at my disposal to keep her mind relaxed and her body sated.

Lips.

Fingers.

Tongue.

Whatever she needed, I gave to her without complaint, while I mentally prayed for her to come back to me of her own freewill.

And without the intervention of another inpatient admission to the psychiatric ward.

ONE MORE SLEEP

Lizzie

OCTOBER 30, 2003

HUGH'S LIPS WERE ON MINE, AND I HAD NEVER FELT A KISS LIKE IT.

He loved me with his tongue.

I knew it was a strange reference to a passionate kiss, but it was the truth.

He had always loved me with his kiss.

All his kisses.

All his touches.

They belonged to me.

All of him, period.

"I want you," I told him, completely reckless with my actions as I straddled his lap and moved into position without faltering.

The driving urge I had to be filled up by him was almost suffocating. I was suffocating and I could only breathe again once he was inside of me.

I wanted to laugh and cry and scream and throw my head back all at once.

The driving force behind my urges felt supernatural because I couldn't be sated.

The agonizing need for more was constant.

It was physically painful to the point where I was willing to fall on my knees to get what I wanted.

What I needed.

I *needed* constant access to him twenty-four seven, and even then, it would never be enough.

As for sleep?

Well, I didn't need to sleep anymore, either.

I was running on magic, like Superwoman.

I was invincible.

Nothing could stop me.

It was so freeing.

It was exhilarating.

"Liz." His voice was torn. "We need to talk."

"No, we don't." I pulled and tore at his chest, fingers digging into his glorious skin. "We need to touch."

Oh God, he looked so good.

I wanted his naked body rubbing against mine.

Without barriers.

Without any clothes.

"Please, baby," he groaned against my lips. He had one hand clamped on my hip while the other was cupping my cheek. "Let's just slow down and talk for a bit."

"You're hard," I replied, completely disconnected from the words coming out of his mouth. I couldn't hear his words. I could only *feel* his body.

Not satisfied with the limited physical touch, I rocked my hips, aligning the softest part of me with the hardest part of him.

Now I could feel him where I needed him to be.

"Have me," I begged, encouraging him to touch my breasts with one hand while pushing his other hand between my thighs. "Have me, Hugh."

"Fuck," he breathed, chest heaving, when his finger slid deep inside me. "I shouldn't be doing this."

"You should," I coaxed, rocking into his touch and tugging at the waistband of his jocks. "It's okay."

Hissing out a moan when I reached inside his boxer shorts, he thrust his hips into my touch when my hand came around his shaft. It was a challenge because there was a lot of *him* to grip, but I knew just how he liked to be touched. "Fuck, Liz…baby, that feels so good."

"Give me more," I begged, riding his hand. "Put more inside me," I urged, needing more in the moment. "One more night and you can put everything inside me."

IT'S SHOWTIME, BABY

Hugh

OCTOBER 31, 2003

To be fair to Mam, she didn't hover or linger when my friends arrived at my house on Halloween night. Instead, she gave us a decent amount of privacy while keeping a watching eye from Mrs. Grady's house across the street.

It was a testament to the trust my mother had in me, and it was wholly undeserved, because inside the top drawer of my nightstand was a three-pack of condoms labeled "extra safe."

"Best foot forward, lads," Gibs instructed, as we all sat around the firepit in my back garden, toasting marshmallows and stealing swigs from a flagon of Devil's Bit. "Tonight, we'll be angels." He grinned mischievously. "But tomorrow night, we'll be fallen angels."

"Devils," Pierce O'Neill corrected.

Gibs looked at him in confusion. "Huh?"

"Tonight, we'll be angels, tomorrow night, we'll be devils," Pierce reeled out.

"Sounds better," Robbie Mac agreed.

"Yeah," Danny laughed. "Way fucking better than fallen angels."

"Stop policing my speech, assholes," Gibsie grumbled, taking a bit of his marshmallow. "I said what I said."

"Don't mind them," Feely consoled, giving Gibs his marshmallow. "You're grand, Gibs."

I tried to keep up with their conversation, I really tried, but it was impossible when my girlfriend was sitting on my lap and circling her hips in such an erotic way that I was painfully hard.

"I need you now," Liz whispered in my ear, tongue snaking out to taste my earlobe.

My eyes fluttered closed and it took the world of strength to hold it together in this moment.

"Be with me, Hugh." Her lips were on my neck then. "Be *in* me."

It was too much and not enough all in one breath.

Unwrapping her arms from my neck, Liz stood up and walked toward the patio door, all the while glancing over her shoulder with a look that said, *here, boy.*

Like a well-trained puppy dog, I obediently followed her, ignoring the cheers and wolf whistles coming from the firepit behind me.

Taking me by the hand once we reached the upstairs landing, she pulled me along wordlessly until we reached my room.

Once inside, she turned the lock and walked me over to my bed; all the while my heart was threatening to beat its way out of my chest.

This was it.

Tonight was the night.

Could I do it?

I wasn't sure.

We both kicked off our shoes, and Liz reached up on her tiptoes to press a hot kiss to my mouth.

"I've been craving this for so long," she admitted, while her fingers made short work of the button and zip on my jeans. "Take it off," she breathed, reaching for the hem of my shirt and pushing it up. "Get naked for me."

"Are you sure?"

"Show me the goods, Biggs," she instructed, as she quickly rid herself of every scrap of fabric on her body.

I was so fucking lost in the moment, so completely hooked on the vision that was her naked body, that I did everything she asked.

"Perfect," she approved, gaze raking over my naked form. "You were made for me."

When she pushed me down on my bed and straddled my lap a few moments later, the pressure was almost too much to take. "Lie down," she commanded, taking the lead by pushing me onto my back. "Mm, yeah, just like that."

Her lips came crashing down on my mouth at the same time her hand fisted my shaft.

"Fuck," I groaned, gripping the sheets beneath us. "Liz…"

"You're always saving me, Hugh," she purred, working me over with reckless abandon, as she peppered my face with kisses. "Let me take care of you for once."

I wanted to.

I really fucking did.

But then I thought of how her eyes looked tonight, all shiny and wild, and the guilt rapidly rose up. "Liz, wait."

We couldn't do this.

Not while she was in the throes of an episode.

"Mm," she breathed, moving her body into position, tracing the head of my dick against herself. "I can't wait to feel this deep inside me."

Slamming the brakes on this was something I wasn't sure another fella my age could do, but I did it. "Wait!" Clamping my hands on her hips, I carefully lifted her off me before bolting to my feet.

"What's wrong?" she demanded, all sexy eyed and breathless. "You're so hard. You were enjoying it."

"I was—I am," I hurried to say, while I pulled my jocks back on. "But we can't do this tonight."

Liz remained silent for a grand total of ten seconds before exploding. "What the fuck, Hugh?" she demanded, climbing to her feet. "You promised we could have sex tonight!"

"Keep it down," I whisper-hissed, pointing to the wall that separated my room from my sister's. "Claire's in bed."

"I don't give a fuck!" My girlfriend continued to seethe, looking almost feral now. "You said you would fuck me, so fuck me, dammit!"

"I can't," I strangled out, willing her to just hear me out. "Not when you're like this."

"Like what?"

"Manic, baby!" I pulled on my jeans and went to her. "Not while you're manic."

Liz glared up at me like she couldn't comprehend a word of it. "I'm not waiting another night."

"You're going to have to," I replied calmly, while I dressed her in my hoodie.

"I'm having sex tonight, Hugh," she said, smacking my hand away. "It's happening."

"Not with me, it isn't."

"Fine," she screamed, stalking toward the door. "If you won't fuck me, I'll find someone who will."

GIVE ME WHAT I WANT OR ELSE!

OCTOBER 31, 2003

HUGH LIED.

He was a *liar*.

He tricked me into thinking he could make me better and then he snatched it all away.

Didn't he understand how badly I needed him?

Didn't he care that I was burning up in flames?

Everything ached and I needed him, dammit!

I couldn't make sense of my thoughts anymore.

I didn't even know where I was going.

All I knew was I felt consumed by rage and *had* to move.

"Hey!" a strange voice called out before a big hand clamped down on my shoulder. "Where are ya going?"

Confused, I swung around to see one of Hugh's rugby pals. "Where am I going?"

"Yeah," he replied slowly, blue eyes one mine. "You okay?" His gaze raked over me and his brows furrowed. "Why are you wandering around the street in a hoodie?"

Was I?

"I'm not sure." Puzzled, I dropped my gaze to Hugh's hoodie that I was wearing and then to the streetlights illuminating the darkness. "I, uh…I don't know."

"Hey," the boy said, holding both my shoulders now. "It's okay. Don't look so sad."

"I am sad."

"Why?"

"Because I…" I blew out a pained breath. "I just want to feel good."

"Feel good?"

"Mm-hmm." Closing my eyes, I swayed from side to side. "I want to be touched."

"You do?"

"Mm-hmm."

"If you want to feel good, I can make that happen for you."

Shivering, I instantly stepped closer. "You can?"

"Yeah." His hands moved to my hips and he pulled me close. "If you want me to."

"Mm." Releasing a frustrated moan, I felt my body sway. "I just want—"

"Liz!"

Confused or not, I *knew* that voice.

Spinning around, I came face to face with those whiskey eyes.

"You can go," Hugh told the other body in a cold tone. "Now."

"Lad, your girl must be wasted," the boy said, laughing nervously as he backed up. "I found her rambling around the street half-naked."

"Yeah, and I'll look after her," Hugh replied, nostrils flaring. "Leave, Pierce."

The boy looked between us before shaking his head and wandering off.

Hugh waited until Pierce was gone before speaking. "What were you doing, Liz?"

"What do you think I was doing, Hugh?" I shot back, tensing.

"I have no idea," he replied steadily. "That's why I'm asking you."

"Why don't you want me?"

"Oh, believe me. I want you."

"Then why won't you fuck me?"

"Because I'm trying to *protect* you."

Fuck, he looked so damn good.

"I can smell your cologne," I groaned, moving my feet until our chests were flush. "You smell so good. Hey—why are you pulling away?" I asked when I tried to kiss him, and he leaned away.

"Come on." He took my hand in his and started leading me away from the street-light. "Let's just get back in the house, okay?"

"No, no, no, I'm not going anywhere with you," I argued, narrowing my eyes at the boy walking me down the street. "You lied to me."

"We can talk about that in the morning," Hugh said, keeping his voice level. "Once you've had a good night's sleep."

"I don't want to sleep," I screamed, instantly furious. "I want to fuck."

He didn't respond.

He just kept walking.

"Stop pulling my arm!"

"I'm not," he replied calmly. "You're pulling on my arm."

I was?

Oh wait, I *was*.

"My bad," I laughed. "That's funny, right?"

"Very."

I rolled my eyes. "You are so cranky."

"Whatever you say, Liz."

"Why are you agreeing to everything I'm saying?"

"Is that what I'm doing?"

"Yes, and it's pissing me off, so stop it."

He remained silent.

"Dammit, stop ignoring me."

More silence.

"I hate it when you do this."

"Do what?"

"Make me feel like a horrible person when I'm only being myself."

"I don't think you're a horrible person, Liz," he replied. "I think you're a sick person."

"That's worse."

"Okay."

"No, you know what? Fuck you." I ripped my hand out of his. "Fuck you for making me feel like it's wrong to be myself."

Hurt flashed in his eyes. "When have I done that?"

"You're doing it right now!" I pushed at his chest. "This is me, Hugh." I held my hands up and twirled around in circles. "This is all me. I'm happy. I'm me. I'm not taking those fucking pills anymore, so if you can't love me as I am, then walk the fuck away."

He stood in the middle of the road with his hands on his hips and shook his head. "You don't mean that."

"You look so fucking sexy when you're pissed with me," I said, feeling a surge of lust hit me. "I'm not the only one who wants you." I closed the space between us. "I see them watching you at school." I reached around and gripped his tight ass and dragged him roughly against me. "Wanting what's mine." I pressed a kiss to his throat. "But you're mine, aren't you?" I kissed him again. "And I'm yours."

"Then fucking act like it," Hugh finally snapped, snaking an arm around my waist. "Because I won't tolerate the kind of bullshit I saw back there." Reaching up, he smoothed the hair off my face and then forced me to look at him. "Do you hear me? If you betray me, there's no coming back from it. Not for me. Bipolar or not."

"I didn't betray you," I breathed. "I love you."

"I'm not a saint, Liz. You can only push me so far."

The angrier he got, the more I wanted him.

"You can make me better." I breathed, capturing his bottom lip between my teeth and tugging. Hugh's eyelids fluttered shut and I felt him grow against me. Releasing his lip with an audible pop, I reached a hand between our bodies and traced the outline of his bulging erection. "I know you can make me better." I squeezed, feeling his resolve weaken with every growing inch. "I can feel it."

Hugh sighed brokenly. "Believe me, Liz, if I could fix you with sex, I would fuck you forever."

"Why can't you just *try*!"

"Because I'm afraid."

"Of what?"

"Of you, Liz. I'm afraid of *you*!"

"So you're afraid to fuck me because you're afraid of me?"

"No, Liz, I'm afraid to fuck you because I don't know which version of you I'd be fucking!"

PART 19

The Great Betrayal

YOU ARE UNINVITED!

Lizzie

NOVEMBER 1, 2003

WHEN I WOKE UP THE FOLLOWING MORNING, ALONE IN CLAIRE'S ROOM, I QUICKLY climbed out of bed and went in search of my boyfriend.

When I found Hugh downstairs in the kitchen, laughing and joking with Thor, I felt immediately incensed.

Why did he look so happy when he was with *him* and not me?

What was wrong with *me*?

Why couldn't he smile at *me* like that?

Thor was the first one to notice my arrival, and I watched him discreetly nudge my boyfriend before standing up and moving for the door. "I'll head home and check on Brian for a bit."

"All right, lad," Hugh replied, smile gone now. "I'll see ya in a while." He waited until his friend left before turning his attention to me. "Morning."

"Morning," I replied, feeling pissed off and out of my depth. "Why didn't you come get me when you woke up?"

"I had things to do," he replied levelly, attention shifting to the mug he was holding. "I was talking to your mam this morning." His gaze cast downwards, and he took a drink from his mug. "She'll be here soon."

"Why?" I demanded, immediately on edge.

"To pick you up, Liz."

"I thought I was staying here?"

"Your mam is going to take you home, okay?"

"Hugh, no!" Feeling devastated, I moved for him and tried to initiate intimacy. "Come on…"

"No, Liz," he replied, immediately shutting me down. "I can't do this right now."

"Why not?"

His shoulders tensed, but he didn't respond.

"Come with me," I begged, wrapping my arms around him. "Please." I kissed his shoulder. "Don't send me back there on my own."

He released a pained sigh. "Liz..."

"Please, Hugh," I begged, feeling frantic now. "Come home with me."

Another heavy sigh escaped him, and he relented. "Okay."

Three hours later, I sat cross-legged on my bedroom floor, facing my boyfriend, and placed another card down, entirely uninterested whether it was a match or not.

Clearly, Hugh didn't care either because he didn't even look down before tossing a card down on the pile.

Instead, he kept his eyes on me the entire time.

Frustrated, I slapped another card down and arched a brow in challenge.

Again, he didn't look at the pile of cards.

He just added another to the pile.

"Are you going to tell me what's wrong?" I finally asked, unable to handle another second of this intense silence.

"That depends," he replied calmly. "Are you going to tell me what you were doing with Pierce last night?"

"Nothing."

"Okay."

"You don't believe me."

"It doesn't matter what I believe, Liz," he replied, tossing another card down. "If you're telling the truth, then you're telling the truth."

"But you don't think I am?"

"I think you need to think really carefully about what you're doing," he replied, tone eerily calm. "And who you're doing it with."

"Oh my God," I hissed, throwing my hands up. "I didn't cheat on you, Hugh."

Hugh shook his head and stood up, and the move sent me spiraling.

"Wait, no, no, no!" Scrambling to my feet, I chased after him, catching him just as he was about to open my door. "Please don't go."

"I'm not doing this with you for the rest of my life," he told me. "Do you understand that?"

"I'm fine, Hugh." Reaching up, I grabbed his face between my hands and kissed him. "See? I'm perfect."

"You're not taking your meds and you're spiraling." His brown eyes implored me to listen. "You're not in control of yourself, Liz, and if you slip next time, I mightn't be there." His nostrils flared. "If you hurt me like that, like the way you almost hurt me last night, I *will* walk away."

"I would never hurt you," I purred, trying to pull him back to my bed. "All I want to do is make you feel good."

"If you want to make me feel good, then *listen* to me," he strangled out, slipping out of my reach when I tried to unbutton his shirt. "Because I am so fucking in love with you that it hurts, okay?" A pained groan escaped him when I pounced on him and pushed him down on my bed. "Liz, please listen to me."

"You want me," I purred, feeling him growing beneath me. "I want you, too. So much I can't sleep at night." Reaching for my shirt, I whipped it over my head. "I touch myself all night and it's not enough." Grabbing his hands, I crushed them to my breasts. "I need this so bad, Hugh."

"I don't know who you are when you're like this," he admitted hoarsely. "And it scares the shit out of me." He sat up, much to my dismay, and gripped my shoulders, forcing me to look at him. "You are scaring me, Liz."

"I would never hurt you, baby," I whispered.

"I'm not scared for myself," he bit out, catching ahold of my face and forcing me to refocus on him. "Look at me."

"Fuck me."

"Look at me, Liz."

"I will when you fuck me."

"And who exactly would I be fucking?" Hugh demanded, chest heaving. "Would it be this version of my girlfriend? The one who rubs herself against other fellas when she's not trying to tear my clothes off. Or would it be the version of her that slits her fucking wrists!"

Wincing, I sucked in a sharp breath, but Hugh didn't stop, clearly on a roll now.

"Would it be the version of her that stays in bed for weeks at a time, or would it be the version of her who attacks anyone that looks sideways? Hmm? Can't tell? Well, neither the fuck can I," Hugh shouted, losing his cool now. "But when the girl I fell in love with pops back up, you let me know, and I'll be more than happy to oblige and fuck *her*." He narrowed his eyes and hissed, "Because that's the only version of my girlfriend that I have any interest in being with!"

"That's not fair!" I screamed back. "You're being unfair!"

"Yeah, well, talk to me about it when you're you again," he snapped back. "I'm uninviting you to the party tonight," he added. "Do you hear me? You are uninvited."

"Bullshit," I snarled, feeling a sudden surge of rage rise up inside of me. "I'm your girlfriend. You can't uninvite me."

"Watch me," he snapped, dropping me onto my bed.

"Hugh, wait!"

"Stay here," he ordered, grabbing his bag and moving for the door. "And take your fucking medication!"

The bedroom door slammed behind him, and I screamed.

Trashing everything in my way, I ripped and tore at the walls, feeling so much fury inside of me, I thought I might kill someone.

"You fucking bastard!" I screamed, leaning out my bedroom window to scream at him. "Fuck you, Hugh!"

"Yeah, fuck me, Liz," he called over his shoulder as he stormed down the driveway.

"I fucking hate you right now!"

He didn't turn around.

Instead, he kept walking until he disappeared from sight.

Until he was gone.

SAY HELLO TO MY LITTLE FRIEND

Hugh

NOVEMBER 1, 2003

"HOLY SHIT," DANNY CALL CHOKED OUT, JOINING US IN THE KITCHEN. "ARE THOSE lads from BCS?"

My house was packed to the rafters, compliments of Gibs, and it took me a moment to track down the group of lads he was referring to.

"Oh, yeah," I mused, instantly recognizing a few of the lads from my time at Scoil Eoin. "I haven't seen those lads in years."

"Well, should we escort them back to their side of town?"

"You're such a fucking snob," Gibs chimed in, looking wholly disgusted. "Escort them back to their side of town." He rolled his eyes. "What a fucking uppity thing to say."

Danny reddened. "Newsflash, we are uppity."

"Your dad is a pharmacist," I reminded him. "Don't get carried away with yourself."

"What's the problem anyway?" Gibsie demanded. "They're not causing any trouble, and besides, they were invited."

Danny gaped. "By who?"

"By me, asshole," Gibs shot back, sounding irritated. "You do realize that we went to primary school with them?"

"And they've been in my house before," I added, brows furrowing. Every birthday party from junior infants to sixth class. "Those lads are decent, and they're more than welcome to be here."

"Only because we had to," Pierce chuckled, joining us. "I thought we left the scum behind in primary school."

This fucker.

He had some nerve showing up tonight.

"You really are a prick, aren't ya?" I seethed, holding on to my self-control by the skin of my teeth. "Get the fuck out of my face before I break your nose."

"Holy shit, Biggsie," Danny exclaimed, looking confused. "What's the problem, lad?"

"The problem is him," I sneered, chest heaving, as I glowered at Pierce. "You better fuck off out of my sight before I take the head clean off ya. Fair warning."

Thankfully, Pierce had the good sense to do just that, disappearing into the crowd with Danny before I lost my shit.

"Care to divulge?" Gibs asked, eyeing me curiously.

"You don't want to know, lad," I replied, still simmering with tension. "Trust me."

"Okie-dokie," Gibs replied, clapping my back. "How about we stop talking and start drinking?"

"I think that's a very good idea, Gibs."

"Here," he said, pushing a shot glass of clear liquid into my hand. "Just knock it back, lad."

Not bothering to question him, I tossed it back. "Fuck," I hissed when the burning sensation clawed at my throat. "What the fuck was that?"

"Say hello to my little friend," Gibs replied in an animated voice, waving a bottle with a sombrero-shaped lid in my face. "Tried and tested by yours truly." Popping the hat off the top with exaggerated flair, he refilled my glass before pouring one for himself. "Guaranteed to numb all feeling."

I eyed him warily as he danced on the spot with the bottle cradled protectively to his chest.

"Trust me, lad." He clinked his glass against mine. "I'm the master concealer."

"Fuck it." Blowing out a shaky breath, I tipped my head back and swallowed it down in one gulp. "This was a mistake."

"On the contrary, my friend, this"—he paused to perch the little hat on his head and down his own shot, before letting out an audible hiss—"is the best decision you've made all night."

"Not the tequila, Gibs, the house party," I explained, accepting another shot from him. "This was a fucking mistake."

"Are you mental?" Still bopping and swaying, he gestured to the jam-packed kitchen. "Look around, Hugo. The house is packed. The drink is flying. The craic is ninety."

He clinked his glass against mine again before tossing it back like a pro.

"Woo!" Hissing out a breath, Gibs continued to dance. "To the first of many parties at your wonderful establishment, Hugo—oh, and don't worry about Old Murphy down the street. If that nosy bastard calls the Gards, I'll take the blame."

And if she shows up? I wanted to say, but the words wouldn't come out. Because I was shit scared of speaking it into reality.

LOSING MY GRIP

I HAD NO MEMORY OF GETTING TO HUGH'S HOUSE WHEN I STUMBLED THROUGH HIS front door, soaked to the skin, with a half-drank bottle of my father's whiskey dangling from my fingers.

Confusion gripped me tight, making it difficult to recognize the smiling faces acknowledging me.

I couldn't make out a word of what they said.

I couldn't even remember the password to unlock my phone.

All I knew in this moment was my clothes were drenched, my head was clouded, and I wanted my boyfriend.

Hugh.

Shaking my head, I stumbled up the staircase, moving on instinct, desperate to find him.

Because I *needed* him.

Because I felt like I was about to *explode.*

Because I couldn't *breathe* without his touch.

Stumbling into his bedroom, I blinked in surprise when my gaze landed on a shaved-headed boy sprawled out on my boyfriend's bed.

Tilting my head to one side, I asked, "What are you doing?"

"Waiting for you," he replied, arms folded behind his back.

"Nuh-uh," I snickered, shaking my finger. "I'm not supposed to be here tonight. Because I've been"—I hiccupped before slurring out the word—"*uninvited.*"

"Yeah, me, too," he replied with a sigh. "I'm on Biggsie's shit list," he added. "Figured I'd hang out up here for a bit and keep out of his way."

"You, too?" My eyes widened as I swung my bottle around aimlessly. "I'm on the same shit list."

He chuckled. "How wasted are you?"

"I'm not wasted," I declared, twirling around in circles. "I'm high."

"You feeling like sharing that whiskey?" he asked, gesturing to the bottle. "That's a big bottle for one girl." His gaze raked over me. "A ridiculously beautiful girl."

"Only on the outside," I slurred, stumbling over to the bed to hand him the bottle. Flopping onto the mattress, I released a wistful sigh. "My insides are ugly."

"I don't believe that for a minute," he replied, rolling on his side to face me. "Fuck, you're even better-looking up close." He took a swig from the bottle before leaning over me to place it on the nightstand. "Biggsie's one lucky lad."

"Oh God, I love him so much." Grabbing the pillow from under my head, I pressed it to my face and inhaled deeply. "But he doesn't want me."

"Of course he wants you," he chuckled, settling back down on his side, facing me. "Every lad at school wants you."

"Not him," I groaned, wanting to cry when his familiar scent from his pillow infiltrated my senses. "Because he's perfect, and I'm not."

"Well, he must be blind to not want you," the boy said, resting a hand on my hip. "And for the record, I think you're pretty fucking perfect yourself."

"You do?"

He nodded slowly. "If you were mine, I'd give you everything you want."

"Like what?"

"What do you want?"

"To be touched," I strangled out. "I want Hugh to touch me."

"He doesn't touch you?" he asked, trailing his fingers up and down my thigh.

"Can you get him for me?" I asked, struggling to focus when his hand moved higher. Clenching my eyes shut, I blew out a shaky breath. "I need to talk to him."

"Why don't you talk to me instead?" the boy coaxed, sending my body into a frenzy when his fingers slid under my dress. "I promise I'm a better listener."

"Mm…" Eyelids fluttering shut, I rolled onto my back and let my legs fall open. "Hugh." Grabbing his hand, I pushed it between my thighs and cried out when I felt his fingers push deep inside me. "Fuck me."

"You want me to fuck you?"

"I need it."

"You sure?"

"I need to feel it."

I was on *fire*.

Burning and blistering and I needed my boyfriend to touch me.

"Mm." Keeping my eyes closed, I nodded eagerly as his fingers moved inside me. "Have me."

Shivering violently, my hips arched upward of their own accord as I stared lifelessly at the wall.

"I'm close," he grunted in my ear, pushing himself deep inside me. "I'm wearing a condom, but I can pull out before I come if you want."

"...*that's it, munchkin, take me in like a good girl...*"

"Fuck, your pussy is gold."

"...*don't fight it, munchkin. Don't be a fucking crybaby like my other one...*"

Shivering violently, I held my breath and waited for it to end.

"Is this your first time?"

"...*see, that wasn't so bad, was it, munchkin? You're a big girl now...*"

"No." My tears trickled onto my pillow. "I'm a big girl."

"Hold up—are you crying?"

"...*keep your mouth shut or I'll slit her fucking throat...*"

"Jesus, I'll stop, okay," he strangled out. "Don't cry."

"No, Hugh, no!" Choking out a pained sob, I reached for him blindly. "Don't leave me."

TURN OFF THE LIGHTS

Hugh

NOVEMBER 1, 2003

"Come on, Hugh," one of the girls from one of my sister's dance groups coaxed a few hours later when she sidled up against me. "Dance with me."

"Yeah, Hugh," Gibs, who was three sheets to the wind and romancing his near-empty tequila bottle, mocked. "Dance with her."

"Sorry, Lisa, I can't," I replied with a shake of my head. "I have a girlfriend."

"Where is she?"

Hopefully at home.

"I have a girlfriend," I repeated, peeling her fingers off my shirt and taking a safe step out of danger. "But he doesn't," I blurted, shoving my teammate Luke Casey toward her.

"Wow, Hugh, how generous," Luke said dryly, while his eyes said, *you better get me out of this, asshole.*

"Oh wow." She exhaled an impressed breath. "You are *beautiful.*"

"He's so beautiful," Gibs agreed, still mimicking her high-pitched voice while batting his lashes. "Such a beautiful, beautiful boy."

Pulling a condom wrapper from her bra, she waved it in front of his face like it was some great prize, and then, before even Gibs had a chance to think of a comeback, she had her tongue down our teammate's throat far enough to touch his tonsils.

Temporarily blindsided, Luke kept his hands up at his sides, completely fucking stunned, and when she slid a hand into her jeans, I had to look away.

"Jesus Christ." Shaking my head, I turned to gape at Gibs. "What did we do?"

"You would think I'd find that sexy, but nope." Shaking his head, Gibs slugged a mouthful of tequila straight from the bottle before cupping his hand around his mouth and shouting, "Lukey, hold three fingers up if you need help!"

Our teammate raised a hand, but instead of showing three fingers, he gave us the middle one.

And then, with his mouth still surgically attached to Lisa Nevin's demon tongue, Luke hoisted her into his arms.

Without missing a beat, she hooked her legs around his waist as he walked them both toward the door.

"Jesus fucking Christ, Hugo." Gibs slapped my chest at the same time I slapped his. "I think he's going to take her upstairs and ride her."

"I think you might be right, lad," I choked out, gripping the front of his shirt as tightly as he was gripping mine. "What do we do?"

"I don't know about we, but you should definitely go upstairs and lock your door, lad." He patted my shoulder. "Unless you want to sleep in another lad's wet patch…"

I was bolting for the stairs before Gibs had a chance to finish his sentence.

Drunk and hazy, I clambered up the steps, not stopping until I reached my room—just in time to catch a glimpse of Luke and Lisa disappearing inside the spare room.

Relieved, I moved for my room anyway, deciding to check it and lock it before any other potential mishaps occurred.

When I reached the door and heard loud moaning and obvious sex noises, I was instantly pissed.

Throwing the door open, I stalked inside and flipped the light on, ready to lay into whatever asshole thought it was clever to fuck in my bed.

When the light came on, I couldn't move.

I couldn't breathe.

Rooted to the spot, while my brain struggled to comprehend what my eyes were seeing, I felt my heart shatter into a million pieces.

MAYBE YOU SHOULD HAVE THOUGHT ABOUT THAT

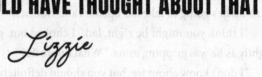

Lizzie

NOVEMBER 1, 2003

"What the *fuck* are you doing!"

"Jesus Christ, I'm sorry, lad!"

"You have one second to get your dick out of my girl before I kill ya."

It took me a moment to register the shouting, and a few more to make sense of why I felt so cold.

"Hugh, I am so fucking sorry, lad. I've been drinking and she was—ah, holy fuck, give me a chance to throw my clothes on, will ya?"

Blinking in confusion, I pulled up on my elbows and watched as Hugh pummeled another boy on his bedroom floor.

What confused me most was the fact that Hugh was the one fully clothed, while the boy getting his face caved in only had boxers on.

"Hugh," I mumbled, feeling confused.

"Cover yourself up!" he roared, pausing mid-punch to point at me. "And don't fucking talk to me right now, Liz!"

Punching resumed, I glanced down at myself, registered my glaringly naked body, and quickly dragged the duvet over myself.

Oh my God.

What did I do?

No, no, no...

What the fuck did I do?

The bedroom door flew inward then, and Thor came bursting in to assess the damage. His eyes landed on mine for a brief moment before he turned away and moved for Hugh.

"It's all right, Hughie, I've got ya." Wrapping his arms around my boyfriend, he dragged him off the boy bleeding on the floor. "He's not worth it, lad."

"Let me go, Gibs." Never in my life had I seen Hugh so unhinged as he wrestled furiously against Thor's hold, desperately trying to lunge at the boy pulling on his clothes. "I'm going to kill that prick."

"Seriously, Pierce?" Thor demanded, struggling to restrain my boyfriend. "Are you that much of fucking turnout?"

"I'm really fucking sorry, Gibs," the boy replied, toeing on his shoes before grabbing his jacket off the chair.

"Yeah, well, sorry doesn't quite cut it, asshole," Thor shot back angrily. "Not when you fuck a teammate's girl in his own bed, you prick!"

"I am so fucking sorry, lads, but she was all over me," the boy protested. "I mean it, Hughie, lad. She told me to have her."

That seemed to register with Hugh, and I watched his shoulders sag in what looked like defeat. "Get him out of here, Gibs," he whispered, sounding broken. "And send everyone home." A deep shudder racked through my boyfriend when he said, "The party's over."

The boy didn't need to be told twice and quickly bolted from the room, followed by Thor. "I'll be downstairs if you need me, lad," he said, glancing back at Hugh before closing the door and leaving us alone.

I braced myself for my boyfriend's wrath, but it didn't come.

Instead, he turned his back on me, gripped the windowsill, and stared out.

"Hugh." Scrambling off the bed, I hurried toward him. "Please, please, please let me explain."

"Put your clothes on, Liz." He didn't look at me when he spoke, choosing to stare out the window instead. "I can't look at you right now."

"I'm sorry," I strangled out, chest heaving. "I'm so fucking sorry, Hugh. Please just *talk* to me."

"Put your clothes on, Liz."

"Okay." Sniffling, I hurried back to his bed and scrabbled to find my clothes. "I am sorry."

Silence enveloped me.

"Hugh, I mean it." My tears were falling at a rapid rate, as the seriousness of the situation started to hit me. "I don't know what happened."

He didn't respond.

"Hugh, please!" Crying hard, I stepped into my underwear and pulled them up my legs. "Say something."

He didn't.

"It meant nothing, I swear. I, uh, I...I thought I was with you." When I grabbed my dress off the bedroom floor, my gaze landed on a used condom. "Oh my fucking

God!" My body shook violently, and I choked out a hoarse sob, while I quickly dressed myself. "What did I do?"

"You can stay here tonight if you don't want to call your parents to come get you," Hugh finally said. Straightening his shoulders, he blew out a breath and moved for the door. "I'm going to crash at Gibsie's."

"No, no, no, please don't leave me," I cried, rushing to intercept him, but it was too late. He was already out of the room and halfway down the stairs. "Hugh!"

"Wait," I cried out, following my boyfriend outside in the middle of the night. "Hugh, please!"

"Go back inside, Liz," he called over his shoulder as he stormed off in the opposite direction of both houses.

"Please, wait!" Running barefoot down the street, I caught up with him and grabbed his shirt. "No, Hugh, don't go." Catching onto his forearm with both hands, I cried hard and ugly when I tried to pull him to a stop. "Please don't go."

Always the gentleman, Hugh obliged and came to a stop, choosing not to drag me barefoot down the asphalt, even though I deserved it.

His entire frame was stiff, and he stared straight ahead in the darkness.

I was holding his arm, but he wasn't giving an inch.

"Look at me."

"I *can't*."

"Why not?"

"Because I don't know you anymore."

"Yes, you do." Sniffling, I reached up and tried to cup his face in my hands. "I'm still me."

"Don't." His voice was broken when he shook his head, reaching up to peel my hands from his face. "I can't have your hands on me."

"I didn't mean it, Hugh." Frantic, I entwined my fingers with his and stepped closer. "I was drunk, okay? I was looking for you. I thought it was you! I love you. I love you; I do. I'm sorry, I'm sorry. I'm so fucking sorry."

"You fucked him, Liz!" he roared, losing his cool. "Pierce O'Neill! My own god-damn teammate! You *fucked* him. So don't stand here and tell me you love me."

"I do love you, Hugh!"

"You don't know the meaning of the word." He seethed, chest heaving. "I loved you, Liz. Me." He slapped a hand against his chest. "I fucking loved you enough to put you first. Even when it was hard to do the right thing. I fucking did it. Because that's what someone does when they love someone. They put that person first."

"I…" shaking my head, I racked my brain to find the words to make this better. To turn back the clocks. "I don't know why I did it." A pained sob escaped me. "It didn't mean anything to me. It's just…sometimes, I get these feelings, and I need…"

"Do you think that asshole cares about you?" he cut me off and demanded, gesturing to the house we had left. "Do you think he gives a shit about anything other than what's under your clothes? Because I'll let you in on a little secret, Liz, he doesn't. Ninety-nine percent of the assholes at my house tonight don't give two shits about anything other than getting their dicks wet!"

"Hugh," I cried, clinging to him for dear life. "I'm so, so sorry."

"You are not a person to those assholes, Liz," he continued to shout, voice cracking with emotion. "They don't care about your heart or your mind or your vulnerability. They don't give a shit about any of that. Because when they look at you, all they're seeing is pussy!"

"I'm so sorry." Violent sobs racked through me. "I just wanted to forget."

"Forget what?" he demanded hoarsely. "Me? Was I so fucking bad to you that you had to do this? You couldn't wait?"

"I'm so sorry. I'm so sorry," I cried, feeling hysterical. "You've been perfect to me. I've never had someone care about me like you have."

"Yeah? Well, newsflash, Liz, it's not all about how you feel," Hugh shot back, chest heaving. "I was in the relationship, too, and *I* wasn't fucking ready for sex, okay? I gave you nine fucking years of my life, and you fuck a randomer in my bed?"

"I don't know how it happened!" I cried out, grabbing my hair. "I just…I wanted to feel good."

"So your need to feel good made it okay to *cheat* on me?"

"Hugh." I couldn't breathe. "I didn't mean to; I swear to God! I think I'm drunk and I just…" I shook my head and cried hard. "I am so sorry!"

"Yeah, see the difference between us, Liz, is that I could *never* be intimate with anyone other than you," he strangled out, trembling. "Drunk or not, I could *never* give myself to some randomer like you just did."

"Just give me another chance, Hugh." Sniffling, I tried to hook my arms around his neck. "Let me fix this, okay?"

"It's too late."

"No." Crying uncontrollably, I held on for dear life, feeling like my entire world was slipping from my fingers. "Please don't say that."

"You can't keep doing this to me," he cried hoarsely, battling to capture my hands that were touching him everywhere. "Liz, you're fucking *killing* me."

"I'm not trying to," I sobbed uncontrollably. "I just…I fuck everything up."

"I thought I knew who you were," he whispered brokenly. "I thought I was what you wanted." A tear rolled down his cheek. "I was wrong."

"Don't say that," I cried, trying to kiss him and feeling devastated when he dodged me. "I do want you. You're all I want."

"You're going to come out of this." Sniffling, Hugh turned his head away and used his shoulder to wipe his check. "And when you do, you're going to hate yourself as much as I *wish* I could hate you."

"Hugh!"

"This is over, Liz."

No.

No.

No, no, no, no, no!

"Please, Hugh," I strangled out, feeling my world fall apart. "Please, I'm begging you!"

"This is *over*," Hugh repeated, voice cracking as he sucked in a shaky breath. "You can stay in my house tonight, and I'll stay with Gibs, but you need to be gone in the morning." He sucked in a trembling breath and roughly wiped his tears away. "And you need to delete my number from your phone."

"Hugh," I cried out, feeling weak. "Please don't stay that."

"It's too late, Liz," he said, backing away from me. "There's no coming back from this."

"I love you!" I screamed after him. "You're my best friend! How am I supposed to be without you?"

"Maybe you should have thought about that" was all Hugh replied before he turned around and walked away.

THIS PAIN WON'T LAST FOREVER

Hugh

NOVEMBER 1, 2003

I COULDN'T BREATHE.

I couldn't think straight.

I couldn't fucking stop *crying*.

How my heart remained beating, I would never understand, because she'd splattered it all over my bedroom wall.

The image of my teammate between her legs, pounding his dick into her made me want to lose my mind.

"I'm going to be sick," I warned, lunging for the toilet bowl as the contents of my stomach left my body.

"I've got ya, brother," Gibs coaxed, kneeling on his bathroom floor beside me and rubbing my back. "Get it all out."

"Pierce," I strangled out between violent hurls. "My fucking teammate."

"He's a bad egg." Gibs tried to console me, while dabbing my chin with a wad of toilet paper. "He'll get his, Hugo. I'll make sure of it."

"She *fucked* him, Gibs."

"I know, lad."

"My *girlfriend* fucked my *teammate*."

"Yeah, and they're both disgusting backstabbers for it," he replied, wrapping an arm around me as I balanced over the bowl. "Fuck them, Hugh. You are worth a million Pierce O'Neills, and you are way too good to for a girl who spreads her legs for your teammate."

"Don't say that about her," I groaned, crying almost as much as I was puking. "Fuck, I can't cope with this."

"You're going to be okay," he promised, cleaning my chin again. "This pain won't last forever."

"It will," I cried, trembling violently. "I have loved that girl since I was seven years old."

"I know you have."

"No, you don't know, lad. You have no fucking clue what I've been through with that girl. I have loved with every fucking beat of heart. I've spent my life completely devoted to her." A hoarse cry ripped from my chest. "How could she do this to me, Gibs?"

"I don't know, Hugh," he replied quietly, remaining faithfully by my side. "Maybe she was drunk?"

"Fuck drunk," I snapped, chest heaving. "I'm drunk, and you don't see me fucking other girls."

Gibs was quiet for a long beat before saying, "Maybe she was having some trouble," he said carefully. "You know, like the trouble she used to have after Caoimhe died?"

"That doesn't excuse shit," I cried, feeling truly broken inside. "Because she had a choice, Gibs, and she chose to ruin us."

PLEASE JUST TAKE HER
Lizzie

NOVEMBER 2, 2003

I COULDN'T REMEMBER FALLING ASLEEP, BUT CLEARLY I DID, BECAUSE WHEN I OPENED my eyes, it was Sunday morning and I was alone in Hugh's bed.

I fell out of bed fully clothed and hurried downstairs and out the front door with only one thing on my mind.

Trembling violently when I crossed the street, I forced my feet up the driveway and knocked on Thor's door. Prickling with anger, I resisted the urge to kick and slap the timber frame while I waited impatiently for them to answer.

When Thor opened the door, he didn't speak. Instead, he turned around and disappeared into his front room.

A few moments later, Hugh appeared in the doorway.

"Hi," I squeezed out, unable to remain still. "Can we talk?"

Hugh looked me directly in the eyes, holding my gaze for a second or two before swiftly shaking his head. "No. We have nothing to discuss when you're like this."

"When I'm like what?" I demanded, throwing my hands up. "What am I doing wrong now?"

"When you're manic, Liz," he replied. "If you want to talk to me, go and get better first."

"Hugh, please." Feeling desperate and irritated, I reached for his hand only to be rejected. "If you just give me five minutes to explain."

"I don't need your explanation." Folding his arms across his chest, he looked down at me with an empty expression. "Like I said: go home and get better."

"I don't know why I did it," I heard myself admit, knowing that I had a whole lot more I needed to say if I had any chance of fixing this but struggling to get my pride to lower. "It was…crazy." Shaking my head, I reached for him again and then blanched when he stepped away. "I don't even like Pierce."

The laugh that escaped my lips was all wrong, wrong, wrong.

I needed to show him how sorry I was, and instead I was laughing.

What the fuck was wrong with me?

Jesus.

"Just go home," he told me, moving to close the door.

"Hey!" Feeling irrationally furious that he wasn't letting me explain, I slammed my hand on the door to block him. "I'm not leaving until we talk."

"You're not leaving until we talk," he repeated in a cold tone. "Okay, Liz." Hugh stepped outside and closed the door after him. I followed him across the street to his house. "Let's talk."

Following him inside, I watched as he pulled his phone out, tapped a few buttons, and pressed it to his ear. "Yeah, it's Hugh. Listen, I have somewhere to be, and I need you to pick Liz up as soon as you can." He kept his back to me as he spoke. "You can be here in fifteen minutes? Yeah, that'll work. Thanks, Catherine. Yeah, bye."

"I'm not leaving," I strangled out when he turned around to face me. "I'm not, Hugh." Tears filled my eyes. "Please!"

"You're not staying," he told me flatly. "Your mam will be here in fifteen minutes, so get whatever you need to say off your chest."

"Why are you being like this?" I said, feeling wounded. "Why are you talking to me that way?"

"What way, Liz?"

"Like you hate me."

"I don't hate you, Liz."

"But you don't love me anymore?"

His nostrils flared but he didn't respond.

"Hugh!"

"I know you're sick, Liz," I heard him say. "I get that, but it doesn't take away what you did."

"What did I do?"

"The fact that you're asking me that assures me that you're even sicker than I thought."

"I'm not sick, Hugh," I hurried to tell him. "I'm fine, I promise. I'm just..." Shaking my head, I choked out an awkward laugh. "I don't know what I am."

Devastation filled his eyes. "I begged you, Liz."

"You begged me what?"

Giving me his back, Hugh walked into the kitchen and stared out the closed patio doors. "I fucking begged you to take your meds, but you couldn't do that one thing for me."

"So because I don't want to feel dead inside, I'm the bad guy?"

"No, Liz, you're the bad guy because you fucked my friend!" he roared, vibrating with tension. "You're the bad guy because you broke my fucking heart last night!"

"Listen, don't overreact." I tried to reason with him, repressing the urge to roll my eyes. "It's fine. It's okay. You didn't want to do it, and I did." I shrugged. "I fixed our problem, so if you think about it, we're in a better place than we were this morning."

"You are un-fucking-believable."

"Oh my God, just stop, okay!" I threw my hands up and screamed. "I said I was sorry! Why aren't you listening to me?" Furious, I tugged on his arm, pleading with him to understand. "Is it really that deep, Hugh?"

His entire frame stiffened, and he reached up to pinch the bridge of his nose. "Ask me that when you're you again, and I'll tell ya."

A car horn honked then, and I started to panic.

"Your mam's outside."

"No, no, no, Hugh, please!" Grabbing his arm, I pleaded with him to not make me leave. "I love you, I do, I swear I do!" Digging my heels in, I tried to stop him from walking us to the door. "Please don't send me away."

"You have to go home now, Liz," he strangled out, physically picking me up and walking outside. "I can't do this," he told my mother, who was waiting at the car. "I'm sorry."

"Oh, Hugh, sweetheart." Mam's eyes were laced with concern. "What happened?"

"Take her, Catherine," Hugh begged, voice cracking. "Please just *take her*."

"Where are you going?" I called after him.

PROMISE ME, LADS

Hugh

CLEARLY, GIBS HAD CALLED FOR REINFORCEMENTS WHILE I WAS GETTING MY HEART broken, because when I made it back to his place, Feely was waiting with a bag of cans and a hug. Collapsing on the couch beside them, I broke down to the two lads that had been by my side since childhood and tried my damn hardest to drink myself into oblivion.

How could she do it to me?

How could give herself away like that?

Why wasn't I enough for her?

I would have understood if I'd been a shitty boyfriend, if I hadn't put her first or had ignored her feelings, but I'd never done any of those things.

"Listen, if you lads value me as a friend, you will never bring what happened with Liz and Pierce up again," I slurred several hours later, a flagon of cider pressed to my lips. "I'll fucking die," I added, both drunk and dramatic. "I'm telling ya, lads, I will drop dead from this pain." Taking another huge gulp of cider, I forced it down and then choked out a pained laugh that turned into a bitter sob. "I need to forget her, and I need you to help me."

"Say no more, my brother," Gibs was quick to offer, slinging an arm around my shoulders. "It has been erased." Drunkenly, he waved his finger around like it was a bloody wand from Harry Potter. "Fresh start."

"Are you sure about this?" Feely asked, cigarette balanced between his lips. "You're making big decisions based on temporary hurt."

"Hurt?" I barked out a pained laugh. "This is so far beyond hurt, lad, I don't know how I'm still standing."

"He is sure," Gibs chirped in, "and he'll be grand." Smiling, he offered me a bear hug. "You're going to drink the shit out of this two-liter bottle of cheap poison and then you're going to puke your soul out and then, once you've slept it off, she'll be out of your system, and you'll be right as rain."

"Maybe I should call her?"

"Fuck no, you shouldn't," he argued, snatching my phone out of my hand before I had a chance to flip the damn thing open. "You should delete her number."

"I should," I agreed and then groaned in physical pain as another flash of torturous images went through my mind.

Images of her *under* him.

Images of him *inside* her.

"I want to die."

"Nope, can't be doing that either," Gibs slurred, sounding as fucked from the drink as I was. "I refuse to allow you to die a virgin."

"What about Cap?" I blurted out, bleary-eyed and three sheets to the wind. "Shouldn't he be here for the pact?"

"Kav?" Feely laughed, joining in on the drunken debauchery now he had loosened up with a belly full of vodka. "No offense, Hugh, and I mean this in the sincerest way, because I love Kav like a brother, but he hasn't bothered to learn any of our sisters' names, let alone girlfriends."

"Don't you be talking shit about my Johnny," Gibsie growled, puffing out his chest. "I'll take the head off ya for that."

"I'm not saying it as a bad thing," Feely said, trying to placate him. "All I'm saying is Kav is interested in a grand total of three things: rugby, the labrador, and Gibs. Anything other than that and he's not taking notes."

"He likes you lads, too," Gibs offered, but the smile on his face assured me that this little tidbit of information had made him feel like a million quid.

"Ah, come on, Gibs," Feely argued with a laugh. "He goes away to camp every summer and the only person he bothers to reach out to is you."

"That's true," I slurred, nodding my head. "You're his favorite."

"At least I'm someone's favorite," Gibs countered. "You two have always been closer than either one of you are with me."

"Because your head is so far up his sister's hole, it's impossible to have a conversation with you that doesn't contain the word *Claire*."

"Because I love her, and she's my intended," Gibs declared before wincing. "Sorry, lad."

"It's grand, lad," I mumbled, batting the air. "At least one of us is happy."

"You'll be happy again, Hugh. I can promise you that, lad," Feely said, clinking his bottle against mine. "You'll find ya a nice, steady girl," he continued, nose scrunching up. "One who won't fuck your teammates."

"Or hate your friends," Gibs chimed in, holding a hand up. "That would be nice."

"True." Feely nodded somberly. "Or go off the rails."

Jesus Christ.

"Promise me, lads," I heard myself beg, feeling my eyes burn with tears. "Promise to God, you won't let me go back to her."

"We promise, lad," they both vowed in unison. "No matter what."

No matter what.

Fuck.

PART 20

Unforgiving Hearts

THIS ISN'T A GAME

Lizzie

NOVEMBER 5, 2003

School started three days ago, and I still hadn't returned.

Dad was *raging* about me being at home, because when he drove me to the hospital last Sunday, he'd been expecting them to keep me. However, due to the lack of beds and because I wasn't an immediate risk to myself, I was released after seventy-two hours.

The doctors told me I was going through mixed episodes, but I wasn't so sure about that, because my highs were getting higher by the day, and I longed for the moment my mind swallowed me whole and I didn't have to think anymore.

Now, I was back under my parents' roof, with my father no longer able to hide his repulsion, which was fine by me because I, too, couldn't hide my lack of shits to give.

I was starting to lose large chunks of time during the day, where I would zone out and have no memory when I came to, and it only fueled the reckless streak inside of me.

It felt like my entire being had been shuffled around and reprogrammed to work on a primal-urge frequency. My senses were in overload, while my empathy was at an all-time low. I found myself rapidly shifting between the craving to have sex and the yearning to slit my wrists.

My parents couldn't seem to stand me, and my father often took my mother away from the house for long stretches of time every evening.

I knew why.

He was giving me privacy to kill myself.

He wanted me dead.

They all did.

Late Wednesday evening, I was alone and pacing the entry hall of my house when the doorbell rang.

Confused, I stared at the door for a long beat, wondering if it was real or just my imagination.

I was hearing more things lately and couldn't tell if the doorbell was another figment of my fucked-up mind. If it was, then it could be the monster trying to get back in and I was *not* falling for his trap.

Tiptoeing toward the door, I stretched up to look through the frosted-glass panel and caught a glimpse of a shadow.

Panicking, I gripped my hair and resumed my pacing.

What if it was the scary lady?

Holy fuck, what if she was coming back for me?

She'd said she would.

She'd promised.

The doorbell rang again, followed by a loud knock.

Yelping in surprise, I hurried toward the door and decided to just open it.

If it was her, then she could have me.

I didn't give a shit anymore.

When I yanked the door inward, my breath caught in my throat.

Whiskey-brown eyes greeted me. "Hi."

"Hi," I breathed, gripping the doorknob as my heart fired up with a thunderous boom. "What are you doing here?"

"I think I left my phone charger in your room," Hugh replied, holding up his trusted Nokia. "I'm on my last bar." He shrugged awkwardly before adding, "Is it a good time?"

Yes!

Yes, yes, yes…

"Yeah, yeah, sure." I stepped sideways to let him pass. "Come in."

Without a word, Hugh walked past me and moved for the stairs.

"H-how are you?" I asked, scrambling up the staircase after him.

"Fine."

"Are you hungry?" Trailing after him, I hovered in my bedroom doorway and watched as he located his books. "I could make you something to eat."

"No thanks, I ate before I came here," he replied in a polite tone, while he continued to search for his charger, eventually finding it beneath the tangled sheets on my bed.

He briefly rolled the cord around the plug before pocketing it and moving for the door. "Thanks."

"W-wait!" I strangled out, feeling panicked at the thought of him leaving me again, as I blocked the doorway. "Please."

Hugh stopped right in front of me but kept his attention on something over my shoulder. *Thin air,* I presumed. It was easier to look at than I was. "I need to go now, Liz."

"Don't leave." I placed my hands on his stomach and slid them up until I was gripping his shoulders. "Stay."

A tremor racked through his big body, but he didn't respond, clearly refusing to look at me.

"I'm sorry, baby." Pushing up on my tiptoes, I pressed a lingering kiss to the curve of his jaw. "Forgive me."

His jaw clenched, right along with his hands, and I knew that his balled fists weren't a prelude for violence. He was battling the urge to love me back.

Reaching up, I gently stroked his cheek and watched his Adam's apple bob in his throat moments before his eyelids fluttered shut.

Stepping closer, I trailed my palms down his chest and then his stomach before slipping my fingers into the waistband of his gray sweats.

His breathing increased, nostrils flaring from the effort it was taking him to not react, but he was so damn stubborn, I knew he wouldn't give in.

Pushing both hands beneath the waistband of his boxers, I reached around and grabbed his hard ass with one hand, while using the other to stroke his rapidly hardening length.

Still, he *wouldn't* give in.

Pushing back up on my tiptoes, I slowly traced the length of his neck with my tongue, not stopping until I reached his mouth and captured his bottom lip between my teeth.

I tugged hard, causing him to finally hiss, before releasing it with a loud pop and then soothing the tender flesh with my tongue.

"We are over," he finally bit out, jaw clenched. "I'm not yours to touch."

"And yet I'm pumping your dick," I purred back, reveling in the fury that shone in his eyes when he glared at me. "Funny little world, isn't it?"

His whiskey-colored irises were almost eclipsed by his dilated pupils, assuring me that while he might very well despise me, he *still* wanted me. Not to mention the fact that he had yet to pull away.

"This isn't a game," he bit out, bracing his hands against the doorframe above my head. "Do you hear me? My life isn't a fucking *game*. You can't keep toying with me, not when I'm trying to move on."

"How's that working for you?" I asked softly, pushing up to nuzzle his cheek with mine, while I continued to pump his shaft *exactly* how he liked it. "Moving on is *hard*, isn't it?"

"Liz, *please*," he groaned, hissing out a strangled breath, as his cheeks grew flushed. "I *can't* do this."

"But you haven't done anything," I coaxed in a voice that was thick with need. "Hmm?" I upped my pace, gripping him tighter, pulling him harder, while I trailed my nails over his glorious ass. "There you go," I purred, working him over better than anyone could. "Let me take care of you."

"I, ah…no, I really…please…fuck!" A raw, male, guttural groan tore from his chest, and his ass muscles tightened, while his hips strained into my touch. "I shouldn't, ah…" His hips thrust again. "You shouldn't…" Another delicious thrust. "Fuck, this is so…"—hissing out a breath, he bit down on his bottom lip and tightened his grip on the doorframe—"…wrong!"

"But it feels so *good*, doesn't it?" I whispered, tracing his neck with my tongue again and then smirking when I felt him nod his head.

"You know I can make you feel better than her," I continued to whisper, tease, and plead, while my hand worked frantically to carry him over the cliff he was clearly avoiding. "Just give in to what you *really* want and let yourself have this, baby." I licked and nuzzled at his neck. "Imagine you're in my bed, exactly where you should be, and you're between my legs, pushing *this* deep inside me, filling me up, and making me stretch to fit all of *this!*"

That did the trick.

The sexiest male growl of approval tore from his throat when his orgasm crashed through him, causing his hips to buck and body to tremble.

Still bracing the doorframe behind me and still trembling from the aftershocks, Hugh dropped his head and sucked in several deep, steadying breaths.

Reluctant to let go but knowing I had to, I slowly withdrew my hands from him and readjusted his boxers and sweats.

His chest was still heaving, and he was still staring down at his feet, and I knew that meant he was drowning in guilt and shame.

His reaction caused a pang of secondary guilt inside of me. Contrary to how I felt about the rest of the world and the people in it, I would rather peel the skin from my bones than purposefully inflict pain on *this* boy.

At least, that's how I felt today.

Tomorrow, who knew how I would feel.

Certainly not me.

But today, I loved him.

Deciding not to make it harder for him, I slipped out of the room and walked into the bathroom.

Closing the bathroom door behind me, I walked over to the sink and washed *him* off my hands.

The seconds ticked by in silence before the sound of his footsteps on the creaking staircase filled my ears, followed by the front door slamming.

Exhaling a strangled breath, I clutched the porcelain sink and stared at my reflection.

A stranger stared back at me.

A whore had stolen my face.

"Good girls stay still and take it. Only whores fight back. You don't want to be a whore, do you, munchkin..."

Unable to stand another second of looking at the person I loathed most, I quickly opened the cabinet door.

Retrieving my faithful razor, I climbed into the bath and draped a leg over the side.

Knowing I needed to do this to stabilize my mind before the switch came, I fixated on a particularly fleshy part of my upper thigh and went to town on myself, carving, cutting, and soothing my soul with every rough drag of the blade.

SOARING IN HER MANIA

Hugh

NOVEMBER 6, 2003

AT FIRST, I WAS NUMB, COMPLETELY AND UTTERLY NUMB AS MY MIND TRIED TO PROCESS the trauma. Nothing I'd ever been through had traumatized me like walking into my room and seeing my teammate pounding my girlfriend.

My Liz!

Pain had socked me so hard in the solar plexus that I had to physically catch myself from collapsing in a heap.

My immediate reaction was to drag that traitorous friend off my traitorous girlfriend and break every bone in his face.

While I managed to rearrange that asshole's nose, it did nothing to make me feel better.

Instead, I just felt hollow and disappointed in myself for not taking the high road. Because Pierce wasn't worth my time and kicking his face in that night only made it look like the scales were even between us.

We *weren't* even, and we never would be.

Yeah, I crushed his nose and caused two fractures in his cheekbone, but he crushed my world and fractured my future.

His bones would heal.

My heart wouldn't.

The logical part of my brain urged me to acknowledge the betrayal, to take it in, absorb the emotions thrashing through me, and then cut my losses and walk away.

Because I *had* to walk away from her.

I could handle almost anything Liz threw at me, but not that.

I couldn't handle *that*.

While Pierce had stabbed me in the back that night, Liz stabbed right through the heart. Unlike the knife sticking out of my back—the one I could survive—Liz's blade shattered inside me like buckshot, splaying and splicing through my heart until there was nothing left.

The worst part of it all was Liz wasn't even sorry.

When she didn't return to school on Monday, I'd half hoped it was because she was crashing down from her high.

She hadn't.

When I realized I'd left my charger in her room and finally worked up the courage to go get it last night, I ended up falling back into the habit of a lifetime.

She put her hands on me and I didn't have the willpower to stop her. It was fucking awful because my body hadn't gotten the memo that her body was off-limits, and it was still craving her.

It was a mistake to go over there, and I would send my sister in the future, but at the time, I'd hoped our interaction would snap her out of it.

But nope.

Like a fucked-up phoenix rising from the ashes of turmoil, Liz sauntered into school this morning still rampant and still soaring in her mania.

School was absolute torture because not only did Liz continue hooking up with my teammate but she was also relentless in her attempt to seduce me.

Sex was all she could think about, and every time I rejected her advances, she ran back to Pierce like a fucking nymphomaniac.

I understood her bipolar had a great deal to do with her sudden hypersexuality, but that didn't ease the sheer fucking heartbreak I was enduring.

I knew this wasn't who Liz was, and I *knew* she was sick, but I was too hurt and too fucking raw to separate the two.

My heart was torn to ribbons, and my confidence was at an all-time low. I felt like an expendable toy that she'd enjoyed playing with for nine years and had grown bored of.

I felt like I was *nothing*.

Nothing but collateral damage in her tornado of emotions.

Images of her face flashed through my mind like a damn projector playing behind my eyes.

I could still smell her on my pillow. I kept finding rogue strands of her hair on random items of clothing.

Jesus, it hurt so bad, it made it hard to breathe.

I wanted to ask her parents what the hell was happening and demand to know why she hadn't been hospitalized yet. I stopped myself from contacting her parents because talking to them wouldn't be good for me, and I had to start putting *me* first now.

I had no idea how to put myself back together, nor did I have the slightest inkling of how to work though the betrayal.

My only remotely productive achievement since the breakup was taking on a part-time job at the pool, and honestly, being in the water was my saving grace. It kept my mind busy and my thoughts *off* her. The fact that our lives were so deeply entwined made it impossible for me to go more than half a day without running into her.

I saw her every day at school.

I saw her at home when Claire invited her over.

I saw her at work, where she was a member.

I saw her *everywhere.*

The worst part of it all was that I *still* loved her, and I *still* wanted to be with her. And I fucking hated myself for feeling that way.

NOT A CARE IN THE WORLD
Lizzie

NOVEMBER 6, 2003

WHEN I ARRIVED AT SCHOOL, I DIDN'T HAVE TO WORRY ABOUT HURTING ANYONE'S feelings because I didn't have a care in the world.

Not even one.

Today, I was as free as a bird, and I could live my life without being plagued by fear.

When Pierce followed me inside one of the toilet cubicles in the PE hall, my mind shut down and my body took over. When he hitched my skirt up and told me to sit on his lap, I did exactly what I was told.

Like a good girl.

Like the monster showed me.

Afterwards, I felt sated, like I didn't need to rub my body all over him or push my fingers deep inside me.

This boy didn't get cross with me for having bad thoughts.

This boy scratched the itch for me.

He made me better with his medicine.

When he left me alone in the bathroom, I studied my reflection in the mirror, fixated on the colors shooting out of my eyes.

Weird lines of gold tracking their way over blue irises.

Fascinating.

My body was sore all over.

Wonderful.

My neck was peppered with love bites.

Glorious.

Dark circles under my eyes.

Ethereal.

Tearstains on my cheeks.

Whore.

Fragments and molecules of dust particles landed on my flesh—I could see them. It was as if time had slowed down just for me, so I could see everything in ultra vision.

Magical.

Drumming my fingertips against the porcelain rim, I tilted my head to one side, trying to make a connection with the stranger staring back at me.

I couldn't recognize her, but I was touching her face.

How unusual.

"So this is where you've been hiding!" Claire growled, blowing in the bathroom door, eyes wild with fury. "What the hell are you playing at?"

"Hi," I breathed, feeling both sated and suicidal. "What did I do now?"

"What did you *do*?" She demanded, eyes bulging. "Liz, you kissed Pierce O'Neill at the lockers this morning. I saw you! And then you scampered off before I could confront you." She narrowed her eyes. "You're supposed to be with my brother, Liz. How could you do that to Hughie?"

"Oh." Devastation hit me like a tidal wave when she said his name. "Yeah, we broke up."

"Shut the front door!" Claire's jaw fell open. "*When?*"

"Last weekend."

"But you were together at his birthday party."

"Yeah, the day after."

"You guys really broke up?" Claire squealed, looking horrified. "Omigod, why?"

"What's your problem?" I snapped, feeling cornered and wounded. "You didn't want me with your brother to start with. Well, you got your wish."

"Lizzie!" Her tone was laced with hurt. "Just because I was uncomfortable about it doesn't mean I wanted this to happen." Sadness filled her eyes. "It all makes sense now. He's been locked in his room for days." She looked at me with a lost expression. "He doesn't come out unless it's for school."

"I need to go," I mumbled, feeling too much in this moment. Emotions were thrashing around inside of me, rising higher and higher, as his face tormented me.

"Liz, hold up," Claire begged. "Let's talk about this."

Ignoring her, I rushed for the door, only to fall over a rogue changing bag and collapse in a heap on the floor.

"Omigod!" Claire rushed to my side. "Are you okay?"

"Peachy." I choked out a fitful, almost hysterical laugh. The more I tried to sober my features, the more I laughed and laughed and laughed.

"Is she high?" another girl asked when she entered the bathroom.

"Who the fuck are you?"

"Liz! Omigod, be nice!"

"Okay," I drawled. "Who the fuck are you *please*?"

"Katie," the redheaded girl said, looking down on me like I was a new breed of alien. "Have you taken something?"

"Nope," I snickered, and choked out another fitful laugh, while attempting to untangle my foot from the strap of the gear bag. "Not that it's any of your business, nosy girl, but I haven't taken up the heroin route yet."

"Liz!" Claire chastised. "You can't say things like that to people."

"Don't worry about it," the girl replied before turning to me and arching a disapproving brow. "You certainly have the heroin-chic look down to a tee."

"Get fucked," I snorted, giving her the finger.

"I'm really sorry about her," Claire said, trying to do damage control. "She's going through a breakup right now."

"Yeah, well, manners cost nothing," the girl huffed before storming out of the bathroom.

"That wasn't nice," Claire scolded, crouching down to help me untangle my feet. "You are acting like a crazy person, Elizabeth Young."

"Indeed, Claire Biggs," I shot back, flopping back on my elbows and watching as she freed my feet for me. "Aren't we all a little crazy inside?"

HATE TO BE YOU

Hugh

NOVEMBER 7, 2003

"ARE YA GOOD, LAD?" CAP ASKED, CROUCHING DOWN BESIDE ME TO TIE HIS LACES midway through training on Friday.

Shaking my head, I blew out a breath and focused on not losing my head.

"Come on," he coaxed. "Take a lap with me."

Considering the prospect of taking a lap meant avoiding the prick wearing number fourteen, I gladly fell into step with my captain.

"You destroyed me in that maths test this morning, lad," he said, not breaking a sweat as he ran alongside me. "I thought I was killing it with 94 percent, but you knocked it out of the park with full marks."

I knew what Johnny was trying to do, and I really fucking appreciated it. He wasn't known for taking an interest in anything that wasn't rugby related, so the fact that he was bringing up test scores meant that he was trying.

While I wasn't entirely sure if he knew what was happening, he clearly sensed the storm brewing inside me, and this was his way of pumping me up.

"Yeah," I replied, jogging alongside him. "It wasn't too bad."

"Not too bad?" Cap laughed, nudging my shoulder with his. "What were you hoping for? A hundred and one percent?"

"I don't know," I replied, shaking my head. "Sorry, my head's in space right now."

"Nah, it's still on your shoulders, ya bleeding brainbox," he replied, tone way gentler than usual.

We ran another three laps and had stopped to stretch out before Johnny spoke again. "Listen, I heard yourself and O'Neill had some kind of falling out over Halloween."

"Yeah," I replied flatly. "We did."

"Care to fill me in?"

My brows furrowed in surprise. "You don't know?"

"Gossip's not really my thing, lad," he replied with a shake of his head. "And I don't go to parties, and this right here is about as much socializing as I have time for." He shrugged before adding, "Besides, I'd rather hear it from the horse's mouth, not the horse's shit shoveler."

"Shit shoveler," I chuckled. "I haven't heard that one before."

He smirked. "So, do you want to tell me what happened?"

"I'd rather not," I admitted, pushing a hand through my hair. "It's, ah, it's just…"

"Fair enough," my captain cut in, holding his hands up. "We'll say no more on the matter, lad."

I arched a brow. "Just like that?"

"What other way would it be?" he replied calmly. "We all have our right to privacy, lad."

"Yeah," I replied, feeling really fucking grateful for him in this moment. "I do want you to know that I won't cause trouble on the team for you."

"That's really good to hear, lad," Johnny replied. "Because the team needs both of ye."

"Yeah, Cap," I replied with a nod, swallowing my pride. "I know."

Liz was sitting on the grassy bank at the edge of the pitch when Coach called it for the day.

Perfect.

I swear I had never walked so fast to get to the changing rooms as I did in this moment.

Ignoring Pierce, who was jogging toward her, I kept my gaze trained ahead and powered on.

"Hugh," she called out when I passed her, but I pretended not to hear.

I couldn't control my emotions right now, and I wasn't about to humiliate myself with her again.

She'd already done enough of that for the both of us.

Wordlessly, Gibs fell into step beside me, blocking my view of her, and for that, I was beyond grateful.

He didn't crack a joke or throw shade.

He just walked beside me, shielding me with his presence.

DON'T HOLD YOUR BREATH

Hugh

NOVEMBER 8, 2003

WHEN I WALKED INTO THE LOUNGE AFTER WORK ON SATURDAY NIGHT, BONE WEARY and ready for bed, I stopped dead in my tracks when my eyes landed on the couch, a.k.a. my makeshift bed since that night.

Holding a finger up to her lips, Mam inclined her head, gesturing for me to come in but didn't move a muscle from her perch on the couch.

I supposed she couldn't, not when she had two girls draped over her lap.

Well, *Liz* was draped over my mother's lap, and Claire was draped over Liz's legs.

It was a whole heap of blond hair and tearstained cheeks.

My fucking heart buckled at the sight.

Feeling like my legs were made of lead, I debated remaining in the archway that led from our kitchen to our lounge before releasing a defeated sigh.

Where else was I supposed to go?

I couldn't leave, could I?

This was my fucking home.

Tossing my swim bag on the floor, I reluctantly joined my mother, taking a seat on the coffee table in front of her rather than risk *her* body touching mine.

Mam waited until I was sitting down before broaching the subject that I knew was on the tip of everyone's tongue. "What happened, Hugh?"

My gaze flicked from my mother to Liz and then my sister before settling back on her. *Always her.* "What did she say happened?"

"Nothing," Mam urged, tone laced with concern. "That's the problem. I can't make sense of a word the girl has been saying all night."

Pain.

It fucking floored me.

Because I didn't want this.

I didn't want her to cry.

I didn't want her to break down again, but I just...I *couldn't* be the one to put her back together this time. "We broke up, Mam."

"That much I've gathered," Mam replied, stroking Liz's cheek like she was her second daughter, and in a way, she always had been.

We'd spent our childhood in this house, in a fortress of love, security, and comfort that my mother had built around us. I knew that's why Liz continued to return. Why she was here right now.

Hell, I didn't even blame her. I'd been in her home. It was like experiencing the funeral on repeat in that house.

Sadness and tears.

Pain and anger playing on a loop like a broken record.

My home had become her reprieve, and breakup or not, I would never take that away from her.

I only hoped she could find in Claire whatever she had found in me because I couldn't give it to her anymore.

"Care to tell me why?" Mam pushed when I made no move to delve deeper. "Something terrible must have happened." Panic flared in her eyes as she put two and two together and came up with five. "Hugh, I know you're in fourth year now, and some of your friends are moving fast with girls, but Lizzie's only in second year. Please tell me you didn't—"

"What—no!" I snapped, cutting her off before she could go there. "That's not me," I bit out, pushing my hair off my face. "I would *never*."

"Okay." Blowing out a relieved breath, Mam turned her attention back to the sleeping girl on her lap. "Then *what* happened?"

"She decided this," I heard myself admit, and Christ did I hate the way my voice cracked when the admission escaped my lips. "She doesn't love me anymore, Mam."

"I don't believe that for a second," Mam argued gently. "Teenage girls don't cry over boys like this when they're not in love."

That hit me hard.

Fucking gutted me.

Tore my heart to ribbons.

"Fuck." Dropping my head in my hands, I gripped my hair so tight, I thought I might rip it from my scalp.

I certainly needed to fuck something up.

Blowing out a frustrated breath, I stood up on shaky legs and inhaled deeply. "Listen, all you need to know is I didn't put a hand on her, Mam. I wouldn't, okay? I'm waiting for her... I mean, I *was* happy to wait."

"But?"

"But she didn't want to."

"Didn't want to what, Hugh?"

"Wait for me."

Awareness dawned on my mother's face, and I could feel the sympathy floating out of her heart and into mine. "Oh, baby."

"Don't say anything," I half warned, half begged. "I don't want you to think badly of her."

Tears filled Mam's eyes. "I wouldn't do that, love."

"I don't want anyone else to think it, either."

"Okay, love."

"Because she's sick, Mam, and whatever she did, she *wouldn't* have done it if she were herself."

"Oh, Hugh."

"Please. I don't want it getting out, Mam," I admitted, rubbing my jaw. "And definitely not back to Claire. So, please just…just put it in a box in the back of your mind and forget about it." Knees bopping restlessly, I added, "Because Liz needs this place." I inclined my head to where the three of them were nestled up. "She needs you and Claire."

"And you?" Mam watched me carefully. "What do you need, Hugh?"

Her.

I shook my head. "I can't think about that right now."

"You'll make up," Mam called after me when I moved for the doorway. "You'll find a way through this. You'll see."

"Don't hold your breath" was all I replied.

RAPID CYCLES AND RACING HEARTS

Lizzie

NOVEMBER 12, 2003

CONFUSION SWEPT OVER ME RIGHT ALONG WITH EXHAUSTION.

I could hardly find the energy to walk.

My head.

Oh God, everything was spinning.

I couldn't keep up with my thoughts.

They were moving too quickly in my head.

Too many thoughts.

Too many feelings.

I was so tired, but I couldn't sleep because my mind wouldn't *stop* tormenting me.

It wouldn't slow down and let me *breathe.*

All the colors and shapes.

All the faces and smells.

Everything was hitting me at once, and I couldn't regulate myself.

Meanwhile, Pierce O'Neill kept talking to me.

Why wouldn't he stop talking to me?

"So, what do you think?"

I stared up at him, confused and annoyed he was *still* speaking to me. "About what?"

"Us making a go of it?"

He reached for my hand, and I was so startled that I didn't stop him.

I was too goddamn stunned.

"A go of what?"

"Us, babe," he chuckled, tucking a strand of hair behind my ear. "How do you feel about us making this official?"

"Official?" I strangled out, feeling physically sick. *"Us?"*

A group of boys walked past us then, and one of them shoved Pierce with his shoulder.

Thor, I noted.

Oh God, Hugh.

He was there, too.

But he wasn't looking at me.

Instead, he was storming down the school hall with his two friends flanking him.

Yanking my hand free, I pressed my fingers to my temples, trying to steady myself, but everything felt *wrong, wrong, wrong.*

But everything *was* wrong.

What the fuck was I doing?

What the hell was wrong with me?

Shoving away from Pierce, I bolted into the girls' bathroom, barely making it inside one of the stalls in time.

Falling on my hands and knees, I heaved as my body rejected the contents of my stomach over and over until there was nothing left to throw up.

Sagging forward, I sucked in a ragged breath, chest heaving, while my mind offered me a rare glimpse of clarity.

Of reality.

All the good in the world was gone.

Erased and replaced with poison.

With sadness.

With unanswered questions and speculation.

All the thoughts.

All the memories.

All the regret I had for decisions I had no memory of making.

I made them, though.

That, I was sure of.

Grief—it swept me up in its cruel wave of suffocation before spitting me out on the beach of guilt and devastation.

I didn't want to be this way anymore.

I *wanted* to get better.

To find the girl I used to be and become her once more.

But she wasn't there anymore, and if, by some small miracle, I found her, the boy she loved with all her heart had been chased off by the demon that had taken on the form of her skin.

What was the point?

I'd already lost everything.

I was *ruined.*

YOU MEAN THE WORLD TO ME

Lizzie

NOVEMBER 14, 2003

LIFELESS, WITH THE EXCEPTION OF A BEATING HEART, I STOOD ON HIS FRONT PORCH and rang the doorbell again. I knew Claire and Sinead wouldn't be at home. They went to mass on Sunday, but Hugh usually spent the morning studying.

I knew I had permission to go inside, but it didn't feel right to intrude on him.

Not after what I'd put him through.

Hold it together, Lizzie.

It might not be as bad as you think.

The moment the front door swung inward and I was greeted by the sight of Hugh, I knew I was lying to myself.

It wasn't as bad as I thought.

It was so much worse.

Hugh folded his arms across his chest, clearly waiting for me to go first.

"I'm so sorry" was all I could come up with.

"For what exactly?"

"Everything." Nervous, I plucked at my sleeves. "I didn't mean any of that."

"No," he agreed with a nod. "*You* didn't mean any of that, but this version of you sure as shit did."

"I'm fine again, Hugh," I croaked out, willing him to hear me. "I'm thinking clearly."

Stepping closer, he reached for my chin and angled my face up to his. His eyes studied mine for a long beat before he released me and shook his head. "Do you honestly think, after all these years, that I can't tell when you're off balance?"

"But I feel steady," I tried to tell him, feeling panicked. "Please, I swear I'm okay."

"Your pupils are so dilated, there's no blue in them, Liz." He folded his arms again. "Are you back on your meds yet?"

I started to nod, but the *don't bullshit me* look on his face had me admitting the truth. "Not yet."

"Then we have nothing to talk about." Unfolding his arms, he reached for the door.

"Can we please go inside and talk?" I begged, feeling the tears sting my eyes.

Pain flickered in his eyes, and he released a frustrated growl before storming away and leaving the door open behind him.

Trailing after him, I continued to plead. "Hugh, I am so, *so* sorry."

"You already said that." Stepping around me, he walked into the lounge, and I quickly followed him, afraid to let him out of my sight in case he changed his mind about seeing me and bolted.

Flopping down on the couch, he stretched out and reached for the remote.

Shivering, I sat on the armchair opposite him. "Are we going to talk about it?"

"What's there to talk about?" He didn't look at me when he spoke, eyes trained on the television mounted over the fireplace instead. "Did you come over to tell me how good Pierce fucks you? Because I'd rather you keep it to yourself."

"Please let me explain."

"No need." He flicked through channels. "I already know what happened."

"Hugh, I was drinking."

"So was I, but I somehow managed to not cheat on you," he replied breezily. "Funny that."

"I didn't cheat on you."

"You let another lad put his dick inside you, Liz. If that's not cheating in your book, then I don't know what to tell you."

"No, I mean I *didn't* do it on purpose."

"Oh." He feigned surprise. "You didn't do it on purpose. Why didn't you say that sooner? That changes everything." Retraining his attention to the television, he continued to rant. "That makes the mental image of my teammate fucking you like a dog *so* much easier to swallow. I can easily forget the image of him fisting your hair while he was pounding his dick into your pussy."

"Hugh, don't…" I choked out, covering my mouth with my hand.

"I'm sorry. Am I not being graphic enough?" He threw the remote at the wall. "Jesus, I'm sorry, Liz. I'd love to tell you more, but I only had a ten-second sneak peak of the party."

"Hugh—"

"In my room, Liz!" Chest heaving, he stormed out. "In my fucking bed!"

"I know, I know, I'm so fucking sorry!" Falling off the armchair in my rush to follow him, I chased him up the stairs and into his room, where he was stripping his bed. "What are you doing?"

"Do you want this?" he asked, dragging the mattress off its base. "Because I sure as shit don't."

With that, he stormed past me, mattress in hand, and flung it down the staircase.

"Sorry if it holds any sentimental significance to you," he sneered over his shoulder as he stomped down the steps and regathered the mattress at the bottom. "I know a girl's first time is special."

"Hugh, please!"

Yanking the front door open, he proceeded to stalk outside and unceremoniously dump the mattress on the front lawn.

Wiping his hands off, he turned on his heels and stomped back inside.

Again, I trailed after him, knowing that I deserved every second of this torture.

"Tell me what to do," I begged, following him back upstairs to his bedroom. "Please, Hugh, just tell me how to fix this."

"Oh, I don't know, Liz. Can you go back in time and un-fuck him? Can you do that?"

"I'm so sorry."

"Two things." He seethed, chest heaving, as his voice cracked. "I've only ever asked you to do two goddamn things, and you couldn't do either one."

"I know, I know," I sobbed, watching him sink to the floor and then recoil from my touch when I moved to go to him. "I don't know what's wrong with me."

"I do," he roared back at me. "You're bipolar and not taking your goddamn medication."

"I'm *sorry*—"

"I can handle the mood swings. I can handle the depression. Hell, I can even handle the mania. And the crazy fucking eyes. And the way I never know if you're going to try to fuck me or hurt me. But I can't handle the cheating."

"I would never hurt you."

"Liar," he roared, tears streaking his cheeks, as he pulled at his hair in utter distress. "Look at me, baby! Take a good fucking look!"

"I'll do anything to fix this," I cried, sinking to my knees beside him. "I'll go back on my meds. I'll go to counselling. I'll do anything, Hugh, anything!"

"It's too late."

"No, no, no, it's not," I tried to plead, feeling frantic now. "It's not too late, baby."

"How the fuck is it not too late, Liz?" He dropped his head in his hands. "You've been fucking him ever since that night." A pained cry tore from his chest. "Whatever hope we had of fixing it before is dead and buried now."

"Yes, we can, we can, Hugh," I cried, touching his arm. "I'm yours. I've always been yours."

"What did you think was going to happen, Liz!" he strangled out, hooking his arms around his knees. "That we could brush it all under the carpet?"

"We can try!"

"No." He shook his head again. "We can't because you publicly shit on us, Liz."

"I didn't mean to do any of this!"

"I know, I know," he groaned, sounding truly conflicted. "I know you're sick. I know you don't mean any of this, but it's still *real* for me. Because I'm here, Liz. I'm the collateral fucking damage."

"Hugh…"

"I don't have a bubble to fall into, baby. My feelings are *real* and I don't have a button to switch it off like you."

Tears streamed down my cheeks as I tried to absorb his words. "Please don't leave me."

"I didn't leave you, Liz," he croaked, lifting his head to look at me. "You left me."

His brown eyes were trained on mine, and I could see everything he was feeling in this moment. I couldn't bear to see the hurt in his eyes, but somehow, I forced myself to do just that.

Because I had to look.

I had to see what I had done to this boy.

The boy I loved with every beat of my heart.

Regret churned inside of me and instantly, I began to doubt myself.

What the hell was I doing?

I couldn't hurt him like this.

You already hurt him, a voice in my head hissed, *you broke him.*

The only person who ever truly loved you, warts and all.

You crushed him.

"It didn't mean anything," I tried to tell him, but I felt so fucking dirty and undeserving. "I don't know why I did it." Pushing his legs apart, I scrambled between them, clutching his big body tightly. "You mean the world to me."

Wrapping my arms around his narrow hips, I pressed my face to his stomach, inhaling the smell of him, needing to feel his skin on mine. Needing to keep this boy in my life.

But it was too late for that.

His touch told me that.

With his shoulders limp and his head bowed, he battled with his hand until he finally allowed it to rest on the back of my head. It was more than I deserved in this moment.

I had broken him; this bright, beautiful, brave soul had been reduced to broken pieces.

They were scattered all over his bedroom floor.

He couldn't take me back, not even if he wanted to.

Because his pride would never allow for it.

I wanted to clean up my image and not be a humiliation to him every damn day, but I was still me. I couldn't erase my past. I was used up and dirty. I always had been. There was no way of fixing that. There was no magic spell to eradicate my memories.

Knowing that I'd given my body to a boy I couldn't bear to remember made me want to hold my breath forever.

It made me want to peel the skin from my bones.

Shame.

That was all I was left with.

LEAVING LIKE A FATHER

Hugh

NOVEMBER 20, 2003

I'D LONG SINCE ACCEPTED THE KNOWLEDGE THAT I WOULD ALWAYS LOVE LIZZIE Young.

My heart didn't have an eject button; therefore, she would never lose her place inside of it.

She just had to change spots if I ever found someone else.

If I ever dared to open myself up to that kind of love again.

If it was even possible.

Something I very much doubted.

I tried to think pragmatically about the breakup, to use logic and reason, but it was so fucking hard when my heart was splattered at her feet.

I couldn't be the better person, and I couldn't turn the other cheek this time.

Because it hurt too much.

Because this was it.

If I took her back, this was how it would be for me, and I deserved more.

I loved her enough to stay, I adored her enough to hang on in there, but until when?

When did this end?

What happened when she had another episode?

Would she cheat on me again?

Would I receive another influx of text messages from concerned teammates, telling me about the rumors they'd heard about my girlfriend?

What if I stayed with her and this continued into college and beyond?

What about when we were married and had children?

Would I still have to live like this?

Would I be able to?

And how was I supposed to explain this to the children we shared?

Where was the line?

This, I suddenly realized.

This was the line, the limit, and the breaking point.

This was where we parted.

This was the part where I left the sinking ship.

After her apology, Liz kept texting, kept apologizing, kept phoning.

I had to turn my phone off because it was breaking my heart to ignore her.

When I told her to erase my number, I hadn't meant it.

But I wasn't strong enough to handle the aftermath.

Everything inside of me wanted to rush back to her, but I couldn't.

"Hugh." My father's voice infiltrated my thoughts, and I spun around from where I was packing my lunch to find him sitting at the kitchen table. "Sit down, son."

"Can't," I deadpanned, retraining my attention on my lunch. "I have to catch the bus for school."

"Please, Hugh," he pushed. "We need to have a little father-son chat. I'll drive you to school after."

Jesus Christ.

This man irritated me to the point where I avoided him as much as possible.

It wasn't hard, considering he spent a good portion of his time avoiding his family like the plague.

Therefore, I found his sudden desire to have a father-son conversation both unnecessary and annoying.

"So," Dad said when I reluctantly joined him at the table. "How have you been doing, son?"

"Fine."

"That's not what I hear."

Mam!

Lovely.

"If you have something you want to ask me, then just go for it." Leaning back in my chair, I folded my arms across my chest. "No need for beating around the bush with small talk."

Pain flickered in his eyes, but I felt no remorse.

He didn't get to check out on me for a decade and jump back in whenever he felt like it, and I vowed to never do that to the people I loved.

My family and friends could always depend on me.

I would never check out like he had.

I would be a man.

I would be honorable and dependable.

I would work hard and never take handouts from a man I had lost all respect for.

649

He would never be able to sway me with presents and impromptu trips away when he had a "good week," like he did with my sister.

He could keep his money.

I would make my own.

"I hear you're having relationship problems?"

"I'm having life problems, Dad," I replied flatly. "Nothing for you to worry about."

"Maybe I can help you."

I scoffed at that. "You can't help yourself, let alone the rest of us."

Dad winced. "That's not fair."

"Yeah, well, life's not fair, Dad, and the truth hurts."

"I know I haven't always been there for you," he began to say, but I cut him off before he could spew another excuse.

"That's putting it mildly," I shot back with a humorless laugh. "You've been a fuck-ing ghost in this house since Joe died. As for being there for me? Well, you haven't been there since my communion." On a roll now, I quickly unleashed my wrath on him. "These pop-up visits might work on Mam and Claire, but don't bother trying it on me. Because I don't need it, ya hear?" Narrowing my eyes, I spat, "I *don't* need *you*."

LIBERATED LIABILITIES

EVERYTHING SWITCHED OFF IN MY HEAD LIKE A LIKE A LIGHT SWITCH.

All the pain.

All the feelings.

All the memories.

Everything just *poof!*

I didn't care anymore, and I fucking loved it.

Hyperalert, I thrived in the madness, completing weeks' worth of schoolwork in just one night.

And my stories?

God, my stories had never been so detailed.

Creativity was pouring from my pen to the pages.

I honestly thought I might be able to do anything in this moment.

They could say what they wanted about me at school.

I didn't care.

They couldn't hurt me.

I was invincible, dammit.

Fuck those bitches.

I would *crush* them with my pen. I would wreck them with my words, and I didn't have to worry about feeling bad about it because I didn't feel anything.

Not a sliver of remorse.

It was the greatest relief.

It was inside of me all along—a wondrous cave to escape inside when the world got too difficult.

Sleep was for the weak, and I was *strong*.

I was forceful and powerful.

No more monsters under my body.

Starved for physical touch, I felt I would die without it.

I was running through a desert, frantically searching for a pool of water. I would die without it. I was so thirsty. I would have consumed contaminated slime if it quenched the thirst, the burning inside of me.

That's how it felt when Pierce was inside me.

He was a means to an end.

I couldn't make sense of it because how could you make sense of madness?

All logic, reason, and moral fiber had checked out.

My body ran entirely on primal instinct now.

It was as if every ounce of goodness inside of my soul had evaporated and been replaced with bad.

I was possessed by the seven deadly sins.

Pride.

Greed.

Lust.

Envy.

Gluttony.

Wrath.

Sloth.

I was consumed by each one and couldn't get enough.

I wasn't rocking in a corner, haunted by voices of the past and crying my life away.

No, I was productive and thriving.

I was taking care of my needs.

Excelling at school and taking what I wanted from life.

If people didn't like that, then to hell with them.

I laughed at how scared I used to be of feeling like this.

All the dread and the worry.

All the panic and uncertainty, and for what?

Because I feared losing what I loved the most in life?

He was already long gone.

I had nothing left to lose now.

Those damn doctors with their fucking pills.

Liars, the lot of them.

When I was on the meds, I was fucking miserable.

And now?

Now, I was *free*.

And I felt *liberated*.

FREUDIAN SLIPS

Hugh

DECEMBER 3, 2003

My heart was broken, my head was in pieces, and my girlfriend was the driving force behind all of it.

Ex-girlfriend, I reminded myself.

Seriously, I couldn't fucking cope with the sudden shifts in her mood.

Every damn day for the past week, Liz had shown up at my house—under the pretense of hanging out with my sister—hell-bent on trying to win me back.

By the time Friday night rolled around, Liz had pulled out all the stops, flashing every inch of her skin in her bid to lure me back to her bedside.

It didn't matter how many times I told her to leave my room, the girl was soaring way too high in the clouds to hear me.

"Why won't you just give in?" she purred, straddling my lap like she had the right to.

It had been twenty minutes since she'd slipped out of Claire's bed and into mine, and I was growing impatient. *And weak.* "Because once I do, there's no going back."

"Ha." Liz grinned down at me, eyes wild and feral. "You said *once* you give in, not *if* you give in."

"You know what I meant." I narrowed my eyes. "It was a slip of the tongue."

"Uh-huh." She winked. "A Freudian slip."

"No, not a Freudian slip, just a regular Hughie slip," I argued back. "Don't go reading into it. You'll only end up disappointed."

"Oh, I highly doubt that," she mused, still pinning me down, still rocking her hips provocatively. "There's certainly nothing remotely disappointing about what I'm *feeling* right now."

"On the contrary"—I paused to buck my hips upward, knocking her off my raging hard-on before continuing—"I hate to break it to you, but not every fella accepts sex as an apology."

"How about just sex?" Reaching for the hem of her vest, she dragged it over her head, giving me a glorious view of her bare breasts. "Minus the apology."

Christ, she had the best tits.

More than a handful but modest enough for her to go braless.

They were damn perky, too, with dusty-pink, rosebud-like nipples that were constantly pebbled and straining.

"Who says I want either?" I taunted, refocusing on the mindfuck straddling my chest, unwilling to give an inch. Even if it caused my balls to drop off from pressure, I would *not* relent.

"Your dick says you do," she challenged, reclaiming her post on my dick.

"And my head says I don't." I pushed right back.

"What about your heart?" she asked, expertly gyrating her hips. Oh yeah, she knew *exactly* what she was doing. "What does your heart say?"

The thought darkened my mood, and I didn't hold back when I replied with, "My heart says don't trust a word that comes out of your mouth."

"Wow," she breathed, quickly concealing her hurt with a narrow-eyed glare. I saw it, though, and it didn't feel nearly as good as I expected it to. "I suppose I deserved that."

"Yeah," I agreed quietly. "I suppose you do."

To give her credit, she recovered the mood from darkening, shifting back into seductress with a relish. Grinning mischievously, she dragged my T-shirt up and trailed her nails down my stomach.

"Mm." She released a sexy moan. "You have the sexiest six-pack."

Repressing a shiver, I folded my arms behind my head and gave her a pointed look. "Pity you didn't think that when you were getting railed by my teammate."

"I can make it up to you." She leaned in so close to my face that her lips brushed mine when she purred, "If you just say yes."

With infinite self-control and the mental image of Pierce O'Neill piledriving her on my bed still fresh in my memory, I arched my chin up, looked her square in the eyes, and said, "No."

SLEEPOVERS AND STEVIE

Hugh

DECEMBER 4, 2003

WHEN LIZ STORMED INTO MY BEDROOM THE FOLLOWING EVENING, SHE MOVED straight for my stereo, CD case in hand. Visibly thrumming with anger, she retrieved the disc from the case before flinging it at me.

"Jesus Christ," Gibs exclaimed, diving out of her way and dropping the ball he'd been balancing in the process.

"Liz." Equally just as pissed, I caught the case midair and quickly recognized it as Fleetwood Mac's album *The Dance*. "What are you doing in here?"

Without speaking a single word, she placed the disc in my stereo and began to flick through tracks before stopping at number twelve.

Then, she held her finger on the fast-forward button, skipping through parts of the song, until releasing it at 3:38.

The moment Stevie Nicks's haunting voice filled the room, my ex-girlfriend turned the volume up to maximum capacity before spinning around to look at me. Again, she never uttered a single word, letting the song do the talking for her.

Instead, she tortured me by standing directly in front of me, chest heaving in such a way that it brushed against mine.

Jutting her chin up in defiance, she locked her eyes on mine and snared me, keeping me captive, as the music ricocheted through the both of us.

She didn't seem to care that we were in full view of my friends, and I couldn't look away from her.

Her eyes were blazing with raw emotion—some of it fury, most of it pain. The intensity of her stare was too fucking much in this moment, bringing with it an onslaught of heartbreak that I'd be working so damn hard on burying.

Jaw ticking, I glared right back at her, feeling every muscle in my body lock up with tension as her eyes screamed the lyrics of the song at me.

Neither one of us moved for the longest time.

I couldn't have if I'd wanted to.

I was trapped.

The more she stared at me, the faster my breathing became until my chest was literally heaving right along with hers.

Because this was too much.

I felt too much for her.

All the pain, all the memories, all the fucking misplaced adoration.

It was crippling.

But I would not falter.

I would not give in this time.

I couldn't.

The song ended and with one final, lingering stare, she ripped her gaze off mine, spun on her heels, and walked out of my room.

Not one single word had spilled from her lips, but she had successfully ruined all train of thought for me.

All I could do was stand there staring after her, while track thirteen began to play.

"I think she was trying to tell ya something, Hugo."

"You think, Gibs?" Feely replied dryly.

He nodded eagerly before clapping my shoulder with his hand. "Definitely."

EARLY MORNING WAKE UPS AND LINDSEY

DECEMBER 5, 2003

I HAD NO IDEA WHAT POSSESSED ME TO DO WHAT I DID IN FRONT OF HIS FRIENDS, BUT I didn't regret it.

Because he wouldn't talk to me and wouldn't listen.

I had nothing left at my disposal.

"What happened?" Claire asked, sitting cross-legged on her bed later that night. "I mean, I know he's my brother, but you can always talk to me, too, you know? I'm here for you, bestie."

I couldn't tell her because I wouldn't have a friend left if she knew the truth.

If she knew how I betrayed her brother.

"It's on me," I forced myself to whisper, because no matter how far it pushed us apart, I couldn't let him take the blame for something he had no part in. "It's all on me, Claire."

"Well, Gerard told me that I'm not supposed to talk about it anymore," she continued to ramble. "He wouldn't say why or explain anything to me, but he made me promise that I wouldn't talk about your relationship anymore. Not to anyone."

"It's okay," I whispered. "Hugh has every right to want to forget about it."

Her eyes widened with sadness. "Forget about your relationship?"

"Me, Claire," I replied, swallowing deeply. "To forget about *me*."

———————————————

Sleep didn't come easily that night, but when I finally drifted off to sleep in the early hours of the morning, I was woken what felt like minutes later by the sound of loud clattering near my head and the sensation of something light and plastic landing on top of the duvet.

Blinking awake, I sprung up in confusion just in time to see Hugh slam his huge stereo system, speakers and all, down on his sister's nightstand. The one on the side of his sister's bed that I was sleeping on.

Once he had the stereo plugged into the electrical outlet behind his sister's night-stand and powered up, Hugh stood back up and quickly set to work on flicking through tracks before settling on number fifteen.

I knew what he was doing the second the historic drum pattern and guitar riff sounded in my ears.

He's responding.

Heart hammering violently, I snatched up the CD case that was thrown on top of me and just stared at him, while Fleetwood Mac's "Go Your Own Way" drifted through the speakers.

He kept his eyes on me when he reached for the volume button and turned it up to its maximum level.

Oh yeah, he was making sure I heard him.

"Omigod, what the hell is happening?" Claire groaned, dragging a pillow over her head while burrowing herself deeper under the covers. "Turn it off, Liz."

There was a better chance of hell freezing over.

Both captivated and ensnared by her brother's eyes, I watched him watch me, unable to move a muscle.

The weight of my regret was pinning me to the mattress, while the force of his resentment was squeezing the air out of my lungs.

I could feel the anger simmering off him; I could feel the hurt and silent accusations wafting out of his heart and right into mine.

This is your fault, he was telling me with his eyes. *You did this to us.*

"Omigod, Hugh!" Resurfacing from beneath a mountain of pillows and stuffed animals, Claire broke our heated stare-down when she flung Garry, her ugly-assed, oversized stuffed bear at her brother's head. "Get the hell out of my room, you weirdo, and take your bloody music with you!"

After one final emotional glance, Hugh tore his eyes off mine and moved for the door, but he didn't turn off the music, leaving his stereo behind him to tell me all of the things his pride would never allow him to say.

I'M MISTER BRIGHTSIDE

Hugh

DECEMBER 12, 2003

OUR SCHOOL RUGBY TEAM WON THE SHEELER'S CUP THIS EVENING AND SOME OF THE older lads on the team decided to throw an impromptu party at Creano's house to celebrate.

I knew coming here tonight was a bad idea, but I somehow allowed Feely to persuade me, only to turn around and *not* show up himself. According to the text he sent me when I'd already arrived, Feely's newfound friend from music club needed his help with something important.

Yeah fucking right.

I knew what kind of help he provided to girls, and it sure wasn't shoveling shite.

The Killers' "Mr. Brightside" started to blast through the speakers then, and I sighed dejectedly, feeling like I was being personally attacked by the lyrics.

If I had just stayed home like Johnny had, then I wouldn't be sitting on a sixth year's couch with a full view of my own personal hell.

Liz was here, rubbing herself all over Pierce as they attempted to dance but kept stopping to maul the faces off each other.

Jesus Christ.

I couldn't catch a break.

I honestly fucking couldn't.

I tried my hardest *not* to look, but somehow my gaze always returned to her.

Dancing with him.

Touching his chest.

Kissing his lips.

"Don't look, lad," I heard Gibsie instruct a few seconds before he sank down on the coffee table in front of me, blocking the horrendous view. "Keep your eyes on me."

"I'm okay, Gibs," I forced myself to say when I felt the complete opposite. "Really, I am."

"Listen to me," he said then, leaning forward to rest his elbows on his thighs. "I know you're in pain, and I know this is killing you, and I am so fucking sorry you have to go through this, lad." He sighed heavily and implored me with his eyes to listen. "But you have to get back up, Hugh. You *have* to pick yourself up and fight, lad."

"I'm trying," I bit out, feeling my heart shatter and thunder all at once. "But I'm just so fucking *hollow*, Gibs."

"I know," he told me, squeezing my knee. "And I know you still love her, but it's over, lad." My oldest friend in the world winced before adding, "You have to let her go."

As painful as it was to hear, it was sound advice from a friend I *knew* had my best interests at heart and would never stab me in the back.

Gibsie was a lot of things, but disloyal was *not* one of them. In my whole life, I had never met a more faithful human being. It didn't matter if we were on the outs or not, he never breathed a word of my personal life to anyone—not even to Johnny and Claire. He had more shit on me than any one of our friends, had lived through the worst of my days with me, and I knew with absolute certainty that he would take all of it to the grave.

It was Gibs who'd picked me up off the ground after the breakup, and he was the one who sat with me during my darkest days—and there had been some dark fucking days. The shit I spurted after the breakup had been unhinged. I didn't dare think about it. Gibs never threw it back in my face, though.

Christ, I was so fucking relieved that I hadn't ruined my friendship with him for a girl who was anyone's girl. Because that's exactly how it had turned out to be.

It still felt sort of strange being here with him, like I was doing something wrong. I suppose I had spent so long getting the head bitten off me for acknowledging the lad that I wasn't used to spending quality time with him.

"It's all good, Hugo," Gibsie interjected, clearly reading my mind. "Water under the bridge," he added with a mischievous wink. "I'm just glad I've got my friend back on a full-time basis. That shared custody of you was triggering bad memories for me." Chuckling, he added, "I'll happily take full custody of you in the divorce, though."

Christ, I was a shitty friend.

"I love ya, Gibs," I decided to tell him, because why the hell not? Liz had already humiliated me beyond all limits. I didn't have any pride left to lose. "I don't know where I'd be right now without you, lad."

"The feeling is mutual, brother," he replied, squeezing my knee again. "You've gotten me through my fair share of dark days, too."

"Do you think I'll be okay?" I whispered, feeling so damaged inside, I needed someone to reassure me. "Will I be able to get past this?"

"Hell yes you will," he replied confidently. "And if you get stuck on the path of getting past this, I'll be right behind you to push you over the line." He smiled encouragingly. "You've *got* this, Hugo Boss-man, and I've your back." His gray eyes shone with sincerity. "Always."

"Biggsie!" Luke Casey called out, weaving through the crowd with several bottles of beer in hand. "That was one hell of an epic drop goal today." Sinking down on the couch beside me, he handed me a bottle and passed another to Gibs. "You won the game for us, lad."

"That he did," Gibs chuckled, instantly falling back into his role of the joker. "Pity about the ball cracking Pierce over the head, though." Gibs winked before adding, "What were the odds?"

"Indeed," I mused, taking a swig from my bottle.

"Biggsie, what's the story with your doll?" Danny Call asked when he joined us with a few more of the lads. "Are ye seriously off and she's fair game?" He inclined his head to where she was grinding all over Pierce and a few others from my class. "Or do ya want me to break his nose for ya?"

"Yeah, I heard about that," Luke muttered, tone laced with disapproval. "He's a fucking plonker."

"Bad form," Robbie Mac added, narrowing his eyes. "It's one thing to razz a lad up, but that's just pure dirt behavior."

"Do you think you should go over there and put a stop to it?"

If I went over there, then she would think I was willing to talk, and if she thought that, she might try to rekindle us, and I honestly didn't have the strength to push her away again.

She already knew I loved her, and she already knew I cared. The only tool I had at my disposal was my condemnation. If I lost that, I'd fall back into hell with her, and I couldn't survive it.

I could handle everything she threw at me, all her episodes and all her moods, but I would *not* tolerate infidelity.

I was pretty sure I could still smell her on the shirt I was wearing. Worse, I had a horrible feeling that said shirt was one she had bought me last Christmas.

Downing the contents of my beer bottle, I made a mental note to wash every stitch of clothing I had.

Everything was tainted, and I needed a clean slate.

"It's grand, lads," I replied, vowing to myself that I wouldn't lose another yard of dignity over them. Not when they'd stripped me to the bone. Shrugging like I didn't have a care in the world, I leaned back and took a swig of my beer before answering, "Nothing sinister happened."

"There's a rumor going around that she fucked Pierce behind your back, lad."

I forced myself not to wince. "Don't believe everything you hear."

"So she didn't?"

"We just decided to call it a day," I heard myself say, lying through my teeth to protect the reputation of a girl who didn't give a damn about mine.

"So, it's like fully off?" Danny pushed, sounding concerned. "As in, permanently?"

"Couldn't be more permanent," I replied, forcing myself to look at her one last time. The minute I did, I wanted to fucking heave up the contents of my stomach.

"Fuck." Danny's tone was serious when he asked, "Are you okay, Hugh?"

"Cally, I'm grand," I shot back, giving him a carefree smile. "Don't worry about it."

"She's not his problem anymore" Gibs was quick to add, taking a hit from a joint one of the sixth year's handed him. "Kum-bay-fucking-ya, Hugo."

"Listen, I'll be honest with ya, Hugh," Luke said when the rest of the lads started up a conversation about today's game. "She's been throwing herself around a fair bit with the lads on the team." Shifting in discomfort, he kept his tone low so that only I could hear him. "Don't worry, lad," he hurried to add, clearly uneasy about bringing this up to me. "Aside from Piercy the turncoat, the rest of the lads have your back."

"I said nothing sinister happened," I replied, feeling sick.

"Yeah, I know you did, lad," he replied, clapping my shoulder in support. "But I'm not as thick as those bastards."

Well, shit.

"I know you're putting on a brave face right now, lad, and fair play to ya, but we've known each other since baby infants, and you've always been a good friend to me, so I just felt like I needed to tell ya that I'll have your back over Pierce's any day of the week."

"Cheers, Lukey," I replied, forcing myself to keep the head. "I really appreciate it, lad, but I don't want her to get any hassle over this." Exhaling a heavy sigh, I added, "We all have school together and play on the same team, so I'm going to take the high road on this one."

"Then you're a better man than him," he replied, squeezing my shoulder. "And you deserve better."

I LOVE YOU, I'M SORRY

Lizzie

DECEMBER 12, 2003

THIS WAS A BAD IDEA FROM THE GET-GO.

I shouldn't have come.

But here I was.

Fucking up another important night of his life.

Because this was Hugh's night, not mine.

He was the one celebrating their team's win, not me.

But when Pierce invited me, I honestly couldn't give up the chance to see him again. A part of me wanted to spy on him, to see if he had moved on, to break my own fucking heart. Because if he was moving on, then I needed to witness it. Maybe then I could get some sleep at night. Maybe I wouldn't keep choking on my regret.

I was drunk.

I knew I was, but the alcohol running through my veins had nothing to do with my actions.

I couldn't blame the vodka for my following Pierce upstairs, nor could I blame the shots for the other parts.

No, it was all me.

Something was broken inside of me, had been since Caoimhe died, maybe even before it, and I was drowning in the aftermath.

Lying down on the mattress, I let the boy I'd ruined my life with do what he wanted to my body.

When he was finished with me, he climbed off the bed, zipped up his jeans, offered me a half-hearted stroke on the cheek, and disappeared back downstairs to his friends, leaving me alone in my thoughts, in my turmoil.

Feeling used and dirty, I quickly grabbed my clothes and bolted into the adjoining bathroom.

The moment I had the lock turned on the door, I sank to the floor in a heap, letting the scalding tears assault my cheekbones.

Fighting back the urge to scream, I bit down hard on my fist and slammed the back of my head against the door repeatedly.

I needed the pain.

It was the only thing that tuned out the noise. Because the noise in my head hurt so much more than any physical pain I could endure.

It wasn't enough.

Nothing seemed to be enough.

All I had was images.

Memories.

His sweaty body.

The fear.

The cries.

The sensations.

The pain.

The weight of him.

The sound of the mattress springs creaking.

Of a different life.

Of an alternate universe.

I needed to stop feeling her pain.

It *didn't* belong to me.

It *wasn't* my trauma.

Feeling the panic blow over into hysteria, I snatched a random toothbrush off the basin and used all my force to crack it in half.

Frantic, I cast the half with the head of the toothbrush aside, using the other piece instead. The rigid plastic wasn't perfect, but it would do what I needed it to do.

Fisting the plastic handle in my left hand, I began to stroke the jagged end against my thigh.

Gently at first, until I built up enough momentum for the sharp, scalding sensation to assault my senses when the sharp ridge tore its way through the upper layer of my skin.

Breaking through the skin was a challenge but one I relished.

Relentless now, I moved my hand back and forth in a ferocious rhythm, biting down on my free hand when the pain became almost unbearable.

But I couldn't stop yet.

Because I wasn't tired.

I wasn't sated.

I wasn't stable.

I needed this.

I needed to make the images leave my head and this was how I accomplished exactly that.

That's how I made *him* go away.

Only when the flesh of my thigh was indistinguishable from the blood dripping from my hand did I stop.

Exhaling a ragged breath, I released my hold on my makeshift weapon and tossed it aside before placing both hands on the cool tiles beneath me.

Closing my eyes, I breathed in deep and slow, letting myself sit with the pain for a moment.

Letting my brain rewire the pathway from mental pain to physical pain.

Taking in a few sacred moments of *peace.*

Lightheaded and broken, I slumped, my back against the door, and held my breath, hoping that if I held it long enough, I might drift off to sleep and wake up back in Hugh's bed.

A little while later, when I was redressed and back downstairs, I was hit with the familiar tsunami of guilt. The moment I walked into the living room and locked eyes with Hugh, I felt my shame swallow me whole.

His whiskey eyes seared holes through my soul, and I wanted to both run into his arms and throw myself off a bridge.

He knew exactly what I had done upstairs with another boy, and it made me feel every bit the whore the monster molded me into.

I could see it in Hugh's eyes that it was over for him, that my actions tonight only solidified his decision to walk away.

I had spent weeks trying to convince myself I did the right thing. That in the long run, Hugh would be better off hating me. If he didn't love me, he couldn't get hurt. If he stayed away from me, he would be safe.

Therefore, I should have been feeling glad about the disappointment in his eyes. It was what I wanted, after all. What needed to happen to set him free from the hell that was loving me.

But when he walked outside, I couldn't seem to stop my feet from following him.

Ignoring the evil glares I received from some of his teammates and the way they muttered the word *whore* when I walked past them, I kept my eyes trained on Hugh's back.

Following him into the night, I trailed every step he took until it led to a stable. When I finally worked up the courage to speak to him, he was leaning against a stable door, with his back to me, scratching a horse's ear.

"Hi," I squeezed out, hovering at a slight distance from him.

His entire frame stiffened and the hand he was using to stroke the horse froze.

"How are you?" I decided to add when he didn't respond.

Exhaling a pained breath, Hugh slowly turned around to face me. "What do you want, Liz?"

You. "I just wanted to say hi."

"Hi," he replied flatly.

I continued to hover, both unwilling and unable to leave. "Are you okay?"

Hugh stared at my face like the question offended him.

Then he muttered something unintelligible under his breath before turning his attention back to the horse. "It's cold out here. You should go back inside."

"I don't care," I strangled out, clasping my hands tightly.

"Yeah," he replied softly, while he continued to give the horse his full attention. "You don't seem to care about a whole lot these days."

"I care about you," I choked out, unable to stop my legs from moving to him. "You're the only thing I care about."

"I know you think you do," he replied, straining away when I tried to hug him.

"I do care," I argued, feeling the familiar scald of tears. "I love you."

"And I love you," he replied simply. "I wish I didn't, but I do."

"Can we fix this?" Sniffling, I used my sleeve to wipe my cheeks.

"Your eyes are black," he said sadly. "You're not well, and Pierce shouldn't be taking advantage."

"I don't care about him," I cried, pulling on his arm. "I only care about you."

"You need to get some help, Liz." He sounded so torn. "You need to do it, okay?"

"If I take my meds, will you take me back?"

"You should take your meds regardless, Liz."

"But would it help?" I choked out, feeling desperate. "Would you take me back?"

"No, Liz." Releasing a broken sigh, Hugh shook his head and stepped around me. "I'm never taking you back."

"Then what's the fucking point of taking them!" I cried out hoarsely, as I watched him walk out of the stable. "Hugh, no, please don't go!"

"Get better, Liz," was all he replied before disappearing in the darkness.

"I love you," I sobbed hysterically, sinking to the ground. "I'm sorry."

THE LION AND THE GAZELLE

Hugh

DECEMBER 18, 2003

"HUGHIE, CAN WE TALK?" WERE THE FIRST WORDS PIERCE SAID TO ME SINCE THE night I caught him in *my* bed, with his dick inside *my* girl.

"You have a lot of fucking nerve coming over here," I replied as I sat on the bench in the changing room and yanked off my boots. Having endured an intense two-hour training session in the pissing rain, I was in no mood for this conversation. Instead, I inclined my head to the other side of the changing room, where his shit was stored. "I suggest you go back over there before I ram these studs up your hole."

"It's *important*, lad," he pushed, continuing to hover near me like an annoying blue bottle. "I wouldn't be here if it wasn't."

Ignoring him, I peeled off my drenched socks before stripping off the rest of my kit and grabbing my towel. When I stood up to head for a shower and saw him follow me, I swung around and glared. "Follow me in there and you won't be coming back out."

Prick.

Storming into the shower stalls, I slammed my palm on the chrome knob and stood directly under the scalding-hot water, trying to warm up from the winter cold and cool down from my traitorous teammate all at once.

I spent longer in the shower than usual, almost thirty minutes, with the hope that he'd be gone by the time I came back out.

Unfortunately, when I returned to the changing room Pierce was the *only* person still there, clad in his uniform and with a dopey expression on his face.

At least he had the common sense to sit on the opposite side of the room this time.

Gripping the towel around my hips, I stalked past him, moving straight for my spot. "What are you lurking around for? Looking for tips? Trying to see how your dick measures up to mine now?"

"I need to talk to you about Lizzie," he decided to start with, which was a bad fucking move.

"Read the room, asshole," I snapped, dropping my towel and reaching for a fresh pair of jocks in my bag. "I'm not interested in what's happening between ya, so just walk away."

"But you're still interested in her well-being, aren't ya?" he snapped back. "Or do you not give a shit about her anymore?"

Every muscle in my body locked up with tension and I had to take a few steadying breaths to calm down.

He had some nerve bringing her up to me.

Forcing myself to take the high road and *not* react, I continued to ignore him while I dressed.

"Listen, Hughie, I'm sorry, okay," he sighed, sounding both remorseful and frustrated. "For what I did. It was bad form on my account. I fucked up, lad. I get that now."

Yeah, I bet he did.

"If you expect me to forgive you for sleeping with my girlfriend of *over four years*, then you're fucking delusional," I reminded him. "The best you can hope for is my tolerance, and you're cutting it fine at that."

"Lad, we've been friends since we were four," he tried to plead. "Surely we can get past this."

"The fact that you're bringing up how long we've known each other only attests to how few fucks you gave about our friendship."

"Hughie, come on, lad…"

"You intentionally destroyed my four-year relationship with the girl I've been best friends with for almost as long as we've known each other." I shook my head in disgust. "The girl you *saw* me with every day for the past decade. So save your excuses for someone gullible enough to believe them."

"She's not spotless in this, either," he shot back in his pitiful attempt to throw Liz under the bus for all of it. "She was the one in the relationship, not me."

"True," I agreed in a level tone. "And because of that, she's no longer *in* that relationship."

"I didn't think she'd do it," he finally admitted, getting to the heart of the truth. "She always seemed so obsessed with you. I was only half messing when I chanced my arm with her that night."

And she was in the throes of mania.

"And you thought it would be somehow amusing to see if you could break us up?" I tossed back. "Or was it jealousy that got the better of you that night?"

"Probably both."

My brows shot up. "Well, at least you're an *honest* degenerate prick."

"Yeah," he muttered under his breath.

"Are we done here?" I asked then.

"Listen, I really think you should talk to her," he had the nerve to request. "She was crying at Creano's party, and she hasn't shown up to school all week."

"Christ." I chuckled humorlessly. "You are something else, do ya know that?"

"She's… There's something *wrong* with that girl," he continued to blurt. "And I am really fucking out of my depth." I could hear the concern in his tone as he ranted. "I think she's having a breakdown or something over the guilt."

The guilt.

"Bitten off more than you can chew, did ya?" I couldn't resist taunting him. "Yeah, I thought that might happen."

"Hughie, come on, lad, this isn't easy for me, either," he snapped. "Having to come to her ex for help."

"I wouldn't piss on you if you were on fire, asshole," I replied, toeing on my runners. "So you forget about me helping you."

"Then help her," he urged. "I know you love her."

"You know I love *her*," I repeated, having heard just about all I could take. "You know I *love* her," I roared, swinging around to glare at him. "If you *know* I love her so much, then why the fuck would you, my friend since primary school, fuck her in my bed?"

"I already told you that I took it too far!"

"No," I snarled, unwilling to let it go once he'd opened the door. "Taking it too far would've been kissing her!" My chest was heaving, and I wasn't sure if I had the ability to not kill this prick. "What you did was taking it to another fucking planet!"

"I was drunk, Hughie," he groaned, flinching. "I messed up. I'm holding my hands up to it."

"And what's your excuse every other time you've put your dick in her?" I demanded, seething. "Well? Have you been drunk for the past forty-eight days, too? Or are you going to use the jealousy card again? Or were you just fucking my girl because she's vulnerable, and you're a piece of shit!"

"I didn't know she was this vulnerable."

"Maybe, but you knew she was *mine*."

"Hughie, come on, lad."

"What the fuck do you want from me?"

"Just go see her or something," he muttered, rubbing his jaw. "Make sure she's okay."

"Why don't you go see her," I snapped back, feeling too damn much, "and leave me the hell out of it?"

"I've been calling her, but she won't pick up," he snapped. "She'll pick up for you, though. She hasn't been to school in a week, and I *know* you care."

"Whoa, whoa, whoa. Let me get this straight." I narrowed my eyes in disgust. "You want *me* to call *my* ex, who *cheated* on me with *you*, because she'll answer *my* calls instead of *yours*?"

"Sounds about right," Pierce muttered, reddening.

My adrenaline was pumping right along with my testosterone, and I could barely restrain myself from the raw, primal urge to rip this prick's head off and put him in his place.

"You know why that is, don't ya?" I said in an eerily cold tone, fully embracing the masculine superiority I had over this prick. "It's because she's mine." Smirking, I prowled toward him like he was a gazelle and I was a lion. "And it doesn't matter how many times she lets you in her bed, she'll never want you more than she wants *me*."

"Oh yeah? Well, she seemed to want me an awful lot more than you that night." Pierce took the bait and snapped, all riled up now. "In fact, if I recall right, she was complaining about how you weren't doing it for her."

"You think because you scratched an itch for her, you're better than me?" Instead of losing it, like he expected me to, I smirked. "You dumb shit. If I wanted to fuck her, I could do it right now, but the difference between the two of us is that I don't take advantage of vulnerable girls. Because I'm a man, asshole, and you're a boy."

"Hughie, relax." His eyes flashed with panic. "Just keep the head, lad."

"Do you know what you are to her, Pierce?" I asked, walking until we were chest to chest, squaring up to each other, with me taking the win in the height department by a good four inches. "All you are to that girl is my piss-poor replacement."

His body thrummed with tension, and he balled his hands into fists.

"You want to throw down?" I arched a brow. "Go for it."

To be fair to him, he thought about it for a good five seconds before cowering away. "I'm not fighting you again, lad."

"Wise decision," I replied moments before my hand shot out and gripped his throat. "Now, you listen." Slamming him roughly against the wall at his back, I leaned in close and hissed, "You're going to stay out of my face, and I'm going to stay out of yours. You don't talk to me unless it's on the pitch or class-assignment related. You keep your hands off her when I'm around, and if I hear a single word of her private business or anything she says or does in your presence getting around school, I will take it as a personal attack on me, ya hear?"

"Ye...ah," he strangled out, turning red.

"You keep your goddamn mouth shut about her being vulnerable or any of it," I threatened. "Because if you ruin her reputation, I will bury you."

I didn't plan to get off at Liz's stop after school today, but when the bus driver pulled in, that's exactly what happened—much to Gibs's and Feely's disgust. Pierce had planted a seed of worry inside of me, and it had continued to fester all day until I'd driven myself half-demented with worry.

Too late to turn back, I made my way up the familiar gravel entrance in the pissing rain until I reached her house.

I was surprised when I found Liz sitting on the front step of her house, but what surprised me more was the fact that she was wearing her uniform even though she hadn't been to school all week.

"Hugh." Her eyes lit up when she noticed me approach and she quickly jumped to her feet. "What are you doing here?"

"Your boyfriend sent me." I kept walking until I reached her. "He wants you to answer his calls."

Her entire expression fell, and a full-body shudder racked through her. "He is *not* my boyfriend."

I couldn't deny the immense pleasure I felt at her reaction, but I hid it well. "Well, whatever you want to refer to him as wants you to answer his calls."

"You're the only one whose calls I'm answering," she replied, looking up at me with big, lonesome eyes. "I'm glad you're here."

"Yeah." I had to clear my throat to keep the emotion out of my voice. "Why are you sitting in the rain?"

She shrugged her slim shoulders. "My body was burning up."

"Are you sick?"

"Nope." She shook her head, and it caused droplets of rain to sprinkle. "Just horny."

Jesus.

"What's with the uniform?" I asked, steering the conversation to safer waters. "You haven't been in school all week."

"Because I've been tired," she admitted, pulling on her drenched sleeves. "And I can't sleep no matter what I do." Shrugging, she pointed toward the meadow and said, "I've been hiding out in the fields all week during school hours, hoping my dad doesn't catch me."

"You should tell Pierce that," I forced myself to say, even though it nearly killed me to do it. "He's, ah, he's *worried* about you."

"I don't want to talk to him," she squeezed out, looking up at me with a guilty expression. "I don't want anything to do with him."

"You just feel that way today," I sighed. "Because you're off your meds."

"I'm afraid to go back on them," she admitted then, giving me the first glimpse of the real her in months. "I'm afraid to remember everything."

"Liz." My heart cracked. "Flipping in and out of reality is no way to live."

"I know." Tears filled her eyes. "But it's better than living without you."

I wanted to go to her.

Despite everything, I wanted to pull her into my arms.

Because I was so damn deeply in love with this girl that it physically hurt to stand here and not *hold* her.

"I love you," she sniffled, using her shoulder to wipe her cheek. "No matter what."

"I love you, too." I couldn't stop myself from responding. And I clearly loved her no matter what because my feelings still stood despite the cheating and heartbreak.

"Do you want to come inside?"

I shook my head. "I can't do that, Liz."

"It's pouring rain," she reminded me, pointing to the dark-clouded sky. "I won't try any funny business."

Yeah, for now. "And what if you change your mind?"

"Then you can leave." She pushed her front door open and stepped inside. "Please?"

I knew I shouldn't.

It was a trap.

A bad fucking idea.

But I found myself following her inside.

Despite the red flags shooting up, I walked up the familiar staircase, eyes glued to her ass that she was intentionally swishing in my face as she walked ahead of me.

When she reached the landing, she did a strange, little shimmy past her sister's door, straining her body as far away from it as humanly possible, before hurrying into her room.

"Where are your parents?" I asked, following her inside the room that had been like my own for years. "Are they out for the day?"

"I'm not sure," she replied, peeling off her drenched school jumper as she moved straight for her bed. "We're not exactly on talking terms at the moment."

My brows shot up. "Even Catherine?"

"Dad doesn't let me get within a ten-foot radius of Mam," she explained with a sigh. "He thinks I'm dangerous."

"You're not dangerous," I replied, walking over to her bed and sitting down without even thinking about it. *Fuck.* "You're sick. There's a difference."

"Why aren't you shouting at me?" she asked, sitting cross-legged on her bed, facing me. "Why are you so nice?"

"I'm not the shouting type," I reminded her. "Well, not usually at least."

"But I deserve it," she squeezed out, gaze cast downwards. "And this hurts because I know what I've lost."

I wanted to tell her that she hadn't lost me, but I would be a liar.

"I want you to be healthy," I said instead. "It's important to me, Liz."

"You're important to me," she breathed, sidling closer until I could feel her hot breath against my ear. "You're everything to me."

And there it was.

The sudden shift in mood.

"No touching," I warned when her hand landed on my thigh. "If you do that again, I'm leaving."

"Really?"

"Really, Liz."

"Fine." Reluctantly, she placed her hand on her lap. "Happy now?"

No, because I *wanted* her hands on me. "Peachy."

"Do you miss me, Hugh?" she asked, eyes growing darker the longer she looked at me. "Like I miss you?"

"You know I miss you," I replied, not bothering to lie. There was no point. She held every piece of my mangled heart. I figured she might as well take the last sliver of my pride while she was at it. "It kills me to see you with him."

"I don't want him." Her voice took on a sultry tone. "I've never wanted him."

"And yet here we are." I shook my head in frustration. "You fucked him, but you fucked me harder."

"Do you want to take your clothes off?" she asked then, shamelessly raking me over with her eyes. "You're soaked to the skin. You might get sick."

"I'll take my chances."

Frustration etched her features. "You're not going to make this easy, are you?"

"Nope." I smirked. "I have my virtue to protect."

"I don't know why I did it," she repeated for what had to be the hundredth time in a matter of months. "I'm not even attracted to him." She touched me again, trailing her finger down my throat, and this time I didn't have the strength to stop her. "You're all I've ever wanted inside me."

Jesus Christ.

"I *could* fuck you," I admitted, feeling both bitter and turned on. "Right here. Just once. For closure. But that would only make it worse for you."

"No, it wouldn't," she said, pressing her cheek to mine and inhaling deeply. "You're all I want."

"It would, because once you've had me, you'll never get over me," I whispered in her ear, deciding to turn the tables on her for once, and then enjoying when she shivered in response. "It'll be game over for you, Liz, and then what?"

"Then we'll keep doing it," she moaned, rubbing herself against me. "Forever."

This was a bad idea, and I needed to stop.

Just...*not yet.*

"Not a chance, baby," I growled, nuzzling her cheek with mine. "You threw away forever with me for temporary with him."

"Let me make it up to you." Peppering my neck with kisses, she reached between my thighs and palmed my rapidly growing erection. "Let me make it right."

"I'm not putting my dick where's he's been," I groaned, unable to stop my hips from arching into her touch. "You need to stop."

"But you love when I make you cum," she teased, tormenting me with her skilled fingers. "I'll give you anything you want."

"All I wanted was fidelity."

"And all I wanted was you inside me." She groaned in frustration. "You're *still* all I want."

"And I still want fidelity," I replied in a guff tone. "But that dream's gone clean out the window, hasn't it?"

"Hugh," she groaned in a pleading tone, flopping back on her pillow. "Stop torturing me."

Fuck, she looked incredible sprawled out on her bed, with flushed cheeks and her skirt hitched around her hips.

"Fine." Releasing a frustrated moan, she parted her thighs, spreading herself completely open, giving me an up-close-and-personal view of her white thong. "If you won't touch me, I'll do it myself."

I had no fucking clue what to say to that, but then she pushed the fabric of her thong to one side, and I quickly lost all ability to speak.

Tracing her slit with her fingers, she slowly pushed two inside her, while she thumbed for her clit.

Holy fuck.

I need to leave.

I need to turn away.

Why the hell am I still staring?

"It's okay," Liz whispered, eyes flicking to mine. "I want you to watch me."

Moaning softly, she kept her eyes on me the entire time.

Jesus Christ.

I couldn't have looked away if I'd wanted to—and I definitely did not want to look away.

In this moment, I could think of nothing but this girl and her perfect pussy.

I knew how she felt.

I'd had my fingers and tongue inside her on countless occasions.

My dick strained against the constraints of my jocks, desperate to have its turn.

The more flushed she grew, the louder her moans became, and the closer I moved. "Touch me."

I shook my head, fucking hating myself for denying myself.

"It's okay," she coaxed. "It can be our secret."

I shook my head again, while my hips gyrated of their own damn accord.

"If you won't touch me, then touch yourself," she breathed in the sexiest fucking voice I'd ever heard.

Holy fuck!

"Show me, baby."

Fuck, I lost my head when she called me *baby.*

A pained groan escaped me as my gaze roamed shamelessly over her.

"Show me that big dick."

A momentary blip in sanity had me unsnapping the button on my school trousers and quickly unzipping.

"Mm," she moaned, rocking her hips into her hand. "Take it out."

Reckless, I did just that.

Fisting my shaft, I quickly worked myself over, while she fucked herself in front of me.

"Come here," she ordered breathlessly, patting the part of the mattress between her legs before resuming rubbing her clit. "I want to see."

Stripping off from the waist down, I knelt between her legs with my dick in my hands.

This was madness.

I was a fucking eejit.

But it would take an earthquake to force me away from her in this moment.

Licking her lips, she flicked her hooded gaze up to me. "Fuck yourself like how you want to fuck me."

Jesus.

Losing all self-control, I went to town on myself, pulling on my dick so furiously that I could feel my balls tighten up faster than usual.

I wasn't unfamiliar with getting myself off, but getting off to the visual of a naked girl beneath me was sending me over the edge way too fucking quickly.

"I'm coming," she cried out, and then her thighs jerked and spasmed, rubbing off my outer thighs and causing me to spill all over her.

Chest heaving, I released with a pained groan, unable to angle my aim away from her face because she was too fucking close.

Mortified, I froze on my knees between her legs, looking at the mess I'd made of her.

Instead of complaining and telling me to fuck off, Liz pulled up on her elbows, smirked, and then traced her tongue over her bottom lip *tasting* me.

Holy fuck!

I'd never seen anything so sexy in my entire life.

And then she reached up from between her legs and held her index finger in front of my mouth. "Open your mouth."

Momentarily losing my ability to form a coherent thought, I did exactly what she told me to and parted my lips.

She slowly pushed her finger into my mouth. "Suck."

Keeping my eyes locked on hers, I did as she asked.

"Taste me."

I *was* and she was even better than I remembered.

"See?" Slowly withdrawing her finger, she pulled up on her knees, chest flush with mine, and smiled. "And we didn't even break any rules."

I choked out a breath, chest still heaving. "What the fuck did we just…"

"Don't worry, brave knight." She pressed a finger to my lips and winked. "Your virtue is still intact."

With that, she climbed off the bed and moved for the bathroom, leaving me alone to reel in my guilt.

YOU CAN HOLD MY HAND

Lizzie

DECEMBER 18, 2003

THE HIGH I WAS RIDING QUICKLY DEFLATED WHEN I RETURNED TO MY ROOM TO FIND Hugh looking utterly devastated.

I couldn't understand why.

He'd blown his load on top of me.

He should have been thrilled.

Instead, he looked like he wanted to cry.

"What?" I demanded, taking in the sight of his remorseful expression. "Don't pretend you didn't enjoy that because the cum I just washed off my face says otherwise."

"Jesus, Liz." Hugh shook his head and started to pace my room. "Can you *not* say it like that?"

"Why not?" I laughed, tracking him with my eyes. "It's the truth."

"Because I shouldn't have done that," he strangled out, looking genuinely torn up. "That was *not* okay, Liz."

"Why?" I demanded, feeling insanely furious in this moment. "You love me, and I love you. You watched me cum, and I watched you. We didn't break your no-touch rule. So where's the fucking problem in that, *Hugh*?"

"Because we're broken up, Liz!" he shouted back at me, hands in his hair as he paced. "Because you aren't *you* right now and I *know* better!"

"Oh, relax!" I sneered, full-on raging now. "You didn't crawl into my bed in the middle of the night and fuck me like he did!"

Hugh gaped at me. "What are you *talking* about?"

"The monster!" I screamed, throwing my hands up. "You know he fucks me in my dreams, don't ya? He's been doing it for years!" I choked out a maniacal laugh. "Oops. Maybe I shouldn't have told you I've been sleep-cheating on you for years!"

"Jesus, Liz." Hugh shook his head and released a furious growl. "I can't talk to you when you're like this."

"Why can't you just love me!" I screamed, stalking toward him when he tried to leave. "Why can't anyone fucking love me!"

"I do love you!" Hugh roared into my face, chest heaving. "If I didn't, I wouldn't be here!"

"Then fix me," I begged, clawing at his shirt. "Make it go away!"

"I've tried!" he strangled out, stepping around me and stalking out of my room. "For ten years! Nothing worked! And I can't keep letting myself feel this way!"

"What way?"

"Miserable!" Hugh shouted. "You're making my life a fucking misery, baby!"

"So you're just going to leave me?" I called after him as I leaned over the banister, watching as he quickly descended the spiraling staircase. "That's how it's going to be, huh?"

"You left me, Liz," he tossed over his shoulder when he reached the ground floor. "Not the other way around."

"Fine!" I screamed, thundering down the staircase after him. "If you don't want me, I'll go find someone who does."

"Liz!" Hugh snapped when I stormed past him in the doorway and ran outside. "Get back here!"

Nope.

I wasn't going back to that house ever again.

Breaking into a run, I bolted down the gravel driveway with only one destination in mind.

Freedom.

When I reached the gate, I thought I was in the clear, but nope. "Don't do this," Hugh growled, grabbing my shoulders before I reached the road. He spun me around to face him and said it again. "Don't *do* this, Liz."

The rain was beating down on us, plastering his halo of dirty-blond hair to his forehead.

Raindrops trickled from his brow to his nose and then his lips, and I couldn't take it.

Looking at him hurt so fucking much.

I wasn't sure if I was screaming or crying, but I knew there were strange noises coming out of my throat.

"You don't want me!" I hissed, breaking free of his hold and booking it toward the road. "He does!"

"He doesn't deserve you," Hugh roared, snatching me back up. "And you don't deserve this demon fucking disease!"

"Let go of me!" I screamed, thrashing against Hugh's impossibly strong hold as he carted me out of the road. "Now!"

"So you can go back to that prick and lay on your back for him? Or worse, go back inside and carve yourself like a fucking pumpkin?" Hugh roared, beyond livid. "Not a chance in hell." He shook his head again and pulled me flush against his chest. "You're coming home with me. Where I can look after you."

"Why would you even want that?" I choked out, roughly shoving him away. "You said it yourself: being around me makes you miserable!"

"Yeah," he snarled, closing the space between us. "And *not* being around you makes me feel even worse!"

His words seemed to resonate with something inside of my subconscious and I felt myself slowly calming.

"Hugh." Shivering, I reached up and brushed his full bottom lip. "I don't want to make you feel worse."

His subconscious reaction was to reciprocate my affection by kissing my finger, only to groan in frustration when he realized his mistake.

Because I was a mistake.

His greatest mistake.

"Listen." Clutching my face between his big hands, Hugh hunched down to lock eyes with me, forcing me to focus on those magical, whiskey-brown irises. "You can't stay here on your own. Not right now, okay? So I'm going to take you home with me."

"You are?"

"Yes." His voice was steady and reassuring and soothed something deep inside of me. "We're going to walk to my place, and you are going to hang there until your parents get back from wherever the fuck they went."

"Just us?"

"Just us," he confirmed gruffly.

"Can I hold your hand on the walk?"

"Yeah, Liz." Pain flickered in his eyes, and he nodded slowly. "You can hold my hand on the walk."

MAYBE WE CAN BE FRIENDS?

Hugh

DECEMBER 30, 2003

"Out," I whisper-hissed midway through showering, when I poked my head around the shower curtain and locked eyes on the blond leaning against the bathroom door. "*Now*."

I was in no form for her antics, not after the last storm I got caught in.

And I didn't have the self-restraint to reject her advances, either.

Goddammit to hell.

Why did it have to be so hard?

Why did I have to fall in love with my sister's best friend?

These sleepovers were *killing* me.

Knowing my ex was sleeping in the room next to mine was the reason I was *showering* at two o'clock in the fucking morning.

"Hi." Reaching behind her back, Liz turned the key in the lock and released a shaky breath. "I heard you come in here."

Of course she had.

My bedroom aligned with my sister's room, which meant we both knew when the other was on the prowl.

Luckily, Claire was a deep sleeper.

Unluckily, Lizzie was *not*.

"So you thought you'd come on in and we'd shoot the breeze?" I bit back a growl of frustration. It was hard enough to handle seeing her at school every day, and my house most weekends, and my dreams at night, but now I couldn't get myself off to the memory of Liz without real-life Liz barging in.

Jesus Christ.

I can't catch a fucking break.

"I needed to see you," she blurted out, hands knotted in front of her. "Really badly."

"Oh yeah?" Huffing out a breath, I dragged the curtain across the rail, purposefully blocking her view of me. "Well, too fucking bad."

"I'm so sorry for losing it on you at my house last week."

"Don't worry about it," I deadpanned. "I'm used to it."

"And for you having to bring me here to look after me until Mam picked me up."

"Like I said," I shot back gruffly. "I'm used to it."

"Well, I'm sorry for being the kind of person you're used to looking after."

I flinched. "Liz."

"Hugh." Her voice cracked. "Oh God, I love you so much."

I knew she did, and her feelings were entirely reciprocated on my end, but that didn't mean what we had wasn't toxic.

"Well then, it's time to stop," I strangled out, quickly bracing the tiles with both hands, while I fought down the decade long urge to go to her. "Because I'm going out with the lads tomorrow night, and I'm going to score with someone." It was complete bullshit, but I needed to arm myself, dammit.

I heard her sudden sharp intake of breath, followed by a smothered sob, and my chest physically heaved from the violent, abhorrent pain that shot through me.

This was too much.

It hurt too hard.

I was too damn deeply in love with her.

Bowing my head, I clenched my eyes shut and willed myself to be strong, to *not* cave, and to have some goddamn respect for myself.

However, all notions of conjuring mental resolve flew clean out of my head when the shower curtain peeled back and Liz stepped inside.

Naked.

She didn't speak a word when she slipped under my arm that was still bracing the wall and wrapped her arms around my waist.

I didn't move a muscle.

I barely took a breath.

Body rigid, I stared down at her blond hair, feeling my heart shatter to pieces, while my body thrummed with delight.

She had her cheek pressed to my chest, and her arms wrapped like a vise around my waist.

We stood like that for what felt like an eternity, with the water pouring down on our joined bodies.

"I'm so sorry," she finally broke the thick silence by saying. "I'm so, so, so fucking sorry."

Again, my chest heaved violently as my heart gunned in my chest. "I know," I managed to croak out, sounding more broken than her.

"I haven't spoken to him." Quietly crying, she continued to nuzzle my chest with her cheek. "I haven't spoken to any boys."

"Liz."

"I love you so much," she strangled out. "I feel like I can't *breathe* without you."

I know the feeling.

"Give me another chance," she begged, welding her body to mine in desperation. "I will do anything—*anything*—to make it up to you, Hugh. Whatever you want, I'll do it." Her cries grew more frantic right along with her pleading. "I won't go out. I won't drink. I'll do the counseling. I'll take the medication. *Anything.* Just…*please* don't leave me."

A stronger man would have been able to hold their ground.

But I wasn't a man yet, and I loved her too much to not comfort her when she was falling apart in my arms.

"I love you, too," I whispered, wrapping my arms around her. "I always have, and I always will."

"No, no, no," she cried, clawing at my back to drag my body closer to hers. "Please don't say it."

"But I *can't* be with you," I strangled out, holding her up when her legs gave out. "We can't get back together."

"I didn't mean it, I didn't mean it," she continued to sob, shaking her head. "I would never do that to you on purpose!"

That was the thing about cheating; whether it was accidental or on purpose, it hurt just the same.

"I don't think you meant it, Liz," I said, voice cracking as my emotions threatened to get the better of me. "But I also don't trust you not to do it again."

"I won't, I won't, I swear, Hugh," she pleaded, reaching up to wrap her arms around my neck. "I'll be good, I promise. A good girl. Like you deserve. I'll be good this time."

"It's not about you being good, baby."

"I'll go back on my meds." Hiccupping another pained sob, she peppered my chest with kisses. "I'll be steady. You know I can do it. You've seen me! So I can be your Lizzie again if you just give me one last chance."

With every ounce of my heart, I wanted to say yes. I wanted that last chance more than she would ever know. But we'd already had so many that I knew in my heart the outcome. "You say that now, but you'll change your mind."

"I won't, I promise," she vehemently protested through her tears. "I will take them every day for the rest of my life if that's what it takes to keep you."

"You'll take them until you start feeling better, you mean." I blinked back my tears. "And then you'll decide that you're cured, and don't need them anymore, and you'll be right back to the beginning. Back to the mania, back to the screaming matches, the not sleeping, and the constant seeking of sex. And then, once you've well and truly fucked yourself over, you'll slip into the depression where you spend weeks at a time in bed, while I spend every waking hour of those weeks wrestling a fucking razor out of your hands."

"*No*, I won't do that this time."

"You do it every time, ba–" My voice cracked, and I had to suck in several heaving breaths to get a handle on myself before I went on. "I can't keep living my life like this." Sniffling, I cradled her head in my hand. "Not sleeping because I don't know where you are, or who you're with, or if you've come off your meds and have another asshole between your legs. Because you're manic and want to fuck anything with a pulse." I shook my head, feeling broken. "I wish I could find a way to make this work, but I can't, Liz. I *can't* do this with you for another decade. I can't plan a future with you when, at any moment, you could switch up on me and fuck someone else." Sniffling, I pressed a kiss to her head. "And it's not fair of you to ask me to."

"I can't live without you," she cried, holding on to me as tightly as I was holding her. "I don't want to."

"Maybe, when some time has passed, we can be friends again," I offered, hating the words as they came out of my mouth. Because I could never be just her friend. This was the girl I wanted beside me every day for the rest of my life. "I'm *always* going to love you."

"No matter what?"

"Yeah, Liz," I whispered, dying inside. "No matter what."

STOLEN BURGERS AND KISSES

Hugh

DECEMBER 31, 2003

Tonight was New Year's Eve, and I had, once again, been coerced by the lads to go on the lash with them. I'd been dreading it all week because this year's one would mark the first in a decade that I wouldn't be spending with Liz.

I missed her so fucking much, I couldn't breathe, and no amount of anything could make it better.

I'd been dreading going out tonight but was pleasantly surprised when Feely suggested we head across town to the disco BCS was throwing at the GAA Pavilion.

Surrounded by mostly strangers, it was a hell of a lot easier to loosen up and enjoy myself. Oh, and the naggin of vodka we each necked in the bushes beforehand hadn't hurt matters, either.

Pissed as a fart, I'd stumbled around the pavilion for most of the night with my three best friends, sometimes dancing but mostly warding off girls.

Johnny, on the other hand, had been lured behind the curtains at the back of the hall by the female *security guard*, who I could only presume, was following through on her promise of *blowing his world*.

Meanwhile, Gibs was too busy falling in love with himself to give anyone else a second glance, while Feely had his eye on a cute, little redhead on the dance floor.

"Goddamn, I'm something else," Gibsie declared, gliding across the dance floor to "Pony" like he was the love child of Snoop Dogg and John Travolta. "The big man upstairs spared no expenses when he made Gerard Gibson, I tell ya."

Gibs was the best dancer in the county, and the fucker knew it. It didn't matter what music was playing, the snake-hipped flanker had the perfect moves for every beat.

"If you were a cake, you'd eat yourself, Gibs."

"Damn straight I would," he wholeheartedly agreed, whipping off his shirt to flex his pecs. "Have you seen me?" Grinning, he kissed his bicep and rolled his hips like a damn porn star. "I'm fucking delicious." And then he pulled out all the stops, dropping to the floor to perform the sluttiest worm move I'd ever seen.

The high-pitched sound of screaming girls was feral, as a horde of them surrounded Gibs, who was dry humping the floor better than any stripper.

"Let's see him get out of this one," Feely slurred, watching our friend get swallowed up by the mob.

Drunk, I leaned against the wall at my back for support, while Feely staggered toward me. "Lad, you're worse than me," I laughed when he started to lean to one side like the Tower of Pisa.

"Did ya get the shift yet, Hughie?" he slurred, resting a hip against the wall next to me.

"Not happening, Pa." Drunk or not, I was nowhere near ready for *that*.

"Yeah, it fucking is," Feely agreed, sidling up to my other. "It's a done deal, lad."

The DJ started the ten-second countdown to the New Year, and it caused a tsunami of pain to rise up inside me.

Fuck.

Liz.

"Ah, you'll have a New Year's kiss," Feely pushed in a coaxing tone, gaze trained in on someone on the dance floor. "Come on, lad." He dragged me onto the floor just as the DJ reached five in his countdown. "Scope out a girl and live a little."

"Four, three, two, one…"

Bleary eyed, I watched as my friend staggered in the direction of the petite redhead he'd had his eyes on all night but was intercepted by a curvy brunette, who swept in and kissed him instead.

I watched as my friend momentarily froze before wrapping his arms around the brunette and reciprocating her kiss.

Ugh.

Christ.

Shaking my head, I turned away from the mauling only to be intercepted by the same tiny redhead.

"Whoa," I managed to say about a millisecond before she pulled my face down to hers and crashed her lips to mine.

Holy fuck.

My immediate reaction was to jerk away, knowing that foreign lips had no business on mine, but then I remembered that my lips didn't belong to anyone.

Breathing hard, I kept my hands on the redhead's shoulders to keep her at bay, while I tried to clear my thoughts.

"Please kiss me," she begged, fisting the front of my shirt as she pushed up on tiptoes. It wasn't an aggressive move. It was a desperate one. "*Please.*"

Big, green eyes shone up at me, looking just as uncertain as I felt.

In fact, her eyes looked like they were close to spilling tears.

Jesus.

I had no clue what it was, but something about this girl's eyes had me nodding slowly.

Relief flashed in her eyes, and she tipped her chin up to meet mine.

And then, for the first time in my life, I kissed a girl who wasn't named Lizzie Young.

The kiss wasn't mind-blowing.

It wasn't fireworks.

It wasn't Liz.

But it *was* nice.

———————————

"I can't figure out if you're waiting with me out of choice or pity," the redhead, whose name I'd learned was Katie, mused after the disco, as we sat on the footpath outside the building. "Because, as grateful as I am to you for saving me back there, I don't think my pride can take another knock tonight."

Her words drifted through the fog in my head, and my eyes snapped to attention. "Huh?"

Her cheeks turned red. "Never mind."

Catching the end of her ramble, I arched a brow and asked, "Why would I be here out of pity?"

She shrugged. "Just know that you saved me from making a massive fool of myself."

"By kissing you?"

"Trust me, Hugh."

"Fair enough."

"Case won't even remember his name," she sighed, gesturing to the wall our friends were getting off behind. "This is what she does."

"You don't approve?"

She shook her head again. "I love her, but that's not how I live."

When she began to shiver, I automatically reached for my jacket. Unzipping it, I shrugged it off and draped it over her shoulders.

"Thanks."

"No problem."

"I'll give it back to you at school next week."

My brows rose in surprise. "You go to school with me?"

"Wow, you really know how to make a girl feel seen."

"No, it's not like that…"

"It's okay. I'm joking." She smiled. "I'm in the year below you guys."

She was in third year. "Since when?"

"I transferred from St. Bernadette's post primary at the beginning of term." Shrugging her narrow shoulders, she tightened her hold on my jacket. "I'm on scholarship."

Now, I *was* intrigued. "What's your poison?"

"Music." She blushed again. "What's yours?"

"Physics," I replied with an apologetic smile. "With a side of chemistry."

"Oh, so you're *that* kind of boy." She winked knowingly. "You're a swot."

I arched a brow. "No offense, but you must be a fair bit of a swot yourself to snag yourself a scholarship."

"Yep, I'm one of the lucky six," she replied with a sigh. "Go me, huh?"

"Why haven't I seen you at school before?"

She smiled. "Maybe after tonight, you will."

"How are you getting home?"

"Casey's older than me," she replied, pointing to the wall again. "One of her friends will drive me home."

"Where's home?"

"A long way from yours." She grinned before adding, "Rich boy."

My brows shot up. "What makes you think I'm rich?"

"Uh, maybe because I've been in your house," she laughed with an eye roll. "Avoca Greystones is a long way from Rosewood."

"Hold up." I tilted my head to study her. "When were you in my house?"

"Your birthday party," she replied, smirking. "Case and I both were." She pointed to her friend again. "Feely invited us."

"Feely."

"Yep. We're both in the school choir."

"No shit." I scratched my jaw, not terribly surprised to learn Feely was in the choir. "You're the special buddy from music club?" I teased, putting two and two together. "Or should I say his bed buddy?"

"Never in his wildest dreams," Katie snapped back, gesturing to where Feely was clearly getting it on with her friend. "She's his bed buddy. *Clearly*."

"Sorry," I muttered, shaking my head. "That was a really rude, not to mention really fucked-up, thing to say to a girl."

"It's okay," she chuckled, nudging my shoulder with hers. "I forgive you."

"Are you warm enough?" I asked, noticing her shiver.

"You're a really nice person," she mused, looking up at me with those big, green eyes. "Did you know that?"

"How'd you figure that one?"

"Just a feeling I have," she replied, still smiling up at me. "I'm really glad I got to talk to you tonight."

"Yeah," I replied, brows furrowed. "Me, too."

"What's going on here?" Feely arrived out of the blue and demanded, as he tried to fix the buckle on his belt. "Well?"

"What does it look like?" Katie shot back in a sickly sweet voice, while she winked at me. "Hugh and I were making acquaintances."

"Are ya all right, Pa?" I asked, feeling a swell of concern rise up inside me when I took in his agonized expression. I stood up and quickly checked him over. "You don't look too good, lad."

Before Feely could get a word out, Casey staggered toward us.

"Hey, you!" Stumbling toward me, she fisted my shirt and roughly pulled me toward her. "Where's your phone?"

Frowning, I reached into my pocket and held it up.

"Thank you," she chirped and then proceeded to squint and tap on the keypad, all the while swaying and staggering.

A few moments passed and a loud ping sounded from nearby.

"Casey," Katie strangled out, looking mortified. "You did not just text me from Hugh's phone."

"I sure did, my sweet-cheeked fox." She winked at her friend before casting a narrowed glance at me. "You." She pointed a finger in my face. "Call my girl." Her words were slurred, but she still oozed confidence. "Contrary to this"—she gestured to herself—"my Katie's a good girl, ya hear? So don't be getting notions about all of us southside girls." She turned to Feely and winked provocatively. "Except for you, preppy." Grinning, she reached up and patted his cheek. "You certainly know how to use what God *generously* gave you, don't ya?"

"Oh God," Katie groaned, physically retching. "I think I'm going to be sick."

"Are you okay?" Feely asked, reaching out a hand to steady her, but she quickly smacked it away.

"Please don't touch me with those hands," Katie grimaced, jerking out of reach, and I honestly couldn't blame her, not when we both knew where those fingers had been.

A car horn sounded then, followed by a lad shouting, "Let's go, Devil-tits. Your chariot awaits ya."

"That's me," Katie said and then quickly backtracked. "I'm mean that's not me. I'm not Devil-Tits." Her face turned almost as red as her hair. "Casey is Devil-Tits. I'm just a girl bumming a lift home in that car."

"Yeah, I knew what you meant," I chuckled.

"Well, thanks for everything." She held her hand out. "It's been a pleasure."

"Yeah." I accepted her handshake and smiled. "The pleasure was mine."

———————————

"Delete it."

"Delete what?"

"Her number."

"Who are you on about?" I slurred, leaning against the side of the mobile chip van.

"Katie."

"Who?"

"That girl back there."

"Which one?"

"The redhead."

I squinted, trying to think her face into memory only to fail and manifest blond hair and blue eyes instead. "Fuck, I love her so much."

"You don't even know her," he snapped back, swaying as much as I was.

"What?" I gaped at him. "Are you mental? I've known her my entire life."

He gaped right back at me, brows furrowed. "Who are *you* on about?"

"Liz!" I groaned pushing my hands through my hair. "Who the fuck else!"

"Oh." He nodded in understanding. "Okay, good. Now, delete her number."

"There's no point, lad," I groaned. "I've had her mobile number memorized since fifth class." I hiccupped before adding, "And her landline number since first class."

"No—"

"Hughie got the shift, Hughie got the shift," Gibsie sang as he staggered and crashed against the leaning tower of Kav. "Good man yourself, Hugo Boss-man! I knew you could do it. It's onwards and upwards from here, lad."

Feely narrowed his eyes. "Who?"

"Who what?"

"Who'd you score with?"

"A corker of a redhead," Kav filled in, joining us at the chipper. "Is she your old doll, Hughie? The one you're always skipping training for? Jaysus, lad, no wonder you kept her hidden away from the team."

I opened my mouth to tell Kav that he had the wrong fucking girl and would know that if he paid one iota of attention to his friends, but was distracted by the fist that smacked into the side of my nose.

"Ow!" I roared as my head twisted sideways and smacked off the metal siding of the chipper van. "What the hell was that in aid of?"

"You!" Feely roared. "Fucking you, Hughie!"

"What about me?" I demanded, beyond confused. "What in the name of Jesus did I do out of the way to you?"

"It's always fucking you," he slurred, shaking his head. "You always come fucking first."

"Lad, I'm not the one who came tonight, so I don't know why you're getting stuck in me," I tossed back. "I'm the virgin in this relationship. You're the whore!"

"Jesus Christ! I *am* a whore," Feely groaned, pushing his hands through his hair like I'd given him some brand-new information. "Why didn't you stop me?"

"Why *would* I?" I demanded back, too confused and too fucking drunk for this conversation. "You never told me to stop you."

"You're my best fucking friend, asshole," he snapped back. "I shouldn't have to tell you."

"Some best friend," I shot back, rubbing my nose. "Domestic fucking battery, Feely."

"Oh relax, pretty boy," he sneered. "You're still every inch the asshole girls fall for."

"Now, now, don't be fighting," Gibs scolded, sliding between us to grab an order from the counter that he neither placed nor paid for. "We're lovers, not fighters."

"Hey! That's my burger," Feely grumbled. "And I'm not his anything."

"Good," I huffed, patting Gibs on the back. "Have fucking at it, Gibs."

"Actually, *I* always come first," Kav interjected, holding a finger up.

"What the hell are you talking about?" Feely demanded.

"You said Hughie always comes first when he doesn't," Kav explained. "Hughie comes second, and *you* come third." Shrugging, he slurred, "Sorry, lad, but the clock doesn't lie."

Feely gaped at him. "Again, what the *hell* are you talking about?"

"Sprints," Kav replied, looking confused. "Why? What are you talking about?"

"Yes," I agreed, eyeballing the lunatic throwing slaps like Vinnie fucking Jones. "What are you *talking* about?"

"Trust you to bring up sport," Feely snapped. "Jesus Christ, Johnny, can't you turn your brain off for one night?"

"Don't take that bleeding tone with me, asshole," Kav snapped back.

"Hold on," Gibs interrupted, holding his burger-clad hand up in outrage. "Why the fuck does your math make me come *last*, Jonathan?"

"Because you *always* come last, Gerard. Now be a good lad and inhale your stolen burger."

"Fuck the lot of ye," I grumbled, snatching up someone else's order from the counter and stalking off, having had more than enough madness for one night. "I'm going to bed."

"Whose bed?"

"My bed, assholes!" I called over my shoulder.

"Tell your sister I'll be home later," Gibs called after. "For my New Year's kiss."

"You keep your lips off my sister!"

WHERE THE HELL WERE YOU, DADDY?

Lizzie

"ARE YOU SURE YOU LIKE IT THIS WAY?" PIERCE GRUNTED, PINNING ME ONTO THE mattress. "I'm not hurting you, am I?"

I would have to feel something to be hurt, and nothing this boy did drew a single response from my body.

I thought it did, but I had mistaken new for good.

He couldn't make me feel good.

He couldn't make me better.

I couldn't *feel* him.

"Just shut up and fuck me," I replied, feeling numb.

When he upped his pace, I felt myself die a little more inside.

Because I did this to myself.

I'd lost everything.

All of a sudden, the big light came on in my room, and my father's voice thundered through the air. "Get your clothes on, ya little bastard, and get out of my house before I kill you!"

"Holy shit," Pierce yelped, scrambling away from me and grabbing his clothes. "I am so sorry, sir."

"Who the fuck are you?"

"Pierce, sir."

"Pierce who?"

"Pierce O'Neill."

"Get the fuck out of my house before I throttle ya!"

"Catherine!" my father continued to bellow, as he hunted Pierce out of my room. "Come here and sort her out before I throttle her."

"*Catherine*," I mocked, rolling my eyes as I climbed out of bed and threw on some clothes. "Get a handle on yourself, will ya? It's not that deep."

"Do you think that's normal?" Dad shouted. "Bringing boys back to the house at your age?"

"I don't give a shit," I laughed. "Besides, he likes me."

"Oh yeah, and he really thinks highly of ya, doesn't he?" Dad sneered, looking furious. "Leaving his load inside of ya."

"Actually, he leaves his load in the condom he always wears, but thanks for the lack of faith, asshole."

"Asshole?" My father's face turned purple. "Who do you think you're talking to?" He glanced over his shoulder and started screaming for my mother to hurry up. "Catherine, you better get in here now before I smack some common sense in that girl!"

"Have at it, Daddy," I laughed, poking his chest with my finger. "Slap some sense into your prodigal daughter."

"Elizabeth, I'm warning you…"

"Maybe if you'd smacked some sense into Caoimhe when you had the chance, you could've stopped her from ruining my fucking life!"

My father's arm reared back, and I felt the full force of his palm when it connected with my cheek.

Instead of crying from the pain, I laughed in his face. "Hit me harder, *Daddy*."

"Stop it, do ya hear me?" Grabbing my shoulders, Dad shook the living daylights out of me, all while tears poured down his cheeks. "Stop doing this to us!"

I knew he was crying.

I could see the tears.

I could hear the agony in his voice.

But I didn't care.

I felt nothing in this moment.

Nothing but intense hatred toward my entire family for allowing the monster in our house.

"Where the hell were you when I was screaming for you!" I tried to scream, only to end up laughing manically, as tears streamed down my cheeks. "You were never there! You never came when I needed you at night! Do you remember, *Daddy*? All the nights I screamed for you? Well, now I'm screaming again, and this time I'm screaming fuck you, you fucking hypocrite!"

"Mike," Mam cried out in the distance, and I turned to see her on the floor in the doorway of my room. "Oh God, Mike…"

"Catherine!" Dad cried out, springing toward her. "Catherine, hold on, love."

I could see her on the ground, holding her arm while my father spoke into his mobile phone.

I couldn't register the sight of my parents.
I just couldn't *feel* anything.

NEW YEAR, NEW ME

Hugh

JANUARY 1, 2004

WHEN I WOKE UP ON NEW YEAR'S DAY, IT WAS TO A BLACK EYE, A WICKED HANGOVER, and a surprisingly upbeat mood.

I had actually *enjoyed* being out with the lads last night, something I wouldn't have thought possible two months ago.

For the first time since the breakup, I didn't feel the immediate urge to bury my head under my pillow and sleep my life away.

Maybe 2004 wouldn't be a write-off after all.

When I came downstairs after showering and filled a bowl with cereal for breakfast, I felt strangely calm. Like I didn't have anywhere to rush off to or a dozen frantic text messages waiting for me.

It was different.

It was...*not* bad.

Tentatively basking in the peace, I sat at the kitchen table, hoofing bran flakes and staring out the window.

I was deep in my thoughts and mentally mapping out my study schedule for the next month when my sister came barreling into the kitchen.

The moment I took in her tear-filled eyes and panicked expression, my body braced itself for trouble.

"What's wrong?" I demanded. "Claire?"

"It's Lizzie's mam," she squeezed out, clutching her phone to her chest. "She had a heart attack last night."

I dropped my spoon. "What?"

"Catherine had a heart attack, Hugh."

"Jesus Christ," I strangled out, immediately jerking to my feet. "Is she okay?"

"I'm not sure." Claire shrugged helplessly and worried her lip. "She's in the ICU."

"Aw, fuck." Gripping my head, I tried to steady my thoughts and remain *calm*, but it was impossible when panic was clawing at my throat. "Was that Liz?" I gestured to her phone. "Did she call you?"

"Oh, uh, no." She shook her head. "It was Helen."

"Helen?"

"A girl in my class," my sister explained. "She's a huge gossiper and literally hears *every* bit of news before—hey! Where are you going?"

"To the hospital," I replied, moving for the door.

"How? Mam's at work."

"Then I'll get the bus."

"Do you think you should?" Claire called out, chasing me into the hallway. "You know, since you guys broke up and all?"

"Her mother had a heart attack, Claire," I snapped back, not giving two shits if it was a good idea or not. "I'm going."

I'LL DO IT

Lizzie

JANUARY 1, 2004

DEVASTATED, I SLUMPED ON THE PLASTIC CHAIR ON ONE SIDE OF MY MOTHER'S BEDside, while my father sat on the other.

With his head bowed and his elbows resting on the side of Mam's hospital bed, Dad cradled her frail hand to his cheek.

My mother looked lifeless, while my father looked truly defeated.

"Your mother fights so hard to be here," Dad said, nuzzling her hand with more affection than I'd ever seen him express. Tears trickled down his cheeks as he spoke. "And every day you don't get better, you push her closer to the grave."

"I'm sorry," I managed to croak out, body trembling violently. "I'll do better, Dad, I promise."

"Promises have to be kept to mean something," my father told me, keeping his attention trained on my mother's sleeping face. He didn't sound angry anymore. Just worn down. "What happened with young Biggs?"

"I hurt him," I admitted, breathing through my nose, as I willed my heart to kickstart in my chest and prayed for a miracle to rewire my fucked-up mind. "And he broke up with me."

"Well, I can't say I blame the lad." Dad sighed. "You've certainly broken my heart and soul—and your mother's, too."

Yeah, I understood that now.

I was seeing the damage up close, and it was *killing* me.

"Dad." Knees bopping restlessly, I pushed my hands through my hair and expelled a quivering breath. "I think I need some help."

"You're damn right you do," he replied, reaching up to brush Mam's hair off her face. "Because your behavior is killing my wife."

Pain.

Guilt.

Shame.

The full force of my emotions punched me so hard in the chest that I momentarily lost the ability to breathe.

"Dad," I wheezed, feeling lightheaded now. "I think you should send me away."

"We'll talk about it later," my father replied. "When your mother is out of the woods."

"No, Dad," I choked out, drowning in my emotions as every part of me shook. "I really think I need to go away now."

"What are you saying, Elizabeth?"

"I don't feel right in the head," I cried, covering my face with my hands. "And I don't want to hurt people anymore."

"You want to go back to the hospital?"

Yes.

No.

Maybe.

"I just want to stop hurting people," I replied, crying quietly into my hands. "I want to be *me* again, Dad."

"Do you mean that?"

"Yeah," I sobbed, nodding my head. "Please help me, Dad."

"All right, all right." I heard the sound of metal scraping on tiles moments before my father's hand rested on my shoulder. "It's okay. I'm here."

"Dad, I'm scared," I strangled out, chest heaving. "I'm so fucking scared of my own mind."

"I know you are." He continued to gently pat my shoulder. "And I'm going to get you help."

"I just want to be okay again."

"You will be." His voice was thick with emotion. "Staying at the hospital helped you the last time, and it'll help you again."

"I'll do it." Sniffling, I looked up at the man who raised me. "I'll do it your way. Whatever it takes, Dad."

"Good girl." Tearful, blue eyes stared back at me. "Now, go for a little walk outside, while I make some calls."

I opened my mouth to respond, only to freeze when the door swung inward.

"Hi." Breathless and panting, Hugh strode into my mother's hospital room. "I came as I soon as I heard."

"Hugh," I strangled out, scrambling out of my chair in my rush to get to him. "Hugh!"

"I'm here, Liz," he said, wrapping me up in his arms when I reached him. "I'm right here."

Clenching my eyes shut, I clung to his body for all I was worth.

He didn't push me away.

He didn't stiffen or recoil.

He fully embraced me in this moment, allowing me to take what comfort I needed from his touch.

"Hughie," Dad sighed, relief flashing in his eyes. "Thanks for coming, son."

"Of course," he replied, keeping a firm hold on me. "How is she?"

"It was touch and go for a while," Dad explained wearily. "But she's out of the woods. The doctors said we got her to the hospital in time."

"That's good," Hugh replied in that familiar steady tone. The one that made me feel like everything would be okay. "Catherine is a fighter," he continued to say, while he rubbed my back. "She'll come back from this, Mike. Stronger than ever."

"Let's hope so, son."

"Here." Hugh peeled the wrapper off one of the granola bars he'd snagged from the vending machine down the hall and held it up to me. We were sitting in the visitors' room on my mother's ward, waiting for my father to come back from making his phone calls. "Come on, Liz," Hugh continued to coax. "Take a bite."

Too weary to protest my lack of hunger, I leaned in and took a small bite.

"Good job," he praised, rubbing my knee. "You look like you haven't eaten in days."

"I haven't," I admitted brokenly, turning to look at him. "Or at least, I don't remember."

Pain flashed in his whiskey eyes. "It's okay." Reaching up, he tucked a clump of my untamed hair behind my ear, fingers lingering on my cheek. "You're going to feel so much better soon."

"Yeah," I croaked out, unable to stop myself from wincing.

Dad was making calls to have me admitted into Brickley House, a private psychiatric and rehabilitation facility on the northside of the city.

I was going away today, and I didn't know when I'd be back.

The fear clawing its way up my throat was terrifying, and the reckless streak inside of me was demanding I run for the hills.

But I wouldn't.

Because I knew I had to take accountability.

My mother was lying in a hospital bed because of me, and my entire world had been blown to smithereens.

I was a fucking mess.

"Hey—hey." Hugh's steady voice broke through the cloud of tumultuous thoughts thrashing around in my head, and I felt his hands on my face. "Look at me, Liz."

Reluctantly, I did.

"It's okay," he said slowly, eyes locked on mine. "Everything is going to be *okay*."

"I'm so sorry," I breathed, tears streaming down my cheeks. "I never meant for any of this to happen."

"I know you didn't," he replied, stroking my cheeks with his thumbs. "And we can talk about everything when you get home." His eyes glistened with tears. "But for now, all you have to do is get better, okay?"

Sniffling, I nodded my head and covered his hands with mine. "I'll never forgive myself for what I've done to you." A pained sob escaped me, and I clenched my eyes shut to stem my tears. "I've hurt you so bad, Hugh."

"I'm here, see?" He offered me a pained smile. "And all I want you to do is take every bit of help those doctors offer you, okay?" A tear fell from his thick lashes to his cheek, and he sniffed his emotions back. "That's how you make this right, Liz—by making you *you* again."

"Your mother's awake, Elizabeth," Dad interrupted, standing in the doorway. "She wants to see you before you go."

LITTLE WHITE LIES

Hugh

JANUARY 1, 2004

SITTING IN HER MOTHER'S HOSPITAL ROOM, I WATCHED AS LIZ AND CATHERINE HAD both an emotional reunion and a tearful goodbye.

In a little while, she would be going away.

She was agreeing to get help.

Finally.

Afraid she would bolt if I left, I remained right by her side, needing her safe more than I needed my pride. I would sit here all night if it meant Liz got the help she needed.

Mike had his car keys in hand, ready and waiting to drive his daughter to the hospital, while his wife refused to let go of her hand.

Fuck, it hurt so bad, I could barely breathe.

Going to Liz when she needed me wasn't something I had to wrestle with.

There was no decision to make.

All the pain and hurt could wait.

I could put the betrayal and resentment on ice.

Because, at the end of the day, I still wanted to be near her, still wanted to hold her hand, still wanted to kiss her lips.

Every inch of me still longed for every inch of her, and I couldn't turn my feelings off.

What I felt for her wasn't expendable, and it hadn't shown up overnight. My love for her had had nine years to deepen and grow, and the roots went deep. It wasn't something that could be rooted out and tossed away.

She was imbedded in the foundations of who I was as a person.

She was ingrained in every fundamental life choice I had made from the age of seven.

Getting over her wouldn't happen overnight. If it took an equal measure of time to unlove a person, then I had nine years of misery to contend with.

I was sixteen now, so that meant I would be twenty-five before she finally left my system.

Fuck, it wasn't even close to being fair.

Because I didn't *choose* this.

I *didn't* want us to end.

I would have spent the rest of my life beside her if she could have just shown me the same commitment.

For a while, I wasn't sure if Catherine and Liz were going to let go, but eventually they did.

"Hugh," Liz sniffled, as her father led her away. "You can't tell anyone where I'm going."

Rising from my chair, I moved to intercept them before it was too late.

I didn't care how pathetic it made me look; I needed to hold her one more time.

"I won't tell, Liz," I said, pulling her in for a hug. "I promise."

"Please," she strangled out, gripping me tightly. "Not even your mam."

"Not even Mam," I confirmed gruffly, feeling my heart shatter in my chest. "Nobody is going to know anything about this." My voice sounded calmer than I felt. Because the truth of the matter was, I was losing my shit internally. I would never let her see that, though. Liz didn't need tears. She needed strength. "You're going to go away for a little while and get some rest," I coaxed, pulling back to smile at her. "And no one in town is going to be any the wiser."

"I'm so sorry," she sobbed, fisting my shirt. "I want to die for what I've done to you."

Somehow, I managed to smile. "Just get better, okay?"

"You'll be there when I come home?"

Pain.

It scorched me.

"Of course."

A few minutes later, when they were gone and I was left alone with Catherine, I heard her say, "You lied to her, didn't you?" Tears filled her eyes. "You won't be there when she comes home."

Shaking my head, I roughly wiped my tears away. "I'm sorry."

PART 21

Turning Over a New Leaf

HIBERNATING HEARTS AND WATERY BRIDGES

Hugh

JANUARY 8, 2004

"I DON'T GET WHY SHE WOULDN'T TELL ME," CLAIRE COMPLAINED, CARRYING ON THE conversation that had started at the breakfast table this morning all the way to the halls of Tommen. "Liz just leaves and doesn't tell anyone?"

"She told me," I reminded her, reeling off my perfectly rehearsed excuse. "She texted me last night."

"But you guys aren't even a couple anymore," my sister groaned, worrying her lip. "Why wouldn't she tell me that she was going to Spain? And what about school?"

"It's only for a few weeks," I repeated for the twentieth time this morning. "As for school, Liz could sit her junior cert in the morning and still wipe the floor with your entire year."

"I guess," Claire replied, sounding uncertain about the whole situation. "It's just… strange."

"Her mam needs some recuperation," I added. "And you can't blame her for wanting to go with her mother."

"No, no, I understand completely," she hurried to say. "I just…wish she'd text me back."

Yeah, me, too. "She'll be back soon."

"Are you okay?" my sister asked then, placing a hand on my arm. "I know you've been super sad since the breakup."

"I'll be—" I was cut off when Feely shouldered past me in the hallway, using the guitar he was carrying to smack against me in the process.

"Jesus!" Claire exclaimed, wide-eyed. "What's his problem?"

"No idea," I replied, readjusting the school bag he'd knocked off my shoulder. "He's been like that since New Year's."

"Why?"

I turned around to glare after him. "Hard to say when he won't fucking speak."

"Well," my sister said, smiling brightly. "At least you still have me."

"And me." Gibsie draped his arms around both of us. "How are my favorite sibling duo?"

It was at that precise moment a pint-sized redhead, with a guitar hanging over her shoulder, came into view. Green eyes locked on mine when she passed me in the hall. "Hi, Hugh."

"Hi, Katie," I replied, feeling a sudden stab in my chest that seemed to come out of nowhere.

She blushed and quickly retrained her attention ahead.

Meanwhile, I craned my head around to watch her pass.

"Well, well, well, it looks like a certain big brother's been holding out on us, Gerard." Dragging my attention back to her with a gleeful cackle, Claire clapped like a fucking seal with excitement. "Hughie has his eyes set on someone new. *Finally!*"

"Claire." I narrowed my eyes in warning. "Before you start, just stop, okay?"

"Your brother had more than his eyes on her on New Year's Eve, Claire-Bear," Gibs replied with a shit-eating grin.

I glared at him.

Gibsie winked knowingly.

"Really?" Claire's eyes bugged in her head. "Omigod! Yay! This is the best news ever!" She swung around to watch Katie's retreating figure. "I think I know her. She started here in September. She's super quiet, but I've seen her talking to Patrick a couple of times."

"Yeah, they're both in music club."

"Aw, what else do you know about her?"

"Nothing, absolutely nothing, because it was just a shift," I warned, attention flicking to my sister. "I was out of my mind from drink."

"You know what they say about the truth coming out when you're drunk." Claire continued to seal clap. "Maybe your heart's ready to come out of hibernation and the booze pushed it along."

"*Claire.*"

"Maybe it's time you gave someone else a chance."

"Maybe it's time for you two to mind your own business."

"Hugh, it's been months." My sister offered me an encouraging smile. "You've got this."

"Too many months," Gibsie agreed, giving me two solid thumbs-up. "And *way* too much water under the bridge."

WHATEVER IT TAKES

Lizzie

JANUARY 10, 2004

"You have to do something for her," Dad begged. "She's whoring herself around and that's not the girl I know." A broken sob escaped him. "She wouldn't do that."

"There's a gap in her medical notes." The doctor eyed my father. "Three years."

"You'll have to talk to my wife about that," Dad replied, sounding weary. "She handles all the paperwork." He cleared his throat before saying, "Please explain to me what's happening here."

"Your daughter is experiencing episodes of full-blown mania—a common factor of bipolar one, however the severity and frequency of her depressive episodes is consistent with bipolar type two."

"What does it matter what type she has? You know she has it, just medicate her, dammit."

"It doesn't work like that, I'm afraid."

"Why the bloody hell not?"

"Bipolar disorder is complicated, Mr. Young," the doctor said. "Children and adolescents with early-onset bipolar can be extremely difficult to treat."

"But you *can* fix her, can't you?"

"We can *treat* her, but it's not as simple as you think, Mr. Young. Lizzie came off her medication without medical supervision," the doctor replied. "She has been rapid cycling between manic and depressive states for several months. She is going to need a lot of supervision and care for the next while."

"How long are we talking?"

"In cases as severe as your daughter's, it usually takes a minimum of two months before progress is seen, but it could take longer."

"I can't handle this," Dad cried, wiping his eyes with his hands. "My daughter is dead, and my wife is sick. I don't know what to do for this one."

"I can assure you that your daughter is in the best possible care."

"What about the shocking?" Dad asked then, elbows resting on the bed I was strapped to. "Could that work for her?"

"If you're referring to electroconvulsive therapy, then no, we don't recommend ECT for patients under the age of sixteen anymore."

"But it *does* happen?"

"Under extremely rare circumstances."

"How extreme does she have to be before someone steps in and does something?" he demanded, throwing his hands up. "The tablets aren't working. She's refusing counseling. Her arms and legs are torn to ribbons. How much more must we lose before somebody helps us?"

"I'll do it," I managed to whisper. "I'll do it, Dad."

Dad turned to look at me. "You will?"

Using every ounce of strength inside of me, I nodded. "I'll do whatever it takes."

Relief flashed in Dad's eyes, and he covered my hand with his. "Good girl."

JUST FRIENDS

Hugh

JANUARY 25, 2004

Today marked Liz's fortieth day in treatment.

It was the longest time we hadn't seen each or spoke to each other in a decade, and every day, I continued to pine for what my soul assured me was its mate.

Unlike Pierce, who moved on within days of Liz's departure, I still found myself thinking up excuses *not* to.

I wasn't unattracted to the girls who asked me out. I was just uninterested.

It had been more than three months since our breakup, and I still wasn't over her, while the thought of being with another girl made my skin crawl.

I knew my behavior wasn't normal for a lad my age, and Feely reminded me of that often, but I just *couldn't*.

Maybe I was programmed differently to the lads on my team, or maybe I was a prude like Liz had labeled me during one of her rampages when I wouldn't have sex.

Nah, you're definitely not a prude, lad.

It wasn't like I didn't want sex—of *course* I did. I just didn't want it with anyone other than the very girl I couldn't have it with…

"Hello again."

I was so deep in my thoughts that I almost ignored the soft-voiced girl who seemed to be addressing me.

Shaking my head to clear my thoughts, I retrained my attention from the locker I'd been staring aimlessly into to the familiar redhead smiling up at me.

"Uh, hey." I turned to give her my attention. "Katie, right?"

"That's right." She smiled. "How's it going?"

"Uh, grand." I shrugged, knowing that I should give her more but not having it inside. "How's it going for you?"

"It's going," she laughed, still smiling up at me. "So, listen, I wanted to apologize again for the whole maiming you on New Year's Eve, while simultaneously thanking you for being so gracious about it." Her cheeks flamed as she spoke. "I was in a really bad place that night, and I'd been… Uh, it doesn't even matter." She shook her head and offered me another bright smile. "Just thank you." She winced before adding, "And sorry."

"You don't need to apologize," I replied, finding her rambling endearing. "And you need to thank me even less."

"Really?"

"Yeah, who doesn't want to be kissed by a pretty girl on New Year's?"

Her breath hitched. "You think I'm a pretty girl?"

Feeling slightly cornered, I nodded slowly. "You know you're gorgeous."

Her cheeks turned the color of her curls. "Wow."

Feeling uncomfortable, I cleared my throat and turned my attention back to closing and locking the door of my locker.

"Hey, would you be," Katie started to say, only to stumble over her words. "I mean, do you want to maybe go to, uh, or, ah, go to the…or just…uh, never mind."

I watched from the corner of my eye as she face-palmed herself, all the while muttering, "Stop talking, Katie," to herself as she trudged away. "You're only making it a million times more awkward."

Smothering a laugh, I shouldered my bag and followed her. "You know, you should really cut yourself some slack."

"I should?"

"Absolutely," I confirmed, falling into step beside her. "That took balls."

"Assertiveness," she explained, tightening her grasp on the straps of her bag. "It's on the top of my list of New Year's resolutions."

"Well, you can tick that off," I mused, holding the door of the main building open for her. "What else is on that list of yours?"

"Oh, you know," she sighed, waiting for me to follow her out. "The usual."

"Humor me."

"Let go of the past, stop worrying about things I have no control of, get over the ass-hole who broke my heart, go to mass every Sunday, kiss a boy, make more friends, and take more risks." She grinned up at me. "Just your stereotypical teenage-girl bucket list."

"Hmm."

"What's the *hmm* mean?"

"Nothing," I replied, shaking my head. "We just have a few things in common."

"The broken-heart part?" She winced in sympathy. "Yeah, I heard about that. Sorry."

"It is what it is," I replied, refusing to lose face.

"Do you want to?" she asked then, stopping in her tracks. "Want to hang out sometime after school?"

I stopped walking and turned back to look at her. "Like a date?"

"Or just as friends," she replied with a shrug. "If you prefer."

"I, ah…" My words trailed off and I fought down a sudden surge of panic. "I'm not, ah…" Another pause while I tried to push down the guilt that I was drowning in.

Stop it, asshole.

You have nothing to feel guilty about.

"I'm not ready for another relationship," I admitted, pinching the bridge of my nose. "I'm, ah, I'm still…"

"Licking your wounds?" Katie said gently. "That's okay. Me, too."

"We could hang out, though," I offered, forcing myself to take the leap. "As *friends*?"

Her green eyes lit up. "I'd like that."

"I like the cinema," I blurted out, sounding like a fucking dope.

"Me, too."

"I'm free on Friday," I added, sounding like a lad who'd never been alone with a girl, let alone spoken to one. I suppose aside from Liz, I hadn't.

"Friday is good for me."

I eyed her warily. "As friends."

Smiling, she nodded. "Friends."

"Okay then." I blew out a breath, feeling cautious and reluctantly hopeful. "I'll, ah, I'll text you later."

"And I'll text you back." Shoving her hand into the pocket of her skirt, she pulled out a phone and waved it in front of me, cheeks reddening. "I have credit."

CLOSE YOUR EYES, SWEETHEART

JANUARY 29, 2004

Remaining motionless on the trolly, I stared up at the nurse and watched as she stuck the pads to my forehead and scalp.

"Close your eyes, sweetheart," she said in an approving tone, stroking my cheek. "You'll be fast asleep soon." She checked the line in my hand and smiled. "Just like last time."

And the time before that.

And the time before that.

Once the anesthesiologist arrived, he would put me to sleep with the mask.

Once I was out, electrical currents would be sent into my brain through the pads, and I would have a seizure.

Closing my eyes when the warm liquid flushed through my veins and the mask was placed on my face, I focused on the mental image of Hugh, while I *prayed* for my mind to never forget a single memory of him.

IT'S NICE TO HAVE A FRIEND

Hugh

FEBRUARY 13, 2004

When I met Katie outside the cinema on Friday night, I was weirdly calm, which was strange because every time I'd met Liz at the same place, every nerve in my body was shot to shit.

Maybe it was a good thing that I didn't feel nervous. Maybe I didn't have to endure heart palpitations around every girl I hung out with.

"No, it's not a date," Katie argued at the counter when it came to pay for the tickets. "I'll pay for my own."

"Yeah, that's not happening," I replied, handing the cashier a twenty before she could. "It's grand."

"You didn't have to do that."

"I know." I frowned at her popcorn-fee hands. "You sure you don't want anything?"

"This is good," she said, waving a bottle of water in front of me. "I'm all set."

Shrugging, I followed her into screen two and sank down beside her.

"This film is supposed to be unreal," she whispered, gesturing to the screen in front of us that was starting to light up. "Casey saw *Meet the Fockers* last week and she's still cackling about it."

It took most of the movie for me to relax.

My muscles were coiled tight with the anticipation of dread.

Like I was waiting for something to happen.

For a fire to put out.

Because there was *always* a fire with Liz.

Not this girl, though.

Katie didn't talk through the film, and she kept her hands to herself.

She was perfectly content to just sit with me, and that threw me.

It honestly felt like she was being sincere when she told me it was company she wanted, and I almost wanted to believe her.

But I had some serious trust issues when it came to hearts that belonged to the opposite sex.

———————

"That was fun," Katie declared later that night when I walked her to her door. "I really enjoyed myself."

"I'm glad," I replied, keeping my hands firmly shoved inside my coat pockets. "I enjoyed myself, too."

"Really?"

"Yeah." I frowned. "I did."

"Do you think it's a bad omen that our first outing landed on Friday the thirteenth?"

"Jesus," I chuckled, shaking my head. "I hope not."

"Yeah, me, too," she replied with a blush. "We should do it again."

"We should," I agreed carefully.

"How's next Friday for you?"

"I'm free on Fridays," I replied slowly, still wary. "I work the rest of the weekend, though."

"Cool." She smiled. "Friday it is, then."

"Yeah." I nodded. "I'll see you then."

"Not if I see you first."

I arched a brow.

She groaned into her glove-covered hand. "I really need to work on that."

"Nah." I laughed, crossing the footpath to head back to the northside. "You're doing all right."

THIS IS ME TRYING

IF THE MANIC STAGE WAS EUPHORIA AND THE DEPRESSIVE STAGE WAS HELL, THEN THE euthymic stage fell somewhere in between.

For a person like me, the third stage was the goal.

For a person like me, the third stage was the hardest.

While the second stage was crippling and the third was mundane, the first was world-shattering.

The sneaky part about being manic was the allure. In the throes of an episode, I felt invincible, like my brain had been switched to an exciting new frequency and I was suddenly seeing the world through a new lens.

An exciting lens.

An addictive lens.

A lens that spared me from feeling empathy and guilt and all the other crushing emotions that consumed me during the depressive state.

It was an altered state of mind that distorted my view of the world and snipped the wire inside my brain that linked my conscience to the consequences of my actions.

The clearer my mind became, the worse my guilt grew. Because with clarity came consequences and I was drowning in mine. Months of fluctuating moods had resulted in my world imploding around me, and the medicine flushing through my veins provided me with a glaring itinerary of proof.

I couldn't run from it.

I couldn't hide.

All I could do was sit on my bed and work through the guilt, shame, and self-loathing.

I wasn't ready to go home yet, not even close, but the urge to race back home, fall to my knees in front of Hugh, and beg for his forgiveness was potent.

He was suffering the consequences of loving a person like me.

I knew I would break him back when we were children. It was the reason I tried so hard to push him away when I was manic. Problem was, I never thought it through until it was too late. I was under some false assumption that I could somehow live without the boy that breathed air into my lungs when nothing had ever been more impossible.

He was brave and honorable, and I had taken that away from him. I had taken his shiny halo and tarnished him beyond repair.

I remembered the boy he used to be before everything went dark, but I had a real hard time remembering the girl I used to be.

She was so faintly imprinted in my memory that I doubted she ever existed to begin with.

The doctors explained the episodes to me and assured me that I wasn't a sex addict, but that I experienced bouts of severe hypersexuality when I was in the throes of mania.

When the depression kicked in, I didn't want to be touched. I didn't want anything to do with it. I didn't want anyone's hands on me.

The doctors told me that was okay.

That these feelings would come in waves.

They wouldn't always be present.

At the hospital, I was screened for a wide range of sexually transmitted diseases, and thankfully, all the results came back clear.

Afterward, I was offered a birth control implant in my arm to prevent pregnancy for three years.

I took it.

Because I was a mess.

The equivalent of a human wrecking ball.

Everyone and everything I came into contact with ended up ruined, and I didn't need to bring any babies into the world and ruin them, too.

COMFORTABLE COMPANIONS

Hugh

APRIL 5, 2004

TODAY MARKED LIZ'S NINETY-NINTH DAY IN TREATMENT, AND LIFE, FOR THE MOST part, had been chugging along steadily. School was a breeze, and work was enjoyable. Our school rugby team was going from strength to strength, while I was consistently breaking my personal best in the pool.

Gibsie and Claire were as happy as clams, dreaming up notions of running their own animal sanctuary, while Johnny continued to bulk up in the gym. The only one slightly off-kilter was Feely, but his issues weren't Liz related.

Meanwhile, *all* my issues were.

I still felt her absence everywhere, and nothing I tried could fill the hollowness under my rib cage.

Liz didn't have a phone in there, which was both a blessing and a curse, because while I desperately wanted to talk to her, I knew it wouldn't be good for either of us.

Mike used to call me every week to fill me in on her progress, but Mam politely put a stop to the calls last month, saying it wasn't *healthy*.

Yeah, Mam knew about Liz being in hospital, but it wasn't because I told her. Mam had overhead one of my phone calls with Liz's dad and put two and two together. She was as supportive as always and had vowed to keep it a secret if I continued to live my life and *not* lock myself away from the world.

I *was* trying.

I hung with Gibs and Claire in the evenings, and the rest of the lads on the weekends when I wasn't working. Oh, and I spent a lot of time with Katie, who turned out to be excellent company.

While we didn't seem to have a lot in common when it came to our chosen school subjects and hobbies—I was a science geek, and she was a musical prodigy—we seemed to enjoy each other's company enough to find a middle ground.

She was surprisingly easy to talk to, and when she opened up to me about her shaky relationship with her musician dad, I found myself divulging details about the shaky relationship I had with my father.

Tonight marked the eighth Friday I'd spent in her company, and instead of going to the cinema like we usually did, Katie suggested we grab a bite to eat.

However, twenty minutes into the first course, I had the distinct feeling this wasn't the usual Friday night catch-up. Katie was dolled up extra nice in a pretty, black dress, with a full face of makeup, and her gorgeous, dark-coppery-red curls pinned up in a fancy style.

Was *this* a date?

Was *I* on a date?

Holy fuck, she'd texted me earlier saying *wear something smart.*

I was on a *date.*

"So, what happened?" Katie continued to probe in the chapter of my life labeled *Lizzie Young,* as she sat opposite me at a table in Spizzico, the fancy Italian restaurant in town. "I know you guys had a bad breakup, but you've never divulged the juicy details."

"Because there aren't any," I replied, taking a sip of water. "We just broke up."

"Bullshit." Katie smirked and took a sip of her water. "So, come on, out with it."

"I don't want to talk about it."

"You know what they say about a problem shared."

I sighed. "It just ended, okay?"

She looked at me. "You're still in love with her, aren't you?"

My shoulders stiffened. "It's over."

"That's not what I asked." Her voice was soft. "It's okay, Hugh. You don't get over a breakup overnight."

Feeling guilty, I exhaled a heavy sigh and said, "Ask your questions."

"Really?"

I nodded. "I'll give you as much as I can."

"Was she your first girlfriend?"

"Yes."

"Was she your only girlfriend?"

"Yes."

"Were you together for a long time?"

"Yes."

"Did you sleep with her?"

"No."

"But you did other things with her?"

"Yes."

"And she's the only girl you've ever been with?"

"Yes."

"Were you in love with her?"

"Yes."

"Did she break up with you?"

"No."

"You broke up with her?"

"Yes."

"Do you plan on getting back together with her?"

"No."

Katie watched me carefully, looking for the lie, and when she didn't find it, she smiled. It was a nice smile. She had good teeth. And freckles. Her freckles were adorable.

"But she's best friends with your sister?"

"She is."

"So she spends a lot of time at your house?"

"She does."

"So, by default, you spend a lot of time in her company?"

"I do."

"And that doesn't tempt you to work things out with her?"

"No."

"Wow." She leaned forward, engrossed in the conversation. "She broke you good and hard, didn't she?"

"Yes."

"That was more of a tactless observation than a question." Katie reached across the table and placed her small hand on mine. "You didn't have to answer that."

"It's okay," I replied, attention riveted to her tiny wrist. Instead of jagged scars donning her flesh, her porcelain skin was littered with freckles.

It was a relief.

It was different.

"What about you?" I turned the tables and asked. "You still haven't told me how you ended up transferring to Tommen."

"I did tell you," she laughed. "I won a scholarship."

"No, I mean, why transfer so late?" It wasn't uncommon. Tommen was renowned for accepting late transfers. They came in all different years, but third year and sixth year transfer students were the most common because those were the exam years, and the academic performance at Tommen spoke volumes. The school had a 98 percent graduation rate, combined with a 400-point leaving cert average rate. There was no doubting the quality of education provided, so it wasn't surprising to see parents moving their children during exam years, and the athletic programs on offer were unlike any others in the province. "If you're smart enough to snag a scholarship, and you clearly are, then why weren't you offered one in first year?"

"Originally, I *was* enrolled at Tommen for first year."

"You were?" My brows shot up. "What happened?"

"My dad happened," she replied with an eye roll. "He was supposed to send the tuition money to my grandparents, but it never happened." She took another sip of her water before adding, "Meanwhile, I never anticipated having to compete for a scholarship to get in—hence the two years at St. Bernadette's."

"Whoa," I mused, intrigued by her backstory.

"Because my skill set rests in music and *not* academics, I had to work incredibly hard to get my grades and portfolio up to a level where I'd even be considered for a scholarship," she explained, still smiling. "It took a while."

"But you did it," I replied, feeling beyond impressed. "That's pretty fucking badass, Katie."

"That's me, all right," she chuckled, blushing.

All I could do was smile in response.

"Do you want to keep doing this?" Katie asked when I walked her to her door after dinner. "On an exclusive basis?"

Repressing the natural instinct to decline, I forced myself to pause and think this through with a level head and *not* follow my heart. It couldn't be trusted to make sensible decisions. It couldn't be trusted to keep me out of trouble.

"I don't know." Mirroring her actions, I shoved my hands in my pockets and studied her face. "What do you want to do?"

"I like spending time with you," she replied softly.

"I like spending time with you, too," I told her honestly.

"But?"

"I didn't say but."

"Yeah," she laughed softly. "But you have one, don't you?"

"I'm not sure what kind of a relationship I can offer you," I admitted honestly. "I'm not exactly back on the horse."

"Yeah, but you're getting there."

Was I?

Maybe I was.

I certainly enjoyed her company. But the thought of going further wasn't even close to being on my radar.

"Don't look so stressed. I'm not going to tear your clothes off," Katie teased, giggling. "I'm nowhere close to being ready for *that*, either."

Feeling relieved, I let out a small laugh. "Good to know."

"But it would be nice to hold your hand sometime," she added, nudging my shoulder. "Or who knows? Maybe we could even kiss again sometime before the next New Year's Eve countdown."

My brows shot up. "You want me to kiss you?"

She blushed. "I thought I made it obvious." When I stared blankly back at her, Katie laughed. "You know, for a boy who's spent most of his life in a relationship, you're as clueless as I am."

"Should I be offended?" I laughed.

"No, it's a compliment." Blushing, she took a step closer to me. "And a hint."

Do it, my brain commanded. *She's lovely.*

Don't you fucking dare, my heart protested. *You know how it'll end.*

Deciding to go with the organ that hadn't led me down a decade-long rabbit hole of *pain*, I closed the space between us and cupped her pretty face in my hands.

Filled with a fucked-up concoction of uncertainty, guilt, and *excitement*, I threw caution to the wind, leaned in close, and pressed my lips to hers.

FRESH OUT THE SLAMMER

Lizzie

APRIL 19, 2004

THREE MONTHS, TWO WEEKS, AND ONE DAY.

That's how long it took the doctors to piece me back together.

Stabilizing my mood, after spending so many months spiraling, took a herculean effort, but I *did* it.

I complied.

I didn't fight the doctors this time.

Instead, I worked with them to crawl my way back to life.

The first several weeks of my admission remained a distorted blur, and I was relieved, because remembering everything hurt. Many of the blackout periods I experienced during mania were still a mystery, and I could only pray they remained that way.

During my stay on the ward, I had ten sessions of electroconvulsive therapy to alter my brain chemistry in the hope of stabilizing my mind and improving my quality of life. I could only hope that it worked because the experience of being repeatedly and intentionally electrocuted wasn't something I would *ever* agree to again.

Daily therapy, along with a carefully selected combination of mood stabilizers and antipsychotics, had brought me to the point of my long-awaited return to society.

Finally.

When I returned to Old Hall House last Friday evening, I felt like a stranger.

Like this wasn't the house I was supposed to come home to.

Like my parents weren't my parents, the bike lying on the front lawn wasn't my bike, and the room I'd spent most of my childhood in wasn't my room.

It was strange, but I handled it.

I worked *through* my feelings instead of running from them.

Mam was thrilled to finally have me home, while Dad was cagey.

I didn't blame him.

I felt exactly the same way.

When I returned to Tommen, it was the first day back after Easter break, and because my mam wanted to ease me back in slowly, I didn't go in until after big lunch.

After suffering a pained one-way conversation with Mr. Twomey in the office, I was ushered off to class with a pat on the head and an invitation to come see him if I needed anything at all. I wouldn't, but at least he didn't get snotty over my absenteeism. The principal seemed to be more concerned with my mental health than my attendance.

Academically, we both knew he didn't have to worry. Before I left, I'd been coasting through my classes, finding the whole junior-cycle curriculum boring. During my hospitalization, once I stabilized, I had completed my schoolwork from my bed. Honestly, I could have missed another three months, and it wouldn't have lowered my grades from higher-level A's.

When I stepped out of the office, a squeal of excitement filled the air.

"Omigod, omigod, omigod!" Barreling toward me, Claire threw her arms around me before I had a chance to say hi. "It's about damn time you came home!" Wrapping me up in her arms, she hugged me with a death grip. "I've missed you like crazy, Lizzie Young."

Shivering, I allowed myself to sink into her hug, allowed myself to consume the warmth she was enveloping me with. "I've missed you, too."

"How's your mam?"

"She's on the mend."

"And you?" Pulling back, she ran her hands all over my hair, searching my face with her eyes. "How are you?"

"You know me, Claire." Swallowing down my emotions, I smiled brightly. "I'm always okay."

Concern filled her brown eyes, but she didn't push.

Instead, she smiled, pulled me to her side, and walked us down the corridor.

"Let me catch you up on all the drama you've missed out on at school—fair warning, there's a *lot*."

"Can't wait," I replied dryly, relieved to fall back into our usual pattern.

"So, I heard the fifth-year girls plotting a scheme called 'operation binding thirteen,'" she announced, before reeling off a detailed account of the conversation she'd overheard in the bathroom at school.

Apparently, the senior girls were participating in a perverted race to get naked with Johnny Kavanagh.

"But the girl can't win by just having, uh, well, you know, with him," Claire continued to explain. "Apparently, she has to make him fall in love with her."

"Ugh." I blanched. "That sounds disturbing."

"And she has to be official with him," she added, scrunching her nose up. "As in *boyfriend and girlfriend*."

"Well then, it's a doomed mission," I replied dryly. "Because the only thing that boy will ever commit to is a rugby ball."

"True," Claire chuckled, nudging her shoulder against mine. "I mean, I get that he's beautiful and popular, but I don't see the fascination."

"Neither do I."

"Like, I know he's polite and all, but he's sort of standoffish." Her eyes widened as she spoke. "And he's big, Liz. Like super *big*."

"He's more than standoffish," I chimed in, rummaging through what was left of my memories. "He's a snob."

"Liz!"

"He prances around the school like he's Tommen's answer to Brian O'Driscoll."

"That's because he *is*," she laughed. "He's the top-ranking outside center in his age group in the country, Liz."

"So that means he gets preferential treatment at school?"

She laughed again. "Yes!"

"Whatever." I rolled my eyes. "I still say he's a snob."

"Gerard says he's just mad that he's still here." She shrugged. "He wants to go home to Dublin."

And that's how I spent the rest of the afternoon, going through the motions with my childhood friend.

It was *nice*.

———————————

When Hugh rounded the corner after last class of the day, I knew I was the last person he expected to run into, which was exactly why I had waited *here* for him.

Hugh was like clockwork. He did what he said he would. Training was something he had committed to and would undoubtedly fulfill because that's who he was.

"Oh shit," he muttered when his body collided with mine and the stack of books I was holding went flying. "Sorry about that," he was quick to reel off, as he gathered up my books that were scattered on the ground. "I didn't see you there."

It wasn't until he stood back up, books in hand, that he looked at me. The moment he did, his sheepish expression quickly morphed into one of surprise, and my books fell to the ground once more. "Liz."

"Hi," I breathed, barely able to stand the pressure in my chest as I watched him watch me, his whiskey-colored irises looking directly into my soul.

An involuntary shiver rippled through my body, and I was almost certain it moved through Hugh because his body seemed to have an almost mirror reaction to mine.

We continued to stare at each other for a long beat before he broke the tension with a shake of his head. "You're back."

"I'm back," I squeezed out, watching as he gathered my books once more. "Can we talk?"

"I have training," he replied, standing up and handing over my books. "Cap will cut my bollocks off if I'm late."

I should have respected his answer.

After all, I had no right to push for more, but I couldn't stop myself from whispering the word *please*.

His feet faltered and I watched the storm in his brown eyes as an internal battle raged inside of him.

Finally, when I had almost given up hope, he relented with a weary nod. "Okay."

He inclined his head in the direction of the picnic tables and relief washed through me.

"So, when did you get back?" he asked, falling into step beside me.

"Friday," I heard myself explain in a much steadier voice than I was feeling. The sensation of his big arm brushing against my shoulder as we walked sent my frazzled nerves on a downward spiral.

Rippling jolts of excitement rocketed through my core, causing my skin to come alive like an electrical current.

Oh God, not here, I mentally prayed, fighting down the familiar disgusting urges and compulsions. *Not now. Be good. Stay fucking stable, dammit.*

"Did it help?" Hugh asked, setting my books down on an empty picnic bench.

"Yes," I lied, taking a seat at the table. "I feel a lot better now."

"Good." He dropped his gear bag on the ground and took the seat opposite mine. Resting his elbows on the table, he plucked at a piece of chipped wood. "I want you to feel better, Liz."

My breath was coming in short, audible puffs when I asked, "You do?"

Hugh stared hard at me for a long beat before blowing out a pained breath. "Of course I do."

"You didn't..." My words trailed off, and I had to look away for a moment to catch my breath before retraining my attention on his face.

It hurt too much.

It didn't hurt enough.

I swallowed deeply, trying to broach the question. "Claire. You didn't…"

"I didn't tell her anything," Hugh interjected in that familiar, assuring tone. "All anyone knows is that you've been in Spain with your parents."

"I'm sorry you had to cover for me," I said, feeling a great deal of shame for dragging him into battles that raged between my mind and me. "I'm sorry for pulling you into my mess at the hospital that day."

"I'd do it again in a heartbeat."

His words threw me. "You would?"

He nodded. "Yeah, Liz. I would."

"Why?"

"Because you're sitting here," he replied simply. "Because you're *you* again." A faint smile ghosted his lips. "That's all I've ever wanted, Liz." Pain flickered in his brown eyes. "I *want* you to be okay." He spoke slowly, enunciating every word with care. "I *want* you to have a good life."

"Yeah." *Just not with you.*

GOODBYE, MY LOVER

Hugh

APRIL 19, 2004

THE MOMENT I LOCKED EYES ON HER IN THE COURTYARD, EVERY HARD-EARNED SLIVER of my battered pride evaporated. As for my heart? It returned to her like a faithful boomerang. Because unlike my brain, it couldn't be tricked into forgetting about her.

I had a million and one commitments after school today, but Liz's unexpected return sent every single one of those clean out of my head.

Sitting opposite Liz at one of the picnic tables at school, I couldn't stop my eyes from raking over her.

She had grown up so much in three and a half months. Her dark-blond hair was shorter than she used to have it, grazing her shoulders instead of the middle of her back. She was a lot thinner now—taller, too. All remnants of her cute childhood features had been replaced by stark feminine beauty.

But it was her eyes that socked me right in the chest.

Those big, pale-blue, lonesome eyes.

Jesus, they were like nothing I'd ever seen before or since.

"You look good," I told her, because it was the truth. "You look healthy."

"So do you," Liz replied, hypnotizing me with those haunting irises. "You look so different." I watched as her gaze raked over me. "You're so tall now, and broad, and *manly*."

My face burned with heat. "That's puberty for ya."

"Listen," Liz said then, and I braced myself for the conversation I knew had to happen. "About what happened—"

"Liz, you don't have to do this," I heard myself cut in, still trying to protect her. "I know you weren't yourself at the time."

"I do," she replied, teary-eyed, as she clasped her hands together on the table in front of her. "I need to get this off my chest and I need you to let me."

Fuck.

"All right." Swallowing deeply, I forced a nod. "I'm listening."

Liz drew in a deep, quivering breath before saying, "I'm truly sorry for the hell I've put you through. For repeatedly breaking your trust and ruining our relationship." Tears continued to fill her eyes, but she blinked them away and kept going. "Coming off my meds was horribly selfish and unfair to you. You've always been there for me, supporting me through everything, and it was incredibly self-centered and unreasonable of me." Another shiver rolled through her as she continued, "I'm really sorry for not taking accountability sooner, but knowing that I hurt you is the hardest pill I've ever had to swallow."

"Liz." My heart cracked clean open. "I don't hold any of it against you."

"Because you're a selfless person," she strangled out. "Because you're *you*." The tears filling her eyes started to trickle down her cheeks. "I know what I did now. Not everything, but the parts I can remember make it clear that I have no right to ask you for a second chance."

"Liz," I strangled out, feeling my chest heave from pressure. "I would do anything to go back in time and change our ending. To stop it from happening. And if there was any way I could get past it, I would, but…"

"You can't," she confirmed tearfully, with a knowing nod. "It's okay, Hugh. I understand." Sniffling, she added, "That's why I'm not going to ask."

"Liz…"

"I know you need to stay away from me," she breathed, body racking with tremors. "And I know why you can't be my friend anymore, but I just want you to know that I am so grateful to have had you in my life." A pained sob escaped her when she said, "I'll never have a greater friend, Hugh Biggs, or a greater love."

"Fuck." I blew out a ragged breath as my heart thundered violently. "Liz."

This was crippling me to the point where my heart was screaming at me to give in.

She's back on her meds.

It'll be better this time.

Give her one more chance.

But then the image of him between her legs flashed in my head, and I held firm.

Because it *would* happen again.

That was the only thing I was sure of.

"I'll never stop being sorry for betraying you," she said, holding her head in her hands. "And I'll never forgive myself for killing us."

Jesus Christ.

I wanted to soothe her.

I wanted to wipe her tears and make her better again.

I wanted *her.*

728

But I just *couldn't*.

"It'll be okay," I strangled out, reaching over and snatching one of her hands up. "We can still be friends."

"No, Hugh, we can't," she replied sadly, entwining her fingers with mine. "You can't be friends with the person you're in love with." Tears trickled down her cheeks. "And I'm always going to be in love with you, Hugh."

I believed her.

I knew this girl better than I knew myself.

I could hear her truth.

I could see it in her eyes.

It mirrored mine.

I knew how she felt because I felt the same way.

It was a hopeless, desperate, frantic feeling.

It was fucking torture.

"We can try," I heard myself offer, feeling panicked at the thought of this being it. *Please, God, don't let this be it.* "Liz, it'll be okay."

"Yeah, it will, because I'm going to take a step back," she declared and the way she said it made me think she had thought about this a lot. "I'll take the sideline bench when it comes to our friendship circle, and I won't interfere in your life."

"Liz." My eyes started to water. "I don't want that."

"Neither do I," she squeezed out, sniffling. "But it has to happen."

I knew she was right; we had to go in separate directions, but that didn't make doing it any easier.

I couldn't be sure if this was her plan, if she intended to break me down like this and shatter my resolve, but it worked.

"I know what you did," she continued, gently squeezing my hand. "How you buried the rumors about what I did with him and covered for the disgusting way I treated you."

"You weren't well."

"And you were the one caught in the crossfire, but you still protected me."

"I'll always protect you." I swiped a tear from my cheek. "No matter what."

Sniffling, she squeezed my hand again. "I want you to have the best life imaginable. Nobody deserves it more than you."

"Liz…"

"And I want you to move on from me," she said, choking on the words like they physically pained her. "I don't want you to feel guilty about it or think you're doing something wrong, because you aren't. Because you are too amazing of a person to spend your life stuck on a fuckup like me."

"What about you?" I could barely see her face through my tears. "How am I supposed to let you go?"

"You didn't let me go, remember?" she sobbed, stroking my hand with her thumb. "I did that."

"Fuck, Liz." I dropped my head on the table, covering it with my free hand while I fought to wrangle in my emotions. "Fuck."

"Claire told me you started seeing someone," she whispered, reaching over the table with her free hand to stroke my hair. "I want you to know it's okay."

I broke down.

I couldn't help it.

Right there in the middle of school, I cried my fucking heart out.

"It's okay," Liz continued to soothe, while I fought to pull myself together. "I *want* you to be happy."

My ears were ringing.

My heart was gunning in my chest.

My heart was insisting I had taken a wrong turn in life and demanding that I turn back.

"It's new," I finally managed to say when I steadied myself. "I, ah…" Roughly clearing my throat, I wiped my eyes with my sleeve and forced myself to look at her. "Her name is Katie."

When her blue eyes met mine, I felt the pull. The undeniable bond that linked my soul to hers. The one that no amount of time or distance seemed to sever. "Is she good to you?"

Sniffling, I nodded. "Yeah, she's really good to me."

The sadness in her eyes was killing me, and I had to fight every instinct inside of me to not pull her into my arms. Because it felt like I had been programmed to protect this girl. The only problem was, I needed protection from *her*. Because no one could hurt me like Liz could.

"I'm happy for you." She tried to smile but choked out a pained sob. "I swear I am," she hurried to say, as she pulled her hand from mine. "It's just h-hard."

I understood.

I knew exactly how she felt.

A wave of panic washed over me when I watched her stand up and retrieve her books and schoolbag.

I wanted to shout *don't go,* but it wouldn't have helped either one of us.

"I'll always love you, Hugh Biggs," Liz said when she rounded the table and stopped in front of me. Inhaling a quivering breath, she leaned down and pressed a kiss to my cheek before whispering, "No matter what."

And then she was gone.

Thank you so much for reading.

Hugh and Lizzie's story is just heating up. Read all about them in the next Boys of Tommen series book, coming soon.

If you or someone you know has been affected by the topics discussed in this story, please reach out to a trusted adult or contact a professional service in your local vicinity.

For support in the Republic of Ireland, please contact the services listed below:

- childline.ie
- jigsaw.ie
- spunout.ie
- cari.ie

For support in the United States, please contact the services listed below:

- National Sexual Assault Hotline 1-800-656-HOPE (4673): hotline.rainn.org
- Substance Abuse and Mental Health Services Administration: 1-800-662-HELP samhsa.gov/find-help/helplines/national-helpline
- National Suicide Prevention Lifeline at 1-800-273-TALK (8255): suicidepreventionlifeline.org

Please speak out.
Do not suffer in silence.
Your voice matters.
Your life is precious.
<3

Thank you so much for reading,

Hugh and Lizzie's story is just heating up. Read all about them in the next Boys of Tommen series book, coming soon.

If you or someone you know has been affected by the topics discussed in this story, please reach out to a trusted adult or contact a professional service in your local vicinity.

For support in the Republic of Ireland, please contact the services listed below:
- childline.ie
- hse.ie
- spunout.ie
- ean.ie

For support in the United States, please contact the services listed below:
- National Sexual Assault Hotline 1-800-656-HOPE (4673)
  hotline.rainn.org
- Substance Abuse and Mental Health Services Administration: 1-800-662-HELP samhsa.gov/find-help/national-helpline
- National Suicide Prevention lifeline at 1-800-273-TALK (8255)
  suicidepreventionlifeline.org

Please speak out.
Do not suffer in silence.
Your voice matters.
Your life is precious.

C2

Song Moments, Feels, and Dedicated Chapters

Amble—Shallow River Run: Patrick singing and playing the guitar vibes.

Zach Bryan—Spotless: stable Lizzie thinking about Hugh after the breakup.

The Moon Loungers—Willow (Acoustic Version): Hugh's feelings for Lizzie all through the book.

George Strait—Check Yes Or No: childhood Liz & Hugh.

Fleetwood Mac—Go Your Own Way: for Hugh in Claire's room in response.

Fleetwood Mac—Silver Springs: for Lizzie in Hugh's room after the breakup.

Dean Lewis—Adore: when Hugh is deep in his feels, cycling home after their date.

Zach Bryan—Something in the Orange: Hugh coping with her manic episodes.

The 2 Johnnies—She Only Rings Me When She's Locked: Pierce thinking about his relationship with Liz.

James Blunt—Goodbye My Lover: Liz & Hugh in the final scene of the book.

Celtic Journey—Lonesome Boatman: at Caoimhe's Funeral.

The Coronas—Someone Else's Hands: Hugh's feelings for Katie.

Avril Lavigne—Hot: Lizzie when she's needy for physical affection from Hugh in the earlier years.

Wrabel—Poetry: Hugh falling for Lizzie when they're young.

Picture This—One Night: when he finds her cheating on him at the party.

Alex Warren—Burning Down: Lizzie when she realizes that Caoimhe let her down.

Zach Bryan—I Remember Everything: Hugh after the breakup, trying to get over her.

Hellogoodbye—Here (In Your Arms): as small children playing.

Mark Ambor—Belong Together: happy & in love as young teens.

Tyler Brayden—Devil You Know: Hugh fighting with Mark.

Freya Ridings—You Mean the World To Me: Lizzie drowning in her devastation over losing Hugh.

Lord Huron—The Night We Met: seeing each other after the breakup.

Grace Cundy—Put Me Back Together: Liz feeling how much he loves her even when she's sick.

Melanie Martinez—Mad Hatter: when Lizzie in unraveling at school.

Phoebe Bridgers—I Know The End: sad moment between Liz and Hugh.

Taylor Swift—Down Bad: after the breakup and Lizzie shredded to pieces.

Thomas Day—not my job anymore: Hugh after the breakup watching her spiral.

Picture This—Smell Like Him: Hugh grieving the breakup.

Tate McRae—you broke me first: Hugh giving it right back to Liz.

Taylor Swift—The Way I Loved You: Hugh thinking about how right Katie is for him but how deeply he loves Liz and how he's torn between his heart and his head.

Avril Lavigne—What the Hell: Liz on a manic episode.

Taylor Swift—My Tears Ricochet: the night of their breakup and Hugh is crushed.

P!nk—Please Don't Leave Me: Liz to Hugh.

Chord Overstreet—Screw Paris: Hugh getting over Liz.

The Script—Nothing: getting drunk with the lads after the breakup.

Snow Patrol—This Isn't Everything You Are: Liz trying to keep going.

Busted—Better Than This: Hugh realizing that he needs to walk away from Liz.

Tom Odell—Another Love: Hugh's turmoil with Katie.

Josh Rabenold—Coney Island: Hugh's mindset and turmoil.

The Civil Wars—Poison & Wine: Hugh and Liz turmoil.

Gwen Stefani—The Sweet Escape: every time Johnny and Gibs are together in a scene, ha-ha.

Ruelle—Carry You: when she sees him at the hospital.

Taylor Swift—no body, no crime: Lizzie's obsession with Gibsie and his family.

Ed Sheeran—Castle on the Hill: the four lads together.

Jamie Lawson—I'm Gonna Love you: the long goodbye.

Ashlee Simpson—Pieces Of Me: Lizzie slowly withering when they're younger and Hugh being there for her.

MARINA—Bubblegum Bitch: Lizzie when she's sleeping around.

Mother Mother—Hayloft: Lizzie getting caught in bed with Pierce.

Ellise—Can You Keep a Secret?: Lizzie coming to her breaking point.

Gretchen Wilson—Redneck Woman: Lizzie and Claire's stark difference.

The 2 Johnnies—Sinead: okay, this one is for Saving 6 but I had to add it because it's giving Joe, Molloy, & Ricey vibes.

Songs for Lizzie

"Always Remember Us"—Lady Gaga

"Spotless"—Zac Bryan

"Hilary Duff"—Beat Of My Heart

"Silver Springs"—Fleetwood Mac

"Hello"—Candice

"Control"—Zoe Wees

"I Love You, I'm Sorry"—Gracie Abram

"Look What You Made Me Do"—Taylor Swift

"Angels Like You"—Miley Cyrus

"manic"—Coleman Hell

"The Reason"—Hoobastank

"Cate's Brother"—Maisie Peters

"You Should Know Where I'm Coming From"—BANKS

"feel like shit"—Tate McRae

"Sirens"—Cher Lloyd

"Mad Hatter"—Melanie Martinez

"This Town"—Niall Horan

"Falling"—Genavieve Linkowski

"Lost Without You"—Freya Ridings

"Shattered"—Trading Yesterday

"Strange"—Celeste

"I'm Sorry Baby"—SkyDxddy

"You Mean The World To Me"—Freya Ridings

"Free"—Rudimental & Emili Sande

"You Are In Love"—Taylor Swift

"Tag, You're it"—Melanie Martinez

"Serotonin"—girl in red

"Heavy"—Citizen Soldier & SkyDxddy

"How Could You"—Jessie Murph

"Pacify Her"—Melanie Martinez

"Like a Prayer"—Madonna

"Don't Blame Me"—Taylor Swift

"Mess It Up"—Gracie Abrams

"Dreams"—The Cranberries

"Breathe Me"—Sia

"I Can't Carry This Anymore"—Anson Seabra

"My Mind & Me"—Selena Gomez

"On Fire"—Switchfoot

"The Good Ones"—Gabby Barrett

"You And I"—Lady Gaga

"Bad Child"—Tones And I

"Nothing in This World"—Paris Hilton

"Shapeshift"—Jenna Doe

"Take Me to Church"—Sinead O'Connor

"Miss Americana & The Heartbreak Prince"—Taylor Swift

"Wings"—Birdy

"Malibu"—Miley Cyrus

"One Last Breath"—Creed

"die first"—Nessa Barrett

"Shadow"—Ashlee Simpson

"Stuck Like Glue"—Sugarland

"Army"—Ellie Goulding

"Try"—Nelly Furtado

"Lithium"—Evanescence

"Helium"—Sia

"I Can Do It With a Broken Heart"—Taylor Swift

"Put Me Back Together"—Grace Cundy

"Close To You"—Gracie Abrams

"I Like Me Better"—Mother's Daughter

"The Doctor Said"—Chloe Adams

"Can You Hold Me"—NF & Britt Nicole

"Warm"—The Coronas

"this is me trying"—Taylor Swift

"Far Away"—Nickelback

"bad guy"—Billie Eilish

"Knockin' On Heaven's Door"—Antony and the Johnsons

"Praise You"—Fatboy Slim

"About You Now"—Sugababes

"I Shall Believe"—Sheryl Crow

"My Skin"—Natalie Merchant

"Unsteady"—X Ambassadors

"no body, no crime"—Taylor Swift

"Motel"—MEG MYERS

"Hypersexual"—Reve

"Take Me Home"—Jess Glynne

"Don't Deserve You"—Plumb

"Salvation"—Gabrielle Aplin

"Bring Me Back to Life"—Ht Bristol

"I'm With You"—Avril Lavigne

"You're Not Innocent"—Codi Kaye

"Hits Different"—Taylor Swift

"Desire"—MEG MYERS

"Manic"—Plumb

"Always Been You"—Jessie Murph

"To You I Belong"—B*Witched

"Loved Me Back to Life"—Celine Dion

"Find Me"—Birdy

"Coming Home Part III"—Skylar Gray

"Nobody Praying For Me"—Seether

"Down Bad"—Taylor Swift

Songs for Hugh

"Go Your Own Way"—Fleetwood Mac

"The Lights of Cork City"—The 2 Johnnies

"If I Gave Myself To Someone Else"—The Coronas

"Break Up In A Small Town"—Sam Hunt

"Without Me"—Alec Chambers

"The Night We Met"—Micky

"Sinead"—The 2 Johnnies

"THE REPLACEMENT"—Kae

"All Too Well"—Taylor Swift

"Bulletproof"—Nate Smith

"Screw Paris"—Chord Overstreet

"A Drop in the Ocean"—Ron Pope

"not my job anymore"—Thomas Day

"Softcore"—The Neighbourhood

"you broke me first"—Our Last Night

"Faith in Fate"—The Coronas

"Another Love"—Tom Odell

"You're Somebody Else"—flora cash

"Walls"—Ruben

"Leave a Light On"—Tom Walker

"Stay Away"—The Honorary Title

"Better Than This"—Busted

"Devil You Know"—Tyler Braden

"Same Old Brand New You"—A1

"I'm the One"—Sunset & Highland

"Ocean"—Martin Garrix & Khalid

"Belong Together"—Mark Ambor

"Cardigan"—Josh Rabenold

"Blackout"—Freya Ridings

"Those Eyes"—New West

"I Remember Everything"—Zach Bryan

"What Have I Done"—Dermot Kennedy

"I Still Love You"—Josh Jenkins

"hate to be you"—Lexi Jayde

"I Got Away With You"—Luke Combs

"Our Story"—Mako

"Before You Leave Me"—Alex Warren

"Adore"—Dean Lewis

"The Burning Heart"—Takida

"Take What I Can Get"—Matthew Mayfield

"Smile"—Uncle Kracker

"Carry You Home"—Alex Warren

"Love Me Back"—Max McNown

"One Night"—Picture This

"Don't Ever Let It End"—Nickelback

"Hold On"—Chord Overstreet

"Beautiful Mistakes"—Maroon 5

"Don't Worry Baby"—The Beach Boys

"Fallen so Young"—Declan J Donovan

"Born To Be Yours"—Kygo & Imagine Dragons

"What's Left of You"—Chord Overstreet

"Suitcase"—Matthew Koma

"Lonely Boy"—The Black Keys

"In Our Own Worlds"—Jamie Lawson

"Firestone"—Kygo & Conrad Sewell

"Baby Don't Cut"—Bmike

"Think Twice"—Eve 6

"One More Night"—Maroon 5

"Never Stop"—Safety Suit

"9 Crimes"—Damien Rice

"Just Looking"—Stereophonics

"Drops of Jupiter"—Train

"It's Not Over"—Daughtry

"Be Still"—The Fray

"For Blue Skies"—Strays Don't Sleep

"When Your Heart Stops Beating"—+44

"Don't Give Up On Me"—Andy Grammer

"Lips Of An Angel"—Hinder

"Only You"—Aaron Krause

"Slow Dancing in a Burning Room"—John Mayer

"Nothing's Gonna Hurt You Baby"—Cigarettes After Sex

"My Tears Ricochet"—Taylor Swift

"Picture Of You"—Boyzone

"Accidental Babies"—Damien Rice

"Whatever Else Happens"—Declan O'Rourke

"Hurricane"—Luke Combs

"Back To You"—Selena Gomez

"This Is Not a Test"—The Coronas

"Robbers"—The 1975

"The Scientist"—Coldplay

"She Will Be Loved"—Maroon 5

"Peer Pressure"—James Bay

"The Weakness In Me"—Joan Armatrading

"Bloodstream"—Stateless

"Wires"—Athlete

"Someone Else's Hands"—The Coronas

"Find My Way Back"—Eric Arjes

"I'll Follow You"—Shinedown

"Kodaline"—Honest

"A Lot More Free"—Max McNown

"Don't Give Up On Me" – Andy Grammer

"Lips Of An Angel" – Hinder

"Only You" – Aaron Krause

"Slow Dancing in a Burning Room" – John Mayer

"Nothing's Gonna Hurt You Baby" – Cigarettes After Sex

"My Tears Ricochet" – Taylor Swift

"Picture Of You" – Boyzone

"Accidental Babies" – Damien Rice

"Whatever Else Happens" – Declan O'Rourke

"Hurricane" – Luke Combs

"Back To You" – Selena Gomez

"This Is Not A Test" – The Coronas

"Robbers" – The 1975

"The Scientist" – Coldplay

"She Will Be Loved" – Maroon 5

"Peer Pressure" – James Bay

"The Weakness In Me" – Joan Armatrading

"Bloodstream" – Stateless

"Wires" – Athlete

"Someone Bless Hands" – The Coronas

"Find My Way Back" – Eric Arjes

"I'll Follow You" – Shinedown

"Kodaline" – Honest

"A Lot More Free" – Max McElown

Acknowledgments

I never know whether to add an acknowledgment section to the end of a book, and a lot of the time I don't, but I decided to add one after *Releasing 10* because I have a few thank-yous to dole out.

Walshy:

It's funny how everything always comes back to you. No matter how many stories I write, when I reach the acknowledgments, it's *always* your name that comes to mind. Because I couldn't write these stories without you.

Thank you for showing me how it feels to be truly loved. Thank you for storming into my world when we were young teenagers and pulling me from the carnage. Thank you for getting me out of there. You took ahold of my hand and never let go, not even when I made it hard to hold on. Thank you for accepting every part of me, the world I came from, and my difficult mind.

Thank you for fueling my love of music with your gifted ability to play *any* instrument placed in your hands. Guitar. Drums. Banjo. Mandolin. Harmonica. Bass. Ukulele. It's insane how you can put your hand to all of them, and your voice? Jesus, don't even get me started on that voice!

Thank you for blowing my world with that guitar you pulled out in class, stunning the shit out of me and the girls with "Johnny B. Goode." I remember looking at Tracy and thinking *what the hell did we just witness?* I still remember sneaking into the pub with the girls to watch you and Madden play your first gig. When you stepped up to the mic and sang "Fall at Your Feet" and you kept your eyes on mine the entire time, I swear I melted. Even our friends knew I was a goner. That was nearly twenty years ago and I'm still a goner, Walshy, so cheers for that. I suppose Angaleena Presley wasn't wrong when she sang about good-looking guitar men and knocked-up girls because we both know what came next. ;)

Thank you for keeping your word, for being the pinnacle of all that's good in a man, and for building us a home I wasn't afraid to lay my head in. Thank you for my babies and for showing me that not all father's leave. Thank you for breaking every generational cycle I was terrified of and changing the narrative. I love you. (For Keeps.)

Slash, Madden, & Al:

Thanks for being Walshy's best friends in the whole world and for always having his back—even if one of you did pass out on top of the head table during the best man speech at our wedding. (I'm looking at you, Ray.)

Thanks for being the best bunch of boys a broken girl could have had in her corner. For the nights I can't remember with the friends I'll never forget.

Thanks for the memories, boys. <3

Nikki Ashton:

They say if a friendship lasts seven years, then it will last forever. Well, we've reached eleven and I can't imagine a world where we don't talk every day. You mean the world to me, and I'll always be down for you, Nik. Thanks for always picking up the phone. For being my loudest defender when the world is cruel. For knowing the person I truly am and having no problem debunking every hurtful lie. Friends like you only come around once in a lifetime, and I only wish that I met you earlier so I could love you longer. If you guys have gotten this far, then check out this lady's books. She is a raunchy, comedic genius with her words. *Roman's Having Sex Again* will always hold a special place in my heart. Thanks for everything, Nik. <3

Caitlin Mahony:

My soul sister from across the pond. Thank you for being the 'dude' to my 'lad.' From the first time we spoke, I realized you were the right person to have in my corner. That I had found more than just an agent but a treasured friend. I also quickly realized that you have the patience of a saint, something required to handle me and my fucked-up mind. Somehow, you persevere with me, and I'm not entirely sure why, but I'm so glad you put your faith in me.

Thank you for standing in front of the world for me when I need to take a breath and for trusting in my ability to do my job. I won't let you down, buddy. Oh, and if you ever go, you better take me with you.

Lexi Campbell:

Thank you so much for coming into my world when I was drowning. I couldn't see straight from panic, and you took that from my shoulders with a snap of your fingers. You stepped up and showed me how to put boundaries down. You put a boundary around me and gave me a chance to heal from the noise. I could thank you a hundred thousand times and it wouldn't be enough. Because I really think you might have saved me for a while there, Lex. From throwing in the towel on a lot of things.

You're so cool and quirky, and I always think it's hilarious when we video call because of how different we are. Even though we're different on the surface, we're so incredibly similar where it counts. (Planners! Just joking, lol.) You're the mysterious and witchy Stevie to my oversharing and holy-medal-wearing Dolly. Ha. Dolly and Stevie. That actually sounds pretty class. You get me, and I get you. And I'm so grateful to have a friend like you in my life. Love you, L. <3

The readers:

I want to thank each and every person who took the time to read this book. It's incredibly humbling to know that so many people want to read my stories. It's been eleven years since I was first published, and it still feels surreal. In those eleven years, I've written many stories and worked hard on each one, but the Tommen series is different. Tommen is *special*. Tommen is the product of ultimate personal vulnerability. I have revealed more of my heart in these pages than I have to people I've known my whole life. Every page I write feels like a cathartic memory torn from the tearstained journals of my youth. Knowing that I have reached others with these stories means the world to me. I only wish I could go back in time and tell that fifteen-year-old girl in that hospital bed to keep breathing. To keep writing. To not be afraid of her mind. That her words mattered. That her story could help others.

Thank you for reading, and please, keep breathing.

About the Author

Chloe Walsh is the bestselling author of the 2018 Boys of Tommen series, which exploded in popularity around the world. She has been writing and publishing New Adult and Adult contemporary romance for a decade. Her books have been translated into multiple languages worldwide. Animal lover, music addict, TV junkie, Chloe loves spending time with her family and is a passionate advocate for mental health awareness. Chloe lives in Cork, Ireland with her family.